It's Always Raining Corpses in Chinatown

IT'S RAINING
CORPSES
IN
CHINATOWN
FRANKLYN E. HAMILTON
© 1989
Don Hutchison

IT'S ALWAYS RAINING CORPSES IN CHINATOWN

edited and introduced by
Don Hutchison

cover by Jerome Rozen

frontispiece by Franklyn E. Hamilton

featuring stories by

Dashiell Hammett

Loring Brent

Sidney Herschel Small

Ralph R. Perry

Russell Gray

T.T. Flynn

Justin Case

John K. Butler

Dane Gregory

Steve Fisher

Emile C. Tepperman

Arden X. Pangborn

William Hines

Frank Gruber

Hugh B. Cave

Frederick Nebel

POPULAR PUBLICATIONS • 2024

TABLE OF CONTENTS

INTRODUCTION

Don Hutchison

REMEMBER FU MANCHU?

With his army of Dacoit footpads, trained killer apes and poisonous creepy-crawlies, Sax Rohmer's maleficent Devil Doctor held the reading world in thrall for half a century.

Fu Manchu's glory years were the twenties and thirties—that fascinating interval between the two "Great Wars." Ignorance and innocence weren't mortal sins then. It was a smaller world, less complex, when houses had attics full of memories and old books where you could sit and thrill to *Tales of Chinatown* and *The Yellow Claw.*

If the worldview these fictions portrayed was simplistic and even jingoistic, it was a factor that seldom bothered homebodies of the Great Depression. For them, such remote and unseen locations as China, the South Seas, India, and the jungled lands of Africa and South America existed as mere backdrops to tales of vicarious adventure.

This was the circumscribed world in which so-called Yellow Peril fiction thrived. The Chinese, or the "Chinamen," as most Americans called them, had come to the New World as coolies to supply cheap labor for mining camps and railroads. By the 1870s, Asian ghettoized communities emerged in the heart of several cities: claustrophobic shadow worlds of serpentine streets and narrow alleys, soon identified as Chinatowns.

While Westerners may have admired Chinese culture and

tradition from a distance, our press chose to emphasize the most superficial and sensational aspects of Chinese life in a process of exoticizing stereotypes. Stories of tong wars, opium smuggling, white slavery, hatchet men and gambling dens appeared frequently in luridly inventive newspaper accounts. The incorporation of these lip-smacking elements into the stew of pulp fiction proved irresistible.

Despite the unprecedented success of his Fu Manchu novels, Sax Rohmer did not invent Chinatown as a story background. Popular literature's romance with things Oriental began as early as the dime novels of the previous century, when fear of the Yellow Peril was fueled not only by Chinatowns—where crime was said to flourish as naturally as disease—but by the clash of merchants and mandarins in the Celestial Empire itself. Early travelers to the Far East returned with anecdotal references characterizing Orientals as being "inscrutable" and "cruel." More significantly, the Chinese were described as so innately fecund as to make their numbers a threat in itself. It was the German Kaiser who first coined the expression that solidified the threat—"the Yellow Peril."

The first Anglo-Chinese conflict—the so-called Opium War—ended in 1842 with the virtuous forces of Western business opening Chinese ports, winning Hong Kong as a British colony, and forcefully encouraging the "Heathen Chinese" to step up drug importation. Not surprisingly, American and European members of the exploitative banquet found themselves prey to acts of retaliation. They were exposed, as the Bishop of Victoria expressed it, "not merely to the ordinary danger of a foreign residence, but to the cup of the poisoner, the knife of the assassin and the torch of the midnight incendiary."

Eventually, Chinese resentment produced the one incident in their long history that is known to the world at large. For fifty-five days in the summer of 1900, some 2000 Europeans and Chinese Christians were besieged in their Legation Compound in Peking by the ferocious secret society known as the Boxers, whose war cry was "Sha! Sha!" ("Kill! Kill!") and whose motto was "Exterminate the foreigners!"

Their swords and clothing dripping red, Boxer terror squads ravaged the countryside butchering missionaries and converts alike. The siege of the foreign legations was no less gory, with eye-witness accounts of "women and children hacked to pieces, men trussed like fowls, with noses and ears cut off and eyes gouged out." It was this thrillingly sanguine image that Western society would long remember.

As usual, popular culture mined bizarre riches from catastrophe. The portrait of the Chinese as sly purveyors of intrigue and cunning was soon spread gratuitously by means of press, plays, radio, film, and most emphatically by popular literature. While much of this was propaganda aimed at justifying commercial exploitation of the East, readers of the period did not balk at descriptions of a duplicitous race heavily involved with dope, poisons, slavery, occult magic and all things unwholesome. Perhaps they found the notion reasonable.

M.P. Shiel, that brilliant but xenophobic Irishman, projected Oriental invasions of the Western world in such pioneer fantasy novels as *The Yellow Danger* (1898), *The Yellow Wave* (1905) and *The Dragon* (1913). The concept of an England overwhelmed by hordes of pig-tailed invaders was Shiel's hysterical contribution to the world of "future war" science fiction. His publishers claimed that Shiel originated the "yellow menace" theme in popular literature. When they reissued *The Dragon* in 1929, they even furnished it with a new title: *The Yellow Peril.*

In Shiel's *The Yellow Danger* the Chinese inject over a hundred of their own troops with cholera and then release the poor souls throughout Europe. The plague destroys one hundred and fifty million Occidentals. In the aptly named *The Yellow Peril,* a diabolical Chinese named Li Ku Yu manipulates the European nations into war with each other to soften them for an Asian mop up. He boasts to the novel's hero: "See if Japan doesn't have Australia—Canada!—and be not surprised if before you die you catch sight of the saffron Dragon Flag of the Manchus flapping from the staff atop of your Parliament house."

American period novels were equally Sinophobic. Charles Foley's *Kowa the Mysterious* (1909) involved a domed Asian city beneath the streets of San Francisco. When the bizarre dome collapses it causes the great San Francisco earthquake. A later novel, *The Earth-Tube* by Gawain Edwards, was a future war epic involving Asian hordes invading America by means of a gigantic tube driven through the center of the earth. A young scientist, King Henderson, penetrates the robotic city of master fiend Tai Majod to save the white race from annihilation. A better-known novel, Floyd Gibbons' *The Red Napoleon* (serialized in Liberty magazine in the early 30s) dealt with a future war instigated by a saffron-skinned militarist named Karakhan, whose battle cry to his Asian invaders was "Conquer and breed!"

Of course, Western literature's anti-foreign animus did not begin or end with the Yellow Peril. Old-style thrillers had long been packed with sinister characters made even more suspect by their strange complexions and funny accents. Literary antiquarian Rick Lai has pointed out that just prior to the so-called Yellow Peril there was an abundance of Italian master villains in British detective fiction. These evildoers had many of the attributes that would come to be associated with their Oriental counterparts. This was not due to any anti-Italian movement but rather to public fascination with secret societies, unusual methods of poisons practiced by the Borgias, and the alleged hypnotic powers of Count Cagliostro.

The best of the pasta perils was Dr. Nikola, a master hypnotist created by Guy Boothby. The sinister Nikola appeared in five novels ranging from *Dr. Nikola's Vendetta* in 1895 to *Farewell Nikola* in 1901. Besides having contact with traditional Italian criminal organizations, Nikola was heavily involved with penetrating the mysteries of a Chinese secret society.

Publication of the Nikola books and the unsettling events of the Boxer rebellion overlapped in time. Soon after, mysterious Chinese characters and Chinese locales began popping up like bamboo shoots in British thriller fiction. Their influence ranged from "boys' paper" heroics involving Sexton Blake and Nelson Lee through the lending library melodramas of Roland Daniels and Edgar Wallace. It was a mystery ploy so widespread that by 1928 the staid members of the Detection Club in London sighed plaintively for "an end to these hordes of sinister Chinamen."

The undisputed king of the Limehouse thriller school was a man born Arthur Henry Ward but known to the world under his inspired pseudonym of Sax Rohmer. A Fleet Street journalist turned dabbler in arcana, Rohmer was that rarity among authors, the creator of a character as mythic as Burroughs' Tarzan and Conan Doyle's Sherlock Holmes.

Rohmer was not the first to exploit the Yellow Peril theme, but he did it with more impact on public awareness. He added his own wrinkle by fusing in one memorable character three major facets of Caucasian paranoia: Oriental mastery of Western technology (a prophetic fear if there ever was one); the employment of occult "Eastern" powers; and the mobilization of a secret international organization consisting of hordes of criminous types representing various "non-white" races and countries.

Tall, thin, with lizard-green eyes, yellow robe and black cap embroidered with coral bead, Fu Manchu was the very picture of warped genius. Such unusual potions as spiders, scorpions and plague-carrying tsetse flies were but part of Fu's prescription to foreshorten the white race's actuarial expectations. Master of super science and creative toxicology, he was the living embodiment of inchoate worries. He was the Yellow Peril.

To confront the Chinese Napoleon and his new world order, Rohmer conceived those strait-laced defenders of the status quo, Sir Dennis Nayland Smith and Dr. Petrie—the Holmes and Watson of Yellow Peril fiction.

Poor old Nayland Smith. The Beatles got their O.B.E. just for singing. Sir Dennis had to work hard for his. During 13 novels spanning nearly half a century he was dumped through trap doors, shot, burned, slugged on the noggin, and subjected to humiliations and tortures too plentiful (and inventive) to enumerate.

There are those who claim that Smith was more nuisance than threat to the brilliant Devil Doctor—that he was, in fact, something of a British bumpkin. Jack Smith, a columnist in

The Los Angeles Times, once noted that the Fu Manchu saga was indeed racist. "It presents Anglo-Saxons as stereotype buffoons," he wrote, "dashing impetuously about, pounding up the wrong stairways, bashing in the wrong heads, getting ourselves popped in the jaw, and all the while delivering the hollow cast pomposities through stiff upper lips. It makes us look like what Queen Victoria would have called horses' posteriors; but then of course we often are."

The instigator of Smith's travails was and is possibly the most famous villain in all popular literature. For nearly eight decades the indestructible archfiend has remained tops in the medical field. Compared to him Doctor No is a mere intern, Crippen a dilettante, and Strangelove a pathetic farceur. Yet he differs from his army of imitators by a nobility of character strangely out of keeping with his macabre methods. In the words of Nayland Smith, "an assassin, a torturer, the most dangerous criminal the law has ever known; but always an aristocrat." Fu began life as a routine Limehouse menace but over time his author came to respect him—even if the world did not.

"I have been worshipped, I have been scorned; I have been flattered, mocked, betrayed, treated as a charlatan—as a criminal," Fu once complained. "Yet always I have been selfless. My crimes, so termed, have been merely the removal from my path of those who obstructed me. Always I have dreamed of a sane world, yet men have called me mad; of a world in which war should be impossible, disease eliminated, overpopulation checked, labor found for all willing hands—a world of peace." High-minded goals for a philanthropist whose tools included giant centipedes, plagues, untraceable poisons, killer mushrooms, and walking dead men!

Rohmer's misunderstood Doctor first appeared in England in a series of short stories in *The Story Teller*, beginning in 1912, just after the overthrow of the Manchu empire in China. The series was an instant hit and was soon picked up by the American weekly *Collier's*, providing a ready-made New World audience. The character was so popular in countless reprint book editions that in later years his author often signed himself $ax Rohmer.

As befits a literary icon, there were numerous movie versions of the Fu Manchu saga, beginning as early as 1923 with several two-reelers featuring stiff-upper-lip English actor Harry Agar Lyons.

In 1929 Paramount cast Charlie Chan-to-be Warner Oland as the wily master fiend in *The Mysterious Doctor Fu Manchu*. In 1930 Oland reprised the role in *The Return of Dr. Fu Manchu* and *Daughter of the Dragon*. Oland, a Swedish star who was known at the time as "the screen's premier sinister Oriental," was hampered in his interpretation by simplistic scripts which reduced the role to that of a powerful Chinese family man out to seek revenge on the "foreign devils" who killed his wife during the Boxer Rebellion.

A slicker version was produced in 1932 when MGM cast Boris Karloff in *The Mask of Fu Manchu*. Shot in the studio's typically lavish style (replete with Art Deco torture chambers) the picture ignored Fu's skewed but high-toned motivations even though it did return him to his rightful place as regal menace to the white race. With Fah Lo Suee, his equally dedicated daughter, Fu is out to recover the lost tomb of Genghis Khan. Nayland Smith warns: "Once Fu Manchu puts the mask of Genghis Khan across his yellow face and takes that scimitar into his hands, all Asia rises!"

A similar plot infused all 15 chapters of Republic Pictures' frenetic 1940 serial *The Drums of Fu Manchu.* As portrayed by youthful actor Henry Brandon, Fu Manchu again sought the Khan's tomb and sacred scepter to achieve his most stupendous crime—the conquest of all Asia. The Republic scripters based their chapterplay on incidents from six of Rohmer's Fu Manchu epics—*Insidious, Return of, Hand of, Bride of, Trail of* and *President*—with the title for the picture being lifted from a Rohmer volume published during production of the film. Because of limited production costs Fu and his faithful Dacoit "men of murder" were forced to confine their urban exploits to California's fictional "San Angeles" rather than to London's fog infused Limehouse.

Republic's dramatization of the Devil Doctor in California was consistent with Rohmer's idea of Fu as the leader of the globe-spanning Si-Fan, "the oldest and most powerful secret society in the world." Rohmer himself had placed Fu Manchu in America, notably in *President Fu Manchu* (1936). The novels were, if anything, even more popular in the U.S. than they were in Britain.

Not surprisingly, Orientals, sinister and otherwise, ran unchecked through mystery and adventure pulp magazines of the twenties and thirties. The voracious pulps seldom failed to capitalize on any theme or trend capable of divorcing coins from thrill-hungry readers. One title, *New Mystery Adventures,* went so far as to promote a series of seven stories involving Wo Fan, a Fu Manchu clone perpetrated by someone identified as "Bedford Rohmer." It is a measure of the Wo Fan series that this Rohmer italicized phrases like "sexual excesses" so that teen-aged readers would not miss them. Despite this splendid service, the stories fell short of enduring literary value.

Authors Lemuel de Bra and Walter C. Brown are forgotten now but each contributed numerous Chinatown yarns to the early pulps. Many of the de Bra stories, more sympathetic to the Chinese than most, were reminiscent of the work of the great British writer Thomas Burke who, in his books *Limehouse Nights* and *Whispering Windows,* wrote powerfully of the tawdry lives of those who lived along "the low-lit Causeway that slinks from West India Dock Road to the dark waste of the waters beyond."

One early Chinese character not so sympathetic was A.E. Apple's Mr. Chang, whose adventures in rascality ran from 1919 to 1936, first in *Detective Story Magazine,* then in *Best Detective.* Chang was no world dominator like Fu Manchu, but a ruthless lone wolf bad guy who killed his first human at the age of nine. Chang was born without emotions; he had the cold blood of a reptile and his pulse stood around forty. Back in China they told stories about him just to frighten children. The Chang novelettes—many of them cliffhangers—were great fun and more original than most other Rohmer-inspired pulp epics.

Not all Oriental fiction was about crime and criminals. Top adventure writer George Worts created the popular Peter Moore series for *Argosy* in 1918. Known as Peter the Brazen as well as The Man of Bronze (Doc Savage fans take note), young Moore faced numerous Oriental foes in the China of decades ago. The character was resurrected in a new series of exploits in 1930 (written under Worts' pen name of Loring Brent) in which Peter once again met up with a variety of Far

Eastern threats, including the fantastic Blue Scorpion and the Eurasian temptress known as The Octopus.

Another hell-for-leather adventurer, Ralph R. Perry's Bellow Bill, brawled his way though *Argosy* and the China seas, taking a toll on Eastern hatchet men and hustlers.

From 1931 through 1936 *Detective Fiction Weekly* ran a well-received series about a San Francisco Chinatown cop named Jimmy Wentworth. Written by Sidney Herschel Small, the stories faced hero Wentworth against the malevolent influence of bad guy Kong Gai and then that of Kong Gai's son, The Nameless One.

Even Robert E. Howard, that rugged chronicler of the Hyborian Age, muscled into fog-shrouded Fu Manchu territory with his popular 1929 *Weird Tales* serial "Skull-Face." A second Rohmer pastiche, "Names in the Black Book," was published five years later in *Super-Detective Stories*. A confessed Rohmer admirer, Howard wrote all or part of three other stories in this vein, but none was published during his lifetime.

Unfortunately, the number of Fu Manchu-style villains far outweighed Oriental heroes in pulp literature. One of the few good guys was Dr. Zeng Tse Lin, a crime-solving physician and scientist who lived in San Francisco's Chinatown district. (The Doctor Zeng stories were written by Walt Bruce and appeared in *Popular Detective* throughout the mid 1940s). However, Dr. Zeng was a white American, Robert Charles Lang by name, born the son of missionary parents in China. One might say that the relationship between Zeng/Lang and a real Chinese hero was strictly occidental.

T.T. Flynn produced an underrated mini-series in *Dime Detective*. These five stories all involved ace Secret Service op

Val Easton versus America's enemies, the sinister Black Doctor and Chang Ch'ien. Another Fu Manchu look-alike, Chang Ch'ien is described as "a myth, a legend, a terror in the under-world of many lands." In a story titled "The Jade Joss" (November 15, 1933) Ch'ien straps Easton to a table and places a wire cage containing a starving rat on Val's naked chest. "When I pull this slide out," Ch'ien says evenly, "he will drop to your chest. There, for a time, fright will keep him busy. But when he begins to think, he will see that the only way out is through your chest. Food and escape in one."

The torture-by-rats bit was a favorite with Oriental fiends of the fictional variety. In the third Fu Manchu novel Nayland Smith had been threatened with just such a fate, and one of the most famous (or infamous) Chinese rat torture yans ever written, "The Copper Bowl" by Major George Fielding Eliot, was originally published in *Weird Tales*, "the Unique Magazine," in 1928.

While sex and suggestiveness were taboo in most pulps of the period, it goes without saying that soft core titillation and torture were staple fare in the so-called "spicy" and weird-menace titles that flourished throughout the 1930s. Many of the slavering torturers were, of course, fiends of the Oriental type. One of the frequent "spicy" contributors was award-winning author Hugh B. Cave, who disguised some of his youthful indiscretions under the wondrous pen name Justin Case. In the interest of moral enhancement and cultural understanding, we include herein a Justin Case torture den epic set in the heart of Boston's Chinatown.

Black Mask great Dashiell Hammett proved himself a writer of his time by casting a sinister Chinese villain in his Continental Op story, "The House in Turk Street." Another Op story, the carefully structured "Dead Yellow Women," served to introduce two of Hammett's most interesting characters—the delightfully duplicitous Chang Li Ching and fascinating Lillian Shan, daughter of a Manchu.

Unlike many pulp writers, Hammett researched his backgrounds firsthand, especially San Francisco's colorful Chinatown, where he often drank and gambled.

"In those days," he wrote, "if you ran a joint in Chinatown, you had a bodyguard whether you needed one or not, just to rate. There was this roly-poly Chinese muscle boy offered to me by a friend who owned a dive down there, to use if I had anybody I wanted pushed around—a leg broken or something—but I was not to spoil him by giving him money for this service. 'Five or ten bucks is okay for a tip,' I was told, 'but no more.' I didn't take advantage of the offer—but I did write the Chinese into a picture later in Hollywood."

Another *Black Mask* regular with personal knowledge of the Chinese was Erle Stanley Gardner, creator of Perry Mason. As a youthful lawyer in Oxnard, California, Gardner was called to defend several Chinese shopkeepers accused of selling illegal lottery tickets.

Swinging into action like hero Mason himself, Gardner had his client, Wong Duck, and other friends switch shops. As a result, the district attorney's agents picked up the wrong shopkeeper. "WONG DUCK MAY BE WRONG DUCK SAYS DEPUTY SHERIFF," a newspaper shrilled the next morning, causing the embarrassed D.A. to drop all the cases.

Thanks to his sensational defense, Gardner attained several Chinese friends and clients. He used this background in writing 73 Ed Jenkins stories for *Black Mask*.

Ed Jenkins, known as The Phantom Crook, was a classic misjudged pulp hero: wanted for two murders, hated by the underworld and hounded by the police. His best friend was Soo Hoo Duck, the undisputed dictator of all Chinese activities on the Pacific Coast. The police could search until doomsday for The Phantom Crook but if Ed could dive through any doorway in Chinatown and claim sanctuary in the name of Soo Hoo Duck, he would elude capture.

Soo Hoo Duck had a name for Ed Jenkins: Sai Yan Pang (Man of the West Who Is My Friend). Gardner also gave Soo a beautiful daughter, Ngat T'oy, who enabled the author to introduce a romantic East-West relationship into the Jenkins saga.

In his autobiographical short story "The Penny-a-Worder" (*Ellery Queen's Mystery Magazine,* September 1958), Cornell Woolrich wrote of a 1930 pulp writer who is forced to spend the night in a hotel room to grind out a 20,000-word novelette to an editor's deadline. The story must be based on a previously commissioned cover painting, which illustrates "a plump-breasted girl in a disheveled, lavender-colored dress desperately fleeing from a pursuer, the look on whose face promised her additional dishevelment."

Woolrich's pulpster protagonist decides that the girl is being pursued because she has been the recipient of a mysterious package—but what's in the package? "There were always certain staples that were good for the contents of mysterious packages. Opium pellets—but that meant bringing in a Chinese villain, and the menace on the cover certainly wasn't Chinese."

Woolrich wrote from experience. Fourteen years earlier in

The Black Path of Fear he had introduced opium dens and sinister Orientals into Havana's Chinatown to stretch his plot to book length proportions.

Even the high-flying air pulps dabbled with themes of Oriental menace. They usually avoided stereotypic Chinese villains in favor of real-life aggressors from the Empire of the Rising Sun—who even then were attempting to shine their light all over East Asia. (One unusual aspect of the Yellow Peril theme was the free-floating transfer of stereotypes from one race to another, resulting in a ready-made bonanza for wartime propagandists).

Arch Whitehouse, himself a Royal Flying Corps veteran with sixteen air victories, unleashed Buzz Benson in *Flying Aces,* home of countless cloudland cavaliers. Buzz doubled as an aviation reporter and undercover agent for the Secret Service. The Benson plots usually involved peril to the US fleet in the Pacific, with Buzz zooming in to wreak havoc on bands of international crooks and not-too-disguised Oriental aggressors.

In December 1934, *Flying Aces* featured a story by Syl MacDowell titled "Armada from Asia." McDowell wrote of a future war in which America was attacked from the air by a motley group of Asians. "The Asian Confederacy," he explained, "was formed of many half-wild tribes, the existence of which civilized America had hardly known before the outbreak of hostilities. They were born warriors. They were Mongols, Abakan Tartars, Kirghiz and many other scourings of primitive people out of Siberia and Mongolia and Turkestan. They were regimented by the powerful nations of the East."

During the thirties *Flying Aces* also featured numerous

non-fiction predictions of a coming war from the East. In their March 1938 number, they printed a cover article titled "How Japan Might Attack America." The article analyzed an amazingly prophetic 1925 book titled *The Great Pacific War*, written by Hector C. Bywater, a noted British writer on Naval affairs. In his book, Bywater postulated a future war in which Japan might use paltry differences concocted in China to declare war on the United States. The *Flying Aces* cover article discussed the possibilities of a war in which Japan might gain first blood and take up key positions in the Pacific.

An earlier *Flying Aces* feature (February 1935) condensed a similar Japanese fictional history, "Dream of War Between the United States and Japan," written by Lieutenant Commander Kyosuke Fukunaga, Imperial Japanese Navy, retired. The book had been distributed previously as a supplement to a 1933 Japanese magazine in an alleged attempt to sow anti-American feeling among populations of Oriental extraction in Hawaii and California.

Despite the odd sympathetic character (Richard Wong in *G-Men* and Dr. Zeng in *Popular Detective* spring to mind) the predominant image of Orientals in pulp fiction was that of the so-called Yellow Peril. Nowhere was this theme more blatantly enacted than in the single character hero magazines. Like their British boys' paper counterparts, the adolescent-oriented hero pulps were awash in Oriental fiends. It was a rare pulp hero who could get through several months without encountering some twisted despot from the East.

The most famous of all pulp mystery men, The Shadow, was no stranger to Chinatowns on either coast. Known as Ying Ko to the Chinese, the Master of Darkness skulked through

New York's Chinatown in "The Living Shadow," "The Fate Joss," "The Chinese Disks," "The Living Joss," and "The Jade Dragon." San Francisco's Chinatown encountered him in "Green Eyes," "The Chinese Tapestry," "Six Men of Evil," "Teeth of the Dragon," "The Chinese Primrose," and finally in "Jade Dragon," the latter not to be confused with "The Jade Dragon" of 1942, which was set in Manhattan's Chinatown.

In fact, the initial issue of *The Shadow* magazine (April 1931) featured a cover painting of a frightened Chinese character and his own vaguely menacing shadow. The cover had been recycled from a 1919 *Thrill Book* to save money. Shadow author Walter B. Gibson was requested to insert a Chinese subplot to justify the cover illustration, inadvertently creating what would become a Shadow standby, the Chinatown locale.

After numerous Chinatown combats it was perhaps inevitable that The Shadow would eventually encounter an Oriental super villain whose abilities and resources—extolled in four Shadow novels—were the equal of his own.

As Gibson explained it, "That was left for Shiwan Khan in *The Golden Master* of September 15, 1939. Since The Shadow in his early years had visited Tibet, there to acquire hypnotic powers that helped him to triumph over fiends of crime, it stood to reason that his nemesis—if he should ever have one— would have to come from that mystic land to challenge The Shadow on his home ground. Shiwan Khan not only came from Tibet, but he also claimed that he owned it, along with outlying territories, which made him formidable, indeed."

Not to be outdone, Popular Publications' The Spider also cut a bloody swath through Manhattan's Chinatown. In "Slaves of the Dragon" (May 1936), *Spider* author Norvell Page reveals that his character had spent many of his early years in the Far East and that he considered the Chinese to be his fiercest foes. The Oriental master-villain of this caper was, as the magazine delicately put it, stripping America of wives, sisters and sweethearts. "I am being paid so much a head" the Dragon explained, "to bring American women, undoubtedly the most intelligent in the world, to mate with the Mongols of Manchukuo. Thus, will a certain nation breed powerful and brainy men-children for its future slaves and wars."

Another Spider caper, "Dragon Lord of the Underworld" (July 1935), featured Su Hsi Tze, "the Arch-Criminal of all time, master of life and death, of disease, of horrible crawling things—the Emperor of Vermin." More Fu Manchu look-alikes arose in "Emperor of the Yellow Death" and "Scourge of the Yellow Fangs." As usual, the white race pulled through.

The Phantom Detective (disguise whiz Richard Curtis Van Loan) encountered Oriental mystery in his second adventure, "The Crimes of Ku Fee Wong (April 1933) and uncovered a Chinese narcotics ring eight months later in "The Yellow Murder." A 1938 novel, "Yellow Shadows of Death," had the chameleon detective practicing makeup skills in San Francisco's Chinatown.

Secret Agent X (the pulp hero without a name) faced the usual Chinatown perils in several book-length adventures. He raided the opium catacombs of China Bobby in "The Golden Ghoul," invaded New York's Chinatown in "Dividends of Doom," and brought hell to 'Frisco's Hong Kong Alley in "Curse of the Mandarin's Fan." What made "X" unique in Oriental settings was that he had the honor of being the Ming Ton's only white member. His initiation took place after he defended one of the tong's outposts against a warlord's band of marauding soldiers.

Nick Carter, the only detective hero to star in dime novels, the pulps and paperback originals, squared off with Oriental villains in all three mediums. In his pulp guise he faced bloody Chinatown warfare in "The Bowl of Tau Su Fo."

Even G-8, Robert J. Hogan's indomitable WWI flying spy, faced his share of Oriental foes in the middle of the Kaiser's War on the Western Front. Chu Lung, a Chinese, was known as the Oriental Master of Death. He threatened the Master Spy eight times in such adventures as "Skies of Yellow Death," and "Red Fangs of the Sky Emperor."

Author Hogan even introduced a Japanese villain to the series—Herr Matzu. While history records that the Japanese entered World War One on the side of the Allies, Herr Matzu preferred the life of a freelancer. "I don't hate anyone," he explained. "I like being friendly with everyone even though I must kill them."

Without question the most politically paranoid of all single character pulp magazines was *Secret Service Operator # 5*. Operator 5 was Jimmy Christopher, a young man of incredible attributes. Like most of the pulpwood heroes, he was a larger-than-life figure absolutely dedicated to the eradication of America's enemies. Month after month throughout the thirties, savage hordes plunged "America's Secret Service Ace" into one overheated fantasy after another. The titles alone were enough to prickle hairs on a reader's scalp: "Invasion of the Crimson Death-Cult," "The Yellow Scourge," "The Coming of the Mongol Hordes," "Corpse Cavalry of the Yellow Vulture." As a surreal social mirror of the collective phobias of its time, the magazine remains unparalleled in the history of popular culture.

Fantastic weaponry abounded in the Operator 5 stories, some of it predating actual World War II devices. The most advanced terror tools were employed by a foe known as The Yellow Vulture—Japanese warlord Moto Taronago.

In each of the Yellow Vulture novels Jimmy's beloved nation suffered a purgatory of conflict and defeat at the hand of Asiatic hordes. Victory came only when all appeared darkest. But even victory was often Pyrrhic. At the end of "The Army from Underground," with Philadelphia, Washington, Knoxville and Baltimore demolished, with giant slaughter machines burrowing out of the ground and carving bloody furrows through the countryside, Operator 5 receives further news: "There is no more Canada," Quillen's whisper cut like a cold wind. "The Japanese have wiped it out… destroyed the remaining cities… annihilated the population. The Dominion is a great wilderness… and the Japanese are using it at this very minute as a base from which to sweep down into New England… coming down to destroy arms… ammunitions…"

That November 1939 issue was destined to become the biggest cliffhanger of them all. Another novel, "Hell's Last Battalion" was announced but never saw publication. Jimmy Christopher's battles were over. America's real war was soon to begin.

If Oriental super-villains were choice antagonists for such pulpwood paragons as Operator 5, G-8, and the Spider, their publisher, the ever-resourceful Henry Steeger, reasoned that a pulp title featuring the solo exploits of such a villain might prove equally popular. When he first decided to do a Fu Manchu-style pulp title he chose as his writer Robert J. Hogan of *G-8 And His Battle Aces* fame. Hogan was no stranger to yarns of Oriental menace, having successfully transplanted the Yellow Peril theme into the Master Spy's Western Front adventures. Editorship of the projected magazine was handed over to young Edythe Seims, who was also a G-8 veteran. Together they came up with something called *The Mysterious Wu Fang*.

In 1935, when the *Wu Fang* magazine made its debut, the name of Fu Manchu was already a household word; the Fu Manchu books were best sellers, and they were usually serialized in such prestigious magazines as *Collier's* and *Liberty*. If the public confused one character with the other, the confusion could only aid the sales of the humble pulp magazine.

Doing their best to add to the identity crisis, the publishers of *Wu Fang* obtained the services of illustrator John Richard Flanagan, a fine commercial artist who had illustrated all of Sax Rohmer's stories in *Collier's* from 1929 to 1935 as well as the American book edition of *The Mask of Fu Manchu*.

Interestingly, the name Wu Fang was not unknown at the time of his pulp magazine debut. Sax Rohmer himself had used the sobriquet for a minor character in *Yellow Shadows* (1925) and Harold Lamb wrote of a Wu Fan Chien in *Marching Sands* (1920). As early as 1915 Arthur K. Reeve, creator of Craig Kennedy the Scientific Detective, had featured an Oriental mastermind of that name in his Kennedy novel, *The Romance of Elaine*. The villainous creation was carried over into the Pathe serial version starring serial queen Pearl White. Silent movie audiences must have responded to the thrill of the Yellow Peril because Wu Fang became Miss White's own saffron menace in a number of early chapter plays.

For a few years there was even a British Wu Fang; his adventures as related by Roland Daniel appeared first in *The Thriller* and in such books as *Wu Fang* (1929), *Wu Fang's Revenge* (1934), *The Son of Wu Fang* (1935) and *The Return of Wu Fang* (1937).

Unlike Sax Rohmer's menace, old Wu seems to have been in the public domain, a sort of unlicensed yellow terror. The character also turned up in comic strips (notably Dan Dunn, Secret Operator 48) and in comic books as well. Even Boris Karloff portrayed a Chinese warlord named Wu Fang in Hollywood's *West of Shanghai* (1937).

Known alternatively as the Emperor of Death and the Yellow Dragon Lord of Crime, the mysterious Wu Fang (pulp version) was described as a tall, gaunt figure with sloping shoulders; his mouth was pinched and narrow, but the upper part of his face above the hideously gleaming green eyes widened to a forehead of great brain capacity. He usually wore a yellow silk robe embroidered across the front with a dragon—and was thus depicted in Jerome Rozen's excellent cover paintings.

Rozen's depictions were true to the mood of the Wu Fang stories, which in turn reflected the entire Rohmerian netherworld of secret passages, dank caves, trap doors, Egyptian tombs, vipers, spiders, bats, and ubiquitous hordes of leering acolytes.

Wu skulked through a series of seven fast-paced novels beginning with "The Case of the Six Coffins." He was killed off in his sixth caper ("The Case of the Black Lotus") but the following month saw him resurrected from his glass sarcophagus. That yarn ("The Case of the Hidden Scourge") sent the saffron scourge packing off to Baghdad hot on the trail of the electrical secrets first developed by Nebuchadnezzar when he illuminated the ancient hanging gardens. Nebuchadnezzar's secret suggested a plan whereby one man (guess who?) could fry every person on earth who uses electricity. True to format, the Hidden Scourge ended with wily Wu once again in shackles, his shocking schemes short-circuited.

It is not certain whether the Wu Fang title was discontinued because of poor sales or because Sax Rohmer may have finally balked at the use of a name so close to that of his famous creation. In any case, the folks at Popular Publications must have retained faith in the idea of an Oriental menace magazine; after a mere two months' breather they introduced a similar title—*Dr. Yen Sin.*

Dr. Yen Sin as portrayed on Jerome Rozen's cover looked suspiciously like his predecessor, Wu Fang. In fact, the cover had been commissioned for the eighth Wu Fang novel, "The Case of the Living Poison," which was announced but never issued. It seemed to matter little since both characters were based on the identical model—Dr. Fu Manchu. (One can postulate a medical college somewhere in Kwangtung that specialized in graduating Evil Doctors *magna cum laude.*)

The editor of the new magazine was Ken White. Interior illustrations were handled by Ralph Carlson, and the novels themselves were written by pulp writer Donald E. Keyhoe— the same man who as Major Donald E. Keyhoe achieved later fame as the author of five best-selling "fact" books on UFOs, including *The Flying Saucer Conspiracy* and *The Flying Saucers Are Real.*

Keyhoe shifted the scene from London's Limehouse to Washington, D.C. It is a Washington that must have seemed foreign to Americans of the year 1936: fog-shrouded, mysterious, deadly, with dark doings in places both high and low. (This was forty years before the Watergate conspiracy; Yen Sin probably ranks as the most prophetic pulp to precede John Campbell's *Astounding Science Fiction*).

From the opening paragraphs of the first novel ("The Mystery of the Dragon's Shadow") we are plunged into an unrelenting world of night, a universe dominated by mystery and murder… and even worse. Burmese blow guns poke from raised coffin lids. Innocent-seeming chair covers conceal Dacoit stranglers. Beams of emerald flame cut through walls and windows. There are torture chambers beneath the Potomac, Tibetan Corpse-flowers, mummies that sing, and corpses with their heads sewn on backwards. It's the formula as before, straight from the special world of magic and menace that only Sax Rohmer could have inspired.

Despite such interesting variations, the new magazine was even less successful than its predecessor. The career of the Crime Emperor was terminated after three brief forays into print. (Sales were not the only reason; publisher Steeger has since related that he yanked the magazine off the stands when someone pointed out that Yen Sin sounded like a sexual reference in another language).

While space limitations preclude the use of Wu Fang or Yen Sin novels in this anthology, we have featured some scarcer (and perhaps more interesting) series characters from yesterday's pages. These include Peter the Brazen and his encounter with the Octopus of Hongkong (sic), Jimmy Wentworth vs. Kong Gai, Val Easton vs. Chang Ch'ien, and Bellow Bill in the China Seas.

Are these stories racist? Who can deny it? Were they meant to be malicious? I think not. Pulp writers produced fiction for two reasons: to earn money and to provide their fans with sheer entertainment. They were vendors of excitement, not significance. When they placed their heroes in Chinatown or the Far East, they were simply mining a tried-and-true formula that offered readers a few hours respite from their own existence.

In his Guest of Honor speech at the 1983 Pulpcon in Dayton, Ohio, author Robert Bloch reminisced:

I don't have to tell you what those magazines meant, particularly to the people who were alive during the depression days. To a man who was unemployed, or perhaps working twelve hours a day if he was lucky and had a job, those magazines gave him a few hours of escape into a different world, a world in which he could live vicariously and experience adventures in places that he'd never hope to see in his lifetime....

People didn't take trips for any great distance in those days. There were no commercial airlines; the only people that were flying regularly were G-8 and the Battle Aces. And so we learned about the world through these sources, and the pulp magazines were a wonderful way to get acquainted. For a few pennies we could indulge in all sorts of vicarious adventures—be guided by a wonderful group of male chauvinist pigs—sexist, racist, completely biased. We loved the characters, we loved all the heroes, heroines—we didn't think in terms of somebody being done an injustice or wrong by being caricatured or pictured as inferior. There was no malice in those stories. They were innocent. And we were innocent.

There, we've gone and said it: the stories in this book were meant to be fun: they should be read in that manner.

Today, Yellow Peril fiction is a quaint footnote in the history of pop literature—an era of adventurous menace that a more tolerant and more sophisticated society can no longer endorse. But the old stories still provide a nostalgic whiff of the past. They conjure up perversely delicious images of a sinister world that never quite existed… except in the wonderland of imagination and in the thrill-saturated pages of those paper time machines we call "the pulps."

Don Hutchison
Toronto

THE HOUSE IN TURK STREET

Dashiell Hammett

*We wouldn't consider an issue complete without
one of Mr. Hammett's stories in it, and after
you've read this tale, you'll understand why.*

I HAD BEEN told that the man for whom I was hunting lived in a certain Turk Street block, but my informant hadn't been able to give me his house number. Thus it came about that late one rainy afternoon I was canvassing this certain block, ringing each bell, and reciting a myth that went like this:

"I'm from the law office of Wellington and Berkeley. One of our clients—an elderly lady—was thrown from the rear platform of a street car last week and severely injured. Among those who witnessed the accident, was a young man whose name we don't know. But we have been told that he lives in this neighborhood." Then I would describe the man I wanted, and wind up: "Do you know of anyone who looks like that?"

All down one side of the block the answers were:

"No," "No," "No."

I crossed the street and started to work the other side. The first house: "No."

The second: "No."

The third. The fourth.

The fifth—

No one came to the door in answer to my first ring. After a while, I rang again. I had just decided that no one was at home, when the knob turned slowly and a little old woman opened the door. She was a very fragile little old woman, with a piece of grey knitting in one hand, and faded eyes that twinkled pleasantly behind gold-rimmed spectacles. She wore a stiffly starched apron over a black dress and there was white lace at her throat.

"Good evening," she said in a thin friendly voice. "I hope you didn't mind waiting. I always have to peep out to see who's here before I open the door—an old woman's timidity."

She laughed with a little gurgling sound in her throat.

"Sorry to disturb you," I apologized. "But—"

"Won't you come in, please?"

"No; I just want a little information. I won't take much of your time."

"I wish you would come in," she said, and then added with mock severity, "I'm sure my tea is getting cold."

She took my damp hat and coat, and I followed her down a narrow hall to a dim room, where a man got up as we entered. He was old too, and stout, with a thin white beard that fell upon a white vest that was as stiffly starched as the woman's apron.

"Thomas," the little fragile woman told him; "this is Mr.—"

"Tracy," I said, because that was the name I had given the other residents of the block; but I came as near blushing when I said it, as I have in fifteen years. These folks weren't made to be lied to.

Their name, I learned, was Quarre; and they were an affectionate old couple. She called him "Thomas" every time she spoke to him, rolling the name around in her mouth as if she liked the taste of it. He called her "my dear" just as frequently, and twice he got up to adjust a cushion more comfortably to her frail back.

I had to drink a cup of tea with them and eat some little spiced cookies before I could get them to listen to a question. Then Mrs. Quarre made little sympathetic clicking sounds with her tongue and teeth, while I told about the elderly lady who had fallen off a street car. The old man rumbled in his beard that it was "a damn shame," and gave me a fat and oily cigar. I had to assure them that the fictitious elderly lady was being taken care of and was coming along nicely—I was afraid they were going to insist upon being taken to see her.

Finally I got away from the accident itself, and described the man I wanted. "Thomas," Mrs. Quarre said; "isn't that the young man who lives in the house with the railing—the one who always looks so worried?"

The old man stroked his snowy beard and pondered.

"But, my dear," he rumbled at last; "hasn't he got dark hair?"

She beamed upon her husband and then upon me.

"Thomas is *so* observant," she said with pride. "I had forgotten; but the young man I spoke of does have dark hair, so he couldn't be the one who saw the accident at all."

The old man then suggested that one who lived in the block below might be my man. They discussed this one at some length before they decided that he was too tall and too old. Mrs. Quarre suggested another. They discussed that one, and voted against him. Thomas offered a candidate; he was weighed and discarded. They chattered on:

"But don't you think, Thomas… Yes, my dear, but… Of course you're right, Thomas, but…."

Two old folks enjoying a chance contact with the world that they had dropped out of.

Darkness settled. The old man turned on a light in a tall lamp that threw a soft yellow circle upon us, and left the rest of the room dim. The room was a large one, and heavy with the thick hangings and bulky horse-hair furniture of a generation ago. I burned the cigar the old man had given me, and slumped comfortably down in my chair, letting them run on, putting in a word or two whenever they turned to me. I didn't expect to get any information here; but I was comfortable, and the cigar was a good one. Time enough to go out into the drizzle when I had finished my smoke.

Something cold touched the nape of my neck.

"Stand up!"

I didn't stand up: I couldn't. I was paralyzed. I sat and blinked at the Quarres.

And looking at them, I knew that something cold *couldn't* be against the back of my neck; a harsh voice *couldn't* have ordered me to stand up. It wasn't possible!

Mrs. Quarre still sat primly upright against the cushions her husband had adjusted to her back; her eyes still twinkled with friendliness behind her glasses; her hands were still motionless in her lap, crossed at the wrists over the piece of knitting. The old man still stroked his white beard, and let cigar smoke drift unhurriedly from his nostrils.

They would go on talking about the young men in the neighborhood who might be the man I wanted. Nothing had happened. I had dozed.

"Get up!"

The cold thing against my neck jabbed deep into the flesh.

I stood up.

"Frisk him," the harsh voice came from behind.

The old man carefully laid his cigar down, came to me, and ran his hands over my body. Satisfied that I was unarmed, he emptied my pockets, dropping the contents upon the chair that I had just left.

Mrs. Quarre was pouring herself some more tea.

"Thomas," she said; "you've overlooked that little watch pocket in the trousers."

He found nothing there.

"That's all," he told the man behind me, and returned to his chair and cigar.

"Turn around, you!" the harsh voice ordered.

I turned and faced a tall, gaunt, raw-boned man of about my own age, which is thirty-five. He had an ugly face—hollow-cheeked, bony, and spattered with big pale freckles. His eyes were of a watery blue, and his nose and chin stuck out abruptly.

"Know me?" he asked.

"No."

"You're a liar!"

I didn't argue the point: he was holding a level gun in one big freckled hand.

"You're going to know me pretty well before you're through with me," this big ugly man threatened. "You're going to—"

"Hook!" a voice came from a portièred doorway—the doorway through which the ugly man had no doubt crept up behind me. "Hook, come here!"

The voice was feminine—young, clear, and musical.

"What do you want?" the ugly man called over his shoulder. *"He's* here."

"All right!" He turned to Thomas Quarre. "Keep this joker safe."

From somewhere among his whiskers, his coat, and his stiff white vest, the old man brought out a big black revolver, which he handled with no signs of either weakness or unfamiliarity.

The ugly man swept up the things that had been taken from my pockets, and carried them through the portières with him.

Mrs. Quarre smiled brightly up at me.

"Do sit down, Mr. Tracy," she said.

I sat.

Through the portières a new voice came from the next room; a drawling baritone voice whose accent was unmistakably British; cultured British.

"What's up, Hook?" this voice was asking.

The harsh voice of the ugly man:

"Plenty's up, I'm telling you! They're onto us! I started out a while ago; and as soon as I got to the street, I seen a man I knowed on the other side. He was pointed out to me in Philly five-six years ago. I don't know his name, but I remembered his mug—he's a Continental Detective Agency man. I came back in right away, and me and Elvira watched him out of the window. He went to every house on the other side of the street, asking questions or something. Then he came over and started to give this side a whirl, and after a while he rings the bell. I tell the old woman and her husband to get him in, stall him along, and see what he says for himself. He's got a song and dance about looking for a guy what seen an old woman bumped by a street car—but that's the bunk! He's gunning for us. There ain't nothing else to it. I went in and stuck him up just now. I meant to wait till you come, but I was scared he'd get nervous and beat it. Here's his stuff if you want to give it the once over."

The British voice:

"You shouldn't have shown yourself to him. The others could have taken care of him."

Hook:

"What's the diff? Chances is he knows us all anyway. But supposing he didn't, what diff does it make?"

The drawling British voice:

"It may make a deal of difference. It was stupid."

Hook, blustering:

"Stupid, huh? You're always bellyaching about other people being stupid. To hell with you, I say! If you don't like my style, to hell with you! Who does all the work? Who's the guy that swings all the jobs? Huh? Where—"

The young feminine voice:

"Now, Hook, for God's sake don't make that speech again. I've listened to it until I know it by heart!"

A rustle of papers, and the British voice:

"I say, Hook, you're correct about his being a detective. Here is an identification card among his things."

The Quarres were listening to the conversation in the next room with as much interest as I, but Thomas Quarre's eyes never left me, and his fat fingers never relaxed about the gun in his lap. His wife sipped tea, with her head cocked on one side in the listening attitude of a bird.

Except for the weapon in the old man's lap, there was not a thing to persuade the eye that melodrama was in the room; the Quarres were in every other detail still the pleasant old couple

who had given me tea and expressed sympathy for the elderly
lady who had been injured.

The feminine voice from the next room:

"Well, what's to be done? What's our play?"

Hook:

"That's easy to answer. We're going to knock this sleuth off,
first thing!"

The feminine voice:

"And put our necks in the noose?"

Hook, scornfully:

"As if they ain't there if we don't! You don't think this guy
ain't after us for the L.A. job, do you?"

The British voice:

"You're an ass, Hook, and a quite hopeless one. Suppose this
chap is interested in the Los Angeles affair, as is probable; what
then? He is a Continental operative. Is it likely that his organization doesn't know where he is? Don't you think they know
he was coming up here? And don't they know as much about
us—chances are—as he does? There's no use killing him. That
would only make matters worse. The thing to do is to tie him
up and leave him here. His associates will hardly come looking for him until tomorrow—and that will give us all night to
manage our disappearance."

My gratitude went out to the British voice! Somebody was in
my favor, at least to the extent of letting me live. I hadn't been feeling very cheerful these last few minutes. Somehow, the fact that I
couldn't see these people who were deciding whether I was to live
or die, made my plight seem all the more desperate. I felt better
now, though far from gay; I had confidence in the drawling British
voice; it was the voice of a man who habitually carries his point.

Hook, bellowing:

"Let me tell you something, brother: that guy's going to be knocked off! That's flat! I'm taking no chances. You can jaw all you want to about it, but I'm looking out for my own neck and it'll be a lot safer with that guy where he can't talk. That's flat. He's going to be knocked off!"

The feminine voice, disgustedly:

"Aw, Hook, be reasonable!"

The British voice, still drawling, but dead cold:

"There's no use reasoning with you, Hook, you've the instincts and the intellect of a troglodyte. There is only one sort of language that you understand; and I'm going to talk that language to you, my son. If you are tempted to do anything silly between now and the time of our departure, just say this to yourself two or three times: 'If he dies, I die. If he dies, I die.' Say it as if it were out of the Bible—because it's that true."

There followed a long space of silence, with a tenseness that made my not particularly sensitive scalp tingle. Beyond the portière, I knew, two men were matching glances in a battle of wills, which might any instant become a physical struggle, and my chances of living were tied up in that battle.

When, at last, a voice cut the silence, I jumped as if a gun had been fired; though the voice was low and smooth enough.

It was the British voice, confidently victorious, and I breathed again.

"We'll get the old people away first," the voice was saying. "You take charge of our guest, Hook. Tie him up neatly. But remember—no foolishness. Don't waste time questioning him—he'll lie. Tie him up while I get the bonds, and we'll be gone in less than half an hour."

The portières parted and Hook came into the room—a scowling Hook whose freckles had a greenish tinge against the sallowness of his face. He pointed a revolver at me, and spoke to the Quarres:

"He wants you."

They got up and went into the next room, and for a while an indistinguishable buzzing of whispers came from that room.

Hook, meanwhile, had stepped back to the doorway, still menacing me with his revolver; and pulled loose the plush ropes that were around the heavy curtains. Then he came around behind me, and tied me securely to the high-backed chair; my arms to the chair's arms, my legs to the chair's legs, my body to the chair's back and seat; and he wound up by gagging me with the corner of a cushion that was too well-stuffed for my comfort. The ugly man was unnecessarily rough throughout; but I was a lamb. He wanted an excuse for drilling me, and I wanted above all else that he should have no excuse.

As he finished lashing me into place, and stepped back to scowl at me, I heard the street door close softly, and then light footsteps ran back and forth overhead.

Hook looked in the direction of those footsteps, and his little watery blue eyes grew cunning.

"Elvira!" he called softly.

The portières bulged as if someone had touched them, and the musical feminine voice came through.

"What?"

"Come here."

"I'd better not. He wouldn't—"

"Damn him!" Hook flared up. "Come here!"

She came into the room and into the circle of light from the tall lamp; a girl in her early twenties, slender and lithe, and dressed for the street, except that she carried her hat in one hand. A white face beneath a bobbed mass of flame-colored hair. Smoke-grey eyes that were set too far apart for trustworthiness—though not for beauty—laughed at me; and her red mouth laughed at me, exposing the edges of little sharp animal-teeth. She was beautiful; as beautiful as the devil, and twice as dangerous.

She laughed at me—a fat man all trussed up with red plush rope, and with the corner of a green cushion in my mouth—and she turned to the ugly man.

"What do you want?"

He spoke in an undertone, with a furtive glance at the ceiling, above which soft steps still padded back and forth.

"What say we shake him?"

Her smoke-grey eyes lost their merriment and became hard and calculating.

"There's a hundred thousand he's holding—a third of it's mine. You don't think I'm going to take a Mickey Finn on that, do you?"

"Course not! Supposing we get the hundred-grand?"

"How?"

"Leave it to me, kid; leave it to me! If I swing it, will you go with me? You know I'll be good to you."

She smiled contemptuously, I thought—but he seemed to like it.

"You're whooping right you'll be good to me," she said. "But listen, Hook: we couldn't get away with it—not unless you *get him.* I know him! I'm not running away with anything that belongs to him unless he is fixed so that he can't come after it."

Hook moistened his lips and looked around the room at nothing. Apparently he didn't like the thought of tangling with the owner of the British drawl. But his desire for the girl was too strong for his fear of the other man.

"I'll do it!" he blurted. "I'll get him! Do you mean it, kid? If I get him, you'll go with me?"

She held out her hand.

"It's a bet," she said, and he believed her.

His ugly face grew warm and red and utterly happy, and he took a deep breath and straightened his shoulders. In his place, I might have believed her myself—all of us have fallen for that sort of thing at one time or another—but sitting tied up on the side-lines, I knew that he'd have been better off playing with a gallon of nitro than with this baby. She was dangerous! There was a rough time ahead for this Hook!

"This is the lay—" Hook began, and stopped, tongue-tied.

A step had sounded in the next room.

Immediately the British voice came through the portières, and there was an edge of exasperation to the drawl now:

"This is really too much! I can't"—he said reahly and cawnt—"leave for a moment without having things done all wrong. Now just what got into you, Elvira, that you must go in and exhibit yourself to our detective friend?"

Fear flashed into her smoke-grey eyes, and out again, and she spoke airily:

"Don't be altogether yellow," she said. "Your precious neck can get along all right without so much guarding."

The portières parted, and I twisted my head around as far as I could get it for my first look at this man who was responsible for my still being alive. I saw a short fat man, hatted and coated for the street, and carrying a tan traveling bag in one hand.

Then his face came into the yellow circle of light, and I saw that it was a Chinese face. A short fat Chinese, immaculately clothed in garments that were as British as his accent.

"It isn't a matter of color," he told the girl—and I understood now the full sting of her jibe; "it's simply a matter of ordinary wisdom."

His face was a round yellow mask, and his voice was the same emotionless drawl that I had heard before; but I knew that he was as surely under the girl's sway as the ugly man—or he wouldn't have let her taunt bring him into the room. But I doubted that she'd find this Anglicized oriental as easily handled as Hook.

"There was no particular need," the Chinese was still talking, "for this chap to have seen any of us." He looked at me now for the first time, with little opaque eyes that were like two black seeds. "It's quite possible that he didn't know any of us, even by description. This showing ourselves to him is the most arrant sort of nonsense."

"Aw, hell, Tai!" Hook blustered. "Quit your bellyaching, will you? What's the diff? I'll knock him off, and that takes care of that!"

The Chinese set down his tan bag and shook his head.

"There will be no killing," he drawled, "or there will be quite a bit of killing. You don't mistake my meaning, do you, Hook?"

Hook didn't. His Adam's apple ran up and down with the effort of his swallowing, and behind the cushion that was choking me, I thanked the yellow man again.

Then this red-haired she-devil put her spoon in the dish.

"Hook's always offering to do things that he has no intention of doing," she told the Chinese.

Hook's ugly face blazed red at this reminder of his promise to *get* the Chinese, and he swallowed again, and his eyes looked as if nothing would have suited him better than an opportunity to crawl under something. But the girl had him; her influence was stronger than his cowardice.

He suddenly stepped close to the Chinese, and from his advantage of a full head in height scowled down into the round yellow face that was as expressionless as a clock without hands.

"Tai," the ugly man snarled; "you're done. I'm sick and tired of all this dog you put on—acting like you was a king or something. I've took all the lip I'm going to take from a Chink! I'm going to—"

He faltered, and his words faded away into silence. Tai looked up at him with eyes that were as hard and black and inhuman as two pieces of coal. Hook's lips twitched and he flinched away a little.

I stopped sweating. The yellow man had won again. But I had forgotten the red-haired she-devil.

She laughed now—a mocking laugh that must have been like a knife to the ugly man.

A bellow came from deep in his chest, and he hurled one big fist into the round blank face of the yellow man.

The force of the punch carried Tai all the way across the room, and threw him on his side in one corner.

But he had twisted his body around to face the ugly man even as he went hurtling across the room—a gun was in his hand before he went down—and he was speaking before his legs had settled upon the floor—and his voice was a cultured British drawl.

"Later," he was saying; "we will settle this thing that is between us. Just now you will drop your pistol and stand very still while I get up."

Hook's revolver—only half out of his pocket when the oriental had covered him—thudded to the rug. He stood rigidly still while Tai got to his feet, and Hook's breath came out noisily, and each freckle stood ghastily out against the dirty scared white of his face.

I looked at the girl. There was contempt in the eyes with which she looked at Hook, but no disappointment.

Then I made a discovery: *something had changed in the room near her!*

I shut my eyes and tried to picture that part of the room as it had been before the two men had clashed. Opening my eyes suddenly, I had the answer.

On the table beside the girl had been a book and some magazines. They were gone now. Not two feet from the girl was the tan bag that Tai had brought into the room. Suppose the bag had held the bonds from the Los Angeles job that they had mentioned. It probably had. What then? It probably now held the book and magazines that had been on the table! The girl had stirred up the trouble between the two men to distract their attention while she made a switch. Where would the loot be, then? I didn't know, but I suspected that it was too bulky to be on the girl's slender person.

Just beyond the table was a couch, with a wide red cover that went all the way down to the floor. I looked from the couch to the girl. She was watching me, and her eyes twinkled with a flash of mirth as they met mine coming from the couch. The couch it was!

By now the Chinese had pocketed Hook's revolver, and was talking to him:

"If I hadn't a dislike for murder, and if I didn't think that you will perhaps be of some value to Elvira and me in effecting our departure, I should certainly relieve us of the handicap of your stupidity now. But I'll give you one more chance. I would suggest, however, that you think carefully before you give way to any more of your violent impulses." He turned to the girl. "Have you been putting foolish ideas in our Hook's head?"

She laughed.

"Nobody could put any kind in it."

"Perhaps you're right," he said, and then came over to test the lashings about my arms and body.

Finding them satisfactory, he picked up the tan bag, and held out the gun he had taken from the ugly man a few minutes before.

"Here's your revolver, Hook, now try to be sensible. We may as well go now. The old man and his wife will do as they were told. They are on their way to a city that we needn't mention by name in front of our friend here, to wait for us and their share of the bonds. Needless to say, they will wait a long while—they are out of it now. But between ourselves there must be no more treachery. If we're to get clear, we must help each other."

According to the best dramatic rules, these folks should have made sarcastic speeches to me before they left, but they didn't. They passed me without even a farewell look, and went out of sight into the darkness of the hall.

Suddenly the Chinese was in the room again, running tiptoe—an open knife in one hand, a gun in the other. This was the man I had been thanking for saving my life!

He bent over me.

The knife moved on my right side, and the rope that held that arm slackened its grip. I breathed again, and my heart went back to beating.

"Hook will be back," Tai whispered, and was gone.

On the carpet, three feet in front of me, lay a revolver.

The street door closed, and I was alone in the house for a while.

You may believe that I spent that while struggling with the red plush ropes that bound me. Tai had cut one length, loosening my right arm somewhat and giving my body more play, but I was far from free. And his whispered "Hook will be back" was all the spur I needed to throw my strength against my bonds.

I understood now why the Chinese had insisted so strongly upon my life being spared. I was the weapon with which Hook was to be removed. The Chinese figured that Hook would make some excuse as soon as they reached the street, slip back into the house, knock me off, and rejoin his confederates. If he didn't do it on his own initiative, I suppose the Chinese would suggest it.

So he had put a gun within reach—in case I could get loose—and had loosened my ropes as much as he could, not to have me free before he himself got away.

This thinking was a side-issue. I didn't let it slow up my efforts to get loose. The why wasn't important to me just now—the important thing was to have that revolver in my hand when the ugly man came into this room again.

Just as the front door opened, I got my right arm completely free, and plucked the strangling cushion from my mouth. The rest of my body was still held by the ropes—held loosely—but held. There was no time for more.

I threw myself, chair and all, forward, breaking the fall with my free arm. The carpet was thick. I went down on my face, with the heavy chair atop me, all doubled up any which way; but my right arm was free of the tangle, and my right hand grasped the gun.

My left side—the wrong side—was toward the hall door. I twisted and squirmed and wrestled under the bulky piece of furniture that sat on my back.

An inch—two inches—six inches, I twisted. Another inch. Feet were at the hall door. Another inch.

The dim light hit upon a man hurrying into the room—a glint of metal in his hand.

I fired.

He caught both hands to his belly, bent double, and slid out across the carpet.

That was over. But that was far from being all. I wrenched at the plush ropes that held me, while my mind tried to sketch what lay ahead.

The girl had switched the bonds, hiding them under the couch—there was no question of that. She had intended coming back for them before I had time to get free. But Hook had come back first, and she would have to change her plan. What more likely than that she would now tell the Chinese that Hook had made the switch? What then? There was only one answer: Tai would come back for the bonds—both of them would come. Tai knew that I was armed now, but they had said that the bonds represented a hundred thousand dollars. That would be enough to bring them back!

I kicked the last rope loose and scrambled to the couch. The bonds were beneath it: four thick bundles of Liberty Bonds, done up with heavy rubber bands. I tucked them under one arm, and went over to the man who was dying near the door. His gun was under one of his legs, I pulled it out, stepped over him, and went into the dark hall.

Then I stopped to consider.

The girl and the Chinese would split to tackle me. One would come in the front door and the other in the rear. That would be the safest way for them to handle me. My play, obviously, was to wait just inside one of those doors for them. It would be foolish for me to leave the house. That's exactly what they would be expecting at first—and they would be lying in ambush.

Decidedly, my play was to lie low within sight of this front door and wait until one of them came through it—as one of them surely would, when they had tired of waiting for me to come out.

Toward the street door, the hall was lighted with the glow that filtered through the glass from the street lights. The stairway leading to the second-story threw a triangular shadow across part of the hall—a shadow that was black enough for any purpose. I crouched low in this three-cornered slice of night, and waited.

I had two guns: the one the Chinese had given me, and the one I had taken from Hook. I had fired one shot; that would leave me eleven still to use—unless one of the weapons had been used since it was loaded. I broke the gun Tai had given me, and in the dark ran my fingers across the back of the cylinder. My fingers touched *one* shell—under the hammer. Tai had taken no chances; he had given me one bullet—the bullet with which I had dropped Hook.

I put that gun down on the floor, and examined the one I

had taken from Hook. It was *empty*. The Chinese had taken no chances at all! He had emptied Hook's gun before returning it to him after their quarrel.

I was in a hole! Alone, unarmed, in a strange house that would presently hold two who were hunting me—and that one of them was a woman didn't soothe me any—she was none the less deadly on that account.

For a moment I was tempted to make a dash for it; the thought of being out in the street again was pleasant; but I put the idea away. That would be foolishness, and plenty of it. Then I remembered the bonds under my arm. They would have to be my weapon; and if they were to serve me, they would have to be concealed.

I slipped out of my triangular shadow and went up the stairs. Thanks to the street lights, the upstairs rooms were not too dark for me to move around. Around and around I went through the rooms, hunting for a place to hide the Liberty Bonds.

But when suddenly a window rattled, as if from the draught created by the opening of an outside door somewhere, I still had the loot in my hands.

There was nothing to do now but to chuck them out of a window and trust to luck. I grabbed a pillow from a bed, stripped off the white case, and dumped the bonds into it. Then I leaned out of an already open window and looked down into the night, searching for a desirable dumping place: I didn't want the bonds to land on an ash-can or a pile of bottles, or anything that would make a racket.

And, looking out of the window, I found a better hiding-place. The window opened into a narrow court, on the other side of which was a house of the same sort as the one I was

in. That house was of the same height as this one, with a flat
tin roof that sloped down the other way. The roof wasn't far
from me—not too far to chuck the pillow-case. I chucked it.
It disappeared over the edge of the roof and crackled softly
on the tin.

If I had been a movie actor or something of the sort, I suppose
I'd have followed the bonds; I suppose I'd have jumped from
the sill, caught the edge of the roof with my fingers, swung a
while, and then pulled myself up and away. But dangling in
space doesn't appeal to me; I preferred to face the Chinese and
the red-head.

Then I did another not at all heroic thing. I turned on all
the lights in the room, lighted a cigarette (we all like to pose
a little now and then), and sat down on the bed to await my
capture. I might have stalked my enemies through the dark
house, and possibly have nabbed them; but most likely I would
simply have succeeded in getting myself shot. And I don't like
to be shot.

The girl found me.

She came creeping up the hall, an automatic in each hand,
hesitated for an instant outside the door, and then came in on
the jump. And when she saw me sitting peacefully on the side
of the bed, her eyes snapped scornfully at me, as if I had done
something mean. I suppose she thought I should have given
her an opportunity to put lead in me.

"I got him, Tai," she called, and the Chinese joined us.

"What did Hook do with the bonds?" he asked point blank.

I grinned into his round yellow face and led my ace.

"Why don't you ask the girl?"

His face showed nothing, but I imagined that his fat body

stiffened a little within its fashionable British clothing. That encouraged me, and I went on with my little lie that was meant to stir things up.

"Haven't you rapped to it," I asked; "that they were fixing up to ditch you?"

"You dirty liar!" the girl screamed, and took a step toward me.

Tai halted her with an imperative gesture. He stared through her with his opaque black eyes, and as he stared the blood slid out of her face. She had this fat yellow man on her string, right enough, but he wasn't exactly a harmless toy.

"So that's how it is?" he said slowly, to no one in particular. "So that's how it is?" Then to me: "Where did they put the bonds?"

The girl went close to him and her words came out tumbling over each other:

"Here's the truth of it, Tai, so help me God! I switched the stuff myself. Hook wasn't in it. I was going to run out on both of you. I stuck them under the couch downstairs, but they're not there now. That's the God's truth!"

He was eager to believe her, and her words had the ring of truth to them. And I knew that—in love with her as he was— he'd more readily forgive her treachery with the bonds than he would forgive her for planning to run off with Hook; so I made haste to stir things up again. The old timer who said *"Divide to conquer,"* or something of the sort, knew what he was talking about.

"Part of that is right enough," I said. "She did stick the bonds under the couch—but Hook was in on it. They fixed it up between them while you were upstairs. He was to pick a fight with you, and during the argument she was to make the switch, and that is exactly what they did."

I had him!

As she wheeled savagely toward me, he stuck the muzzle of an automatic in her side—a smart jab that checked the angry words she was hurling at me.

"I'll take your guns, Elvira," he said, and took them.

There was a purring deadliness in his voice that made her surrender them without a word.

"Where are the bonds now?" he asked me.

I grinned.

"I'm not with you, Tai. I'm against you."

He studied me with his little eyes that were like black seeds for a while, and I studied him; and I hoped that his studying was as fruitless as mine.

"I don't like violence," he said slowly, "and I believe you are a sensible person. Let us traffic, my friend."

"You name it," I suggested.

"Gladly! As a basis for our bargaining, we will stipulate that you have hidden the bonds where they cannot be found by anyone else; and that I have you completely in my power, as the shilling shockers used to have it."

"Reasonable enough," I said, "go on."

"The situation, then, is what gamblers call a standoff. Neither of us has the advantage. As a detective, you want us; but we have you. As thieves, we want the bonds; but you have them. I offer you the girl in exchange for the bonds, and that seems to me an equitable offer. It will give me the bonds and a chance to get away. It will give you no small degree of success in your task as a detective. Hook is dead. You will have the girl. All that will remain is to find me and the bonds again—by no means a hopeless task. You will have turned a defeat into more than half of a victory, with an excellent chance to make it a complete one."

"How do I know that you'll give me the girl?"

He shrugged.

"Naturally, there can be no guarantee. But, knowing that she planned to desert me for the swine who lies dead below, you can't imagine that my feelings for her are the most friendly. Too, if I take her with me, she will want a share in the loot."

I turned the lay-out over in my mind, and looked at it from this side and that and the other.

"This is the way it looks to me," I told him at last. "You aren't a killer. I'll come through alive no matter what happens. All right; why should I swap? You and the girl will be easier to find again than the bonds, and they are the most important part of the job anyway. I'll hold on to them, and take my chances on finding you folks again. Yes, I'm playing it safe."

And I meant it, for the time being, at least.

"No, I'm not a killer," he said, very softly; and he smiled the first smile I had seen on his face. It wasn't a pleasant smile: and there was something in it that made you want to shudder. "But I am other things, perhaps, of which you haven't thought. But this talking is to no purpose. Elvira!"

The girl, who had been standing a little to one side, watching us, came obediently forward.

"You will find sheets in one of the bureau drawers," he told her. "Tear one or two of them into strips strong enough to tie up your friend securely."

The girl went to the bureau. I wrinkled my head, trying to find a not too disagreeable answer to the question in my mind.

The answer that came first wasn't nice: *torture.*

Then a faint sound brought us all into tense motionlessness.

The room we were in had two doors: one leading into the hall, the other into another bedroom. It was through the hall door that the faint sound had come—the sound of creeping feet.

Swiftly, silently, Tai moved backward to a position from which he could watch the hall door without losing sight of the girl and me—and the gun poised like a live thing in his fat hand was all the warning we needed to make no noise.

The faint sound again, just outside the door.

The gun in Tai's hand seemed to quiver with eagerness.

Through the other door—the door that gave to the next room—popped Mrs. Quarre, an enormous cocked revolver in her thin hand.

"Let go it, you nasty heathen," she screeched.

Tai dropped his pistol before he turned to face her, and he held his hands up high—all of which was very wise.

Thomas Quarre came through the hall door then; he also held a cocked revolver—the mate of his wife's—though, in front of his bulk, his didn't look so enormously large.

I looked at the old woman again, and found little of the friendly fragile one who had poured tea and chatted about the neighbors. This was a witch if there ever was one—a witch of the blackest, most malignant sort. Her little faded eyes were sharp with ferocity, her withered lips were taut in a wolfish snarl, and her thin body fairly quivered with hate.

"I knew it," she was shrilling. "I told Tom as soon as we got far enough away to think things over. I knew it was a frame-up! I knew this supposed detective was a pal of yours! I knew it was just a scheme to beat Thomas and me out of our shares! Well, I'll show you, you yellow monkey! And the rest of you too! I'll show the whole caboodle of you! Where are them bonds? Where are they?"

The Chinese had recovered his poise, if he had ever lost it.

"Our stout friend can tell you perhaps," he said. "I was about to extract the information from him when you so—ah—dramatically arrived."

"Thomas, for goodness sakes don't stand there dreaming," she snapped at her husband, who to all appearances was still the same mild old man who had given me an excellent cigar. "Tie up this Chinaman! I don't trust him an inch, and I won't feel easy until he's tied up. Tie him, up, and then we'll see what's to be done."

I got up from my seat on the side of the bed, and moved cautiously to a spot that I thought would be out of the line of fire if the thing I expected happened.

Tai had dropped the gun that had been in his hand, but he hadn't been searched. The Chinese are a thorough people; if one of them carries a gun at all, he usually carries two or three or more. (I remember picking up one in Oakland during the last tong war, who had five on him—one under each armpit, one on each hip, and one in his waistband.) One gun had been taken from Tai, and if they tried to truss him up without frisking him, there was likely to be fireworks. So I moved off to one side.

Fat Thomas Quarre went phlegmatically up to the Chinese to carry out his wife's orders—and bungled the job perfectly.

He put his bulk between Tai and the old woman's gun.

Tai's hands moved.

An automatic was in each.

Once more Tai ran true to racial form. When a Chinese shoots, he keeps on shooting until his gun is empty.

When I yanked Tai over backward by his fat throat, and slammed him to the floor, his guns were still barking metal; and they clicked empty as I got a knee on one of his arms. I didn't take any chances. I worked on his throat until his eyes and tongue told me that he was out of things for a while.

Then I looked around.

Thomas Quarre was huddled against the bed, plainly dead, with three round holes in his starched white vest—holes that were brown from the closeness of the gun that had put them there.

Across the room, Mrs. Quarre lay on her back. Her clothes had somehow settled in place around her fragile body, and death had given her once more the gentle friendly look she had worn when I first saw her. One thin hand was on her bosom, covering, I found later, the two bullet-holes that were there.

The red-haired girl Elvira was gone.

Presently Tai stirred, and, after taking another gun from his clothes, I helped him sit up. He stroked his bruised throat with one fat hand, and looked coolly around the room.

"So this is how it came out?" he said.

"Uh-huh!"

"Where's Elvira?"

"Got away—for the time being."

He shrugged.

"Well, you can call it a decidedly successful operation. The Quarres and Hook dead; the bonds and I in your hands."

"Not so bad," I admitted, "but will you do me a favor?"

"If I may."

"Tell me what the hell this is all about!"

"All about?" he asked.

"Exactly! From what you people have let me overhear, I gather that you pulled some sort of job in Los Angeles that netted you a hundred-thousand-dollars' worth of Liberty Bonds; but I can't remember any recent job of that size down there."

"Why, that's preposterous!" he said with what, for him, was almost wild-eyed amazement. "Preposterous! Of course you know all about it!"

"I do not! I was trying to find a young fellow named Fisher who left his Tacoma home in anger a week or two ago. His father wants him found on the quiet, so that he can come down and try to talk him into going home again. I was told that I might find Fisher in this block of Turk Street, and that's what brought me here."

He didn't believe me. He never believed me. He went to the gallows thinking me a liar.

When I got out into the street again (and Turk Street was a lovely place when I came free into it after my evening in that house!) I bought a newspaper that told me most of what I wanted to know.

A boy of twenty—a messenger in the employ of a Los Angeles stock and bond house—had disappeared two days before, while on his way to a bank with a wad of Liberty Bonds. That same night this boy and a slender girl with bobbed red hair had registered at a hotel in Fresno as *J.M. Riordan and wife*. The next morning the boy had been found in his room—murdered. The girl was gone. The bonds were gone.

That much the paper told me. During the next few days, digging up a little here and a little there, I succeeded in piecing together most of the story.

The Chinese—whose full name was Tai Choon Tau—had been the brains of the mob. Their game had been a variation of the always-reliable badger game. Tai selected the victims, and he must have been a good judge of humans, for he seems never to have picked a bloomer. He would pick out some youth who was messenger or runner for a banker or broker—one who carried either cash or negotiable securities in large quantities around the city.

The girl Elvira would then *make* this lad, get him all fussed up over her—which shouldn't have been very hard for her—and then lead him gently around to running away with her and whatever he could grab in the way of his employer's bonds or currency.

Wherever they spent the first night of their flight, there Hook would appear—foaming at the mouth and loaded for bear. The girl would plead and tear her hair and so forth, trying to keep Hook—in his rôle of irate husband—from butchering the youth. Finally she would succeed, and in the end the youth would find himself without either girl or the fruits of his thievery.

Sometimes he had surrendered to the police. Two we found had committed suicide. The Los Angeles lad had been built of tougher stuff than the others. He had put up a fight, and Hook had had to kill him. You can measure the girl's skill in her end of the game by the fact that not one of the half dozen youths who had been trimmed had said the least thing to implicate her; and some of them had gone to great trouble to keep her out of it.

The house in Turk Street had been the mob's retreat, and, that it might be always a safe one, they had not worked their game in San Francisco. Hook and the girl were supposed by the neighbors to be the Quarres' son and daughter—and Tai was the Chinese cook. The Quarres' benign and respectable appearances had also come in handy when the mob had securities to be disposed of.

The Chinese went to the gallows. We threw out the widest and finest-meshed of drag-nets for the red-haired girl; and we turned up girls with bobbed red hair by the scores. But the girl Elvira was not among them.

I promised myself that some day....

THE OCTOPUS OF HONG KONG

Loring Brent

The most mysterious and dangerous woman in
China challenges Peter the Brazen in a deadly game

1

MYSTERIOUS MESSAGE

WHEN THE SWIRLING warm waters of the Canton River meet the cold incoming tide of the China Sea in Lyeemoon Pass, the city of Hong Kong vanishes into fog. Streets become tunnels of wet gray vapor which cling to window panes, trail pedestrians and rickshaws in ghostly plumes, change street lamps to sickly glowing pearls, and give that fabulous Oriental metropolis a quickening sense of mystery.

Thieves and footpads creep into the streets, bold as wharf-rats. Familiar objects become strange and sinister in the damp gray shroud of fog at nightfall. Familiar sounds are amplified or dimmed. The whistles of steamers feeling their way into or out of the harbor are far-off melancholy mooings—the muffled bellowings of lost souls. The very gurgling of the water along Connaught Road, which is the bund of Hong Kong, takes on a sinister meaning.

Peter stared in fascinated disbelief.

On this evening, the business life of "The Pearl of the Orient" was drawing to a close, and the gay life of a Hong Kong night was beginning. American and British bars, snug and warmly aglow, resounded to the merry clatter of cocktail shakers, of voices already a little boisterous.

In the native quarters, iron shutters were raised, cooking smells mingled with the fumes of incense from brooding temples and the more acrid pungence of smoldering spicewood from the braziers of closing bazaars. And China proceeded about her mysterious nighttime affairs.

The weird harmonics of a stringed instrument, plucked by the chilled fingers of a Burmese beggar, twanged across the velvety refrain of the latest American foxtrot played by the Colony Hotel's orchestra—smartest hotel, smartest orchestra in Hong Kong; the West meeting the East on the common

"Banish them! Make slaves of them!" Susan cried regally.

ground of music, meeting but never blending.

The sensitive ears of the tall young American who emerged from the waterfront offices of a trans-Pacific steamship agency singled out the foxtrot through the twanging of the lute. He tucked into an inner pocket a pair of steamship tickets, snapped up the collar of his raincoat against the damp chill, and strode through the fog toward the Colonial, whistling.

He was unquestionably the happiest man in Hong Kong tonight. Tomorrow he was marrying a girl who, in his opinion, was not only the most beautiful girl in the world, but the most charming and the gayest. He had reserved the best suite on the *King of Asia* which, at noon, would up anchor and away to America. And the honeymoon of Mr. and Mrs. Peter Moore would have begun!

He was happy on a number of grounds. To marry the most attractive girl on earth, to return to America was enough. But there were other reasons. Tonight was his last night in the seething, tumultuous Republic of China. He was through with China forever; its intrigues, its dark and sinister lure. China was in his blood, in his very attitude toward life. It was time to go. A married man had no business in China. And Peter Moore had been an expatriate long enough. On to America! Home!

Phantoms slithered past him on the wet sidewalk. Rickshaw boys clip-clopped past him on the thin, muddy slime on the cobblestones. Their measured strides ticked out a refrain, repeated it over and over, made it ring above the velvety strains of the Colonial orchestra, the weird melody of the Burmese lute. Go-ing home! Go-ing home!

One of the phantoms brushed the American's shoulder, almost bumped him into the gutter. But this one did not pass on. He was a tall, thin figure in gray, as gray as the very fog. A gray hood cloaked all of his face but the eyes, which peered at the American, bright as a snake's. He might have been a passenger on the grisly craft that crosses the River of the Dead.

Not a beggar. The gray cloth was of too fine a texture for a beggar. The eyes danced over the American's face and a thin, whispery voice uttered in the tongue of North China:

"Those who know do not tell, and those who tell do not know."

Peter Moore gave a slight start. That ancient saying of China's wisest philosopher had once, far in the hazy past, had a dangerous significance. But the actual significance, the time, the place, the occasion evaded him. It recalled suddenly the blaze of an equatorial sun, the whispering of palms, the beating of long, slow waves on a white beach.

The apparition whispered, "I will meet you in your hotel

room in precisely ten minutes. It is of the utmost urgency. Leave word that I am to be admitted."

"Wait a minute! *Hai-yah!*" the American called. But the gray ghost had vanished into the fog.

"This," Peter Moore addressed himself, "is damned nonsense." It was a dream in the mist. And yet the man in gray had been there, his voice had been as actual as the sidewalk.

UNEASILY, THE AMERICAN wondered what this might portend. He was sure he had cut off his past as if with a knife. Was this voice from a vague niche of that past—a ghostly tendril linking him with some forgotten obligation, some unfilled threat?

"Those who know do not tell, and those who tell do not know." What was the rest of it? "By many words, luck is exhausted. A little stream if not stopped may become a great ocean."

He was perplexed and a little worried. He walked slowly the rest of the way to the Colony, trying to spur a hazy memory. At the desk he hesitated. He left word that a Chinese caller was to be sent to his room.

He took the elevator to the seventh floor, proceeded down a wide corridor and let himself into his room. He locked the door, opened a handbag and removed from it a blue Smith & Wesson .38 revolver. He loaded it, unlocked the door, left it fully ajar and waited.

Without key to the identity of the man in gray, but highly suspicious, he was taking no chances. Tonight was his last night in China. And he was determined that it would be his last night in China. No forgotten old episode of the past would enchain him!

He heard felt soles padding down the maroon carpet runner and slipped behind the door. The deadened footsteps hesitated, turned into his room.

Peter Moore slipped out from behind the door, held the revolver on his unknown caller, and shut the door.

In the bright light of Mazdas, the gray cloak proved to be waterproof, finely-woven Shantung.

The unknown pulled off the cape, revealing to Moore the head and face of a Chinese some sixty years of age, gray, gaunt, unsmiling. Only the lively eyes possessed youth. Green-black, they glowed and gleamed.

The gray, gaunt, unsmiling face was unfamiliar.

"Master," the old man said, "I come to serve, not to harm."

Peter Moore had lowered the revolver.

The old Chinese said, "You do not know me, master." The green-black eyes were sparkling now. "But you have become, in the house of my heart, the most welcome of all guests. You do not recall what happened in Saigon?"

Moore said cautiously, "Many things have happened in Saigon."

"You saved the life of my oldest son in the Temple of the Nine Hundred and Seventy-Four Winged Serpents. He was left there to die of cobra bite. You tricked him away from his enemies. You hurried with him to the French Hospital. You imperiled your life to save his!"

"His name," Moore said quickly, "is Chay Gah."

"Mine is Chay Quon. I am your slave. I come here at greatest personal risk to give you a warning. My life, the life of my sons and my little grandsons are endangered by this rash visit. I can, with honor, say only this: Your betrothed is in danger. You will meet with bitter disappointment unless you act swiftly."

Chay Quon had backed to the door. His hand fumbled for and found the knob. His other hand had disappeared into the folds of the gray Shantung robe. It appeared again. The yellow, clawlike fingers clutched a thin white object that softly glowed.

"Take this," Chay Quon said. "It is the key to no riddle, but it may assist you out of peculiar troubles—if you are the man you were."

He thrust the slender white object into Moore's hand, opened the door and departed.

Somewhat bewildered, the American adventurer did not move for a moment. He looked at the white object. It was a phial of white, translucent jade. The contents appeared to be lavender or purple. It meant less than nothing, at present, to him. He dropped it into his pocket and yanked open the door.

He shouted: "Chay Quon!"

The clanging of an elevator door answered him. The corridor was empty. Chay Quon was gone, leaving behind him the very aroma of ominous mystery.

2

"WASHED UP!"

MOORE CLOSED THE door and started across the room with the intention of returning the revolver to the handbag. Thinking better of it, he dropped the weapon into a hip pocket.

Versed as he was in the deviousness of the Oriental mind,

he did not know quite what to make of Chay Quon's visit. Moore's fiancée, Susan O'Gilvie, was having dinner tonight at the Luxor with two young women of her acquaintance, an old friend and a new one—Jane Henderson and Marcia Pool. Moore and Miss O'Gilvie had agreed to spend this, their last unmarried evening, separately. After tonight they would never be parted—not for a single hour! They had agreed that she was to dine with Miss Henderson and Marcia Pool, while he was to dine with Marcia Pool's fiancé, Terry Teeple, an amusing young American who was the wireless operator on the ship on which Miss Pool had just arrived in Hong Kong.

What Chay Quon had said perplexed and worried Moore. He would go to the Luxor, make sure that Susan was safe and spend the evening, not with Terry Teeple, but in taking steps that no harm befell her.

The head waiter had once been the steward of a ship on which Moore had made a run as wireless operator.

Moore went to the fashionable night club. It was crowded, but he did not see Susan O'Gilvie or Jane Henderson.

The head waiter came over to him. "Alone tonight, Mr. Moore?"

Moore said that he was looking for Miss O'Gilvie. "I don't see her here. She made a reservation for a table for this evening."

"When did Miss O'Gilvie make the reservation?"

"This morning. She phoned."

"I don't recall it, Mr. Moore."

"That's queer. Perhaps I've made a mistake." But he hadn't made a mistake, and it wasn't, in light of other minor things, quite so queer as it might have been.

Somewhat grimly the young man returned to Queen's Road,

hailed a rickshaw and directed the coolie to the Henderson mansion, on Upper Elbert Road, near Government House.

Reaching the Hendersons', he told the coolie to wait, ran up the steps and rang the bell. The Hendersons' English butler opened the door. Moore asked him if Miss Henderson was home.

"No, sir."

"Do you know where she's dining?"

"Yes, sir. She is attending a dinner dance at the Recourse Bay Hotel, with Captain Mac Alister."

"Has Miss O'Gilvie been here?"

"No, sir."

Moore thanked him and returned to the rickshaw. Why had Susan lied to him? He was uneasy. It was unlike her to lie, to practice deceit in any form. Rather, it had been, until very recently, unlike her. She was frank, honest, sincere to a fault. A girl with her type of courage never resorted to lies or deceit. Yet, in the past few days, he had discovered her in a number of petty lies and little deceits.

Under ordinary circumstances he would have suspected that Susan was up to some mischief. She was a thrill-hunter. Yet he was sure that she was now as anxious to leave China and its intrigues forever as was he. Her recent nervousness and evasiveness he had supposed was natural in a girl soon to be married. But that hardly explained her small lies and petty deceits.

He dismissed the rickshaw at the Colonial and went directly to Susan's suite. He was about to knock when he heard the murmur of voices. He hesitated, then knocked.

THERE WAS A delay of perhaps ten seconds before the door was opened. Susan opened it. She was charming, beautiful in a negligee of orchid. She looked strange. She looked excited. Her eyes were brilliant, the pupils dilated. Her cheeks were feverishly flushed. Her lips had a bright, feverish look.

He was conscious, as he anxiously regarded her, of two distinct scents—the delicate French perfume she used, and an exotic spiciness, not incense, not perfume; a heady smell, a somehow sinister aroma.

She did not fly into his arms. Her eyes, which were not blue but a deep, lovely violet, stared at him almost wildly, as if he were a stranger, as if she were terrified. But he knew that the brilliance in them was anger.

Susan said in a vexed voice, "What do you want?"

He could have been no more surprised if she had slapped him.

"Good Lord, Susan," he said. "What's wrong? You said you were dining with Jane Henderson and Marcia Pool at the Luxor."

"I changed my mind." She was staring at him with defiance. And he suddenly had a strange feeling, a feeling almost mystical; that Susan was gone, that she had slipped away from him forever, that in her place was a strange, soulless woman.

"Who's here?" he asked.

"No one," she answered, in the same defiant voice.

"I could have sworn I heard voices."

"You're mistaken, Peter. I—I wanted to be alone."

"You didn't want to kiss me."

"Not now. Please go."

It didn't quite come off. This wasn't mere nervousness. There was trouble. It was that exotic, spicy aroma.

He said grimly, "Let me in."

Susan stood her ground a moment, then stepped aside. Peter Moore went into the room. It was the parlor of her suite. The spicy smell was stronger. He sniffed it and said, "What is it?"

"I don't know what you're talking about, Peter."

He looked at her, troubled. Lying again. He wanted to take her into his arms, to smash down this barrier, whatever it was, that had come between them. Susan was small, slim, dark-haired. Her size had deceived him before.

"Susan," he said gravely, "you're lying to me. You're up to mischief."

She had not closed the door; was still standing on the threshold, with arms folded on breast, chin up, eyes strangely brilliant.

He asked, in a somewhat shaken voice, "Where's Marcia Pool?"

"I'm sure I don't know."

"But you had a dinner engagement with her, if not with Jane Henderson. I heard you ask her this noon at lunch if she would have dinner with you tonight. You'll have to admit this is pretty mysterious. What happened?"

"Am I responsible for her?" Susan cried angrily.

Moore shook his head with a baffled air. "I don't understand you, Susan. In a way, it seems to me you are responsible for her. You know China. She doesn't."

"She got away from me," Susan said sullenly.

Moore's blue eyes sharpened. "What do you mean?"

"We did start out for dinner," Susan replied, still with that sullen air. "We took rickshaws."

"To the Luxor?" Moore interrupted in a surprised voice.

"We changed our minds. We decided we wanted to have a real Chinese dinner. We were going to the native quarter. We were going along Tung Road when she suddenly stopped her rickshaw and jumped out. She'd seen some one she knew—an old friend."

"A man or a woman?"

"A man. I think it was an old beau. I don't know. And she yelled at me to go on without her."

MOORE STARED AT Susan O'Gilvie. "That doesn't sound like Marcia Pool," he said. He did not, to be sure, know Marcia Pool very well. He had known her only a couple of days. She was a charming, delightful blond girl of about twenty— very much in love with tall, dark Terry Teeple.

"Naturally," Susan said, "I was furious. After all, we did have a date. And when she dashed off like that—"

"Susan," Peter said firmly, "you're lying again. What happened to Marcia Pool?"

"I told you!" Susan cried. "She saw this man—"

"Nonsense. You're making it up as you go along. You broke your date with her, didn't you? You didn't see her at all this evening, did you?"

"Have it your way," Susan said stonily.

Moore shook his head. "It—it's pretty puzzling," he said. "You—you've changed so. Something is going on that you're not telling me about. Don't you want to talk things over? If I've done anything to offend you—"

"I have no desire to talk anything over."

"But can't you tell me what's going on? When I came to this door a moment ago, I'll swear I heard voices. All this—this subterfuge, all these deceptions—"

She cried, "How dare you spy on me?"

"Good Lord, Susan, I wasn't spying. I was worried. I wanted to make sure everything was all right. An old friend told me there was trouble brewing. He said you were in danger."

As if she had not heard, she said angrily, "You were spying! I'm sick of you!" She licked her bright, dry lips. "You—you fortune hunter!" she cried.

Peter's face went grim and white. Then the crimson of anger mounted into it. It had always been a bone of contention between them, that fabulous fortune of hers, but never before in this sense.

Susan, for two years, had maintained that she was too modern, too sensible, to let love slip by when she was sure she had found it, and that in Peter Moore she had found the one man she could ever love. Until very recently he had stubbornly refused to marry her because of her great fortune. The problem had finally been solved to their mutual satisfaction. They were to live entirely on his income, to touch none of her own.

He said, feebly, "Susan, you're joking, aren't you?"

"Am I?" she cried. "Look at me!"

He was looking at her. And again, he was swept by the feeling that this girl who faced him was a stranger. She had often been angry at him. She had flown into rages. But she had never, at her angriest moments, lost her charm. He had the feeling of mysterious, dangerous fires. She had suddenly become a haughty little princess.

He went to the door and said quietly, "Okay, Susan. The wedding bells are off."

He hesitated. It was very much like a nightmare. In the

two years he had known Susan they had shared adventures, dangers, hardships and fine, exalted moments. He knew her only for a charming, delightful, generous gay companion whose only fault was an insatiable thirst for adventurous thrills. He presumed now that she had found an adventure more desirable than himself.

There was no relenting in her eyes. They remained brilliant, hard.

AS HE STARTED down the hall he heard her door close with a sharp click. He hesitated, went on. He was too hurt, too angry, too baffled to think clearly. He went to his room and tried to think it out. He dismissed the theory that he might have done something to offend her.

He gave way briefly to fury. He told himself that she wasn't, never had been worth it. And he knew he was lying to himself. She was worth it. She was the most charming, most attractive, the most lovable girl he had ever known.

And it suddenly occurred to Peter that he had been a blind, stupid fool. She was in danger! They had been through so many scrapes. She knew the ropes. There had been some one, a dangerous enemy, hiding in the room, prepared to shoot him if she had not done precisely as she was instructed!

It was the only logical explanation for her sudden, complete reversal of character. She had not dared warn him; had trusted to his cleverness to guess the truth, to save her from some unimaginable danger. That explained the murmurs he had heard. That explained her startling change toward him.

He was running down the hall. He passed the elevators, ran to the stairs and took them three at a bound. At her door, he paused and listened. He heard nothing. He decided against knocking and tried the knob. The door was unlocked.

With revolver ready he threw open the door.

The parlor was empty. He tiptoed to the bedroom door, threw it open. The bedroom was empty. The bathroom door was open, the lights were burning. Both rooms showed evidences of Susan's hasty departure. The dresser drawers were pulled out. A powder puff and a few dark hairpins were scattered across the dresser. Otherwise, everything she possessed was gone. She had evidently dressed the instant he had left, had packed and gone!

Where? Why? What had happened?

He stared about the abandoned bedroom with a sickly thumping heart. His guess had been wrong. She hadn't been in danger. She had meant what she had said.

Peter Moore saw, at that instant, his image in the long French mirror on the back of the bathroom door. He saw a tall young man with rumpled blond hair, stricken eyes, ashen face. He looked pretty awful. He felt pretty awful. He could not believe that Susan meant what she had said. Only yesterday she had impulsively thrown her arms about his neck, clasped him tight, and told him how deliriously happy she was. They were, at last, to be married! Wasn't it wonderful?

Or had it been the day before yesterday? When had the change in her begun? A man in love is apt to be blind.

He felt sick. He thought of the steamship tickets in his pocket. Well, that was off. Everything was off.

He was suddenly aware of the perfume she used. A faint breath of it lingered in the air, made her seem vividly near.

The face in the French mirror was no longer gray but darkly red. Peter Moore gave his reflection a hard, bitter grin. Jilted!

HE WAS ABOUT to leave the room when his attention was attracted by the glint of light on metal or glass under the bedside table. He bent down and picked up a small empty phial of carved crystal with a carved kingfisher jade stopper. No more than a drop of thick, purple liquid remained in the bottle. He pulled out the stopper and sniffed it. And the smell which rose sweetly, spicily into his nostrils was the same that he had detected in the air on his earlier visit.

He held the phial to a light and, with narrow, dreamy eyes, inhaled the exotic fragrance again. Then he took from his pocket the jade phial Chay Quon had given him. He removed the stopper and sniffed the purple contents. It was the same sweet, spicy stuff! Unquestionably, it was a drug, some potent Oriental concoction, more sinister in its fragrance alone than opium!

Peter rejected the impulse to taste the stuff. He had had experience with Oriental drugs.

He placed both phials in his pocket and returned to his room. He tried to think clearly. There was no question in his mind that Susan, on the very eve of their marriage, had fallen under the power of some sinister influence. He had, in the past, helped her escape from a number of dangerous predicaments, but on those occasions he had had Susan's cooperation. Now she was his enemy.

His mind flashed back to some of their past adventures. Their most dangerous enemy had been Mr. Lu, the monstrous genius who lived in a marble palace at the bottom of the Lake of the Flying Dragon in the cobalt mountains of Szechwan. In Annam, a few weeks ago, Peter had succeeded in destroying Mr. Lu's vast power, and had, he believed, killed that mythological figure.

This, he was certain, was not the work of that fantastic giant with the jade brain.

There was a knock at his door. He opened it. A Chinese boy handed him an envelope. In one end of it he felt a small, hard lump. The envelope was addressed to him in Susan's vigorous handwriting. He tore it open. The small hard lump proved to be the emerald engagement ring he had given her. The note was brief.

Dear Peter:

We are absolutely washed up. I mean it.

Susan.

That was all. He was staring grimly at the ring when a sudden explosive shattering of glass occurred at the window. The lower pane had been burst. He flattened himself back against the wall and watched the jagged hole. His room was six stories from the street, four from the roof. There was nothing beyond the window but swirling gray fog.

As he stared, a small white-and-red object fluttered in through the jagged aperture.

It was the creamy petal of a flower. He bent down and picked it up. It was a lotus petal, one end of which was dripping with blood!

3

INTO THIN AIR

MYSTIFIED, PETER EXAMINED the lotus petal for a mark, a symbol of some kind. Finding none, he placed the blood-dipped petal in the envelope with Susan's note and returned the envelope to his pocket. The lotus petal was, presumably, a warning. Presumably, it implied, according to his knowledge of China and its devious methods, that he was to keep his distance. But from whom or what?

The warning, so delicately conveyed, helped to clear and crystallize his thoughts. It was no longer a question of hurt pride, of being jilted on the eve of his marriage. Susan's very attitude was a cloud over the issue, a cloud cleverly devised by Susan's—his—latest enemy.

His job was clear-cut: he must remove Susan from an ingenious, diabolical influence before both their lives were ruined.

Peter descended to the lobby and made inquiries. Miss O'Gilvie, he learned at the desk, had paid her bill and checked out. At the mail desk he learned that she had left no forwarding address. And from the Sikh doorman he learned that Miss O'Gilvie had left in a black sedan chair.

"A public chair?"

"No, *sahib;* a private one."

"Numbered?"

"I saw no number, *sahib.*"

"Did you recognize it?"

"No, *sahib;* it was a strange chair."

That was that. Susan had been called for. A strange sedan chair had spirited her—to what fantastic fate? At all events, the trail was broken.

He watched the tide of vehicles in the street for a moment—wraiths emerging from and vanishing into the sea of fog. Rickshaws, sedan chairs, wheelbarrows with enormous wheels, each having for a cargo a fat, prosperous-looking Chinese. Always fat, always prosperous.

He returned to his room. He wanted to inspect the broken window, to attempt, if possible, to pick up this other trail.

Moore was half out the window, staring upward into fogbound darkness, when his door burst open and a young man's voice cried, "Hey, Mr. Moore! What's going on, anyhow?"

Moore backed out of the window and into the room. A pair of sparkling black eyes in a flushed, handsome young face stared at him. Terry Teeple was a tall man of about twenty-four, with thick, curly black hair.

"I've been waiting down there in the bar for an hour," Teeple said. "Anything wrong?"

"Yes. Plenty." Moore told him briefly of Susan O'Gilvie's strange behavior, her disappearance, and showed the wireless operator the lotus blossom.

He had hardly concluded his account when Teeple interrupted with, "Where's Marcia?"

Moore told him what Susan had said. The sparkle left the young man's eyes. His face became grave.

"That's funny," he said. "It doesn't sound like Marcia. She doesn't run out on dates. And she's crazy about Miss O'Gilvie—thinks she's wonderful."

Moore said: "I don't believe the story. I don't believe Marcia started out with her. But we'll check it up."

He picked up the phone and called Marcia Pool's room.

When she did not answer, Moore hung up the receiver and said, "Something queer is going on. I'd like to have a look at Marcia's room."

THEY SECURED A pass key from the desk clerk, went to Marcia Pool's room and let themselves in. It was in the condition that a pretty, frivolous young woman like Marcia Pool might have been expected to leave a room in. Clothing was flung over chairs. Powder had been spilled on the dressing table. The air was warm and sweet with the fragrance of bath salts and perfume.

Evidently Marcia Pool had bathed and dressed to go out to dinner in the rush and hurry that seemed characteristic of her.

"She went out to dinner with somebody," Terry Teeple said quietly. He looked sad. "Maybe Miss O'Gilvie was right, after all. Maybe Marsh did meet somebody she knew—an old beau."

Peter was thinking rapidly, wondering where would be the best place to begin looking. He was more worried than he seemed. He was sure that Susan had been lying. He was sure that Marcia Pool had not rudely left her and gone off with some old friend, even an old beau.

But he said briskly, "They may have gone to dinner somewhere in that neighborhood. We'll look-see."

The two young men took rickshaws to Tung Road. It was a narrow, dark little road, with street-lamps widely spaced. There were several native restaurants in the neighborhood, but none of them was the kind of restaurant to which you would take the kind of girl Marcia Pool was.

In the fourth of these dank little eating places Moore found a telephone. He called the hotel and asked for Miss Pool. To his great relief she answered the phone.

Her voice was hysterical.

"Oh, it's Mr. Moore!" she cried. "I've just got back here after a perfectly horrible experience! Have you seen Miss O'Gilvie?"

"Yes."

"Is she all right?"

"I believe so. What happened?"

"We started out for dinner," the hysterical girl said. "We were going to the Luxor, but we changed our minds. Miss O'Gilvie thought it would be more fun to go to a place where we could get real Chinese food. She said we knew just the place.

"We went down Queen's Road—I think that's the road—and turned into a dark little alley. Halfway down the block both our coolies stopped. A horrible looking Chinaman stepped out of the shadow of a building and grabbed my hand. Miss O'Gilvie was on the other side of me—I mean, our rickshaws were stopped side by side.

"When I screamed she grabbed my other hand and said, 'Don't yell! It's all right.' I don't know why she said that. I thought it was terribly mysterious. This—this man was trying to drag me out of my rickshaw. There was a closed sedan chair near him—a dark red one. He said something to me in Chinese—and I hit him in the face. I jerked my hand away from Miss O'Gilvie. I jumped out of my rickshaw—and ran toward Queen's Road.

"But I heard this man after me. I think there were several others. I dashed into a narrow little doorway and hid. They ran on past. I don't know how long I hid there. It seemed ages. I was too terrified to come out. I knew they were looking for me, and I was afraid something had happened to Miss O'Gilvie. But I didn't dare move! I was never so scared or bewildered in my life. And finally, when I was sure they'd gone, I sneaked out and ran every step of the way back to the hotel. I only got in a few minutes ago. Where's Terry?"

"Right here."

"Is he all right?"

"Yep."

"But it's so mysterious," Marcia wailed. "Why did Miss O'Gilvie grab my hand? What was it all about?"

"I'll explain everything when I see you," Moore answered. "Terry and I will be up to your room in about ten minutes. Keep the door locked. Don't let any one in. Understand?"

"Yes. But what on earth is it all about?"

"We'll try to clear things up when I see you."

PETER MOORE HUNG up and turned to Terry Teeple. "She's okay now," Moore said. He told Terry Teeple what Marcia had told him on their way back to the hotel.

At the Colony entrance they paid off their coolies and went to Marcia's room. There was no response to their knocks.

Terry Teeple said, in a shaking, husky voice, "They've got her! They got in there and grabbed her! Who is it?"

"I don't know."

Terry Teeple went down once again for the pass key. The two young men let themselves in. Since their previous visit the scene had drastically changed. The room was now in the greatest disorder. Two chairs had been overturned. The dressing table had been pulled out at one end about a foot from the wall. The rugs showed evidences of a scuffle. But what interested Moore most at the moment was the window. It was open. It was open upon a fire escape.

He went to the window and looked out, up, down. He found a shred of jade-green chiffon dangling in the fog from a sharp point on the fire escape railing.

Terry Teeple identified it. "She was going to wear that green dress tonight," he whispered.

Moore said, "I don't know anything about Marcia Pool. You'd better tell me what you can. Is she wealthy?"

"Her father's a millionaire."

"Where is he?"

"New York."

"She was traveling alone, wasn't she?"

"Yes."

"Did you know her before this trip?"

"No. I met her the day after we left Frisco. Look here, Mr. Moore. You know China like a book. You know how these Hong Kong gangs work. I haven't much money, but I'll guarantee her father will pay any price!"

Peter replied grimly, "This isn't an ordinary kidnaping." He suddenly felt sick. There was no question that Susan was somehow involved in the disappearance of Marcia Pool. That meeting with the Chinese in Tung Road had been, he was sure, a rendezvous. Otherwise, why would Susan have grabbed Marcia's wrist and tried to detain her—and warned her not to yell?

He felt sure that Susan, acting under some one's orders, had attempted to deliver Marcia Pool into the hands of some dangerous and wily Oriental. Moore had, he believed, reached Susan O'Gilvie's room in time to hear her discussing a new plan with some member of the conspiracy—some woman. This new plan had just been executed.

If Susan had been poor it might have been a little easier to understand. But Susan was not poor. She was fabulously wealthy in her own right. Granted that she might have lost her senses through the use of some mysterious drug, why should she take part in any plan involving the kidnaping of another wealthy girl?

No, it was not an ordinary kidnaping.

He began to look about the room carefully, sniffing the air as he moved about. He expected to find a trace of that mysterious scent which, he was now sure, had been Susan's undoing. But he detected no other odor in the room but a faint, springlike fragrance—an old-fashioned fragrance, the one that he had noticed on his former visit here.

"Geranium," he said.

"It's the only kind of perfume Marcia uses," the tall, agitated young wireless operator said.

IN HIS THOROUGH examination of the room—an inch-by-inch search—Peter had reached the dressing table. It was littered with a jumble of toilet implements—gold-backed brushes, a comb, a hand mirror, a manicure set, several dozen small, gold-topped jars and little bottles.

Half-hidden by an edge of the hairbrush, he found what he had been fearing he would eventually find.

It was a note on a sheet of white rice paper, painstakingly written in purple ink.

Mr. Horatio Pool:

Your daughter will die tonight of a thousand tortures in a thousand exquisite agonies. Perhaps you will be sorry now for that night in Yokohama in 1914.

There was no signature, but pinned to the bottom was a lotus petal, one end of which was black with dried blood!

Terry Teeple read it over his shoulder, and burst explosively into a seagoing man's profanity. He was going to crack Chinese skulls and fracture Chinese jawbones until the streets of Hong Kong were knee-deep with his victims.

"It isn't going to be as simple as that," Peter warned him. He removed one of the phials from his pocket and took out the stopper. "Smell this," he said. "Is it familiar?"

"It smells dangerous," Terry Teeple said. "No. It's new to me."

"Are you sure you've never smelled anything like it in Miss Pool's presence?"

"Positive."

"She hasn't acted strangely, or differently, in the past day or two?"

"Not a bit. I saw her less than two hours ago. We had a cocktail at the American bar. I brought her here, kissed her so-long. No, she was just the same."

"You say she was traveling alone?"

"Yes. She was making a trip around the world, and was meeting her brother Gregory in Manila. We became engaged the night before we put in at Yokohama."

"Does she know any one in Hong Kong?"

"Not a soul. Some of her father's old friends live here, but she hasn't looked them up. We've been together practically every waking minute of the time. The *Vandalia* only got in last night."

Peter glanced at the note again. "Was Miss Pool born in China?"

"Yes. In Peking. But her family—her father, mother, an older sister and Gregory moved to New York when Marcia was five, and have lived there since."

"She wouldn't recall any of her father's old friends—or enemies," Peter said thoughtfully. "Has she mentioned any of them?"

"She mentioned a few people he knew in Shanghai and Hong Kong—all old friends. But she didn't look any of them up. We were too busy."

"Know her father's address in New York?"

"No. He has an apartment there and a summer place at Southampton, Long Island."

PETER PICKED UP the telephone. He said to the operator, "Get me Mr. Horatio Pool, in New York City. If he isn't at his apartment try his place at Southampton, Long Island."

While he waited for the call to be put through, Peter looked about the room for further clues. He was still looking without success when the long lines operator advised him that Mr. Pool was on the circuit.

A gruff voice ten thousand miles away said sharply, "Hong Kong? All right, all right. Is it you, Marcia?"

Peter explained himself. At the end of fifteen minutes, at approximately ten dollars a minute, he was still endeavoring to make a frightened, suspicious, angry millionaire in New York understand that his daughter had been stolen from her hotel room in Hong Kong, China, and that only from his lips could the necessary helpful information be obtained.

The connection was good, Mr. Pool's voice was clear, but he was almost hysterical.

Peter said: "Think hard, Mr. Pool. What happened in Yokohama in 1914?"

The frantic father at the other end cried, "Good Lord, man! I was there a dozen times that year. That was the year of the War. Nineteen years ago! A thousand things happened—deals of all sorts. I met countless people under every possible condition."

"Enemies?"

"I've got enough enemies in the Far East to start a war!"

On an inspiration, looking at the note, Peter hazarded: "Does the name Lotus suggest anything?"

The man ten thousand miles away answered: "Hold on! Wait! Let me think! Lotus! Lotus Burma!"

Something clicked in Peter's memory department. Lotus Burma. Shanghai. Some four or five years ago he had seen a Lotus Burma, a fascinating, beautiful Eurasian woman at a party given by a Japanese exporter.

Horatio Pool was saying, "She came to one of our parties that summer in Yokohama—a party in honor of the American Ambassador. She wasn't invited. She insulted Mrs. Pool. I had the servants put her out. Lotus Burma was a notorious woman—one of the richest women in China, an opium fiend."

"That's all for now," Peter said, cutting the hysterical man off. "I'll report later."

He replaced the receiver and turned to Terry Teeple.

"It still doesn't make sense," he said. "The only incident he can recall happening in Yokohama in 1914 concerned a half-caste named Lotus Burma. This Lotus Burma is a hellion—but it doesn't seem to hold water. We'll get busy. Have you a gun?"

"In my room."

"Get it and meet me outside."

4

THE WISE ONE

PETER'S OBJECTIVE WAS the House with the Black Door on Wing Lok Street, a place known among the select as the Mansion of Divine Contentment, and to tourists and most white residents of Hong Kong, known not at all.

A grimy, one-story stone building with corrugated steel shutters at the window, the Mansion of Divine Contentment gave no indication that it led a charmed life.

Peter told the wireless operator to wait. He advanced to the black door, knocked twice, then once, then twice again. The door swung open. An elderly Chinese in the servile blue of the Chinese lower classes peered into his face and said, "Ah, master, it is you!" and stepped aside for Peter to enter.

He went through a labyrinth of rooms and corridors without hesitation, and came at length to a finely polished brass door, carved beautifully and ornamented with laughing lions and sneering tigers. This he opened without ceremony, entering a room with walls of golden silk and an atmosphere of the finest sandalwood incense.

A fat, living Buddha squatted on a teakwood stool in a corner. He was sipping, from a silver goblet, a decoction which Peter recognized as rice gin flavored with whompee juice and pomello seeds.

He stared at Peter with his tiny, shoebutton eyes and set the goblet down with a clink on the mother-o'-pearl taboret beside him.

"By Buddha's toenail," he cried, in a thin squeal of a voice, "I heard, once again, that you had leaped the dragon gate. Clacking tongues in the heads of fools told me you had entered the holy contests for the high priesthood of the temple of the Blue Skull with the Living Brain in Annam, that you locked horns with Lu the unconquerable and were cast to his black leopards for tiffin! You are a man of rubber and steel indeed. How many lives has a cat of your caliber?"

He peered uncertainly at the American adventurer. "I grovel and abase myself in the muck of this miserable room in the presence of your magnificence. I am flattered that a man of your high purposes has crossed the sill of my wretched abode. I am the slave to your bidding. Command!"

"I'm here for some information, Yat Gow," Peter said crisply. "Let's dispense with the formalities."

"O man of many troubles," Yat Gow piped, "in the Taoist heart there is no place where mercy cannot be exercised; in the Taoist brain no corner that is not illuminated with sympathetic wisdom. Command!"

Peter withdrew the full white jade phial from his pocket. He advanced on the fat, flowery Yat Gow with the phial unstoppered, but he held it firmly in the muscles of his fingers.

"Smell!" he said.

But the pudgy little nose of Yat Gow was already working, wriggling like the nose of an excited rabbit.

"By the whiskers of Buddha!" he squealed, making a snatch for the phial. "One thousand Taikwan *taels* for that!"

Peter withdrew it from the range of the fat, clumsy hands and dropped the stopper in place.

"Not for sale," he said. "What is this stuff?"

"It is the drug of sublime joy and utter self-fulfillment and magical power!" Yat Gow cried. "Where did you steal it?"

"Tell me more about it."

"A thousand Taikwan *taels*," Yat Gow cried, "for the name and address of the man from whom you got it!"

"Is it as rare as that?"

"It is rarer than the sixth toe of a dragon! It is rarer than the essence of life! It is rarer than a fleshy appearance of the King Gautama Buddha!"

"What is it?"

"Alas, would I beg for a drop, a merest taste, if I knew what it was? It is a secret. It was lost with the last of the Mings. I tasted it just once. The Grand Eunuch in the household of the Empress Dowager gave me two drops on my tongue years—years ago! In the summer palace, in Peking. I would have given my right and my left eye for two more drops. But the Grand Eunuch was disappointed in the pickled rotten eggs I brought to him. I incurred his disfavor. It was my last taste."

"What was the effect on you?"

"A sense of utter power and dominion, a deadening of my damnable conscience. One loses all sense of scruples. One becomes a superman with not the slightest principles. And one hates magnificently."

"What would be the effect on a lover toward his or her beloved?"

"Beautiful contempt and scorn!"

PETER HAD SUSPECTED as much. But now that his suspicions were confirmed he felt sick and defeated. Susan's strange hostility was now painfully understandable. One taste of this magical stuff and she had become its slave. He could fight through an army of enemies for her, but how could he compete with a drug that turned love to poisonous hate?

Peter returned the phial to his pocket. "Yat Gow," he said, "you are the smartest man in Hong Kong. You see all, know all—"

"—And say nothing," Yat Gow finished complacently. "Yet my brain is a storehouse, a *godown* of riches, at your complete disposal—for five drops of the Drug of Divinity!"

Pete said firmly, "No. You have enough bad habits, with your black smoke and your whompee juice. Isn't it true that this stuff is more responsible than anything else for the downfall of the empire?"

"Who takes that drug," Yat Gow answered, in the manner of a man coining an epigram, "cares not what falls."

"What do you know about Lotus Burma?"

The beady little eyes lost their shimmer and squinted at him steadily out of their folds of fat.

"We gaze vainly at the mountain's brow," Yat Gow answered.

"Yet behind us, like wild horses, come flashing our misdeeds," Peter said threateningly, "prepared to overtake us at the smallest misstep."

"This is more blackmail," Yat Gow sighed. "Let me think a moment. What do you wish to know about Lotus Burma?"

"Is she still a madwoman, with dreams of horrible revenge on those who slighted her in the past?"

"With advancing years," Yat Gow answered, "the capacity

to love diminishes, but the capacity to hate discovers no horizons. You refer to the mysterious lady known as The Octopus."

"Tell me what you can about her."

"*Hai-yah!* What is there to tell? She is beautiful, fascinating—a creature of mystery. The man who has dealings with such as she does well to write a prayer to the lord Gautama Buddha on a scrap of red paper, chew it rapidly and swallow it. Otherwise, his digestive operations may cease entirely—at the source."

"You mean, a slit throat."

"You are too literal, master. I know nothing whatever of Lotus Burma. She is as mysterious as the heart of an opal, as secret as the ways of a serpent. All I can say—" Yat Gow hesitated, made a slashing, complex gesture in the air with one finger—the Chinese symbol for great danger.

"Where is the den of this octopus?"

"Will my judicious answer furnish the key to your riddle?"

"Answer the question, you fat pig," Peter answered. "You are too full of whompee juice and poetry."

Yat Gow lifted hairless brows and pudgy hands in gestures of futility. "The Octopus," he said resignedly, "lives in the great black vulture of a house spraddling the tip of the Peak. You know the house well."

"The house that Lak Chak built?"

"The same. Now," Yat Gow said covetously, "do I merit a drop of the drug—one little drop?"

"Your soul will doubtless rot in a thousand hells," Peter answered, "but you shall have the drop." And he gave Yat Gow the nearly empty phial.

"Dangerous stuff—very dangerous," a low voice said.

Peter wheeled about. A man was standing in the doorway—a tall, thin, dark-skinned man of about forty; a red-haired man who closely resembled a caricature of Satan. He had the sharp, angular features, the V-shaped smile, the cynical, dark eyes. His hair was of a dusky shade of red—it resembled the play of fire in smoke.

Moore grinned, walked over and shot out a hand to clasp the other's. "Dan de Sylva!" he cried.

THIS SATANIC INDIVIDUAL was an old friend, the companion of more than one dangerous adventure. Daniel de Sylva was a gem dealer—the brains, in fact, of the great de Sylva Corporation. He and his agents in the Far East purchased rare gems, sold them to European and American clients at fabulous profits. He lived an exciting, dangerous life. Peter Moore had not seen Dan de Sylva since the completion of a certain little episode in Bangalore, India, about a year previously.

"How long," Peter asked, "have you been standing there?"

"Long enough to realize that two dogs are barking up the tree at the same tiger. My notion is that the two dogs might be blended into one. I happen to be looking for Lotus Burma myself. That's why I came here. I knew that Yat Gow was the one man in Hong Kong who can honestly be described as a two-legged Hong Kong directory. Well—do you want the job, Peter?"

"My plans for getting married tomorrow have been upset," Peter answered. "But I still have hope."

"This job," the Satanic individual said in his low voice, "is a dandy. Pardon us, Yat Gow. All of this will leak into your storebin eventually, anyhow. Listen and learn! Three weeks ago, Peter, one of my most trusted men was robbed of two million dollars' worth of diamonds—Malay water diamonds—in Buitenzorg, Java."

"By Lotus Burma?"

"Now, don't be vulgar, Peter. Does one arm of an octopus know what another arm is doing? You may have gleaned that Lotus Burma is mysterious and dangerous beyond ordinary reckoning. There is a possibility that she knows about the diamonds. And there is a possibility—slight—that she knows my man was murdered. I can't let my men be murdered, Peter. You know that. This matter must be thoroughly investigated by a man who knows his Far East. In brief, you have fairly walked into the job. There's a little ship pulling out at dawn for Buitenzorg. It's a dangerous job. Want it?"

"I intend," Peter answered, "to be sailing for San Francisco at noon tomorrow."

"With a bride on your arm?"

"If my night's work is successful."

"Pardon my curiosity, but is the bride-to-be involved in any way with the eight-armed mystery?"

"Yes."

"Then, knowing you, I can guess that you are paying The Octopus a visit this evening. You might kill two birds with one stone. Bring Lotus Burma back alive! That's all. If you're the man you used to be, you'll deliver her neatly wrapped—if kicking—to my hotel room. All I want is my diamonds—or her life. But I intend to take it myself."

He stopped. Both men looked at Yat Gow. The fat Chinese was convulsed with mirth. His yellow face was pink.

"What's the joke?" Satan asked.

"You have not met The Octopus," Yat Gow explained himself.

"No, but I've seen Peter the Brazen in action," de Sylva said, almost angrily. "Will you help me, Peter?"

"I'll do my best."

"I am staying at the Colony, too. Room eight nineteen. If you don't bring The Hong Kong Octopus back alive, my offer is good all night."

PETER THANKED HIM and returned to Terry Teeple who waited with impatience on Wing Lok Street before the House with the Black Door.

"Are we on the right track?" he eagerly demanded.

"We're on the track," Peter answered, "of the most mysterious and dangerous woman in China—The Octopus. We may be trailed. We'll walk."

They took back alleys to the foot of the great black hill which rises majestically from Hong Kong. The rest of the way was up steep, tortuous mountain trails, carved along precipices by the English in the early years of their occupation of the island.

During pauses for breath, Peter told Terry Teeple what he knew of Lotus Burma and what he knew about the house that Lak Chak built.

"Yat Gow could tell me little about her," Peter said. "She's a woman of mystery. All I know is that she's Eurasian—half white, half yellow. But I think we're rapidly learning why she's called The Octopus."

"If she's got Marcia," Terry Teeple said wrathfully, "I'll wring her damned neck!"

"You'll be lucky to save your own," Peter said. He had little faith in the successful outcome of this expedition. For many years, he had heard dark rumors concerning a woman who was known as The Octopus.

"This house in which she's living," he went on, "is known as The Palace of the Ninety and Nine Black Dragons. It was built some years ago by Lak Chak, the king of the thieves—the grand potentate of the great Thieves' Guild of China. I was Lak Chak's guest there for a month. He wanted to impress me with his superiority.

"Actually, I was his prisoner—with the freedom of the house. He wanted a house with dozens of mysterious exits. We'll reach one of them in a moment. The most amazing spectacle I ever saw in my life was a banquet he gave one night to four hundred of China's Number One Thieves. There were a thousand sing-song girls, twenty native orchestras. The food was served from great lacquered vats, and rice wine and *samshu* and *arrack* came into the banquet hall in hogsheads."

That had been long before he had met Susan. He stopped talking, fell to thinking of her again, her loveliness, her gayety, her wonderful companionship. Off to his right stretched a sea of fog. Above them the stars of China sparkled clearly. Below, nothing of the city was visible. A faint wind stirred the branches of the beefwood grove they were approaching.

In the center of it Peter stopped. In the starlight, on a great bald knoll beyond, sprawled, or crouched, a low, black structure—the Palace of the Ninety and Nine Dragons.

Peter kicked aside an accumulation of leaves and exposed a plate of blackened bronze about four feet square.

"This is our entrance," he said. "Keep your gun ready."

"What's your plan, Mr. Moore?"

"First, to find if our guess is correct."

He lifted the bronze plate. A breath of damp, moldy air floated up to the two young men. Peter's heart was beginning to thump. His senses became preternaturally alert. This was the danger line. Beyond lay trouble, danger, possible death.

A narrow stone staircase wound down into the bowels of the earth. At a depth of perhaps forty-five feet the stairs ended upon a long and narrow tunnel, damp and slippery underfoot, the walls, by matchlight, arched, rankly green with moss, flecked here and there with splotches of lichen.

At the end of the arched tunnel, at least two hundred feet from the staircase, was an iron door. Peter opened it cautiously. Beyond the door the tunnel forked. He deliberated a moment, took the left fork, advancing with all possible stealth. Behind him, gun in hand, face white and grim, tiptoed Terry Teeple.

Peter struck another match, held it high while it blazed into flame. The way ahead was clear, but he felt uneasy. Some indefinable change had been made in the arched tunnel since he had been a prisoner in this fantastic house.

The match flame expired. With renewed darkness came a sudden chill breath of air. He was conscious of the soft beat of it upon the side of his face and neck. And, before he could strike another light, powerful arms encircled his head. He was caught into a viselike grip. A knee jabbed him expertly in the solar plexus. In the same instant Terry Teeple's Colt automatic exploded twice in his ear. Then there was the thud of a falling body.

WITH THE WIND knocked out of him, Peter went to his knees. Strong hands grasped his shoulders. His hat went spilling off. He was jerked to his feet. A bag of harsh cloth was jammed down over his head. He heard Terry Teeple's cursing suddenly end on a gasp.

Hands were grasping Peter's elbows. He was being walked in a new direction. He knew that a door, cunningly concealed, had been built in the side of the tunnel since his previous visit. He was being urged, half-carried up a steep incline.

A lock rattled. A door opened, clanked shut behind them. Then came a short flight of stairs, a brief excursion over a floor that had the feel of polished marble. Another door opened, closed behind them.

The procession now halted. The captors on either side of him still gripped his elbows.

He was still short of breath, and his heart was beating in measured strokes of disgust.

His senses busied themselves. His skin felt a greater warmth, and through the coarse black cloth over his face he saw the gleam of lights and smelled the fragrance of Number One temple incense. Through this, like an insidious thread, crept the odor of the magical purple drug.

A girl's cold voice said, in English: "Remove the coverings."

The bag was snatched from Peter's head. He blinked in a sudden golden irradiation. The room itself, regally large, might have been carved from a block of purest gold. Walls and ceiling were gilded. Priceless golden Afghan rugs were strewn about the gilded floor. He had a quick impression of old Mongolian tapestries, of great gilded braziers sitting about, redly aglow with charcoal.

Then all of his awareness became concentrated on a richly carved iron-wood chair with a high back. It was like a throne.

A young woman, in the imperial red and blue brocade, with the dragon flowers of the old empire, was seated there. Her dark hair was done in fantastic swirls, oiled and doubtless scented, for it was in the old Chinese fashion. Her lashes were heavily beaded, her mouth was garishly painted. Her fingernails were lacquered a bright blue.

Her head was held imperiously. Her eyes, liquidly brilliant, stared down at him with hauteur. The pupils were dilated.

Peter Moore gasped, "Susan! Good Lord! What does this mean?"

5

CONDEMNED

THERE WAS A glassy little smile at the lips of the thrill hunter. And Peter, sickened, realized that she had found the ultimate thrill. Only one plan presented itself: To spirit her away from this place somehow, to deprive her of the devilish purple drug until she recovered her senses, her sanity.

Yet he was hopelessly outnumbered. His captors were powerful black men, naked except for sarongs, which fell straight from uniformly flat hips to naked heels. Mighty chests, shoulders and arms were discouraging.

He guessed they were Abyssinians. There were six of them, one at each of his elbows; one at each of Terry Teeple's elbows.

Terry Teeple was straining in the hands of his two black captors. He was panting through clenched teeth.

Susan was staring down at Peter with haughtiness. His heart

was beating a dirge now. In that barbaric costume she was more beautiful than he had ever seen her. She was a little princess.

In a cold, regal little voice she said, "Why did you come here? I told you I never wanted to see you again. You are a fool!"

Terry Teeple burst out savagely: "Who the hell is this?"

"My fiancée," Peter said grimly.

"Where's Marcia?"

Susan was staring coldly at the wireless operator. Her eyes narrowed with displeasure. And suddenly Peter, watching her, wanted to shake her until her teeth chattered; wanted to spank her—this girl who was playing such a dangerous game of princess.

"Where is she?" Terry Teeple shouted.

"The little blond girl," Peter said.

The princess imperiously answered, "I do not know. I am not interested."

Peter uttered an outraged growl. Then a gilded door opened. A woman came in. And no possible question could exist as to the newcomer's identity.

She was tall, slender, queenly in a gown of royal purple. It was as if Peter had never seen Lotus Burma before. She was the most barbarically beautiful woman he had ever seen. Her features were as symmetrical as a porcelain Buddha's. Her eyes were large and lustrous. Her skin was like cream—not white, not yellow, but a soft and amazing shade in between. She had the slim perfection of a goddess. She was ageless. She might have been twenty or forty.

She moved with a sinuous grace that was fascinating. A slim, graceful arm moved in languid gesture as she placed a stiletto of an amethyst cigarette holder to her red lips, puffed and breathed out the smoke in an enchanted vapor.

There was something hypnotic about this woman—a dangerous, secret charm. In her was perfectly expressed the exotic lure of all Eastern lands. Peter could understand a little better how Susan might have been captivated, fascinated by this strange woman. In spite of his danger, the real possibility of his losing his precious life, and in spite of his heartbreak, he was stirred. For the beauty of Lotus Burma was of the kind that challenges the masculinity of any man.

Mysterious, beautiful, more dangerous than any hamadryad cobra, this woman known as The Octopus entered the golden room.

PETER, INSTANTLY ON guard, took in other details. Pearls. She was evidently a lover of the rarer breeds of pearls. She wore blood pearls at her ears—pearls as large as dimes, as red as blood. She wore a rope of blue pearls about her slim neck, and ropes of black pearls were wound about her wrists.

Lotus Burma only glanced at Terry Teeple. He might have been, according to the value of her gaze, an unimportant piece of furniture. Her large, dark, lustrous eyes returned to Peter Moore.

As she came nearer he became more amazed. Only in this woman's mouth was the legend of her cruelty confirmed. It was a beautiful mouth, a sensuous mouth, a mouth capable of infinite barbarity. And the lips were as vividly red as the lips of a mythological vampire.

Lotus Burma advanced to within a few feet of Peter Moore. Holding the long, thin amethyst holder to her amazing lips, she stared at him boldly, without reserve; at his eyes, his blond hair, his mouth, and so on deliberately to his slightly muddied shoes.

The astounding black veil of her lashes lifted. Her eyes glowed at him. She lowered the amethyst holder and looked into his eyes with a faint, mysterious smile.

In a sweet, husky contralto she said, drawling, "So this is Peter Moore—Peter the Great—the Man of Bronze! I am Lotus Burma."

Peter only tightened his lips a little.

In that sweet, sensuous, remarkable voice, Lotus Burma went on. "I have heard of your exploits, your power over my people. We should have met long ago. Perhaps we should have combined forces." Her eyes narrowed. "You think not?"

A cat was toying with a mouse. Peter, the mouse, had nothing whatever to say to Lotus Burma.

"Who knows?" drawled the most dangerous woman in China. "We might have ruled the world. But I think not. We were born under warring stars. Oh, I knew that sometime we would meet—enemies!"

In spite of himself Peter was fascinated. Her languor, her very sensuousness made her as dangerous as a lazily awaking python.

"I know your life in China, your adventures," Lotus Burma went on in that seductive drawl, "in the smallest details. But what do you know of me?" Her voice had become fuller, stronger, with a promise of dynamic power. "What do you know of me?" she cried. "I, goddess of vengeance! I, instrument of Destiny!"

Her eyes had lost their soft lustre, were brilliant with waking fires. Her voice, losing none of its rich beauty, had lost its huskiness, become clear and hard. Here, in soft, alluring flesh, was a thing of steel or jade.

"You look on a woman who has been vilely wronged by your contemptible race!" she cried. "Scorned and insulted and wronged because of the yellow blood flowing in my white body! Humiliated! Treated like the dust beneath your feet! Ah! Who dares insult Lotus Burma today? No man! No woman! I am the mysterious, the ruthless! I am The Octopus! Those whom I hate, those who have wronged me, I crush!"

She was, Peter reflected, utterly insane. Beneath her amazing, beautiful eyes he saw the telltale marks of the opium addict. And from her very creamy flesh was breathed the scent, the familiar, malignant sweet spiciness of the purple drug. Yet these signs of weaknesses only enhanced the sense of her mysterious, ruthless strength.

SHE SEEMED SUDDENLY to soften. Her voice, issuing again from that cruel, lovely mouth was soft music.

"You do not know my story. I am the daughter of a princess. I do not speak of my white father. He was of the race that humiliated, wronged me. My mother was a princess of the old regime—an intimate of Her Imperial Highness Tsze Hsi—the last ruler of the greatest race ever to occupy the earth! And yet your race, your stupid race has scorned me, has called me half-caste—Eurasian!"

The rich, beautiful voice had risen again. It was like an instrument of the very devil, ingeniously calculated to sway the feelings of its hearers.

Terry Teeple, with jaw belligerently outthrust, was nevertheless staring at Lotus Burma with utter fascination.

"Your stupid, blind race," the voice went on, "refused to acknowledge that the blood of conquerors, of emperors, flowed in my veins. When I appealed to the white race for companionship I was insulted and scorned and humiliated. Did I not have the right to move in the highest circles of white or yellow? Yet was I received, was I accepted, was I treated according to the exaltation of my ancestry? No, no, no! I was a half-caste, a Eurasian!"

Lotus Burma puffed at the amethyst holder. The cigarette had gone out. With pantherine grace she bent over one of the gilded braziers, thrust the end of the cigarette into the coals, inhaled deeply. Returning to Peter she blew a thin stream of hot, scented smoke into his face.

But this was not an insult. It was a gesture of mystery and despair. It was the period at the end of a sentence. She could not express herself further in words without demeaning herself.

She continued in an altogether strange manner. The fire of resentment was gone from her eyes. A faint flush of pleasure stained her creamy cheeks.

"I have had my revenge on this one and that. I have dedicated my life to punishing those who had the effrontery to insult and humiliate me. Tonight, I am repeating a pleasure of which I never tire. I am striking the dagger of lifelong agony into the heart of Horatio Pool, who, on the night of July ninth, 1914, in Yokohama, Japan, insulted me, humiliated me—had me ejected by servants from his house!"

"Where is she?" Terry Teeple snarled.

Lotus Burma as if for the first time, seemed to become aware of the wireless operator's presence. She regarded him with an air faintly repugnant, faintly amused.

"Ah," she breathed. "You. You are her lover, are you not? Perhaps, if it pleases me, I shall let you see her die."

"You slimy rat!" Terry Teeple roared. The black men held him firmly. His complexion was almost blue with fury.

Delicately, contemptuously the woman known as The Octopus contemplated him.

"Yes," she purred. "I have decided I shall let you see how horribly the sons and daughters of the men and women who have affronted me can die. I shall let you carry back to Horatio Pool a vivid word picture of her agonies, her tortured screams— the sight of her bloody little carcass palpitating its last!"

Terry Teeple uttered an inarticulate snarl. He tried frantically to free himself; relapsed to ripe shipboard profanity, and fell to futile panting.

Lotus Burma had turned to Susan.

"You—Tsi Lo Lan—what is your opinion?"

Susan had been staring at Peter. A change had come over her. Her pupils had lost most of their dilation. She seemed sobered. The beginnings of terror were in her lovely violet eyes. Her small hands were clenching the arms of the great ironwood chair, as if she were preparing to spring out of it.

THE OCTOPUS SAID sharply, "Tsi Lo Lan!" It was Chinese for "violet," a name by which Susan had come to be known in China because of the rare, beautiful coloring of her eyes.

Susan said feebly, "Peter! Peter! What am I doing—"

"Tsi Lo Lan!" Lotus Burma cried harshly. From the fold of her dress she had whipped a little phial. She took out the stopper. She stood threateningly over Susan. "Open your mouth!"

"Don't do it!" Peter shouted. "Don't take it!"

But Susan had, like a girl in a trance, opened her mouth. Peter, struggling against the powerful black hands, saw the purple drop fall on her small pink tongue. Lotus Burma was holding Susan's hands. Seconds passed. Watching Susan's eyes, Peter saw the pupils begin to dilate again. It was horrible. On the very verge of normality, she had been snatched back, driven back into the vile mists of the purple drug.

Satisfied, Lotus Burma stepped back. Insidiously came her rich, beautiful contralto: "What is your opinion, Tsi Lo Lan?"

Susan straightened in the ironwood, thronelike chair.

"Let the two of them see the little blond girl's agonies?" The Octopus insinuated.

Susan made an imperious little gesture. The haughty smile was back.

"Kill them, too?" Lotus Burma purred.

"Banish them. Make slaves of them," Susan regally answered.

The Octopus sent a thin smile of contempt at Peter.

"How splendid that I have delivered this charming, beautiful young woman from your clutches!" she said.

"I want them out of my sight," Susan cried.

"But to witness the delicious murder of the sweet little blond one?" Lotus Burma suggested.

"No. I don't want to see either of them again—ever."

"Very well."

The Octopus made a gesture of dismissal with the amethyst cigarette holder. In Chinese she said to the black men, "Lock these swine in a strong room. Guard them well."

Peter sent a final glance at Susan. She was still regarding him with that air of princely scorn. The black men pushed Peter and

Terry Teeple out of the room. Peter recognized the great black marble hall into which they were inducted, and the Alley of Jade down which they were taken. This was one of Lak Chak's many incredible extravagances—a long corridor panelled from floor to ceiling with slabs of green jade.

Fine Ming tapestries partly covered the walls. Below the tapestries were Chinese war chests of red and blue lacquer—each one a museum piece.

Conducted briskly down the Alley of Jade, Peter's mind was working as briskly. Somehow, he and Terry Teeple must contrive not to be locked in a room.

Under his breath, very softly, very tunelessly, Peter began to whistle. Terry Teeple stopped his cursing and gave Peter his closest attention. When Peter had whistled a tuneless measure, Terry Teeple began whistling, too, softly, without melody.

What Peter had said, in a short whistle for a dot, a longer stream of tunelessness for a dash, was, in terms of the International radio code: "Get ready for action. I will make them release us in a moment. Fight hard."

And what Terry Teeple had whistled tunelessly in answer was, "O.K. All set. Make it soon."

To the black man on his left Peter said loudly, in gutter Chinese: "What price a bottle of the Divine Drug?"

The black man on his right answered in pidgin: "Pay my look see!"

"Can do," Peter said. "But how can do with arms allatime tight?"

His arms were released, but Terry Teeple's were not. However, the six black men managed to crowd close about Peter.

He removed the white jade phial from his pocket. He held

it up, gripping it firmly. Next instant, six pairs of black hands were snatching, clawing for that precious phial.

Peter doubled the phial into his fist and struck mightily at a black jaw. He heard a skull behind him crack against a jade panel, the war-growl of Terry Teeple as his two hamlike fists sought more jaws. Peter occupied himself with a yelling black man, knocked him senseless and assaulted another.

In perhaps forty seconds the two belligerent young Americans had vanquished six surprised black enemies.

Peter yanked at a tapestry, but only the white silk lining came away. He made strips of it.

He panted, "Work fast. Bind hands and feet and gag each one." He knew that the great war chests were empty.

The two young men tied the hands and feet of the six blacks, gagged them, lifted them one by one into six chests.

There was a sudden shout at the far end of the Alley of Jade. Peter and Terry Teeple slid behind one of the fabulous Ming tapestries.

The jade panel behind them gave way with sickening suddenness. Magically it swung wide, a gleaming green hinge. And both young men fell backward into a room dimly lighted by a single lamp suspended by fine brass chains from a dark ceiling.

A voice sadly intoned: "Ah! Though a man never trips over a mountain, he may trip over a clod!"

6

THE PIT

A WIZENED OLD Chinese in the black of lounging was kneeling on cushions at one end of the small dark room. Before him on a little teakwood taboret were a tray, a spirit lamp and implements with which years in China had made Peter Moore familiar.

Chay Quon did not seem surprised or at all agitated by Peter's and Terry Teeple's startling entrance. Peter removed the phial of purple drug from the pocket to which he had restored it at the conclusion of the shambles; held it into the feeble rays from the lamp, and said, "Chay Quon, I am indebted to you for still another chance at trouble."

The old Chinese who had accosted him in the fog and later come to his hotel room with a dire warning, nodded his gray head with indifference.

"The friendships of the day," he said sadly, "are those of self-interest alone. Yet I am indebted to you."

Calmly, he proceeded with his ritual. He selected a pipe from the collection on the taboret—a satinwood pipe with a brown tortoise-shell tip. He plied needle, blew on flame, kneaded amber-colored *chandoo* cube and inhaled the biting smoke deeply. The opium sizzled, melted, evaporated in dense fumes.

Chay Quon laid the pipe aside, brushed his hands with the gesture of a man satisfied, and took on generally the air of a man refreshed and stimulated. Having finished what is, to a

Chinese, the equivalent of a cup of bracing tea, he was now prepared to discuss matters.

"A man burning with passion," he stated serenely, "follows the undulations of a thought. Master, I am indebted to you for my life. But I must warn you that I am this woman's slave. If I am detected in the act of betraying her trust, not only I but my sons, my little grandsons will rot in the death tower of Macao. As a man of great honor, I shall do your bidding. Perhaps a man can ride two tigers, despite the warnings of the Wisest One of all."

Terry Teeple interrupted impatiently: "What's he saying? Is he a friend?"

"Yes. He'll help."

"Ask him where Marcia is."

Peter put the question to Chay Quon, who answered: "The little blond one is locked in a room. She is to die tonight. She is the nineteenth."

"We have come to take her away," Peter said.

"Master, it is impossible."

"To a man of merit and honor," Peter said swiftly, "the word impossible is nothing but a challenge. What is your purpose in this shameful place?"

"I am in charge of the ceremony—the death ceremony. It is to begin in twenty minutes."

"Then there is no time to lose," Peter said briskly.

Chay Quon shook his head. "At risk of my own life, I will escort you and your friend to safety."

"No, Chay Quon. We have come for the little blond girl."

The eyes of the old man narrowed again.

He made a hissing sound through his teeth.

"There is little hope, but I am a man of honor, I am indebted to you for my life. I will think." He meditated a moment, staring intently at Terry Teeple, then at Peter.

"The little blond one is to be given to the octopus in twenty minutes," he said.

"Then there is truth in that fable?"

"Yes, master. She lets her victims be crushed and sucked to death by a giant octopus. I can think of no way to save this girl, master. She is doomed."

Terry Teeple impatiently broke in: "What's he say?"

"He says," Peter answered, "it's a pretty tough assignment."

"Is there any hope?"

"Sure, there's hope."

CHAY QUON HAD risen, was pacing to and fro, his eyes dark, his brows knit.

He said finally, "Master, there is but one way. You will wear my ceremonial costume. I will give you a Malay dagger and a revolver. I will give your friend a revolver. The young man may wish to use it on himself before this night is done."

Chay Quon had produced from a rosewood cabinet the three weapons—two revolvers and a long, curved dagger.

"What does he say?" Terry Teeple asked.

"We may be able to shoot our way out of here with these guns."

"What's the dagger for?"

"Emergency."

"Come with me," Chay Quon said. "There is little time."

The old Chinese touched the surface of the near-by wall. A square aperture appeared in the floor at Peter's feet. Below this opening, stairs of stone led down into darkness.

Chay Quon started down the stairs. Peter and Terry Teeple followed. Peter was familiar with this secret stairway. It led directly into Lak Chak's famous banquet hall.

But the door at the end of the stairs opened upon a surprise. The great room, once paneled in varicolored *nara-wood*, had been converted into a hideous enormity of purple. More than two hundred feet in length, by a hundred in width, the one-time scene of gargantuan revels had been done over according to Lotus Burma's strange preferences.

She was evidently infatuated with that color of the old royalty. It was as if her very soul had been tainted with the purple of the malignant drug.

The color, laid on boldly, seemed to writhe and squirm in the flood of brilliant electric illumination. Peter gazed about him with startled amazement. Here, he had been privileged to gaze on that astounding scene—the Number One thieves of China gathered together, stuffing their bellies with bird nest soup, pickled rotten eggs, broiled rats, toasted octopus tips; swilling these delicacies down with rice wine and whisky and *arrack*.

But the massive furniture had been removed. The great purple hall was bare save for a half dozen huge jars of the Kiang S'u period—great porcelain containers in which the bodies of emperors had once been preserved in honey and mercury. Some of these were eight feet in height.

A dais had been erected against one wall. On this, in a row, stood six heavily carved teakwood chairs.

Peter's eyes wandered quickly to another object of greater interest. This was a length of slender ladder made of some translucent pink stuff, which hung from the ceiling by bronze chains. The upper end of the ladder vanished into a round hole in the ceiling. The purpose of the chains was apparently to lower the ladder from this hole.

The lower end of the ladder came within about thirty feet of the purple-lacquered floor. And just below it, suddenly, Peter saw the white lip of the tank.

He walked quickly over. The tank was set in the floor, like a kind of cistern, and it gave off a pearly glow. Going close, he looked down shining white walls of a substance which appeared to be alabaster, and into crystal clear water. Fastened to one side of this round alabaster cistern, or tank, was another ladder of rose quartz. The top of the ladder came to within about six feet of the top of the alabaster cylinder.

And in the clear water at the bottom of the tank was sprawled a shapeless black mass.

Peter, staring with horrified fascination, could not repress a shudder. He could see the little ice-green eyes of the octopus, the tangled mass of its arms, the beak with which it disemboweled its victims.

TERRY TEEPLE, STANDING beside him, suddenly seized his arm.

"Good Lord, man! Is—is that how Marcia is supposed to die?"

Chay Quon was rapidly explaining to Pater, who translated.

"The victim is sent down that ladder from the hole in the ceiling. The ladder is lowered until it connects with the ladder fastened to the wall of the tank. The victim climbs down into the tank. When she is on the lower ladder, the upper one is raised. She cannot possibly escape. Then the water is slowly, very slowly raised in the tank until—"

Peter stopped. Terry Teeple was cursing. Peter explained the rest of it. Then:

"Chay Quon says the victim is given a so-called chance. Immediately below the ladder, do you see the square of alabaster fitted in? It's a door. A push opens it. If the victim can dive under water, escape the octopus and open that door—she is free. A tunnel leads to safety outside. But no victim has lived to reach that opening. This octopus, Chay Quon says, has never tasted anything but human flesh since Lotus Burma secured it. If we can't prevent it, your fiancée will be the nineteenth human being who has been fed to that horrible monster."

"It is nearly time, master," Chay Quon finished.

Peter said: "Frankly, I can't see much hope, fellow. But we'll do our best. I will wear Chay Quon's costume and take charge of the ceremony. From now until the time is ripe to strike, you will hide yourself in one of these jars. Don't be impetuous. Control yourself. A false move means you'll lose Marcia— and we'll lose our heads! We're hoping that Lotus Burma will forget our existence—believe we're safely locked up—until after this matter is attended to. Climb into that jar. At the right moment I'll shoot the guards, you'll jump out of the jar, we'll grab Marcia—and make our getaway through that window. Be ready to shoot, be ready to fight—but don't lose your head."

"How many guards will there be?"

"Chay Quon says only three."

Terry Teeple grimly climbed into the great vase, and Peter and Chay Quon returned to the latter's quarters, where the ritual of the death-by-octopus was explained to Peter while he donned the strange, fantastic garment devised by Lotus Burma for the occasion.

It consisted of a purple satin robe with a sash of gold brocade. The headdress was a miniature octopus, carved beautifully of black onyx. Fortunately, it came down over the face, as a mask, with slits for eyes and mouth. And even more fortunately, Peter Moore and Chay Quon were sufficiently of a size so that both robe and headdress fitted well or well enough.

"Now, master," Chay Quon said, "there is time only to bind and gag and mutilate me. Do not hesitate. The knife is sharp. Do not forget: Lotus Burma is diabolically shrewd. If I am found here, only bound and gagged, how can you have come into the possession of the ceremony? I must have the appearance of torture. I am a man of honor and great merit. I have no fear. Proceed, master!"

Peter swiftly bound Chay Quon's hands and feet, gagged him, and then picked up the knife. He shuddered at the prospect of deliberately inflicting hurt and injury, yet, as Chay Quon had said, there was no alternative.

Chay Quon closed his eyes. Peter made a series of shallow cuts in the old man's muscular forearm, others, as Chay Quon had directed, on the calves of his legs. None of these slashes was deep enough to cause serious bleeding, but they gave Chay Quon a gory appearance.

IN THE DISTANCE a bell clanged softly. It was, Peter knew, a command for his appearance as master of the death-by-octopus ceremonies in the hideous purple hall.

He threw a light cloak of yellow silk over Chay Quon, as a safeguard against his premature discovery by guards or Lotus Burma, and descended the narrow stairway into the purple chamber of horrors.

Peter's heart seemed to have climbed; was banging furiously somewhere in the region of his ears. His mouth was dry. He was shaking with apprehension, with expectancy. He went into the purple hall knowing that a single wrong gesture would result not only in the ordained death of Marcia Pool, but in his and Terry Teeple's.

He steadied himself; told himself to stop this damned shaking—and boldly walked into the hall. He was thankful for the mask, thankful that the ceremony called for no speeches on his part. Throughout, it was to be conducted in silence.

He advanced slowly, with measured strides, to the edge of the alabaster pool. There, with arms folded on chest, he sharply executed an about-face. This brought him face to face with the occupants of the dais.

Only three of the chairs were occupied. In the center sat Lotus Burma. On her right sat Susan. On her left sat a fat, middle-aged Chinese with black wisps of mustache, worn in the mandarin style.

A door on the side opened. Black men filed in. Peter, counting them, felt his heart give a sickening thump, a chill dance along his backbone.

Five—six—seven!

Chay Quon had said there would be only three! One at the valve which caused the water in the alabaster cylinder to rise, and two at the tank with the master of ceremonies, to seize the victim in case she attempted to leap from the ladder to the floor in an attempt to escape her exquisitely horrible fate.

Eight—nine—ten!

Ten black giants! With the sickness of despair, Peter

wondered if Chay Quon had betrayed him, if Lotus Burma were suspicious—if she had discovered that he and Terry Teeple had escaped their guards and were dangerously at large in this black palace!

He watched her face. It showed no suspicion. It was tranquil. She was gazing expectantly at the aperture in the ceiling from which hung the rose-quartz ladder.

Her eyes darted here and there. She was wearing her secret smile—a smile of anticipation. A greedy, pleased little smile. You might almost see her lick her lips with relish.

Peter waited, watching her. The black men filed about the room. One took his place at the valve. The remaining nine formed a semicircle on the side of the tank farthest from the dais, in order not to obstruct Lotus Burma's view.

THE PREPARATIONS WERE complete. Lotus Burma raised her right hand to a level with her slim, beautiful, creamy shoulders. Peter unfolded his arms, commanded them not to tremble, and made a sweeping salaam. He wondered again if this whole ceremony, in its hideous entirety, were not based on some old and secret ceremony practiced by the Chinese emperors—a secret of Lotus Burma's royal mother.

He made a curt gesture to one of the black men, who promptly knelt and pursed his lips and blew upon a potbellied brass incense pot which stood beside the tank like a metallic pig. A cloud of dense blue smoke rose into the air. It was, of course, the finest of sacrificial incense.

Then Peter made a circuit of the tank, lifting his feet slowly, bobbing his head each time a foot went down. This was presumably for the purpose of driving certain unfavorable devils from the scene, to give the octopus every fair chance at enjoying his human meal.

Completing a circuit of the tank, he stretched his arms high over his head, a gesture made difficult and hazardous by the eight glassy black arms of the octopus headpiece which projected in as many directions.

This was a signal to eyes at peepholes in the ceiling that the victim was to be sent down the ladder, Peter sent a glance at Susan. In spite of drugs, he could not believe that she could stomach this proceeding. She was gazing with fascination at the hole in the ceiling.

A girl's whimpering voice came floating down; a protest. There were sharp interjections in Chinese, then a little wail came down, "But why?"

Peter steeled himself; hoped that Terry Teeple was doing the same, would not lose his control and run amuck.

A small pink foot appeared at the ceiling aperture, then another. Then the small blond girl started down the ladder. She came slowly but with apparent certainty. Not until she was a dozen feet down from the ceiling did she look down.

She seemed to look square into Peter's face—that black glossy mask. Her blue eyes were large with horror. Her golden hair was disheveled. Her face was white, her lips gray.

Peter's heart was thudding. Marcia Pool was going to her death as a slave girl of the old summer place in Peking. She wore white silk crepe pajamas—the tight jacket and skimpy trousers of all Chinese girls. She was so small, so innocent, so childlike that Peter ground his teeth to control himself.

For a long moment she stared down at him, down into the tank. For the first time, she realized what her fate must be.

Suddenly she screamed—a shrill, heartbreaking sound. And Peter, with sickly thumping heart, hoped she would not fall. The victim who fell went to a swifter doom—plunging into the very center of the tank, within easy reach of those eight horrible arms.

But Marcia Pool did not faint. For a moment she stared, then she started down the ladder. Looking up, Peter saw why she did not try to go back up. The ladder had been slowly lowered until the top of it was now about five feet from the ceiling. And the round aperture was closed.

She came down a few steps, hesitated, stopped.

Clinging midway down the ladder, she clutched at the rungs, stared down and trembled. She did not cry out again. Slowly, the ladder came down until the lower end was level with the floor. It continued to go down until the lower end touched the top of the ladder that was fastened to the wall of the tank.

MARCIA POOL DID not attempt to leap off the ladder to the floor, to escape her hideous fate. Black guards had been stationed there to prevent that. If she had leaped, they would have caught her—thrown her into the tank without ceremony.

But the small blond girl did not attempt to escape. And Peter could guess why. She was paralyzed with terror. Her little hands were fairly frozen to the rose-quartz rungs. The sight of that deep-sea monster in the tank, the knowledge that she was to be its victim, had stupefied Marcia Pool.

Watching her, Peter tried to keep his thoughts in order. The attempt to rescue her must be made soon. He darted a glance at Lotus Burma. The smile at her vampire lips had brightened. Her eyes were avid with expectancy. Clearly, Peter could see into her twisted mind—could see there the gloating hideous soul of this woman, could glimpse her insane joy in seeing this innocent, delicate girl clasped and devoured by the hungry sea monster.

He glanced sharply at Susan. She seemed to be coming awake again. Her lovely mouth hung ajar, her eyes were round and large and dark with a quickening terror.

A Negro with a long black whip in his hand had stepped forward. Peter made the gesture for the blond girl to climb down. She must go part way down before he could act. In another moment bullets would begin to fly, and she would be directly in their path.

The blond girl looked at him piteously, too dazed to understand, too frightened to move. Yet she must climb down onto the lower ladder.

The black man with the whip advanced. She saw him and recoiled. She was shaking so violently that Peter wondered how she had strength enough to climb to the rungs.

The Abyssinian lifted the whip. He flicked it at her. The tip struck the flimsy silk stuff at her shoulder. The girl uttered a little cry. The black man pointed down. She looked down. Her breast was rising and falling with little gasps.

The black man lifted the whip again. Peter heard a low, soft burst of laughter. He looked toward the dais. Lotus Burma was laughing. And for the first time in his life, Peter wanted to shoot a woman.

Marcia Pool was going down the ladder. She reached the lower one. Her great blue eyes stared at the monstrous mass at the bottom of the tank. She clunk to the lower ladder, her slim body, so slightly clad, silhouetted against the glowing alabaster.

The upper ladder went up.

Peter backed away from the tank, reached inside the purple robe and grasped the handle of the revolver Chay Quon had given him.

Before he could fire the shot which would apprise Terry Teeple that the time to act had finally come, Susan uttered a shriek.

She screamed, "No! No! This can't go on! Stop it! Get that girl out of there!"

And out of the tail of his eye, as he flashed out the revolver, Peter saw the black man give the valve a twist, and he heard the sudden gushing of water into the alabaster cylinder.

Near by occurred a sharp, ponderous crash. One of the massive Kiang S'u vases had toppled over. The priceless blue neck of it cracked. Out of it crawled Terry Teeple, snarling robust curses, shooting as he came.

7

HYPNOTISM?

PETER THREW OFF the grotesque black headgear and stepped backwards out of the purple robe.

He heard Susan shriek, "Peter!" as he fired at the first black man who started toward him. This one collapsed and slid face down along the purple-lacquered floor and Peter pulled the trigger a second time, aiming squarely between the eyes of the man at the great bronze valve.

Long knives had appeared as if by magic from the black

men's *sarongs*. One of these knives whistled past Peter's ear. He shot down the man who had thrown it.

Terry Teeple had shouted, "Hang on, Marcia! We'll get you out!" His revolver had disappeared. He had evidently gone too primitive for firearms. Peter saw him seize two ebony necks; saw him send two gleaming black skulls cracking together; saw him pick up, in the following split second, a third Abyssinian and, lifting him over his head, kicking and shouting, hurl him down into the tank.

Peter saw, to his horror, that the water had risen; that the blond girl had climbed as far up the ladder as she could, and that one of the eight black arms had reached up to coil about one slim pink ankle.

The octopus had so far ignored the black man, who kicked and blubbered, who could not swim, who threshed the crystal clear water into foam.

The enemy had been reduced to two. Terry Teeple was taking them both single-handed, unarmed, dodging their knives, trying to reach them with his tremendous fists.

Peter, running to his assistance, stopped at the bronze valve, to twist it in the opposite direction.

A woman was screaming. It was Susan.

One of the two remaining black men slipped. Terry Teeple sent a fist crashing into his face. The remaining enemy sprang at him with knife uplifted—and Peter shot him accurately in the forehead!

Terry Teeple picked up the man he had just floored and threw him into the alabaster tank as Peter started toward the dais. In another moment, he was certain, this great hall would swarm with reinforcements. This was his last chance to get

Susan away. It was his only chance to seize Lotus Burma—to deliver her to Dan de Sylva.

Lotus Burma, the fat Chinese and Susan were standing at their chairs, in petrified attitudes, when Peter started toward them. The plump Chinese decided on instant departure. He vanished through the arched doorway behind the dais.

Lotus Burma also vanished, but more swiftly, and with all possible mystery. She dropped through the floor. When Peter reached the dais she was gone—had vanished, leaving behind no clue as to the manner of her escape. An ingenious trap-door had, of course, accomplished it.

He had lost his chance to help Dan de Sylva. He said grimly, "Come on, Susan," and seized her hand.

She wailed, "I can't go—not yet!"

He bent down, swept an arm about her knees, swung her to his shoulder and strode toward the alabaster tank.

WHEN PETER REACHED the tank, an octopus and five black men were actively engaged in the water. Five black snakelike arms were busy, each with the largest morsel of food the monster had perhaps ever contemplated. But the sixth arm still clung, with its sucking disks, to the slim, pink ankle of the intended victim.

Terry Teeple, on his knees, was shouting advice and encouragement. "Hang on, honey! It won't be long now!"

And the little blond girl cried, "I can't! I'm fainting!"

Peter picked up the other gun from the floor where Terry Teeple had dropped it. He saw there were three unexploded shells in the cylinder. He fired them in the octopus's head, aiming at the eyes. This had the effect only of aggravating its threshings. Such monsters die hard.

Peter said, "We've got to go out that way. No other is safe." He had taken the long, curved dagger from his belt. "Don't let Miss O'Gilvie get away."

"What are you going to do?"

"Going down there. The water's below that door now. That's how we get out of here—with luck!" He picked up the golden sash of the ceremonial costume he had worn. Terry Teeple held fast to one end while Peter slipped down to the ladder. He said to the blond girl, "Hang on a little longer. We'll all be out in a minute."

She whimpered, "I—I could die! Can you get this horrible thing loose?"

Peter slid down past her. He bent down, slashed at the tentacle. It held fast. He could hear, above the splashings and shouts below him, the sucking sound of the black disks against the girl's ankle.

He hacked at the black arm, finally hacked it almost through before it uncoiled and fell writhing into the water.

There were two bullets left in his own revolver. At closer range he aimed again at the icy-green eyes of the monster, fired with deliberation, saw both eyes, in turn, vanish.

Blind, if not dying, the octopus was no longer so dangerous.

Peter called: "Send down Miss O'Gilvie. Don't let her get away from you!"

He heard Susan's shriek of fury. He reached down and pushed at the oblong of alabaster. As Chay Quon had promised, the alabaster block swung away from his touch. He bent down and looked into a tunnel of gray stone, round, no greater in diameter than four feet.

Peter said, "Okay, Miss Pool. This way!" He gave her his

hand, helped her down the ladder, through the oblong open-ing, and into the tunnel. Susan, angrily protesting, came down the ladder and followed the blond girl. Then Terry Teeple let himself drop. His feet struck the upper rung of the ladder, fractured it, found safety on the second. And Peter, reaching out, prevented him from swaying and falling into the water.

The two young men followed the girls into the tunnel. On hands and knees they followed it until it opened into another, larger corridor, which they followed, always in the same direc-tion, for perhaps an eighth of a mile.

Peter did not recognize this exit as one of Lak Chak's until it ended in a clump of bushes.

They were on a knoll. Below them, at the foot of the Peak, the lights of Hong Kong sparkled with the brightness of diamonds. The fog had gone.

Peter said uneasily, "We'd better keep moving. We may have outwitted her, but she's still the most dangerous woman in China."

Yet he could not have guessed, as he said it, in just what shocking way his semi-prediction was to be fulfilled.

MARCIA POOL WAS giving way normally to hyster-ics. Laughing and crying, she was reliving an experience that would no doubt haunt her as long as she lived. Terry Teeple, with an arm about her, was trying to comfort her. They started down the trail.

Peter, firmly holding Susan by the elbow, waited for her to speak. She had, so far, said nothing.

Now, she said, "Darling, you'll never forgive me. You'll never understand."

But she made no gesture, no move, to go into his arms.

He said quietly, "Are we sailing tomorrow?"

"Of course!"

"Do you still feel you want to marry me?"

"Of course, darling!"

Peter said nothing. New doubts were rising. He was certain that Susan was no longer under the influence of that baleful purple drug. Its effects were apparently short-lived, despite their drastic power while they lasted. Yet something was wrong. He held her arm firmly.

She said impulsively, "I'll always love you. There never will be any one else. But—"

His heart was beating a dirge again.

"If I could only make you understand!" Susan cried.

"That you don't actually mean what you've been saying," Peter said. "That you don't love me, that you don't want to marry me."

She panted: "I can't! I can't marry you. I can't leave China!"

"That woman has you hypnotized."

"Ah, darling, you don't understand."

"I know she's had you doped with that damned drug for days!"

"It isn't that!"

"Then, good Lord, Susan, tell me what it is!"

He could feel the soft sobs shaking her.

She whispered, "If—if I only knew!"

Peter knew that she wanted to put her face into her hands. He reasoned that hysterics would clear the air. But she didn't have hysterics. She cried only a moment, and she quickly freed herself of his arms.

"We'd better go back to the hotel," she said.

They took sedan chairs down the hill; rickshaws from the base of the hill to the Colony.

The night clerk said, "Miss O'Gilvie, all of your baggage came a moment ago. We sent it up to your old room."

Susan thanked him. She and Peter entered the elevator and went up to her suite.

At the door, she said, "I don't want you to come in. I want to be alone—I want to think."

"We're going to be married in the morning," he said grimly. "We're sailing for America at noon."

"You'd better come in," Susan said.

They went in and she closed the door. Peter thought she had relented. He took her hungrily into his arms, but when he tried to kiss her, she averted her head and pushed him away.

"I can't make you understand," she said wearily.

"Then we'll talk it over until one or the other of us does understand." He pulled her down beside him on a settee. He picked up one of her hands and held it. "You know China as well as I do," he said. "You know there are people here like Lotus Burma—dangerous people. We've always managed to avoid these traps. Let's try to reason this out."

"You can't reason a thing like this out," Susan said. She pulled her hand away and jumped up.

"You saw her try to kill that poor girl by means of that octopus."

"It's like a nightmare," Susan said. "Oh, how horrible!"

"Then why do you want to go back to her?"

"Do I want to go back to her?" Susan cried. "Did I say I wanted to go back to her? I have no intentions of going back to her!"

"Are you contradicting yourself? Do you want to marry me— go back to the States?"

"No!" Susan cried. "Never!"

Peter got up and went to the door. She was staring at him almost pityingly.

As he went out, she wailed, "You don't understand, Peter!"

Peter said nothing more. He had recalled seeing on the streets of Hong Kong a liberty party of sailors from an American battleship in port.

A LITTLE MORE than an hour later, Peter Moore, Terry Teeple and a small mob of American sailors, thirsting for a fight, went up the Peak, surrounded that black vulture of a house, battered down the doors and rushed inside.

Emptiness met them. Lotus Burma had evidently decided on immediate flight. The great, bizarre structure was empty. Even the furniture and furnishings were gone!

Peter returned to the hotel. It was now a little after four o'clock. He proceeded directly to Room 819. He banged on the door.

It was promptly opened by a man with a gun in his hand. The Satanic de Sylva stared at him a moment, then smiled his V-shaped smile. He lowered the revolver, opened the door, and drawled: "You didn't bring her back alive."

"No."

"I have just learned, from one of my most trusted observers," Satan said, "that The Octopus and her entourage are aboard a small steamship that is sailing at dawn for Java. That's less than an hour away."

Peter said nothing.

"This agent of mine who was rolled for two million dollars' worth of diamonds," de Sylva said, "was murdered in a peculiarly cruel way. He was hung up by his toes and stabbed to death by infinitesimal degrees with a sharp hairpin. In case this job still appeals to you, it seemed only fair to warn you—"

"I'm taking the job," Peter said.

KING COBRA

Sidney Herschel Small

*Locked in the Depths of Kong Gai's
Lair, Jimmy Wentworth Is Doomed to
the Strange Death of the Snake*

1

"ARE YOU SATISFIED it's suicide?" demanded Captain Dunand. He stared down at the dead man on the floor as if asking him to solve the riddle. "Are you, Jimmy? If you aren't, now's the time to say something, before the newspaper boys are tipped off to what's happened."

"Not any more satisfied than you are," Wentworth said.

The two detectives were in a ninth floor-apartment high on Nob Hill, San Francisco's exclusive residence district. From the windows, had either man raised his eyes, could be seen the bay, and, nearer, the tiled roofs of Chinatown.

"I don't like empty safes," Dunand muttered.

"Clean as a whistle," agreed the Chinatown detective. The safe, hidden in a recess made to hold a radiator, had been concealed with a bright Oriental painting made on silk. It was closed, but not locked, when they had discovered it. Closed and without a scrap of paper inside.

"And yet this man Carrington might have been broke," the

captain of detectives said. "Perhaps he'd spent every dime he ever owned. Maybe he had papers in the safe and wanted 'em destroyed before he shot himself—"

"He must have shot himself," Wentworth said, thinking aloud.

"Of course he did, Jim! The gun's clenched in his fist. That's unusual, but I've seen it once or twice before. And his head's powder burned. He must've shot himself. Every window in the apartment was locked. The entry door in the rear was locked. O'Malley had to smash the door down to get in, and it was not only locked, but the chain bolt was in position. As if—"

"As if he were afraid of something?"

"Maybe, Jim. I wish I knew."

The dead man lay face downward on the floor. The cold hand gripping the heavy automatic in its stiff fingers had aimed well. Undoubtedly the muzzle had been pressed against Carrington's forehead when the trigger had been pulled. And the result was not a pretty sight.

"Want to talk to the elevator boy?" Dunand asked. "O'Malley's waiting in the hall with him. The manager of the place is running the elevator until we're done with the kid. He's a Chink kid. You might get something out of him."

In a pea-green uniform, buttoned to the neck, the nervous elevator boy looked very yellow.

"I bring number ninety-seven topside," the boy said unhappily. "I hear gun shoot. Number ninety-seven, Mr. Johnson, go telephone police. Tha's all I know."

Wentworth, born in China, could have questioned him in any one of a dozen dialects, but since the Chinese knew him only as patrolman, and not as Dunand's right-hand man in the district, he continued speaking in English.

"You were on this floor when you heard the gun?"

"I open elevator door," the boy nodded. "Gun he go bang."

"And then Mr. Johnson called the police?"

"He say, 'Something funny,' and telephone."

"You didn't try to open the door, or ring the bell, of this

apartment?"

The China-boy appeared unnecessarily uneasy as he said, "No. I not want see," his eyes faltered, dropped, to the dead man. "I not want see Mr. Carrington dead."

"How'd you know he was dead?" Wentworth snapped.

"I heard gun."

"Didn't you think he might have been cleaning a gun and it discharged?"

"I not think what happen," the boy shuddered. "I very afraid."

Wentworth's question darted out. "Why were you afraid?"

"The shot," the boy said.

Jimmy was back where he started, and knew it. There was every reason why the Chinese boy should have been fearful at hearing the discharge of the weapon in a sedate apartment house. Wentworth understood well that fear, in a time of crisis, meant neither guilt nor concealed information.

"I'd like to talk with this Mr. Johnson," he said to Dunand.

"Know the firm of Johnson, Blalock and Freeland? Johnson's the retired president… O'Malley! Will you go to Mr. Johnson's

apartment and ask him to step over here? And don't grab him by the arm, either, O'Malley!"

Mr. Johnson was a tall, spare man in his late seventies.

"Messy way to die," he commented. "Want me to tell what little I know? Gladly. Charley"—glancing at the elevator boy—"was running me up. Just as he opened the door, we heard a shot. Whether or not I actually heard poor Carrington fall I am not certain. I may have erred in not attempting to open the door—not that it would have done any good—but it seemed that the police should be notified instantly. And after I telephoned, I found Mrs. Johnson—she is in ill health, gentlemen—rather upset, and did not want to leave her. And that is all I know… except…"

The detectives said, with one breath, "Except what?"

"Mrs. Johnson said that she heard some one scream. Our apartment is next to Carrington's, you know."

"The top of his head was blown off," Dunand grunted. "He couldn't have yelled. Your wife was nervous. She imagined it."

"The funny thing is that she said she heard the scream about two or three minutes before she heard the shot, captain."

"From Carrington's apartment? Or a noise in the street?"

"She insists that it was Carrington's voice, and that he cried out in agony. As a matter of fact, Mrs. Johnson was trying to get my son, at the office, to tell him, when I returned from my after breakfast walk. I spoke with her, gentlemen, and she is absolutely positive the scream came from this apartment."

"Only a few minutes before the shot?"

"Less than five minutes. Probably only two or three."

Wentworth whirled on the elevator boy. "Who've you taken up to Carrington's apartment this morning?" he snapped.

"Eight o'clock, I take downstairs Mrs. Cohn's maid and dog," the boy began in a singsong voice. "Next, Mr. Hotchkiss he go office. Mr. Wilson he go office. Miss Chase, she go get hair fixed pretty. She gave me fo' bits to find taxi. Mr. Murphy, he go work too. Mrs. Murphy, she go with him. Only two I bring back up on elevator. Mrs. Cohn's maid and dog, she come back. Mr. Johnson, he come back from smoke cigar and walk. Nobody else. Nobody for Carrington."

"Charley's got a pretty good memory," Johnson said. "He even remembers our guests' names, especially if they give him a quarter."

"Is there a service elevator in the rear?" Dunand asked.

"Packages taken to apartments six to seven thirty, eleven to twelve, in morning," Charley said, as if repeating a ritual. "Six to seven thirty, I take up. Next time, porter take. Not yet next time. First time, nobody go up with me."

"Which is that," Wentworth said. "There's a fire escape, but even so—"

"The doors were locked, and the windows were locked, and the gun was his own, and it was in his hand," Captain Dunand growled. "We're a pair of fools, maybe, Jim. But… that scream! That may mean something."

"What do you suspect, gentlemen?" the retired merchant asked. When neither of the detectives replied, he added, "I had always thought that the police were well pleased if a death appeared to be a suicide."

"We like to make work for ourselves," grinned Jimmy.

"I wish the young men in my firm felt the same way. If you tire of the detective bureau, come and see us. Now, if you gentlemen are finished with me, I'll run along."

"May we ask Mrs. Johnson a few questions, later?"

"We're both at your service. All we knew about Carrington is that he was very quiet and kept to himself, and that he was apparently a man of means." Johnson waved a hand toward the furnishings of the apartment. "This cost a pretty penny," he commented. "My firm's in the importing business, and I can assure you that these paintings and ornaments are genuine. I've never seen finer, even in China."

When the talkative old merchant had gone, Jimmy said, "Got an offer of a job, anyhow, chief." And then, without warning, he turned on the elevator boy. "Who did you take up to this apartment this morning?" he snapped.

"Nobody."

Since the Chinese was startled, he said the single word in his native tongue, and was forced to repeat it in English. Wentworth was now satisfied that the elevator boy had spoken the truth.

2

CARRINGTON'S BODY WAS taken to the morgue. The apartment in which he had lived was searched from floor to ceiling. There were no finger-prints on the gun except those of Carrington. There were no finger-prints at all on the door of the safe. Every window fastening was examined, to make certain that none of the locks had been tampered with. The rear door—the service door, leading to a small hallway and the second elevator—was locked. Like the front door, it was fastened with a chain bolt. The chain of the front door had been ripped down, and the lock broken, when O'Malley had burst his way inside.

George Carrington had blown his brains out. He had been alone when he had done it. Suicide. But why was the safe empty? And what had made the dead man scream out in agony before he had fired the fatal shot?

Carrington had been alone when the trigger was pulled. Both Dunand and Wentworth were convinced of that fact. As they left the apartment at last Dunand said, "We haven't missed a bet, Jim. The circumstances are unusual, that's all. As far as the scream goes, he may have gone batty before he shot himself. And the empty safe only means that he'd destroyed all of his papers."

"Ever see the knob of a safe without finger-prints, chief?"

"Yes," said Dunand. "I know a man in the city here who always opens and closes his safe with gloves on. Then if he's robbed, we'll be able to get the prints of the thief without the man's own marks being in the way. This fellow may have had the same habit, and did it that way this morning because he'd always done it that way before. May have been just nutty enough."

Carrington's out-going telephone calls revealed nothing out of the ordinary, and finally Dunand said, "Go down to your beat, Jim, or the Chinks will miss you. I'll have Carrington's past examined, but unless something unusual comes up, you might as well forget this."

The two men separated at the front door. Dunand went back to his office. Jimmy walked thoughtfully down the hill, and just as the clock of Grace Cathedral struck noon he started to pace his beat. Every so often a Chinese merchant bowed to him; here and there Jim stuck his head into the doorway of a bazaar and said good morning to the placid proprietor. When he finally came to the bowl shop of the Wangs, a father and son who had at times tipped him off to impending trouble in the Oriental district, he went leisurely inside.

Young Wang Chen-p'o, in American clothes, was smoking a cigarette behind the counter.

"James," he said immediately, "I think we've been put on the spot."

Wentworth knew the indomitable courage of the Wangs, who had been threatened before for being friendly with the police.

"I'll lock you up for sixty days for vagrancy," he said. "That'll keep you safe."

"Don't like your prison diet. Not enough rice. My honorable father has gone to see the priest, who is even more versed in Chinese lore. Perhaps when he comes back we will know what the trouble is."

"What happened?"

"An hour or so after we opened the store this morning, we found a little snake made out of paper fastened to the inside of the door. It is probably some sort of a warning. But we don't know what kind."

"Who put it there?"

Wang Chen-p'o shrugged. "It may have been stuck on the door yesterday, and we didn't see it until this morning, when the light was better. Who? Your best friend may be your worst enemy if sufficient gold is placed in his hand. I—here comes my honorable father, Jimmy."

Old Wang shuffled slowly into the shop. Behind him were two slender Chinese in black. Wentworth knew that both were hatchetmen hired for protection by the Wangs. The ancient Chinese bowed gravely to Jimmy, walked behind the counter and then drew himself painfully to a high stool.

"I learned nothing," he said in Cantonese to his son. "However, it will be well if you stay at home after dark."

"The priest knows nothing, honorable father?"

"He says he has never heard of a snake warning."

Silently, he forestalled Wentworth's request by drawing out a little paper snake from his coat and handing it to him.

"A cobra," Jimmy ejaculated.

"A king cobra," said old Wang. "The deadliest serpent in the world."

"And," said his son, "I have just observed a man walk past our miserable store. He looked inside. With interest. If he saw you examining the snake, Jimmy, we are in for trouble, having shown it to you, and you are in danger for having seen it. Watch your step, James."

Wang the elder smiled for the first time. "Jimmy is now happy. Danger, to him, is food, shelter, temple and women. However, the little snake may have been a joke. Chinese humor is sometimes devious. It may mean any one of a thousand things. Or it may mean—"

"Death," said his son.

"Or Kong Gai," said Wentworth.

At the evil name, old Wang's head lowered. "The same thing," he muttered. "Kong Gai the deadly. In my unworthy opinion, I should say that the cobra would be the symbol Kong Gai would select with which to warn men of his displeasure."

The three were silent. Kong Gai, the mysterious and ferocious legendary figure of Chinatown, feared by all, who knew that Wentworth was more than a patrolman. About Kong Gai nothing was known. Jimmy had crossed his evil path several times, and each time had come away with one of Kong Gai's tongmen as a captive. But all Wentworth knew of Kong Gai was that the Chinese had a voice as sweet as a gentle summer breeze; a voice like a girl's. Whether Kong Gai were a dwarf or a giant, Jimmy had no idea.

Kong Gai was back of every evil happening in Chinatown. His tentacles were always reaching out. He controlled the opium importing, the opium smoking. He exacted tribute from respectable merchants. What was Kong Gai up to now?

"The king cobra," said Wang thoughtfully, "warns once before he strikes. *He* never warns before striking. I think I will employ another hatchetman, Jimmy. I am too old to stand the excitement of an unhappy death."

"If you could tell me who might've put the warning on the door, I might be able to help."

Wang bowed courteously. "Chen-p'o and myself have talked over every visitor to our shop," he said. "All were honest men. All men are honest, until it is worth more to be the opposite. We have no idea who left the little snake."

"Let me know if you learn anything," Wentworth said. "I'll drop in later—"

"At twenty minutes past one," grinned young Wang. "We set our clocks by you, Jim. Well, don't take any money with holes in the middle."

Wentworth stepped boldly out of the shop, giving his uniform belt a hitch, but before he started northward along his beat he gave one swift look southward. So far as he could see, all was serene. The Wangs were in for something. Jimmy knew how useless it would be to report anything to headquarters. If the Wangs' lives were saved, he had to do it himself. How? He had no idea. If Wang and the priest did not know exactly what the snake warning meant, no white man—not even one who knew much of Chinese lore—could hope to solve the mystery.

As Jimmy passed the curious shops—in one a live octopus, with its suckery tentacles reaching up the glass water-filled tub in which it was kept, and where, under water, it would be butchered to provide feasts for wealthy Chinese—he dismissed the Wangs, and wondered if Dunand would discover anything about Carrington which would be interesting. No finger-prints on the safe. The scream of agony.

Because of the snake warning, Jimmy thought, "Not even a snake could have got into Carrington's apartment. The man committed suicide. That's all there was to it. I'll bet Dunand finds out Carrington lost his shirt in the market, and went haywire."

As he came to a corner of Dupont Street, and stood idly a moment watching two Chinese youngsters sidle up to a fruit stall, coaxing each other to get nearer to a tempting pile of lichee nuts, some one on the side street cried out wildly, in terror.

Wentworth's body tensed. He was running westward even before he actually saw what was happening.

In the street, halfway up the block, lay a Chinese. A second Asiatic was bending over the prostrate form. As Wentworth raced up the steep street, the second Oriental, seemingly warned, jumped up, and began to run. The fleeing Chinese was lame, and ran slowly. Wentworth had no need to shout, nor to draw his gun.

The narrow street, a moment ago filled with Chinese was emptied miraculously. Even the blind beggar propped against a sunny wall opened his eyes and scuttled away. There remained only the man lying in the street, the fugitive Chinese, and the detective.

Jimmy's long legs drew him nearer with every bound. The fleeing Oriental, perhaps warned by a confederate, turned.

He saw how close the blue-clad officer was. With an instant's hesitation, he twisted sidewise and darted down the nearest dark cellar stairway, with Wentworth less than twenty feet behind him.

As the detective leaped down the rickety stairs, he jerked out his small electric torch. It was dark as the pit in the cellar. Wentworth, as he ran, pressed the button of the torch instantly, and light flashed. But not from the torch. Stars danced once before Jimmy's eyes, stars whirling and dazzling, and then everything went blacker than the silent cellar, and the detective, smashed over the head, fell to the dust of the floor, unconscious.

3

BEFORE JIMMY WENTWORTH opened his eyes, he knew several things. Firstly, he was bound. Secondly, he had been the biggest fool in the world, to have followed the Chinese into the cellar after Wang's warning to watch his step. Thirdly, his head felt as if somebody were hitting it with hammers. And lastly, he was in a room where lights were lit.

The thought, and the pain throbbing through him, must have made him blink, for a sweet, lovely voice said, "You are awake, detective? I was growing impatient. Your head aches. That I regret, but it was necessary to strike hard. If you will open your eyes, I promise a most unusual feast of beauty, which will make you forget the pain. In addition, you have wanted to see me. Here I am. The man who is rightly feared. Kong Gai."

The sweet, melodious voice trembled on the last word. Wentworth shivered, and then slowly opened his eyes.

Facing him was a wizened Chinese, seated on a teakwood stool. Kong Gai's evil eyes watched the white man with delighted content. On one silk clad knee was a thick writing pad. In the Chinese's right hand was a pencil studded with one blue jewel.

Strangest of all, kneeling at Kong Gai's slippered feet was a Chinese girl. Although Jimmy Wentworth knew only too well the sort of fate in store for him, he was unable to avoid staring at the exotic figure. The girl was dressed in magnificent brocaded silks, pale blue and orange. Her face was almost Caucasian. In her smooth black hair was a white gardenia, no paler than her cheeks. Her eyes, somber as pools of ink, were fixed on the bound detective.

Kong Gai's pencil moved. He handed a sheet of paper to the girl, and she read, softly, "How do you like my voice, Mr. Wentworth? If you thought to find me, by means of it, that would have been difficult, wouldn't it? It is a useful voice."

Did the girl hesitate an instant before she continued? Did Kong Gai's yellow eyes darken at the infinitesimal pause? "Since my daughter was educated in a mission, she speaks both English and Chinese. What do you think of the little idea of my mouthpiece?"

"I think," said Jimmy, "that in a few minutes you'll have a lot of police breaking in here when I don't report at headquarters."

The deadly face wrinkled with enjoyment as Kong Gai's fingers scrawled the next message.

"In where?" read the girl.

Jimmy knew that his feeble, obvious bluff hadn't worked. Where? He had not the slightest notion. After he had been slugged, Kong Gai's hatchetmen had probably carried him, through underground passages, to this room. And it was undoubtedly a long way from the cellar just off Dupont Street.

"Anyhow," Wentworth said coldly, "I wouldn't mind a cigarette."

Kong Gai scribbled a few words on his pad; the girl read them aloud—"Get the white man cigarettes"—and then, like a sleepwalker, went to an ivory box on a carved stand and brought Wentworth one of the paper tubes. She knelt beside him, put the cigarette between his lips, and lit it with a bit of twisted paper. Wentworth, when she was close, saw that her eyes were entirely blank.

A clap of Kong Gai's hands brought her back to him. She read what he had written on the pad.

"Those are very good cigarettes, detective. I bought them in India. There is a very little opium in them for flavoring." The girl puzzled over a word, and then continued, *"Papaver somniferum*—which is opium—is a boon to all Orientals, detective. In bringing much of it into this country, I am doing good. Don't you think so?"

Wentworth wondered how much Kong Gai would boast. Not that it made any difference now! Instead of answering the question, he said, "The cigarette tastes fine, Kong Gai. I suppose you learned about the little cobra you put on Wang's door in India, also?"

The ugly Chinese snarled a word, and then smiled. He wrote swiftly. The girl read, "I was afraid you had been told about the snake in the Wangs' shop. It is a warning from the King Cobra—Kong Gai! Soon you will see how it works."

"Just as soon die that way as any other," Wentworth told him.

He knew that Kong Gai was amused, and that the Chinese had watched him when he looked about the room, searching in vain for some means of escape, some plan. "When it comes to a tough way to die, Kong Gai, you won't like the noose. We'll get you."

Wentworth was trying to anger the Chinese again, but couldn't do it.

Kong Gai had been writing, his eyes shining as his pencil moved. When he had finished the girl voiced his message.

"You are mistaken, detective. Since this is your last day to live, let me point out your error before you learn it yourself. I have seen a coolie bitten by a cobra. He felt burning pain at once. Within a minute he began to lose power over his legs. In a few minutes more his lower jaw began to fall. Froth and saliva ran from his mouth. He was in agony. He moaned and twisted his arms. Then they, also, became paralyzed. Only his brain was clear, to feel the pain, to know that death was coming. That is how the Wangs will die. It is how you will die."

Wentworth stared at him, as if Kong Gai were really the King Cobra. The evil snake-like eyes fascinated him, and it was a full minute before he was able to say, "If the police don't get you for killing me, they'll hang you for murdering the Wangs."

Again the horrible pause while Kong Gai scribbled his retort.

"I think I will leave the Wangs where your learned police can find them. The post-mortem appearance is not distinctive, detective. I do not believe your blundering surgeons will find out what really took place. It will amuse me to read your newspapers. 'Mysterious death dealt to Chinese merchants.' And who would expect a cobra bite in San Francisco?"

Jimmy supposed that once Kong Gai had ceased enjoying

the situation, it would be his own finish. What a way to die! Bound! Caught by his own foolishness!

"Why, dear detective," the pale girl read, "the poison from a cobra is so terrible that when a white man, of any intelligence, knows what has happened, he blows out his brains rather than face the agony—"

"Like Carrington," Wentworth snapped.

Kong Gai himself, proof that he could talk, screamed, *"Hai! How did you know?"*

Jimmy hadn't known. Some strange intuition had forced him to say the words.

The wizened Chinese had slipped from the teakwood stool. He came directly in front of Wentworth.

"You know too much," he snarled. "It is a good thing I have you here! How much more do you know?" His eyes darted at the white man venomously. "Who have you told about the cobra poison—about the death of the snake?"

Wentworth spat out the end of the cigarette.

"If you do not answer, I will give you only a little cobra poison! Just enough so that your tongue becomes motionless, and grows large until your mouth is filled with it, and you choke to death—"

"That'll be a fine way to make me talk," said Jimmy.

Kong Gai struck him in the face.

"Bring on your snake," the white man suggested. "Let's get this monkey business over with, Kong Gai. I'm not going to tell you how much I know, nor who else knows about anything."

The Chinese fumbled in his coat and drew out a hypodermic. "Many a cobra has been killed to give me this poison," he boasted. "It is pure cobra venom. I can keep it for years, and by adding water, have something as poisonous as when the venom came from the cobra. The death is lingering, and very painful. I will thrust the needle into your vein—"

"Is that what you did to Carrington?"

Kong Gai rocked back on his heels. "So the great detective doesn't know so very much? No, that is not what I did to Carrington. It is not what I will do to the Wangs. You talk too much, detective. You give yourself away."

"So do you," said Wentworth. "You talk like a mission Chino who went to an American college—"

"And was laughed at! And saw the woman he loved stolen by a white man! But there has been revenge, my friend! Little Rose-blossom"—he waved his hand toward the girl—"should have been my child instead of Carrington's… and now she is indeed mine! To do with as I wish! She has no will but mine—"

"Or your drugs—"

"Her father finally discovered my trail. I was ready for him. His own hand spattered his brains on the walls, and you, oh, fool, thought he had killed himself. I was not there, but my hand pulled the trigger! Just as I will kill the Wangs, the father and the son! *Hai-ya!* To-morrow they will see a little spider, perhaps, that symbol of ill luck. One of them will squash it with his hand. And inside the spider, made so carefully from paper by a man I know, is a tiny bit of spun glass, and beneath the glass is a little capsule which breaks… and into the veins goes the venom of the king cobra!"

"Carrington wouldn't have hit a spider with his hand."

"Ah, no. A friend of mine went to see him. Yesterday! And when my friend departed, he carefully placed a capsule, and a bit of spun glass in it, on the door knob! And when Carrington went to open the door this morning he knew—within a fraction of a second, when his palm began to burn—that Kong Gai had found him! And you, white fool, thought he had committed suicide!"

Kong Gai laughed shortly.

"I have boasted," he said, "but it will not do you any good, Wentworth."

He clapped his hands loudly three times, and in a moment a thin, silent hatchetman padded into the magnificent chamber. Kong Gai scribbled on his pad, and handed the note to the blank-eyed, dazed girl.

"Drag the white dog before me," read Carrington's daughter. "We will put the serpent mark on his chest and listen to his screams." In the same lovely, monotonous voice, she went on, "Little Rose-blossom has been a good girl. She may stay and see the entertainment, after which she will be given the pale violet drink she loves so much."

For the first time the girl showed animation. She turned gratefully toward Kong Gai, as if thanking him for his kindness. Knowing the terrible drugs of the Orient, Wentworth was positive that the girl was kept under the influence of one of them, a mixture with opium as its base, which destroyed reason and senses.

The hatchetman jerked Wentworth to his knees, and dragged him directly before Kong Gai. Then he padded over to the brazier, and put a thin silver opium pipe into the red coals. He seemed happy. He hummed to himself as he watched the end of the pipe slowly turn bright.

When it was white hot, he stepped to Wentworth's side. A knife, delicately wielded, ripped through the white man's uniform and bared his chest.

Jimmy's arms strained against the thongs; they cut into his wrists, but the soft, pliable leather did not give at all. If only his hands were in front of him!

One hand smoothing the girl's hair, Kong Gai, the girl kneeling at his feet close to Wentworth, leaned forward. His eyes shone brighter than the coals. He looked, and was, a king cobra ready to strike.

The hatchetman smiled at Wentworth, as if it were the greatest joke in the world, and, still humming, went to the stand, returning with brazier and pipe. He cut pieces of Wentworth's heavy blue uniform coat into strips, and made a handle for the pipe.

He said, "For your honor, oh king of all the cobras!" to Kong Gai, and then picked up the heated pipe.

"First trace the body, and last of all the hood," Kong Gai hissed. "And then, highest of all—near his throat, where the flesh is delicate—the symbol of Kong Gai!"

Wentworth felt sweat burst from his forehead as the heat of the pipe neared his skin. True to his nature, the hatchetman did not hurry. He, like his master, wanted this white dog to anticipate the pain. Jimmy's lips were a thin gray line. Every muscle from head to foot was as taut as steel. They wouldn't get a sound out of him. He wouldn't move. He wouldn't even shut his eyes against the agony. He'd grin. They couldn't wipe that grin from his face as long as he was alive.

Then, almost before he felt the pain sear his chest, the stench of burning human flesh—his own—rose to his nostrils. The torture had begun.

4

WHAT MADE JIMMY Wentworth, isolated and bound, drive his head into the hatchetman's middle he never knew. Escape was impossible. What the Chinese actually wanted most of all was to have him try escape; to have him beg and plead and writhe before them. Perhaps he saw, for a fraction of time, a flicker of intelligence in the girl's dazed eyes. Perhaps he hoped to make the hatchetman pick up his discarded knife and bring instant, painless death.

Into the thin hatchetman's belly Wentworth drove, with all the force of his long, powerful body. The unexpected assault, with no warning cry, no telltale movement of an eyelid, drove the Chinese back. He fell against the girl, against the high stool of Kong Gai. The three fell backward together in a heap, with Kong Gai and the hatchetman spitting anger.

Wentworth rolled to his side. Once his blind aim missed. Then welcome pain shot to his head from his wrists.

The hatchetman was on his knees struggling to free himself from Kong Gai's flowing robe. Instinctively, the Chinese sprawled forward toward the knife on the rug. Wentworth, half blind with pain, jerked his arms wide, and the thongs, burned partly by the coals, snapped.

The two men came together just as the Chinese reached his knife. Wentworth had no second to lose. Any instant Kong Gai would clap his hands and bring men. If only the devil didn't want any one else to see what had happened! The knife was high in the air. Wentworth's fist swung with terrific force, and the hatchman's head was almost snapped from his body.

Kong Gai was swooping down now, his face a mask of demoniac rage. In his hand flashed a long, double-edged blade. On his knees, Wentworth had no possible chance to parry the blow. Death was close, and he had asked for it before. Now his hands were free, and he was ready to fight for life.

He snatched up the heavy, coal-filled brazier, caring nothing for the anguish the hot metal brought, and hurled the fiery weapon straight at Kong Gai's face. The Chinese screamed once, terribly. Before he could cry out a second time, to summon aid, the detective was all over him at once, and bore him to the floor.

With Kong Gai's own robe the detective bound and gagged him. The hatchetman was stirring; voices outside chattered and questioned. Wentworth glanced at the girl. There was a little pucker of doubt between her eyes, but she stood motionless beside the overturned stool. Here and there coals began to smolder on the rugs. Wentworth kicked them together swiftly, and then emptied a flower bowl over them.

He dragged the hatchetman beside Kong Gai, and bound them back to back. Then his face lit. He cast about the room until he found the pad of paper, and wrote on it rapidly.

When he handed it to the girl, she said aloud, clearly, "When I clap my hands, I desire that one of my servants secure an automobile. Have it wait for my honorable self at the door below."

Wentworth hoped the door was below! He listened to the girl's lovely voice sing the command in Chinese. He wished that he could take Kong Gai along with him, but that was impossible. Not only must he rescue the girl, but he must take no chances in doing it.

Beside Kong Gai Wentworth knelt.

"I'm going to borrow your clothes, oh, great Kong Gai," he said. "I do not suppose you will wait for me to return, or, if I did, your hatchetmen would let us in before you escaped. So I say good-by, oh, boaster! First"—releasing one of the makeshift bonds—"I am going to borrow your clothes." Expertly, Wentworth stripped the Chinese. "Probably you wear a different costume when you go riding," the white man said cheerfully. "If you lose face for appearing in the street in silks, I'm sorry. I'd ask you where your street clothes are, but I don't suppose you'd tell me. Thanks for your hospitality, Kong Gai. I'll return it just as soon as I can."

Gagged, Kong Gai could only make inarticulate noises, akin to the venomous hiss of a viper.

In Chinese attire, the lean white man seemed to have suddenly shrunk in size. He stooped. His shoulders bent forward. His knees, under the silks, bent also. He appeared no taller than Kong Gai. Last of all, he unlaced his shoes. After he had slit the heels of Kong Gai's slippers, he pulled them over his own feet.

Kong Gai and the hatchetman he dragged to a far corner, and covered them with a rug. He had a moment's hesitation: he could carry Kong Gai easily enough, but would Kong Gai ever carry anything—and Wentworth, to the servants outside, must be Kong Gai. No, it wouldn't work. The first job was to save the girl, if it could be done.

Wentworth padded Orient-fashion, over to her. He took her hand and patted it gently. Then he wrote on the pad again. There was a way he might be able to return! But that would mean bringing the girl with him. Out! He tore up the sheet, and wrote on it: "I expect several white men. If they return before I am back, bring them to this room without question." That would bring several of the Chinatown detail inside… and perhaps nab Kong Gai!

He wrote a few more words, and handed the paper to the girl, guiding her toward the spot where the hatchetmen had entered earlier. In her sweet voice, associated with Kong Gai's presence, she said, "Open the door. Kong Gai departs," and added the order concerning the admission of white men.

The door opened. Wentworth's head was hidden in the silks. Even this precaution was unnecessary. In the dim, sandal-wood-scented hallway, servants bowed low. None dared lift their eyes to the dread figure of their master, Kong Gai, the cobra king, whose very touch was death. Even the half dozen slim hatchetmen lined against the far wall averted their eyes in superstitious fear. Kong Gai was a generous master. His commands, spoken through the white maid, were rewarded with gold and the juice of the poppy. But who could tell what might happen if the Evil One were addressed without permission? Hence it was considered wise to look the other way.

One cringing old Oriental shuffled ahead of Wentworth and the girl. The aged Chinese opened doors, and slid back secret panels, for the "master" and his white slave girl. The hall was long. There were stairs to be mounted. Lights were snapped on, and off, by the old man. Runways had to be carefully descended. For a full five minutes Wentworth and the girl followed the servant. Once the air grew cold, still, and damp, as if they must be underground. Once, when the lights were on,

Wentworth saw an apparatus designed to collapse the walls. He guessed that they were in some deep tunnel, far below the streets. Up and down they followed the servant, around corners, sometimes doubling back on themselves.

At last, his hand on a great iron bolt, the servant bowed low, and said, "The hire-machine is outside, according to your command. I am your slave, Kong Gai. I live as you live. I dare your anger. Oh, Kong Gai, is it wise to go into the street in bright silk?"

"It is wise," Wentworth said in the same dialect.

He was ready to throttle the Chinese if the man detected the different voice, but all the servant said was, "Go in peace, oh, Kong Gai, and return safely. I will go to your room now, and pray to your great idol."

Wentworth wanted to keep the servant out of that room! So he said, in a husky tone, "Wait here for me. I return soon."

It was very dark where they were standing. Behind him, Jimmy caught the flicker of pale yellow light. He heard the thudding of feet in the passageway. Some one must have entered the room and found Kong Gai!

"Your blind servant hears something, oh, Kong Gai," muttered the old Oriental.

"Open the door!" Wentworth growled in Chinese.

"Perhaps it is a message for you—"

Wentworth shoved the servant away from the barrier. The Chinese, having guessed that something was amiss, screamed, "It is not the voice of the master! Come quickly, brothers!" The blind servant tried to push Wentworth back, clawing at him with long, jagged nails.

Thrusting the old man back, Jimmy fumbled for the bolt.

Would it push back? Yes! But was there some other lock, to which the servant had the key? If the door didn't open, Kong Gai's horde would be on him in another minute. And then Wentworth, holding to the bolt, jerked the door open. The sunlight streamed in.

Hurrying the girl ahead of him, Wentworth saw a taxi waiting in the narrow alley. The driver jumped from his seat and opened the door.

"Get going," Wentworth snapped. "Step on it!"

"Say, what's this?" the driver asked belligerently as he saw the girl. "I ain't gonna get mixed up in no funny business."

"If you don't snap into it, you'll get a bullet in the back! Police headquarters on Kearny Street. Hall of Justice. Come on!"

The driver hesitated. He was behind the wheel now, trying to puzzle things out. Who was this Chink speaking like a white man? And what a swell looking jane he had with him, all dolled out in Chink clothes! "I don't want none of this," the driver growled. "The pair of you get out!"

Wentworth, knowing how every second counted, urged, "You can't go wrong taking us to the Hall of Justice, man! This's life or death! I'm on the detective bureau, hurry it up!"

The driver started to say that he himself was the chief of police when the first shot roared in the narrow street. No car ever leaped forward any faster than the taxi. Wentworth, thrown back against the cushions as the machine swayed down the street, said to the girl, "You're safe, Miss Carrington."

She stared straight ahead as if she heard nothing. Jimmy looked directly into her sad, dazed eyes. "Damn Kong Gai!" he muttered.

5

EVEN OLD DENNY, seeing his last years of service as doorman in the Hall of Justice, who had seen many strange things in his long life, was startled when Wentworth and the girl passed through the door. A girl, white, beautiful, dressed in silks bright as the sun, with a flower in her black hair, with kingfisher-jade on her fingers—that was a sight to stare at! But Jimmy Wentworth! Old Denny could see the young Chinatown detective's blue patrolman uniform under a silk Chinese robe and, where the uniform was ripped apart, could see a long seared red mark on his chest.

A hundred thousand questions were in Denny's mouth, but all he said was, "Captain Dunand's in his office. An' there's a couple o' newspaper hounds waitin' to see him as usual."

"Thanks, Denny," Wentworth grinned. "I'll give 'em something to think about, won't I?"

The three newspaper men, waiting for a statement concerning a bootleg raid, stood in front of Dunand's door when they saw the pair approach. "What's up?" they chorused.

"Go outside and you'll see," Jimmy told them. They vanished toward the elevator before Jimmy opened the chief's door.

Dunand was alone. He turned, and then stood up when he saw Jimmy's silent companion. Wentworth led the girl to a chair, and forced her gently to sit down. Then he walked close to Dunand.

"This slave raid business's bad, Jim," Dunand said quietly. "One of the missions tip you off? You'll find that she's the legal wife of somebody now, even if she wasn't when you rescued her. That's what always happens. Before you tell me about it, there's something doing on the Carrington case—"

"I know," Jimmy said. "She isn't a slave girl, captain. She's Carrington's daughter."

The grim captain of detectives leaned far back in his chair. He looked briefly at the lovely girl, sitting so silently, and then said to Wentworth, "There was mention of a daughter in Carrington's safe deposit box. But that isn't all. We've learned how Carrington died—"

"Cobra poison."

Dunand ejaculated, "How'd you know? The chemists just found out!"

"Kong Gai told me."

"Talk," Dunand ordered.

Swiftly, Wentworth explained.

"I told Dr. White he was crazy," said the captain. "Told him there was no cobra in the apartment, and no way one could've got in. What a fiend that man is!"

Dunand fingered some of the reports on his desk—charts of absorption bands from the police chemist in many colors: dark violet for codein, violet-red for caffein, a pure violet for strychnin; there was a full spectroscopic test which discovered the animal poison from the cobra venom; there was even a photograph of the venomous effect of the poison on the blood of the dead man. The customary mucous membrane of the stomach was missing, proving that the chemist had not been fooled for a minute.

"The blood'd turned black, and was very fluid," Dunand said quietly. "White was on the right track at once." Soberly, "I'll call a matron, and then I suppose she'd better take Miss Carrington to a hospital to rest up. Carrington was a very rich man. He's got a sister living in Oregon. We'll wait until she comes before deciding what to do." Dunand was all crisp decision now. "The taxi driver's waiting? Right. He'll remember the exact location. We'll rip Chinatown apart to get Kong Gai this time."

"I was five minutes walking out. There are walls which can be collapsed. You'll never find his real den. Even if you did, chief, you wouldn't find him there."

Dunand drummed on his desk. "Don't like bein' beaten!"

"Neither do I. And the longer I stay here the better chance there is of missing the actual murderer of Carrington."

"What?"

"Kong Gai 'll attempt to carry out his threat to kill the Wangs. That's where I'm going."

"Somebody 'll be waiting to knife you—"

"Can I have a coat, chief? And a gun. Kong Gai got mine."

"Better have the nurse fix that burn."

"It doesn't hurt now." Jimmy grinned at Dunand. "Want to come, chief? We'll get into the Wangs' shop without being seen."

Dunand reached instantly into his drawer for his own automatic. "If the newspaper boys get hard boiled, Jim, tell 'em we're goin' out for lunch."

"Sure," Jimmy agreed. "They saw me come in. That 'll satisfy 'em perfectly!"

The station nurse knocked. Inside, she took one look at the girl, saying shrewdly, "Drugged. Little doses all the time, probably. She's temporarily deaf, I think. It will be some time before she is better."

"Take her to a hospital. Send out for whatever things she needs," Dunand ordered. "I'm… going out to lunch."

Jimmy, buttoning his coat, went to the silent girl's side. "Everything's all right now," he smiled. He reached down and patted the lax hands lying on the silk of her gorgeous robe. The girl's eyes lifted slowly, and Wentworth thought he saw a flash of recognition in them. For some reason he did not understand this pleased him very much.

The newspaper men were waiting. "Look here, officer," one of them said. "You told us if we'd go outside we'd find out what was the matter."

Dunand yanked at his detective, but Jimmy stopped.

"No," he objected. "You asked what was up, and I told you if you went outside you'd see."

"We didn't see anything! What was up?"

"The American flag," Wentworth grinned, and hurried after Dunand to the elevator. The newspaper boys didn't think it was funny, and went downstairs to pump Denny, which did them no good at all.

Wentworth dismissed the taxi driver after the cab had taken them just to the shadow of old Grace Cathedral, on the edge of Chinatown. The Oriental district teemed with Chinese, with tourists; the windows of the bazaars displayed wares of the East; the guide on the corner promised: "See the mysteries of Chinatown. Singsong girls. Tong men. Joss house"… and Wentworth, suddenly, drew Dunand toward a little stand where coconut candies and lichee nuts were sold; where china lilies bloomed in blue pots.

The old vendor murmured, "Peace to the friends of the house of Wang." He ducked aside. The two white men stepped past him. A door, seemingly a part of the wall, opened, and closed at once as the detectives went through it.

"We'll come out in the back of Wang's shop," Jimmy said. He reached, in the darkness, upward, and took down a flash light. "I don't see how we can be too late. I left Kong Gai pretty unhappy. It'll take him time to get after the Wangs, but he'll do it as soon as he remembers he boasted to me about it. And then we ought to nab the actual murderer of Carrington—the man who did the deed—if not Kong Gai. And that will hurt him, and hurt his reputation."

As they walked along the damp passageway, Wentworth told his chief briefly of the reason for the Carrington girl's capture, of the other things he had learned about Kong Gai.

"The man is a fiend," Jimmy said. "He wants power. He hates white men. I think he controls the opium traffic now. And he has a finger in the pie of smuggling Chinese into this country. In a short time every merchant in Chinatown will be paying him tribute. We've got to get him before that happens."

"There were some letters in Carrington's safe deposit box which bear out what you believe, Jim. Kong Gai thought to destroy all the evidence by having the little safe rifled. By the way, I jumped the Chink elevator boy; asked him—or had one of the men do it—who was in the apartment yesterday. He insists no Chinese went to Carrington's rooms at any time. He's lying—"

"Maybe. Kong Gai's wealthy now. No telling who he has working for him. Well, we'll see in a moment or two, if we're lucky."

A door, thick wood and steel, blocked the way. With a coin, Wentworth knocked against it, and metallic sound filled the tunnel. Four times Jimmy tapped on steel, then once, then four times again. A singsong voice, dim and muffled, said:

"How long a time is fixed for the life of man?"

Wentworth answered instantly, in the same tongue, "It is limited to the time that suffices to emit a breath."

The guard tapped twice on the door. Wentworth answered with two taps, and then with four and one, short and sharp. The barrier swung slowly open.

"Honorable younger brother," the detective said, "there is no time to be lost. Are the august Wang and his son Wang Chen-p'o above?"

The guard slid back the bolts. "Come," he invited.

The detectives followed the gaunt hatchetman around sharp turns, until they were in a simply furnished room. Here a relative of the Wangs, busy with writing brush, went into the shop to return with young Wang.

"Still alive?" Jimmy asked.

Wang Chen-p'o, dressed in American clothing, offered cigarettes before replying. "So far, so good," he admitted. "Alive, James, but a trifle nervous."

"Why?"

Chen-p'o shrugged. "The warning of the snake."

Dunand was glancing curiously about the room. He guessed how valuable some of the simple bowls and ornaments must be; but what interested him more was the rack of rifles against a wall, and the three lean Chinese playing some game on the floor beneath the weapons.

"Anybody come in you're doubtful about this morning, Chen-p'o?"

"The usual tourists. That's all."

"You're sure?"

"Positive."

"Then all we need to do is wait."

Young Wang puffed deeply on his cigarette. "For… Kong Gai?" he asked slowly. "For his vengeance?"

"Correct."

"I suppose you don't care to tell me what's in the wind?"

"Not time, old man. Only this—and tell your father also—don't touch anything, anywhere. Especially not a spider. Got that right?"

"A spider should be instantly killed—"

"You'll be, if you smash it! Got it straight?"

The Chinese nodded soberly. "I suppose you want to get where you can look out into the shop, or did you just come to warn us?"

"We want to watch."

The younger Wang went to the wall, and slid back a small peephole. "In front of this, Jim, is a cupboard," he explained. "I'll open the cupboard when I return to the shop. There are some bowls on the shelves, so arranged that you can see the door, and most of the counter. My honorable father will sit where you can see him. That O.K.?"

"Fine. Remember, don't kill any spiders!"

"Not me. If there is any supplementary killing to be done, James, why not let one of our hatchetmen do it? The boys really need exercise. They'd enjoy a little recreation."

"We want to capture the man, or men, alive."

"It seems so silly; you want to catch a man alive, just to be able to hang him. It is not logical. However, I am your friend. Far be it from me to criticize your strange customs."

6

———

WHILE JIM WATCHED and listened, he and Dunand spoke together in whispers. They followed the curious trail which had started at Carrington's apartment; followed it step by step until it brought them again to Wang's shop. Dunand was positive that a trace of the cobra poison would be found on the door knob of Carrington's room. The police chemist has said that it dried to yellow crystals, and retained its deadly properties for a long time. If the Chinese came to play the same prank on the Wangs, with a poisoned artificial spider, the similarity of method should be sufficient to convict the murderous attendants of Kong Gai.

Wentworth knew Chinese habits and the Asiatic mind well enough to be certain that Kong Gai would attempt to carry out his boast. He hoped that the King Cobra would do it as speedily as possible. When he thought of Kong Gai's vengeance striking at the lovely, defenseless white girl, Carrington's daughter, his lips thinned to a white line. Kong Gai was a devil. He had really killed Carrington three times: once, by stealing his child, the second time by poisoning the white man, who knew the awful death in store for him, and thirdly when Carrington had blown out his brains rather than let the fire of the venom burn through his veins. Wentworth knew he would face Kong Gai again. If only, when that time came, he had a gun in his hand!

Several customers, men and women, entered the shop—all Americans. Wentworth watched them all. They made their purchases, and departed. Two white men came in; they bought a Canton ginger jar. While one of them paid for the porcelain, a sedate Chinese merchant waddled in.

Wentworth, recognizing the Asiatic as a respected merchant, relaxed as the conversation began. The two white men, waiting for young Wang to wrap the jar, stood listening as if enjoying the—to them—unusual scene.

"On the tenth of this month, honorable Wang," the merchant said, "a feast is to be given in my poor house. We need new bowls for tea. Is it permitted for me to select from your admirable collection?"

"I have only miserable bowls, none suitable for a man of your taste, Po Ling. If I show them, I beg that you overlook their many defects."

Captain Dunand, peeping out, whispered to Wentworth, "That fellow in the gray suit. I've seen him. I know. He was mixed up in some robbery. We couldn't prove it on him."

Wentworth nodded, and watched closely. He slipped his gun from its holster, in case either of the white men made a motion toward the Wangs. The fact that the two Americans remained in the shop—young Wang had handed them the package—was now suspicious. Different patterns of porcelain were brought. Po Ling selected a design. The interminable argument about price began. Penny by penny Po Ling raised his offer, penny by penny Wang dropped his demands. Finally they met.

"It is agreed," Po Ling smiled, and stroked his face. Immediately one of the white men stepped away from the counter, and started to examine porcelains on the shelf opposite. On the counter, where his hand had rested, Jimmy saw a little brown spot. The spider. "I am a poor man," Po Ling grieved, "but my guests must have proper bowls."

He drew out a silken coin sack, and, in opening it, stared at the top of the counter. "Honorable Wang!" he cried, as if disturbed. "I see a spider! I cannot make a purchase where such an unlucky and evil insect lives!"

Old Wang said placidly, "I will kill this spider," and raised his hand.

Wentworth and Dunand rushed into the shop almost side by side. Although no word had passed between them, Dunand covered the white men, and Wentworth had his gun squarely at the Chinese merchant.

"Do not move," Jimmy commanded in Chinese.

Dunand's men were white as sheets, although both tried to laugh. The merchant's jaw dropped. He did not move. Instead, before Wentworth could cover his mouth, Po Ling wailed nasally, loudly, "Help! Help!"

Before he repeated the word, a shot ripped through the window of the shop. Jim fired instantly, over Po Ling's shoulder, as four hatchetmen, who had been lurking outside, slid like black shadows into the bowl shop. Captain Dunand whirled toward the door, and one of the white men smashed him with his fist behind the ear.

Old Wang, behind the counter, stroked his wrinkled face. Chen-p'o shouted a command in Chinese.

In the split second of time possible, Wentworth saw everything happening before him. The merchant Po Ling was scuttling for the door. The two white men had both drawn guns, but did not seem to want to use them. But the four hatchetmen slipping forward had no such scruples. Three edged toward the detective; the fourth bent over Dunand's prostrate body.

Wentworth fired at him, his hand as steady as if he had been at pistol practice. The Chinese squealed, and fell half across Dunand's body. Two more Asiatics, both waving automatics as if they were knives, raced into the shop—the hatchetmen who had been acting as observers from the other side of the street.

"Do not kill the white dog! Kong Gai wants him alive!" one shouted.

Instead of backing away, Wentworth, his gun blazing, rushed forward. Some Chinese would knife Dunand at the first opportunity. A knife whirled at Jimmy as he fought to reach the prostrate captain. Hands clawed at him. Wentworth felt hot pain in his shoulder. He fired his last shot point blank into a snarling, spitting face.

"Drag him down!" some one screamed.

The hatchetmen forced Wentworth sidewise by sheer weight of bodies. A shelf of bowls crashed to the floor. Jimmy knew he could never hold them off. They'd rather take him back to Kong Gai than anything else. They'd rush him out of the shop, to a basement somewhere close, and that would be his finish!

From the rear of the room the Wang guards came. In their hands, swung like clubs, were heavy rifles. Skulls cracked. A guard cried aloud as a Kong Gai knife reached his heart. The bowl shop became a terrible place of battle, of blood and agonized screams and death.

Po Ling, the old merchant, had vanished. The two white men were moving cautiously doorward, intent on leaving. Kong Gai's hatchetmen now had their hands full. The detective managed to batter his way after the pair.

"Get 'em up!" he roared about the frightful tumult. "Drop

your guns! Turn around! Face the wall!"

One of Kong Gai's men screeched, "Let us depart, brothers of the snake! This is no longer good!"

Nor was it. Although Kong Gai's two gunmen had shot three of the Wang guards, Captain Dunand, lying on the floor, was now up on one elbow. Very precisely he was crippling one after another of the hatchetmen. Considering that he had been knocked unconscious before, his aim was miraculous.

The place was a shambles. Only old Wang was a spectator. His son, Chen-p'o, had grappled with a Manchu hatchetman, a man with jagged fangs showing over his lower lip. The hatchetman bore the slight Chen-p'o toward the counter. Step by step, inch by inch, Chen-p'o resisted, but the hatchetman bore him back until Chen-p'o's hips were against the wood. Then, using his legs as levers, the Manchu began to exert real pressure. His jaws dripped. Backward went Chen-p'o. In another few seconds his back would be broken.

Old Wang, without unseeming haste, selected a pair of ivory chopsticks from beneath the counter. Dunand dare not fire, lest he kill Chen-p'o. Jimmy's gun was empty. The guards were too engrossed in their battle to see what was taking place. But old Wang deliberately picked up the artificial spider from the counter. He looked at it quizzically and then leaned forward. When the spider was on the cheek of the hatchetman, old Wang pressed it against the skin.

For one second more the Kong Gai hatchetman tried to snap Chen-p'o's back, and then his hand raked at his cheek.

"The cobra!" he wailed. "The cobra poison!"

"Exactly," said old Wang, and smiled.

Two of Kong Gai's men were dead, and two of the Wang

guards. The Manchu was going to die. He dropped to the floor, and was reciting as many prayers as he could remember. There were bloody shoulders from Dunand's shots. The two white men kept their hands high. Captain Dunand, sitting up, was now complete master of the situation.

"Jim," he said contentedly, "this was great! Have young Wang call the wagon. It's a grand haul."

Wentworth lined up the wounded hatchetmen, and, taking no chances, ordered the Wang guards to watch the door, lest a rescue be attempted. Jimmy did not think it would occur. Kong Gai must have figured that he had sent enough men for a simple task. Also, the King Cobra was probably either fortifying his own lair, or finding a new one.

The street outside remained still as death. Only a few white tourists walked along it, gazing into the windows, and wondering why there were so few Chinese about. Chinatown knew what was happening. At such a time a man hid deep in his own cellar.

"Turn around, you two," Dunand commanded the pair of white men, after Chen-p'o had called the Hall of Justice. "A pair of rats," he decided.

"Hop-heads," Wentworth said shortly.

"It's gettin' pretty tough when a man can't go into a store an' buy somethin' without havin' the cops pull a gat on him," one of the men blurted.

"Sure. It's a rotten shame," Jimmy agreed. "In a minute I'm going to start crying."

"You got nothin' on us," the second whimpered, appealing to Dunand. His hands were shaking. It was obvious that Kong Gai's hold on him was through opium. "You gotta leave us go."

"Concealed weapon," Dunand reminded him. "And you can't deny you cracked me on the jaw."

"I was scared, cap. Honest, I was scared. Suppose you was buyin' a cup in a Chink store, and th' bulls come rushin' in. You'd be scared, too, cap. I ask you. Wouldn't you be scared?"

"I would, if I were you," Dunand said. His voice became colder. "Cuff 'em, Jim."

Wentworth did it. "We are holding you," the captain of detectives said grimly, "for the murder of one Walter Carrington."

The second man began to tremble violently. "We… We… I…"

"Shut up," snarled his companion. "That's all boloney, and you know it. Carrington blowed off his dome. I read it in th' papers—"

"You just went to Carrington's apartment to see the view out of his windows," Dunand suggested.

"Who says we was there?"

"The elevator boy'll say so," Dunand snapped. "Don't talk. Anything you say will be used against you."

The patrol wagon roared down the street. The shop filled with blue-coats.

"Careful with that Chink," Dunand said, pointing to the man inoculated with cobra venom, who was writhing on the floor. "Doc says he's got a fancy serum, and he wants to try it out. If only Carrington had known there is a way to save life after a cobra bite!"

"Is that true, chief?" Wentworth asked. "I didn't know it."

"Doc says so. He used a lot of fancy words. Sometimes the serum works. Say, Jim, what's the matter with old Wang? What's he waving his arms about?"

"He's telling his son that when he himself was young, he could have killed all of the hatchetmen single-handed," Jimmy grinned.

THE WRONG MOVE

Ralph R. Perry

*They didn't know Bellow Bill, if they thought he'd
stand for being shanghaied in a Chinese coffin*

1

CHEN FU ADDS A PIECE

CHEN FU OWNED and directed a gambling hell, along
with many other enterprises less openly conducted and more
criminal. Yet he himself played no game save chess.

Day after day he sat in a small alcove overlooking the main
floor of his establishment, but concealed from the players by a
screen of gilded wood backed by curtains of faded and dusty
crimson silk. To his ears rose the muffled thump of dice and
the rattle of roulette, the slap of cards from the poker tables,
and the click and murmur of *mah jong*. By turning his head,
he could watch through a slit in the curtain the bartender and
the dealers of a dozen games.

In his veins ran the gambling fever that is the heritage of
the Cantonese. Yet those who entered the alcove to whisper
reports of other enterprises, scattered through the pearl islands
east of Cape York, invariably found the old man with a chess
board across his knees.

His opponent was an even older, more withered Chinese in a black coat; a man who had the gentle face of a scholar, whereas Chen Fu's features possessed the sharpness of the fox. The games between them were incessant. Were pearls to

be pirated around Thursday Island? Was wool or opium to be smuggled? Could a planter with a crop coming into bearing be driven from his land? Was there a place where a trader could make a legal profit, and no trader there?

The wrinkled fingers of Chen Fu hovered over the ivory chessmen while he listened to such propositions. He would move a piece—and offer money or ships or men or advice. Whatever he said, and whatever bargain was agreed upon, the black-clad scholar remembered word for word. They were brain and memory, and the most prosperous freebooters in the South Seas owed allegiance to the pair. Chen was shrewd. He knew how far to venture, and with whom. Even at the chess, he won more often than not.

He was winning as usual, seated alone with his familiar, late one afternoon, when a booming voice drowned the sounds of the gambling room. Chen Fu turned and peered through the slit.

"The big pearler with the voice of a dragon, he who is tattooed from shoulder to wrist and from neck to waist, is back," he said.

Bellow Bill gave a roar like a roused lion.

"Bellow Bill Williams," reminded the scholar in a whisper. "He is honest, or you would make him rich."

"He is drinking whiskey—half the bottle of whiskey before he sets it down," muttered Chen. "Yet his step is steady, and his eye bright! Now he will play stud poker—and he will win, because he is not afraid. Then he will drink more whiskey, and go back to sea."

"Men seek profits, and monkeys fun. But which do the gods call the monkeys?" the scholar paraphrased maliciously. "It was Bellow Bill who killed your kinsman's hatchetmen."

"My kinsman pitted a pawn against the queen," Chen growled.

He moved a chessman, almost at random.

"When a tree grows big enough to shade a garden the wise farmer cuts it down," he added.

"But if the tree grows on the land of another, the farmer can only bite his thumbs," whispered the scholar maliciously.

He moved, also, and exchanged a bishop for Chen's queen.

"You will lose," the scholar remarked dryly, "because you were thinking that fewer pearls come from the north, and fewer smugglers need our help. The tree that shades us grows, and the farmer is even now building a high wall which we cannot cut down."

"Aie!" Chen Fu agreed.

He hardly seemed to notice the loss of the most important piece in the chess game. He lifted a wall phone, and spoke softly to the bartender on the floor below. Then he bent intently over the board.

"My mother's—!" gasped the scholar in consternation.

He leaped up and ran to the peep hole. Concealed behind the bar, the bartender was shaking a pinch of white powder into a glass of whiskey. The boy set the glass by the huge, tattooed hand of the tattooed giant, who was well over six feet in height and two hundred pounds in weight. And with the toss of a curly, coppery-blond head, Bellow Bill downed the drink, too intent on his cards to look at it.

INSTANTLY THE PEARLER was up, with a roar like a roused lion. His chair was hurled back. One mighty heave sent the poker table flying, the players sprawling before it. Ten men could not have stopped his rush at the bartender—but knockout drops work swiftly.

Half-way across the big room, Bellow Bill swayed, stumbled to his knees, and slid gently onto his face.

Like buzzing flies, the Chinese attendants gathered around him, lifted him up and bore him through a side door.

"Aie!" shrilled the scholar. "What have you done? When the drug wears off he will not leave one stick of this place together—nor your pigtail on your head!"

"Honored uncle, it is your move," said Chen Fu, placidly.

The scholar fumbled with the pieces.

"But you dare not kill him!" he shrilled. "Even the police know he is honest! That he would spit in your face—"

"That is true," Chen Fu muttered regretfully. "Each man moves in his own way. The paths of the rook and bishop cross—but they cannot move together. And yet I needed a man who was honest—and unafraid." He smiled slightly, and taking advantage of the scholar's blunder, he moved a pawn into the king row. "Give me back my queen, honored uncle," he commanded.

When this had been done, Chen said:

"I shall not hurt Bill. But it came to me that we could send the opium by another schooner, and that *he* might go north in the big box, in the opium's place."

Amazement drained the scholar's face of blood until it was the color of ivory long buried in earth.

"And then?" he gasped.

The face of the gambling proprietor was bland.

"One cannot foresee the end of the game; only the moves," said Chen Fu placidly. "Both games were lost—and see! I have brought back the queen onto the board!"

2

—

THE BIG BOX

BELLOW BILL WILLIAMS awoke with a splitting headache. He lay in darkness; he smelled the bilge water of a ship's hold; he felt the plunge and heave of a schooner sailing close-hauled in a moderate breeze.

The sensations were too vivid to be a nightmare, but they made no more sense than a dream—unless he were the victim of a practical joke. Bill recalled Chen Fu's place, the taste of the last drink, and the expression of the bartender as Bill started after him. The joke was a damned poor one, and the men who had played it were going to find that out—pronto. With an anger sharpened by the racking pain in his head, Bill raised himself and collided with something padded but unyielding, four inches above his nose.

Frantically, he lashed out with arms and legs.—He was in a box.—No! He was in a padded coffin! He was being carried out for burial at sea!

Bill's courage was as hard as his muscles. Cold sweat broke out on his forehead, yet he made but that one convulsive move-ment. By an effort of will so great that it was physical as well as mental, he changed a yell of horror into a strangled grunt. Every muscle was rigid, yet he forced himself to lie still.

He was in a coffin, but why was the coffin in the ship's hold? At sea, dead men are buried from the deck; not shipped to some other spot. Besides, Bellow Bill had no home to be shipped to.

If he had been judged dead, the people who had carried him where he was had gone to a great deal of unnecessary labor.

Moreover, if this was a coffin he was lying in, why could he breathe so easily, and smell the bilge so strong? His rigid muscles relaxed. With his fingers Bill commenced to feel the sides of his prison, inch by inch. He was confined in something the size and shape of a coffin, and lined like a coffin, though the lining felt more like a cotton quilt. There was a pillow under his head, but it was lumpy and uncomfortable. Bill explored— and touched—first the blade of a heavy knife, and second the barrel of a revolver.

The box was too narrow to permit him to grasp either of the two. Again he lay rigid. Weapons had been provided; but hardly that he might commit suicide, unless he became utterly panic-stricken. Otherwise, the gun would have been put into his fingers. He had been armed, which implied that he was expected to fight, but that conclusion still made no sense.

Though Bill had enemies in plenty, none of them, as far as he was aware, were also enemies of Chen Fu's. In fact, the contrary was true. Bellow Bill had often aided the officials in the South Seas, and the criminals never. The puzzle was unsolvable, but he felt around the inside of the box with renewed confidence. Eventually he discovered an iron knob. When he pulled on this, he heard the lid of the box slide open an inch or two. Reaching upward, he enlarged the gap until he could sit up.

As he rose, his face scraped against sailcloth, but there was no weight upon the canvas. An old sail must have been tossed over the box to conceal it. The darkness was still absolute, from which he inferred that the sun had set, since the hold of a schooner is seldom light-tight. Bill had matches, but first he reached for the fine cut chewing tobacco which he carried loose in his hip pocket.

He chewed slowly, extracting the full measure of solace and enjoyment from the quid. That was typical of him. He stopped wondering why he had been shanghaied; he stopped guessing about the destination of the schooner and the character of her skipper.

All of these things would be important—later. For the next half hour they were immaterial.

Here he was, almost certainly without the knowledge of the skipper, and probably unwelcome to the crew as well. And so what? He might be compelled to work his passage, merely. He might find himself involved in some highly nefarious enterprise, and in order to save himself he might be forced to aid it, with all his strength and his vast experience in the South Seas. Anything he planned in advance, as likely as not, would be wrong. Therefore, he must not plan; he could only prepare. Bill thrust the quid under his lip and struck a match. He was no longer excited or tense. He had a job to do, and he was even able to grin at the rather grisly humor of his predicament.

THE FAINT LIGHT revealed a schooner hold such as he might have seen in a thousand ships. There was very little cargo, so little, in fact, that it could not be that the schooner was engaged in legitimate trade. Planks and wooden billets used for dunnage littered the lower deck, and Bellow Bill also marked an iron-shod handspike which had been left in the hold for stowing or shifting cargo.

There were two exits. The main hatch in the deck overhead was battened down. The crew must open this before he could climb out, and while he was climbing out he would be at their mercy. On the other hand, he could easily overpower any sailor who climbed down. The thing was fifty-fifty.

The other possible exit was the cargo port, a door built in the side of the schooner and held shut with iron dogs. This he could open, but it led to the sea; and though he might reach up, catch the rail and climb over the side, he would be likely to make some noise which would attract a sailor to the spot. Bill would be as helpless as though he climbed out of the main hatch, and he would leave behind him an open port which might fill the hold with water.

He struck another match, and examined the big box he had just left, hoping that he might find a letter which would give him a hint. There was nothing. The box was obviously of Chinese workmanship, probably designed to smuggle aliens into the United States or Australia. Bill grinned. He needed no further evidence that Chen Fu had tossed him into this mess.

The old chess-playing crook had evidently expected him to get out by himself.

Bill concealed the knife and revolver under his coat, picked up the iron-shod handspike, and began to pound mightily on the side of the schooner. The sound of the blows reverberated through the hull—and under the cover of the noise, the pearler opened all the dogs on the cargo port except one.

For ten minutes he made racket enough to wake the dead. But nothing happened.

He shifted his attack to the main hatch then, and pounded so hard that the tip of a handspike splintered a plank. Still there was no response from the top side.

Bill ceased, suddenly. Had he been sent out to sea on a derelict, with the helm lashed? The idea was illogical, but vivid. He listened, and among the noises of the sea heard a new sound—the rasp of a bit boring through the deck, close to where he stood.

That was all. But Bill was almost relieved to learn he was not aboard a flying Dutchman.

"AHOY! OPEN THE hatch!" he roared in the great voice that boomed like surf.

Scrith—scrith—scrith went the bit. No other answer.

Then, with a snap of splintering wood, the drill broke through the three-inch deck planks into the hold. Instantly it was withdrawn.

"No, I won't open that hatch!" rasped a voice on deck. But it was not addressing Bill. "What the hell difference does it make to us who it is? We know who it *ain't*, don't we?"

"It's Bellow Bill Williams!" thundered the pearler.

"He says he's Bellow Bill, and he roars enough like a bull to be telling the truth," rasped the voice.

It was an edged and sneering voice. Never before had Bill disliked an unseen man to the same degree. He fingered the revolver—but the deck planking would take most of the force away from a bullet.

"Give me the funnel and the bellows, Moa," rasped the voice. "We ain't done this in too long, anyhow!"

Bellow Bill moved swiftly away from the auger hole. He heard the wheeze of a bellows—and instantly a sharp whiff of burning sulphur was forced into the hold. The place was being fumigated—to kill rats!

With an oath, the pearler whipped off his coat. The cold-blooded deviltry of the deed infuriated him. They knew who he was, and they didn't ask a question. They were just going to keep on pumping in the gas until his skin was burned out of his throat and lungs—until he choked, turned black in face, and died!

Bill wadded the coat around the handspike. He could plug the hole, temporarily.—*Temporarily!* Then they would knock out the plug, or bore another hole! And gradually the hold would fill with those biting fumes. As yet, the sulphur only made a smell.

Bill unwound the coat from the iron-shod club. He had a better use for it than that.

"A rat, am I, hey?" he bellowed, knowing the men on deck could hear. "Okay!"

CURSING SOFTLY, HE stumbled across the hold to the big box and ripped out the quilted lining. He dragged the sail to the side of the schooner, close to the cargo port. He hoped they could hear him stumbling around, and that they would believe he was seeking an exit.

He lifted the revolver, and fired—at the sound of the pumping bellows—and then, in five slow, evenly spaced shots, he emptied the gun. He hoped that first bullet had stirred them up, and that they would believe the other five had been aimed the same way. They'd be wrong, of course, for with the muzzle held against the side of the schooner, Bill had sent the last five bullets crashing through the planking, blowing a ragged hole about an inch in diameter.

Swiftly, he put his lips against this orifice, and sucked in fresh air—for already the fumes in the hold were making him cough. Grimly he touched the single dog that held the cargo port shut. He would turn that—but not now; not while they were waiting for him.

He grasped the handspike and attacked the bulkhead that separated the hold from the living quarters of the schooner. He might have broken through—the first blow, struck with all his strength, cracked the thick oak planks. But they would be waiting for him to stick out his head. Between his own strokes, he could hear a hammering somewhere aft in the schooner. That puzzled him, though he put the sound down to more deviltry.

Little by little, he let his assault go feebler. The sulphur choked him. He coughed more and more.

The blows of the handspike now would scarcely have cracked a box. They ceased—only to begin again with the frantic, aimless hammer of a dying man.

Bill's coughing, the harsh gasps torn from his great lungs, were not assumed.

He was half strangled when he let the handspike slip through his fingers, wrapped the coat and the quilt around his head, flung himself down with his lips against the bullet holes, and drew the old sail over his body.

Some of the sulphur fumes seeped through. He shut his eyes against the smart. At least, he was breathing fresh air, and he believed he could hold out until long after those on deck believed him dead.

Rat, was he? Well, those who corner a rat had better make sure that they kill it! An immense, cold rage filled him— against a man with a nasty voice, another called Moa, and a chess player named Chen Fu.

3

—

THE NOOSE

THE RUSH OF the water along the sides of the schooner drowned every other sound. Bellow Bill could only guess when the bellows ceased to force gas into the hold. He endured a pain that seemed to press under his eyelids and into his eyeballs; he had a throat that was like sandpaper.

He tried to remember how long a sulphur candle burns. He had fumigated a hold hundreds of times himself. You lighted one of the sulphur candles; closed the hatch, and went away. In the morning, you opened the hatch again.

In time, these devils would cease plying the bellows. In time, there would again be but the one man at the wheel who was awake on the deck of the schooner. That man would know when Bill flung open the cargo port. His nose would warn him, if his ears did not, but he would not be able to leave the wheel instantly. When he did run to the rail, over the open port, Bill planned to be elsewhere. He visualized every projection along the side of a schooner which would afford a handhold. He could get aft—if he could see.

He was in dread lest the fumes were injuring as well as torturing his eyes, and that fear ended Bill's endurance at last. He breathed deep and leaped up, throwing off the quilt and the old sail. He wrenched back the last of the dogs, pushed the port open, and swung out on one of the doors, as a child rides a swinging gate.

His eyes were still tight shut when he crashed against the side of the schooner. Had they failed him he would have climbed the rail, but through streaming tears he managed to locate the scuppers—small, oblong slits cut through the rail at the level of the deck, to permit sea water to run off. They were three feet apart, and they offered no more than a finger hold; but for Bellow Bill's steel-sinewed fingers that little sufficed.

Like some huge gorilla, he swung himself aft. Though the rushing sea tore at his feet, which dipped at every roll, he was not shaken loose. With an amazing speed, he went the length of the schooner without showing so much as his head above the rail. Though he saw the man who had been at the wheel, when the latter leaned over the rail, the sailor looked down-ward, at the cargo port, instead of aft.

"Peltz!" the sailor yelled, "*Peltz!* He ain't dead! Get up here!"

Bellow Bill swung under the stern, located with his feet the preventer chains on the rudder, and let himself slip into the water, seizing the chains and letting the schooner tow him. The overhang of the stern concealed him, and the salt water cleansed his eyes. For an expert swimmer, that spot was safe, since he could not be shot at from the deck. Later, he would reboard the vessel; but at the moment, two men were looking for him, guns in hand, and when he rushed them he preferred to have the revolvers back in the holsters at least.

"I say! Who shanghaied you?" came a whisper.

It was faint—almost drowned by the rush and gurgle of the water—but the shock of hearing a whisper at all almost made Bellow Bill let go of the chains. No one could see him here! There was no possible way....

He looked up. No one was leaning over the taffrail, but

underneath the stern itself, not two feet from his head, what should have been an immovable glass dead-eye was an open hole which framed the pale blur of a face. How a man could cram himself into that tiny compartment under the stern, and how he could have unfastened the dead-eye flashed through Bill's mind while his hand was flashing to his waist for the knife. He struck—and the face dodged, escaping the steel.

"OH, I SAY!" came the whisper—excited, protesting, and barely audible. "I'm shanghaied myself, y'know! Didn't you hear me pounding when you did?"

"Shut up!" Bill rumbled.

For there was talking on deck.

"—you'll damn well go down, sulphur or no sulphur!" snarled the voice Bill hated. "You're at sea now, Moa, I'll have you know! I'll see Bill's body, or by the Lord, I'll heave to till I find it floating!"

"There's no time to waste! If he did jump overboard, he must drown! How can he make shore, across the barrier reef?"

"He must have choked in that hold, too, but he didn't!" snarled Peltz. "You damn sheep-stealin' landlubber, Bellow Bill Williams's name is a byword! He's *known* at sea, lemme tell you! An' Smiler Peltz ain't takin' chances with tykes like *him!* Leave the wheel in the becket and get below! I'll hold the deck with my gun till you find him!"

Bellow Bill listened, but Moa made no further protest.

There was a thump as Moa started to raise the hatch. Bill raised himself till his lips were close to the pale blur of a face in the dead-light.

"How many of them are there?" he rumbled.

Whisper he could not, but he could lower his voice until the growling sound deep in his chest was pitched in key with the gurgling water.

"Just two. Moa and Peltz.—I say!" the answering whisper was excited and eager. "I'm John Harris, of Sydney, you know—the heir."

"I don't know; besides, what of it?" Bill rumbled. "Make some kind of noise. Pound on the door—yell for help."

"But they'll see I got the dead-light open—with a spoon. They wouldn't even give me a dull table knife to eat with!"

"Yeah, I hope they do see it," Bill growled.

He could hardly repress a grin. Harris was a kid, proud of himself—and indignant.

"Don't stop them from shutting it, either," Bill added. "They've got to shut it, or they'll sink when the wind changes. Yell bloody murder, buddy. We've got to get that damn sure-thing player of a Peltz excited.—Damn the guy that invented guns! I'll bet that bozo's sitting aloft, waiting patient for me to stick my head up so that he can pop it!"

"But I *want* the schooner to sink! They'd have had to let me out!" Harris retorted. "And if I yell, they'll find you!"

"Don't you ever obey orders?" Grim laughter rumbled in Bellow Bill's chest. "You yell, buddy. Make believe you're scared. It won't hurt you. Or I'll go and get myself shot, and when you sink this boat you'll have fifty miles to swim, startin' from a locked room!—Let you out?—Peltz? You're thinking of another sort of skipper."

"Oh, all right!" Harris whispered disgustedly.

His face disappeared from the dead-eye. With fists and feet, he hammered on the door; and the scream he uttered was so shrill, and so long drawn out that Bill winced. Only a dying horse, or an utterly terrified woman, can put that maddening quality into a scream. It was hard to believe that a man could do it—especially a man who didn't believe in the idea.

"Ay-eeeee—eeeee!"

On and on, shriller and shriller, till Harris's voice broke. A gasp for breath, and then a choked, despairing wail.

"Sinking!" Harris yelled. "We're sinking! Oh, God, look at the water!—Let me out!"

Bellow Bill took a better grip on the rudder chains, and lifted himself close to the dead-eye, the knife poised. He heard the click of a lock, the thud of a blow.

"Shut up!" Moa snarled. "Leak, eh? Huh! You wanted one!"

"Don't kick me!" Harris sobbed.

"No?"

Three measured thuds, and silence.

"Whew!" Moa snorted. "Cheap London soft-belly! Where the hell's the dead-eye?—Oh!"

And in the opening under the stern appeared, not a face, but the heavy circle of glass!

BELLOW BILL WAS as quick. His knife did not make a thrust, but a whipping circle. The blade grated on the glass, and slashed around upon the fingers which held it. Moa screamed and dropped the dead-eye. Bill drove the knife through the opening as far as he could reach, but the blade met nothing. Within the schooner there was a brief grunting and thrashing. On deck, Peltz demanded sharply what the matter was.

"I say! I've his gun!" Harris's whisper, exultant and triumphant. "I laid doggo, and snatched it when he lifted his hands!"

"Pass it out!" Bill rumbled fiercely.

"Oh, but I say—"

"Then lock the door, you damn young fool!" Bill roared, with all the power of his lungs.

The chance for surprise was gone, tossed away by an over-zealous and inexperienced kid. With the knife in his teeth, Bill caught the taffrail and swung himself onto the deck. He expected a shot, but Peltz had evidently been too cold-blooded to rely upon the uncertainties of marksmanship at night.

The slide of the cabin companionway was thrown back, and the light of an oil lamp beat upward.

From below, there was a burst of revolver fire—shot after shot. Grim-lipped, Bill leaped from the darkness down into the light. He landed in the cabin like a cat. No man alive could have located Peltz quicker, where he stood backed against the cabin bulkhead, revolver in hand. A cat could scarcely have whirled quicker than Bill, or made a greater spring. The pearler hurled himself across the cabin like a living spear with a knife tip. And he knew in that split-second both that he was a split-second too slow, and also that Peltz could not save himself either.

No bullet could stop Bill's lunge. The knife drove through Peltz's body. Bill crashed against the bulkhead, and the skipper toppled upon him. Blood deluged the pearler. For an instant he was not aware that the blood was not his own. Peltz's revolver lay on the deck beside him. Bill had not seen the blaze of powder; had not heard the shot. *Peltz had not fired!* And there had been time for Peltz to shoot.

In a daze, Bill stood erect, mechanically feeling his body for a wound. The pearler stared down at the lifeless body. In addition to the gash of the knife, blood welled from a bullet hole in Peltz's chest. He had lost his chance because he had already been shot through the lungs.

Under the stern a door opened. Moa staggered into view—a swarthy, powerfully built half-breed, but dressed in the ducks of a white man instead of the Melanesian *lava-lava*. Against his back Harris, fair-haired and crimson with excitement, held a smoking gun.

"Peltz fired through the door and I fired back!" he crowed.

"That so?" Bill rumbled.

Annoyance struggled with amusement.

"Then go get a bucket and a swab and clean up this mess, kid," he said. "You've had your beginner's luck. From now on you're the deckhand."

"But I say!"

"*You listen!*" Bill contradicted. "You came so near grandstanding me dead that I can't start in too soon to teach you to leave something to the other guy!"

4

SPIDER TO FLY

MOA SAT AT the cabin table. His right hand was bandaged, and his lips were locked in stubborn silence. Bellow Bill pushed back an empty plate that had been piled four inches high with slabs of bread and slices of canned corned beef half an inch thick.

"We could make him talk, but why bother to get rough?" he rumbled. "I'll take an observation of the stars and find out where we are. By morning, we'll be back in port. Then we'll turn him over to the police on a kidnapping charge, and that will settle him."

Harris squirmed in his chair.

"To-morrow will be too late for me," he said. "If I don't take active charge of my grandfather's sheep station by to-morrow at noon; I forfeit my inheritance under the will. I say, I'm not objecting to your plans, Bill!" Harris added hastily. "But I can't possibly reach the station from the port in the time that's left—and you know, the coast is inaccessible from the sea, what with the barrier reef and all. I've just been shang-haied out of ten thousand acres of good Australian land. It's gone and all that, and so I'm not beefing about it! Only Moa is an under-overseer, and he taught me to ride when I was a nipper. I know who bribed him to shanghai me, and why. But it's really very little satisfaction to me to put Moa in quod. He's just a pawn, y'know!"

"Whose pawn?" Bill boomed.

"Oh, my cousin's. Named Harris, christened Ben. You couldn't possibly understand, unless you were an Australian from the back blocks yourself. You see," Harris declared with perfect candor, "my great grandfather was a convict—trans-ported and all that. He went into the Never-never country when any one could have ten thousand acres for the asking; and three generations of Harrises made a sheep ranch out of the bush. It was bally hard, and out in the sun and the dust and the smell of sheep dip, we wanted to prove we weren't scum—that we were just as good as the men who'd stayed in England. We were, y'know. But we fair wanted to make them admit it.—But you can't understand!"

"Your *cousin's* pawn?" Bill rumbled, as softly and heavily as far-distant thunder. "And what does that make me? Go on, buddy. I'm from the States, but maybe I'll savvy."

"I was the fourth generation, and I was the Harris that got to England. Ten years ago that was. I was but a little nipper—with something to show." Harris's fair face glowed reminiscently. "I showed them," Harris said. "I spent more money than some. I took prizes others wanted. And still others I jolly well punched in the nose, because that was all they could understand. All grandfather wanted was letters from me that told every detail. Every time I made a good showing, he increased the size of my monthly draft. It was his triumph—the family's triumph, y'know. He'd never been in a town bigger than Melbourne. He'd never seen the inside of a cabaret or a university. And yet he got more of the old bounce out of hearing what I did than I got in the doing."

"The checks got larger and larger," Bill purred. "Doesn't that strike you as strange, with the price of wool on the toboggan?"

"Why—er—the clip might have been larger," Harris replied vaguely.

"Unlikely!" Bill grunted. "But perhaps your grandfather showed your letters to Chen Fu?"

"Who?" Harris demanded, open mouthed. "I say, what are you leading to?—Show family letters to a Chinese? Bally nonsense! Grandfather wouldn't have a Chink on the station!"

BELLOW BILL GLANCED at the swarthy face of the under-overseer. Moa's features were wooden—too wooden.

He knew who Chen Fu was. Bellow Bill could see, and he was uneasy.

"Your grandfather died?—Suddenly?" Bill rumbled.

"I say, will you please let me explain!" Harris snapped. "Not at all! He was sick for weeks, though all the time he was sure it was nothing serious. The actual news was unexpected, of course. I'd just time to catch a steamer. Real Australians, you know, hate absentee landlords in England. The understanding was that when Grandfather died, I must come back at once and manage the ranch. His will give me only thirty days, so I wouldn't have time to hem and haw. Of course," said Harris candidly, "I did want to stay—rather. But ten thousand acres was too much to give up. My cousin Ben must have thought so, too. For when I reached the port—with just twenty-four hours left to get to the station—Moa was waiting for me with the car. He suggested a drink to celebrate, and the next thing I knew, I was crammed into that compartment aft."

"Did you drink in a Chinese gambling house?" said Bill.

"I drank out of Moa's flask!" snapped Harris. "Are you hipped? You keep trying to involve Chinamen in my affairs! Don't you see that if I fail to fulfill the provisions of the will, Ben gets possession of my property? I might go to law, claiming that I was shanghaied, but Ben would have money to fight the case, and I wouldn't. He's stayed on the land and I haven't. He's likely to win, or enjoy the income of the estate for years, while the case dragged along. Whereas if he cut my throat, questions would be asked. There'd be lots about me in the papers. But I could disappear like—like—"

"Like a tattooed old roughneck pearling skipper," Bellow Bill chuckled.

He shifted his quid and continued to address Harris.

"I thought you were kidnapped," he said, "but you haven't the money to pay a ransom, so that's out. I can see why your cousin would prefer to have you alive, but I can't see why he wants two sheep stations. Financially, a station to-day is nothing but a pain in the neck. Yours managed to pay dividends, and that's miraculous. Two men—strangers—get shanghaied on the same schooner. Me they try to kill at the drop of a hat, though they were aware that some one would know who murdered me, and when." Bellow Bill stared at Moa with narrowed eyes. "The case is too complicated for us, kid," he rumbled, "and so we'll go back to port and lodge a complaint of attempted murder against Mr. Moa here; then we'll go to law to recover your station."

"Without money?" Harris snorted.

"No, buddy," said Bill softly. "With all the cash you need—supplied by an old chess-playin' Chink named Chen Fu. Chen's interested in you. That's the one thing that's clear. Don't ask *me* why! I'm going to ask *him*—by dawn to-morrow. *And I'll find out*—eh, Moa?" Bill bellowed, sudden and loud as a clap of thunder.

"Yes!" rasped Moa. The wooden mask of his features broke suddenly. His lips twisted into a snarl like that of a wolf who feels the jaws of a trap close. "Chen will hang me, and send the constables to put your cousin and my brother in jail. Chen will catch them red-handed, without even a warning, and then he will laugh and give you your worthless land!"

Moa leaned toward Harris with vicious, savage delight.

"Did you think that wool paid for the drafts you got?" he sneered. "You fool! The price of wool was in the paper every day, and you thought the clip was larger!—Opium paid the drafts! Stolen pearls and smuggled aliens! Your grandfather, your cousin, my brother and me are the biggest fences in Australia! We've taken the cream of Chen's business, and so he hates us!"

"Supplanted Chen? How?" Bill roared.

Moa flung himself back in his chair, exhausted by his outburst.

"There's a channel through the barrier reef, in front of the station," he snarled. "I'll pilot the schooner in before noon to-morrow—if you choose!"

5

NEEDLE'S EYE

TO RIGHT AND left, surf roared over shallow reefs of coral. A mile ahead was the low line of the shore, grayish-green under the morning sun. Beneath the bow of the schooner a narrow ribbon of smooth water twisted erratically toward the land.

Harris had chosen, and Bellow Bill had acquiesced.

Forward, Moa pointed out the course. His arm swung like a weather vane. At the wheel, Bellow Bill exerted all his seamanship. The bowsprit followed Moa's arm as though the two were actuated by a single will. The pearler no longer wondered that this channel was not shown on the charts. Rather, the marvel was how the secret had been discovered, for no sane sailor would have thrust his ship into such a narrow lead, with a two-mile wide belt of surf thundering around. Despite his skill, Bill expected at every instant to feel the keel scrape on the coral. He was not quite sure that Moa had not elected to drown rather than rot in jail.

And if the schooner reached a harbor, what of Harris and himself? A channel through the barrier reef was like a rat hole in a granary that was otherwise locked and guarded. No coast guard patrolled the barrier reef. The constables ashore watched for contraband along the routes which led into the interior, and not along the roads which skirted a coast supposedly without a harbor. Though this channel was too crooked and too narrow to have any commercial value, to thieves it was priceless.—And thieves would be certain to guard the secret as something beyond price.

Bill glanced at Harris. The lips of the younger man were bloodless, and stubbornly set. The pearler both admired and pitied him. With one savage speech, Moa had smashed Harris's ideals and his pride in his family. The kid had rocked to the blow, but instantly he had elected to fight back.

Seek Chen Fu's aid and betray his cousin to the police Harris would not. To give up his rights to the sheep station and disappear was a step that he refused to consider. The station was his. By his grandfather's will he had become the head of the family. He insisted that he would go on, assume his inheritance, and act as the master. Stolen goods should flow through the Harris station no longer.

How would he stop the flow? John Harris did not even attempt to answer that question. He had no plans; only determination and courage. His cousin, Bill pointed out, had shanghaied him in order to force him to join the others, and to be in a position to get rid of him in case he refused.

Yes, quite so. And though Chen Fu might be anxious to rid himself of dangerous rivals, he would be indifferent to the fate of Harris, personally. The Chinese had been careless enough about the risk Bill ran, hadn't he?

Yes, quite so. Nevertheless, blood was thicker than water. Did Bellow Bill want to leave the schooner before it entered the channel? He could row away in the dinghy. Some passing ship would pick him up.

Bill had greeted that suggestion with rumbling laughter. He was aware that courage, unless backed by experience and craft, would only put Harris into an unmarked grave. He had not saved the younger man to let him throw himself away. Nor did the pearler care to be a cat's-paw for Chen Fu. The scowl on Bill's face was not caused wholly by the perils of the tortuous channel through the reef. He had been played with. He was embarrassed, and he was angry, which made him doubly dangerous.

BY THE TIME the schooner came within a quarter of a mile of the shore, Bill had decided that Moa's pilotage could be trusted. Very soon they would cease to thread through the reef and would enter the deep, calm, safe waters of the lagoon which lay between the coral and the beach.

Moa, at that moment, was signalling to put the wheel hard up. With a tight-lipped grin, Bill spun the spokes—hard down! The schooner crashed against a hidden reef, and while the masts were still vibrating from the shock, Bill whipped out his knife and slashed through the main sheet and the halyards. The boom swung outboard and snapped at the gooseneck as the schooner pounded on the reef. The falling sails buried the deck.

"Oh, but I say!" Harris gasped.

Moa came running aft—to stop short, and glance in desperation at the surf to port and to starboard. Bellow Bill had drawn a gun. He was taking careful aim at the buckle on Moa's belt.

"You ain't useful any more!" he boomed. "Get down below!—Follow him, Harris!"

The two descended to the cabin, covered every step by the gun. No sails hid the deck of the schooner from the shore. Bellow Bill crossed the deck erect, cat-footed, grim. The sight of his face as he swung down into the cabin made Moa shrink.

"But why?" Harris mumbled in horror. "Why do you have to kill him—now?"

"That's up to him!" Bill boomed. "Moa, have you got that flask that Harris drank from?"

The muscles of the under-overseer's throat worked convulsively. He managed to nod.

"Get it!" Bill commanded. "And drink it—all of it!"

Moa moved to obey like a man already drunk. The drug was so powerful that he was unable to finish the draught before he swayed and collapsed. Bellow Bill snatched the flask from his hand as he fell, knelt beside him, and raised his eyelids to examine the pupils. Moa lay with only the slightest rise and fall of his chest to indicate that he lived. Bill nodded in grim satisfaction.

"There'll be no more trouble with him for hours," he rumbled. "And so.—Can you take orders, Harris?"

"I—think so!"

"I can knock you out," Bill rumbled. "I'd have knocked him out—with a belaying pin—if he hadn't been willing to take that drink. But drugs and discipline are safer than a knockout, and they last longer."

The pearler drew his revolver and fired twice into the deck, with a distinct pause between the shots.

If possible, Harris's eyes stuck out further than ever.

"But I say! Are you balmy? What do you want?" he mumbled.

"From you? Nothing. Don't speak—and don't move," Bill boomed. His face was cold and hard as bronze. "That'll give you practice."

He turned on his heel and ascended to the deck.

THERE HE FIRST swung the dinghy into the water. Next he carried out of the hold the big box in which he had been shanghaied, and tumbled it down into the cabin. Last, he cut three large squares of canvas from the sail and provided himself with a coil of rope. He moved without haste, for he knew that he was being watched from the shore. He hoped he was being watched closely. Just one thing Bill hoped had escaped observation—the fact that Moa had been pointing for uphelm when the helm went down.

In the cabin, Harris was poking gingerly at the big box. For the first time, Bellow Bill let a dancing, reckless twinkle creep into his eyes. Harris appeared to be relieved.

"You realize," the pearler boomed abruptly, "that we can't row ashore without giving the men who may be waiting for us a dead, cold drop? Therefore—all this. I ain't crazy, buddy. I'm just getting ready to fight, with a chance to win."

Harris frowned.

"This schooner can't be floated easily or quickly," Bill explained. "Some passing ship is going to see masts where the masts of a wrecked ship couldn't possibly get to, according to the charts. There'll be a report, an investigation by the coast guard; and within a week at most this channel will no longer be a secret. Then the flow of contraband stops."

"But I say! That's clever!"

"The bozos ashore will think it's something else," Bill boomed curtly. "Take a look at your gun, and make sure it's in damned good working order."

While Harris complied, the pearler wrapped Moa's unconscious figure in canvas, leaving the feet exposed, and lashed the bundle with rope.

"You see," he purred, "it'll look as if Moa steered me wrong and wrecked the schooner. Therefore, I took him down here in the cabin and shot him."

"But you didn't!"

"Don't he look like a corpse?" Bill boomed. "Stick that gun under your shirt where it will be handy, and lie down in the big box. I'm going to cover you with canvas and put Peltz in on top of you. *He's* dead enough!"

Involuntarily, Harris recoiled.

"Lie underneath—" he gasped.

"Lie under a stiff and make believe you're one, too!" Bill boomed. "That's orders, buddy! You see, I'm supposed to have taken you down here and murdered you, too. Because I figure that was what your cousin Ben would want me to do, once the secret of the channel was discovered."

Stiffly, Harris climbed into the big box. He repressed a shudder when Bill laid Peltz upon him. Yet for several seconds he did not speak, and in the end all he said was:

"It'll be a bit hard to lie still."

"Aye-aye, buddy!" Bill agreed. "And it's hard to put your life in another man's hands, too. But at least you won't be shot in cold blood as you walk across the beach, and a corpse that jumps from a coffin waving a gun is—surprising. Use your head, and listen for a cue from me. Then jump up, run for the thickest brush, and hide. You know the country. You ought to be able to remain hidden, and in a day or two no one will stop you from taking charge of your station."

"But I say! How about you?" Harris protested through the canvas.

"Oh, I'll have a gun in each hand." Deep, reckless laughter bubbled in Bill's chest. "I don't think they'll shoot till they find out what I've got in the big box. And afterward—I'll be looking for trouble, you see!"

6

SUN—AND SAND

BELLOW BILL STOWED Moa's canvas-wrapped body in the bow of the dinghy, letting the feet stick up to be identified. The big box with its double load he balanced across the stern sheets, and took his place at the oars.

He was forced to row slowly, for the little boat was loaded almost to the water's edge, and to swamp, or to jar the box off the stern, would be fatal. As he pulled away from the schooner, the beach lay yellow and empty under the sun, and though the hair rose on the back of his neck and his heart hammered as he approached the land, he did not look around until the dinghy grated on the sand. He must not appear nervous.

As a matter of fact, he wasn't. The suspense merely keyed

him to concert pitch. If they shot him, they shot him. In every campaign there is bound to be one step, one moment, of pure gambling risk. There is no use in worrying how the dice will fall. Bellow Bill merely wondered whether he would have a chance to show his stuff.

That he was allowed to land was in his favor. Turning, he saw—one man, waiting alone, half way between the shore and the dense, gray-green underbrush. A scout? Bill thought so. The beach was fifty feet wide. The man appeared to be unarmed. A tangled golden beard concealed his features. He was middle-aged. His complexion and the set of his shoulders had a definite resemblance to those of John Harris.

"Are you Ben Harris?" Bill boomed confidently.

"Aye, mate.—And who the hell are you?" The tone was bitter, impersonal.

Ben's eyes were on the big box. He scowled.

"Name's Williams. Peltz's new deckhand," Bill boomed. "And damn me, mate! I've never have signed on if I'd known the cargo! I'm like to swing!"

"Aye, you've played hell!" was the bitter retort. "Don't lie, you Chink-loving bush-loper. Peltz never had a deckhand. I know what you are. Take those stiffs back and dump them into the hold. Then burn the schooner, and them along with it. After that, come back and get yours—and I hope to God it's a rope at the last!"

For an instant Bill's blood was ice. So he wasn't to have even a chance? So Ben Harris was another Peltz, who played sure? Bill's huge tattooed hands closed on the revolver butts at his belt. Ben hoped he would get a rope. Why "hoped"? Ben could knot it round his neck!—"Chink-loving"? The big box was obviously Chinese, and yet—

"Light a fire and burn a ship. Sure!" Bill roared. "Have them find charred bodies in the hold? Not me, mate—and that's flat! We'll stick them in the ground ashore. And as for swinging"—Bellow Bill drew both revolvers—"we'll see about that!"

He paused, watching the underbrush.

"Peltz double-crossed you," he added. "He was going to let Harris go free—in return for a deed of gift to the station. Moa got wise and shot him, but I guess Moa decided Peltz's idea was good, after thinking it over. He ordered me to come about and go back to sea—and I guess you saw what happened! There was nothing in that for me, so I gave it to them. I didn't figure you'd care.—And now get your mates out of that brush!" The roaring voice rose to thunder. "I know they're there. Are they too yellow to shoot it out with one man?"

Ben Harris smiled bleakly, and half turned.

"I wouldn't have cared—much," he muttered. "Though I just wanted to put the screws on the young fool." He raised his voice. "Well?" he called questioningly.

OUT OF THE bush came the dry, throaty chuckle of an old man who seemed to be well pleased. Bellow Bill's guns wavered. In a flash, he knew part of the answer.

"That was well done, Bellow Bill!" called Chen Fu softly. "Let us talk no more of ropes and bullets, but of gold."

The old Chinaman thrust the foliage aside and stepped out on the sand, his black-clad secretary at his elbow. Chen Fu was so pleased that he was shaking hands with himself in his wide sleeves.

"The queen," he chuckled to his chess-playing companion, "is a mightier piece than the knight or the rook. I never doubted it would be you who swept Peltz and Moa from the board; and throughout the South Seas, all men know that Bellow Bill never asks to see his profit in advance."

"Oh, aye?" Bill purred. "What's the spider doing out of his web, Chen?"

"The spider hoped that the wasp would bring home a fat fly to another web," Chen explained softly. "I thought that you could remove Peltz. But what would you do here, with him?" A long-nailed forefinger pointed contemptuously at Ben Harris. "He is a fool who chanced upon a valuable secret. But he's no match for me—or you. The thing was very simple: I had promised him opium. I brought it—and seven men. The knives of my men were at his throat before he was aware that he had reason to fear me. He should play chess." Chen Fu chuckled. "The king is not dangerous, except when other pieces prepare his attack. And so I will put the screws on a young—pawn. To whom I intend no harm."

"I don't get you. The game's ended," Bill boomed.

He wondered swiftly whether Chen counted his secretary as a man or not. Probably not.—In that case, there were seven tough Chinese in the bush to be dealt with.

"For you, Bellow Bill," Chen Fu chuckled softly. "You played well, but I was not deceived. Men move according to what they are, whether the men be flesh or ivory. The eagle bites—but not like the snake. And *you* did not murder John Harris.—Peltz? Yes!—Moa? Perhaps.—But never the lad. For he would have been shot only through fear, and you have never been afraid, Bellow Bill."

Bill caught his breath. Chen's shrewd, wrinkled face mocked him, banishing any idea of bluff.

"You are right, Chen," he rumbled. And added more loudly, lest there be a movement in the big box. "And yet John Harris— is dead. Men are as they are. Yet they blunder. And I blundered. I wished to frighten Moa, and he read in my face the death that he would have given me if he had held the gun. When I swung below, he snatched the other revolver I wore in my belt. I shot him, but he pulled the trigger and Harris stood in the path of the bullet." Bill shrugged. "Afterward, I tried to profit by an accident.—I did not expect you here."

The sun burned down upon the yellow sand. Little waves lisped at Bill's heels as he stood beside the dinghy, staring across the big box at Chen. Chen's beady black eyes searched the pearler through and through.

"Look for yourself!" he boomed. "Dead men will—wait."

Chen smiled shrewdly, and spoke in Cantonese. A burly hatchetman shouldered out of the underbrush and crossed the sand toward the boat.

Bill smiled slightly. Seven minus one left six.

"Suspicious, Chen?" he mocked. "There is no need. I'll help your man."

HE STEPPED TO the bow, lifted out Moa with one hand, and sent the canvas-wrapped figure rolling across the sand.

The effort made Bill stagger. He lurched against the dinghy, at least pushing it a foot backward toward the sea by a thrust of his hip. Bill was grinning, and his eyes danced with golden flecks. With both hands, he lifted up Peltz so that all might see the gaping wounds, and dropped him carelessly—into the bow, where Moa had been.

"A living shield is better than a dead one!" Bill boomed.

Inwardly he blessed John Harris for his fortitude.

The hatchetman had stopped six feet away. Bill caught the canvas that covered young Harris, and swung it into the air with a wide flourish toward the hatchetman's face.

Behind the flying canvas, Bellow Bill leaped. A huge tattooed hand closed on the hatchetman's throat; another gripped the sash at his waist. With a terrific heave, Bill swung the man into the air, whirled, and slammed him bodily down into the big box.

"Hold him there, Harris!" Bill thundered, and dove headlong for the stern of the boat.

With a roll and a twist he was crouched in the shelter of the hull.

"Plug him if he moves! Not unless!" he ordered Harris.

Rifles cracked in the undergrowth. Bullets whined around the dinghy, but they flew high. Instinctively, the marksmen tried to spare their comrade in that first fire. Bellow Bill caught the stern of the dinghy and braced his heels in the gravel. Only for an instant was he exposed. With one long, steady pull, easy for his vast strength, he drew the dinghy off the sand and dropped beside it again—into water that was knee-deep.

Reaching upward, he tipped over the big box, and knocked the hatchetman senseless with the butt of a revolver as he came tumbling out. Next, Bill caught young Harris by the collar. Bill threw himself on his back in the shallow water and kicked furiously with his feet, swimming with the dinghy as it drifted toward the sea.

Chen Fu screamed with rage. At sea was the schooner, with another dinghy, provisions and water, that offered a safe means of retreat. And the beach was empty of boats! Shrilly, the old voice cackled orders.

A volley sent splinters flying from the dinghy. With high-pitched yells, the Chinese charged, firing as they ran across the beach and plunged into the shallower water. There were six of them, but Bill uttered a satisfied grunt.

"Keep your head down, Harris!" he boomed. "We've got to get the dinghy out, buddy! That's the job!"

Bill rose himself in water that was now waist deep, to fire over the stern. He had never been a good shot. He scarcely aimed, but blazed away into the thick of the charge. One man pitched forward on his face at the water's edge and lay still. A second dropped, howling, to clasp his shin in both hands. The other four dashed into the water.

Bill ducked under the surface and swam back to meet them. A pearler and a deep sea diver, he was as much at home under water as a shark, and his knife was more terrible than a shark's teeth. The foremost Chinaman screamed horribly, and toppled over in a swirl of water that was suddenly red. The second saw a huge dim shape swimming at his legs; he yelled Bill's name, and turned to run. Before he had made two strides, however, the knife overtook him. The others waited for no more. In mad panic they splashed for the beach.

For a moment they ran alone. Then Bill, seeing no more legs beneath the water, sprang up and gave chase. One Chinaman still clung to his rifle, but his eyes were tight shut. And the crack of a revolver as Harris opened fire lent the man wings. Screaming, he crossed the beach and plunged into the bush, heedless of the thorns. His comrade was not a yard behind.

BEN HARRIS STILL lay in the sand where he had thrown himself at the first shot.

Chen Fu was in flight, like his Chinese gunmen, but the transition from victory to defeat had been swift, and his old legs were not equal to the emergency. He slipped in the soft sand. The black-clad secretary, with a courage and loyalty that did him credit, was trying to lift him when tattooed hands caught both by the pigtails and bumped their heads together. They dropped, half stunned.

Bellow Bill shoved the knife back into his waistband and picked up the nearest rifle. He covered Ben Harris. John Harris was already wading ashore.

"Well, Ben?" Bill thundered.

"I don't give a damn whether it's the Chinks or you or him!" growled the blond-bearded man. "I'm dusted out!"

"Yep!" snapped Bill. "And lucky at that! I ought to drill you for hiring a squid like Peltz. But you're just wooden-headed, I guess; and I'm just your cousin's partner. He'll want to let you go. If—"

"If what?" Ben growled, for Bill was grinning down at Chen Fu, who now blinked up at him, half dazed.

"—if you'll show me where this one put the opium he said he brought," the pearler finished grimly. "Ben, I'd advise you to turn King's Witness. If you help to put this old chess-playin' devil where he belongs, I think the authorities will let bygones be bygones. And as far as you're concerned—"

"But I say! Can't we keep the whole mess quiet?" the younger Harris interjected.

"This quiet?" Bellow Bill swung an arm at the stranded schooner, and the bodies on the beach. "No, buddy. You can save your family, but damned if you can whitewash 'em! You run your station, and the talk will die down in time. It always does, unless a man tries to be too smart. Eh, Chen?"

"No can be too smart," the old man contradicted with a firm, gentle dignity. "I play a game, and I lose. I smuggle opium forty years, and I go to jail over a paltry twenty tins. All right!"

Chen touched the base of his pigtail with a wry grimace. "From the classics you have learned wisdom, honored uncle," he remarked to his secretary in Chinese, and added, in English, "but not because I was too smart, I said to him, 'I have added a queen to the board'; but you not only move every way—too far and too fast, like a queen—you jump, too.—Next time, I know—I get out of jail some day. I play more chess. But next time, I say to bartender, 'There comes Bellow Bill. Give him very best whiskey; nothing more, nothing less.'"

IT'S RAINING CORPSES
IN CHINATOWN

Russell Gray

*The trail of mince-meat corpses grew longer,
vaguer and bloodier, as it led its way toward
Chinatown.... When Ethan Burr, ace crime
investigator, took the case, he had a hunch he
was licked before he started—for even the
Practitioner of Death couldn't be expected to
win out against a dragon league of fiends!*

1

The Thing in the Sack

THE SUN SLANTED through the Venetian blinds and lay
on the bar in streamers of light. George Simms blinked at the
tables which stood in shadows, then turned to the bartender.

"Have you seen Ethan Burr today?"

The bartender appraised Simms suspiciously. He saw a flabby
man in a derby who looked like a motion picture version of a
detective. But appearances, the barman had learned, didn't mean
a thing. Once, a meek-looking little guy had come in. Nobody
had paid any attention to him until he had opened fire on Ethan
Burr, who had been sitting at his usual table drinking beer.

The bartender liked to tell how in spite of the advantage of surprise, the meek-looking little guy hadn't been able to shoot more than one bullet, and that hadn't quite hit the mark. Burr's .44 had leaped into his hand, out of nowhere it had seemed, and another corpse had been marked up for the private detective whom the newspapers referred to as the Practitioner of Death.

The Chinese slashed with his knife at the same time that Burr's gun came up.

The bartender played safe with Simms. "He ain't here," he said cagily, "but if you wait maybe I'll find out where he is."

HE FADED TOWARD the end of the bar and disappeared. Half a minute later he beckoned to Simms from the back of the room. Ethan Burr was seated around the L of the saloon, his back against the wall, a half-empty glass of beer on the table.

"Hello, George," Burr greeted. "Sit down. Two beers, Al."

"Fine," Simms grunted. He sank into a chair.

As Burr drank down the rest of his beer, Simms eyed him. He remembered Burr, years ago on the force, when Burr had been a carefree, exceptionally clever, first-grade homicide dick who was set to go far in the department. Then his charming young wife had died because Burr hadn't been able to afford the necessary surgical and medical expenses to save her life.

The blow had permanently removed any smile from his hard, thin mouth and his steel-gray eyes. He had quit the force, opened an office as a private investigator, determined to make enough money so that his two young children would never know want. His services came high, and if one wanted an utterly ruthless and fearless machine of justice, his fees were worth it.

The bartender brought the two beers. Simms took a deep gulp, smacked his lips, then his eyes went to Burr's face.

Burr leaned back in his chair. "You're jittery, George. Is chasing divorce evidence too much for you?"

"I was a fool," Simms said. "I should have stayed on the force. But when I saw all the dough you were making in private law, I got greedy."

"Not making out?"

"Well, the agency is getting on a good footing. But a couple of days ago I bit off more than I think I can chew. Frankly, Ethan, I'm a little nervous. I sank every cent I possess into the agency and borrowed up to the hilt. If I pass out, my wife and daughter will be absolutely destitute."

Burr said nothing, his face remained impassive. Simms sighed. "What do you know about Chinamen?"

"I know that they don't like to be called Chinamen. They prefer Chinese. Their colony in this town is nothing in size like New York or San Francisco, but it's fairly large."

"Would you trust 'em?"

"In their personal lives they are the gentlest and most honest people I know," Burr stated. "There are exceptions among them, but perhaps not so many as among our own people. Frankly, I like 'em."

"Yeah," Simms grunted. He stared at the wall above Burr's head. Then he said, "Look here, Ethan, how'd you like a piece of a case."

Burr nodded. "That depends."

"Five hundred," Simms said. "I'll do all the leg work."

"Sorry, George."

"One thousand."

Burr fingered the jagged scar which ran down his left cheek and disfigured his mouth. That had been caused by a blackmailer's knife. He'd got ten thousand dollars for that case.

"I'm not in this game for the fun of it, George," Burr said.

Simms sighed again and stood up. "Maybe a grand isn't money to you. I can't go higher without stepping out altogether, and I need that dough."

He moved away, his feet lagging, his shoulders bowed. Burr opened his mouth to call after him as Simms turned the corner of the L. He changed his mind and lifted the beer glass to his lips....

THE FOLLOWING MORNING Ethan Burr visited the city morgue. He handed the attendant a pass.

"I'd like to get a look at George Simms," he said.

The attendant screwed his face. "There ain't much to see. He hasn't been sewed together yet."

"I can take it, Higgins."

Higgins shrugged and led Burr into the autopsy room. The various parts of George Simms' body were laid out on a table. It was as bad as anything Burr had ever seen. The head was separated from the torso, and the rest was in a number of pieces. The eyes were open, staring up at Burr.

"I told you," Higgins said, as he followed Burr out.

"What's the dope on his murder?" the detective asked.

"Just like the morning papers said," Higgins told him. "A cop comes across this sack on the sidewalk at about midnight. He sees something seeping through that looks like blood. He opens the sack and in it he finds what you just saw. That's all that's known."

Burr left the morgue, got into his roadster and drove to a neat little cottage in the suburbs. A girl answered his ring. She was tall and easy to look at, in spite of the fact that there was little color in her face and her eyes were red from weeping.

"Mrs. Simms?" Burr asked, not quite able to believe that anybody so young and lovely could have been George Simms' wife.

"I'm Zelda Simms, her sister-in-law. I'm afraid she's in no condition to see anybody."

"My name is Ethan Burr," he said. "I was a friend of George."

Her eyes fixed on his scar. "Oh, yes. George spoke about you. Won't you come in?"

He stepped into a foyer. Through a side door he saw a small woman sitting stiffly in a chair. With a handkerchief she dabbed at eyes which seemed to have no life. Seated on a footstool was a girl of seven or eight—a pretty little thing with a tumble of blonde curls.

Zelda Simms took his hand and led him into a big kitchen. "It's best that you don't disturb them," she said.

"You live here?" he asked.

"Yes. My brother was good enough to let me share his home." She bit her lips. "I don't know what we're going to do now. We'll have to move, of course. George rented this house. And I understand that he did not leave a cent. Fortunately I have a job."

"How much do you make?"

She looked up at him angrily. Then she smiled wanly. "Having been my brother's friend, I suppose you'd like to help. I make only twenty a week, but we'll manage. We'll have to. I don't want to accept favors."

He thought of the widow and child in the other room. Three women left destitute. And in a way, he thought, it was his fault, because conceivably he might have saved Simms' life. Simms had been slow, a good routine man but nothing more. He had had no business taking a case which called for hair-trigger thinking and action.

He said, "I don't want to give you anything that doesn't rightfully belong to you. George approached me yesterday and asked me to take a piece of the case which brought about his death. I accepted, so the fee rightfully belongs to you three. It's five thousand dollars."

She stared doubtfully at him a moment. Apparently satisfied that he was telling the truth, she said, "Why, that would be a windfall."

Then she frowned. "But we're entitled only to half."

"Of course. The entire fee is ten thousand…. Well, I'll be pushing on."

She gripped his hand warmly, her eyes lighting up. "I can't begin to thank you," she started to say. Then he was gone, an embarrassed look on his face.

THE LOVELY VISION of Zelda Simms stayed with Ethan Burr as he drove to the local Chinatown. He finally submerged it with an effort.

The Chinese quarter consisted of three blocks of the oldest slum area in the city. Nearing it, Burr parked his car some distance away and walked the rest of the distance. In tiny shop windows along the crowded narrow street placards exhorted: "Smash Japanese Aggression!" Farther down the street a huge painted sign announced, under Chinese characters:

SAM MING

IMPORTER

That was his destination.

Burr happened to be glancing up when the thing came hurtling off the roof. For an instant he thought it would hit him and he jumped backward. But it landed a good fifteen feet beyond, narrowly missing an ancient Chinese who had been stolidly plodding along. The old man emitted a wail and his aged legs started pumping. The street cleared instantly.

It required only a glance to show Burr that the object which had fallen was a gunny sack fastened on top with wire. Blood was seeping through the coarse weave.

Then Burr was running into the house from which the sack had been dropped. He had his gun out. The stairs were poorly lit and rickety and there were five flights of them. No sound issued from any of the doors he passed.

He was panting when he reached the roof. Four buildings had roofs precisely the same height as the one he was on. All were deserted. Whoever had hurled the gunny sack could have gone down into any one of the houses.

Almost at once his eyes fell on the blood which stained the tar and pebbles covering the roof. The trail led to its edge. Obviously the gunny sack had been dragged along and then pushed over.

He followed the trail of blood back, found that the sack had been brought up to the roof from the house immediately to the right. He went down the stairs. No blood was here or in the top floor hall. Either the blood hadn't started seeping through the weave until the sack had reached the roof, or, more likely, the sack had been wrapped in canvas to prevent a telltale trail from revealing its source.

Burr knew that it would be futile to make a search of the apartments of that house. There were at least six on a floor, twenty-four in all; and anyway, there would be no way of telling who the killer was.

When he reached the street he found a patrolman standing next to the gunny sack which he had opened. There wasn't another person in sight.

"Burr!" the cop grunted. "You would be around when there's a corpse."

"Who is it?"

"Only a Chink," the cop said. "Chopped up with one of their nasty little hatchets. We'll never find out who did it. We never do. They shut up like clams."

Burr didn't have much stomach for it, but he forced himself to spread open the mouth of the sack.

The head was on top. He looked into a thin yellow face—a young, sensitive face. The tattered remnants of tortoise-shell eye-glasses still clung to the ears. The bulging eyes and contorted facial muscles spoke of the horror the young man must have felt just before the death blow had struck.

A prowl car screamed up the street. Burr turned away from the gunny sack and strode rapidly toward Sam Ming's establishment.

2

The Hatchet Murder

SAM MING WAS slim and suave and completely bald. A younger man, who was formed like a round ball, with a button on top for a head and sticks for the arms and legs, showed Ethan Burr into the lavishly furnished office.

"Ah, Ethan Burr," Sam Ming purred as he came from behind

his desk to shake hands with the detective. "It is always a pleasure to receive you." He spoke with an Oxford accent.

Burr took the chair which the fat young man pushed toward the desk. He said, "I'm looking for somebody who wouldn't find it a pleasure to see me." He stopped and glanced significantly at the fat man.

"Lin Fu is my confidential secretary," Sam Ming assured him. "You can speak your mind plainly in his presence."

Burr shrugged. "I trust very few men, Sam Ming. That's one reason I'm still alive. You're one of the few. If you say he's all right, let him stay."

Lin Fu bowed his head. Burr loaded his pipe and went on: "Sam Ming, you're known as the unofficial mayor of Chinatown. You've caused the tongs to make peace. You act as judge and arbitrator of disputes and your word is considered final. There's little goes on here that you don't know about." He paused to light his pipe. "Why was George Simms murdered?"

The faces of Sam Ming and Lin Fu remained impassive. But Burr expected no visible reaction and waited for Ming to speak.

"I have read of the unfortunate incident in today's newspapers," Sam Ming drawled. "Why do you expect me to have special knowledge of his demise?"

Burr rose and went to the window. A little way down the street there were a lot of uniformed cops and plainclothesmen. No Chinese were to be seen.

"You know what happened downstairs a couple of minutes ago," Burr said. "And yet you two didn't even appear interested when I came in. That shows that you are. I had an idea from a conversation with George Simms yesterday that Chinese were involved in the case. There are the chopped up pieces of a poor Chinese boy in a sack downstairs—killed the same way as Simms was. He looked like a nice boy; the kind you'd have working for you."

Keenly he searched the two yellow faces to see what effect his shot had had.

Burr walked around to the front of the desk. He leaned toward Sam Ming. "Look here. I promise to stay away from the police. Simms left a wife, a daughter and a sister who were dependent on him. He had been working for somebody and the fee he would have received would do them a lot of good. I'm willing to take over for the same fee he was supposed to get, so that I can give it to his family."

Sam Ming closed his eyes. Lin Fu sat as solid as a rock with his fat hands on his knees. Burr waited.

FINALLY SAM MING'S eyes opened again. "George Simms was employed by me," he admitted. "The boy whose remains are now being examined by the police was in my humble employ. More than that I cannot tell you. You have pledged your word that you will not go with this information to the police."

"Afraid?" Burr mocked.

"No," Sam Ming purred lazily, and Burr knew that he told the truth. "We shall settle this our way. It is necessary." His lips twitched at the corners. "There will be no fee for you, Ethan Burr."

"But if I get to the bottom of this, there will be a suitable reward?" Burr inquired.

"I cannot say." His eyes closed.

Burr glanced at Lin Fu who had not moved. He went out. In

the street he found Sergeant Howell of Homicide in charge of the Chinese boy's murder.

"Make way for the Practitioner of Death," Howell sneered. "What do you know about this, Burr?"

"I did it with my little hatchet," Burr said. "If you want a civil answer, try acting human, if it isn't too much of a strain."

Howell's heavy face turned purple. "You damn money-grubber! We know Simms was murdered because he was working on something. His wife hasn't any idea what it was, but now we know that Chinks are tied up in it in some way. Simms got the business in the same way as this Chink. It's clear you figured it like that and now you're in Chinatown trying to cop the fee he'd been working for. By God, if you get under my feet I'll break you."

"You'll be miles behind me if you follow the trail," Burr snapped.

He strode away in the opposite direction.

The following street was not as deserted. But Burr sensed that the Chinese were going about their business furtively. When he looked at them, their eyes shifted quickly. The only ones at ease were the white people who drifted into Chinese restaurants or peered into the windows of curio shops.

A Chinese girl of about ten was moving slowly toward him, rattling coins in a collection can and chanting in a shrill voice: "Chinese relief. Please help the Chinese people."

A small man, dressed entirely in white, dropped a quarter into the can. He whispered something to her and she smiled up at him. She was extremely pretty. Burr fumbled in his pocket for change as she spied him and started in his direction.

She never reached him. As she passed close to the doorway

of a house, she pitched forward on her face. The hatchet had come so quickly out of the vestibule that Burr hadn't seen it in midair. But he saw it now, buried in the girl's skull. Blood gushed from the hideous wound, flowing over the sidewalk.

The collection can had fallen from her hand and rolled into the gutter. Across the street a white woman screamed.

Burr was already moving toward the vestibule from which the hatchet had been thrown. The door leading into the hall was closed. Gun gripped in his right hand, he turned the knob with his left and kicked the door open.

A narrow, smelly hall stretched in front of him. Daylight streamed in from a partly open door in back of the hall which led to the backyard. And through the back doorway a yellow face momentarily appeared. Then a hand shoved out below the face and a gun roared.

THE BULLET CAME nowhere near Burr. He snapped a quick shot at the face, but not before the door had slammed. His slug smashed through the door panel.

Burr started forward in pursuit, then stopped as a warning click in his mind told him of a possible trap. He continued toward the rear of the hall again, going more carefully now, until he reached the back of the staircase. A man was standing there, a hatchet raised above his head.

Burr shot from his hip. He pumped three bullets in a row to make sure, then leaped toward the back door. There was nobody in the littered backyard which was enclosed by a high board fence.

His eyes stopped at a sugar barrel which stood against the fence. He clambered up on it, saw a pair of broad shoulders dropping over the fence of the next yard. Quickly he shot at the shoulders. A man screamed in agony; the shoulders dropped from sight.

Burr jumped into the next yard, pulled himself up on the opposite fence. The third yard was empty. The wounded man couldn't have kept climbing fences; he hadn't the time and his bullet-torn shoulder wouldn't let him. He must have run into the back door of the third house.

Although wounded, the Chinese was armed and could pick Burr off in these dimly lit halls. Burr went through all the halls of the house and finally reached the roof without coming across anybody. When he had fired his gun in the backyard, no heads had poked out of windows as they would have in any white community. And this house, in which nearly a hundred people lived, seemed a house of the dead. No sound, no audible hint of life, reached him. And yet he was conscious of human beings huddling in terror in their apartments. In one of them was the killer.

Looking down from the roof, he saw the street crowded with cops. They'd been only a block away when the girl had been murdered. Burr went to the back of the roof and saw other cops and plainclothesmen scampering about in the backyards. He attracted their attention and necks craned up toward him.

"I got one of them in the shoulder," he called down. "He's in this house or an adjoining one. He's Chinese, a big fellow."

"We'll block off the street," a detective shouted back.

Burr realized that he couldn't do any more. The rest was up to organized police routine. He went down to the street.

The body of the pretty little Chinese girl lay where it had fallen, covered now with a shawl. Burr's facial muscles tightened.

Sergeant Howell was patiently listening to the little man in white linen who had dropped a coin into the girl's collection can just before the murderer had struck.

"THERE'S THE MAN I was telling you about," the little man said, nodding toward Burr. "She was going toward him when she fell with that horrible hatchet in her skull. He rushed into the hall and then I heard shots."

"Burr," Howell growled. "I thought so when I heard that the beggar who killed this girl was dead in the hall with a couple of slugs in him."

"Ethan Burr?" the little man said. "The one they call the Practitioner of Death?" He thrust out his hand. "Permit me to congratulate you. I'm S. Hartley Kern, the attorney. You may have heard of me."

Burr said to Howell: "I winged the second one. Your men are combing the block for him now."

"These damn Chinks and their damn hatchets!" Howell raged. "And now they go slaughtering little girls!"

"The hatchet man was white," said Burr dryly. "The other one was Chinese, but he carried a gun."

Howell gulped. "White? Did you get a good look at him?"

"Good enough. Did you?"

"I was questioning witnesses," Howell said. "Come on."

Howell and Burr went into the hall. A couple of detectives were standing over the man Burr had killed. They had turned him over on his back. A brutal, unshaven white face looked up at them.

"Let's hear your version, Burr," Howell said. His attitude was truculent.

"I'm sure they knew I was coming down the street," Burr told him. "They killed the girl in front of my eyes because they knew I'd go chasing into the hall after them. The white man hid behind this staircase with another hatchet ready to lay my head open when I rushed past. The Chinese was stationed at the door to draw me on. They weren't eager to trade shots with me, and a hatchet can be more certain at close quarters.

"I suspected the trap when the Chinese let me see him and when he shot so quickly that there wasn't any possibility of hitting me. He didn't have to take the chance of aiming more carefully because he figured this lad would be sure to get me. He would have, too, if the whole thing hadn't struck me as having been a perfect set-up for a trap."

Howell's eyes bulged a little. "You mean to say they killed that girl just to draw you into a trap?"

"I doubt it," Burr said. "They wanted to kill the girl anyway. If their scheme had worked, they would have killed two birds with one gesture."

"But why?" Howell asked. "What could anybody have against a little girl like that?"

Burr packed tobacco into his pipe and lit it. "I don't know," he said slowly, watching the smoke float in the sunlight which streamed in through the open back door. "But I intend to find out."

3

Garroted!

POLICE KEPT POURING into the district. For a while Burr followed them around as they searched for the wounded man and questioned the inhabitants of the airless hovels.

The Chinese simply stared at their questioners with the bewildered, hopeless expression Burr had seen on the faces of Chinese peasants after a flood or famine or the passing of the Japanese war machine. They shook their heads and repeated dully in English, or through interpreters, that they had seen no wounded man, that they did not know why anybody should want to kill a Chinese young man and little girl and a white detective.

Some of them must have been lying. All of them were scared.

A detective plucked Burr's sleeve. "Captain Rowland wants to see you downstairs."

The chief of the Homicide Bureau was a big man with a florid face from which jowls sagged like empty bags. He was savagely chewing on a cigar as he stood on the sidewalk listening to Sergeant Howell.

"Here's Burr," Captain Rowland said. He poked a pudgy finger into Burr's chest. "Look here, Howell tells me that the Chinaman and the one you plugged laid a trap for you. There's only one reason why they'd want you out of the way and that's because they thought you were onto something hot. What is it?"

"They flattered me. I'm as much in the dark as you are."

Rowland thrust out his jaw. "Want me to believe that? You're playing a lone hand, as usual, so that you can cop a fee. And what brought you into Chinatown?"

"George Simms was a friend of mine," Burr said.

"Huh!" Rowland hooted. "How'd you know Chinamen were involved?"

"From a talk with him yesterday. He didn't say another thing about the case."

"You're lying, Burr!"

Burr shrugged. Not lying as much as Rowland believed. He had simply failed to mention that he was after a reward.

"Here's what I know," he said. "You're wasting your time looking for the wounded Chinese. It's plain that he got away. Even if you caught him, he wouldn't talk. There's nothing you can do to make a Chinese talk when he doesn't want to. And he's not important anyway. He's only small fry. It's the head of the outfit you want to get after."

"Outfit?" Captain Rowland said. "What outfit?"

"I don't know. But obviously there's some sort of an organization. The deaths of Simms and the Chinese lad and the girl are related. We know why Simms was killed—because he was getting too close to something."

"And I suppose the little girl was a member of the rival gang?" Rowland sneered.

"She has to fit in somewhere," Burr said quietly. He had an idea, but he wasn't telling Rowland until he was sure. "Now go ahead and solve your own case."

He turned on his heels and strode away. Twilight seeped softly down into the narrow street.

"MR. BURR," A voice called and a hand gripped his arm.

He turned to look into the lovely face of Zelda Simms.

"What are you doing here?" he demanded.

"I read in the afternoon paper how that sack containing the poor Chinese boy was dropped almost on you. And now I heard how a little girl was also murdered and you were almost killed," Her hand tightened on his arm. "I know that you're doing this for my sister-in-law and my niece and myself. Please drop it. We don't want the money if it means endangering your life."

He said, "Look, sister, you said you'd heard about me. You must have heard that I don't care for anything but money. Danger is my business, and I'm after my half of the fee. The other half will be turned over to your sister-in-law. She's legally entitled to it."

"Oh." She shrank away from him. She had come here to plead with him to drop the case, but his hard, mercenary manner filled her with contempt. He could see it in the firm set of her mouth. He felt almost sorry he had taken this easy way to get her to return home.

"I'm sorry I bothered you," she said stiffly. "I shall demand an accounting of every cent to be divided evenly between you and my sister-in-law."

"Sure," Burr said. "Now be a good girl and run home."

He watched her tall, attractive form moving down the street. Later he would have to find some way of getting back into her good graces. He realized, suddenly, that he felt it very important that she think well of him.

Burr climbed up two flights of narrow stairs to see Sam Ming's office. The outer office was furnished in the most modern and efficient manner. None of the dozen or so Chinese employees who had been in the office earlier were there. It was long past working hours. The only occupant was Lin Fu, whose roly-poly body was hunched over a Chinese newspaper.

He bounced up to his feet at Burr's entrance. "Unfortunate events are occurring in our wretched community," Lin Fu said. "I assume you wish to see my honored employer. He is in his office contemplating the tragedy of our people."

"I suppose you got that line of lingo out of a book," Burr observed admiringly.

"Please?" Lin Fu frowned.

"Skip it," Burr said, going to a door on the far side of the room.

He pushed open the door. There was no light in the office. In the dimness of what remaining light came in through the windows he saw Sam Ming slumped over on his desk.

Burr jumped forward, lifted the head of the Chinese. Sam Ming was dead. A thin circle of indented skin ran completely around his neck where a silken noose had been drawn tight.

"Lin Fu!" Burr called, his voice hard.

The fat secretary appeared in the doorway. A cry gurgled in his throat. He waddled to the desk in the closest thing he would ever come to a run.

"Slain!" Lin Fu exclaimed. "Garroted!"

"Yeah," Burr said. "Who was in here since you last saw him alive?"

"Nobody. About an hour ago Sam Ming expressed a wish to be alone. I dismissed the employees for the day, then picked up the paper and read."

BURR WENT TO the window. "No fire-escape on this side

of the building," he mused. "A man could climb down from the floor above, but not with all those cops in the street. The only entrance to this room was through the outer office in which you say you were sitting all the time."

Lin Fu blanched. "My dear sir, surely you do not suspect that I—" He broke off. "Now I recall. For the space of sixty seconds—surely no more—I stepped into the washroom."

Burr said, "Sam Ming must have seen his murderer come through the door. He would have made an outcry, put up some sort of struggle. On the contrary, he gave the murderer a chance to step behind him while he sat at the desk and slip the noose over his head. That means he knew and trusted the murderer."

Lin Fu swallowed hard. "Willingly would I have laid down my life for him." His eyes, sunk in layers of fat, swept about the room. "Perhaps the slayer is still in this room. I returned too soon to allow him an opportunity to escape."

There was a closet in the room. Burr pulled out his gun and went to it. "Pray that he's here," he told Lin Fu, "or you'll have to make up another yarn."

He opened the door. As he had expected, nobody was in the closet.

Then Lin Fu screamed. Burr spun around and glimpsed a dark form bolting out from behind a row of letter files. The shape smashed into Lin Fu, knocking him down, and Burr had to hold his fire for fear of hitting the fat Chinese. A moment later the shape was through the door.

Burr stepped around Lin Fu. In the outer office he saw a slim Chinese scampering between the desks toward the hall door.

"Stop or I'll shoot!" Burr ordered.

The man kept running. Burr had enough time to put a bullet

precisely where he wanted it. Just as the Chinese reached the door Burr squeezed the trigger. The man's leg gave way under him, but he continued to throw his body forward, groping up for the doorknob.

Burr ran over to him and dug his fingers in his crop of thick black hair.

"Relax," he said. "You won't get far with a .44 slug in your leg." He turned the man over on his back. Malevolent black eyes glared up at him.

"Lai Soong!" Lin Fu exclaimed.

"You know him?"

Lin Fu was wringing his bands like a frantic woman. "He was one of our most trusted employees." He stood over Lai Soong and hurled a stream of Cantonese invectives at him.

"Why did you kill Sam Ming?" Burr asked.

Lai Soong closed his eyes and pressed his lips firmly together. Burr knew that nothing could make him talk. He stood up.

"Now what's it all about?" he asked Lin Fu. "You know as well as I that this fellow didn't kill Sam Ming on his own hook. He's got somebody over him. Do you want the real killer of your boss punished?"

Lin Fu tugged at one fleshy cheek. "With the honored Sam Ming gone to join his ancestors, I am in command. Yet the responsibility is too great."

"Do you want these killings to go on?" Burr repeated. His tones were harsh.

Lin Fu took a deep breath and straightened up. "Yes, I will assume the responsibility. Perhaps you can succeed where George Simms failed. Apprehend the murderers, Ethan Burr, and you will be paid well."

"Five thousand dollars."

"It is high, but we can afford it."

"Now give me the low-down," Burr said.

Lin Fu shook his head. "That I cannot do. First, because I do not know the identity of these creatures of infinite evil. Second, because publicity will nullify our laudable work. I must request, as part of our bargain, that you withhold from the newspapers, and even the police, any knowledge you may gather concerning your venture."

Burr studied Lin Fu keenly. "I think I'm pretty close to knowing what it's all about. From your point of view I guess you're right."

Feet padded in the hall outside. The door flew open and Sergeant Howell and a couple of plainclothesmen rushed in.

"One of my men said he heard a shot coming from—" Howell broke off and gaped down at Lai Soong who lay flat on his back, his eyes still closed, no sign on his face of the pain he must be suffering from his wound. "What's the matter with him?"

"One of my bullets is in his leg," Burr said. "He just murdered Sam Ming. I saved him for you even though he won't talk."

"My God!" Howell cried. He strode toward Sam Ming's office.

4

Invitation to Hell

AN HOUR LATER Ethan Burr, after having eaten an elaborate Chinese dinner, left the restaurant drawing languidly on his pipe. A man clad entirely in white hurried across the street toward him.

"You remember me, Mr. Burr? S. Hartley Kern. I was an eyewitness to the brutal murder of the little Chinese girl."

"Well?" Burr said.

S. Hartley Kern bit off the end of a slender cigar. "I was deeply shocked by the murder, Mr. Burr. For hours I have watched the police milling about without any signs of coming nearer a solution. I know your reputation, and I have supreme confidence in your ability. While I am not a rich man, I am willing to pay to have the murder of that poor girl solved. Some of my best friends are Chinese. I admire not only their food and their intelligence, but also—"

"Are you trying to hire me?" Burr broke in.

"Exactly. I will pay you two thousand dollars if you capture those responsible for the death of the girl. I realize that they are also responsible for other murders, but I am not concerned with that. Seeing that girl so brutally—"

"It's a deal," Burr interrupted again.

He pulled a notebook and pencil from his pocket and drew up a contract. "This will require two witnesses," he told Kern. "I think we'll find them in here."

He led Kern into the restaurant he had just left. The Chinese proprietor who stood behind the cash register, and one of the waiters, solemnly read the contract and affixed their names. Burr watched them closely, but their faces told him nothing.

That, Burr told himself as he stuck the contract in his wallet, made his third client on the same case—if he included George Simms' family; and it was for them he was really working.

"I'll be around for your money tomorrow, Mr. Kern," he said. "I'm prepared to make arrests within an hour. There might be some casualties. Our contract, you notice, specified that the leader of the culprits be captured, dead or alive."

Everybody in the restaurant heard him. He wanted to be heard.

S. Hartley Kern smiled benignly. "Knowing your reputation, I hardly think there will be anything but corpses."

Outside the restaurant a Chinese boy of seven or eight was waiting for Burr. He thrust a sheet of paper into Burr's hand and scampered away.

The note was written in small capitals with a brush. It read:

This message will be your first intimation that Zelda Simms never reached her home. We are prepared to enter into an agreement with you in return for her release. If we can come to terms, she will be handed over to you unharmed. If you ignore this note, Zelda Simms will be made extremely uncomfortable. Come alone to 17 Elm Street.

There was no signature. None was necessary.

"A message concerning the case?" S. Hartley Kern breathed at Burr's side.

Burr crumpled the note and shoved it into his pocket. "It's personal," he murmured. "Very personal."

He walked over to a cigar store down the block and glanced through the city directory. Then he stepped into the phone booth. Mrs. Simms, her voice thin and weary, answered.

No, Zelda Simms was not at home. She had left the house several hours ago, and although she had said she would be home for supper, she had not yet returned. Mrs. Simms was obviously worried.

BURR'S EYES WERE chips of gray-blue ice as he dialed police headquarters. He asked for Lieutenant Wade Kirk of Homicide.

"Burr?" Kirk's voice presently came excitedly over the wire. "Say, you're having quite a time for yourself in Chinatown. Sorry it's out of my district."

"So am I. Listen, there are plenty of cops outside in the street, including Captain Rowland, but I don't want to be seen talking to any of them. Can you relay a message to Rowland?"

"Let's have it."

Burr read the contents of the note he had just received.

Kirk laughed derisively. "That's the most childish kind of trap I've ever heard of."

"Sure. But maybe Zelda Simms is really at that address."

"They're not that dumb."

"Probably not," Burr agreed. "But why hand me the message? And why abduct Zelda Simms if the killers don't intend to use her as bait? There's a chance that a quick raid on 17 Elm Street might net something."

"Okay," Kirk said. "Good hunting."

Burr remained in the booth making social calls to acquaintances in order to kill time. He had an idea that he was being watched. Ten minutes passed. Then through the store window, he saw sudden activity in the street, and he left the phone booth.

All the police who had flocked into Chinatown converged simultaneously on 17 Elm Street. The note had given, simply, an address. Actually it was a four-story tenement building with a fish store in the basement. The raid was so sudden and thorough that hardly a fly could have escaped.

After twenty minutes the police were convinced that Zelda Simms was not in the building. They had searched every square inch, had lined up scores of terrified Chinese.

Burr leaned against a lamp-post, sucking abstractedly on a dead pipe. There were weary lines about his eyes and mouth. The scar on his cheek seemed to be throbbing with subdued fury. He did not stir as Captain Rowland strode up to him.

"Let's see that note you said you received," Rowland demanded savagely.

Burr handed it to him. The captain read quickly and scowled.

"Since when do you go to the police with information?" Rowland barked. "I have a notion you knew it was a gag."

"There's a girl with whose life I don't want to take any chances," Burr replied quietly.

"And you took a phoney note like this seriously? Don't tell me that you've gone soft in the head."

"The note didn't say the girl would be here," Burr answered. "It said that I should come here. I didn't because I thought there might be more possibility of getting her back alive through a sudden raid. I'm afraid I was wrong."

"I'll say you were," Rowland growled.

The police drifted away. Burr stayed there, leaning against the lamp-post, puffing stolidly on his pipe. Perhaps Zelda Simms had been killed before the note had been sent, or perhaps she had been killed after the raid. Any minute her lovely body might be found in a gunny sack—if nothing worse than that had been done to her.

HOURS PASSED. THE police were slowly leaving the neighborhood. Stores were closing for the night. Lights blinked out in the windows. And still Ethan Burr remained there like a graven figure. Once he ran out of tobacco and went to the cigar store for a fresh package and returned to the lamp-post.

Then Burr saw the Chinese boy who had handed him the message turn the corner and come running toward him. The boy thrust another slip of paper at Burr and hurried off.

The second note read:

As we had expected you to communicate with the police and so were prepared, we are not as angry as we might otherwise have been. Zelda Simms remains unharmed—until ten minutes after you have received this message. It will take you half this time to reach 256 Market Place. Enter the curio shop. If you do not go there directly, or if you stop to make a phone call or exchange a single word with anybody, the place will be empty when you arrive, and you will never again see Zelda Simms—alive.

Burr nodded glumly. This was what he had been waiting for.

He started to walk casually toward Market Place. It might not be a trap. There was a good chance that the writer of the notes really wanted to deal with him. There was no doubt in Burr's mind that the terms would be impossible for him to meet, but of the most immediate importance was for him to reach Zelda Simms.

The window of the curio shop at 256 Market Place was filled with the usual teakwood Gods of Happiness and Buddhas and back scratchers and photos of Chinese movie stars. Reed blinds in back of the window and the door prevented him from seeing into the store. The place seemed dark.

He tried the door with his left hand. It opened. A spring swung the door shut behind him; he heard the click of a snap-lock. His gun dropped into his right hand.

The large store, filled with Chinese curios and bric-a-brac, was empty. A bulb dangling over the counter seemed to have hardly the power of a candle. Burr stood motionless, tense, his eyes roving. His gun jerked up as, near one row of shelves, he saw a shadow which was the size and shape of a man.

Then he laughed soundlessly to himself and moved over to the thing. It looked like a fossil of what might have been a dragon. From each side of its spine jutted six curved append-ages. A heavy chain hanging from the ceiling held it upright. Obviously it was no real fossil, but cleverly constructed of steel.

Burr hadn't taken more than a couple of seconds to look at it. He turned away from it, looking for a door to the rear of the store. He found it next to the end of the counter and took a single step toward it.

Then he heard a scraping sound behind him and started to swing around. Something long and hard hit his side. The chain rattled and, before he could make a move, twelve steel, skeleton-like arms wound themselves about him. He lurched forward, twisting, but almost at once he knew that he was hopelessly caught.

The dragon had swung against him and its steel arms had imprisoned him in a relentless, crushing embrace.

5

The Lair of the Dragon

FEET SCRAPED BEHIND Ethan Burr. Glancing down, he saw a yellow hand reaching from behind the dragon. He squirmed, tried to swing his gun toward the hand. A sharp blow struck his wrist, numbing his arm all the way up to the shoulder. Then the hand snatched the gun away from him. A harsh voice laughed in his ear.

The laugh was echoed by another in the rear of the store. Then there were several long minutes of silence. Burr ceased his struggle to free himself from the gripping arms of the dragon. He knew when he was licked: it was futile to waste energy.

A scream for help might be heard in the street, but it would mean instant death. And it was doubtful if much attention would be paid to a scream. He waited. There was nothing else that he could do.

Presently the door near the end of the counter opened and a small man in white linens stepped into the front section of the shop.

Burr's thin lips curled. "S. Hartley Kern! I thought it might be you. You were entirely too solicitous about the death of that little Chinese girl. You would have known that your interest would endanger your life, and I tabbed you as the kind of person who wouldn't take any needless risk for a principle."

S. Hartley Kern smiled and said: "I suppose you realize that I could have had you killed a few minutes ago. You are completely at my mercy. Yet I do not mock the dreaded Practitioner of Death over his plight. I salute you for your courage. I admire you. It required a great deal of nerve for you to come here alone into the very jaws of death."

"Wouldn't it be funny if I collected two thousand dollars from your estate for killing you?" Burr said. "I believe I could, legally, by virtue of our written contract."

"Two thousand dollars!" S. Hartley Kern snorted contemptuously. "And that's how you earned your reputation for being in love with fat fees! How would you like to earn five thousand a week, every week, with a substantial bonus at the end of each month?"

"What you're trying to say is that you want to hire me as a professional murderer?"

The little man shrugged. "Why should that disturb you? You have killed many men for money. Here is your chance to get into the real money you seem to want so badly."

"And if I don't accept?"

S. Hartley Kern sighed. "Isn't that a rather unnecessary question?"

Burr straightened up in the grip of the steel arms. His eyes remained emotionless. He said nothing.

"I see you need additional inducement," Kern said.

He clapped his hands. A Chinese stepped into view from behind the dragon. The door in the rear of the shop flew inward and another Chinese came through. Then Burr heard the girl whimper.

Seconds later Zelda Simms appeared in the doorway. Thin wisps of her blouse trailed from her hips; evidently it had been ripped from her when she had put up a fight during her abduction. Her bare shoulders were hunched forward, her arms crossed over her breasts which were covered by a skimpy brassiere. Her tall form was trembling violently, and from her lips whimpers trickled piteously.

Then she saw Burr and she stopped dead. The whimpers turned to moans.

A VOICE BEHIND her ordered: "Come on, keep moving." A foot lashed out through the doorway and she plunged heavily forward. Before she hit the floor, invisible hands seemed to twist her around and hurled her down. Her mouth was open wide, but no sounds came from it. She rolled on the floor, tearing at her throat.

Burr pounded at the steel arms, cursing harshly. A fourth man, white and gaunt, came into the room. In his hand he held a long silk cord. And then Burr saw that the other end of the cord was tied in a noose about Zelda Simm's neck, which was drawn tight when she had fallen.

The white man left enough slack so that her fingers could tear the noose loose. Then he kicked her again. Coughing and gasping for breath, she stumbled to her feet and stood shivering.

Like a beaten dog on a leash, Burr thought with cold fury. He noticed bruises on her white skin where she had been kicked and beaten.

S. Hartley Kern said, "We have been comparatively merciful to her. I have more or less held my men off. You may have heard that Chinese are masters at refined torture. They would enjoy practicing their art on her."

"Will you release her if I accept your proposition?" Burr demanded.

Kern smiled smugly. "I have gone to a great deal of trouble to get you and the girl here. Possibly, if you accept my offer, the prospect of that much money every week will prevent you from betraying me. Perhaps you plan to accept only long enough to obtain your release. I have too much at stake to take a chance. The girl will be removed to a place which you will never be able to discover. If you betray me or if anything happens to me, the girl will die an extremely unpleasant death. I will give you proper assurances that while you live up to your bargain she will receive every comfort. Undoubtedly she must mean a great deal to you or you would not have run so much risk for her."

"Don't!" Zelda Simms wailed. "I'd rather die at once."

"Not at once, my dear," Kern said softly. "My men kill slowly—ever so slowly. And as for Burr—"

He made a motion to one of the Chinese. The man stepped behind Burr and there was the grinding sound of chains turning on a windlass. The twelve arms of the dragon tightened still further, constricting his ribs. He could breathe only with difficulty.

"Let's get this straight," Burr gasped.

Kern waved a hand and the twelve arms relaxed somewhat. Burr drew air into his lungs.

"I know that your racket is concerned with the raising of relief to war-torn China," he said. "That's why the little girl

who was going around with a collection can was murdered—
as a warning to the organization which had sent her out. Sam
Ming was head of the group which was collecting these funds.
Whites as well as Chinese are contributing lavishly. You got
together a gang of killers, including at least one of Sam Ming's
employees, Lai Soong, whom you no doubt bribed, and set
about trying to take control of the organization through terrifying those in charge."

BURR'S EYES WERE hard. "I suppose you began by sending threats. When they were ignored, you went into action.
Perhaps you killed one or two whom the police did not hear
about. You were in a pretty good position because Sam Ming
was anxious that the public did not hear of the bloodshed over
the control of the relief organization. It would be too demor-
alizing. People would not be sure which was the legitimate
organization, and eventually would begin to doubt if any was.
Many of the contributions would be withheld.

"You didn't care, because there would still be plenty coming
in. But Sam Ming cared. He was devoting himself to sending help to his people. Instead of going to the police, he hired
George Simms. You got rid of him. One of your men saw me
entering Sam Ming's office. You suspected that Sam Ming
had hired me to take George Simm's place, and I flatter myself
that that made you nervous. You arranged a trap for me in the
hall of a house, at the same time killing that girl. When you
failed to get me, you had Lai Soong kill Sam Ming, thinking
that would take the heart out of the leadership of the group.
Maybe you've succeeded. For all I know, Lin Fu might also be
working for you."

S. Hartley Kern chortled. "A man has to be good for me to want to hire him and pay him a fortune. You're good, Burr—not only with a gun but with your head as well. After we have complete control of the China relief organization here, we will branch out into the real gravy in New York and San Francisco. There's no reason why we shouldn't succeed. Haven't many similar organizations been taken over by the rackets? Oh, we'll send some money to China, but a large part of it will go into our own pockets. Yours and mine, Burr. With a man like you in with us, we can't be stopped."

Ethan Burr's mind was racing wildly. He had been in desperate predicaments before, but never in one as apparently hopeless as this. If he accepted Kern's offer, Zelda Simms would be taken away before he was released and Kern would make sure that he did not find her. In addition, he would at once be given a task to perform, probably to kill somebody, and if he did not carry it out, Zelda's fate would be too frightful to think about.

There were long moments of silence. Zelda Simms was looking at Burr with a dull, haunted expression. She stood huddled as if against a storm, her fingers digging into the flesh of her upper arm. The noose was tight about her throat, but it allowed her to breathe. The Chinese who had taken hold of the other end of the cord jerked it every now and then, straightening her up, and his eyes were smouldering embers as they moved over her.

"Well?" Kern snapped impatiently. "Take it or leave it, Burr."

Ethan Burr moved; only his arms, it is true, which were free from the elbows down. But that was enough to permit him to reach the Chinese who had been turning the windlass which constricted the arms of the dragon.

He got his hand on the Chinese's shoulder and yanked him close. He had seen the bulge in the left jacket pocket where the yellow man had put his gun. His free hand dipped for the weapon.

Only a second or two had passed before he felt the hard, comforting stock of his .44 against his palm. The yellow man was shrieking, squirming to break his grip, and his hand held a knife he'd produced from under his gown. Before Burr's eyes flashed a picture of the second Chinese, winding the windlass taut with his left hand, his right jerking at the string around Zelda's neck.

THEN BURR HAD his gun in his hand. The Chinese slashed with his knife at the same time that Burr's gun came up and crashed against his head. Burr felt the blade glance off his shoulderbone, saw the yellow man sink.

Meanwhile the other Chinese was pulling a gun from some-where in his clothes. And Burr saw that Kern had his gun out and the white man also had a gun, and he knew that he couldn't get all three of them.

Somewhere glass smashed, but he paid no attention to it. Standing in the grip of the dragon's arms, Burr triggered his gun. Kern went down first, and next the white killer. Kern hadn't had a chance to shoot; the white man had sent one slug into the hideous skeleton head of the dragon.

Then he swung his gun around toward the second Chinese. He found him writhing on the floor, although he knew that he couldn't have shot him. A gun roared, and the wounded man lay still.

Burr looked up with astonished eyes. Lin Fu was waddling

into the store. Behind him the glass door was smashed. A contented smile formed a wreath on his fat face. In one pudgy hand he held an enormous pistol.

Abruptly the smile vanished and, with a little cry, Lin Fu heaved his roly-poly body forward in what vaguely resembled a leap. He lowered himself to the floor, and Burr, following him with his eyes, saw him kneel beside Zelda Simms who was once again tearing at the noose about her throat. The man who had held the noose had pulled it tight just before he had gone for his gun.

Lin Fu knocked Zelda's frantic hands out of the way and set to work with his own plump fingers. In almost no time he was pulling the noose over her head. Then he helped her up to her feet.

"There is a compensation for everything," Lin Fu observed. "If that despicable individual had not tightened the noose and pulled you off your feet, you might have been pierced by one of the flying bullets."

"Never mind philosophizing now," Burr said. "Get me out of this hellish contraption."

Lin Fu waddled over to the windlass and turned the chains. As the arms loosened their grip, he explained: "As a humble creature with tremendous responsibility since the lamented death of my honored employer, Sam Ming, I considered it my duty to keep an observing eye on your activities. For the space of hours I watched you lean against a lamppost with infinite patience. I followed you to this miserable hovel. The door shut behind you, and I was forced to listen from without. I overheard the boasting of yonder lowest of insects. Perhaps I should have broken in at once, but I had to hear all; for what is the life of one or two compared to the good we can do my unhappy people by sending them what little relief we can afford?"

"You came in just about in time," Burr said, stretching his cramped muscles. "Thanks."

Zelda Simms was rubbing her throat and coughing. When she felt Burr's touch on her arm, she looked up and smiled. Then, without warning, she fainted.

Burr caught her in his arms.

"You will turn over my fee of five thousand to the widow of George Simms," he told Lin Fu. "As a favor to me, you will say that the fee was ten thousand and that the five thousand was her husband's share. You will do this without arousing suspicion?"

Lin Fu bowed his head. "I understand." His eyes widened. "You are content to be satisfied to go without compensation after the magnificent work you have done?"

A ghost of a smile flickered on Burr's lips. He thought of the contract for two thousand dollars, signed by S. Hartley Kern, which was in his pocket. If his lawyer succeeded in collecting the sum, it would be a grand joke. The thought made him chuckle.

Zelda Simms stirred in his arms. He threw a shawl over her and held her close to him as he carried her out to the street. He was still smiling.

THE JADE JOSS

T.T. Flynn

It was only a chunk of green tomb jade, but Carl Zaken—the dread Black Doctor—was eager to commit murder for it. And Val Easton—ace Secret Service op—went willingly into the grisly torture chambers of Chinatown to steal it back. For on it depended the success or failure of the Doctor's ghastly plan. Its possession could either kindle or quench a world-wide horror blaze.

1

The Woman in Black

THE DRONING DIN of predinner traffic was loud in Herald Square, ten stories below, when Val Easton straightened from his traveling bag and said: "That's that, Bradshaw. I'll reserve a berth on the night train before we dine."

His companion, tilted in a chair against the wall, ran a palm over a gray blaze in otherwise black hair, and grunted: "You chaps are always on the move. Might as well be traveling salesmen."

Bradshaw snorted as Easton turned to the telephone. He was faultlessly dressed, without an ounce of spare flesh on his angular frame. His trim mustache was as black as his hair. He looked like a clubman in the middle thirties, without a care in the world, But Bradshaw was forty-eight, a deputy police commissioner, up from the ranks, at home in all the shady corners of the underworld.

Val Easton was harmless looking, seldom hurried, amiable. His slender figure was not one to attract attention. Few people were aware that behind that amiable face was the full power of the American Intelligence Service, sometimes loosely called the Secret Service.

Having reserved a berth on the midnight train to Washington, Easton turned to Bradshaw. "First spare evening I've had to myself in weeks," he commented. "Dinner's on me, and a thousand thanks for the help you've given me."

Bradshaw raised a deprecating hand. "Not at all," he protested. "It's been a pleasure. Fact is, I'm damned envious of your work. I'm looking forward to future contacts with you."

Val Easton chuckled. "Never can tell what's around the corner," he said.

At that moment the phone rang.

"Pardon," Val murmured, and answered it…. "Yes, this is Easton," he said…. "Put him on."

HIS FACE SETTLED into an expressionless mask as a gruff voice came over the wire. It was Gregg, talking from Washington. Gregg, that heavy-set, saturnine man who stood at the right elbow of the State Department, as unknown and overlooked by the public as the actions of that subtle force which he controlled. Gregg—the Chief.

Gregg's voice rasped out: "I was afraid I wouldn't catch you. Got something for you to do: Go to the home of Cartier

Beurket on Fifth Avenue. They're having a reception tonight. Formal, I'd say. See Beurket himself. Show him your identification badge. Get from him a sealed envelope—and any personal comments he may make—and bring them here to me in Washington. Want it all the first thing in the morning. It's important. Got it?"

"Yes," said Val. "Who is he?"

"Cartier Beurket," said Gregg gruffly, "is an antiquarian, a collector. Specializes in Oriental art. He's just back from a six months' collecting trip in China. Been doing some special work for me. I want his report. Come straight to the office from the train."

Val hung up. He was smiling wryly as he turned to Bradshaw. "Sorry," he said. "The dinner's off. Got

Val leaped up on a chair, shouted, "Keep away from that man!"

an evening's work before I make the train."

Bradshaw threw up his hands. "I was afraid of it. Any help I can give?"

"Guess not. Know anything about a Cartier Beurket, on upper Fifth Avenue?"

Bradshaw nodded immediately. "Who doesn't?" he said. "The Beurkets are an old New York family. Filthy with money. He's a bachelor. Used to be rated a great catch, if I remember correctly. Fooled the women. Only interested in his collection, I understand. He's on the board of the Metropolitan museum, and all that.

"I'm familiar with him because his place is one of the danger spots we keep an eye on. He has a collection worth several millions in a private museum built into his house. Beurket's gone half the time; and the place is an open invitation to all the big time crooks who hit town. He takes all the precautions, of course. Special wing built on the house—iron bars, steel shutters, latest in burglar-alarm systems. I've inspected the place."

"Seems to be safe enough," Val agreed.

"More or less," Bradshaw stated. "The house is wired also. Special guards are on duty day and night. It's harder to get into than the Sub-Treasury. But it's a bet that some day some smart crooks will crash through and make a clean-up. And then we'll have Beurket and the insurance people on our necks to settle the thing. The department's detailed a couple of plainclothesmen for the evening. Well—"

Bradshaw shook hands and departed.

THE FALL EVENING was crisp, cool, bracing when Val came out on the street. He shook his head at the carriage starter's lifted hand, and walked over to Fifth Avenue, turned north with long strides. Always, when there was time he walked. His best thinking was done then; and there was much to think about.

Carl Zaken, the Black Doctor, was on his mind now. And

Chang Ch'ien, that tall, golden-skinned Oriental. Through the shadowy paths of international espionage tales of Carl Zaken, the Black Doctor, had for years seeped like fantastic nightmares. Master spy, incredibly clever and ruthless, he had been always a menace to those governments he worked against. And Chang Ch'ien, who had come out of the underworld of France a myth of terror, had proved no less dangerous in company with the Black Doctor.

The Black Doctor and Chang Ch'ien were still at large. American Intelligence had no reason to believe that they were not still plotting. So from high quarters had come orders to hunt them down. And it was this hunt that had brought Val Easton to New York, following a slender thread of information which had petered out when fully investigated. In the morning he would be back in Washington, admitting defeat.

He was almost to Forty-sixth Street when the astonishing thing happened.

A taxicab was parked at the curb, motor idling softly. He was abreast of it, paying no heed, when a woman's arm thrust out, beckoning to him. He heard his name called in a clear, vibrant voice.

"Mr. Easton! Mr. Easton!"

Startled, Val stopped, turned. He saw the small black hat, the heavy black veil swathing her features; and the furred coat, collar turned up around her neck, mantling her figure effectively. Black gloves covered her hands. A woman all in black. And a woman of mystery.

Then her voice metamorphosed into quick, vibrant seriousness. "Mr. Easton—don't go to that house tonight! Go back to your hotel! Go to Washington as you intended!"

There was a haunting familiarity about her voice. Nothing that Val could put his finger on definitely; and yet it was there.

He said: "How do you know who I am, or where I am going? What makes you think I intend to start for Washington tonight? And—pardon me—but how the devil did you know I'd be along here at this time?"

Only one man in New York knew that he was going to Washington tonight. Only one man knew he was going to Cartier Beurket's home.

Only Bradshaw knew that.

But not even Bradshaw knew that Valentine Easton would be walking along here at this time of the evening!

Val himself had not known it twenty minutes before. He had passed through the hotel lobby and come out on the sidewalk, half minded to take a taxi. Not until the bracing night air was on his face had he decided to walk. And now this woman in black was here across his path with full knowledge of his plans!

She laughed again behind the veil, that haunting, vibrant laugh. "It doesn't matter, does it? I know many things about you, Valentine Easton. I know you are going into danger tonight if you go to this house. Turn back. Go to the train. Let someone else carry out this order for you."

Val moved a step nearer, stooped, peered intently at her. But the shadows were thick inside the cab. "You know too much," he said crisply. "You say too little. What house am I going to?"

That was merely to keep her talking while he racked his brains and listened avidly for some slight clue to her identity.

She gave him none. There was no laughter in her voice now. It was sharp, serious. "You know what house. You know I tell the truth. Turn back! One who wishes you well warns you."

THERE WAS A foreign inflection about her voice. It smacked of Russian, and that baffled him still more. He had met many women in many countries; some Russian women. But of all these he could think of none who might be in New York now; who might know his movements as this woman did; who might be waiting here at the curb, mysteriously uttering her tense warnings.

"I'm interested," Val told her. "What else have you to say?"

"I have said enough. Good-bye."

"Not 'good-bye,'" Val informed her curtly. "We'll go into this further." He reached for the door handle—and suddenly stopped, moved back a step. The small blunt snout of an automatic had slid over the windowsill.

"Don't do that!" she warned.

The motor of the cab speeded suddenly. It lurched out from the curb, swept down the outer traffic lane and left him standing there. The tail-light was dark over the license plate and the curb lights gave too little illumination for him to get the number. The cab swung right on Forty-fifth Street—vanished.

And Val Easton, standing there, swore under his breath. The next moment he was exploding: "Follow that cab that just turned on Forty-fifth!"

A second cab had swerved in to the curb, unnoticed, its driver's hand raised inquiringly. Val wrenched open the door, leaped inside, the machine started with a jerk.

"Ten dollars if you trail it without being discovered!" Val called.

The man threw up a hand in assent, and swung into Forty-fifth Street.

Only one cab was before them. The drawn rear curtain

marked it as the machine they wanted. It whirled to the left under the elevated on Sixth Avenue.

Val's driver swung in under the El pillars too. The two machines zig-zagged across town, swung south on Third Avenue.

Through the gray-black shadows they sped downtown. The cross streets fell back in swift succession. Twenty-third—Fourteenth—Cooper Square—and then into the Bowery. Other machines shifted in and out ahead of them as they rolled along the Bowery. And ahead of them, beyond Bayard Street, the cab they followed turned sharply to the right and vanished.

Val knew this district. That cab had turned into Pell Street, into the compact, warrenlike area of Chinatown, lying just off the Bowery.

Val suddenly exclaimed angrily: "What are you doing? Follow that cab!"

The driver had whirled to the right on Bayard in seeming disregard of the machine they followed. He threw over his shoulder now: "Got a hunch, mister. It woulda been too raw, tearin' into Chinatown after them. If they ain't wise yet we're tailin' they'd be plenty quick after we did that."

"Something in that," Val admitted.

The driver shot to the second block with his accelerator down on the floor boards, and with a reckless swerve headed south again, turned and doubled into Pell, slowing to an idling pace. And they rolled sedately into the heart of Chinatown.

To right and left the balconied fronts of the grimy old buildings rose five and six stories. Lighted windows gleamed. Leisurely figures padded along the sidewalk. An elevated train thundered past on the Bowery straight ahead of them. They were approaching the head of Doyers Street.

"Looks like they've turned into Doyers!" he threw over his shoulder; but the next moment broke out. "That's the hack over there, ain't it?"

They rolled past a taxi pulling out from the opposite curb. Its driver glanced at them without interest. Across the sidewalk a woman was just entering a dimly lit door. A slender woman swathed in a fur coat, with a small, perky black hat visible above the upturned collar. The door closed behind her.

A sign on the window at the left of the door said—*Li Fui Shan, Importer.*

"How about it?" the driver asked over his shoulder.

Val relaxed in the seat and reached for a cigarette. "You win the ten," he declared. "Drive me back uptown."

2

The Face at the Window

THE HOME OF Cartier Beurket was on Fifth Avenue opposite the southeast end of the Park. It was of substantial brick, three stories high, imposing in its disregard of the modern world which had grown up about it.

A new wing, of brick also, had been built on one side, two stories high. The windows of the new wing were set high above the street level, barred on the outside, curtained inside.

It was well after nine o'clock when Val Easton settled with his driver, and sauntered across the sidewalk. Two machines had just pulled away as they drove up.

A man loitered beside the steps, hands in his topcoat pockets. His glance slid over Val unobtrusively, went on to a machine at the curb. Val grinned to himself as he crossed the small portico to metal-grilled gates standing open. That plainclothesman had paid little attention to this arriving guest.

The door swung open and Val entered a spacious hall, octagonal in shape, floored in ebony parquet. At the back a sweeping staircase curved up to the second floor. In the next room a string orchestra was playing. He glimpsed couples dancing. Guests in evening clothes were eddying through the hall. Through an undertone of laughter, animated conversation, a black-clad manservant said blandly: "Your name, sir?"

He was all of six feet tall, this manservant. His shoulders were broad, his face lean, hard. His firm, bald politeness held no trace of servility, and his eyes were direct as he waited.

A small table beside the man held a sheet of typed names.

Beurket, Val thought fleetingly, was amply protected here. This man was a guard, probably a detective, sifting the guests carefully.

"I'm not on your list," Val told him. "I'd like a word with Mr. Beurket, please. I'm Valentine Easton."

A tall man, with a snowy mop of white hair, talking with some guests a few feet away, turned. A murmured word to the others and he stepped across.

"I am Cartier Beurket," he said.

For an instant Val's palm held a small gold badge so that only Beurket's eyes could see it. The other nodded. "I've been expecting you, Mr. Easton. The men's cloak room is at the front of the hall upstairs. I will join you there in a few moments."

Val left his topcoat and hat in the upstairs room, lighted

a cigarette and strolled out. Cartier Beurket met him at the head of the stairs. Beurket was half a head taller, thirty or forty pounds heavier. His face was tanned mahogany color, bespeaking long periods spent outdoors in all kinds of weather. He had a hard, fit look, with his aquiline nose, high forehead and steady blue eyes.

Unspoken liking leaped between the two, hinted at only by mutual smiles.

Val said: "I'm a bit foggy about all this. I was ready to push off to Washington tonight when Gregg called me."

Beurket nodded. "I was to go down there myself, but I find I can't make it for a few days. Gregg doesn't care to wait. The papers I am sending to Gregg aren't quite ready. I'll slip up to my study shortly and finish them. Can you spare an hour or so?"

"With pleasure," Val assured him. "Just so I make the night train."

"No trouble about that," Beurket replied. "While you're waiting, join the guests. I am going to open the gallery shortly. You may find it interesting."

AS THEY TURNED to the stairs Val said: "Have you any reason to anticipate trouble tonight, Mr. Beurket? I was warned not to come here."

Beurket glanced at him from eyes suddenly frosty, alert. "Who warned you?" he asked.

"I don't know. A veiled woman. I can't place her. I understand you're just back from the Orient. You've evidently been doing some intelligence work for the department. Did you bring back any enmities that might come to a head here tonight?"

"No," Beurket said positively. "I'm certain of that. In China I kept my eyes open for certain things Gregg was interested in. But no one over there had any reason to suspect such was the case. You weren't told what trouble to expect?"

Val shrugged. "Sorry—no. But the circumstances were so unusual I have no reason to believe the warning was not given in good faith."

They were halfway down the staircase now. Beurket's laugh was that of a man without nerves.

"I doubt if there's any cause for alarm, Mr. Easton. The place is well guarded. This is not an elaborate evening. There are no jewels or valuables among the guests worth stealing, I'm certain. My collection has never been bothered. The most valuable pieces are kept in a special vault to which my sister and I alone have the combination. It would take at least twenty-four hours for the best equipped cracksman to penetrate it. It is impossible to short circuit the alarm system or circumvent it."

Beurket chuckled. "Enjoy yourself while you're waiting. Ah, here's my sister, Adelaide. May I present Mr. Easton, who is going to save me a trip to Washington, Adelaide?"

Swift comprehension flickered in Adelaide Beurket's eyes. She was almost as tanned as her much older brother. Not more than twenty-four or -five, this girl. She was tall, slender in a sheathlike evening gown of wine-colored velvet. Brown tints made her eyes deep and shadowy. Her hair was waved close along her head and caught low in a knot at the base of her neck. A wide, generous mouth, a direct look, and a healthy, alert manner made her as likeable as Cartier Beurket himself.

For all of ten minutes he was with her, strolling about, meeting the guests, chatting briefly. Adelaide Beurket apparently knew who he was, why he was there. She mentioned that she had been to China with her brother, acting as secretary.

Val told her of the warning, watched her reaction. Adelaide Beurket quirked her lips, frowned, shook her head. "It's Greek to me," she stated. "But if Cart says there's no reason to worry, I suppose there isn't. We're rather well guarded here."

She left him presently. Val moved about alone, thinking. He could not rid his mind of that black-veiled woman who had vanished into the shadowy shop of Li Fui Shan. The name of Li Fui Shan was not familiar. But it sharpened memories, released a flood of conjectures. A vague, disquieting sense of impending disaster was taking possession of him.

CARTIER BEURKET HAD vanished, in his study, probably, finishing his report to Gregg. Now and then Val caught a glimpse of Adelaide Beurket playing the perfect hostess, smiling, animated. The guests had about all arrived. Shortly they would be admitted to the *piece de resistance* of the evening—Cartier Beurket's latest acquisitions.

Then with no more warning than that, Val's premonitions were borne out.

Val was standing at the foot of the staircase in the big octagonal hall when the girl descended rapidly and stopped before him. He had met her—a Miss Elston. She had a dry, dusty, bookish look about her, despite the soft white evening gown she wore. Shell-rimmed glasses seemed to belong on the face.

"Where," she gasped, "is Mr. Beurket?"

Her face was chalk-white. Her eyes wide and frightened. Her fingers were crumpling and uncrumpling a handkerchief, and she gave every indication of an unnerved, terrified woman.

"I can't say exactly," Val told her. "I think he's busy. Is something wrong?"

"I saw a face!" she told him breathlessly. "It was near the window when it appeared. Horrible, ghastly! It looked in, saw me and vanished!"

Val put a reassuring hand on her cold fingers. "What did it look like?"

Miss Elston gulped. "I can't tell you," she replied uncertainly. "It—it was ghastly! He wore black, I saw that. A hat was pulled low over his face. The face was grinning as it looked in. I could see teeth in the horrible mouth. And the eyes seemed to glitter. When they saw me the face was gone instantly."

Val said to Miss Elston calmly: "What room were you in?"

"The back bedroom on the right side of the hall," she babbled. "I stepped in there to see how it was furnished. The light was on when I entered."

"Quite so," Val said calmly. "I'll attend to this, Miss Elston. I suggest you mingle with the guests and forget it."

She shuddered, forced a smile tinged with relief. "I will," she agreed.

"And don't say anything about it," Val cautioned.

"No," she promised, "not a word."

ADELAIDE BEURKET HAD gone into the next room where they were dancing. Val found her in there, at the back, talking to an elderly man with a Vandyke and glistening prince nez. She looked up as Val approached, caught his eye, came toward him with a questioning smile.

"Where is your brother?" asked Val.

"In his study. Why?"

"Miss Elston saw a face at one of the back bedroom windows. The room at the right of the hall, I believe."

She became grave instantly. "Impossible! Unless someone had a ladder—"

"Perhaps someone has."

She shook her head. "No—I can't see how. The outside of the house is guarded. It always is at night."

"Queer," Val admitted. "But she seems positive that she saw something outside the window. I say—would you mind showing me the back of the house before you disturb your brother?"

She took him through French doors at the rear of the room, through a big dining room where a white-aproned maid was busy at a sideboard; and on back to a butler's pantry, and a spotless green-and-white kitchen where other servants were working. She closed the back door behind them.

It took some moments for their eyes to get accustomed to the darkness. She said under her breath: "One of the watchmen should be back here somewhere."

A tiny formal garden lay behind the house, L-shaped. The newer wing built to hold Cartier Beurket's collection did not extend back as far as the house itself. On the right an apartment house towered high; on the left were the higher walls of another great building. Inexorably the city had closed in, until now this old mansion with its tiny walled back yard was an oasis in a wilderness of stone, brick, steel. The traffic out on Fifth Avenue sounded muted, far away.

"I'll look them up while you go back in," Val suggested. "It's a bit cold out here, and you're not wearing a wrap."

"No. I'd better go too," she decided. The men won't know you."

So they went together along a flagstone walk; and as they went Val looked up at the back of the house, rising three stories above them. There was no back porch. Just the house wall, three sheer stories. Windows on the second floor glowed with light. Those on the third floor were dark. Along the whole back of the house was no spot where a man might peer into one of the windows.

They turned the house corner along a fringe of low-trimmed bushes in the shadowy ell behind the annex. Adelaide Beurket walked slightly ahead, confident, unhurried.

But suddenly she wavered, lurched forward. A sharp little cry burst from her.

Val jumped forward, exclaiming: "What is it?"

"Look out! Don't step on it!"

But her warning was too late.

3

The Crimson Lotus

VAL'S FOOT STRUCK something soft, yielding. He recoiled from the feel of it, caught in his pocket for matches.

A man was lying there on the flagstones. Lying face down, arms stretched out limply above his head.

Adelaide Beurket uttered a low exclamation of dismay. "It's one of the guards!" she cried under her breath.

Val held the flaring matches close as he bent, and turned the figure over. It came limply, slack dead weight. Curly black hair lay damp and close to a bare head. A pallid face turned up to them, ghastly in the matchlight. The open eyes gleamed white in a fixed stare.

"He's dead," Val said, straightening.

Val bent again, looked; frowned. "He seems unmarked. It's queer… wait."

As the matches died out Val hastily lighted others. He held them close to the coat front, and the yellow glow limned a damp, darker stain against the dark fabric of the coat. In that stain a half inch slit through the woolen threads was barely visible.

"Better not look," Val urged quietly.

He lifted the coat collar and looked beneath. The tiny slit was over the heart. A crimson stain, splotched the shirt. And the shirt was slit too, where a thin, keen blade had driven through to the flesh beneath.

"He was stabbed!" Val told her. "We want the police. Take me in to your brother. Can we go around by the front and notify the detective on duty there?"

She did not question his decision. "This walk leads to the front. But—but there should be another man on duty back here."

"I'll have the man out front look for him. Don't want to waste any time."

They were already skirting the side of the annex. As they went Val noticed it had no windows in the back or on the side. They walked on cement beside it, and a high brick wall rose at their right. Beyond the wall towered the big apartment house.

They came out through a stout iron gate into the semi-glow of Fifth Avenue, where pedestrians trod the sidewalks, and automobiles and lumbering busses passed.

Automobiles were parked along the curb; chauffeurs idling in some of them. And near his post at the foot of the house steps the detective still loitered unobtrusively.

"There's a dead man at the back of the house," said Val. "One of the guards. May be another back there also. A guest claims she saw a face outside one of the second-story windows."

The transformation in the other was amazing. His lethargy left him like a discarded coat. "My partner went back there a few minutes ago!" he jerked out. "I've been waiting for him. Lord! I'd better telephone the precinct station."

"I'll do that," Val said. "You search the back yard and look for that man who was outside that window."

He spoke more crisply than he should. He knew it at the quick stiffening of the other; but there was no time to explain. He turned to the steps before the detective had time to reply.

THE BIG OCTAGONAL hall inside was strangely deserted. The orchestra was playing softly, but the guests were no longer dancing. A faint hum of voices over the music in the next room marked where they were.

Adelaide Beurket said to the guard at the door, "Has Mr. Beurket taken them into the wing?"

The guard looked down at her alertly. Despite her remarkable control one could see that she was under a strain.

Val spoke: "Where's Mr. Beurket?"

A shrug answered him. "I can't say, sir. I have not left the door here. I heard Jennings, the butler, announcing that Mr. Beurket wished everyone to come into the gallery."

Adelaide Beurket said quickly: "We'll find him in there."

"Watch this front door carefully," Val instructed the guard.

"Let no one in or out until you are sure who they are. A man has been killed at the back of the house."

He left the doorman gaping after him, and followed Adelaide Beurket inside. A number of the guests were bunched at one side of the room.

On the wall there, a long, silver-embroidered tapestry curtain had been drawn aside, revealing a low doorway. By standing on tiptoe when he reached the edge of the jostling group Val was able to see the massive steel edging of the door Bradshaw had mentioned.

It was open now, and through the entrance the guests were filing slowly. Soft, shaded light was visible in the annex which housed Cartier Beurket's treasures.

Short of shoving rudely there was no way to get through the jam in the vault doorway. Adelaide Beurket raised her voice. "If Mr. Beurket is in the gallery, will someone please ask him to step out here?" She took Val's arm and drew him back where her words could not be overheard. "I don't believe Cart is in there!" she exclaimed under her breath. "If he had been down here he certainly would not have asked the butler to invite them into the gallery. Cart would have done it himself."

"Probably busy in his study," Val suggested. "He promised to finish the report I came for as soon as possible."

She caught his arm, said with an apprehensive catch in her voice: "I—I'm afraid. It isn't like Cart to do a thing like this. Will you come up to the study with me?"

"Of course."

SHE LED HIM to the front hall where the black-clad door man was standing flat-footed at his post, shoulders hunched and one big fist clenched as if expecting trouble momentarily. He spoke to them with suppressed excitement. "D'you need any help, Miss Beurket?"

"None, thank you, Wilkins," she refused.

She tapped swiftly up the stairs ahead of Val. She hurried to the front of the hall, opened a door. The room was pitch black. Val was at her shoulder when she clicked the light switch.

For the space of half a dozen heart beats she stood there staring, while Val moved in beside her. On all four sides shelves of books reached clear to the ceiling. In the opposite wall a fireplace was topped by a carved mantel on which sat three slender, graceful Chinese vases. To the left of the fireplace, before the drawn drapes of a window, was a small, flat-topped desk and a chair. Before the fireplace, was a massive, leather-covered easy chair; and on the other side of the chair was a low mahogany table, stacked with books, periodicals, smoking jar, pipes and an ash tray. Those were the physical details of Cartier Beurket's study—but Cartier Beurket himself was not there.

Then Val saw what she saw; was already starting across the room when she exclaimed: "Those papers on the floor! Cart never left them like that!"

The desk top had been swept clean of all papers. They littered the floor around the chair. Envelopes, typewritten sheets, bills, documents, scattered in confusion.

Adelaide Beurket stopped at the corner of the desk. "These were all in order on the desk two hours ago!" she burst out. "I saw them! Cart's mail had accumulated. He hadn't had time to go through it yet. And now—and now, look at that!" She pointed.

The desk drawers had been opened and closed carelessly.

Val looked in one and found it looted. The aroma of tobacco smoke was still strong on the air. A pipe lay on the green desk blotter with a scattering of ashes at the mouth of the bowl, as if the pipe had been dropped hastily, Val bent, blew the ashes and uncovered two charred spots on the blotter, touched the pipe bowl and found it still warm. He scowled at the jumbled mass of papers on the floor as he lifted the telephone receiver off the cradle and dialed police headquarters.

A few crisp words to headquarters sketched what had happened, and Val turned away from the telephone.

"Your brother was here a few minutes ago," he said. He didn't make this mess, of course. He probably went down to the gallery after all, and someone went through his desk after he left. You go down," Val urged, "and look for him in the gallery. I'll poke around up here before the police come."

"No!" she refused flatly. "I don't think he's down there. I'll stay up here."

Silently Val turned and scanned the room.

TWO WINDOWS WERE set in the bookcase at their right. They looked down on Fifth Avenue, he saw, when he pulled the drapes. Both windows were locked on the inside. No hiding place in here. Val's eyes dropped to the great blue-and-white rug covering the floor. It was a beautiful lotus-flower design.

Val lifted his head, nodded at a single door set in the wall opposite. "I'll have a look in there," he said casually. "Be out in a minute."

He walked to the door without looking at the rug again. He did not want her to see what he had seen. It was plain enough, and yet the design of the rug masked it from the casual glance. Two tiny dark stains by one of the lotus flowers. Two little stains, red against the white, where there was no red in the design.

There was another drop, and another, and another, widely spaced across the soft background of the rug, drawing a gruesome trail to that single door set in the bookshelves. Adelaide Beurket moved toward the door as Val did. She obviously intended to enter the room also. Val did not try to stop her. She sensed something was wrong; and to tell her might anticipate more than the truth.

The door opened to his touch. The switch clicked. The room was flooded with light; a bedroom masculine, severer with dark, hand rubbed furniture, a few Chinese prints on the walls.

"He's not in there," she said, and there was sudden relief in her voice.

A gruesome trail was on this side of the door also. One drop—another drop—and still another, leading inexorably to a second door across the room.

Val said: "What door is that?"

"The closet."

"I think," said Val, "you'd better go back."

"Why? Why do you think so?"

Their mutual restraint made the growing tension more electric. Val drew and expelled a regretful breath. "I'll tell you in a moment," he replied—and stepped to that closet door, whipping out his handkerchief as he went. He laid the white linen square over the knob and opened the door. At his shoulder Adelaide Beurket whimpered suddenly.

"It's Cart! Oh dear Lord! He too!"

IT WAS THERE almost as Val had expected to find it. A huddled form on the floor of the closet. A motionless form as lax and still as that lifeless body in the night behind the house. The shining patent-leather shoes, the formal evening clothes, and, dimly, the shock of white hair back in the closet marked Cartier Beurket at first glance.

He used scanty ceremony in dragging Cartier Beurket out of that cramped hideaway into which he had been thrust. Val was red-faced, panting as he lay Beurket face up on the bed and examined him swiftly.

Adelaide Beurket cried fiercely: "He's been murdered!"

"No," Val objected. "No, I don't think so." For when his fingers settled on Beurket's wrist they detected the faintest beat of a pulse.

Val rapped: "Get an ambulance at once!"

She fairly flew into the next room. As he bent over Beurket again, he heard her sharp, imperative tones at the telephone.

Beurket's shirt front and waistcoat were bloody. The same tiny, familiar slit was visible in the cloth. Beurket too had been stabbed over the heart with a long, slender blade. But this stroke had not gone true.

Nothing could be done now. Skilled medical attention was needed. Val went into the next room.

"Is there a gun up here?" he asked Adelaide Beurket.

"No… what are you going to do?"

He was already leaving the room, grim-faced, quick-moving. "Keep an eye on him," Val directed from the door. "Better lock yourself in."

He ran to the stairs. Short minutes had elapsed since they had hurried up with foreboding; now, as he ran down two steps at a time, more foreboding gripped Val. He barked to the big guard at the door: "Has anyone come down since we went up?"

"No. What's the matter?"

"Plenty. Beurket has been stabbed. Police and ambulance are on their way. Collar anyone who comes down."

Wilkins' hard face set. He dropped his perfect grammar. "Won't do me a hell of a lot of good to watch these steps. There's a back flight too."

"Damn!" Val exploded. "I didn't know about them. Try to watch both stairs."

4

The Black Doctor

VAL WENT SWIFTLY across the polished floor to the vaultlike door of the treasure gallery. The orchestra was still playing softly behind the palms. Val smiled mirthlessly, stepped into the humming life that filled the gallery.

Two stories high the vaulted roof swept overhead. Great bronze chandeliers hung from the ceiling, and through intricate frill work backed by colored glass the light dropped in a soft, even glow.

Cartier Beurket's wealth had drained every corner of the Orient. Marvelous old tapestries hid the entire expanse of wall space. Great glass cases held the beauty of long dead dynasties. There was pottery and porcelain, enamel ware and glass, bronze, lacquer ware, and marvelous carvings in wood and ivory and jade. There were textiles of beautiful silks and embroideries.

Val pushed in among the well-dressed guests, grouped about half a dozen big glass cases in a single row.

He glimpsed the contents of one case. Jade. Dozens of pieces, intricately carved, superbly colored. Mutton-fat jade, milky and opaque; and light-green jade, and lavender jade; bright apple-green jade and white jade, spotted with the same green. Bowls, vases, bells, amulets, necklaces....

Moving through the crowd Val looked to right and left sharply. He saw a tall, portly butler standing apart, and went to the man. "Are you Jennings?"

"I am, sir?"

"Did you let these people in here?"

"I did, at Mr. Beurket's request, sir," the butler answered with growing frostiness.

"You saw him in his study?"

The butler shook his head. "Mr. Beurket sent word by one of the maids. He was busy and requested me to open the gallery door and admit the guests."

"I see," said Val—and suddenly whirled around as a woman cried out: "What is this man doing?"

Her voice had come from the end of the row of cases. At that spot the people suddenly began to mill in confusion, jostling together. Some were trying to get away from the case, some pressing in toward it.

Standing on tiptoe, Val could see over the heads to where that cry had been uttered. He saw a figure straighten beside the end case, a tall figure dressed in formal black evening clothes. The man stepped from the case, snarling.

For an instant, over the milling heads, he and Val looked at each other. And for the first time that night Valentine Easton felt his blood run cold. In all the world only one man could be that tall, stooped figure with the pale, bony, cadaverous face and blazing eyes. Only one man could have penetrated among two score carefully sifted people within this guarded domain of Cartier Beurket. There had been some attempt at disguise, a little padding of the cheeks from inside, a few lines carefully changed on the face by clever shading; but Val would have known that face anywhere.

It was Carl Zaken, the Black Doctor!

VAL EASTON WAS perhaps the only man in that softly lighted gallery who realized the terror among them. Master spy, incredibly clever, cold blooded and ruthless, the Black Doctor killed without the slightest hesitation. Clear now was that dead body of the guard; the savage knife thrust dealt Cartier Beurket. How Carl Zaken had entered, what his purpose was did not matter. It was enough that he was here.

Val was unarmed. He reached for an ebony pedestal on which sat the small bronze figure of some Chinese god. He caught it up, leaped from his perch and started for the crowd of milling guests. The heavy bronze weight was comforting.

He caught a glimpse of the Black Doctor still backing away; grinning now that pale, ghastly grin that could be so terrifying, serving as it did as a window for the soul beneath. Zaken carried something in one hand and with the other was reaching inside his coat.

"Get back from that man!" Val cried out. "He's dangerous!"

But in the confusion ahead of him his words were lost. He passed the end case where the Black Doctor had been standing. A small powerful instrument had ripped the lock and hasp clear out of the wood. On a bed of soft black velvet in the case one single object had been displayed. It was gone now. The confusion was increasing.

"Let me through!" Val shouted, as he pulled and shoved.

And suddenly without warning the lights went out.

An instant later in the pitch blackness a woman cried out, choking. Men strangled, gasped. Val felt a sudden smarting in his eyes and nostrils.

Tear gas had been loosed. Already he could feel the burning sensation in his eyes, the sudden flood of tears; and he started to gasp and strangle.

Val won past the last staggering figure, careened off a case and went forward three paces before he opened his eyes. The big gallery was still in tomblike blackness. Wild confusion lay behind him as he plunged forward. As he had guessed, there was no gas here back of where the Black Doctor had been standing. The weapon, a small fountain-pen gas gun, had shot the deadly fumes into the crowd of guests; and for some moments it would not drift back of its point of origin.

Zaken apparently had vanished.

Val lost his way. It was some time before he located the door and passed through, leaving behind mad confusion in which women's screams, men's oaths were lost in general strangling helplessness.

Midway of the polished floor he met another figure coming toward him. A brusk voice barked: "Who's it?" A big hand clapped on his shoulder.

"That you, Wilkins?"

"Yeah. Oh—Mr. Easton!"

"Hell's busted loose! Beurket's collection has been raided. Anyone gone out the front door?"

"Nope. But somebody just lammed upstairs in a hell of a hurry. Didn't stop when I asked who it was."

"Let's have your gun, Wilkins!… Don't argue! I need it! That was the crook going upstairs! He's a killer!"

"Here you are then." Wilkins thrust his automatic into Val's hand.

WILKINS WAS SWEARING with amazement as Val made for the stairs. He was halfway up when he heard a shrieking siren. The police, long overdue, or the ambulance had arrived.

Panting, Val stopped at the head of the stairs and listened. In the dark close by Adelaide Beurket burst out: "Who is it? What is wrong downstairs?"

"Easton. Trouble in the gallery. A thief used tear gas. Did you hear anyone come up these steps?"

"A few moments ago someone ran up, made no answer when I called, and went on to the third floor."

"What's up there?"

"Bedrooms, bath, guest rooms. The servants who live in have their rooms up there too."

A fist hammered loudly on the front door.

"Better go down and take charge!" Val urged. "If that's the police, tell 'em to surround the house. Have the master light switch investigated. The current must have been cut off there."

The third floor stairs were close. Val took them more slowly, warily. He still had the heavy bronze statue in his left hand, Wilkins' automatic ready in his right.

Zaken must be on that third floor. And it was dark too—still, deserted. The quiet up here was ominous. Val slipped toward the back of the hall, guiding himself by an elbow brushing the wall.

He moved deliberately toward the back room on the right side. The dry, bookish Miss Elston had seen the face just below it. Her description now was understandable and like a guiding signpost.

She had seen the Black Doctor there on the sheer outside wall. How he had gotten there was still a mystery. But Carl Zaken must be leaving by the way he had entered.

The bedroom door was closed, but not locked. It opened to Val's touch. Fresh air blew against his face. Gun ready, he edged into the room.

Something sinuous and snakelike jerked across the window as he looked out.

Val put the bronze statue on the floor and grabbed out the window. His hand closed on a ladder made from thin, strong silk cord and light bamboo cross pieces, not more than six inches wide; a ladder that could be rolled up into a small bundle, carried easily, and yet by which a man could descend and mount a sheer wall like this with no trouble.

He looked up. The ladder was still swaying, jerking. He was in time to see a dark figure clambering over the edge of the roof. Leaning out, Val shot at it—once—twice....

Thundering reverberations crashed on the night and echoed back from the high apartment walls nearby.

He could not tell whether he had hit. The figure disappeared. A moment later the silk and bamboo ladder was jerked up. Val caught it, held on. The drag above ceased instantly. A moment later the ladder fell down about his hands.

Val yanked it in, left it lying across the window sill. From the edge of the roof above a voice spoke.

"That will be you, Valentine Easton."

Without answering, Val shouted from the window: "Anyone in the yard?"

He was not answered.

On the roof Carl Zaken laughed at him. "Good night, Easton. Next time I'll deal with you more thoroughly!"

"You're cornered up there," Val called. "The police are here. The house is surrounded. I'll deal with you myself in a few minutes."

"An incurable optimist," Carl Zaken mocked him. "I was expecting you, Easton. I'm sorry you didn't get in my way. Give my regards to Gregg, in Washington." And the Black Doctor was gone.

Val hauled the ingenious ladder into the room, slammed the window down, locked it, and hurried downstairs.

There was no attic to the house. A man could not leave the roof without a ladder. Zaken's ladder was locked inside. Those were the facts, but Val was not sure of them. That cunning mind on the roof would not walk into a trap.

CANDLES HAD BEEN lighted on the first floor. The suffering guests had fled from the gallery, were overflowing outside. Val saw them milling on the sidewalk, wiping their eyes, choking.

An ambulance stood at the curb. A police patrol car was parked behind it. Patrolmen were pushing among the guests inside the front door. A white-coated interne, flashlight in one hand and black bag in the other, hurried to the stairs with Adelaide Beurket.

Val said to a uniformed officer: "Watch the outside of the

house. The killer's up on the roof! He won't be down this way!"

The stalwart patrolman, ignoring a weeping woman who caught at his arm, said: "If he's on the roof, we'll go up after him, mister."

"You can't. He went up on a rope ladder and then cut it at the top and threw it down."

"Ain't that nice? Then he's up there until we grab him."

"I doubt it," said Val through his teeth. "He had to get up there some way before he could fasten a rope ladder, didn't he? He can come down the same way." Val left the puzzled cop wrestling with that idea and shoved outside.

An arm's length from the open gate at the corner of the annex, he found the detective who had been standing guard at the front steps.

"Why the devil aren't you in the rear?" Val snapped at him. Again, without thinking, he used the wrong tone. The man took quick offense.

"What business is it of yours?" he retorted illnaturedly. "I've been back there! My partner's dead and another one has the back of his head caved in. No one else in the yard. No way to get out of it over that high wall. I'm waiting to collar anyone who tries to come out this way."

Val pocketed the automatic which he had carried in his hand from the third floor. "All right," he said. "Come on back with me."

"Nix!" the detective refused sourly. "I'm watching this gate until things clear up some."

Val went alone. The back yard was as he had left it, quiet, still, isolated from the teeming city. The dead body still lay on the flagstone walk. The brick wall surrounding the yard was all of fifteen feet high. A quick circuit of it showed no way a man could have climbed it. The house remained dark. But the back door was open; he heard low excited voices there; and then the harsher tones of authority. "This the back yard? Anybody come in this way?"

Val went toward the rear steps, made his presence known, said to the patrolman who emerged from the house: "Watch the roof."

The patrolman moved out into the yard, looked up, grunted: "If there's a man up there he's still there. No way he can get down."

"Looks that way," Val agreed. "If he does try it, shoot first and talk later. He'll do the same." Leaving the officer there, Val went out front.

5

The Mask of Kuan Ti

THE SIDEWALK WAS jammed with guests and a curious crowd. More police arrived. No man could leave that roof without discovery.

The ambulance drove off with a warning twirl of the siren. A second siren swept along Fifth Avenue and swerved in to the curb. It was a hook and ladder truck from the fire department. An extension ladder was placed against the front of the annex. A detective and two patrolmen went up the ladder with guns ready in their hands. Flashlight beams glinted, wavered on the annex roof. A fireman took a scaling ladder up. They were on the house roof a few minutes later. Val pushed through the crowd on the sidewalk to the front steps. He was starting into the house when a hand caught his arm.

It was Bradshaw, deputy police commissioner.

Val said, "Come inside. I want to talk to you." And there, Val hastily outlined what had happened.

Candles were still burning in the big octagonal hall. Bradshaw studied Val shrewdly in their wan, flickering light. "You know who the thief was?"

"Yes. Carl Zaken, the man I've been after for the past week."

"Hell!" Bradshaw exclaimed, startled. "He's not a man to make a play like this."

Bradshaw fingered his trim black mustache, frowning. "How the hell did he get up the roof if all he had was a rope ladder?"

"You tell me," Val suggested.

Bradshaw snorted. "We'll sweat it out of him when they get him."

"I doubt," said Val slowly, "if they get him. I've got a hunch he's not up there on the roof now."

The lights flashed on suddenly. A helmeted and rain-coated fireman carrying an electric lantern tramped out of the rear regions of the house. He recognized Bradshaw, lifted the light in greeting and said: "Somebody snatched a fuse out of the fuse box down in the cellar."

Val grinned wryly at Bradshaw. "A little more mystery for you."

A plainsclothesman bustled in, saw Bradshaw, came to him. "No one up on the roof," he stated.

"What!" Bradshaw exploded.

"Nope. The boys have been all over it with their lights. It's clean."

"Search the house!" Bradshaw snapped. "Every part of it!"

SO FAST HAD the business moved that the confusion had not quieted yet. The guests were still milling around in bewilderment. Through them came Adelaide Beurket. She was wiping her eyes as Val went to meet her, followed by Bradshaw.

"How is your brother?" said Val.

"The doctor says he will probably be all right. The wound isn't as bad as it looked at first sight. Cart evidently fell against something and was knocked unconscious. I thought I had better stay here."

"What did you find in the gallery?"

She made a wry face; she was hard hit, but trying not to show it. "He got one of the most valuable things we have," she said simply.

"What?"

"Cart managed, by a marvelous piece of luck and the expenditure of a staggering sum, to bring out of China this time a thing so valuable, so revered by millions, that it would undoubtedly have been taken from us by the Chinese government had anyone suspected we had it. The jade death mask of the Emperor Kiang Hsi."

She looked at Val and Bradshaw as if expecting some startling reaction; and when they both only looked blank and questioning, she explained patiently.

"Kiang Hsi was the greatest emperor of the T'ang dynasty, the mightiest China has ever known. Under it the Chinese empire reached its highest state of prosperity. Kiang Hsi was the War Emperor, following in the footsteps of Kuan Ti, the War God. Objects of great value are buried in the tombs of the Chinese emperors. Kiang Hsi, among other things, was buried with a jade mask of Kuan Ti on his face. It has become legendary as a source of mighty deeds and power."

"I suppose," Bradshaw commented politely, "it must be valuable."

"Valuable!" she flashed in indignation. "Priceless!" In the first place, *han yu*, ancient jade or tomb jade, has an appeal all its own to the Chinese. The mask of Kuan Ti was carved from a flawless block of mutton-fat jade, speckled with emerald green, the most precious jade of all. It is darker now, as tomb jade becomes from contact with the body."

Bradshaw asked: "What's it worth today?"

Her eyes looked past them, through them to far things. "Rivers of blood," said Adelaide Beurket slowly. "Thousands of lives. No money could buy the death mask of Kiang Hsi— unless it was purchased from a thief who was also under great obligation, as happened in this case. Kiang Hsi's memory is revered by millions. His jade death mask of the War God, recovered from the tomb long ago, has become a god-thing in itself. The superstition has grown up about it that some day a man will come to fill the shoes of Kiang Hsi and wear the jade mask of the War God, and bring back to China the glory and power of his reign."

"You mean," Val said shrewdly, "that the mask is worshipped as a joss?"

"Joss," she said, "is the name for any of the gods to whom prayer sticks and prayer papers are burned, and prayers are said. The jade mask is like any other statue of Kuan Ti, the War God; only ranking far above mere statues because of its association with the Emperor Kiang Hsi. It was one of the treasures of the

Forbidden City. During the looting that followed the Boxer rebellion it disappeared. It has been lost to the world since, until, Cart, who had been running down rumors of it for years finally got it on this trip."

Bradshaw looked at Val inquiringly. "Will you tell me," he asked with asperity, "what Zaken wants with that mask? It's no good to him. He couldn't dispose of it in this country or on the continent. Besides," queried Bradshaw, "since when has Zaken taken to anything like this? According to you, he's playing for far greater stakes than larceny could bring."

"The mask is associated with the War God," Val said under his breath. "That right, Miss Beurket?"

"Exactly, Mr. Easton. Millions believe the mask carries the power of Kuan Ti."

"And if a leader turned up with the jade mask?"

"It would depend on the man."

"I think," said Val slowly to Bradshaw, "I understand now why Zaken came tonight for the jade mask."

LESS THAN HALF an hour had elapsed since that first tragic moment in the back yard. Val looked at his watch, slipped it back, said to Bradshaw: "I'm going up to Beurket's study. The butler let the guests into the gallery under mighty suspicious circumstances. He told me one of the maids brought orders from Beurket to do it. It sounds fishy. How about checking it while I'm upstairs?"

Bradshaw agreed grimly. "I'll see him. If he's holding out, he'll come through to me."

In Cartier Beurket's study Val went at once to the scattered papers on the floor. "Perhaps you'd rather look through these yourself," he suggested to Adelaide Beurket. I want to see if any of that report is here."

She shook her head. "Go ahead. I'm keen to know. Cart was secretive about this. I haven't the slightest idea what he was doing."

Val picked up a double handful of the papers and laid them on the desk. "Your brother is just the type of man we need. Most people talk too much."

Val leafed rapidly through the papers. "Don't know myself exactly what he was doing for the government," he admitted. "But it was all to be in his report."

Ten minutes later they looked at one another. Cartier Beurket's papers had yielded no sign of a report.

"Stolen?" she asked helplessly.

Val nodded glumly; then suddenly snapped his fingers. "The wastebasket! Should have thought of it before!"

He lifted the small metal basket to the desk chair. Discarded paper filled it almost to the brim.

Val opened the crumpled sheets, putting them on the desk. Out of the first dozen he put two aside. Numbered three and seven, they were written in bold, heavy strokes.

Page three—

... most of the inland provinces I found a strong undercurrent of dissatisfaction. Different from anything I have encountered in twenty-seven years' contact with the country. Distinctly different from the old hatred of the foreigner. Incoherent in most cases unless one probes carefully and deeply. Distinctly ominous. In the province of Shensi....

Page three had been stopped at that point, crumpled, thrown away.

Page seven—

… the same condition existed. Little realization of it among the western population there. They all considered Shanghai guarded and docile, as a standard. But they're a stiff necked lot for the most part, unable, or unwilling, to see much beyond their own corner. From sources in Shanghai I checked further. Much money is available to influence native feeling. Heard again and again of a certain Chang Ch'ien, whose prestige seems great among those who spoke of him. The man is not now in China, I gather, and could not discover where he is. Secret bases mentioned in the Marshall Islands, now under….

Adelaide Beurket returned the papers. Her tanned, frank face was a study. "I see," she said simply.

Val put them in his pocket. "I wish everyone saw as well," he said briefly. "Shall we go down?"

They were both silent as they left the study and descended to the first floor. The shadow of things apart, beyond the evening's happenings, lay over them.

A DEGREE OF order had been restored in the house. Patrolmen and detectives were everywhere, taking names and addresses, searching, standing watchful and ready. A word to one of the officers guided Val to the big dining room. Bradshaw was in there, facing a perspiring and distinctly uncomfortable butler, and a chic little maid, now flushed, defiant, and slightly frightened underneath.

"It's the truth!" the maid was insisting as Val entered. "You can do anything you please, but I didn't know about it! I delivered the message, and that's what I'm paid to do! And I'll go into court with the same story! My references are good and I've never had any trouble before."

"That's right, sir," the butler seconded hastily. "She came here with the best of references."

"Blast her references!" Bradshaw grunted. "Oh—hello, Easton." He turned disgustedly. "This girl admits bringing the message from Beurket. She claims she was at the head of the stairs when Beurket's study door opened and a man, one of the guests she thought, looked out and told her Beurket wished her to tell the butler to open the gallery. The man went back in the study. She delivered the message; Jennings here opened the gallery—and that's all these two claim to know."

Val eyed the flushed girl thoughtfully. "What did he look like?" he asked her.

"Why—why, tall, and—and stoop-shouldered. He was in evening clothes like all the guests, sir. His face was thin, and—and ugly. I felt queer when he looked at me. But I knew Mr. Beurket was in there, so I took the order to Jennings at once, sir."

"Let them go," Val said under his breath. And when Bradshaw dismissed them, and they were out of earshot, Val said: "She's telling the truth. Zaken gave her that order. He came in through that upstairs window, finished with Beurket, and entered the gallery with the guests. Everything planned and carried out methodically. Even to his escape—he knew what he wanted, came for it, and he got away with it. Your men can question the guests and search all night and they won't find much else.

"Zaken is one of the most dangerous men in the world today. He has been a professional spy for years. More than one government has tottered because of state secrets he has stolen."

"The devil!" Bradshaw exclaimed.

"Quite. And now Zaken is starting something so monstrous and incredible that if he is not stopped he'll throw the world into chaos."

Bradshaw's hand poised at his mustache. He stared.

"Asia," Val said, "is a heap of powder waiting for the spark. And Carl Zaken," in grim conclusion, "is that spark!"

BRADSHAW THREW UP his hands. "I know you people have information the public doesn't get. And I can understand the possibility of an international angle. But the jade mask? Where does it come in? Why is he wasting his time on a small thing like that?"

"Zaken knows what he's up to—and I think I do, too. We've got to get it, Bradshaw. And get those papers stolen off Beurket's desk. Without delay, too."

Bradshaw protested quickly: "You don't want much. You've been looking for some trace of this man for a week, with all the assistance we could give you. And now you say he's got to be found in a few hours. He'll duck for cover."

"Naturally," Val agreed. "We'll have to smoke him out. Suppose you leave orders for fingerprints to be taken off the doors in Beurket's study and bedroom, and come along with me. Zaken's through with this house. And I think I know where he's gone. Where we can pick up his trail anyway. In Chinatown!"

"Then I'll throw men into Chinatown and search every rat hole along Pell, Doyers and Mott Streets!" Bradshaw burst out.

"Then you can't go with me," Val told him flatly. "No more publicity on this, if you please. If Zaken has gone there you'll frighten him away. He won't be expecting me. Come along if you care to, but just we two go."

Bradshaw considered and then shrugged reluctantly. "All right," he assented. "I'm taking it for granted you know what we're doing. But don't forget we have the responsibility of clearing all this up."

"I," said Val Easton grimly, "have something a damn sight bigger to clear up. Got a gun?"

"I'll get one from a dick."

"Get two. I don't want to have to go to the hotel and dig into my bag. And Bradshaw—no publicity about the mask."

"Right," Bradshaw agreed.

Val had a brief word with Adelaide Beurket while Bradshaw was getting the weapons. She looked less grief-stricken; told him that the hospital reported her brother would recover. He had gained consciousness for a short time and was now sleeping easily.

"That's great!" Val said with relief. Then to her he made the same request he had of Bradshaw. "Don't give out any information about the mask," he begged. "Newspaper reporters are out there already. They'll question the guests, get to you without doubt. Tell them a valuable piece was stolen from the collection. Say it was jade if you must. But nothing about the history of the mask, or the missing report."

"Of course," she agreed, "if it will help you any."

6

Fog Night

A THICK FOG had descended on Chinatown. It swirled before the headlights in gray opaque waves, poured cold and damp into Bradshaw's car as it raced down the Bowery.

"I haven't the slightest idea what we're running into," Val admitted. "But I know Carl Zaken. I assure you he'd like nothing better than to see me out of the way."

They rolled slowly, carefully into Pell Street through muggy soup that all but blotted out a big banner in Chinese characters swung above the street. The old iron balconies on the dingy building fronts, the few parked machines at the curbs, the lighted windows in the very street before them were barely visible.

They crawled past the shop of Li Fui Shan. A light glowed dimly inside the window. Pedestrians were few.

Bradshaw parked the car half a block beyond the shop and they got out. "Now what?" he demanded.

"I'm hoping a young woman will be in the shop of Li Fui Shan. Where she is, Zaken should be tonight. If he isn't, she'll know where he is."

"Is that all? We've got a man down here who knows every corner of this district. Charlie Gong. Born in Frisco; been on the department here in New York for ten years. He's just the man to help on this. I can call the precinct from the nearest corner box and find out where he is."

"Good idea. Go ahead. But no cordons. Intelligence has to be *sub rosa*. And a whole squad out tonight couldn't escape notice. Carl Zaken isn't worried about the police. He's proven that. He's slippery, and the only way we can nab him is by being just twice as slippery."

"Slippery it is then," Bradshaw agreed as they came into Doyers Street and the police box.

Bradshaw unlocked it with his key, rang in, said into the mouthpiece. "Commissioner Bradshaw talking… hello, that you, Garrity? Where is Charlie Gong?… Gone to Li Fat's restaurant?… Call Li Fat's, Garrity, and tell Charlie Gong to hustle over here to the box… no nothing wrong. Just need him, and I want him quick."

Bradshaw hung up, closed the box. "Charlie'll be here in a few minutes," he said. "Nice boy. Smart. And knows how to keep his mouth shut. You can tell him anything and not be afraid it'll leak all over this district."

They waited less than five minutes near the call box. A short, slender figure, with topcoat collar turned up and slouch hat brim turned down, materialized suddenly out of the fog. Grinning, he shook hands with Bradshaw.

"Regret ten thousand times keeping honorable commissioner waiting," Charlie Gong said in smiling apology. "My unworthy head bows low in shame, while pride swells me near to burst at this chance to shake one commissioner's honorable hand."

"Still the little humorist, I see," Bradshaw chuckled. "He speaks better English than either of us, Easton. And with a Harvard accent when he forgets. I can never quite forgive him that. Charlie, this is Mr. Easton. We've got a bit of delicate work on tonight. Want your help and all the smart thinking you can give. And it may be dangerous; got your gun?"

"Delighted, Mr. Easton," Charlie Gong said, shaking hands. "I am at your service, gentlemen. And I always go armed at night, commissioner. Too many in this district resent my being a member of the police, and my humble efforts on behalf of the law. My tong had made it plain that they cannot take up quarrels incurred while working at my job. That rather makes an open season for me, you see. I shall probably get a knife in the back one of these days," he finished quite cheerfully.

CHARLIE GONG CAME only about to Val's shoulder. He had the usual high cheek bones, the slant eyes, the general conformation of his Canton countrymen from the south of China. His lips were full, his nose broad, his eyebrows black and heavy beneath the down-turned hat brim; but his eyes, twinkling, direct and shrewd, coupled with a distinct firmness of his mouth and chin, marked him as a man to be depended on.

"There has been robbery and murder uptown, Charlie," Bradshaw stated. "Mr. Easton has reason to believe the man who did it can be found here in Chinatown. Or at least some trace of him. It's vitally important we get him tonight if possible. And there must be no publicity if we can help it. Not a word to anyone."

"I understand," Charlie Gong nodded. "Who is this man, and what reason have you for believing he may be found in Chinatown?"

"The name is Zaken," Val said. "Carl Zaken—sometimes known as the Black Doctor."

No recognition appeared on Charlie Gong's face. "I'm sorry, gentlemen; if he's here I have not heard of him. Will you describe him?"

Val did so.

"No," said Charlie Gong. "I don't believe I've seen him."

"Have you heard of a man called Chang Ch'ien?" Val asked quickly and bluntly. And he watched the other's face closely.

No expression appeared on Charlie Gong's face. He returned Val's gaze unblinkingly, gravely.

"I have heard of Chang Ch'ien, Mr. Easton. Just a word here and there. Those who speak of him do so furtively. He is not a topic of public conversation. What he is or who he is I am unable to tell you. I gather that he has power and wealth; that those who mention him are afraid of him. But if a man by that name is here in Chinatown, I don't know it."

"Do you know anything about a man named Li Fui Shan, who owns the shop back there along Pell Street?" Val asked then.

Charlie Gong's face lighted up. "Li Fui Shan, eh? Can do, Mr. Easton. I know Li well. He's been here in Chinatown for over twenty years. One of our most respected merchants. He is a man who has prospered by hard work and honesty. His gifts to charity are extensive. He sits high in the councils of the On Leong Tong. I cannot speak too highly of him."

"Is he married? Does he have any daughters?"

"His family is in Kwangtung Province in China," Charlie Gong smiled. "His sons are being educated in Canton, I believe. Like many Chinese in this country he does not see his family for years at a time."

"No women at all?" Val insisted.

"There is, I believe, a niece, Mr. Easton. She does not live with Li Fui Shan, but she has been there frequently of late. I have seen her one or twice entering or leaving; and I have heard her mentioned. Things like that get around. A very beautiful girl, as I recall her."

"I thought so. I want her. She entered Li Fui Shan's shop several hours ago. If she knows she's wanted she'll escape or hide. Have you any way of gaining access to Li Fui Shan's living quarters?"

"I'm afraid not," Charlie Gong said. "Without a search warrant I couldn't go back. And if Li Fui Shan is hiding someone, he would not be apt to invite me into the rear."

"All right," said Val. "We'll go in. You watch the rear of the house. Collar anyone who tries to leave. And watch out you don't get a knife or a bullet in your ribs."

As the three of them talked they had moved over in the shelter of the nearest doorway. Now, as they stood there, one of the infrequent pedestrians came along the sidewalk, materializing out of the fog. His head turned, staring, as he came abreast. Val saw a man of about his own size, stooped, thin-chested, with a head too big for his body. There was something about that head that caught the eye. It seemed to move, hunched forward, like a disembodied member, detached from the slighter body beneath. It had a prognathous jaw, a wide, cruel slit of a mouth, a great hooked nose and staring, burning eyes. Certainly one would not be apt to forget it in a long time.

Recognition glinted in those burning eyes. A dry, harsh voice threw out, "Hello, Gong," and the furtive figure went on without slackening its pace, vanishing in the swirling fog as suddenly as it had appeared.

"Sweet-looking customer," Bradshaw commented. "Who is he, Charlie?" Charlie Gong, who had not answered the other's greeting, said impassively: "That is Emile."

"The devil! I heard of him."

"The honorable devil would be ashamed of his company," said Charlie Gong blandly. "Emile is a dangerous man. I've had my qualms about crossing him."

"Creepy fellow," said Val. "Who is he? What's his last name?"

"Just Emile. That is all anyone knows him by. We are certain he is a leader in one of the biggest dope rings, with ramifications in England and on the Continent; but so far none of his activities here in Chinatown has given us proof of that. He lived," said Charlie Gong, "in China for some time, and all over the East, I believe. He speaks the Mandarin dialect of the north, and has a fair smattering of Cantonese. Ostensibly he is an importer, and I've never been able to prove anything else.

"Queer," continued Charlie Gong reflectively, "that he should be walking on a night like this. He has a ten-thousand-dollar car if he chooses to ride in it."

"Look into that some other time," Bradshaw suggested. "Right now we have other business."

"Give me ten minutes to get behind Li Fui Shan's building, commissioner, and then deal with the venerable Li as you see fit."

PELL STREET WAS oddly quiet, deserted. But in the shop of Li Fui Shan there was still a light. The door was locked.

"Hell!" said Bradshaw. "But we're going in!" He knocked.

Curtains parted at the back of the shop and an elderly man shuffled to the door as Bradshaw knocked again. He peered through the glass at them, and then unlocked the door with obvious reluctance as Bradshaw gestured.

Looking out, he said severely: "My shop closed till tomollow, gentlemen. You come back then."

"We're in a hurry," said Bradshaw. "We won't be here tomorrow. Are you Li Fui Shan?" And Bradshaw pushed inside as he asked that.

His abrupt entrance was met with composure. "I am Li Fui Shan," the old man said with dignity. "What you want, gentlemen?"

With Charlie Gong's words still fresh in his mind, and Li Fui Shan, the man, there before him, Val found it hard to believe that there could be anything wrong in this modest shop. Li was indeed a venerable man. His scanty hair was snow white. Whatever garb he wore during the business day had been set aside for the dignified comfort of a long black silk coat, swathing silk trousers and thick-soled felt slippers. An old man, but not wrinkled, emaciated, as so many of his countrymen became. Li Fui Shan's face was plump, kindly, dignified. One could visualize him smiling often, always courteous.

He was courteous now as he bent his head after Bradshaw said: "We'd like to look at some pottery."

"You catchee," said Li Fui Shan, dropping into pidgin English. "I give you light." He gave them the freedom of his shop with a gesture and padded leisurely three steps to a light cord hanging from the ceiling.

The shop was filled with a heterogeneous collection of Chinese craftsmanship. Pottery, bronzes, rugs, silks, porcelain ware, statuary, and trinkets of all kinds. Some of the stuff was good and some obviously bad, for the tourist trade. Li shuffled behind one of the cases and began to take down samples of pottery from the wall shelves. He ranged half a dozen on the case and looked at them inquiringly.

Bradshaw examined them with a show of interest.

Val looked about, listening.

The smell of the Orient was strong in here—musk, sandalwood, incense. The shop was very quiet. The faint roar of the Elevated over on the Bowery sounded, died away. Then, fainter still, far off, a fog whistle on the river moaned rhythmically. Beyond the heavy tapestry curtains at the back of the shop no sound was audible. If anyone was in there they were keeping very quiet.

Li Fui Shan waited behind the counter like an impassive Buddha.

"Show me some more," Bradshaw requested. "I'm afraid these aren't suitable."

Li inclined his head and turned back to the shelves. "You wanchee numbah-one vase, eh?" he inquired over his shoulder.

"I suppose so," Bradshaw grunted. Then he turned his head and shot a look of inquiry at Val; a slightly baffled look as if he were beginning to be convinced that this was wasted time.

Val himself was wondering. If he had not so plainly seen that veiled woman in the black fur coat enter here, he would have given this Li Fui Shan a clean bill of health. But she had come in here. She was known to Charlie Gong, if only by heresay. Li Fui Shan, for all his kindly venerable appearance traced directly to Carl Zaken, the Black Doctor.

And where Carl Zaken's influence reached there was danger.

Thinking so, Val swung about suddenly—and caught the barest flutter of the tapestry curtains at the back of the room.

Someone was standing behind them looking into the shop!

And suddenly the quiet and peace took on the ominous look of watchful waiting. Li Fui Shan's kindly Buddha-like face became a mask, hiding breathless tension. Val went to the counter, picked up one of the vases and examined it. He caught the old man behind the counter sliding an imperceptible glance toward the back. Old Li knew there was someone back there.

"It's up to you, Bradshaw," Val said casually. Maybe I can find something else back here that will do." He idled slowly back along the counter, inspecting the contents within.

Li watched him for a moment and then, hurried back. You likee see nice silk?" he questioned. "You come up front; I show."

The curtains had not moved again.

"All right. Get out your silk," Val said—and as Li started back toward the front Val turned away from the counter—and made a quick jump for the curtains.

He was certain that he heard a quick scurry of movement beyond, and the soft click of a latch. But when he jerked the curtains back he found only a small alcove, backed by a door, closed now.

Li Fui Shan's indignant cry filled the shop. "What you do? You come away!"

7

Tai Shan

VAL TRIED THE door. It did not open, bolted inside apparently. He drew back two steps and lunged at it. The bolt was not strong, nor the door either; it shivered, cracked, gave. Val drew back and struck it again.

Li Fui Shan's rising crescendo of indignant cries broke off suddenly. Bradshaw's cold voice said: "Steady, old-timer. We're from police headquarters. Get violent and I'll call the wagon!"

And Val struck the door a third time, driving it in with a rending of screws from wood. He staggered through the open doorway, peering intently. There was a hall beyond; a dark hall, seemingly deserted. But no—

The light striking past him through the doorway showed a thick-set, black-shirted Chinese crouched against the wall. He sprang out as Val saw him, crouched in the middle of the hall, a short knife glinting in his hand. Still crouching, he moved a step forward, holding the knife ready for a slashing up-stroke. And somewhere in the darkness at the back feet pattered hastily; a door closed furtively.

In the shop Li Fui Shan expostulated shrilly: "What for you bleak in my house this way?"

And Bradshaw said gruffly: "Shut up or I'll crown you! What is it, Easton?"

Val dragged his automatic from his coat pocket. And, as if realizing quick action was the only thing to meet a gun, the crouching figure before uncoiled in a swift rush, slashing up with the knife.

Val stepped back, whirling aside before the silent savagery of that rush. The gleaming blade struck a button on his coat, slid off, and ripped through the cloth, slashing deep, at an angle. He felt the cold slither of it clear through to the skin as he struck the wall. And then, as the knife flashed out from under his upraised arm for another stroke, Val chopped down hard with the gun barrel.

The crunch of steel against bone was the loudest thing about that brief, silent scuffle. The stocky Chinese lurched over against the side of the passage, sank to his knees, crumpled in a limp little heap.

Val witnessed this with relief. He wanted no gunfire, no killing if it could possibly be avoided. For the plain facts were, he and Bradshaw were in this building without a search warrant. A shooting might make it awkward.

Bradshaw yanked the curtains clear back and snapped through the alcove: "Everything all right?"

"So far," said Val shortly. "I had to slug this fellow, but he'll come out of it. Nasty beggar. He slid that knife along my ribs. Would have put it in my stomach if I hadn't jumped quick. Watch him and the old man, Bradshaw. I think someone we want is back here. We were being watched from behind the curtain when I made a jump for it."

"Go ahead," said Bradshaw. "I'll back you up. When they start drawing knives, rough 'em."

Val went back along the hall into thickening blackness. Doors opened to right and left. It was a squalid, grimy hall.

The worn floor squeaked miserably under foot. A staircase,

starting from the back of the hall, slanted to black silent regions above. A door on the left showed light underneath and through the keyhole.

Val opened it, blinked with amazement.

He looked from the sordid hall into beauty, richness and excellent taste. The furniture was carved hardwood, dark, polished, intricately inlaid with mother-of-pearl. Heavy silk covered the windows. Gold-embroidered tapestries hung on the walls. Several beautifully carved and painted screens cut off corners of the room.

It was empty now; but it had been occupied short moments before. Blue hazy smoke drifted before a silk-shaded floor lamp. A hammered brass ash tray on a small red-lacquered table held several cigarette ends and one still sent up a faint curl of smoke.

VAL STEPPED IN swiftly, gun ready in his hand. He made a circuit of the room, looking behind the screens. They hid no one. There was a door in each end of the room, but before he could try either a commotion in the hall drew him quickly. There was enough light in the hall now to see a strange and welcome sight.

Charlie Gong, short and placid, was shepherding two figures in from the back. A man and a woman. Charlie saw him, and panted: "Here's two who came flying out. I don't think there were any more."

The man was Emile, that grotesque-faced figure who had passed furtively in the fog.

And the woman—in all the world there could be only one such pale, soft, beautiful face framed in jet-black hair, like an alabaster cameo. Her mouth was a vivid red; red as the color of an East Indian flame tree, and her strange, striking beauty had all the lure of a lotus flower in full bloom.

Bradshaw had come into the hall, bringing the now uneasy Li Fui Shan. He whistled softly between his teeth. "Some catch, Charlie. What have we here?"

Emile hunched there, his wide-slit mouth snarling. His big head swayed about as he looked at them. "I'll make somebody sweat for this!" he threatened furiously. "When a citizen can't call on friends without a bunch of cops surrounding the house and crashing in this way, it's time to go high up about it! I'll have Gong's shield before I'm through! Who are you two?" he barked at Val and Bradshaw.

Charlie Gong clucked regretfully, and succeeded in looking very much like a mischievous youngster. "Honorable Emile makee run flom doah, likee dragon chop-chop his pants seat; so me catch'm and ask how come."

"Lay off that pidgin talk!" Emile snarled malevolently. "I know you can speak as well as I can!"

Charlie Gong chuckled. "Better, old chap," he agreed. "But I'll wager five to one I can't get out of a house half as fast as you left this one. You went down those steps as if you had greased shoes."

Val faced the girl. She was furious, scornful. But even in anger her voice was oddly musical, vibrant. "You—you do this to me, Val Easton! After—after…." She broke off, bit her lip.

Bradshaw stared. "You know her?" he asked Val in astonishment.

"This," said Val, "is the lovely Tai Shan, sister of Chang Ch'ien. Tai Shan, may I present Deputy Commissioner Bradshaw?"

She ignored Bradshaw. "I am not interested in the police," she said indifferently, and again her voice was clear and musical in that dim, dark hall.

"I haven't thanked you for that warning tonight, Tai Shan. You had me fooled for a time. That Russian accent—I'm still wondering how you knew where to find me on Fifth Avenue."

"I would not lift a finger to save you from anything!" said Tai Shan scornfully. "You are not worth it. But if I wanted to know where to find you, I would have someone sit in a hotel room next to yours and listen to your talk."

"We live and learn," Val sighed. "I should have been watching for that."

"What do you want with me?" Tai Shan demanded.

"Where is Carl Zaken?"

"Ah—so?" Her anger left suddenly. She smiled faintly. And in that dim, sordid hall she was like a figure in some lovely old Chinese print. Her exotic beauty was a flame, heightened if anything by the grotesque ugliness of the snarling Emile.

"You want Carl Zaken?" Tai Shan mocked. "Why come to me, Val Easton?"

"We might search the place," Val mused, watching her.

Tai Shan shrugged indifferently.

Li Fui Shan had been standing beside Bradshaw in dignified silence. He burst into shrill protests. "This my place! You no search without paper!"

"Don't waste your breath," Bradshaw counseled the old man curtly. "We're in now and we'll do what we blasted please! And if you're hiding this Zaken, you're in for a rough time."

TAI SHAN MELTED suddenly. "He can tell you nothing," she said to Bradshaw. "No one you want is in this house. I know. I've been here all evening. I pledge you my word. Li Fui Shan is merely an old friend who has been repaying an obligation two centuries old by giving me a roof when I need it. Don't bother him. His hospitality has been abused enough tonight. Let me get my coat and hat. Take me out of here. I will talk to you some other place."

Li Fui Shan's face softened. He made a slight graceful bow. "My daughter," he said, "this humble house is yours."

Charlie Gong spoke to him in Chinese. Li Fui Shan answered. Charlie said to Val and Bradshaw: "This is not his niece. There is a blood debt between the families dating back eight generations. She is more than a niece to him; she is his blood, his daughter. Such things are done among my people. He assures me there is no one else in the house. I believe him."

"Take us out of here," Tai Shan insisted. "To the police station if you will. I will talk to you there. You see," and her smile at Val was suddenly dazzling, "I am a tractable prisoner."

Val studied her a moment, and smiled thinly. "Too tractable, Tai Shan; too very tractable. You're beautiful, you're lovely— and you've got the heart of a tiger back of it. But there is no hurry. Let us first speak about this Emile, who, I understand, is in the dope game. What business has he with you, Tai Shan? I've thought hard things about you, and I've fought you—but I always supposed you were clean. I've admired you. I never thought you were mixed up with dope."

A slow red flush crept up to her high cheek bones. "Dope!" Tai Shan repeated, and her musical voice was suddenly off key, harsh. "This man a seller of drugs?"

"Yes."

Emile raised a hand whose fingers were short, thick, and rubbed his bulging jaw. He was in no way disturbed. His wide slit of a mouth grinned at them. "Prove it," said Emile comfortably. "Just try to prove it." He acted like a man who had been accused often before and rested secure in the knowledge that he could not be reached.

Tai Shan's dark eyes rested on him inscrutably. "Then it is true?" she said in a dull, metallic voice.

Emile shrugged. "I told him to prove it. My private life has nothing to do with this. I didn't come talking dope to you, young woman. Forget it."

And Val was suddenly sure that this lovely Tai Shan had had no inkling of her visitor's profession. Yet that was no help to the mystery of Emile's presence here with her. Emile had come alone, afoot when he might have ridden in his expensive car; he had come late and clandestinely; and both of them, at knowledge that the police were in the front shop, had thought of nothing but escape.

"It might be better," Val said to her, "to tell what his business is here."

She bent her head thoughtfully, looked disturbed, seemed to weaken. "I—I will," she nodded. "Take me to the police station, Val Easton. I'll get my coat." She wore a black dress, tight-fitting, sheathing her slender figure closely. She was lovely, exotic, touching in her surrender.

But Val said to her cynically: "You should be an actress, Tai Shan. Before we leave here I'm going to find out why you're so anxious to go to the police station, to get away."

And the words had hardly left his mouth when a telephone rang sharply in the room behind him.

TAI SHAN STARTED; her head came up. It struck Val then that she had been listening for something ever since Charlie Gong had brought her back into the hall. He grinned as the telephone rang again and Tai Shan offered hastily: "I'll answer it."

"You'll stay right here," Val told her gently. "Charlie Gong will answer it. It may be someone who speaks Chinese."

Her meek submission vanished in a breath. "You have no right to take that telephone call!" she burst out angrily. "We are entitled to some privacy!"

"You're getting all you're entitled to, Tai Shan. And if it's an important message you shall hear all about it."

Charlie Gong was already in the room. They could hear him answering the call in English—which shifted to Chinese a moment later. Tai Shan was pale, tense. Her little fist clenched at her side. She was straining to hear. The grotesque Emile was standing taut also, listening. In contrast Li Fui Shan seemed little interested in who answered the telephone.

Charlie Gong spoke in the sing-song cadences of his native tongue—listened—spoke again; and a few seconds later hung up and returned to the hall. He glanced at a wrist watch.

"It is now seventeen minutes after eleven," Charlie Gong said. "At five minutes to twelve an automobile will call for Tai Shan and her friend. Everything, I am informed over the telephone, is all right. And she is not to fail to bring the foreign devil."

Tai Shan bit her lip; her eyes were blazing, but she said nothing. Emile looked uneasy. His burning eyes went from Charlie Gong to Bradshaw, to Val as if trying to read their minds.

"Who was it?" Val asked the little Chinese detective.

Charlie Gong shrugged. "I don't know. I was afraid to ask questions. I merely said that the high born lady was busy. It was evidently taken for granted that since I was here in the venerable Li Fui Shan's home I spoke with authority. I should not be surprised," said Charlie Gong, "if I was not mistaken for that pig lying on the floor inside the door; who is stirring now by the way. I will get him."

Bradshaw smoothed the end of his small black mustache and smiled with satisfaction. "If there's a car coming for these two, we'll grab it, Easton. It should give us something to work on."

Val had been standing, frowning to himself. The frown passed as suddenly as it had come. He grinned. "The car was going to take them somewhere. I'll slip into Emile's coat and hat and take his place."

"But the woman?" Bradshaw objected. "You can't get by with it with this girl."

"No," Val agreed. "But I know one who can take her place—if she is still in town. I haven't seen her for a couple of days. Just a minute—while I telephone."

The telephone was on a lacquered stand in the corner of the big room he had searched. The directory was underneath. He leafed through it, found a number, gave it. It was answered almost at once. He spoke rapidly, finished: "Hurry up! There's no time to lose!"

And back in the hall to Bradshaw, Val said: "She's coming. Nancy Fraser who's worked with me a lot. She's the one woman in the country who could go through with this. I hate to drag her into it—but I can't pass up this chance."

TAI SHAN LOOKED suddenly like an enraged cat; a

beautiful cat, but dangerous. Her hand flicked out without warning inside the bodice of her dress, came out with a tiny gleaming blade. Val's hand shot to her wrist. He had the knife, had her subdued a moment later. "I was looking for something like this," he said reproachfully. "It's no use. We're going. Take it sporting."

"Go then!" said Tai Shan breathlessly. "Go with my blessings, Val Easton. And remember—my blessings." She began to laugh.

"Over-wrought," said Val to Bradshaw. "She'll have to be handled carefully. I suggest you get several plainclothesmen here to watch these people. No use taking them to the station house. I'm sure Li Fui Shan would rather have it that way."

The old man nodded in silent agreement.

"I'll do that," said Bradshaw briskly. "And Charlie and I will tail you in another car."

"Good. But you'll have to work fast."

Bradshaw used the telephone hurriedly. And in an incredibly short time three plainclothesmen entered the shop. Bradshaw gave them directions; they took Tai Shan, the grotesque Emile and the browny native who had stood guard in the hall; took them into the big lighted room, handcuffed the man, put Tai Shan in a chair firmly despite her indignation.

Then Nancy Fraser came into the shop, breathlessly, her cheeks pink from cold and haste. Nancy Fraser, whose daring and ingenuity was known all through the Intelligence. In spite of that she stood there inside the door, softly feminine, a little beauty with fine, clean cut features, sun-tanned, chin firm, and mouth wide and quirked humorously at the corners.

Val thought again with admiration that she had the deepest

and bluest eyes he had ever seen; and her platinum hair cut short and waved close to her head was as beautiful as ever when she stripped off her little felt hat and smiled at him.

"Here I am, Val. What's the bad news?"

Swiftly as they went back into the hall, he gave it to her.

"Exciting," said Nancy gaily. "I've been famishing for something like this." She met Bradshaw and Charlie Gong composedly.

"Are you sure it's all right to take her, Easton?" Bradshaw queried doubtfully.

"Have to," said Val. "She understands. It's part of the game. I'd rather have her than most men. I'll get Tai Shan's coat and hat, Nancy. They'll be a little big, but I guess you can manage them."

In a few moments more they were both ready, Val in Emile's coat and hat; Nancy in Tai Shan's.

"Got your gun?" Val asked.

"Never go out without it at night," said Nancy airily. "We girls are fragile, you know."

Bradshaw and Charlie Gong left the shop for the police car parked down the street. Val and Nancy waited in the front. The hands of Val's watch crept toward twelve—and suddenly there was a soft purring motor outside, headlights gleaming dimly through the fog. A horn blew once.

"Here we go," said Val. "Chin up and keep your hand on your gun."

Coat collars turned up, hats shading their faces as much as possible, they left the shop of Li Fui Shan and walked out into the damp swirling fog.

8

House of Hooded Men

A LIMOUSINE STOOD at the curb, big, black, powerful, fast. Two figures were in the front seat, and as Val and Nancy came out of the shop of Li Fui Shan one of the men leaped out, opened the rear door and stood stiffly at attention. He was a short, slender Oriental, wearing a chauffeur's uniform. As Nancy came abreast of him he said something to her in rapid singsong Chinese, finishing his speech with a rising interrogation.

Val stiffened; his hand in his coat pocket clutched tight on the automatic. Was their masquerade to be penetrated at the very start of this mysterious journey?

But Nancy acted quickly, as she always did in moments of stress. Her little gloved hand came up in a careless gesture of assent. She stepped into the limousine without speaking.

It was evidently enough. When Val sank into the deep luxurious seat beside her the door closed, the fellow entered the front, and the driver pulled away from the curb at once.

Val reached out and touched Nancy's hand. He had to grope to find it; for the rear inside windows were curtained, and there was even a curtain lowered behind the two men in the front seat. They were in complete blackness, unable to see where they were going.

"Emile was slated for a blind ride," Nancy said under her breath.

"But I am not Emile—and you are not Tai Shan to keep an eye on him. We'll cheat a little."

Val lifted the curtain at his side and looked out. They were rolling swiftly out of the fog-filled tangle of Chinatown. They passed under the forest of Elevated pillars, criscrossing Chatham Square, rolled along Division Street under the Elevated and turned north with it. In a few minutes they were on First Avenue, speeding north. They crossed the Harlem River on the Willis Avenue bridge, turned on the Westchester road.

The fog thinned out, but as they neared Westchester, it began to thicken again. The limousine rolled faster toward its mysterious destination. Nancy peered out for some moments. "I wonder where we're going," she whispered.

Val had sketched to her the evening's happenings in a low tone; he said now, "I wish I knew. I don't like it. I had no idea we were going so far out." He lifted the rear curtain, looked behind. The headlights of several cars were visible. Back there somewhere were Bradshaw and Charlie Gong.

"At least," said Val, "Bradshaw and Charlie Gong are our ace in the hole."

"Makes me feel better," Nancy confessed. "I'm not afraid— but Carl Zaken is a horrible person. I can't forget him as he was in Washington."

They turned off the Avenue. Val lost track of the streets and directions there. He was in unfamiliar territory, and the still thickening fog was no help.

Nancy lifted the rear curtain, looked back. "I don't see anyone following us, Val."

In the swirling mist behind, no car was in evidence.

Val tapped a cigarette on the back of his hand and lit it. "We're in for it now," he said slowly. "We're on our own."

"I've been that way before," Nancy said philosophically. But her voice had a slight tremble.

And suddenly they were there....

FOR SOME MINUTES there had been no street lights, no sign of houses, and the wheels had left the pavement. The limousine made a sharp turn. Looking out they could see bare, ghostlike tree trunks looming eerily through the fog. The car stopped; the motor died. The man who had let them into the car opened the door and the cold night air swept into their faces as they got out. Fresh air, tangy with the salt and fish smell of the open sea. The hoarse blast of a fog whistle vibrated through the night at no great distance away.

The car door closed. The little Chinaman spoke again in his native tongue to Nancy. And again she did not reply. There was not even light now to gesture. They stood in blackness, complete and abysmal, except for the dim cowl lights, fog-smothered before their glow reached the front bumper.

But again luck saved them. A powerful flashlight in the hands of the saffron-skinned footman glowed out before them and swept ahead, piercing the fog. It shone on steps of stone, and piercing on beyond brought up against a house wall covered thickly with ivy. It picked out a shuttered window, stark, forbidding. And then the footman walked up the stone steps, keeping the light down so they could see as they followed.

There was nothing else to do but follow. Where they were, what this place was, what was expected of them, was mystery, dark, sinister. They mounted five steps—Val counted them—

and crossed the porch to a boarded door. The flashlight showed it clearly, dark, weathered boards, guarding a deserted house against intruders.

And the house seemed deserted. Their steps scraped loud, harsh; there were no sounds, no lights, no signs of life. And yet, when, stopping before those weathered boards, their guide said in a voice that sounded startling loud:

"*Hola!*" The weathered storm door swung out silently on oiled hinges.

A second door of heavy bolted planks stood open inside it, and beyond, in a high-ceilinged reception hall, a faint red glow streamed out to meet them.

Their guide stepped back as a second figure materialized in that dim ghastly glow, bowing welcome. This was another Chinese, bland, inscrutable, wearing black trousers and silk jacket. He bowed a second time as they entered.

The dim red light came from an inverted globe high up against the ceiling. It was so faint that what small part of their faces was visible could hardly be seen.

The doors were closed behind them. This second man bowed a third time and padded ahead of them on noiseless felt soles. He stopped at a table against the side wall, picked up a piece of black cloth, and said something to Nancy in Chinese, at the same time moving behind her for her coat. Val watched, slit eyed, his hand on the gun in his pocket. Nancy shook her head.

Her wish seemed to carry weight. Muttering a singsong something, the fellow lifted his hands and brought the black cloth down over her head.

Nancy's hand was in her coat pocket also. And for a moment Val thought she was going to step from under the cloth and bring her gun out. Then he saw, with a foolish surge of relief, that a black mask with eyeholes and a place to breathe had been placed over Nancy's head.

A second mask was handed him from the table. Val slipped it on, pushing his hat off as it went on, so that at no moment was his face entirely visible. He too refused the offer to take off his coat.

The hood felt close and warm about his face. Through the eyeholes he could see Nancy, grotesque and rather horrible in the ghastly red glow. But for all the eeriness of this little bit of stage play there was relief too. Their faces were hidden.

THEIR YELLOW-SKINNED ATTENDANT bowed, walked noiselessly to the rear of the hall and opened a door, going through ahead of them. They were taken to the left along a second hall, through profound quiet. They came to a door. Their guide knocked. It was opened. Incense, thick, heavy, cloying, rolled out to meet them. And behind his mask Val almost uttered an exclamation.

A great hall-like room opened before them.

Here was Asia, mysterious, inscrutable, beautiful. The high ceiling was vaulted, braced by great carved timbers. And from those timbers, hung silken lanterns, their gay colors dimly visible.

A dais at the far end of the room was backed by a marvelous tapestry covering half the wall. One single throne-like chair rested on the dais. And in each corner of the dais a bundle of joss sticks in brass containers sent up thin wavering spirals of smoke. Nancy's fingers dug into Val's arm again as the scene burst on them; and it was not the room but the two score

figures in it that were so startling. Figures masked like themselves in black, some seated on the chairs against the wall, some
standing and moving slowly about. A very few were engaged
in conversation. The most of them were sitting silently.

It was a strange, uncanny scene. The eyeholes in those loose
enveloping hoods gave the impression of life without emotion
through the eery red glow of the lanterns. Such voices as were
speaking were low, muffled. They were all men, all but Nancy.
Further than that one could see nothing. What manner of
men they were, what nationality, what they were doing here,
was all a mystery.

Their guide had closed the door behind them, leaving them
on their own. Nancy spoke from behind her mask in a muffled
whisper. "Val, what is this?"

"Your guess is as good as mine," Val husked back.

Black-shrouded heads turned, stared at them as they entered.
Some turned away after a moment, others continued watching them. The thick cloying atmosphere, of the room, for all its
silence, was electric with an undercurrent of tension.

No one came forward to greet them, no one spoke to them.
And after a moment, Val sensed that the gathered company
had no cohesion. Each man was apart from the others. No
man could tell what lay behind the shrouding hood next to
him. Val Easton had been many places in a somewhat hectic
career, but never had he been a part of anything like this. He
kept in mind that he was Emile, a power in the big dope rings,
and that besides him should be the lovely Tai Shan. It still did
not make sense.

And the next moment his pulses leaped; he went tense and
watchful. The crashing notes of a great gong vibrated through

the room. The seated figures came to their feet abruptly, turning toward the dais behind which the gong was booming. And before the last vibrant note died away, the great gold and silver tapestry curtain parted in the middle—and Carl Zaken, the Black Doctor, stepped out on the dais....

THERE WAS NO applause or greeting. The Black Doctor was not masked. He still wore the evening clothes in which he had appeared at Cartier Beurket's.

The notes of the gong seemed to echo and re-echo, farther and fainter into the distance, until finally they were vibrant no more. And in those long seconds the tall stooped figure on the dais was imperceptibly bathed in a brighter red glow, while the rest of the room grew dimmer, darker. The pale, ghastly, cadaverous face of the Black Doctor stood out in blood-red relief until it and only it, was a focal point for all eyes. The emanations of that silent figure reached out and dominated the room. And then:

"Voila, you are here!" His dry grating voice reached into every corner of the room.

"You are here," the Black Doctor repeated, looking slowly about. "From Europe, from China, from India, from this country. You have been called here for your reports, and they are pleasing. No man among you knows his neighbor. Your identities are safe tonight. But all of you know toward what you have been working. Your rewards will be magnificent, your power unlimited. Once in a thousand years the current of history is reversed and one part of the world rises to master the other. That time is here. Asia, so long eclipsed by the white man, is ready for the spark...."

Carl Zaken paused; and his flaming malevolent eyes stared through the blood red halo about him. He smiled; and to Val Easton who knew the man, it was the smile of a monster, indescribably vicious and dangerous.

"*You* will be the spark," Carl Zaken's dry grating voice told those standing hooded figures. "Tonight you will see that which will put the power into your hands. Gentlemen...."

Carl Zaken lifted a hand, half turned to the great silver and gold tapestry curtain at the back of the dais.

Crash....

The hidden gong thundered its blood chilling reverberations through the silence of the room.

The curtains parted—and a gasp ran through the room. Standing there, stiff, erect, was a great tall figure clad in a magnificent dragon robe of Imperial yellow; an Oriental, a member of the Celestial Kingdom unmistakably. A round silk hat with a yellow button on the crown topped the giant figure's head. But not that brought the gasp, not that sent Val Easton's pulses hammering and brought Nancy Fraser closer to his side. For covering the face of the figure was a life size dull amber mask of jade.

Life size and lifelike, that jade mask shaped in the perfect lineaments of a man that had never lived; The features of a god, stern, haughty, with a small beard cunningly carved on the chin.

"Is that it?" Nancy whispered.

"That's it," Val said through his teeth.

And though he had never seen a jade mask before, he knew it for what it was. The death mask of the great Emperor Kiang Hsi. The mask of Kuan Ti, the War God. Once beautiful mutton fat jade speckled with emerald green, it had darkened to its present colors, in the tomb, where, for centuries, it had covered the face of an emperor who had made his power felt over most of his known world. By the hundred thousands men had died in the name of Kuan Ti. By the millions men would die in the name of that cold jade mask, given life and meaning by the deeds of one man thirteen centuries dead.

Already, tonight, blood had stained that beautiful jade. The future promised rivers of it in the name of hatred, greed and lust for power.

AND NOW THE great golden figure in the Imperial dragon robe paced sedately to the gilded, carved throne chair and seated himself, hands palm down on his knees, erect, stiff, regal.

Carl Zaken's voice rang through the great vaulted room.

"Gentlemen, the death mask of the great Emperor, Kiang Hsi. The god mask of the War God Kuan Ti. A joss that will make its wearer infallible. Gentlemen, Chang Ch'ien, the war leader who will inflame all China, will lead the yellow race as conquerors of the world. With this mask he cannot fail."

The great gong crashed out about them once more. And Chang Ch'ien sat there, stiff, immovable, hands on his knees and the god mask staring at them without expression, as it had stared for thirteen centuries. And the golden robe on that golden figure seemed to take on some of the blood tinge of the ghastly light which drenched it from above.

It was high drama, cunningly staged. And yet Val Easton's palm was damp about the handle of his gun as he witnessed it from among those black-hooded figures. For there was menace here too. Menace, danger and death for Nancy Fraser and himself. And for scores of thousands of unsuspecting people who tonight were sleeping peacefully in well-sheltered homes. Here, all about them, in the great room was something so vicious and threatening to the peace of mankind that it must be stamped out quickly, as one would destroy a venomous snake. And Val realized with a sickening feeling of helplessness that he could do nothing against this mad man who desired to rule a world. His own life, Nancy Fraser's life, hung by threads— the thickness of the threads forming the black cloth over their faces. If they were discovered it meant the end.

Something of that must have been running through Nancy's mind also. For she crept close to Val. He could feel her arm rigid against his. Silently he berated himself for drawing her into a thing like this. And his eyes riveted on that gilded throne chair; for Chang Ch'ien spoke from behind the jade mask….

"Go back and whisper what you have seen. Tell all your people that the spirit of the great Kiang Hsi has returned again. Tell them to make ready. Plans of which you know nothing are maturing. A few more moves, a little patience, and we shall be masters of the world—'For he who aims the bow that kills is master!'"

The calm, clear voice speaking in perfect English had an uncanny rhythmic purring quality that was half hypnotizing. One felt that the mind behind it was a mighty thing, projecting out, enfolding the will to which it was addressed. One felt that here were depths beneath depths, and a man whose power, ruthlessness, and cunning could sway a multitude, set a world at war. Val felt it. And those motionless black hooded figures about him felt it too. They stood like statues, spellbound.

Chang Ch'ien spoke again. "There is among you one whose beauty is no less than her sagacity. She has guided here tonight a man whose power reaches into strange and vital places. A man unknown by the world. A man who can bring disgrace and fear to those high in government circles in half a dozen countries. By his connections and his knowledge he can help us undermine where other men would fail. A dealer in drugs, gentlemen, whose victims are his slaves. His face you shall not see until his work is done and Asia rules the world. But she who brought him here shall be known to you all."

Val heard the uncanny purring voice with quick horror. Unexpected disaster had fallen on them. He sensed what was coming, even before the great golden Chang Ch'ien said distinctly:

"Tai Shan, my sister, come forward and show yourself.…"

NANCY STOOD BREATHLESS and unmoving by Val's side.

A hush of expectancy held the room. The black hooded heads turned toward them. All eyes were on Nancy, waiting, waiting.…

Chang Ch'ien spoke again with a sharper note of authority, "Tai Shan, come forward!"

"What shall I do?" Nancy's tight whisper came from beneath her mask.

There was nothing she could do; nothing. If she went forward and removed that black hood she was doomed. If she refused to obey she was lost. The real and lovely Tai Shan would never have refused. The brief fleeting seconds seemed endless. Carl Zaken, on the edge of the dais, bent his head forward and stared through the blood-red glow suspiciously. A queer ripple of tension stirred the hooded figures about them.

Chang Ch'ien's voice cracked like a lash. "Tai Shan!"

"Val!" That was Nancy, whispering her helplessness through the black cloth.

"I'm sorry," Val whispered back.

And even as the words passed his lips Chang Ch'ien came out of the gilded throne chair in one catlike movement. His hand lifted, pointed. His purring voice rang out from behind the mask. "Hold her! Hold that man with her! My sister would never disobey my order like this!"

"We're on our own, Nancy! Do what you can!" Val threw that at her as he jerked the automatic from his coat pocket. They had no hope of escaping. Their lives at this moment were running out as fast and surely as the last grains in an hour glass.

"Stand back!" Val cried out to those black-hooded figures about him.

Carl Zaken's harsh voice cried from the dais, "Stop him!"

They were dangerous, desperate men hand-picked by the Black Doctor and the golden Chang Ch'ien. They closed in from every side. Val pumped the automatic twice savagely; and heard Nancy's gun bark at his side. They both would die—but they would die dearly....

A man staggered, fell; another lurched—but still they came in. Hands caught at him from behind. Val's next shot struck the floor as his arm was knocked down. He heard Nancy cry out. And then, struggling futilely, he was jerked back and borne to the floor. The black hood was tightened about his face, his neck. Fingers choked. The weight of many bodies crushed him against the floor—and a red haze dosed in. Red, blood-red, like that halo bathing Chang Ch'ien and the Black Doctor on the dais.

And then the blackness of death….

LIGHT STRUCK INTO Val's eyes. Bright light, coming from a floor lamp somewhere to the left of him. His throat was dry, sore, painful. He felt sickish, dizzy. Then memory of all that had happened flashed over him. The Black Doctor—Chang Ch'ien—Nancy Fraser.

He was on his back, looking up at the ceiling as thought of Nancy cleared his head like a dash of cold water. He tried to sit up—and couldn't. He was held rigid by a strap over his throat. His wrists and ankles were strapped down tight. Rolling his eyes, Val saw that he was on some sort of table raised above the floor. He could lift his head an inch or so, turn it from side to side. He was in a small room whose walls were hung with black silk embroidered at intervals with writhing golden dragons. With difficulty, he made out a cabinet, a couch, and over against one wall a bookcase about the height of a man's head.

Under the table on which Val lay suddenly sounded the shrill hungry squeal of a rat, the rapid chattering of tiny, sharp teeth.

Val's heart beat faster at the sound. Alone, rats in the room! His coat was off, shirt sleeves loose. Helpless, defenceless—and rats in the room! The rat squealed again, but remained under the table. And in the minutes that followed Val heard it again and again, always directly beneath him. He puzzled for a little and then ignored it, thinking of Nancy Fraser. Where was she? What had happened to her?

Movement beyond his feet caught his eye. Neck strained

against the strap across his throat, he saw a bookcase across the room swing out noiselessly on hinges at one end, revealing an opening behind it. And from that opening a tall, powerful figure wearing a green mandarin coat and a round hat with a yellow button, stepped into the room. He closed the bookcase, came to the table where Val lay and looked down at him. The uncanny purring voice of the man called Chang Ch'ien said:

"I have waited for this, Valentine Easton."

Chang Ch'ien's words were without emotion—and chilling and foreboding for the very lack of it.

Without the ancient jade mask Chang Ch'ien was just as impressive. The shades of that golden dragon robe he had worn on the dais seemed still to linger in his golden-tinted skin. His full-lipped mouth, his stabbing slant eyes, with a small sickle shaped scar at the corner of his right eye, his smooth black hair sweeping back from his forehead as he lifted the hat for a moment gave him the appearance of a tall yellow god. The scar drew his eye up into the slightest sardonic cast. And then he smiled; and cunning lay behind it, and ruthlessness, and cruelty. And one saw how this man had become a myth, a legend, a terror in the underworld of many lands.

Beneath the table the rat squeaked again and chattered its teeth. Chang Ch'ien smiled broadly, without humor, said:

"Where is my sister, Tai Shan, Valentine Easton?"

"Where is Nancy Fraser?" Val countered huskily. His throat was swollen, tight.

"A beautiful girl, Miss Fraser; and spirited. She's been asking for you."

"Damn you!" said Val thickly.

"Where is Tai Shan? Miss Fraser came here wearing Tai

Shan's coat and hat, in the car that should have brought Tai Shan. What have you done with her?"

And a fierce joy burned through Val's veins at the sudden break of anguish he caught in Chang Ch'ien's voice. The man was vulnerable in one spot at least.

Val said bluntly: "She's guarded. You can't help her."

Chang Ch'ien looked down at him without moving a face muscle. "I believe she is, Easton. You found her at Li Fui Shan's. How, I don't know, but I would have heard from her by now if she were free."

"Quite," Val agreed. "Suppose we talk business. Nancy Fraser, myself, Cartier Beurket's jade mask, and, say—Carl Zaken, for your sister."

"You fool!" Chang Ch'ien purred. "*You* bargain with me!" One hand with long tapering fingers came out of a coat sleeve and caught the front of Val's shirt. Calmly, methodically, Chang Ch'ien ripped the cloth away until Val lay on the table bare from the waist up.

"You fool!" said Chang Ch'ien again. "Once before you crossed my path and got away. You were a dead man when you entered this house. But before you die, you will tell me where Tai Shan is. You will write the order that will release her."

Val laughed at him. It was all he could do.

"You will scream for the privilege of releasing that girl whose foolish interest in you probably betrayed her this evening," Chang Ch'ien said without emotion.

CHANG CH'IEN STOOPED, reached under the table, and when he straightened he held a small wire cage in his golden tapering fingers. A wire cage filled with scurrying frantic movements, shrill keening chatters of fright and rage, and a brown furry body that dashed from side to side in the upper half.

At first Val was puzzled. Two straps dangled from the bottom of the cage. It was partitioned in the middle. In the upper half, bounding about on the partition which formed a floor, was the gaunt hungry body of a great savage rat.

"He has been starved for a week," Chang Ch'ien purred. "He is frightened, angry, desperate for escape." Speaking, Chang Ch'ien set the cage on Val's chest, passed one of the straps beneath Val's bare torso and buckled it on the other side, holding the cage firmly in place. There was no wire in the bottom; nothing but space between his flesh and the partition halfway up in the cage.

"When I pull this slide out," Chang Ch'ien said evenly, "he will drop to your chest. There, for a time, fright will keep him busy. But when he begins to think, he will see that the only way out is through your chest. Food and escape in one." Chang Ch'ien smiled lazily, but his eyes were flaming. "Before he has won free," he said, "you will be a madman, Valentine Easton."

And Val knew that it was so. Only an Oriental could devise such ghastly, terrible torture. He shuddered; cold perspiration broke out on his forehead as he visualized those hours of agony in which sharp rodent teeth gnawed through flesh, nerves, bones on their way to freedom and satiated hunger.

The rat had quieted now, was staring nervously about from little beady, blinking eyes. The tapering fingers of Chang Ch'ien's left hand caught the slide and drew it slowly out. The rat balanced precariously on it, and as the opening into the bottom of the cage widened before him he thrust his head down, staring at the bare expanse of flesh below. Rigid, Val waited for the impact of tiny cold feet on his chest—and the horror that would quickly follow.

And suddenly that ghastly taut moment was broken into by the swift slide of books in the bookcase. Raising his head, Val saw volumes falling out of the second shelf from the top; volumes thrust aside by a hand that shoved through, holding a large caliber revolver!

9

Slashing Blades

CHANG CH'IEN STARTED back from the cage, turned as if to flee. But a crackling command in singsong Chinese from behind the bookcase stopped him rigid. The voice of Charlie Gong said: "Good. Now unstrap him. The cage first, and perhaps we'll put it on you. Quick, before I shoot, my friend!"

The sickle-shaped scar at the corner of Chang Ch'ien's right eye flamed with silent passion. Silently he turned to the table, fumbled with the straps, and set the wire cage down on the floor again. Still silently he freed Val's neck, arms, ankles. Val swung to the floor, swayed a moment, and turned to the bookcase. The smiling face of Charlie Gong peered through at him.

"Search him," said Charlie Gong. "Quick!"

Val did so, found a long knife tucked in the waistband of Chang Ch'ien's trousers, but no gun.

"Now watch him!" Charlie Gong directed. "I'm coming in. I

would have shot him but I was afraid it would bring the house down on our ears."

Charlie Gong withdrew his gun, pushed open the bookcase and stepped into the room. Chang Ch'ien waited, hands in his sleeves, face impassive once more. He had spoken not a word. Charlie Gong closed the bookcase and stepped toward the table. One step he took on a small Chinese rug lying on the floor—and the rug suddenly dropped beneath his feet and Charlie Gong vanished in a yawning hole in the floor. Vanished silently, his gun flying up above his head, and on his face a look of unutterable amazement.

And as Charlie Gong dropped from sight Chang Ch'ien's hand came out of his sleeve holding a second knife. He whirled on Val like a great golden-skinned cat.

"Now!" Chang Ch'ien said, and the word came like a whip lash as he lunged forward, sweeping the knife up before him.

Val was cornered against the table, hemmed in, unable to dodge. Chang Ch'ien rushed suddenly, his knife upraised. Val did the only possible thing. He countered instantly with the knife he held. His gleaming blade slashed out, down, counter-ing with the skill of one who had fenced much.

The blades clashed metallically. With a quick twist Val threw himself to one side, pivoting his weight on the clashing blades. Chang Ch'ien's knife was deflected, sliding on up past Val's blade at an angle. Its keen point ripped skin and flesh above the elbow of Val's left arm as the blow swept on past into space. The force of Chang Ch'ien's rush brought him hard against the edge of the table, his green mandarin coat brushing against the blood welling from Val's arm. And, catlike, the big Chinese recovered himself and swung about for another stabbing blow.

Val's right arm was free. He reversed his palm and smashed it toward Chang Ch'ien's head. The solid, heavy end of the knife handle caught the big fellow squarely behind the ear. Chang Ch'ien dropped like a poled ox. Dropped and rolled over on the floor, his knife clutched in nerveless fingers. He never moved. The fresh scarlet blood from Val's arm stained the front of the green mandarin coat; and close beside it the great gaunt rat bounced in fright from side to side of the small wire cage.

PANTING, SUDDENLY WEAK from the nervous reaction, Val laid the knife on the table and picked up the torn fragments of his shirt. He mopped the blood off his arm. He had a gash several inches long and a quarter of an inch deep, bleeding freely. Quickly he wrapped the shirt around it, tied a quick rough knot as best he could and stepped to the square yawning hole in the floor.

"Charlie Gong!" he called down cautiously.

From the black well-like hole Charlie Gong's voice came up, surprisingly cheerful. "Astonishing! I thought you would be dead by now, Easton."

"Still kicking. Our friend is out cold."

"You should have killed him," said Charlie Gong cheerfully. "Sorry I can't help you. Better get out of the house as quickly as you can—if you can. Don't know how many men they've got."

"Where is Bradshaw? How did you get in? I thought you'd lost us. I'd given you up."

"We had a puncture," Charlie Gong explained. "Last we saw of you the car was heading into Westchester. We came on, looked around. No sign of you. Bad business. Bradshaw was stumped. And then we suddenly ran into a string of cars leaving some place hurriedly. We found the drive they were coming out of and walked in to investigate. And bless you," said Charlie Gong in his flawless English, "there was the car we had been following, standing in front of the house. The driver was behind the wheel. I surprised him. We took him off in the fog and I talked Cantonese to him. After I had knocked his front teeth out he talked to me as one brother to another. There was trouble inside, he said. His partner had blundered and would perhaps die for it. Two strangers had been caught in the house."

Charlie Gong's voice floated up out of the darkness, calm and careless, with no hint of the drama and bravery he was recording.

"There was no time to go for help. I doubted if you were alive even then. I slugged the fellow after he had told me all I wanted to know, took his cap and coat and walked to the front door. The man at the door let me in, thinking I was the driver. We Chinese have moments of reason. It wasn't difficult for me to persuade him to bring me upstairs to you. Our friend Chang Ch'ien was talking when I arrived on the other side of the bookcase. I let him finish before I rudely interrupted his modest pleasures. You will find the doorman on the other side of the bookcase on the floor."

"Where is Nancy Fraser?"

"I don't know. I wanted to get you first. Better get out of here quick and send Bradshaw for help. From what Chang Ch'ien said I doubt if she's harmed—yet."

"How about you? Can you get out of there?"

"No," said Charlie Gong casually. "I am underground, I think. The walls are stone, and damp. Leakage from the beach probably. I must be below water level. Besides, my leg is broken."

And not until then did Val have the full measure of that little Chinese detective.

VAL LOOKED ABOUT. There were no windows in the room. Impossible to try to get Charlie Gong with his broken leg out of the house. He would be safer down there.

"I'm going," said Val. "I'll do the best I can."

"Good luck. And by the way, I understand you're mystified about how that chap got off Beurket's roof. The chauffeur was driving the same car for that job. He kindly told me before I broke his head that your man swung down from the seventh floor window of an apartment they had rented in the building adjoining. The space between it and the roof edge of Beurket's private gallery was two or three yards. By pushing hard this Zaken crossed the gap, stood on the roof. One of his men followed him and slid on down the rope into the back yard. After disposing of the watchmen there, he entered the back door when no one was looking and slipped down into the cellar.

"After putting the lights out he left without discovery in the darkness, climbed up to the roof again and swung across the space into the third-story window of a second apartment they had rented. This Carl Zaken followed in the same way. They walked out of the door of their apartment house, around the corner to their car and drove away. Everything had been planned, I understand, from the moment word had come from China that the mask of Kuan Ti had been smuggled out of the country. Chang Ch'ien's agent had been looking for it there.

"I tell you all this," Charlie Gong's cheerful voice floated up out of the darkness, "in case I am unable to talk when you find me again. Good luck."

Val left him there, that gallant little fellow. And naked to the waist as he was, with blood-stained arm and side, he opened the bookcase and stepped through. He could have asked Charlie Gong to try to throw his revolver up. Deliberately he left that comfort to Charlie Gong.

The bookcase was double, with books facing out on both sides. Val found himself in a bedroom. He stepped over the inert form of the doorman, crossed the room, opened the door into the hall and was greeted by an exclamation of astonishment. Coming toward him two paces away was a blue-clad, saffron-skinned servant, carrying a big leather kit bag in one hand. He dropped the kit bag and turned to scurry along the hall.

Val caught him in the first step, succeeded in throttling most of his squall of fright. With a full armed sweep he shoved the fellow against the wall and smashed him in the jaw. The first blow didn't do it—but the second and third did. He left the fellow there on the floor.

The hall turned at both ends. No stairs were visible. It was impossible to tell which way to go. Val went in the direction from which his victim had been coming.

He made the turn to the left, found steps a short distance beyond—narrow steps that turned at right angles as they went down. Blood was dripping from Val's arm, staining his torso. He still carried the knife in his right hand. Hair rumpled, face set, blood-smeared, he was a startling and savage sight. At the bottom of the stairs he found another hall. This big old stone house seemed to be a tangle of rooms and halls.

Fate decided his direction this time. A door slammed to his left. He went to the right. Another door slammed behind him.

He heard steps shuffling in his direction, men talking excitedly in Chinese. Val opened the first door he came to; it happened to be on the left. He stepped through—and stood stock still, nerves tense.

He was in the big vaulted room where he had been throttled unconscious. The dais, the thronelike chair, the great silver and gold tapestry and all the other furnishings were still in place; but the room was empty. His own cautious steps sounded loud.

Val hesitated, stared. He knew now how to get to the front entrance to leave the house. But what would happen while he was gone? Could he get back in the house, find Nancy Fraser....

VAL TURNED HIS back on the door which led to the open, free night outside; turned his back and went to the dais. Carl Zaken had disappeared from behind that great tapestry. He might still be found beyond there. Val clutched the knife ready as he stepped nimbly upon the dais and approached the tapestry. The Black Doctor would get short shrift if they met— and Val sought that meeting.

Silently, he slipped through the tapestry and found an open door in the alcove behind it. He went down the steps at the back of the dais, through the door, and found himself in another hall. The great brass gong that had been struck hung from two uprights by the wall. The striker leaned beside it. The hall was empty.

Walking carefully along, Val suddenly heard a muffled voice saying: "It will be too late in a few minutes. Too late. It's your last chance to help him. Who knew you were coming here?"

And Nancy's voice, shaken, desperate, denying, saying

bravely: "No one knew. Let me think. I—I can't think. Give me time. Don't do anything to him—yet."

"Where is Tai Shan?"

"I don't know."

And Carl Zaken's harsh voice: "I have a way, Miss Fraser, of stimulating memory. Perhaps this will do."

Nancy cried out with pain.

Val sprang into the room through a red haze of anger. There, opposite the door, sat Nancy tied in a chair. And standing over her was the tall, stooped figure of the Black Doctor, twisting one wrist cold-bloodedly and methodically.

On a table close by them rested the jade mask of the Emperor Kiang Hsi!

Nancy saw Val enter the room. Her eyes widened, her face puckered in astonishment through her pain at sight of his blood-smeared figure. Carl Zaken saw her face and whirled.

One look—and Zaken grabbed under his coat, under his left arm....

Val leaped at him, swinging the knife. The Black Doctor met him with a gun snapped out from a shoulder holster; a gun that roared, caught Val in mid-stride.

Val felt the shock of the bullet striking his shoulder, spinning him off balance, so that he staggered. That saved him from the second hasty shot that roared from Carl Zaken's gun, point blank; for this shot went between Val's arm and side. Val heard Nancy cry out with fear. And then he was on that tall, stooped figure whose pale cadaverous face was snarling like a death mask. Val knocked the gun away as the third shot roared out, slashed across and down with the knife.

The keen edge cut deep to the bone across Carl Zaken's knuckles.

The Black Doctor cried out with the pain of it. His nerveless fingers opened. The gun fell to the floor. Zaken scrambled back away from the menace of that flashing knife. He struck the table, knocked it over. The jade mask fell to the floor with a ringing sound. But such was the quality of that ancient jade that it did not break.

At the moment however Val had no thought for it as he followed that scrambling figure across the room. Carl Zaken caught a chair in passing, swung it around. Val threw up an arm. But the chair struck him heavily, drove him back, stopped him dead for a moment, dizzy with pain.

And in that moment the Black Doctor plunged to the side wall of the room bolted through a second door, slammed it. When Val reached it the door would not open. A bolt had been shot on the other side. The Black Doctor was gone. His voice, shouting, could be heard receding on the other side.

Val swung quickly, shaking his head to clear it. Quickly he cut Nancy loose from the chair.

"You're wounded! You're bleeding!"

"Never mind!" Val panted. "Come with me quick! We've got a chance to get out! A bare chance! God knows how many of them are in the house here!"

On the way to the door he scooped up the jade mask and the gun Zaken had dropped.

The hall was empty as he burst out into it ahead of Nancy.

But somewhere to the back voices were answering the Black Doctor's shouts.

"This way!" Val threw at her.

He led her to the end of the hall, past the great gong, up the steps to the dais, through the tapestry curtain and down across the big room where they had been trapped. Those three roaring shots, the Black Doctor's shouts had brought life to that ominously quiet house. As they neared the door which they had passed through earlier in the night, it opened and two blue clad Orientals, knives in hands, rushed through.

Val shot the first one without slackening his pace. The second one squealed with fright, doubled back through the door, slamming it—but not locking it. Val jerked it open, rushed through. The clamor behind them grew louder as more men joined in the pursuit.

That run to the front door seemed endless. But they made it without further opposition. The guard was gone. Charlie Gong had taken care of him. Val jerked the door in, kicked open the storm door—and suddenly they were both out in the dank, dark, fog-filled night.

The big ivy-covered stone house loomed behind them, black, seemingly deserted—but with the rising cacophony of furious pursuit sounding inside like a hive of bees erupting.

They stumbled down the steps. Headlights suddenly glowed through the fog ahead of them. Val raised the gun, shouting:

"Bradshaw! Bradshaw—where are you?"

And where the headlights were the voice of Bradshaw called: "Here!"

Bradshaw was by the car. It was Bradshaw who took in the situation in a flash, slid behind the wheel, stamped on the starter; and as they tumbled in the back started the big limousine with a lurch. They roared off into the fog just as pandemonium burst out of the house.

And the fog which had veiled its mystery earlier, now saved them. It blotted out the trouble and pursuit behind. Bradshaw left his own car where he had parked it and drove swiftly to Westchester Avenue, to the first light, the first telephone.

And it ended that way. The house was deserted when the police squad got there. Charlie Gong, broken leg and cheerful grin, was in the well-like prison into which he had fallen. But Chang Ch'ien and Carl Zaken, the Black Doctor, were gone. There was no trace of Cartier Beurket's report. But Beurket was alive, could write another shortly.

And the mask, the precious jade mask of Emperor Kiang Hsi, was safe. No mad leader would incite yellow-skinned millions to follow the god of war!

IN THE DRAGON'S LAIR

Justin Case

Turned to stone while still alive! Oriental
cunning and Oriental lust may exist in
the very heart of an American city!

1

THE SIGN ABOVE the shop's doorway said K'UNG TZU, ORIENTAL ANTIQUES AND CURIOS, and the words were repeated on the rain-smeared oblong of unclean window to the left of it. Uptown a clock was tolling eight.

Big Bill Cleaves, salesman for the Carmody Manufacturing Company, stood there in the drizzle and muttered savagely: "Well, here goes for the fourth assault, and this time by God—!" Then, pushing open a door which was seemingly the means of ingress to rooms above the shop, he climbed a flight of unlighted stairs and put his thumb hard against a bell.

The door opened. A slant-eyed Chinese girl stared out and said with an air of impatience: "K'ung Tzu is not at home. It will do you no good to keep returning here."

Bill Cleaves grinned at her. She was a good-looking girl, if one went for that sort of thing. She was young and dark-haired and slender, and her somber colored tunic revealed lovely feminine curves. She was attractive enough, yes—but the cold glint in her unblinking eyes would have warned Bill Cleaves to keep his distance, even had he been otherwise inclined.

"Sure, sure," he grunted. "Only I was talkin' to K'ung Tzu this afternoon, see? And I got an appointment to come here." He pulled a folded envelope from his pocket and thrust it forward. "Here's my passport, sister."

The envelope bore neatly penciled words which read: "Mr. Cleaves, of the Carmody Manufacturing Company, will call this evening at eight o'clock. Allow him to enter and await my

arrival." It was signed with the name K'ung Tzu and with a Chinese symbol which made that name authentic.

The girl nodded, said stiffly: "Please, then, to come in." She led Bill Cleaves through two dimly lighted rooms and into a third which was obviously the curio dealer's private sanctum. "Please," she said, "to wait here."

The door clicked shut. Bill Cleaves was alone.

A THIN SMILE twisted Bill's generous mouth. Hell, it hadn't been so difficult to get into this joint, after all, despite the fact that K'ung Tzu had thrice refused to see him! It was risky business, of course, and the Chink might be sore when he arrived. But that was a chance any salesman had to take.

It was a chance worth taking, too. This K'ung Tzu was an important guy. He ran no less than a score of "antique and curio" shops in the Chinatowns of a dozen large cities—shops where dumb tourists, thrilled to the ears, paid large money for stuff they thought genuine.

Most of that stuff was manufactured by novelty companies and then cleverly doctored by K'ung Tzu's own master craftsmen. And K'ung Tzu bought a lot of it.

Well, if the Chink would listen to reason he'd find out that he could buy better stuff, for less money, from the company which had sent Bill Cleaves to call on him.

Bill grinned again and glanced at the note which the Chinese girl had handed back to him. It had been a cinch to frame that note, after messing around the offices of a rival company and obtaining a sample of K'ung Tzu's handwriting and signature. Sure—a cinch! And now all Bill Cleaves had to do was wait here for the eminent Oriental to walk in.

He looked around him. It was a small room, furnished in most expensive Oriental splendor. Small statues of Confucius and Mencius sat complacently on a mantel above the ornate fireplace. Embroidered silks adorned the walls. There were large water-color paintings of men and women, nude, which made Bill Cleaves want to look closer.

He wandered around, stood a long while before some of the pictures. "A hell of a lot of interesting things," he mused, smiling, "come under the name of art. This K'ung Tzu, if he's as old as they say he is, must sure have young ideas!"

He took down the statue of Mencius and examined it. It was worth something, that statue; its base was fashioned of very old and very valuable cloisonné enamel. Gingerly he put the thing back, strolled curiously around the room again, and then returned to the statue for a second look.

This time, in lifting it from its place on the mantel, he leaned against the elaborate brick facing of the fireplace. He lost interest in the statue of Mencius. Instead, he stared with widening eyes at a narrow section of paneled wall which was slowly swinging open.

He himself had opened it, by leaning against some concealed mechanism....

HE TOED FORWARD, leaned low in the aperture, and peered into what seemed to be a small, windowless chamber beyond. He stared harder, took a slow step forward, and thought better of it. Amazingly light on his feet for a man so big, he paced across the private sanctum of K'ung Tzu and locked the door by which he had entered.

Then, with a scowl twisting his lean face, Bill Cleaves slid through the opening in the paneled wall and entered the secret chamber beyond.

The room was dark, furnished only with an ancient, dusty carpet that covered every inch of its square floor. Its only light came through the narrow aperture behind him; but that light, dim and diffused as it was, revealed enough of the room's contents to raise short hairs on the nape of Bill Cleaves' neck and sap color from his face.

Against the far wall, facing him, stood a woman. Bill walked slowly toward her, his fists clenched against the wave of cold horror that crawled through him.

The woman was almost completely naked. Above and behind her loomed the head of an enormous wooden dragon—a thing so luridly painted, so grotesquely hideous in the room's dim light that Bill Cleaves wanted suddenly to back away from it, to wheel and lurch back to the door before the monster's glittering eyes could drag him closer.

A master craftsman had carved that thing. A mind steeped with opium smoke had conceived it. And the girl—the young girl whose body was an exquisite creation of the greatest Craftsman of all—was caught horribly in the clutching embrace of the monster's wooden claws.

Bill Cleaves' eyes were monstrous in his head as he went closer. He gaped at the dragon's red-and-yellow arms, saw that they were hinged to the huge wooden body and fitted with thumbscrews by which the movable claws could slowly be forced inward against the creature's spiked torso.

The girl had been flung against that spiked body and bound there. Her head had been forced back, her hair coiled and knotted around an out-jutting spike. She had been forced to look up into the monster's gaping mouth—a cavernous yellow maw filled with sharpened teeth.

And then, probably while she screamed for mercy, cruel hands had slowly turned the thumb-screws which had caused those long, needle-keen claws to curl inward and bury themselves in her cringing flesh.

God!

Bill Cleaves wiped cold sweat from his face and took a faltering step backward. But the horror of the thing fascinated him; he continued to stare. It was too late now to do anything else. The girl was dead....

Dead! There could have been no death more agonizing. Bound there in the embrace of that fantastic wooden torture-dragon, forced to stare up into the creature's fanged mouth and into its huge, glittering eyes, the girl had been gored to death by wooden claws which even now were buried from sight in her blood-smeared flesh.

Hot blood had coursed down her satin-smooth legs to form a crimson pool at her feet. Her face was a frozen mask of torment, her rigid hands clenched, as if still fighting for freedom, on the wooden talons which had penetrated, to the depths of her body.

"Like—like a wax figure in a chamber of horrors at some beach-resort museum," Bill Cleaves thought dully. "Only it's not made of wax...."

FOR A MOMENT he was not sure of that. The girl's body did look like a figure carved of wax. Its breasts, unstained by the blood that drenched waist and legs, were white and smooth as fine-grained gypsum. No ravaging hands had ever mauled their pale loveliness, Bill was certain.

He reached out slowly and touched one milky shoulder. As abruptly as if he had touched fire, he jerked his hand back, stood stiff with amazement. It took him a long time to sway forward again, to make sure that his questing fingers had not sent a false impression to his numbed brain.

He gripped the girl's shoulder more tightly, slid his hand down across the pale protrusions below. The flesh encountered by his trembling hand was hard as stone!

"What the hell—" Bill Cleaves muttered.

He shook his head, stepped back. This sort of thing was out of Bill Cleaves' line entirely. Through his mind flashed the story of the Russian princess who had made statues for her garden by pouring water over nude, living girls in the dead of winter. But this was something different. This girl had been tortured to death and then, in some hellishly ingenious manner, her agony-racked body had been preserved against decomposition.

But why?

He peered again into the girl's face. Scowling, he bent closer, trying hard to remember where he had seen that face before. And then, eyes narrowed with sudden understanding, he shrank back, turned on the balls of his feet and strode silently to the aperture through which he had entered.

There had been photographs in the newspapers, not long ago, of a girl who had been reported mysteriously missing....

Bill Cleaves strode across the expensively furnished sanctum of K'ung Tzu and unlocked the door. He no longer desired to talk with K'ung Tzu about curios or antiques—or about anything. He wanted only to get out of the Oriental's sinister abode, as quickly and as silently as possible. His fists were clenched and his mouth was set in a thin, colorless slit.

He strode through the two rooms through which the sloe-eyed servant girl had led him. The girl herself, her face utterly empty of expression, came silently out of shadows and stood with her back to the door which gave access to the street.

She stared straight at Bill Cleaves and said quietly: "You are leaving?"

Bill stood quite still, sensed trouble, and said with assumed indifference: "Sorry, but I can't wait. Another appointment—"

"The eminent K'ung Tzu will be here at any moment."

"Sorry, but—"

"And you will wait."

"Now listen. I tell you—"

THE GIRL'S OCHRE-HUED hand came out from under the folds of her tunic. The hand held a small, pearl-butted revolver. "You will wait," she said ominously, "because

you entered here under false pretenses and with a note of intro-
duction which was not written by my master. K'ung Tzu will
be most interested in meeting you. Please to sit down."

Bill Cleaves forced a short, mirthless laugh from his lips,
shrugged his shoulders and stepped backward. The girl smiled,
moved quietly away from the door. She should have known
better, but then, she did not know Bill Cleaves.

For a six-footer, Bill Cleaves was uncannily fast on his feet.
He tore into the girl with his head down, fists flailing. The
gun went out of her hand and clattered hollowly against the
wall behind her. Hurled off balance, the girl crashed with a
spine-jarring thud against the doorframe.

Bill Cleaves' head had slammed hard against the firm, quivering pit of her stomach. His hands, sweeping higher, raked the
flesh of her thighs, bruising as they went, and smashed against
her mouth as her thin lips opened to scream.

The blow would have felled a horse. It lifted the sloe-eyed
girl from the floor and dumped her in a limp heap across the
seat of a chair.

Bill Cleaves slammed the door behind him and went snarling down the stairs.

AN HOUR LATER, Bill said "Thanks, mister!" to the
morgue attendant on the third floor of the *Tribune* building,
stuffed a handful of newspaper clippings into his pocket, and
hiked up one flight of stairs to the editorial rooms. Men in
shirt-sleeves glanced at him and nodded. Before becoming a
mighty good salesman, Bill Cleaves had been a fair-to-mid-
dling news hound.

He paced quietly across the big room and steered a straight

course toward a desk where a good-looking brunette was using a dictating machine. He put a hand on the girl's shoulder, took a cigarette from the box of flat fifties on the desk and said: "You almost through for tonight, Ruth?"

She looked up at him. "I can't make it. Bill," she said in a low voice. "Mason has been after me all evening—"

"You mean to tell me you're going out with that lug?"

"No, no—of course not. But I had to tell him I was going straight home, and if he sees me walk out of here with you—"

Bill nodded, glanced savagely across the room. Even before looking, he knew that Matt Mason, number one re-write man on the *Tribune's* staff, would be leaning sloppily over the desk in the corner, glaring at him. He was right. Mason, with unwashed flesh bulging against the unbuttoned collar of a dirty shirt, was staring holes in him.

"Okay," Bill said quietly to the girl beside him. "Get out soon as you can and meet me at the Green Rooster. I got something for you that will boost you high enough in this dump so you'll be able to spit in Mason's filthy face the rest of your life."

THE GREEN ROOSTER, on Medford Street, had a postage-stamp dance floor, a three piece orchestra, and innumerable lamplit booths where patrons drank bad liquor and consumed good Chinese food.

Bill Cleaves sat alone in a corner booth and smoked endless cigarettes. While waiting, he looked again at the clippings he had taken from the morgue-files in the *Tribune* building.

When Ruth Werner slid into the booth at quarter past ten, Bill shoved the clippings across the table and said quietly: "Ever seen those before?"

She glanced through them, looked up at him quizzically. "Of course, Bill. Why?"

He stared at her. It was not the first time he had done that, either. She had the sort of form that went well in a white bathing-suit—tall, slender, beautifully proportioned. Some day, maybe, she would agree to give up being the best-looking girl in the newspaper business and condescend to be the glorious wife of a certain damn-fool salesman. But right now—

"I'm a nut for letting you in on this," Bill said, scowling. "It may be dangerous as hell. But it could mean a lot to you." He leaned closer, flattened one hand over the newspaper clippings. "Listen. This girl is supposed to be missing. Only tonight I found out different, see? I stood as close to her as I am to you, and—"

He stopped talking. Very slowly he swiveled in his seat and glared into a flabby, loose-cheeked face that leered down at him. "Well," he said curtly, "what do *you* want?"

The man who had come so silently to the booth, and who stood now with his hands resting on the table-edge, was Matt Mason. *Tribune* re-write man. There was nothing lovely about Mason's twisted face as he leaned forward and aimed the gaze of his smouldering eyes at Bill's companion.

"So you had to go straight home," Mason snarled.

Ruth Werner stood up, her face suddenly pale, one hand pressed hard against her heaving bosom. When she did that, Mason voiced a short, guttural laugh and leaned closer, his sleeve brushing Bill Cleaves' shoulder.

"Listen, babe," Mason said. "For God's sake get wise to yourself. I like you, see? And I'm a regular guy. I'm anxious to do big things for you—swell clothes, an apartment, good times. Be sensible and tell this mug, Cleaves, to pack his bag and take a trip for himself."

He pawed the girl's shoulder, with his big hand—perhaps intentionally, perhaps because he was leaning off-balance over the booth table. With utter loathing in her wide eyes, Ruth Werner shrank from his touch. And then Bill Cleaves stood up.

Bill Cleaves said quietly: "You came looking for this, Mason." He put his left hand on Mason's shoulder, swung the man around with a savage jerk and drove his right fist with sledge-hammer force into the middle of the re-write man's flushed face.

That started it. It was a good scrap while it lasted, and would have been better had not a couple of jabbering Chinese waiters rushed to the booth and separated the two combatants. The waiters were backed up by an excited manager and by a trio of big, silent, evil-eyed giants who stood by while the manager did a lot of tight-lipped talking.

"I will not have fighting in my establishment," the manager declared acidly. "You come into the back room and settle this argument where you will not annoy my other customers."

RUTH WERNER PUT a trembling hand on Bill's arm and said: "No, Bill. Please!" But Bill Cleaves was sore. Bill glared into the bloody face of Matt Mason, then looked at the Chinese manager and growled sullenly: "Okay. Lead the way."

The manager walked stiffly through swinging doors and through a kitchen. Bill trailed him. Ruth Werner protested in vain. Matt Mason, wiping blood from his snarling mouth, walked between two silent giants who gently but ominously took hold of his elbows.

The Chinese manager held open the door of an inner room and said: "You will come in here, please." Bill strode over the threshold, with Matt Mason and the girl behind him.

Then, with a sudden gasping suck of breath, Bill Cleaves stiffened and stood staring.

The room was already tenanted. It contained an even half-dozen robed figures who obviously constituted a prearranged reception committee. The shapes closed in with swift, silent precision, blocking Bill's sudden attempted retreat to the door. Behind Bill, Ruth Werner uttered a low cry of terror and Matt Mason, snarling, said gutturally: "What the hell is this?"

Bill Cleaves knew what it was, knew that it hinged somehow on the ghastly thing he had discovered in the secret chamber at K'ung Tzu's house, a short while ago. Knowing that, he flung out a hoarse warning shout and hurled himself in a headlong rush for the door.

He almost succeeded in getting there, did succeed, at least, in hurling aside two of the menacing shapes that swarmed over him. Then a gun-butt in the hands of a saffron-skinned giant crashed down on his head and spilled him to his knees.

With strangling fingers at his throat. Bill Cleaves lost consciousness.

IT WAS A strange room, and at first, when he labored sluggishly back to his senses, Bill Cleaves thought he was dreaming. The floor that stretched away from him was carpeted in black, and in the center of the black was woven a huge yellow dragon whose frightful body seemed to have no end.

Other dragons, with fanged mouths and glittering eyes, were embroidered on expensive silk draperies that covered the room's four walls. The ceiling was a writhing mass of color.

Subdued lights glowed in four corners, and hanging braziers at the far end of the chamber illuminated a raised platform whereon stood the thing which Bill Cleaves had encountered, eternities ago, in the abode of K'ung Tzu. He stared at the nude, torture-twisted body which to his touch had seemed so like a thing carved out of white stone. He shuddered, strained against the soft but unyielding cords which held his aching body in an upright position against the wall.

The dead girl in the clutches of that grotesque wooden dragon did not seem so horrible now. There were other things to stare at—other things to curdle the blood in Bill Cleaves' pounding heart.

Statues, they seemed to be, but he knew better. Illuminated

by indirect lighting in niches along every wall, they gleamed in ghastly detail for him to gape at. Nude women—one of them nailed horribly to a wooden frame, her tongueless mouth wide open, her body impaled on a long, threaded lance of metal which apparently had been slowly turned by means of outjutting handles, until its point had penetrated through the girl's body.

Another of those pale, wax-like figures lay supine, her arms and legs and head bound to a baseboard painted bright scarlet. There were numerous raw cavities in the blood-smeared flesh of her body where monstrous sleek-bellied rats had been feeding. The rats were frozen in death now—just as was the girl herself—yet they seemed horribly alive as they crouched there on tortured flesh, their feet and fangs still imbedded in the girl's marble body.

Another—but Bill Cleaves had seen enough. He closed his eyes, fought to subdue the horror that coursed through him. Up there on the dais a door had opened, and from the opposite end of the chamber robed figures were slowly advancing toward a curved row of carved teakwood chairs.

With dark dread icing his flesh. Bill Cleaves stared.

ON THE PLATFORM, two silent giants had led Ruth Werner forward, were holding her now where the avid eyes of the assembled robed figures could drink in the beauty of her half-clad body. Pale light spilled over the lilting sweetness of her breasts, on the glossy velvet of her slim waist. Yet the girl did not cringe from the intensity of those stares. She seemed to be enjoying them.

When the ochre hands of her captors released her, she stood there on the edge of the dais and swayed her body sensuously, lifting her own hands, turning slowly, and stroking her hips, her thighs....

In horrified amazement, Bill Cleaves watched her.

There was sound in the room now, where before there had been only nerve-racking silence. A crimson-robed figure had advanced from the rear of the platform and was softly addressing the assembled congregation. Bill Cleaves stared into a slant-eyed face and tried hard to place it, and then, with a start, realized that he was peering at the man whom he had four times tried unsuccessfully to interview—the eminent Chinese merchant, K'ung Tzu.

"Brothers of the Dragon," K'ung Tzu intoned softly in a sing-song chant that curdled Bill's blood, "we are assembled here tonight for a double purpose—to provide the final statue for our new meeting chamber, and to destroy a too-curious white man who succeeded tonight in entering my home and discovering certain of our secrets.

"Look upon this woman. She is by far the loveliest of any we have brought here, and I am assured by the eminent Doctor Weng, who has just concluded his examination of her, that she is virginal. Therefore she is acceptable to us.

"With her tonight we were successful also in capturing a man whose body is corpulent and sensual enough to complete the theme which we have planned for the niche of honor. That statue, as you know, is to represent lust. Everything is in readiness. Doctor Weng is waiting."

K'ung Tzu stepped back into the shadows, but Bill Cleaves was staring wide-eyed at something else—at a small red spot of blood on the bare arm of Ruth Werner. The needle-sharp point of a hypodermic syringe had made that wound, he was certain. Some hellish drug was even now running in that lovely body, transforming Ruth Werner into a hungering, sensual creature whose drugged mind delighted in her own shamelessness.

FROM THE SHADOWS K'ung Tzu silently reappeared, leading a second figure to the center of the stage. A snarl rose in Bill Cleaves' throat when he saw the flabby, terrified features of Matt Mason—features even now discolored by his own fists. Mason, too, had been shorn of his clothing and supplied with a pair of wrestler's trunks and he stood now like a pale fat statue fashioned of dough, a sweat of fear oozing from his heavy flesh.

"We are ready now?" the voice of K'ung Tzu intoned, and the answer came in a murmuring wave of assent from the robed shapes below.

"Doctor Weng, if you please—" K'ung Tzu raised a hand, motioned to a white-garbed Oriental who stood waiting at the rear of the platform. The doctor came forward with short, quick steps, nodded, seized one of Matt Mason's hands and plunged a small gleaming needle into Mason's arm above the elbow.

Mason voiced a hoarse cry of pain. K'ung Tzu smiled, said softly—so softly that Bill Cleaves barely heard the words: "It is nothing, my friend. It is merely an aphrodisiac, to stimulate your natural desires. The drug you need fear is that which will come later. That drug was conceived by the eminent Doctor Weng himself, and will rush through your veins, destroying you, solidifying your body to stonelike hardness...."

The Chinese stared quietly across the room at Bill Cleaves. "That drug," he murmured, "will be used upon our troublesome friend also, but only after he has been made to suffer the torments of the clutching dragon. He has seen what the dragon did to a certain young woman whom he discovered in a secret chamber at my home. For him the torment will be even greater, because death will be denied him until the very end of his agony."

Bill Cleaves snarled a lurid answer and strained savagely against his bonds. Terror and rage were fighting within him. Right now, rage was uppermost; his face was flushed, curled mouth drooling hot saliva. Later, perhaps, terror would water the blood in his veins....

ON THE PLATFORM, the Oriental was leading Matt Mason forward, and Mason, though unbound now, offered no resistance. His avid eyes drank in the loveliness of the girl who stood there. And K'ung Tzu said softly: "She is yours. All yours!"

Matt Mason needed no urging. Huge and loathsome in his gross fatness, he reached out and dragged Ruth Werner toward him. K'ung Tzu stepped aside, smiling. The white-robed Doctor Weng, holding now a twin-tubed syringe and alert for the moment when his instrument of death would be needed, stood waiting.

Bill Cleaves, white with terror, raged futilely at his bonds and bellowed curses that drew no answers.

There on the platform Ruth Werner had gone into the arms of a man she despised. But she no longer despised him—not with that hellish virus roaring deep in her supple body and lashing her to a frenzy! Her arms were around Mason's neck, her lips glued hungrily to his.

Bill Cleaves, helpless to intervene, uttered a groan of despair and felt the sledging of his heart grow sluggish. This was the end.

He knew what would happen, what had happened to other young women whose bodies were displayed throughout this chamber of torment. Those women had been ingeniously tortured. At the height of their agony, they had felt the prick of the odd-shaped hypodermic which lay now in the hands of Doctor Weng.

Some hellish fluid in those twin glass tubes had instantly solidified their agony-twisted bodies into stonelike statues for the adornment of the clan's meeting-room.

And he himself, Bill Cleaves was scheduled to face the same ghastly fate! But the girl on the platform would be forced to endure no such torture. Her fate was to be different. She and

Matt Mason, together, were to pose for a statue representing the madness of passion, and that statue was to occupy a niche of honor....

EVEN NOW K'UNG Tzu had steered Matt Mason onto a broad wooden pedestal, and the girl was in Mason's thick arms, crushed hard against him. The insurgent drug in her veins had driven her to madness. She was enjoying it!

Every fiber of that lovely body quivered, and the slithering hands of Matt Mason served only to feed the flames of the girl's insanity. Her head was tilted back, her mouth fastened hungrily on the lips that seemed now to be drinking the soul from her body—lips which under other circumstances would have revolted her.

Then, raging frenziedly at his bonds, Bill remembered the undulating words of K'ung Tzu. "She is virginal... therefore she is acceptable to us...."

"Listen!" Bill bellowed. "Listen, you fools! You're making a mistake! Ruth Werner's not the kind of girl you think!"

It was a deliberate, hoarsely screamed lie, but it took effect. K'ung Tzu, staring, strode to the edge of the platform and raised his hand for silence. He glared at Bill. He said acidly: "What do you mean?"

"I mean I don't give a damn what your Doctor Weng says— that girl isn't what you think! My God, I ought to know!"

K'ung Tzu's yellow face became slowly convulsed with rage. "You lie!"

"What the hell good would it do me," Bill growled with strange, savage coolness, "to lie at a time like this? It won't help *me* any, will it?"

K'ung Tzu stood quite still for a moment, seemed to be indulging in deep thought. Then he turned, rasped an order to two saffron-skinned giants who stood at the rear of the dais. The men strode forward and dragged Ruth Werner from the embrace of Matt Mason.

K'ung Tzu, descending from the platform, went into conference with the robed figures below.

Bill Cleaves, rigid against his bonds, waited with rising terror for the verdict.

"I'm listening," Bill muttered.

"The situation is this, my friend. Our program must be carried through tonight, because tomorrow the eminent Doctor Weng departs for the Orient. Therefore we must obtain tonight another woman to replace the one who stands there on the dais. Do you understand? Even if you are lying, we can take no chances on the wrong kind of woman."

"I get it."

"It is our belief that you may be able to assist us. In return for that needed assistance, we offer you your freedom."

"You mean," Bill said, scowling, "you want me to bring the right kind of girl here, so you can…?"

"Precisely."

"To hell with you!"

K'ung Tzu's shoulders moved with a slight shrug. He said softly: "Apparently your life means little to you." He turned away, motioned to the two sloe-eyed giants who stood waiting on the platform. "Prepare this fool," he ordered gently, "for the extreme torment of the great dragon!"

Bill Cleaves' eyes bulged in their sockets. Sweat oozed from the pores of his ridged forehead. "No, no!" he croaked. "My God, no!"

"Then perhaps you will reconsider your decision."

"I—I'll get a girl for you," Bill groaned. "I'll do it. My God, anything but—but—" His voice broke; hot tears rolled from his bloodshot eyes and stung his lips. "Let me get to a phone," he mumbled. "I'll find a girl...."

K'UNG TZU'S THIN lips curled in a smile of triumph. He nodded to the two giants. They stepped closer, released Bill Cleaves and led him, stumbling and retching, across the room. K'ung Tzu followed slowly.

"The young man's spirit is quite broken," K'ung Tzu said mockingly. "He has—what do you call it?—lost his nerve. That is indeed a pity."

A door swung open, clicked shut. Bill Cleaves raised his head, stared, and saw that he was being escorted along a dimly lighted corridor. Offering no resistance, he allowed his giant captors to lead him up a short flight of uncarpeted stairs, along a second narrow hall and into a small, gloomy office.

A telephone stood there on a desk. Bill sank into a chair beside it, fumbled the phone into his hand and then stared into the hovering faces of his persecutors.

"Listen. I can't go through with this! My God, I can't do it!"

"You prefer the dragon, my friend?"

Bill groaned, bent over the instrument. Beads of sweat dripped from his face and splashed on the table-top. He dialed a number, sat like a man stricken with some deadly disease, and waited for an answer.

"I—I want to talk to Rosie," he mumbled a moment later. "Yes—to Rosie." Then: "Listen, Rosie. This is Bill—Bill

Cleaves. Listen, I'm in a spot, see, and I need a swell kid like you to—to help me out."

"Tell her," K'ung Tzu whispered softly, "to come alone to number fifty-two Medford Street, which is a shop run by one Ming Wu. You will be waiting for her."

"Listen, Rosie," Bill Cleaves mumbled. "I'm at fifty-two Medford Street, see? It's a place run by a guy named Ming Wu. I—I know it's late, kid, but I just got to have help. I guess I've done favors for you, haven't I?" He licked his lips, glanced frantically at the men who stood watching him. "Listen," he mumbled. "I'd ask your brother Tommy—yeah, Tommy—only they wouldn't let him in here. You got to help me, Rosie."

He hung up, pushed the phone away from him, and put a trembling; stiff-fingered hand to his perspiring face. "She— she's coming," he groaned.

After that, they took him back to the torment room.

K'UNG TZU AND his confederates again went into conference. The conference lasted a long time. Bill Cleaves, securely bound again, stared dully at the dais, where ochre-hued giants stood guard over Ruth Werner and Matt Mason.

Whatever hellish drug had been fed to the girl, she seemed now to be getting over the effects of it. She seemed bewildered by her own near nakedness, horrified by the avid gaze of Mason's hungry eyes. Her ivory-smooth breasts rose and fell with rapid gasps of breath; she tried to cover them with her hands, tried to hide the rest of herself by twisting sideways in the grip of the yellow men who held her.

Then K'ung Tzu was pacing toward her, smiling evilly, and Bill Cleaves stiffened in his bonds, suspecting the worst. K'ung

Tzu nodded, turned quietly to the giants who held her.

"This woman is useless to the Brothers of the Dragon," he said quietly. "You may take her and do with her what you will. She should provide good amusement."

Ruth Werner screamed, fought frantically to free herself. Worms of horror crawled in Bill Cleaves' staring eyes. He raged at his bonds, bellowed hoarsely: "You can't do it! Damn you, leave her alone!"

K'ung Tzu turned, smiling, and said softly: "Soon the woman named Rosie will be here, and you will see what we are capable of doing, both to her and to you."

Yellow hands had dragged Ruth Werner across the dais, were pulling her now toward the door at the rear of the chamber. She moaned for mercy, battled furiously to break free, but the fiends who escorted her had dealt with women before and knew every hellish trick of enforcing obedience.

Long-nailed fingers gouged her sensitive flesh, bit into the hollow of her back, and forced her forward. Her screams brought only mocking laughter from the fiends who stared gloatingly at her pale beauty.

Against the wall, Bill Cleaves fumed like a caged jungle beast, while the girl he loved was dragged toward a door through which she might never return.

And then K'ung Tzu and others of the almond-eyed clan were advancing toward him, and K'ung Tzu was saying softly: "It is time, my friend, for us to meet the woman whom you so graciously sent for. We have only to go upstairs into the shop of Ming Wu...."

A pearl-handled revolver came into the Chinaman's hand, lay there, its muzzle pointing at Bill's chest, while other hands released the white man's bonds. Hard fingers curled on Bill's arms, drew him forward.

"I hope for your sake," K'ung Tzu said, "that you have not attempted to deceive us."

Bill Cleaves stood rigid. Wide-eyed, he stared at the door where the girl he loved was being dragged to a fate worse than the death which originally had been planned for her. His trembling body clamored to go hurtling forward, but the gun in K'ung Tzu's yellow hand sobered him.

WHITE-FACED, WITH FISTS clenched and his heart beating violently, he allowed them to lead him across the room.

"The woman's name," K'ung Tzu murmured, "is Rosie? And she is beautiful?"

Bill nodded heavily. "Yes, her name is—"

He failed to finish. Another voice had answered, and that voice, booming hollowly through the room, stiffened Bill Cleaves as abruptly as though an electric current had passed through him.

"Sure," the booming voice rasped. "Sure! The name's Rosie. And if you yellow-skinned rats want to see how beautiful Rosie is, take a good look!"

Bill Cleaves shot one startled glance at the dais. One glance was enough. It showed him a lean, unkempt figure standing there wide-legged under the red glow of a hanging brazier. It showed him a snarling masculine face under a ragged mop of black hair, and a pair of bony hands curled around a Thompson sub-machine gun.

Big Bill Cleaves waited for no more. The pearl-handled revolver in K'ung Tzu's fingers had wavered. Bill whirled, swung a pile-driver fist that shattered flesh and bone and brought spurting blood. The Chinese staggered sideways, screaming curses. Scooping the gun from the floor. Bill lunged with insane fury toward the fiends who were dragging Ruth Werner across the rear threshold.

He was too well occupied then to see the rest of it. He heard shouts of rage and amazement behind him, heard the voice of the man on the platform bellowing to the Brothers of the Dragon to "come and get it!"

A revolver barked, was answered by the deafening, ear-splitting thunder of the Tommy gun. Yellow men were screaming. The man on the platform was yelling words of derision. Back in a corner. Matt Mason was seeking cover.

In the room's rear doorway, Bill Cleaves hurled himself upon Ruth Werner's captors. And the Bill Cleaves who did that was no longer a human being, but a snarling beast gone berserk with red rage.

The pearl-handled revolver belched in his fist, spewed death. When it was empty he made a murderous bludgeon of it, swung it blindly, with superhuman strength, against bloody fists and faces that loomed before him.

Behind him, the machine gun was still thundering, and the thunder ceased while Bill exchanged blows with the last of the fiends who had sought to drag Ruth Werner away. The gun in Bill's hand raked a snarling face; his fist, clenched hard, crashed with bone-splintering force into features already ripped and gouged and smeared with blood.

The last of the sloe-eyed giants went down. Bill leaped over him, caught Ruth Werner's trembling body in his arms and whirled.

But it was finished. The Chamber of the Dragon was a bloody horror-room, its floor covered with bullet-riddled, contorted shapes who would never again gloat over screaming victims.

TOWARD BILL CLEAVES strode the lean, unkempt figure which had descended from the dais—and Bill said gratefully: "Thanks, Rosie. Thanks a lot."

Later, when he had removed a robe from one of the dead Orientals and draped it around Ruth Werner, he and Ruth and the man named Rosie, with Rosie's machine-gun for a passport, marched out of the horror-chamber, Mason shuffling behind.

Bill looked down at Ruth, who clung so close to him that the warmth of her thinly clad body stirred strange desires within him. He said quietly: "This is Solly Rosenthal, honey. Fifth Precinct Homicide, and a pal of mine."

"And this, I suppose," Rosenthal grinned, fondling the hot Tommy gun, "is my brother Tommy."

"Yeah. I figured you'd understand."

Later, when the streets of Chinatown were behind them, Solly Rosenthal waved a hand and said indifferently: "See you later, you two. I gotta get some sleep." And Bill Cleaves signaled a prowling cab, letting Mason find one for himself.

On the way to Ruth Werner's apartment, he leaned back in the seat and held the girl very close to him. When he kissed her, she melted against him and held her hot, moist lips against his for a long time….

BLOOD ON THE BUDDHA

John K. Butler

Out of the Frisco fog came death that night, for the Laughing Buddha had played a grim jest on those who sought to desecrate his shrine. Now three men lay in pools of their own blood at the idol's feet, while the joss-sticks mingled their perfumed smoke with killers' cordite and Rex Lonergan, ace op from headquarters, sought to crack the wall of mystery around that temple of terror.

1

The Girl at Maxie's

REX LONERGAN SAT at the far end of the bar, hunched over his fourth beer. He was waiting for the Peeper to show up. He'd been waiting for almost an hour past the appointed time and now he'd begun to doubt that the Peeper would show.

It was at Maxie Hymer's Waterfront Club. They served the beer in vase-like glasses, each big enough to hold a bunch of sunflowers—and it was a terrible brew. You could smell it as soon as you walked in. You could also smell the stale smoke, sawdust, and most of the customers who patronized Maxie's.

"Want me to put a little head on that?"

Lonergan shook his head at the bartender. "I know when I'm licked, Mike."

"Well, you know how it is." Mike grinned, "you got to cater to your trade. These fellows like all they can get for ten cents. After the second, they don't much care whether it's good or not."

"I can understand that," Lonergan said drily.

Maxie Hymer came along the outside of the bar. He sent Mike out of earshot with a slight movement of his bald head and leaned close to Lonergan. "A lady to see you, Rex. She's upstairs in Room Ten."

"What lady?" Lonergan asked, because he wasn't expecting any lady.

"I don't know, Rex; she didn't say."

Lonergan said, "Thanks," while getting off the high bar-stool, and added: "If the Peeper shows up looking for me, tell him to wait."

Blood covered the idol's bronze baldness.

He walked on sawdust to the other end of the bar. The thin, pasty-faced man at the tinny piano was still playing *Mother Machree* and singing it in a hoarse throaty voice. Tears streamed down his face. A bunch of sailors had been buying him beers.

LONERGAN WENT DOWN a short hall past the restrooms and opened a door into another hall. Steep worn steps went up. There was also a narrow side door to the street but that was kept padlocked so Maxie's tenants wouldn't try a slip without paying rent.

Lonergan climbed to the second floor, rapped knuckles on the door of Number Ten. A woman's voice called, "Come in," softly.

He went in and found himself looking into the dark muzzle of a small automatic. When he looked over the top of the gun at the woman's face he said: "Hello, Sue."

She lowered the gun. "Shut the door, Rex."

He shut it but the singing of *Mother Machree* still came up loudly through the floor. Everybody in the place seemed to be singing it down there.

"Better lock it," Sue suggested. She was sitting on a plush sofa that showed bits of stuffing through many torn places. She held the blue-black gun in her lap.

Lonergan turned the key in the lock. "Why all the firearms?" he asked.

"I'm scared, Rex. Honest to God. I'm scared clean down to my socks."

She was; he could see it. Fear showed in her overbright eyes, in the puffiness under them, in the tremble of her full lower lip.

Police work hardens a man to fright in women and Lonergan had seen plenty of it. In his whole career, though, he'd never seen a scare like this. It took her body in a tight grip and shook her, all over.

"You've got the willies, Sue. What is it? What's the trouble?"

Her shivering became a quick hard shudder. "I can't tell you,

Rex—I can't tell anybody. That's *it,* see? I'm going nuts! I'm going clean nuts!"

It came from her lips in a tense, desperate sob; it forced big shimmering drops of water to her eyes. And these weren't the tears of a frail feminine creature who finds herself in her first trouble and wants a shoulder to cry on. That was just the point.

Lonergan knew Sue. He'd known her all her life. They'd been raised, neighbors, in the Mission District. She'd been in plenty of trouble through the years, had taken many hard knocks. But hard knocks had never made her afraid. She'd always taken the worst as it came, with a cynical sneer and a burst of profanity. Now she'd gone all to pieces.

"You've got to help me, Rex. I never asked you before. You helped me lots of times but I never asked—you know that."

He had helped her, often, because he'd known her for so long and because he'd known her father—and because he thought there was some good somewhere in Sue. He said: "You tell me what the spot is and I'll lend a hand."

She stared across the room and didn't answer him.

"The Peeper," he probed casually, "had a date to meet me here tonight at nine. Know anything about that?"

"He won't come"—her lips hardly moved except for the trembling—"he's dead."

Lonergan didn't speak, didn't show anything. The Peeper was Sue's brother, ten years older.

"He's naked—sliced in ribbons," she said in a voice as flat and dead as the Peeper must be. "In an empty fruit gondola in the S.P. freight yards."

"Cops there?" Lonergan inquired softly.

SHE NODDED STIFFLY. Then her spine went limp and she bent over with her face in her hands to shut out a picture nightmarishly hideous.

"I saw it," she said dully into her hands. "I heard it. We were taking a powder together—not from the law, from—worse. We went into the freight yards to grab a rattler south. We got in this empty fruit car—but they came after us."

She hesitated. That shudder took hold of her slim body again.

"Peep couldn't get the door to slide shut. He put me in the empty ice compartment that they got built into those cars. I thought he was coming in after me. He couldn't make it—no time. He shut the door. It only went part way, like the gondola door. I was hiding there. Peep made a run for it. He wanted to lead them away from me, I guess. They caught him."

In the pause, Lonergan asked: "Who?"

There wasn't any answer to that. "They brought Peep back into the gondola and they was stronger than Peep so they closed the doors. They lit flashlights and went to work on him. You can't hear nothing from inside a closed fruit car."

Lonergan kept attentively silent, waited.

"They tore his clothes off and went to work with knives. I wanted to yell and I couldn't even breathe or they might hear me. Peep wouldn't talk—he couldn't. Then they wanted to know where I was and Peep still wouldn't talk. They cut him and I had to see him, hear him, all the time they killed him. He passed out a lot of times but they brought him to and worked on him. Finally, he died. They opened the door and a yard dick yelled from over the tracks—and they scrammed. The dick put his flash in the car and saw Peeper and then ran for help, blowing a whistle. I got out while he was gone. I knew Peep was supposed to meet you here, so I sneaked over."

She still didn't look at Lonergan whose face had gotten very hard. Knotty little muscles along his jaw throbbed in tight rhythm. His fists were big and white-knuckled against his thighs. He moved to a wall telephone and got Mike downstairs at the bar. "Rye," he ordered in a deep toneless voice. "Make it good. Two glasses. Send it up to Room Ten."

He went back to the sofa, sat beside Sue Steiner's hunched form and placed a big hand on her shoulder. "Anybody know you came here?" he asked.

She was a moment answering, her face in her hands. "I—I wouldn't—I'd be dead like Peeps if they did. I used two taxis and a streetcar and went through a movie show, getting out through a side exit. I rang Maxie's night bell from the street and he unlocked the door and brought me up here."

Lonergan said: "Sue, what do you expect me to do for you if you won't talk?"

"I want you to do what Peeper and me first thought of. That's why he made the date for you to meet him here. I want you to pinch me for something, anything. Send me up for a stretch at Tehachepi or else—"

He shook his head slowly. "You'd have to talk if we pinched you, Sue. Even if I laid off, the boys at headquarters would make you talk."

She met his eyes. Her hand groped for his. She was desperate, pleading. "They don't have to know I got any connection to the Peeper's spot if you don't spill it. You can cover me, Rex. I'll go out and bust a window or something. You can grill me at the can and I'll spill something, any old thing that'll win me a stretch—"

The singing downstairs got louder. They were all singing some navy song and stamping their feet.

"You sure your spot's as bad as the Peeper's?" Lonergan asked.

"Foreigners—a bunch of tough foreigners that won't stop at nothing." She broke off.

Mascara ran down into her eyes and she put the gun on the sofa and fished in her purse for a soiled handkerchief. A ring came out with the crumpled linen, dropped into her lap—a big shiny ring. Her fist closed over it, instantly returned the ring to the purse.

"That damn singing," she mouthed bitterly. "Crazy drunken lugs!"

It was a steady roar of voices downstairs, a thunder of stamping feet. Lonergan could hardly hear the knocking at the door and the voice—"Here it is, Mr. Lonergan."

He left the sofa to unlock the door and let in Mike with the rye. Only it wasn't Mike with the rye.

Behind Lonergan, Sue Steiner let out a wild, high-pitched scream. A man elbowed the door back and slammed a long-barreled gun at Lonergan's head. Lonergan didn't have time to duck or to snatch out his revolver. The steel barrel took him on the side of the head, just above the ear, and he staggered sideways and down.

The crash of shooting came loud above the singing and stamping at the bar below. Lonergan, half blinded by his own blood running into one eye and pain-tears flooding both, struggled swiftly to his knees, wagging the fogginess from his brain. A second blow thudded dully, viciously at the top of his skull. There was an explosion like dynamite in a closed room— and he went under.

LONERGAN BLINKED STICKY film from his eyes, and the bartender's white scared face came into focus. "Geez, I thought they gotcha!" Mike said.

"I'm not shot, huh?"

"No, but there's a gash plowed over your ear. I poured rye on it."

Lonergan sat up and dug knuckles into his eyes, looked around groggily. "Somebody shot awful close, Mike," he said.

The bartender nodded. "It was two guys. I walk into the lower hall with the rye and there they are by the steps. One socks me down with a gun, but I don't go quite out. I can hear shooting up here and then they both come down lugging a dame."

Lonergan shot a swift glance toward the sofa. Sue Steiner wasn't there. He saw a dark wet spot on the rug—but no gun, no purse.

"I don't think she was dead," Mike said. "One of the guys had a hand on her mouth. They went out the street door. Must've been unlocked."

Lonergan got to his feet and went over to the sofa. He stooped over the dark heavy stain on the rug, the wet drops that led away from it. "She tried to shoot it out, I guess," he said. "Poor kid…."

He'd started to turn away from the sofa when something caught his eye and he bent quickly, scooped a hand into the tight space between the seat cushion and the plush arm-rest.

He looked at the heavy ring in his palm. Gold, like a signet ring, but instead of initials it bore, fitted into the gold, an onyx emblem—a double-headed eagle. This was the ring that had fallen from Sue's purse when she drew out her handkerchief, the ring she'd hastily concealed from him.

There was something else—it had been wedged with the ring—a crumpled newspaper clipping. He read it.

RUSSIAN PRINCESS VISITS CITY

Sometime last week Princess Tanya Andreva arrived from New York, slipping quietly into the city and taking residence at the Golden Gate Apartments where, until recognized yesterday, she was known merely as Miss Grace Hill.

When pressed for an interview the Princess explained that she is here only for a rest and prefers to remain incognito.

The Princess came to this country very recently from Paris, where she has spent most of her life since the Russian Revolution. She was accompanied by Alexander Southerland, her fiancé, a retired Virginia tobacco grower.

The beautiful Tanya has had a glamorously exciting life. The daughter of the Grand Duke Stanislas, cousin of the last Czar, she was a mere child at the time of the revolution, she fled Russia with her father and the twenty-three-year old Prince Ivan Meledoff, a cousin.

The fleeing party was led through Siberia and part of the Gobi Desert by a faithful Chinese servant. Attacked by bandits in the Gobi, the Grand Duke lost his life but the servant brought the Princess and Meledoff safely to Shanghai. Later the servant organized a party to return to the Gobi for the Grand Duke's body. Prince Ivan was lost on this expedition and was never heard from again.

It was rumored at that time that Princess Tanya was heir to a fortune in jewels, among the collection a priceless head-piece which had belong to Catherine the Great. It was never determined whether the jewels had come out of Russia with the escaping party.

Lonergan folded the clipping and stowed it in his vest pocket along with the ring. A frown knitted his brows in a shaggy V.

"You find something?" Mike prodded.

Lonergan didn't answer, but he'd found something all right. Sue had wanted him to find it. She'd tried to shoot it out with the men who'd crashed the room, failed, and got hit. In that brief moment of confused fighting she'd planted the ring and the clipping for Lonergan or investigating officers to find. It was all she'd had time to do. The tip was pretty vague.

LONERGAN CROSSED THE room to the hall. Downstairs Maxie Hymer stood by the street door, his hand at the padlock. He glanced up as Lonergan's foot creaked on the top step and grinned—too casually. "Hello, Rex. I was just making sure the door was locked."

Lonergan came down the stairs and walked over close to Maxie. The singing and stamping in the bar had stopped; there was only a low drone of talk.

"You just locked it," Lonergan accused flatly.

Maxie's eyes shifted from Lonergan's stare. He ran the tip of his tongue nervously on dry lips. "Why, no, Rex. I always keep—"

"You always keep it locked, sure. But you left it open a while ago, so some guys could get in. Now you're covering up for them. Who were they, Maxie?"

Maxie's eyes got big with innocence. "Did something go wrong, Rex?"

Lonergan took hold of Maxie's necktie. He didn't try any

rough stuff, just gripped Maxie's tie and drew Maxie's face toward him with a slow determined pull. "Let's not kid each other, Maxie. You know me pretty well and you know I can't take kidding."

He let that sink in, and Maxie squirmed a little and said: "Sure, I know that, Rex—"

"Now get this, Maxie. You had an eye out for Sue Steiner to show up tonight. As soon as she got here you tipped somebody. You unlocked that street door. Two tramps came in, shot Sue, tried to rub me, and scrammed with Sue. Who'd you tip, Maxie?"

Maxie began to crawl. "Honest to God—"

Lonergan's face had frozen into a grim half-smile. "I want to find who got Sue and who got the Peeper. You're going to help, Maxie. My friends never hold out on me and I only have friends in Frisco. The others—well, they go away, Maxie. They go lots of different places, but they go."

Maxie Hymer broke all at once. "O.K., Rex, I'll play. You got to cover me, though, Rex. It was Red Nolan. He said he was having all the places spotted for Sue, and to call if she came in. When I called he said to leave the street door open. You know how I stand with Nolan. I take his beer and I take his orders—I got to, Rex! You know that!" Maxie Hymer's voice took on a desperate whine. "I'm telling you this man to man, Rex, not to a cop. I can't afford to cross Nolan!"

Lonergan let go of Maxie's necktie as though it had become suddenly a slimy thing. "Ought to throw away that blue tie, Maxie. Yellow's your color."

He walked down the hall to an outside phone, called headquarters and told them he'd walked smack into a job. He told about Sue Steiner and ordered a radio broadcast on her, said there might be a connection to the Peeper's death. He didn't say anything about the newspaper clipping and the heavy Russian ring.

2

The Princess Tanya

THE MANAGEMENT AT the Golden Gate Apartments was careful about letting people in—especially late at night. Especially big men with dried blood on their collars. But Lonergan got in.

The woman who opened the ivory door to Apartment 13-B was tall and white-blond and shapely. She didn't look as if she had been raised in a convent. She didn't look coarse, either. She stood very straight-backed and full-curved in a long green gown. The tilt of her chin was aloof, confident.

"Princess?" Lonergan inquired.

Her china-blue eyes were cool and unsurprised as she frankly studied the dried blood on his head and collar. She bowed, only slightly.

"I'm from the police. It's important, or I'd come at another time."

The cool eyes moved away from his stained collar, took in his face. There was a little surprise now—a mild, unruffled surprise. She didn't invite him in with words but stood aside with an aloof attitude, and he walked into a long livingroom with marble fireplace and furniture that was artistic and probably frail.

"From the police," the princess explained to a tall, wide-shouldered man at the fireplace. The man was smoothly polished in a dinner jacket. He spoke to Lonergan in an accent that certainly wasn't Frisco and gestured to a chair. "Brandy?" he inquired. "Cordial, perhaps?"

The princess seated herself with supple grace on a small gilt stool and said to the tall man: "Whisky, Alexander. Policemen drink whisky."

Lonergan had a feeling she was kidding him. She did it with dignity, easily, but he still didn't like it. "Nothing for me, thanks," he said. Then, "It's about a young San Francisco girl. Her name is Sue Steiner. I'm not sure whether you know her or not, but—"

The princess leaned forward. "Sue? Do you mean my maid?"

"Maid?" Lonergan asked. Sue Steiner had done a lot of things in her life but he could never picture her in the role of maid to a Russian princess.

"A slim little thing. Very American. Dark hair. Speaks in a sort of slang."

"That sounds like Sue," Lonergan admitted.

"She has a brother," the princess went on. "Herbert Steiner was my chauffeur."

Lonergan was amazed again. "You mean the Peeper…." He broke off, adding: "When did you employ them?"

Princess Tanya looked away from him to the tall groomed man. "A day or so ago, wasn't it, Alexander?"

ALEXANDER BOWED AN agreement. Alexander, Lonergan thought, would probably bow agreement to anything the princess said. Alexander, he thought further, was probably a stuffed shirt.

"Find them through an employment agency?"

Lonergan asked that of the princess. She glanced at Alexander. Alexander said: "I employed them. Got them for the convenience of the princess during her stay here. Some party at the Mark Hopkins recommended them."

"Do you happen to remember who?"

Alexander shook his head. "Sorry. This party seemed respectable enough. Some gentleman. Met him at the bar."

"Oh," Lonergan said, because you could meet anybody at a bar.

"We are both strangers in San Francisco," Tanya explained. "I have never been here before. Mr. Southerland is from Virginia."

"Oh," said Lonergan again. "I thought Mr. Southerland would be French. His accent—"

Alexander flushed as though from an insult. "I have lived in Paris a good deal," he bit out.

"What do you wish to speak to us about?" the princess asked. "What about Sue?"

Lonergan had no patience with word-fencers. His methods were direct. He said: "Herbert Steiner, known to the police as the Peeper, was tortured and murdered tonight in a fruit car in the Southern Pacific freight yards. His sister, your maid, was a nice kid that could never keep from slipping off the straight-and-narrow. Sue was shot in a beer joint on the waterfront and carried away by a couple of gunmen."

The brows of the princess, those neatly penciled brows, drew together in a quick frown. "Surely," she said, "you don't think—"

Alexander moved away from the fireplace, waved his hand slightly as he interrupted: "The princess, of course, isn't concerned with the personal lives of her servants."

Princess Tanya Andreva looked at Alexander with languorous, satisfied eyes. Lonergan fished the heavy gold ring with the Russian double-headed eagle from his vest pocket and held it in his palm, his palm extended to the princess.

Her breath drew in sharply past parted lips. The languorous, satisfied look vanished from her eyes. "Why, that belongs to me!"

She was about to take it when Lonergan closed his fist on it. She looked startled. He said: "It'll be returned to you in due time. Just now it's evidence in a murder and kidnap case."

"Sue!" The princess faltered. "Sue must have stolen it. I missed it. I—" She didn't go on. Alexander Southerland said nothing but appeared very interested.

"I don't know how true it is," Lonergan said, "but I happened to read in the paper that you might have brought some important jewelry out of Russia at the time of the revolution. Now if this ring is part of a collection and you lost anything else, I suggest you let the police help you."

The princess tossed her white-blond head. "There was no collection," she stated flatly. "Rumors only. I have lost nothing but this ring which was one of the few things my father gave to me."

"You have nothing to report?"

"Nothing," she said, and Alexander Southerland echoed, "Nothing."

Lonergan got to his feet, flipped the heavy gold ring into the air as though tossing a coin; caught it "Thanks very much," he said. "Sorry to bother you this way."

THE STREET WAS cold, dark, and wet with fog. Lonergan paused on the brick stoop at the lighted entrance to the Golden Gate Apartments and fixed the collar of his overcoat closer around his neck and ears.

His roadster stood a little way down the block, on the other side. As he crossed the street a rhythmic rumbling came from the cable-slot between the narrow car tracks. A fog siren out on the Bay moaned dismally.

Lonergan stepped up off the cobblestones to the darkly glistening sidewalk. A tiny spark of light that might have been the tip of a cigarette vanished instantly. Yellow glow from a street lamp didn't penetrate the deep shadow of the delivery alley where the cigarette spark had vanished.

Lonergan's heels clicked on pavement as he passed the dark mouth of the alley. He wheeled sharply and went back. A flashlight in his hand sent a hard bright beam into the little canyon and shone on the man standing there.

"You want anything?" the man asked sourly. His face was sickly white in the beam of the flash; his hands were sunk deep into the full side pockets of a trench coat.

"No," Lonergan said. "I thought maybe you did."

"Not a thing. Got everything I need."

"How about smokes?" Lonergan asked in a flat husky voice. "That one you just put out in such a hurry—that your last?"

"No. You want to bum one?"

Lonergan ignored the question and then asked his own. "Suppose a cop came along and wanted to know what you were doing here? What would the answer be?"

"The answer?" A slow confident grin spread over the thin face that was so white in the flash-beam. "It'd be that I'm waiting for the boss, a Mr. Carmody. I drive for him. That Cadillac at the top of the hill is his. I'd show my license. I might even produce Mr. Carmody."

"And Mr. Carmody," Lonergan finished casually, "who is a tin-horn politician under Red Nolan's thumb, would say anything you wanted him to say." He snapped off the flash. "Well, so long, chauffeur. No hard feelings?"

"Not at all," came sourly from the dark. "Me, I like the friendly spirit in Frisco. Guys stop and ask if you want anything. I like that. Very nice."

Lonergan went down the street and got his roadster, drove to an all-night drug store around the block. He called head-quarters, got Hu Rawlins on the phone.

"Listen, Hu, want to work?"

"No," Hu Rawlins said firmly. "It's twelve o'clock. I'm not a doctor, just a cop. I quit—"

"Meet me," Lonergan went on briskly, "at the drug store, California and Hyde Streets. Ten minutes. Want you to shadow a guy that seems to be shadowing somebody else."

Hu Rawlins began, "Hey—" and started to add a lot of other things, but quit with an oath when he found he was expressing himself into a dead telephone.

RED NOLAN, BEER baron of the Bay Cities, had a big ugly house near the Presidio. Lonergan gave his name to a Chinaboy in a starched white jacket.

"You wait, pliz, thank you, Missa Lon-ey-gon?"

He didn't have to wait. From an archway down the hall Red Nolan's voice boomed cordiality and welcome. "This way, Rex! Just in time, fella! We're having a little fun!"

Lonergan stepped through the archway. The fun was a poker

set-up with drinks on a tea-wagon rolled close to the game table. Red Nolan shoved his chair away from the table and shook hands with Lonergan, grinning broad friendliness.

"This is swell, Rex. Guess you know the boys?"

Carmody, the politician, nodded casually. Judge Weseen of the Municipal Court smiled a "Hello, Rex," and Edward J. Cohen, Nolan's attorney, began to build Lonergan a highball on the tea-wagon. There were three other men at the card table, all "business" associates of Nolan.

"How about sitting in?" Nolan invited.

"Not on my salary," Lonergan told him.

"Hell, Rex!" Nolan pulled a fat wallet from his breast pocket, spoke to Cohen crisply. "Give Rex a stack. This is on me."

Lonergan shook his head slightly, his eyes stayed on Red Nolan. "A couple of guys tried to erase me tonight down at Maxie Hymer's. I thought they looked like a pair of your boys, Red."

Nolan fingered a stack of chips on the table, appeared very surprised. "Rex," he said, "you only have to name them. Tell me who they are and they're canned. I don't have much to do with how my staff spend their evenings, but if they get drunk and monkey with my friends—well, they're washed up, Rex. I mean that. I won't have it."

"That's damned nice of you," Lonergan said. "Guess I'll be shoving off."

"Don't rush," Nolan objected. "Hell, you haven't even told us why you dropped in."

"I'd be wasting my time if I did. Even a cop can see that. If I asked about Sue Steiner and the Peeper, you wouldn't know them. If I asked about sending some boys to Maxie's—hell, you and these poker-pals've been playing the pasteboards for twenty-four hours without interruption. For instance"—Lonergan's eyes went hard and demanding on each man at the table—"Red Nolan hasn't had any telephone calls, has he?"

Judge Weseen cleared his throat pompously as though about to deliver a legal decision from the bench. "I don't believe we've been bothered with the phone for twenty-four hours." He smiled fraternally around the table. "We take our poker seriously, eh, gentlemen?"

Lonergan hadn't removed his hat. Now he yanked the brim low over his brows, shrugged his big shoulders deeper into his overcoat. He turned his broad back on the men at the poker table, said between his teeth, "My turn's coming," and walked out of the room.

3

The Laughing Buddha

KYLE'S SHIP CAFÉ on Market Street has a central location. Rex Lonergan often used it for his personal headquarters. It was approaching one o'clock in the morning when he barged through the steamy glass doors and strode into the small bar off the foyer.

Hu Rawlins, who'd gone to work shadowing the man Lonergan had discovered in the delivery alley opposite the Golden Gate Apartments, was supposed to phone the dope to Kyle's if he got anything.

The phone rang as the bartender nodded a greeting to Lonergan. "Bet this is for you again," the man said, answering. He nodded, handed the receiver to Lonergan. Hu Rawlins' voice came over the wire.

"Listen, Rex, I'm calling from the Tuey Far Low Restaurant in Chinatown. Tailed that guy down here from the Golden Gate Apartments. He stayed holed up in that alley till a woman came out of the Golden Gate. She's a beauty, Rex, sort of a Greta Garbo. Long green dress under a white coat—"

"Yeah," Lonergan cut in, "the Russian princess."

"I dunno about that. Anyway, she got in a cab that pulled up for her. Right away this punk sneaked out of the alley and ducked into a Caddy sedan he had parked at the top of the hill. He trailed your princess and I trailed him. He's still in China-town. It's all crazy. Know where the beauty went?"

"No."

"Sing Kee's laundry on Grant Avenue! Sent the cab away and walked right in. The punk stayed outside. I parked down the street. In a minute she came out of the laundry with an old Chinaman. The two of them walked down the street and went up the hill by the Green Dragon. They turned down the alley above Grant and went in a door. They're still there."

"How about the punk?"

"He seems as dumb about it as I am. He keeps walking up and down the alley, smoking."

"Listen, Hu, we can't tail them into Chinese places," Loner-gan said. "We need help. Go over to Sing Kee's, he's a friend of mine—and tell him to lend us a good Chinese. Snap into it. I'll meet you in front of the Tuey Far Low in five minutes."

HU RAWLINS AND the slim, wiry little Chinese that was

Sing Wong, eldest son of Sing Kee, head of the Five Families Tong in Chinatown, were waiting when Lonergan got there.

"They're still in there," Rawlins said. "Know what it is? A Buddhist temple."

"A what?"

Sing Wong, very American-looking in a dark business suit, spoke with a clear educated English. "That's correct, Lieutenant. It's called the Temple of the Laughing Buddha."

"You mean it's on the up-and-up?"

"Absolutely. The temple has been kept secret only because the priest, Chung Yuk, has wished to avoid the influence of Occidental religion. Chung Yuk is sincere. For six years the temple has been a sort of branch of the Buddhist faith."

Lonergan stroked his chin. "Can you think of any reason why a Russian princess would go there?"

"Curiosity, perhaps?"

Lonergan grinned. "Not after one o'clock on a foggy morning."

"You'd like to look in the temple?"

"Yeah, but I can't. I'm known to this princess as a cop. I don't want her to know I'm watching her."

"I can," Sing Wong offered, "allow you a look into the temple in an unusual way. You won't be seen."

It was an unusual way, all right. Up a flight of dim musty stairs to a Chinese rooming-house, then down a narrow corridor, through two heavy wood doors that were not locked.

Only Lonergan followed Sing Wong. Hu Rawlins had remained at the head of the alley above Grant Avenue to keep an eye on the shadow, and to be ready to follow in case the princess and her old Chinese companion left the temple.

"I must ask you," Sing Wong said in a whisper, "to close your eyes to suspicions of unlawful doings in this building. It is run independently of the temple. The lower classes of Chinese rent these rooms for pipe-smoking and other things. I am known to the proprietor as a friend."

Lonergan nodded, and Sing Wong tapped knuckles on a door that was all red, gold, and green in intricate dragon and serpent designs. The door opened. Sing Wong talked to a fat little Chinaman, money changed hands and a key was given to Lonergan's escort.

Still another door had to be passed, this by the key. Lonergan followed Sing Wong along a dim silent corridor into a small room.

"At one time," Sing Wong explained, "the quarters now occupied by Chung Yuk and his Buddhist temple were part of this rooming-house. A passage still connects. You will see."

They entered a closet, went through a spring-panel into darkness. Sing Wong's hand touched Lonergan's arm, guided him on soft carpet only a short way into pitch-blackness. Then there was a light, soft, yellow, the wavering light of candles. Sing Wong had parted a curtain and they were looking through a carved teakwood grill into the temple of the Laughing Buddha.

THE FLOOR WAS some feet lower than the one upon which the two men stood spying. A short flight of steps led down to the temple floor-level. The grill, the curtain, was to shut off the disused connection to the rooms above, but there was a metal catch and hinges on the door-like grill.

The priest, Chung Yuk, droned weird prayers. His altar was a bronze figure on a heavy table, a figure of a Buddha some three feet high, two feet broad. The statue sat with fat legs crossed and fat hands resting on the knees. The round naked belly had a bloated look.

But the thing about the bronze figure that held Lonergan's eyes was its face, a full-cheeked, grinning face, ugly, stiff. In the moment that he studied it, he had a feeling that this Buddha had once been a living thing; that, living, it had seen some cruel joke of man and had broken into hard lewd laughter. Then some magic had turned it to bronze and the laugh remained molded in greenish metal through the ages.

Sing Wong's hand made a slight pressure on Lonergan's arm, but the cop had already seen what the young Chinese wanted to call to his attention.

Princess Tanya Andreva knelt before the altar. Her white-skinned beauty, her shapely vital body as she knelt, and the bright worldliness of her expensive clothes made her appear out of place in the temple, a Twentieth Century woman thrust back into ancient China. Joss sticks burned before the Buddha. Incense floated thick and blue in the stagnant air, its warm perfume strong in Lonergan's nose.

The other person kneeling at the altar was an aged Chinese, thin and bent. Under a black skull cap his face was the texture of dark leather, wrinkled, sunken in deep hollows under his high cheek bones. His eyes seemed unimpressed with the ceremony before the Buddha.

Chung Yuk, the priest, ceased his droning prayer. The long brocaded robe swished on the dusty floor as he went through the narrow archway behind the altar.

As soon as he had gone the old Chinese and the Russian woman glanced nervously at each other. Tanya reached out a soft white hand and touched the cold green base of the Buddha. Almost, it was a caress, as though the fat figure were a thing alive, or a thing that symbolized a living memory.

The old man reached out, too. There was nothing of a caress in his touch. His bony yellow hand was a claw, reaching out to clutch.

Immediately, Chung Yuk returned through the arch with fresh joss sticks. The Russian princess and her companion had drawn in their hands swiftly, and the priest didn't notice anything as he began to burn the sticks in continuation of the ceremony.

Then it was over. Tanya Andreva and her Chinese companion rose to leave.

Instantly, Sing Wong dropped the curtain into place over the carved grill and the weird temple scene was gone from Lonergan like the abrupt end of a dream.

OUTSIDE, ON GRANT Avenue, the fog was as thick and wet as ever, but it seemed somehow invigorating after the incense of the temple and the decay of the doubtful Chinese rooming-house.

"The lady's Oriental companion," Sing Wong explained to Lonergan, "is called Gin Lem. He is a stranger to the city, having arrived perhaps two months ago. He is employed as a night-worker in my father's laundry."

"Will you keep him spotted for me?"

"My honorable father and his family," Sing Wong said sincerely, "always look for opportunities to be of assistance to you, Lieutenant. America is our country. We respect its law and its officers."

They were at the mouth of the dark alley above Grant. A shadow loomed out of deeper shadow in a doorway and became the bulky figure of Hu Rawlins.

"They just came out that alley door from the temple," Hu advised. "The lovely lady went one way and the Chinaman went back to the laundry. That punk, the shadow, put in a phone call from the Tuey Far Low. Now he's hanging out front. Seems to be waiting for somebody. I think the dame's gone to her cab; it's still waiting up Grant."

"Tail her," Lonergan snapped. "Wong will hang on Gin Lem, the Chinese. I'll watch the punk."

4

They Serve—and Die

DAWN IN CHINATOWN came imperceptibly. The roof of fog hanging heavy over buildings changed to a cold gray mist through which thin daylight filtered into the narrow street.

Lonergan, having posted himself around the corner from the Tuey Far Low, stamped chilled feet on the pavement and kept rubbing circulation into his hands. Long ago Hu Rawlins had left the Quarter following the Russian woman, and long ago Sing Wong had gone into his father's laundry to keep an eye on the old man known as Gin Lem.

Lonergan continued to watch the small thin man he called the "punk." There had been a number of phone calls from the Tuey Far Low and finally a return call.

Twenty minutes after the punk received this call an

old-model Packard Touring cruised down Grant and stopped. Black side-curtains with cracked yellow isinglass partially concealed the two men inside. The punk had a talk with them. Then he went down the street, entered his Cadillac and swung it around so it faced in the direction of Market Street and the Packard. In the short block between the two cars that pointed toward each other, waiting, was the laundry of Sing Kee.

Lonergan didn't take chances on a lone play. The situation called for help. He'd gone in the kitchen of the Tuey Far Low and phoned headquarters the license numbers of the two cars and complete descriptions. All around Chinatown, cops in radio cars would be cruising.

The strap watch on Lonergan's wrist showed 5:14. A dairy truck rolled by toward Market. A light car passed with bundles of morning papers. The starter on the Packard across Grant growled briefly. The motor sputtered to life.

Lonergan sauntered around the corner, unbuttoning his overcoat and slipping his right hand to the revolver butt at his left armpit. Walking north on Grant Avenue, gray and cold with daybreak, he saw the Cadillac further along pull away from the curb and start his way in low gear.

The Packard Touring headed slowly toward the Cadillac. In between, a stooped old Chinaman shuffled along the sidewalk, one claw-like hand holding the collar of his black jacket close to a thin yellow throat to keep out the morning fog. He had come out of Sing Kee's laundry. The night's work was over. It was Gin Lem shuffling home.

The Packard swerved into the curb with a squawking of brakes. Across the street the Cadillac slid to a stop.

Gin Lem shot fearful eyes at both cars. He began to run.

Then he stopped still. His hand left his collar, jerked to his waist, digging under the loose black jacket, hesitating.

A big man in a cloth overcoat jumped from the Packard to the sidewalk with a sawed-off shotgun in his hands. "Hey, Chinky! Get in the buggy!"

Lonergan ran four long strides and shifted sideways, ducking into the doorway of a closed meat market. He had his gun out. "Hold it!" he shouted. "Police!"

The shotgun came up. Lonergan threw himself backwards. Two blasts from the shotgun shattered glass in the front of the meat market.

LONERGAN, ON HANDS and knees, stuck his head from the doorway. Down the sidewalk old Gin Lem went into a swift crouch. Something like dull silver flashed from his hand with credible speed.

The man with the shotgun jumped back and folded into the gutter, a knife-hilt sticking from his belly. The other man in the Packard got out, halfway, hammered at Gin Lem with an army automatic.

The bullets jerked the body of the old Chinese, twisted it around. His legs locked together at the ankles and buckled at the knees. Before he collapsed to the pavement, Lonergan banged four shots at the man with the automatic. At least one was a hit. The man sat down, quickly and dazed, on the running-board of the Packard. Across the street in the Cadillac, the punk lifted up a heavy shotgun, sighted.

Lonergan fired twice, too fast, and crawled back in the doorway just in time. The shotgun, automatic, threw lots of lead in rapid dynamite explosions. More glass went out over

Lonergan's head and jagged pieces showered his overcoat and tinkled on the concrete under him. Somebody's hard voice yelled unclear orders.

Lonergan fingered fresh cartridges into the empty chambers of the revolver, snapped the swing-cylinder into the frame. Out of sight, two pistols made echoing noises in the street.

The punk in the Cadillac raced by the meat market in low gear. He drove with one hand, firing at Lonergan in the doorway with a pistol as he drove. None of the shots were any good.

Lonergan kneeled erect and blasted twice at the car. It kept going. He tried again. It still kept going. He leaned around the edge of the doorway. The Packard was pulling away from him fast. The man Gin Lem had knifed wasn't in the gutter. His buddy must have picked him up.

Sing Wong was in front of the laundry, hunched over with his forearms clamped to his abdomen but still on his feet. He walked around in small circles, wobbly-legged, the muscles of his face bunched and contorted, and a revolver hanging limply to a finger by its trigger-guard.

Lonergan ran forward into the middle of the street so Sing Wong wouldn't be in the way. He sighted high, not at the gas tank. He wanted to blast right through the top fabric for the driver.

When his gun clicked empty a siren many blocks away screamed authority. The Packard swerved on screeching tires, skidded, righted itself, and roared down the hill to the waterfront.

Lonergan walked toward Sing Wong who still staggered in smaller and smaller circles, hunched over, pressing his abdomen. "Wong…" he began huskily.

Sing Wong checked his staggering, avoided Lonergan's helping arm and drew himself very straight and confident. "I am sorry, Lieutenant. I came from the laundry too late. Very stupid. My father will get a doctor for me and then apologize to you for his son's wooden stupidity."

Lonergan stood still, his hands at his sides. Sing Wong said again, "I am sorry, Lieutenant," and walked erect and unsteady into the laundry, leaving a trail of red wet spots behind him.

Lonergan blinked his eyes twice and rubbed his left hand across his hard face. The knuckles of his right hand, gripping his empty revolver, got white, and he said something profanely determined between clenched teeth. Police sirens seemed to be wailing all over Frisco.

RAIN SPATTERED STEADILY on the windows. Lonergan stood spread-legged in the hall outside the morgue, smoked a cigarette without ever taking it from his mouth, and watched Hu Rawlins who was coming toward him, alone.

"Where's Tanya Andreva?" Lonergan asked.

"On her way, Rex. She's got a guy with her—a dude. Big tobacco-grower or something."

"Alexander Southerland," Lonergan explained. "She's going to marry him."

Hu Rawlins said: "I didn't get anything out of tailing her. She went to the Golden Gate Apartments straight from Chinatown. This fellow dropped in on her this morning just after you got in touch with me about bringing her down…

Rawlins broke off and added: "Say, that was an awful mess I heard about in Chinatown. Do you think the princess met the old Chinaman and went with him to the temple just to put the finger on him for the punk?"

Lonergan shrugged.

Princess Tanya Andreva, dressed strikingly in black fur, was coming down the corridor on the arm of Alexander Southerland. Her eyes were cool blue under a black turban-like hat.

"You wished to see me, officer?" she inquired.

Lonergan nodded curtly. "We'd like an identification, if possible."

Hu Rawlins held the door open. Lonergan gestured politely, and then followed the princess and her escort into the morgue. From behind their backs he gave a high-sign to the attendant who was sitting on a chair eating a ham sandwich. The attendant got up with the sandwich still in his hand. With his other hand he opened a cabinet door, one of many along the wall. Iced air rushed from the compartment. The attendant tugged out a roller slab and flipped back the sheet from a corpse.

"It's Gin Lem!" The princess moaned. All natural color went from her cheeks, but she gave no other signs of faintness. "What…?" she began.

"Shot," Lonergan told her. "This morning in Chinatown. We happen to know that you paid him a visit at the Sing Kee Laundry."

Alexander Southerland appeared very calm and dignified. He could be that way, even in a morgue. One of his arms was about the supple, black-furred waist of the princess—in case she needed support.

"Is this the—ah, servant?" he asked her.

Blue eyes, no longer cool, rather hot and resentful, remained fixed on the leathery face of the dead Gin Lem.

"May we go outside?" the princess suggested.

"Certainly," Alexander Southerland said, as though he, rather than the law, had authority there. They went to the corridor.

"Would you mind telling us what you know about this Gin Lem?" Lonergan asked the question directly of the princess Tanya Andreva, his back to Southerland.

THE WOMAN HESITATED. She arranged the full collar of her fur coat close about a smooth white throat. Her eyes had a far-away look. "It goes back—so many years. I was just a little girl and we had to flee from Russia."

She paused again, her mind, apparently, crammed with distant pictures and memories.

Lonergan said: "I believe I read something about that."

"We had to escape. Gin Lem was young and strong, a servant to the Grand Duke Stanislas, my father. Gin Lem knew routes through Siberia and China. He was our guide. With him we felt safe from assassins and bandits and adventurers.

"No. It was not the fault of Gin Lem. One night—I remember well—we had taken shelter in a deserted monastery on the edge of the Gobi Desert. China was so big and desolate. Bandits came. My father stayed to fight them, to hold them off. We fled in the night with Gin Lem."

"We?" Lonergan asked.

"Myself and an older cousin, Prince Ivan Meledoff. We got safely to Shanghai. Later Gin Lem returned to the Gobi with Prince Meledoff and a party. My father was dead—the bandits. Prince Meledoff became lost. We never saw him again, and I was almost alone except for Gin Lem."

"Servant?" Lonergan prompted.

She nodded. "Yes, for many years. After I came out of the convent in France he became more guardian than servant. A year ago he left Paris to come to America. He came finally to San Francisco. When I traveled here, it is natural that I should see him, the old friend. I saw him last night at the laundry."

"You don't know what enemies he had?"

Southerland stepped between Lonergan and the woman. "Of course not," he put in. "The princess, as we mentioned before, is not concerned with the personal lives of her servants."

No, Lonergan thought bitterly, not concerned with the personal lives of her servants.… Yet, Peeper Steiner, employed as her chauffeur got tortured to death. Sue Steiner, employed as her maid, had been shot and kidnaped. And Gin Lem, servant from the past, guide during the escape of a royal family from Russia during the revolution, had just been shot to death in Chinatown.

Lonergan said: "I hope you're telling everything."

"It would be absurd to think otherwise," the princess replied haughtily.

"An insult!" Southerland added. Lonergan ignored him.

"I would like," the princess said, "to have the body of Gin Lem. I would like to arrange in the Chinese quarter the kind of funeral my servant would have wanted. His body must be returned to native soil for burial."

"We can release the body most anytime," Lonergan informed her. "A careful autopsy isn't necessary in this case. I saw the cause of death."

"Thank you, officer," the woman said briskly.

Southerland bowed. They walked together down the corridor, turned off.

Hu Rawlins, leaning against the door to the morgue, grinned. "And that's that."

Lonergan didn't grin. "Tail her," he ordered. "If she won't tell us the whole story, we'll dig it out. Don't let that princess stuff get you."

5

Burial Party

AS AN ORIENTAL spectacle, the funeral of Gin Lem was a flop. Fine rain fell in a steady drizzle. It soaked the banners across Chinatown's narrow main street, made the cloth hang limp, soggy, and it ran together the colors in the paper lanterns.

Not many people turned out. The Chinese of the Quarter watched casually from shop doorways as the procession went by and then returned to business. After all, Gin Lem was new to Frisco, and while his death made a splash in the papers, it was only of passing interest to the slant-eyed people who lived huddled in the district surrounding Grant Avenue.

Princess Tanya Andreva followed the procession. That was why Rex Lonergan followed it. The princess rode in a green Chevrolet sedan driven by Alexander Southerland. Lonergan strolled along the sidewalk in the thin rain, his coat collar high and the brim of his wet felt hat yanked low. He had to dodge his head now and then to avoid the umbrellas of a scattering of white spectators who lined the curb.

Rex Lonergan reached the intersection where California street leveled off briefly on Grant Avenue before plunging again into its steep descent Bayward. He was just ahead of the procession. He ducked into a doorway and shook rain from his hat.

Out on the intersection a traffic cop in a shiny raincoat put up his hand to halt a cable car that had come down the hill to cross Grant.

"It's sure a tame funeral."

That came from Hu Rawlins as he joined Lonergan in the doorway. Lonergan didn't glance at him, his eyes fixed on a sedan that was parked over the edge of the hill on California. A man had leaned his head from the driver's seat to look back up the hill. His face, in the instant Lonergan saw it, brought back a sharp memory of that room over Maxie Hymer's Waterfront Club and a big man who had socked Lonergan with a gun.

"What's the matter?" Rawlins asked.

"Where's your car, Hu?"

"Just around the corner. Why?"

"Get to it," Lonergan said crisply. "Watch that sedan parked across from the church. This funeral may not be as tame as you think."

Hu Rawlins started to ask a question. He didn't finish it. The hearse had moved slowly into the intersection. Up the hill on California Street, brakes screeched. A light coupé came down fast, skidding almost sideways on the slippery surface of California. The driver worked his wheel in quick strokes, skidded clear of the halted cable car, gunned his motor and crashed head-on into the side of the white hearse.

The impact of the collision spun the hearse as though it had been on a turntable. The coupé bounced away from the crash, teetered on two wheels, rocked, and fell heavily to its side with a raining tinkle of broken glass.

EVERYBODY NEAR THE intersection surged toward the scene. Lonergan bumped into a couple of running people, got jabbed in the cheek with an umbrella.

The head and shoulders of the driver of the coupé appeared out of the side window that was now pointing skyward to the rain. He blinked his eyes, gaped foolishly at the cop. "Too much-a da rain," he said in an Italian accent. "Too much-a da brakes."

Lonergan glanced over the heads of the crowd and saw the man who was parked in the sedan over the edge of the intersection wave slightly to a pedestrian. The pedestrian, a tall lean man in belted tweed overcoat, nodded a reply and pushed briskly through the crowd to the overturned coupé. He presented a small white card to the Italian.

"Mark J. Hancock," he clipped. "Attorney-at-law. Don't say a word."

The Italian grinned. "You betcha my life, Mr. Hancock. I don't say da word."

The police officer glanced angrily at the lawyer, said: "He's pinched for reckless driving."

Hancock smiled in a smug way. "Anything you like, officer. This accident…."

Instantly, then, two pistol shots cracked sharply over the chattering voices of the crowd. It was not on the intersection. The shots came from a block back on Grant, from the funeral procession that had been halted.

Lots of things happened swiftly. The man over the edge of the hill apparently took the shots as a signal. He released his brake. The sedan coasted away from the curb, going down the hill. He threw out his clutch and added his motor to the car's momentum.

Hu Rawlins, driving alone in a squad car, raced across the intersection, scattering the crowd with his siren, and sped over the edge of the hill in pursuit of the sedan. Back on Grant Avenue startled cries, shouts of surprise and terror, came simultaneously from dozens of throats.

Lonergan ran back. No people got in his way. The spectators at the funeral, professional mourners, who'd remained in the procession even at the time of the accident, had scattered to the protection of doorways, and Lonergan had a clear view of the avenue. He saw the rear of a big car as it sped away from him, saw it skid wide at the next corner and disappear off Grant.

Its going left the avenue deserted except for the green Chevrolet in which the princess and her escort had followed the procession. This car was stalled down the block, empty.

Alexander Southerland sat on the sidewalk curbing, bent over, pressing both hands to his head. His hat was gone and blood oozed from between his fingers, dripped to the pavement and diluted itself in rain water.

Lonergan said: "What happened? Quick!"

"Abducted," Southerland clipped. "The excitement down the street—I started to get out. A big car was at the curb. They came and grabbed the princess. They took her. I tried…."

Alexander Southerland took his hands from his head and looked at them. The sight of his own blood sickened him, frightened him. His face got suddenly white. Lonergan knew the sign; he put out both arms and caught the sagging body as Southerland fainted.

ALL THE REST of that rainy day newsboys shouted extras on the streets. At the Civic Center officials were red-faced with temper and worry. Hannaman, the D.A., gave out vague statements to the press that his office would prosecute the criminals to the full extent of the law. Chief Ryan, of the police department, passed cigars to the reporters and said that these puzzling crimes undoubtedly were due to out-of-town gangsters.

After the reporters left, Ryan mopped his forehead and muttered to Lonergan: "Just when election's coming up, too. We got to nail these birds, Rex. What a tangle! The papers—"

"The hell with the papers." Lonergan sat up in the chair. "We released Alexander Southerland. He doesn't know any reason why the princess would be kidnaped unless it's for ransom. He never saw Gin Lem till he came to the morgue; he doesn't know anything at all. On top of that, there's still no word from Hu Rawlins—not a word since he started chasing that sedan."

BY LATE EVENING there was still no word from Hu Rawlins. Then, for the fifth time, Lonergan went around to Kyle's Ship Café, and the bartender said: "That Rawlins phoned. He's at the same place he was before—in front of the Tuey Far Low in Chinatown."

Rawlins was there, all right, waiting in the dark and in rain that had become a downpour. "Listen, Rex," he hurried, "I was chasing the guy in the sedan down the Penninsula, see? I wanted to nail him. Then I switched on my short wave and got a broadcast that the princess was snatched from the funeral procession. I put two and two together and figured a stooge crashed into the hearse just to make a little excitement and cover up while some other guys nabbed her."

"Right," Lonergan agreed. "Whoever the outfit is, they must've been tipped the woman had police shadows."

"This guy in the sedan was parked there to see everything came off O.K. Now I began to figure it probably wouldn't do much good to nail him—he wouldn't talk. I decided to tail him around and see if he wouldn't lead me to the snatch set-up."

"Well?"

"Well, I trailed him to Palo Alto. He ditched the hot sedan and spent all afternoon covering his tracks. He thought he'd ditched me but I followed him here. I think this is the end of the trail."

"Where'd he go?" Lonergan asked.

"That Chink rooming-house where you went with Sing Wong to get your peek at the screwy Chinese temple. About twenty minutes ago."

Lonergan took Hu's arm, walked him down the deserted sidewalk in the heavy rain. "We'll do it this way, Hu. I'll get some Chinese from Sing Kee's tong to smuggle me into the rooming-house. You throw out a net of radio cruisers in the Quarter. I'll take a gander at the set-up in the rooming-house. If the princess is held there, I'll give the high-sign for a raid. If she isn't, we'll send the cops away. No use stirring up a hornet's nest till we find her. If I don't come out in half an hour bust in with the boys."

"Hell, man!" Rawlins objected, "you can't go in there! If those guys nab you—"

"Call headquarters," Lonergan clipped.

"You punks won't call nobody!"

The command came from behind them as they walked—a harsh voice. Lonergan started to turn his head and something hard jabbed into his spine. "Keep that mugg around! Keep walking, or you both take it in the back."

They kept walking, their faces grimly frontward. Behind them heels clicked on the pavement.

"Across the street, muggs. We go upstairs."

The two police detectives walked side by side through the rain. They might have been just a couple of friends out for an evening's fun in the Chinese Quarter.

Up the flight of musty stairs, down the dim corridor. Lonergan, jabbed in the back with a gun muzzle, opened both the unlocked doors. Then they stood before the heavy door that was painted red, gold, and green, with dragon and serpent designs.

"Knock," the man behind Lonergan ordered.

He knocked and the door opened. A fat Chinese started to close it again, but a white man stuck out a hand and held it back. It was the thin, pasty-faced man—the punk.

"Look what I found, Bert. Dicks, smart guys. Wanted to call their buddies but I thought different."

The punk nodded slowly, a wise smug grin on his thin lips. "Come in, boys," he invited coldly. "Why is a cop a cop? I been wanting to know for a long time."

"It's the fun," Rawlins said sourly.

"With me, it's the salary," Lonergan said.

As he said that he whipped his fist in a sharp swing at the punk's face. Out of the corner of his eye, he saw Rawlins follow up the lead and turn on the man behind them.

The punk's head jerked back. Lonergan sent in a quick left-right, but somebody had gotten behind him with a sap. He went down, groggy. The blackjack thudded continuously on his skull. From far away came the voice of the punk, hard, vicious. "Out of the way, you! It's my turn at him!"

6

The Buddha Bleeds

A FLAT YELLOW surface above him got clear as Lonergan stared up at it. It was a ceiling; the dark jagged lines were cracks in the plaster.

"Hi, Rex," said a low voice.

Lonergan tried to turn over, couldn't. He discovered, with returning consciousness, that his arms were folded under the small of his back, his forearms pressed parallel and lashed together. He tried to move his legs; they were held securely at the ankles.

He rolled his head to one side on the dusty bare floor and saw the prone figure of Hu Rawlins. Hu said, "Hi," again, smiling. He'd had a bloody nose, and in the dim light of the room his face was a mess. "Whatever we're going to do," he began, "we better hop to it, Rex. I think most of them have left the joint."

Lonergan rolled his aching head the other way. Lying on a stained mattress was another person, a woman. She was in a bad way, moaning deep in her throat as she slept. He recognized the profile—Sue Steiner.

Hu Rawlins said: "They were in the next room—I could hear 'em through the wall. They had a woman in there, the princess, I guess. From what they said I figure they've been torturing her ever since the snatch at the funeral. I think one of the guys in there was Red Nolan. He said, 'I know something the lady won't like', and she screamed. She began to talk. I guess it was what they'd been waiting to hear. Nolan says, 'Where is this temple?' and I guess she spills it because he says, 'Fine, you can take us there right now.' They went out. Then you came to."

Lonergan explored the binding on his forearms by moving his fingers. It was adhesive tape. "How strong are your teeth?" he asked.

Rawlins grinned. "Like a bull pup's."

Lonergan arched his back and threw himself into a side roll that carried him over the floor to Rawlins. He lay propped on his side, his taped forearms within reach of Hu's teeth. Rawlins worked the end loose, then rolled the other way to unwrap the tape with his free fingers.

The whole operation didn't take over a couple of minutes. Lonergan sat up, tore the tape from his ankles. While he was releasing Rawlins, Sue Steiner groaned to wakefulness.

"Rex," she murmured, "I left those things for you. I knew you'd come for me." A crying laugh caught in her throat. "You'll get them, eh, Rex?"

"You bet, Sue."

She was unconscious again as Lonergan helped Hu Rawlins to his feet. Lonergan moved silently to the closed door and dropped his right hand under his left armpit, on an empty shoulder holster.

Hu's jaw dropped. "You still got a gun?"

"No," Lonergan said, "but maybe I won't need one."

His left hand turned the doorknob soundlessly. The door wasn't locked. He drew it inward by slow inches. Before him was part of the dim hall. He took a careful step forward.

DOWN AT THE far end of the corridor a man read a newspaper under a cobwebby electric bulb. He sat on a low stool, his profile to Lonergan. It was the punk.

Unarmed, you can't rush a man who's nearly fifty feet away—not when the man's coat bulges with a holstered gun. Lonergan didn't try it. He took another quiet step into the corridor. His left hand found a loose cigarette in his pocket and put it between tight lips. All his movements were calm and deliberate. His right hand stayed a fist concealed under his coat where his empty holster was.

"O.K., punk," he snapped coldly. "Pull it."

The punk looked up from the paper, shivered in surprise. His hands didn't move except to let go of the newspaper. Then he stood up, very slowly, still not moving his hands.

Lonergan faced him down the long hall. "I said, pull it!" he challenged again. "Civilian always gets the first shot—police regulation."

The punk didn't move. Lonergan's mouth curved into a cynical smile. The unlit cigarette tilted with the curve of his mouth. He drew a match from his pocket with his left hand, flared the head with a scratch of his thumbnail. Slowly, confidently, he lifted the burning match to the cigarette, his eyes never leaving the punk and his other hand not moving from its ominous hiding-place under his armpit.

"What're you waiting for?" he demanded.

The punk's thin face twitched. The punk's right hand trembled a little, became a tense claw.

Lonergan flipped away the match and started down the long hall in slow firm steps, closing the distance between them. Smoke from his cigarette crawled up his cynical, challenging face, drifted back from his head in fine swirling streamers.

The punk shifted his feet uneasily, awkwardly. He watched with narrow blinking eyes as Lonergan made his steady, confident advance down the hall.

"Geez…" he muttered weakly.

"It's not easy to kill a man with a gun," Lonergan told him calmly. "A lot of punks think it is. They think all you got to do is pull a trigger and another redskin bites the dust. A punk tried to rub me in a room over Maxie Hymer's; he was right on top of me—and missed. A punk never learns. Give him a rod and a man to shoot at, and he thinks he's a killer."

Lonergan's slow deadly march came to a halt only three feet from the punk. The punk repeated, "Geez!" not weakly now, but desperately, from a tight nervous throat. Still his hand didn't move toward the gun under his coat.

Lonergan smiled and bowed. "Maybe you like it still closer?" he inquired with mock courtesy.

He took another step. He took a swing. The swing came from his idle left hand, brought a hard-knuckled fist against the punk's narrow jaw. The punk was slammed back to the wall. Lonergan gave him a right, and then another left.

Feet pounded on the floor. Hu Rawlins came up, saying: "What's the charge for that show?"

Lonergan had caught the falling gunman in his arms. A long-barreled Mauser automatic left the punk's holster and became Lonergan's.

He said, "Gutless son"—and yanked a snub-nosed revolver from the punk's coat and gave it to Rawlins along with the sagging weight of the punk himself.

"Tie the guy, Hu. Scram for some law. Be sure they cover that alley by the temple."

LONERGAN PALMED OPEN a door. Frail yellow light filtered into the empty room and showed him another door, opposite. It was a closet door; he'd been through it before.

He went through it again now, through the spring-panel into the black passage which had once been a connecting way between these musty rooms and the place that was now the Temple of the Laughing Buddha. His shoes were soundless on old carpet. He groped his way forward, his left hand guiding him along a plaster wall. Voices came to him from the temple.

A woman's voice, astonished—"Alexander!"

And a man's voice, growling—"Thought you wanted me to handle this. Thought you wanted to keep clear and trick the dame?" That was the deep husky voice of Red Nolan.

There was no answer. Red Nolan spoke again. "Figured we might double-cross you, eh? Wanted to be on hand for the blow-off, eh? Well, get this, you phony Russian! I don't double-cross, see? When I—"

A few words snapped briskly in a language Lonergan didn't know. It was a man's voice. A woman's voice cut into it, crying wildly: "Alexander! You speak Russian! You—"

Gun-shots interrupted that. The temple, hidden from Lonergan by the heavy curtain across the grill, thundered with guns. Lonergan groped along the dark passage wall, the round butt of the Mauser gripped in his fist.

The shooting from the temple ceased as Lonergan found the curtain. The woman cried out again. There was a ringing blow of metal against metal.

Lonergan held back the curtain and peered through the grill-work into the soft yellow light of the temple. He saw Red

Nolan's body sprawled grotesquely on the floor. Another man sprawled, there, too.

He glanced off to the temple altar, hazy in the blue smoke of incense, and his body went instantly rigid from what he saw. Alexander Southerland stood before the greenish-bronze idol, swinging a Chinese battle-ax in ringing blows against the metal. But it wasn't that sight which held Lonergan in frozen astonishment. It was the apparent result of the ax.

Blood covered the idol's bronze baldness. Crimson that looked warm and thick enough to have come from the broken veins of a living thing stained the head of the statue, made glistening red trickles on the Buddha's molded face, and formed tiny rivers on its naked bronze belly.

Princess Tanya Andreva, long hair tumbled, golden, was crouched on her knees before the altar and at the feet of the man with the ax. Her smooth white arms came up the man's body to his chest. He ignored her, swinging his weapon.

"Don't!" she cried shrilly. "Don't strike! Don't strike again!"

Lonergan had released the catch on the grill-work. His feet made a dull thud on bare planks as he ended his jump to the temple floor.

Southerland turned abruptly at the sound, knocking the blond woman away from him and hurling the ax in a vicious downward sweep. The flying weapon just cleared Lonergan's head as he ducked; it chunked its steel blade deep into the wall behind him.

Tanya Andreva crawled out of the way. Southerland, at the temple altar, snatched up a revolver that was on the table. And Lonergan matched him, shot for shot.

Searing fire streaked across the cop's chest. Southerland

doubled up, suddenly boneless, and collapsed in front of the Buddha altar; he pulled the trigger aimlessly as he crumpled but the revolver only made an empty clicking sound.

Lonergan walked forward with the Mauser dangling at his side, approached the altar and stared, still incredulous, at the blood on the bronze statue. Then he glanced down and saw the body of Chung Yuk, the temple priest. Something had severed the jugular vein of the old man's throat.

Tanya Andreva came to the altar. Her fingers nervously explored all over the bronze designs at the Buddha's base. She forced something, her fingers white with the strain. A small bronze plate dropped down and sifted a shower of sand to the floor. Hard things sparkled in the sand. She worked a hand into the opening and brought out a jeweled headpiece, gold-linked, flashing colored stones.

"Oh," Lonergan said cynically. "So that's it. That's why you yelled for him not to hit the statue. You were afraid he'd break it. But it could've been put together again. Diamonds don't crack easy."

She held the headpiece tenderly in her hands. Her eyes shone with a warmth and emotion he hadn't seen before.

"You are American," she said. "You value things by money. It is beyond you to understand my feelings toward this head-dress. I would shed blood to protect it. It is the same as it was with this poor Chinese priest who lies there dead at the altar; something more to him than money. It is his blood on the bronze Buddha. He shed his blood over the altar trying to keep them from touching the thing he worshiped." Then she forgot Lonergan, her eyes hot on the jeweled piece in her hands. "Great Catherine," she murmured.

Lonergan said, half to himself: "Chung Yuk isn't the only man who shed blood for this Buddha."

7

Wind-Up

HANNAMAN, THE D.A., took a cigarette from a silver case and inserted it in Lonergan's mouth. Lonergan sat in an office chair with his hands at his sides. Bandages crossed his chest, under his clothes, and the doctor had forbidden him to lift his arms for a time.

Hannaman put fire to the cigarette and said: "Anybody who wants to take a sock at Rex has a swell chance; he can't even put up his guard!"

Chief Ryan, sitting heavily at the side of the D.A.'s desk, grinned broadly, advising: "Rex had better keep off the streets for a while."

Hannaman inclined his head toward Princess Tanya Andreva. "The princess has come down here to help us out," he said. "Let's get the whole thing straight. Did Sue Steiner talk, Rex?"

Lonergan nodded. "So did Southerland—I mean Meledoff. What they didn't say I can guess. The case runs back a long ways. It picked our town to come to a head."

"All the Russian jewelry," Ryan put in. "The appraiser just told me the stuff from the Buddha was worth over half a million bucks—I mean broken up and cut."

Tanya Andreva tilted her chin scornfully, snapped: "Broken up! Cut!"

Hannaman smiled at her politely. "We understand the historic value of these pieces, the value to the collector, the priceless value to you. Chief Ryan was referring to the worth from a criminal's viewpoint."

"Sure," Lonergan said. "Anyway, here's the sketch. At the time the princess escaped from Russia under Gin Lem's wing and the party was attacked by bandits, the old Chinaman tried to save them by taking them to an abandoned Buddhist temple, or monastery. Gin Lem had been there before and he knew all the statues; knew about the phony bottom in the Laughing Buddha. So they hid the jewelry in the idol, and while the girl's father fought off the bandits, Gin Lem slipped away with the young princess and Meledoff.

"When Gin Lem got the little girl safely to Shanghai, Meledoff said he went back to find her father and the jewelry she was supposed to inherit. The bandits had killed her father, and the bronze Buddha was gone. They found out some explorer had come along and taken a fancy to the collection of statues in the monastery. The explorer lifted the whole works. But Gin Lem figured he'd be able to get the jewelry; there wasn't a chance in a million the explorer would find out what was hidden in the Buddha unless somebody told him.

"On the way back to Shanghai, Ivan Meledoff got the idea he was a sap to go hunting for the jewelry just to turn it over to his kid cousin. So he ditched Gin Lem and went on his own. Gin Lem figured Meledoff had got lost. He hadn't. Meledoff started on his hunt for the Buddha, changing his name a dozen times and finally calling himself Alexander Southerland. I got next to the guy when he tried to pass himself off as a Southerner—I know a Southern accent when I hear one."

"The hunt took all this time?" Ryan asked.

The princess shrugged cynically. "Time? What is time?"

LONERGAN NODDED. "WHAT'S a few years of searching if you can snag onto loot worth around a million in a collector's market? The princess grew up in France. Then she began to help Gin Lem trace down explorers. Right?"

That last he asked of Tanya Andreva. "Yes," she said, "oh, yes. It was slow, took years. We had to stop to get money. But we finally got on the right track. In Paris, we heard of an Englishman who explored China and the Gobi desert. We went to see him about the Laughing Buddha. Of course we did not let him know why we sought it—never could we let anyone learn the truth—not even the police. We had to keep our secret until I had my jewelry. The Englishman told us he had given the Laughing Buddha away ten years ago to some Chinese in New York City. So Gin Lem went to New York. I had no money so I remained in Paris. The next day it was in the paper that Princess Tanya Andreva and Gin Lem sought a strange Buddist idol."

"Yeah," Lonergan interrupted, "and that's where this Alexander Southerland enters the picture again. He was in Paris, driving a cab for a living. He read about the princess being on the trail of the Buddha, and he figured the way to beat her now was to follow her leads. He went to see her. She didn't suspect he was her own cousin, who used to be Ivan Meledoff. She couldn't remember him, being just a kid at the time. He put up a nice front. She liked him. She said she wanted to get to America but she didn't tell him why. He knew, though. So he got some dough together and brought her here. Gin Lem had traced the Laughing Buddha to this temple in our Chinatown.

"Southerland tried to pump the dope on the Buddha out of her, I guess, but she wouldn't tell him anything. He had to keep track of her, so he contacted Red Nolan and spilled the story. Red planted Sue Steiner in the apartment as Tanya's personal maid. He planted the Peeper as her chauffeur. They were supposed to spy on her, but they weren't told the real low-down on the jewels. They were in the dark on that angle.

"Gin Lem had a job in a laundry. He pretended to be a Buddhist, and every time he was alone for a second at the temple he got the statue open and swiped out a piece of jewelry for the princess—I guess it wasn't swiping; the stuff was hers anyhow. Well, the princess got one of the rings and had it at her apartment. Sue Steiner was tired of working at a maid's salary and stole the ring. When Southerland saw her with it, he figured Sue had found out where the Buddha was and was double-crossing him. He sent Nolan's boys out after her. They went after the Peeper too, because they figured her brother was in with her on a double-cross. Sue and the Peeper tried to skip town. They got the Peeper and tried to make him talk. He couldn't talk because he didn't know what it was all about. They killed him. They didn't get Sue till she was with me at Maxie's. They snatched her and gave her the works. They wouldn't believe her when she said all she knew about the Russian ring was that she stole it from the princess."

"So Nolan was in it all down the line, eh?" Ryan put in.

"Sure. Nolan was to split fifty-fifty with Southerland on the jewelry-haul when they found it. Nolan did all the dirty work, using his boys, and Southerland kept his face clean and was nice to the princess. Nolan had the punk trailing the princess all the time. The punk saw her meet Gin Lem in Chinatown and go to the temple. He didn't know it was the temple, of course; these Buddists kept it secret. Anyway, he reported to Nolan and Nolan had a pow-pow with Southerland. They figured it was best to pick up Gin Lem and make him talk. I busted up that play but they killed Gin Lem and slipped my radio net.

"So with Gin Lem dead there wasn't anything left for them to do but snatch the princess herself. Down at the morgue Southerland picked up the idea we had police shadows on her. That would make a snatch a tough job. But Nolan said he could fix that. They picked on the funeral of Gin Lem for the time and place. They knew a lot of sightseers would be hanging around and hold up our fire if it got to a gun-fight. So they hired that Italian to ram his car into the hearse at California Street. They even had a lawyer waiting to back up the Italian. The fake accident made a lot of excitement and they used it to have some birds snatch the princess. They kept Southerland in the clear by tapping him on the bean.

"Well, it all came off according to schedule except that I sent Hu after a guy in a sedan. This guy was parked on the scene to supervise. Hu did some nice police work and trailed this bird all day till he got back to Chinatown. Hu and I were all set to close in, but they had the street spotted and a guy picked us up. About that time they tortured the princess into telling where the Buddha was. Hu and I got loose and picked up the pieces."

Hu Rawlins, standing by the door, said: "He means he picked up the pieces. Rex's modest," he added kiddingly.

"Shut up," Lonergan ordered. "This Southerland, or Meledoff, got to figuring he ought to be on hand for the pay-off so Nolan couldn't skip with the whole loot. He traced them to the temple where Nolan was about to get the Buddha. Southerland turned real greedy and rubbed out his partner, Nolan, one of Nolan's bodyguards, and the Buddhist priest who was trying to save the idol. Southerland didn't know how to open the trick bottom in the statue, so he went at it with an ax. That was where I barged in."

Lonergan quit talking. His throat had gotten hoarse. He got out of the chair, said he was going home.

Hu Rawlins winked. "How about me buying you a drink first, Rex?"

Lonergan made a snorting noise in his nose. "Listen to the guy, will you? Here I am all tied up with bandage—can't bend an elbow, can't get my hands to a bar, can't lift a glass higher than my belt-and Hu says he'll buy me a drink! Tie that!"

"Some other time, then," Hu Rawlins said, and added, not irrelevantly: "My mother's maiden name was MacTavish."

THE MANDARIN'S THIRTY-THIRD TOOTH

Dane Gregory

Each night in Charlie Kee's Fragrant Almond Chamber the beautiful, golden dancing girl, Bho Kum, tossed a red rose to the youth she loved… and a scathing prophecy to the one she didn't. But this night, while the Mandarin Ko Kim smiled broadly and wept large tears, Bho Kum tossed… murder!

1

With a Gift of Roses

CALL IT A study in gold. It began with death and ended with death, but in Chinatown murder is sometimes cloaked in a tissue of imagery and glamour. And this particular tissue is wrought of the purest leaf-gold: gold for the color of Bho Kum's dancing slippers; gold for the mandarin's thirty-third tooth; and gold for the wicked lantern that bloomed one night in a cupola where there should have been no light at all.

And gold for Ti-Yam, god of moonlight, who had graced the sky with an extravagant golden moon through the celestial courtesy of one Yun-Ten-Tin—the Supreme Ruler of the Somber Heavens.

The tale begins rightly with Bho Kum, though. The scenic moon and that evil golden lantern in the Yan Yuap tonghouse were simply stage props for the third act of a melodrama that had started some time before. And it had started with the girl Bho Kum, whose transcribed name would be Purse of Gold and whose small golden body ticked out suave rhythms to the moon-fiddles that sang nightly in Charlie Kee's Fragrant Almond Chamber.

Sergeant Lou Grandon of the Chinatown detail had heard of the girl before he saw her. And that was principally why he saw her. When a dancing girl's beauty was such that bizarre tales of it ran the entire length of the little Orient, the exigencies of office compelled Grandon to take something more than a passive interest in the girl herself. It was strictly a matter of duty.

In Chinatown as in other places, trouble usually began with a woman. The sanguinary tong-wars of the twenties had usually begun that way, and in four cases out of five the woman had been a dancing girl. And because no man can live twenty years in a world of pageantry without himself becoming a part of the pageant, Grandon was worried about Bho Kum. When hardened old hucksters assured him that the girl was like music clothed in flesh, vague warnings crept into Grandon's mind.

The warnings intensified when the dilettante columnist on an uptown newspaper wrote that Bho Kum was "the Oriental Gypsy Rose Lee"—and when his unfriendly rival reported in a half-column of type that Gypsy Rose Lee was only the Occidental Bho Kum.

So Grandon went to Charlie Kee's, smelling trouble.

Grandon snapped two shots... And the knife flashed through the air....

THE CRIMSON NEON piping scrawled EATS, blatant Yankee acknowledgment of fact; but the golden calligraphs below the neon said that this was Charlie Kee's Fragrant Almond Chamber and his Balcony of Joy and Delight. In reality, it was a Chinese supper club that differed in one important respect from the gaudy tourist-traps on either side. For it was exactly that—a Chinese supper club—and one at which all tourist trade was received with little enthusiasm.

Grandon sat down at a palm-screened table across from the

drunken philosopher Fow Gat, a gaunt man peering owlishly
into the lees of his wine glass.

It was a bowl-ceilinged room of subtle lights and strange
contrasts: of dissonant music and of porcelain girls whose
silken raiment shimmered against the hard formalism of
dinner clothes. But there were men as well as girls in Oriental
dress. At one table squatted a mountainous mandarin clothed
in flowing turquoise robes and the conventional flat skull-cap;

and Grandon observed with sudden surprise that the mandarin was weeping. His gold teeth made a rind of brilliance in his huge innocent face, but there was a steady drip of tears from the low-lidded eyes.

"My God," Grandon mumbled, "surely the jokes can't be that funny."

"Perhaps," said the drunken philosopher Fow Gat, "he weeps for Chinatown, sinjin."

Grandon recorded the comment automatically, but he was listening to the two buffoons on stage—a Weber and Fields act in pure Cantonese.

The tall comic had just whacked the short one across the buttocks and remarked sagely that punk-sticks would be burned in his honor the next time Tsai Tin Tai Shing took a vacation from the joss-house. The remark seemed singularly unfunny until Grandon remembered that Tsia Tin Tai Shing was one of the more jocular gods in Chinese mythology: a deified monkey that had learned the language of men.

Even then, it seemed rather unfunny; but the mandarin's teeth splashed golden joy and fat tears of mirth rolled down cheeks.

"And who," said Grandon, "is the weeping man?"

"The Mandarin Ko Kim, illustrious. Always he smiles broadly and weeps great tears when he smiles. I think that, being fat, he must smile; and being sad, he must weep."

Grandon held his hard gray gaze on the drunkard's fuzzy eyes. "And why should he weep for Chinatown?"

Fow Gat gestured to a little structure of ebony sticks on the table in front of him. They might have been toothpicks, but they were not. "You interrupted an important conversation, sinjin," he said severely. "When you spoke to me, I was holding converse with a poet who has been dead since the year 905."

GRANDON DID NOT laugh. There were certain enigmas beyond his comprehension, but he knew what he knew about the game Fow Gat had been playing with those little ebony sticks.

It was an occult pastime whose mysteries, the learned Confucius had written, he might perhaps begin to penetrate were he granted fifty more years of intensive study. And Grandon knew from the tales he had heard that it was not a pastime for children or drunkards.

Easy enough to try, though.

You simply cast the sticks like a handful of dice and they fell into one of fifty seven possible patterns. You fixed the pattern in your mind and visualized it on the panel of an imaginary door. And if you waited long enough, the moment inevitably would come when your inner mind broke free of all physical bondage: and then the imaginary door would swing wide before your eyes so that you could pass through it into the equally fictional world beyond.

Grandon did not like it. Though he tried to agree with the Western savants who called it an ordinary form of self hypnosis, he still did not like it.

He drummed the table and said, "You bring your toys to an odd place, Fow Gat. Does a drinker see doors in the bottom of his *sam-shu* glass?"

"Always," the philosopher said shrewdly. "Otherwise he would not drink. I played the game of the ebony stick, sinjin, and I met the poet Li T'ai Po. Have you forgotten it is mid-September?"

And Grandon remembered that it was. It was the festival time called Distribution of the Moon Cakes, when all Chinatown honors the bibulous poet who dived out of his rowboat in an effort to capture a sublimely beautiful woman. The woman turned out to be only a reflection of the autumn moon; and the poet Li T'ai Po was drowned.

"And what," said Grandon, "did you find to talk about?"

"He wept, sinjin, as the melancholy mandarin weeps. He wept for himself and for Chinatown."

Grandon leaned over the table, entranced in spite of himself. "Why?"

"He said that when the water-roots tangled in his lungs, he knew beauty for what it was—an evil and deadly illusion. And he wove a new poem for me, illustrious."

Fow Gat burped into one hand and tapped out cadences with the fingers of the other. "Here is the poem, sinjin," he chanted.

"If I had thirty-two enemies, I would not bite each enemy with one of my thirty-two teeth.

"I would carry a thirty-third tooth in the shape of a beautiful woman, for beauty is a fang so deadly that it can slay thousands yet leave no trace."

Grandon moved his square shoulders uneasily. He said, "It sounds like pure bilge-water to me," not quite certain that it did. "If he can't do better than—"

Fow Gat raised a dramatic forefinger. *Hoya!* The dancing girl comes."

As at a signal, the overhead lights dimmed to a sleepy half-light. The moon-fiddles sang sudden wild dissonances that dissolved curiously into those dulcet harmonies to which no Occidental ear is ever quite attuned. The curtains that draped the proscenium broke apart like scarlet fog: and to the ticking, ticking, ticking of her tiny golden slippers, the girl Bho Kum came dancing.

SHE COULD NOT have been more than sixteen. Her loose dark hair, worn in an Oriental version of the page boy bob, tossed gaily about a child's immature bosom. Her high-arched feet, delicate as a doll's, grew into fragile golden legs that flashed in and out of the broken *kimona* she wore—dancing and dancing as a child's legs dance to the hurdy-gurdies.

A kid, that was all. A bright rose shook color from her hair; a round scarlet spot quivered on her upper lip and each of her eyelids; but these were adornments that served only to stress the wistful gravity of her face. And it was even a childish game she played: tossing a rice fortune-cake aloft while she moved with the fiddle-song.

"Tonight," Fow Gat said softly, "will be different from last night. She will throw the rose to young Thomas Loong and the rice fortune-cake to young Sam Lau. Everyone here will envy Thomas Loong and laugh loudly at Sam Lau. Then the lights will go out for a moment and two men will hate each other in the dark."

Grandon's big hands locked together. He saw the handsome youth Thomas Loong, seated stiffly at a table close to the stage; and he saw the equally handsome Sam Lau, only a table away from Loong. He remembered that the fathers of those two were chieftains in powerful nation-wide tongs that had once warred bitterly over a sing-song girl from Ceylon. Friendly tongs now, forgetting old scars in the unity patriotism demanded of them—but how long would friendship last if there were trouble again?

Grandon said curtly, "Tell it."

Fow Gat said, "Why, it is only a little game this artless child plays, sinjin. And perhaps the game is as artless as the child, but in all the gambling parlours of Chinatown there is no gambler ready to wager that it will not end in bloodshed. Do you understand?"

"Tell it."

"Both young men love the girl Bho Kum—as who does not? But few men know which of the two the girl Bho Kum loves. One night she flings the red rose to Loong and the next it is captured by Sam Lau… The rose, you see, is a symbol of her admiration. But the rice fortune-cake holds a strip of rice paper inscribed with a very insulting fortune, and it is the symbol of Bho Kum's contempt. You see?"

"I see," said Grandon. He stared at the grim Bho Kum, somehow expecting her beauty to have altered in the face of this revelation. But it had not, and strangely it seemed more evil by virtue of its changeless purity.

"Does she love either?" he said.

"She loves Sam Lau," said Fow Gat.

Bho Kum tossed the rose.

It fell in the hungry fingers of Thomas Loong; and the fiddle-song snapped apart to leave a little tense hush while Loong smiled triumphantly and pinned the petalled badge over his heart.

Bho Kum spat on the fortune-cake. She threw it scornfully. It fell in the center of Sam Lau's table and shattered there.

GRANDON WATCHED YOUNG Lau's shaking fingered extract the strip of paper. He held the fortune up to his eyes and then wadded it into a tight little pellet between his palms. The pellet slipped out of his fingers. There was laughter, and Grandon could see the dark blood rising in Sam Lau's cheeks.

"So she loves Sam Lau, does she? And what makes you think so?"

"Illustrious," Fow Gat said mournfully, "I am both a wise man and a drunkard. A wise man knows whom his loved one loves, and a drunkard knows she does not love him." He put his face in the crook of one arm and went to sleep.

The moon-fiddles screamed.

Bho Kum threw out her hands. The broken kimona fell away like the wings of Icarus, and for a heartbeat she stood thus in the center of the stage—slender and nearly naked.

Then the fiddles sobbed *towsey-mongelay*—the words that mean eternal farewell—and all the lights in the Fragrant Almond Chamber dissolved into darkness. There was only a perfumed silence, as if everyone here were caught in the same unaccountable dread that held Grandon motionless in his chair.

The overhead lights blinked on again.

And nothing, it seemed, had changed. The dancer Bho Kum was gone from the stage, but in the cabaret room itself the dinner-coated men and porcelain girls meshed in a familiar pattern. Fow Gat still slept with his face in the bend of one arm. The enormous mandarin smiled his smile and wept his pear-shaped tears.

Thomas Loong looked down at the rose on his breast.

But Sam Lau was gone. Only the crumbled rice-cake remained where Sam Lau had sat; and Grandon came to his feet with the sudden sure knowledge that something had happened.

A porcelain girl screamed. She pointed at the rose on Thomas Loong's breast and then dipped her face into hollowed hands.

Grandon shouted, "All right! All right! Just hold your places everybody—I'll take over from here!"

He stared down at the rose.

The rose was enormous. It covered the entire left lapel of Thomas Loong's dinner jacket, and it was brighter and wetter than any rose should be.

Pinned dead-center in its scarlet calyx was the double-edged blade of a Han knife: and the hilt of the knife was embossed with a symbol terribly familiar to Grandon. It was the benevolent dragon of the Yan Yuap tong, the organization of which Sam Lau's father was chieftain.

He held his fingers up to Thomas Loong's face.

The boy stared at the fingers but did not breathe on them, and Grandon knew that he was no longer interested in such temporal things as a dancer with golden skin. Like the drowned poet Li T'ai Po, he had found that beauty can be lethal.

2

Offerings to Kwan Tai

CAPTAIN ED GUNTHER of Homicide was a fretful centaur in run-down carpet slippers and lemon-striped pajamas. He pulled at the fingers of one hand so that the joints snapped. "Tong-trouble," he said bitterly. "My God! The tongs have been at peace for more than ten years, and then all of a sudden this thing has to break open a month ahead of my retirement. Lou, couldn't you possibly have stopped it?"

"It happened in the dark," Grandon said heavily.

"Oh, I know. Damn it, would have to happen that way, now wouldn't it? The Chinese can't do things like other people—they've got to have their melodrama at any price."

Grandon shook his head in bleak negation. "You're wrong. The average Chinese isn't melodramatic. The occasional melodrama is the only part of Chinatown that touches your life, that's all."

"Oh well," said Gunther, not convinced. "Well, we've got to keep this thing from slopping over if we can. You've talked to Charlie Kee and the girl?"

"Yes. Kee's as much in the clear as any other night-spot operator that hires slightly off-hue performers. Bho Kum packs em in, that's all. And we can't hold the girl for throwing a fortune-cookie at somebody and a rose at somebody else."

"She says what?"

Grandon made a wry mouth. "Her eyes say she's scared—

but I'll be damned if I know of who or what. Her lips say she's a dancing girl from Soochow and that her mother was a bound-foot woman who taught her to dance with a piece of split bamboo. That's all."

Captain Ed Gunther tugged at his fingers and looked reprovingly at them when they failed to crackle. "This Lau kid can't have got very far away, can he? Well, pick him up and sock it to him as soon as possible."

"No," said Grandon.

"What?"

Grandon rocked slowly and stared at the floor, trying to put the impossible in words. "That's what I wanted to see you about, Captain. For God's sake, let me handle this! I don't know where Sam Lau is, but let me find him and talk to him before you do anything at all."

Gunther stared.

"OH, I KNOW. It's a homicide case and all that. Technically, it's out of my province now. But Ed, I know these people. I know Sam Lau. He's second-generation Chinese, and he was the valedictorian in his high school class. Some of the old Chinese cling to the old customs—but Ed, Sam Lau didn't plant that tong-knife in Tommy Loong's heart."

Gunther jumped. "Say that again."

"I mean it. He was the only man in the room close enough to have done it, and he was the only man in the room with an obvious motive. And—"

"And the only man in the room who disappeared."

"Yes," said Grandon. "It was as neat a frame as anything I've ever seen. But still a frame. You can pick up one of those old tong-knives in practically any curio shop."

He rocked and waited, still looking at the floor.

Gunther said, "And suppose it is a frame? Let the kid clear himself when and if we bring him in."

Lou Grandon went to the window. He braced his body against the sill and stood there looking out into the night.

He said, "Do you happen to remember the trouble between the On Leong and the Hip Sing tongs in New York's Chinatown, Ed? It happened in '24, I think. Well, it spread. It spread to other tongs and other towns, and before it ended there were plenty of new-mown corpses. A tong-war is like a European war, Ed—it just won't stay in one place."

"And what?"

"The same thing is about to happen again. If you hold Sam Lau on a murder charge, it'll be interpreted as an official proclamation that a Yan Yuap tongster knifed a Jok Lem tongster. Tommy Loong's father is head of the Jok Lem, and he'll have to demand a blood reprisal. That's the layout."

Gunther was silent.

Lou Grandon said, "Give me a few hours, Ed—that's all I'm asking. Meanwhile, tell your boys to look busy and do nothing—and to keep that tong-knife angle out of the papers. I'm not saying I'll break the case, but Homicide can have the credit if I do."

Gunther sat in silence and worried his hair into a fawn-like crest. His pointed ears twitched nervously. He lit a cigar and said, "It's the craziest thing I've ever done, but I'll tell the boys to give you a few hours. Just a few hours, that's all. Lou, have you got anything at all to work with?"

Grandon put on his hat. "Yes."

"Hey! You have? What—"

Grandon said, "A tip from the poet Li T'ai Po, who was drowned in the year 905. He thinks the real murder weapon was somebody's thirty-third tooth."

"Oh," said Captain Ed Gunther; and sat down again. "Honest to Hannah, Lou, I don't quite know what to make of you. Sometimes I'd swear you're three parts Chinese yourself."

Grandon turned in the doorway. "I'll bet you say that to all the boys, Captain, but thanks just the same. A Chinese was discovering America along about the time your ancestors and mine were picking nits out of each other's fur." *

IN THE PEACOCK-FEATHERED interior of the old joss-house on Plum Street, there are fourteen pampered deities who are rarely without votary offerings from their disciples. Barren wives pay homage to Ni-Lung, twelve goddesses of motherhood. Chinatown's gambling claque woos Choi-Sun, goddess of finance, and is even more attentive to that jovial god who is the darling of the entire galaxy. Before Quan Yin, joss of good fortune, the tea-cups are never dry.

But as there is a cat that walks ever alone, so is there a lonely and saturnine god who smells the smoke of crumbling punk only in those rare intervals when Little China is about to smell the smoke of cordite.

He is Kwan Tai, god of war.

---

* Author's Note: With all due credit to Columbus, five gets you ten the sergeant is right. In A.D. 499, a Buddhist priest named Hui Sh'n announced the discovery of a new continent which appears to have been a reasonable well-drawn facsimile of this one. Though many historians scoff at the claim, Hui Sh'n's story was plausible enough so that it was into the official annals of the Empire.

Lou Grandon stood in the shadowy joss-house and watched smoke wreathe Kwan Tai's face as the vapors from a soup tureen might wreath a hungry man's. He had expected to find punk in the censers, for Chinatown at high noon should be noisier than this. It was quiet with a watchful and prayerful quiet against which the various scattered sounds were like pebbles striking a cloisonne bowl.

Heavy with trouble, he turned away.

The mandarin Ko Kim stood at the threshold, so huge a man that the sunlight could not break past him into the joss-house. The mandarin kowtowed and gave Grandon a great bright smile, but tears squeezed out of his lidded eyes so that his cheeks were glossy with them.

"Eh-yeh!" he chanted. "It is bad. The two tong-leaders pay obeisance to Kwan Tai, and only a little while ago I saw a poor coffin-maker looking at the finest jade."

"It is bad," said Grandon with utter sincerity.

"You have found no trace of the boy Sam Lau?"

"No trace."

"Eh-yeh! May Father Tao speed you in your search. We must preserve Chinatown from bloodshed, honorable one. I am a man who smiles often, but only because my bright teeth blind me to the fact that we Chinamen are an unhappy people."

"The boy will be found," said Grandon. "And whenever or wherever he is found, illustrious, there will be no blood reprisals."

He cut across Chinatown and went to the Temple of Heavenly Harmonies, the chemist's shop where Sam Lau's father waited in withered sorrow.

He said slowly, "I have seen your offering to Kwan Tai, honorable. Is it wise?"

"War," said the old man, "is only as wise as the fools who wage it. I did not place the first punk stick there, and unless my son is harmed the Yan Yuap tonghouse will not be the first to flaunt a golden lantern from its cupola."

"Your son has not returned?"

"He has not returned."

"You do not know where he has gone?"

Old Lau said, "My son is an honorable youth. Having no knife, he would not have killed; and having killed, he would not have fled. I think that the Jok Lem tongsters seized my son and that he is now dying under slow torture."

Grandon said, "You are wrong, venerable, believe me. The Jok Lem tong and the Yan Yuap tong once signed an eternal peace treaty over the blood of a white rooster. Since then you have played chess with Thomas Loong's father."

The old man drew a somber silence around him and then let it fall away like a garment. He said with sudden terrible intensity: "Go to Wai Loong, sinjin. Tell him that I know many good chess-players but that I am possessed of only one first-born son."

IN THAT MEAT-SHOP known as the Gateway to Inner Concord, smoked ducks dangled along the walls like bleak monuments to themselves. And the death of his son had dried all the juices out of Wai Loong so that he was as bloodless as one of his ducks: an old man whose skin lay like yellow paint on a skull.

Grandon said, "I mourn with you, Wai Loong, but I also mourn with the fathers of those who are about to die. I have seen your offering to Kwan Tai. Is it wise?"

"War," said Wai Loong, "is a liquor that tastes sweet only before it is drunk. Yet a man lost in a desert of despair does not question the quality of the oasis."

"You mean, then, that other men's blood must be spilled for the blood of Thomas Loong."

Old Wai Loong shook his head. "I ask only that which is any father's due. There will be no war if Sam Lau is surrendered by his tong to the tribunal of justice. And not to tong-justice, sinjin, but to the law you represent."

"It is a fair request," Lou Grandon said, "and it does you credit, wise one. But Sam Lau has not returned to his father's home, and the leader of the Yan Yuap tong believes that he is held captive by yours."

Wai Loong was silent.

"Is it true, Wai Loong?"

The old man looked at him levelly. "It is not true, sinjin, nor do I believe that the honorable one believes it. When the tiger's whelp has made his first kill, he returns to the den of the tiger."

Grandon sighed heavily and went out into the brittle reverie of Chinatown.

Along its parrot-hued midway he went: and into those crooked by-streets where old garments swung like an army of the hanged and there were shadows that never moved.

He talked to children with enormous sad eyes. He talked to hucksters and to tavern-keepers. He talked to bright-plumed little dolla-dolla girls and to a wrinkled trot whose tongue clacked endlessly against gums the color of gunmetal.

He set the whisper rolling through Chinatown: Sam Lau must return. Wherever the boy Sam Lau may be, tell him he must come home very soon.

But when the lamps burned orange holes in the night, Sam Lau had not returned. And Grandon's few hours had expired. Homicide had broadcast the pickup order, and throughout the city there were cop-cars beating the streets for the apothecary's vanished son.

Grandon went to Charlie Kee's Fragrant Chamber.

It was packed to the gunwales as he had known it would be, for blood lends an awful enchantment to beauty already enchanted. But there were two empty tables near the stage: and when Bho Kum danced on her golden toes, men glanced strangely at one another as if they were hearing the tick, tick, tick of a death-watch beetle.

Tonight she wore no rose in her hair. Tonight she tossed no fortune-cake and there was no blackout at the end of the number. But she danced as guilelessly as before, flinging her child's body about so that she was like a little swallow of swift dartings: a little golden bird of murder.

3

The Gorgon Has One Eye

GRANDON HAD SPENT twenty years on the Chinatown squad, and he was all but inured to those paradoxes that confound other men. At one time, he had watched highly-placed Occidentals lend their financial support to the slave trade while condemning it virtuously in the newspapers. At another time he had seen the city health department concern itself with a chicken-pox scare while two eyeless lepers begged in the streets of Chinatown. But here was something else again, a contradiction in physical terms that appalled him because it was new. Death and innocence danced hand in hand.

He went out again. He went to the establishment of Sam Lau's father and knocked three times on the weather-beaten panel.

Old Lau opened the door and nodded gravely. Somewhere in the lamplit darkness beyond, a woman's grief made a thin, unending minor.

"Perhaps I come at a bad time, venerable," Lou Grandon said. "I take it your son has not yet returned."

The ancient regarded him with no sign of emotion. Out of a long silence he said deliberately, "Sam Lau has returned to his father's household."

It was the unforeseeable. Grandon settled back on his heels and drew in a small, tight breath. "It is well. But I am a police officer, illustrious, and the charge is murder. I must speak to your son,"

"You may speak to him, sinjin," the chemist said.

He led the way through a room of rattan furniture and dark brocaded walls. He said, "Quiet, woman," to the bodiless voice; and then a three inch panel of teak moved inward under his hand. He gestured wordlessly.

Grandon went into the room, letting the door click shut behind him. Old Lau did not follow.

Four black candles swung their dull blades like sleepy warriors. Grandon's shadow moved jerkily across the wall and then was motionless as a stain.

He said, "Sam Lau."

Sam Lau did not speak.

Grandon bent low, letting the breath sigh out of him so that the candles tossed their spears. "Sam Lau?"

Old Lau's first born son lay with his long hands folded tranquilly across his dinner coat. Two brass coins weighted his shut eyelids.

Under Grandon's square fingertips, the boy's cheek was cold and wet from the distilled vapors of the night.

He was many hours dead: and driven deep into his heart was a Han knife inscribed with the symbol of the Jok Lem tong.

Grandon's big hands fumbled awkwardly in the empty coat-pockets, searching for the thing he had not found at the Fragrant Almond Chamber last night. He found it lodged in the cuff of the right pants-leg—a tiny ball of rice-paper that whispered in his fingers as he spread it to the candlelight. He read Sam Lau's fortune and then tucked it carefully into his vest pocket.

Old Lau was still waiting beyond the door, his hands hidden in wide silken sleeves and his face expressionless as an egg. The woman's voice wailed again.

Grandon said, "I am educated in pain but not in words, venerable. I can only say that I am sorry."

The chemist bowed his head. "From you, sinjin, the words are as eloquent as a poem by Tu Fu. Your eyes speak for your heart."

"The boy was delivered at your threshold?"

"Yes."

"By whom?"

"I do not know. I can only guess."

"Remember, venerable, that a slayer can always sign somebody else's name to his crime. When did this happen?"

"Perhaps an hour ago. Who can say? Time is an immeasurable thing when it measured by sorrow and hatred."

Grandon said gently, "I know. It is my duty to report this to headquarters, and the boy will have to be turned over to the homicide detail. You understand that, don't you?"

And the woman in the dark cried, "Aiee! Aiee!" like a long-held note on a weeping fiddle.

IF ONE BUT knows the legendry behind them—and Lou Grandon knew better than any man on the city payroll—there are portents more ominous than the sulky crawl made of smoke into Kwan Tai's nostrils.

On the fringe of Chinatown stands the Yan Yuap tonghouse, an old landmark thrusting its slanted-roof cupola high above all other houses in the immediate district. The only route to the cupola is an antiquated outside fire-escape.

Not in two decades had any man scaled the stairway; and not in two decades had there been war.

But tonight the Yan Yuap tonghouse was jeweled with an ornament of baleful splendor, a great unblinking gorgon's eye that stared dourly across the crooked rooftops below. And its stare was fixed on the dark tower of the Jok Lem tonghouse, where shortly another huge golden lantern would burn like a gorgon's eye.

For these are the lanterns of war.

En route from the call-box where he had reported Sam Lau's murder, Grandon saw the light in the Yan Yuap belfry. He had known, of course, that the lantern would be there; for the old chemist's frightful poise was that of a man who has yielded himself at last to the inescapable. He stopped in front of an old gabled house that pushed at the cobbles of Plum Street. A few pale windows hung there in the sketchy outline of a child's boxkite, but no sound from within touched the edges of Chinatown's quiet. It was a transient rooming-house.

He went up a rutted flight of stairs and came to stop at the first-floor landing. He knocked.

"Who?" called a little voice.

Grandon beat the door again.

A thin fan of light cut the darkness, growing by cautious degrees. In the slot of the doorway, a small oval face widened its amber eyes at him. Under the face one coral-tipped hand made a nervous brooch at the throat of a peacock-blue jacket.

"Go 'way, you. Go way plitty soon."

"No," said Grandon.

It was a narrow oblong room in which rickety Occidental furniture clashed with the bright trappings of the tenant's personality. Grandon looked into the empty bathroom and then swung around to face the girl again.

He said, "All right, Bho Kum—where is he? Where can I find your boss-man?"

She pressed her shoulders into the wall and bit the back of one hand. "Me cly cop-cop," she assured him. "Po-leetz! Me scleam bloody hell and say you tly love me."

"I'm police myself," said Grandon, "and you know it. Talk your own tongue, little tea-blossom—I understand. Where is your master?"

"I have no master."

"You need not be afraid of him, Bho Kum—nor of me."

"I have no master," the girl tinkled. "My mother taught me—"

Grandon said, "I've heard it, Bho Kum. She taught you to dance with a bamboo switch. And then you were sold to somebody, weren't you?"

The girl's eyes grew round and lambent above her clenched hand. "No, my lord."

Grandon said, "When your mother taught you to dance, Bho Kum, did she also teach you to make brush-writing?"

"No, my lord."

Grandon smiled a sudden bleak smile. "I thought not, little thrush."

He took from his vest pocket the strip of rice-paper and spread it in one palm. "Yet your message to the boy Sam Lau is in excellent brush-writing, Bho Kum."

THE GIRL GAVE a little fluttering cry. Her hand fell from her mouth, and all her defenses fell with it. She moved slowly toward Grandon, staring at the fragment of paper.

"It is not yours! It is Sam Lau's—Sam Lau's! My lord, where—"

Grandon looked deep into her eyes. "Yes. It is Sam Lau's. But you didn't know the contents of the note, did you? You were simply told to throw it to Sam Lau in the fortune-cake."

The dancing girl went deathly still.

"I think," Lou Grandon said heavily, "you didn't even know the meaning of the game you played. Your master told you it was an innocent game, didn't he, Bho Kum?"

Bho Kum's hands fitted themselves together in a little ivory puzzle-lock. She shut her eyes and spoke with the monotony of one who repeats an ancient promise. "Sam Lau will not be hurt. It is not a wicked game, policeman. And soon my benevolent master will give me to Sam Lau so that he can make me his wife."

A great pity softened Lou Grandon's face. "Your master lied to you, Bho Kum. It was the most evil of all games, and he never intended to keep his promise."

Her eyes flew wide. "My lord?"

Grandon said very gently, "The fortune-cake held sorry fortune for Sam Lau, little one. It held this love message signed falsely with your name, and Sam Lau's heart asked his mind no questions."

Bho Kum said with a catch in her voice: "You tell me the truth, policeman? By the peace of your *amah* and your honorable father, you do not lie?"

"By the peace of all my ancestors," Grandon swore sombrely. "The note asks Sam Lau to leave the Fragrant Almond Chamber when the lights go dark. It asks him to wait for you at the alley door of his honorable father's shop. But it was not you who met him there, little dancer from Soochow. It was a great ugly shadow, and the shadow carried a knife."

Bho Kum's heart beat in her voice. "My master is a laughing man. He is kind. He does not whip me."

"There are beasts," said Grandon, "that laugh over the torn flesh of the dead. And weapons more cruel than any whip, Bho Kum. No, your master is not kind… In the alley back of the chemist's shop, there is a refuse bin where no one would think to look for a boy's body." He rolled the paper between his palm. "Do you understand now where I found this note, little Bho Kum?"

GRANDON COULD NOT face the awful entreaty in her eyes. There had been no contradiction, after all: she was only a frightened child in the dark. He said slowly, "I am not a laughing man, Purse of Gold, and so I can grieve with you. And with Sam Lau's worthy parents, to whom your master delivered the body this evening."

Bho Kum cried out only once: but it was a sound more eloquent than the dreary minor of Sam Lau's woman.

Grandon said, "Bho Kum?"

The oval face was passive now, shut in mysterious calm. "My lord?"

Grandon said, "You do not believe any longer that your master is benevolent?"

"I have never believed it, honorable one. I lied to you."

"And will you help me? You will not be afraid?"

Bho Kum spread her hands on a great emptiness. "It was only for the boy Sam Lau's sake that I was ever afraid. He told me Sam Lau would die unless I obeyed."

Grandon turned to the window. He raised the smoky yellow blind and then let it sag back into place. Moonlight dusted the narrow room and the dancing girl's dark hair; but brighter than any moonlight was the great golden lantern that glowered from the Yan Yuap belfry.

"You saw the light, little one?"

"Yes, my lord."

"Do you know its meaning?"

"No, my lord."

Grandon said, "It is the beacon your master hoped to see in the tonghouse, Bho Kum—for the beast that laughs over the flesh of the dead is the same beast that fattens in time of war. It is a death-light, little flower. It means that the Yan Yuap tong has put a price on the head of every Jok Lem tongster in Chinatown."

"Because Sam Lau is dead?"

"Yes, Bho Kum. And being innocent of Sam Lau's murder, the Jok Lem tong will meet the challenge with a light of its own. Much blood will be shed because your master has taught honorable men to distrust each other again."

"It is an evil light, my lord."

"A very evil light," said Grandon. "Nor will the war stop there, Bho Kum. The two tongs have their branches throughout the country—and so it will spread, and spread, and scores of young men like Sam Lau will be shot down."

"The light must go out, my lord."

"Yes, it must go out forever, Bho Kum. You and I will—"

She swayed backward against the wall and said huskily: "Great one! The door! The door!"

Grandon smiled a lean hard smile, took out his service gun.

4

Hide in the Dark

THE DOOR MOVED noiselessly, letting darkness into the room inch by inch. In the darkness, a rind of golden brilliance flashed once then receded into a huge innocent face. Grandon centered the service special on the place where the smile had been.

He said, "Close the door quietly behind you. And let your hands be empty of steel when they come out of your sleeves, fat one. Both my gun and I know your skill with a knife."

The mountainous mandarin kowtowed politely, great tears

glistening on his lashes. He pressed the door shut with his shoulders and cautiously removed his dimpled hands from wide turquoise sleeves. He looked from Grandon to Bho Kum; and his smile would have been less frightful had it been less benevolent.

He said to Grandon, "I did not hear the conversation, illustrious, but I can guess its nature. You know now why my eyes weep even when my teeth smile. *Wah!* Better that a man's soul transmigrate into a pig than that he have an unnatural daughter who lies about her father."

Grandon said, "She does not lie. And she is not your daughter. And that is not why you weep."

The fat man's eyes swung reproachfully to the girl. "Little quail, how could you have told such tales to a trusting foreigner? For money? *Eh-yeh,* I know now why silver ingots are sometimes cast in the shape of a faithless woman's foot."

Grandon's index finger tightened in a muscular reflex. "The threat is not too subtle to be read by this foreigner, fat one. I have heard the story of the slave girl whose foot was shod in molten silver because she betrayed her master. But this time the master will be in the police *yamen* awaiting a trial on a double murder charge."

"Hai!" said the giant. "Murder?"

"The murder of young Loong and of Sam Lau."

An enormous tear trembled on the mandarin's nose. "But surely you make humor, sinjin. I did not even know of Sam Lau's death, and I was at least a stone's throw away when the boy Loong was slain."

"One may cast a knife as far as a stone."

"And place it accurately in the dark?"

"If one is a man who weeps in the light. I know the nature of your affliction, fat one. It is a disease called nyctalopy, and the light of day is torture to your eyes. But there are compensations, aren't there? You see with a cat's eyes in the dark."

The fat man wept. "May Quan Yin turn his face from me forever if this tale is true! Why should I wish to bring evil on my unfortunate countrymen?"

"They are not your countrymen."

"*Ho?*"

Grandon moved slowly toward him. "You are neither a true mandarin nor a true Chinese. I knew it today when you said, 'we Chinamen are an unhappy people.' It is a term never employed by the Chinese themselves."

"*Ho?*"

"From the size of your bones," said Grandon, "I think you are a renegade Manchu. But your nationality is of little moment, enormous one, since your services belong to any country with an open purse. You are simply a professional agent provocateur, and any schoolboy could guess the name and motives of your present employer."

The giant put his shoulders to the wall, smiling through his tears. "It is a theory, sinjin."

"And fact as well. Divide and conquer! Your employers know that millions of American dollars are pouring into Chinese hospitals and the war chest of Generalissimo Chiang Kai-Shek. They know that the Chinatowns of this country are the conduit pipes through which a great deal of that foreign gold passes. And they know that the disunity and terrorism of a national tong-war would do far more than stem the flow of gold—that its net psychological effect might very well cost

China as a nation much of the favor its expatriates have won for it here… Is this pure theory, fat one?"

"It is pure theory," smiled the weeping man: and with one great swing of his arm he sent the nut-oil lamp to the floor.

The flame sketched a pale calligraph and died in tinkling glass.

The girl Bho Kum moaned in the darkness. "Great one! He will kill you now!"

THE SERVICE GUN struck at Grandon's palm. Above the girl's voice he heard his bullet drive solidly into fat and bone; and reviled himself in the next instant for the subconscious impulse that had shifted the gun-barrel.

He said, "Bho Kum! Run!"

Bho Kum's feet made a fugitive skirl of sound. Somewhere in that intense darkness the fat man laughed cheerfully though his pain. "But not too far, small one," he said. "Perhaps I shall want to punish you later."

The dancing girl's heeltaps ticked in the hallway.

Grandon clipped two shots at the voice; and knew on the next heartbeat that only the shock of recoil had saved his life. The point of a thrown knife passed along his rib-cage and sank trembling into the wall.

"*Hai!*" said the fat man. "Do you, too, see in the dark? Well, I have other knives."

"You had better use them fast," said Grandon, "or you will be out of blood before you are out of knives."

"There is much blood in a fat man."

Grandon took two forward steps and swung the gun-barrel hither and yon. In that unbroken darkness it was like trying to impale an evil spirit on the point of a pin. A man in his natural element at last, the Manchu seemed to move as noiselessly as vapor for all his elephantine weight. Twice more Grandon shot at the disembodied voice, and twice the fat man's genial chuckle came to him across the dying echoes.

"I am saving my knives," he said, "but you are prodigal with your ammunition."

"I carry two guns," lied Grandon, "and plenty of shells for both."

THE FAT MAN swung his arm. It made a silken whisper no louder than the clash of a butterfly's wings, but all Grandon's ancestors shouted in warning. He sat on his heels. The blade of another Han knife quavered eerily in the wall. And this time the fat man did not laugh. A cryptic silence folded over the room. Grandon's wrist-watch went chickety-chic-chic in an explosive little burst of sound.

A woman downstairs coughed into her palm, reminding them discreetly that this game could also tax the endurance of those who only stood and listened.

Grandon's fingers clasped a chair leg.

"*Hoya!*" said the fat man. "A strange weapon, sinjin—and you make an excellent target."

"But I think," said Grandon, "you will save your last knife until I make a perfect one."

He feinted with the chair and swung it at the window rather than the fat man.

It was a stratagem that caught the window, the fat man and the woman downstairs by surprise. The woman trilled like a bird. The window chattered hysterically. The fat man cried

"Hai!" in a voice of pain and surprise.

Moonlight cut an oblong hole in the wall and laid its bright lacquer on everything in the room; and for three chics of Grandon's wrist-watch the Manchu stood utterly still. Bemused by the light in his vulnerable eyes, he stood like a great black cutout against the riven window-shade.

The fat man threw the knife.

Grandon ducked under the blade and shot its owner with a complete economy of effort putting his sixth bullet where the first should have gone.

Grandon went out into the street.

"BHO KUM!" HE shouted. "It's all right, Bho Kum."

There was no *"Ai?"* from the shadows around him. Chinatown's hush was a thousand miles deep, and his voice shattered against that silence and came back to him with questions in it.

He tried it again. "Bho Kum?"

Grandon looked up at the infinite archway above him. "Hell!" he whispered feelingly; and broke into a sudden run.

Where the Yan Yuap tonghouse drove its spearhead cupola into the moon's bright path, there was no sign of the great golden lantern that had been brighter and more wicked than any moon.

Grandon came to a stop in the shadow of the tonghouse.

"Bho Kum," he said; and this time there were no questions in his voice.

He remembered then that the girl Bho Kum had been as literal-minded as any other child. And that he had told her that the golden lantern must go out or there would be war in Chinatown. And that the iron stairway up the building-side was steep, steep—perilous, it might be, even for a dancer's sure feet.

Or had the stairway betrayed her footing, after all? He remembered too, that her face had been shut in a certain mysterious calm…

Lou Grandon said, "Well, there will be peace in Chinatown, Bho Kum," and spread his coat very gently over the patch of darkness where she lay. For the girl Bho Kum lay across the shards of the great Yan Yuap war-lantern: and the golden flame in the lantern and the girl had gone out into the darkness together.

THE BLUE COFFIN

Steve Fisher

"I shall return and bring death to Honolulu…"
As the dying Chinese hissed those words Mark
Turner smiled coldly. He didn't think he would
ever recall that weird threat in horror—
didn't guess he might have to pit steel bullets
against the cunning of the living dead!

THE ARMS OF approaching darkness slid a crimson shaft of light across the old and twisted road that was River Street. In that swollen stream of stagnant water that rumbled ruthlessly toward the sea, was all the dirt of Honolulu. It was a river of filth and slime, and River Street was no better—sidewalks broken, cobblestones out of place, the odor of garbage everywhere about it.

A tall shadow leapt across the road as the lone figure of a man blocked out the monotony of the barren street; his heels crunched in a sure step. A breeze rustled past him, whispering, perhaps, a mordacious tale of murder; or echoing a grim warning to the white man who was daring to intrude upon the streets of the godless yellows of Oahu. The breeze died away. A hushed stillness suggesting death descended slowly, hovering with the stifling heat. There was only the swish from the gutter called River Street, now—that and the abated breath and crunching steps of the white man.

He was over six feet tall. His shoulders were straight and his body tapered down like the body of a swimmer. His arms and legs were thick and well muscled. His service automatic rose and fell on his hip with each step he took. He alone in Honolulu dared anything at any time. He alone could walk up River Street and live. To the Orientals and all the other races and mixtures of races in the Hawaiian Islands, he was "Red Eyes."

Mark Turner's eyes were not really red. But his face being a strong bronze in color, his hair a vivid red and a trim red Van Dyke beard being on his chin, the natural contrast made the somber brown of his powerful eyes appear dark red. When he was angered, fire seemed to flash from those optics—it was a fire the natives both admired and feared. To them Mark Turner was more than a captain of Honolulu detectives, he was a white superhuman.

In spite of his powerful reputation, however, Turner had no qualms about the mission he was now bent upon. Nor did he flatter himself that he was so feared that some Oriental wouldn't send a blade hurling into his back as he passed by.

He was on dangerous ground, and no one knew it better than he. He was here, he hoped, to see the worst Asiatic fiend who had ever come to the Islands and stayed out of jail, draw his last miserable breath and die.

Turner would take no chances in a mere coroner's report of this death.

Two men had been killed in Honolulu streets within the past week. One had been an individual who was prominent in

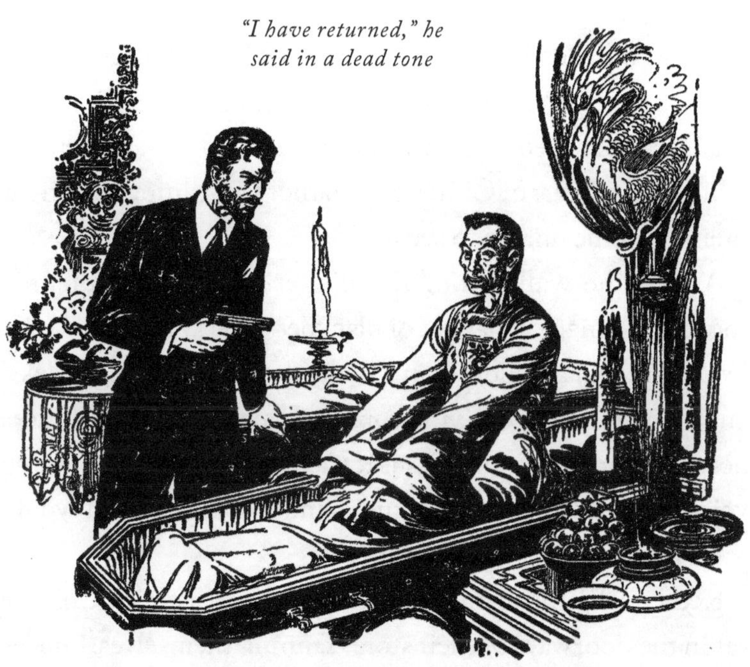

island business. The other had been only an illiterate Hawaiian who had raved about a "rat" springing at him, just before he died at the hospital. He had been walking down the street, he said, when this giant rodent with gleaming eyes and long fangs suddenly appeared. The wounds on the neck of the Hawaiian were identical to those found on the dead businessman.

Turner had fretted over the case. He had stayed up with black coffee, and his astute mind had attacked it from every psychological angle. When he had at last arrived at the conclusion that the old and powerful Su Lee was behind the killings, and had started his men gathering evidence to that effect, the case was suddenly shattered by a personal call from the Asiatic, which stated that he was dying and that he wished to die "clean" so that he could join his most honorable ancestors.

It sounded like hokum to Turner. A lure into a death trap,

perhaps. But Red Eyes had been in those kind of places before. Being a dick never was an easy job, and no one ever said that it was. If Su Lee died, Turner would see him do it—and perhaps while in the heart of Chinatown gather some information his men would be unable to secure.

And so he walked on. The flickering shadows merged together to make a blanket of blackness that was pierced only by the grotesque yellow lamps in the doorways of "pig shacks" and miniature pagodas. The confused buzzing of the Chinese became louder; it seemed as if it was a rising flood of droning voices that was circling around, climbing higher, and would soon break in mad oriental tumult.

Red Eyes Turner came to a narrow alley of a street. Chinese sat in the doorways of their stores fanning themselves. Graceful Oriental females dressed in alluring robes lingered as near to their windows as they dared. There was the stench now of cheap incense, and the noise of voices was a mad babble. In the distance the tall house that belonged to Su Lee loomed like a monster among midgets.

Turner's heels cracked along the road. He looked to neither his right nor his left. His arms were swinging free, but they never wavered too far from his unhooked automatic holster.

His blood chilled as the thought came to him that behind any corner—lurking in any doorway, on any rooftop—the rat that had already murdered two men might be waiting to strike down another. Perhaps, feeling Turner on his trail, it would try for him. He tried to grin. But the atmosphere was too heavy for gaiety. Death was too close.

He was hating the unending noise more than ever. Squawky music, rattling pans, voices, voices. The *slap-slap* of slippers. The veiled and burned-out laughter of Manchurians. The excited cry of the coolie class. All blending together, rushing through the darkness. All confusing, combating, and then—

A shrill gong screamed out.

There was an immediate silence. The quiet wings of death swept low, and the ghastly shadow of murder hovered near. Silence. No movement. Frozen yellow faces. Evil, gleaming eyes. The incense was heavier, the air stickier.

MARK TURNER STOPPED in his tracks. His hand slid back to his automatic. Gripping the gun in his palm, he moved forward again. His reddish eyes were narrowed. His lithe body was as tense as that of a cat. The trim red Van Dyke etched his face in grim lines.

He went up the steps to the large house of Su, rapped upon the gold-colored panel with the butt of his gun. He was breathing faster when the eye-panel slid back. The door slipped open. A servant bowed.

"Master very low. Gong mean death of master soon. Three gong mean master then dead."

It was always that way, and Turner knew it. One gong when a man approached death, and three when his spirit joined that of the others in whatever heaven Confucius promised. There could be no faking about that. It was evident that Su Lee was very ill.

"Does Su wish to see me?" Turner asked low.

The sleek servant clasped his hands and bowed. "If honorable master of detective will honor Su Lee—"

"Lead the way," Turner snapped. "If he is sick we have no time to waste."

The Chinaman turned and started down the corridor. Red Eyes was taken through first one room and then another. All were designed with fine Oriental tapestries that showed a taste most discriminate to lovers of exotic beauty.

The death room, however, had black walls. Ebony they were, and they glistened like the top of a coffin and made the withered figure of Su Lee, who was on a large white-covered bed, stand out weirdly.

A tall Manchurian stood in one corner of the room. His arms were folded. He was Low Sam—Sam Low to Americans who patronized his herb business in the central parts of Honolulu. Turner had often believed that the tall and ghostly looking Sam Low was interested in more than herbs, and now he knew it, or at least felt that he did.

Low had a bony face with slant eyes that seemed to haunt one. Two ugly snags of teeth protruded over his lower lip. His fingernails were long and black looking. The yellow skin of his face was taut.

"I am glad to see you join us in the mourning for our brother who is about to depart," he said in a whisper.

"Yes, and I'm rather glad to be here," Turner answered, eyeing the Manchurian coldly.

The slim and lovely figure of a girl was at the foot of the bed. Her face was waxen. Turner thought he had never seen anything so reposed or tranquil as the expression that she now had. From her position he realized that she was the only living child of Su Lee. It was customary for the son to stand at the foot of the bed, but Su Lee had no sons. Perhaps this was why he had called in Turner. He thought he was dying in shame.

"My honorable father is about to descend into a better

world," the girl said quietly.

Turner glanced down at the sick man. His fingers were gripped tight. A red agate ring, large and beautiful, was the only ornament that he wore. His cheeks were sucked in and the lids of his slant eyes looked as though they were heavy, laden with the lead of time.

"I am going to die," he hissed. "I am quite ready now. But I have something to tell you all first. Come closer."

Turner leaned over the side of the bed. The aged Chinaman continued.

"I am coming back. I am earth bound. I have been slaving all my miserable life to discover the formula for eternal living, and now it is mine." His old and burning eyes stared up into Turner's. "I was not a gentle and peaceful soul during my span of living. I had and still have the diabolic powers of a devil. I shall return after death and bring hatred to Honolulu." His fists grew tight. His face was strained a little, and suddenly he jerked as if some kind of a shock had shuddered through his body. "I shall return to kill," he went on, his voice hoarse and ghastly, "because I hate—I hate—"

He sucked in his breath. The dry, rasping air sent a shivering sound throughout the room. Then Su Lee relaxed. The heavy lids of his eyes closed. His daughter moved forward and covered his face. The one white man in the room moved back. He faced Sam Low.

"What did he mean by what he said?"

A trace of grim, deathlike smile flickered across Low's yellow face.

"Su had been preparing for this end. All his life he has dealt with chemistry; with herbs that even I knew nothing of; with bits of life—"He ended his explanation with a weary shrug of his shoulders. "He says that he is coming back to kill. I hope that that is not possible, but I am afraid."

"You're an idiot," Turner snapped. "Men don't return from the dead."

The same inane smile shadowed itself on Low's thin lips.

"Perhaps not, my honorable friend," he said. "But remember that the Chinese race is the oldest in the world. We know secrets that you and your modern-minded scientists would not believe. Everything and anything is possible." He looked away, then his narrow black eyes returned to Turner. "In the event that his death is a permanent one, however, I am taking charge of his gambling casinos. He has left them to me."

Red Eyes Turner's lips grew tight. "You'd better stay out of the racket, Low," he said, "if you know what's good for you." As he spoke he was thinking of the marks in the necks of the men who had been murdered by the huge rat.

"I am the new and defiant king," Low continued in a monotone, "unless Su Lee comes back." His fanglike teeth flashed ominously.

"Suit yourself," Turner said. "But it's not going to be so easy for you. I'm clamping down on you babies. These oriental charms of yours have lasted too long. Much too long, Low. Tonight—"he jerked his thumb toward the corpse—"with his death, the end has come to everything concerning Chinatown's crook world."

"One grows weary of such talk," Low said.

The Chinese girl turned on them both. Her lower lip was tight.

"Get out. Please, both of you get out. You don't seem to realize that my father has just died. You two stand here and—"

"My humble apologies."

"I don't want to see you anymore, Mr. Low. Please go away from here."

Sam Low moved toward the door. Turner took a last glance at the corpse and followed.

A PORTLY BUSINESSMAN stopped in front of the Honolulu court house and lit a cigarette. He glanced at the bronze statue of King Kamehehi. His hand shook as he dropped the match to the sidewalk. Beads of sweat were cropping out over his brow.

He began walking on. Then suddenly a brown form flashed from the heavy shadows. It looked no larger than a huge dog, but it leapt with the spring of a gorilla.

The fat man screamed hoarsely.

"The rat!"

"THEY ARE THE same damn marks, sir," the detective reported.

Captain Turner stared down at the corpse that was lying just in front of the statue. He rubbed his Van Dyke beard slowly. The high cheek bones of his face contrasted with the iron hardness of his jaw.

"I ordered no one to touch the next victim of this so-called rat," he said slowly.

"I didn't touch it, sir, but I can see those marks. They're as plain as day when you flash your light down. It's the same two."

Turner's reddish eyes were like stone. He bent over the corpse. With a quick glance at the two jagged marks on the back of the neck, he quickly turned the body over.

"Lewis Smith," he breathed, "he's one of the big shots on the real-estate board." He said it more, it seemed, to assure himself that a third murder had occurred and that once again an important man was the victim.

"The papers will eat this up," the young detective said.

"Never mind the papers. Turn your light down here. Smith didn't die without a struggle, I don't think, even if he was practically scared to death."

Turner went over the body carefully. He found scratches. They didn't look much like the scratches of a rat. He was about to give up until the body was taken to the morgue, when he saw something in the grass just below the statue; something with a hard tinny glow.

The captain of detectives snatched it up immediately. He turned it over in his hand. As he did so his lips grew tight again. Fire seemed to erupt from his reddish eyes. He got to his feet.

"Have them take the body away," he said in a low voice.

THE SUN GLINTED its late afternoon shadows in through the window, spreading a golden blanket across Mark Turner's mahogany desk, which was littered with various kinds of papers. His elbows jammed on top of them and his head resting on his fists, the detective captain presented a picture of concentration.

Several other men in the room sat motionless, waiting for some word from their chief. A clock on the wall ticked ominously. Evening would be coming again—and with it the hour of the rat.

Mark Turner lifted his head. His hard, reddish eyes scanned the faces of the other detectives, then he glanced down at the scattered papers. "All of these," he said, "bits of evidence; stuff we practically stole to get—and it all points toward Su Lee as being behind this rat racket."

"And Su Lee is dead," said a lieutenant.

"He's dead and I'm crazy," Turner replied. "Lewis Smith had been blackmailed by the rat. The first two murders scared him. He decided to kick in with the dough. He went to the statue last night according to instructions to leave the money demanded. The money was wrapped in a paper package; his secretary told us that. The package is gone—and Smith is killed."

Turner lit a cigarette. He stroked his Van Dyke soothingly and went on talking.

"Other members of the realty board on which Smith served have received similar blackmail threats. They are scared stiff. If they don't pay, they will be killed; if they do pay, they will be killed—"

A tall sergeant leapt to his feet. "It can only be one guy, chief. This Sam Low. He's the most powerful."

Turner shook his head. "It couldn't be Sam Low. He's crook enough but he wouldn't go in for that stuff." Red Eyes pounded his fist on the desk. "It has to be Su Lee!"

"But Su Lee is—"

Turner jumped up. "Damn it, I know it. He's dead and I'm nuts trying to figure this out. You guys beat it. I'll do some investigating on my own."

But Turner couldn't help remembering the hoarse and rasping voice of the dying Su Lee. "I shall return from the dead and bring death to Honolulu because I hate—I hate…" The diabolical warning shrieked back into the detective captain's eyes. Somehow he couldn't shake it from his mind.

The sergeant remained at the door as the others filed out. He turned to Mark Turner.

"I checked up on Sam Low's store," he said. "Low hasn't been there all day. I thought you might like to know that."

Turner had been staring down at the red thing he had picked up near the corpse last night. He glanced upward now.

"Low hasn't shown himself today?"

The sergeant shook his head grimly.

Turner puffed on his cigarette, then suddenly he threw it down and stepped on it. His high cheek-boned face grew as hard as stone.

"I've got an idea," he said, "a helluva good one. If I'm wrong I'll report in at the asylum, in the meantime—"

"Where you going, chief?"

"To Chinatown again," Turner replied.

MARK TURNER'S AUTOMATIC was leveled on the Chinese girl. He was entirely unconscious of the exotic tapestries around him; even of the mystic perfumey incense that wafted in the air. His burning eyes were on the girl.

"I was told that Sam Low is here. He didn't go down to his business in Honolulu today. For that reason I want to see him."

The girl shook her head. "He is not here."

"Where is your father's corpse?"

"The prayer room is honored with his old and respected body, but—"

"No burial?" Turner snapped.

"He desired to rest in this house until he could return to life."

"I want to see this prayer room."

"You may not," the girl said firmly. She moved her hand toward a hidden gong.

Turner snatched the stick from her hand. "Call any of your slant-eyed friends," he warned, "and I'll have to get rough with you. I really wouldn't want to have to do that. I'd be a good girl, if I were you."

She was breathing faster. Her face was stoic with disguised hatred.

"We are going to this prayer room," Turner told her. "Do you understand?"

Suddenly she leapt back. Her elbow whipped into the gong. She stood straight then, her lips twitching defiantly. Turner backed up. He felt the wall; knocked on it, and found it solid. He weighed his body against it.

Presently there were three Chinese in the room. Turner's automatic had them covered, but that seemed to make no difference. They began approaching him.

"Get back, you coolies," Turner barked. "I'm not fooling you."

They kept on coming. Turner fired, hitting one of them in the shoulder. They had been waiting for that. Five others sprang out. Gunfire roared out into the room. A knife slashed into Turner's side.

His automatic spat bullets with the rapidity of a machine gun. He counted the yellow men going down, laughed madly at the contorted, grotesque looks on their faces.

And then he barged forward, swept past the girl. He stampeded through two rooms, took the winding steps to a second floor. The hall at the top of the steps was dark. One glimmering blue light flickered at the very end, and that was all.

From downstairs the girl screamed. "Stay away from that room—it is the room of the living dead!"

Ignoring her, Turner rushed forward. He threw his weight

against the door; it smashed open.

The sight inside was pretty in a way—if death can be called pretty. There were half-coffins there. They were the shape of coffins—two of them, one on each side of the room—and they were blue. Over each one there was a blue light. It was a ghastly illumination that showered radiance upon the two dead men.

Turner stared down at Sam Low. The tall Manchurian's hands were folded peacefully. His face had lost the strained look. The snags of teeth that protruded over his lip seemed to be harmless. The detective felt his hand. It was stone cold. Sam Low was dead.

His red eyes burning to pierce the dim blue light, Turner swung about. He gazed at the other coffin. He saw the still corpse of Su Lee.

And then he saw something that made the blood in his veins run cold. Su Lee's hand moved. Slowly, surely and stealthily it moved. Gradually the whole body of the ancient Chinaman began rising to a sitting position.

The weary old eyes popped open. Glassy blackness stared through the misty light and into Mark Turner's grim white face. Parched and whitened lips moved; a withered yellow face became contorted.

"I have returned—" Su Lee said in a dead tone. "I told you I would, Turner." His words were slow and deliberate.

Turner leveled his automatic. It was empty now, and he knew it.

"Lay back down," he barked, "or—"

Su Lee got up from the coffin. He seemed like a spectre as he slithered across the room and toward Turner. His arms were outstretched. His glassy eyes were glittering. The white death powder on his face was streaked and ugly.

Turner dropped his empty weapon. He reached out both hands and clutched Su Lee's shoulders. He shook the Chinaman.

SUDDENLY THERE WAS a human fury. No longer was there a dead, walking corpse. It was a mad animal. A beast at bay. Clawing fingers tore at Turner's throat. A kicking leg tripped him back. Smashing fists beat into his face.

Stumbling to the floor, Turner was for a moment at a disadvantage. The attack had come as a complete surprise. The detective lunged, his powerful arms out. The strength he put into the punches knew no limit.

But the attacking thing seemingly felt no pain. It bit and scratched and gouged, and its energy was without limit. Turner felt his head being bashed back against the floor. He jerked his body, twisted it around. Throwing out his arms he struggled to release himself from the thing.

At last, his breathing coming shorter and hot sweat streaking his bronze face, Turner was successful in throwing the attacker from him. He leapt to his feet. When the thing rushed again, his quick right smashed to the jaw.

A left followed in. He sent Su Lee reeling back. Turner stepped forward. He jerked out his handcuffs and slapped them on Su Lee's wrists.

The old Chinaman shook his head. His eyes were wild. He was no longer reposed or calm.

"All right, all right," he said, "it was you, Turner, or it was me."

"It might have been me, had you not been so stupid in your deception of death," Turner said. "I was convinced at first that you had really died. Then when they didn't sound out the three gongs for you—like they did that first one—I began to wonder. Even in trying to make the fake look real you hated to break the rules of centuries and lie in the gongings about death."

"I was afraid you'd think of that," Su Lee breathed.

"The whole set-up was," Turner went on, "that you were extorting money from wealthy businessmen by threatening death by the 'rat' if they didn't pay up. You killed a couple of men to show that you meant business. When I got wise and sent the boys out for evidence, you knew I'd find out if you didn't do something, so you invented that phony death.

"The flaw there was that Sam Low was in on your scheme, and when I thought you were dead, he decided to double-cross you, thinking you wouldn't be able to show your face around Honolulu to claim what was yours. So you killed him, too. Then you killed another businessman so that I would think that the rat was someone else, because you were already dead."

"Talk—talk—" Su Lee murmured. He pricked his arm with his thumbnail.

"The main thing that'll hang you in court though," Turner rasped, "is this." He pulled something from a pocket and waved it in Su's face.

Su Lee nodded. "My lily—my daughter, she did not know. She believed me able to return from the dead. Do not harm her, will you?"

Turner was silent a moment. He had in his hand the big red ring that had been on Su Lee's finger—the same ring he had found by the statue. He was examining the two jagged points that extended when the ring was squeezed properly.

"So the rat," he breathed low, "was Chinese, and the fangs, tin ones."

Su Lee slumped to the floor. Turner had been so busy presenting his evidence that he hadn't seen the thumbnail prick in Su's wrists. He saw it now, however, and he understood.

He sucked in his breath, and turning, left the room. He circled the stairway and descended slowly. The girl was still where he had left her. She had been afraid of the room with the coffins. Her slant-eyes were wide.

"He is a corpse that lives, isn't he?" she breathed. "I didn't want you to know. I—"

"What about Sam Low?"

"He went to feed my father herbs that gave him the power of a giant. Didn't you see him up there?"

Turner nodded. Stooping, he picked up the clapper to the gong and handed it to the girl.

"Remember this," he said firmly, "the dead don't return. Now take this and ring it three times, and then three times more."

TONG TORTURE

Emile C. Tepperman

They warned Nick Ronson to wash his hands of the case—so he stuck with it like a leech. But when he got mixed up with a Tong revenge gang, it looked as though he'd bought a one-way ticket to hell.

THE BODY OF the dead Chinaman was the first thing that Nick Ronson saw when he came into the library of the wealthy Gregory Deming. Next to the Chinaman was another lumpy form.

The man from the medical examiner's office was just starting to work on the body of the little yellow man. He was not pleasant to look at; he had been shot through the head, and the bullet had come out in back.

Nick turned an inquiring glance at the others.

McGuire, of homicide, was sitting in a straight-backed chair and talking confidentially to Gregory Deming. Deming, the well-known collector of jade, seemed to be all broken up.

Not so, McGuire. The homicide man was smoking one of Deming's expensive cigars with evident relish. His trousers were pulled up at the knees, and the cuffs were an inch or so above the tops of his purple socks, which he wore without garters. He glanced away from Deming, and his self-satisfied look changed to a sulky frown when the manservant preceded Nick Ronson across the room—taking care to give the bodies a wide berth—and announced to the jade collector, "Mr. Ronson, sir."

Deming pulled himself together, arose with a word of apology to the homicide man, and offered his hand to Nick.

Nick shook hands with him, then said to the police detective, "Hello, Mac. How's tricks?"

McGuire scowled. "Pretty good till you showed up. Anybody send for you, or did you just smell trouble?"

Deming smiled apologetically at McGuire. "Sorry. I've been so upset I forgot to mention it before. I thought it best to hire a private detective as a bodyguard. These Orientals, you know—"

"Sure, sure," McGuire growled. "It's your privilege, Mr. Deming."

Nick said, "I didn't understand that you only wanted a bodyguard. I could have assigned one of my men for twenty-five a day. I don't usually—"

Deming interrupted. "I know, Mr. Ronson. But I don't want an ordinary operative. I know you're worth more than that yourself—but I'm ready to pay it. You can write your own ticket."

Nick shrugged. "All right, if that's the way you feel about it." He glanced across at the bodies. "Who did all the shooting?"

Deming said nervously, "I did." He pointed to an open wall safe. "I got back earlier than usual tonight, and found the Chinaman at the safe. He had stabbed Frayner." Deming closed his eyes hard as a surge of emotion swept over him. He indicated the body under the sheet, next to the Chinaman. "That's Frayner. He was my secretary; been with me for five years; just been married—and he has to be stabbed to death protecting my jade collection from a common thief!" The collector turned back to Nick, his chin quivering. "That Chinaman must have had the combination, because the safe was open the way it is now. When I surprised him, he came at me with a knife—the same knife he killed Frayner with. Luckily, I was armed, and I shot him."

McGuire got out of his chair. "Everything checks," he told Nick. "There's the knife on the table. The Chink's prints are on the safe. I called downtown, and Inspector Glennon said it wouldn't be necessary to bring Mr. Deming down now. It's a plain case of robbery and murder."

Nick said. "So what am I supposed to do around here? What're you afraid of, Mr. Deming?"

The tall, graceful jade collector was looking at the body of the yellow man with somber eyes. "I'm afraid there may be—reprisals. These Chinese—"

NICK WALKED OVER to the body. The medical examiner was through, and was making out a report. On the dead man's middle finger was a wide gold band. Nick bent and saw that there was an inscription in Chinese characters etched in the gold. He could read the hieroglyphics almost as well as he could read English; he had spent many eventful years in the East. That particular inscription he had seen often before. Translated, it meant roughly, "Respect the gods, but have as little as possible to do with them."

Nick arose from the body, and faced Deming. "Did the Chink get anything out of the safe?"

Deming nodded. He produced two pieces of jade from

his pocket. Each piece was five and a half inches long. There were jagged edges on one side of each. Nick took them from Deming, and fitted them together. The jagged edges fell into place, the two pieces became as one, forming a little icon, or image, representing a man squatted upon a low pedestal.

Across the front of the pedestal was engraved the same inscription as on the dead man's ring!

Deming was saying, "That's a figure of Confucius, carved in nephritic jade. The workmanship is consummate; the piece is perhaps two thousand years old. It is absolutely impossible to estimate its value in dollars. I wouldn't sell it for a million."

McGuire took the cigar out of his mouth to say, "The Chink had both pieces in his pocket. That's all he was after."

There was a thoughtful expression in Nick's eyes as he handed the image back to Deming. "Looks to me," he said, "like you'll need more than protection—you'll need life insurance. This image comes from a shrine of Kung Fu-tsu, which is the Chinese equivalent of Confucius. The shrines of Kung Fu-tsu are under the special protection of the Kung Tong, and the dead Chinaman there is a member of it." He shook his head. "No thanks, Mr. Deming. I can't take the assignment. When those boys have it in for you, it's just too bad."

McGuire said sneeringly, "Just yella, huh?"

Nick glared, was about to say something nasty, when Deming interrupted hastily. "Look here, Ronson. From what I've heard of you, you're not the man to turn down a job because it's dangerous. That's why I called you in. I want to keep this jade, and I also want to stay alive. I'll pay you five thousand dollars to fix it so I don't have to worry about this Kung Tong any more—and I don't care how you do it!"

Nick considered for a moment. Then he said, "They may want indemnity—for him." He nodded toward the body.

"I'll pay it—whatever they ask. And the fee to you for arranging it."

"All right," Nick agreed. "You keep to the house—don't go

out till I see what's what. I'll send a couple of my men over to take care of you in case these boys start something prematurely."

Deming said, "You want a check?"

Nick nodded. "In advance. I don't guarantee results, and I'd hate to have to sue your estate for it."

Deming made a wry face, but he sat down and wrote the check.

Nick took it, grinned at McGuire, and went out.

In the street he hailed a cab, and said, "Corner of Race and Marley."

WHEN HE GOT out of the cab he walked down a half block, and stood for a moment, looking up at the bleak brownstone facade of the house on Marley Street.

He made sure that his .32 Special slid easy in the holster beneath his armpit, walked up the five steps of the stoop, and rang the bell.

Almost before he had his finger off the button, the door was opened by a short, skinny Chinaman, who, when he saw Nick, bobbed his head and said squeakily, "Hello, Misteh Lonson. Come lite in. Charley Mee waits for you."

Nick said nothing, but his eye went to the gold band on the middle finger of the Chinaman's right hand. It was the same kind of ring that the dead Chinaman in Deming's living room had worn.

Nick stepped into the dark hallway, and the servant closed the door. Then he turned and led the way toward the rear, saying, "Please to follow me, Misteh Lonson."

Nick thought he detected a subtle gleam in the skinny

Chinaman's eye, but he had long ago learned the futility of trying to read any sort of meaning into the expression of a Chinaman's face. He went along behind him till they reached a massive oak door at the end of the corridor.

The servant rapped in a peculiar way—twice, then once, then three times very swiftly. Almost at once there was a click, and the heavy door started to swing open.

The room within was only dimly lighted by a single low lamp that stood near the door.

In the middle of the room was a long table. There were chairs around this table, but none was occupied except the one at the head, facing the door. In this chair sat a very fat, motionless Chinaman.

Nick stepped into the room, and the door closed mechanically, leaving the skinny servant on the outside. Nick noted that the fat man was manipulating a row of buttons on the table. These, doubtless, controlled the door—also, perhaps, various other gadgets in the room.

Nick walked up to the end of the table opposite the fat man and said. "Hello, Charlie. How did you know I was coming?"

The fat man spoke impassively. His countenance, which was almost entirely in shade, hardly seemed to move, except for his lips. His English was as good as Nick's, with the exception of a slight lisp. "This poor offspring of a snail," he said, "is overwhelmed with humiliation that he cannot rise to fittingly greet the eminent Mister Ronson. But the disabilities of old age weigh heavily upon me. I—"

"Can it, Charlie," Nick interrupted him, unceremoniously. "I know you're a fraud, so why waste all the words on me. How did you know I was coming?"

Charlie Mee did not move. His voice took on an edge of sharpness. "You are the same old Nick Ronson—always getting to the point. What difference does it make how I knew? You are here. You have something to say?"

Nick nodded. He put both hands on the table, leaned forward. "I have, Charlie. And this is it. You're the head of the Kung Tong. I know it, because I learned it once when I did you a service. I was well paid for that service, and we are quits. I ask nothing for that. But I have come now to offer you something."

Charlie Mee said nothing, did not move. He waited in silence, the epitome of the patient Oriental.

Nick went on after a moment. "Today, one of your brotherhood broke into the home of Gregory Deming, the jade collector. He stabbed Deming's secretary to death, and attempted to steal a jade figure of Kung Fu-tsu, Deming surprised him, and when this member of your Tong attempted to attack, Deming shot him in the head."

Still the fat man maintained silence. Only his eyes were now glittering dangerously.

Nick continued. "Deming was justified in shooting your Tong member. But he's afraid the Tong may be out for blood—so he's engaged me to keep his skin whole. I have taken his money, therefore it follows that I must fight his enemies. I should be very sorry if you felt that you had to avenge this member of yours who killed Deming's secretary."

Nick stopped. He had made his position clear.

For a long time Charlie Mee gazed at him impassively down the length of the bare table. Nick wondered what devious thoughts were going through that Oriental mind.

Finally Charlie Mee stirred and spoke. "The laws of the

Tong forbid me to speak freely to one of an alien race, Mister Ronson. But I am sorry that you have taken this man Deming's money. For it is written that Deming must die—and you must fail in your task. Let me give you a warning—return this money and wash your hands of it. There is safety for you in that course. Otherwise, much as I regret to say it, death waits for you, as well as for him."

"You don't understand," said Nick. "Deming is willing to pay a cash indemnity to satisfy the Tong. You can practically name your own price."

Charlie Mee answered him, speaking very slowly. "There is no indemnity, Mister Ronson, that will satisfy the Kung Tong. Deming's life is forfeit. We will purchase the jade image from his estate."

NICK TOOK HIS hands off the table and stood up straight. His hands hung loosely at his sides, and he nudged the armpit holster a trifle forward with his left arm. "Then it must be a war between us, Charlie. You know I never back out of a job."

The fat man nodded. "I know that, Mister Ronson, and that is why I took precautions when I learned that Deming had sent for you. I knew that you would come here first, for you are a straightforward man, a worthy opponent. But you are beaten. Deming is beaten. It is regrettable that you, whom I truly admire, must go down to destruction with your client."

Nick smiled crookedly. "All right, Charlie, we understand each other fine—you love me, and I love you—like brothers. In fact we love each other so much we're gonna have a little private war."

The fat Chinaman nodded. "Reluctantly, I agree with you.

It is war!" He leaned forward a little, his eyes staring opaquely along the table.

"When," Nick asked, "does this war start—when I leave your house?"

Charlie Mee's fat lips twisted into a smile. "I am so sorry, Mister Ronson. The war must begin—now! Even though you are a guest in this poor house of mine, I cannot afford to allow you to leave it alive. You are the only white man who knows of this house. Now that you are an enemy, you must die!"

Nick scowled. His hand flashed to his armpit holster, but stopped when Charlie Mee rapped out an imperative, "Wait!"

The fat man raised a forefinger on which the elongated fingernail gleamed to a claw-like point and indicated a section of the wall at Nick's right. "I told you," he went on, "that I had taken precautions."

Nick, standing rigid, his hand within an inch of the gun butt, flicked his eyes to the right, and started.

There was a panel in the wall which must have opened soundlessly. Framed in the opening, knelt a raw-boned, high-cheeked hatchet-man. He was dressed in black, with a black skull cap. Beady eyes were sighted along the barrel of a Browning rapid-firer which was trained unswervingly on Nick's middle! A yellow hand fingered the lever tautly.

Nick swung his eyes back to the fat man. He still kept his right hand taut, and spoke through thin lips. "It won't do, Charlie. Your playmate will get me, all right, but I'll crease you, too, for sure. You know I can do it; right through the heart."

Charlie Mee smiled. "Indeed, you are renowned for your skill with a gun. But I have anticipated that, too. These buttons on the table are not the only ones. My feet—"

Even as he spoke, his feet moved, and a sheet of steel shot up from what had looked like a groove in the table. The steel snapped up to a height of about four feet, effectively screening the fat man from Nick's view.

At the same time, from behind the barrier, Charlie Mee uttered a short string of commands in Cantonese.

Nick rolled away from the table, his hand snaking out the gun at the same moment that the Browning in the hands of the hatchet-man began to spit flame and to chatter wickedly in the semi-gloom.

Nick heard the wicked spat of the slugs tearing into the floor just beyond the spot where he had been. If the raw-boned Chinaman had been more adept at handling the quick-firer, he could have raked the room and torn Nick to pieces. As it was, though, he kept his finger on the trip, and exhausted the entire drum before he could shift; it takes a lot of practice to swing a Browning, even in a short arc, before the drum is empty.

The hatchet-man didn't realize his ammunition was out, and finally got the Browning around so that it bore on Nick. But it no longer spouted lead. He looked down at it with an expression of puzzlement.

The quiet in the room after the smashing chatter of the gun was oppressive.

Nick was on his knees on the floor. The hatchet-man raised his head in sudden panic as understanding came to him that he was without ammunition. He dropped the rapid-firer, and his hand darted to his sleeve, came out with a glittering, curved knife. But Nick was on his feet, grinning and yelling, "Oh Boy!"

He darted quickly across the room, and brought the barrel of his gun down on the Chinaman's skull. Yellow skin cracked, and the hatchet-man dumped forward on the floor, face down on the Browning, the knife still clutched in convulsive fingers.

Nick swung around, stepped toward the far end of the long table where Charlie Mee had been. Charlie Mee was no longer there!

He had evidently slipped out through another panel when the shooting started.

Nick came back to the open panel. The hatchet-man lay across the opening, and the panel, which had started to close, had stopped its motion when it hit him.

Nick stepped through and found himself in a long, dark corridor. The walls were of some sort of metal, lined with asbestos. Sound proof. Which accounted for the absence of police after the shooting.

The dim light from the room behind left the far part of the corridor in blackness. Nick went along slowly, gun at his hip, left hand feeling the wall.

Suddenly, up ahead, a door in the left side of the corridor opened; a shaft of weak light illumined a form that leaped into the corridor; the door was closed.

Nick knew that he was outlined by the light behind him for the benefit of whoever had come into the narrow corridor. Instinctively he crouched, just as a gleaming knife flashed through the air above him. The knife caromed against the partly closed panel behind and clattered on the floor.

Its tinkling clatter was only an echo, though, of Nick's heavy gun roaring in the darkness. He shot three times toward the one who had thrown the knife, and then lay flat on the floor for a moment. At first there was no sound from up ahead, then a slight shuffling noise, and a groan.

NICK RAN FORWARD; getting out his flashlight. The man he had shot lay half reclining against the wall. He was small, yellow, with deep sunken eyes—another hatchet-man. Three distinct bubbles of blood spurted from his chest. Nick's shooting had been perfect.

Nick threw the light in the Chinaman's face, and even as he did so, the man's eyes glazed and there was a death rattle in his throat.

Nick's back was to the door that the hatchet-man had come out of, and he hastened to rectify that by hurrying away down the corridor. He glanced back at intervals, expecting the panel to open again, but it didn't. At last he reached the end of the corridor, and felt a door knob; turned, and found the door locked. He wasted no time, putting a bullet right smash into the lock between the jamb and the door. He tried the knob again, and the door swung free. Nick stepped out into the night and found himself in a back yard.

There was a litter of garbage cans around, and he started to make his way through them. He heard a window creaking open in the house above him. If he were spotted now, he could be picked off with ease. He looked about for cover. His hand rested on one of the garbage cans, and he saw that it was empty. Just as the window came up, he vaulted into the can and ducked his head.

From his retreat he heard Charlie Mee say in Cantonese, "Do not shoot; it is not desirable to attract attention to ourselves at this time. Go down into the yard and search. He has not had time to escape from there."

A moment later a voice from down in the yard near the door called out, also in Cantonese, "He has come through here, master; the lock is shot away!"

Charlie Mee ordered, "Search the yard carefully, then. Look in all the trash cans. Do not let him escape!"

Feet scurried in the yard. Nick held his gun steady, barrel pointing up toward the sky. He could see a single star above him, and a slowly moving cloud that was moving up to obscure the star.

Suddenly a gaunt yellow face hid the star and the cloud from his view. The face started to shout, and Nick fired. The face disintegrated, and Nick jumped straight up, put a foot on the edge of the can, and vaulted over.

A chorus of shrill yells came from various parts of the yard. Flashlight beams flitted about. Nick stepped over the body of the Chinaman who lay alongside the garbage can, and darted across the yard.

From the window above, Charlie Mee shouted in shrill sing-song dialect, "Shoot! Shoot now! He must not escape!"

Nick swung his gun up and took a pot-shot at the sound of Charlie's voice, and knew that he had not hit him, for wood splintered in the framework of the window up there.

Lead winged past him, a slug tore at his sleeve. But the Chinese are notoriously poor shots, and he reached the fence unwounded. A dark shape hurtled at him, and Nick straight-armed that shape with the hand that held the gun. The shape uttered a pained yelp, and collapsed.

Nick hoisted himself up on a garbage can alongside the fence and jumped. Shouts rose to a tumultuous crescendo behind him; a gun barked from the window above, and just at that moment Nick's foot caught on a projecting nail as he was clearing the fence. His arms went out wildly into the air, and he hurtled over into the next yard. He landed heavily on concrete, the breath knocked out of him for the second.

He heard one of the Chinese in the next yard call out, "He is killed, master. Your aim was true!"

Charlie Mee replied from above in his unhurried voice, "Come up, then, quickly. Leave his body. We must abandon this house before the police come."

Nick got up and felt about for his gun which he had dropped when he fell, picked it up, and sped away through the yard, down an alley.

He saw the back of a policeman who was just turning the corner on the run from Race into Marley, and he walked away rapidly in the opposite direction.

At the corner of Claremont Avenue he hailed a cab and gave the address of Deming's home. Just as the cab got under way, a police radio car tore down Claremont and rounded into Race, with siren shrieking.

The driver called back through the open sliding window, "Must be another shooting. The way these cops ride, you'd think there wasn't nobody on the streets but them!"

Nick didn't answer; he was busy loading his gun.

A LITTLE SURPRISE was waiting for him in front of Deming's house. There was a police radio car at the curb, a headquarters' car, and an ambulance. A small crowd was being held back from in front of the entrance by a couple of bluecoats.

One of the cops stopped Nick as he shoved his way to the front row of the crowd.

"What's happened?" Nick demanded of the cop.

The uniformed man didn't vouchsafe him any response, but pushed him back into the crowd. Nick lunged, shoved the cop out of the way, and sprang up the steps of the house.

The policeman roared, "Hey, you!" and leaped after him.

Nick gained the entrance, and bumped into a giant of a man in plain clothes who was just coming out.

Nick gripped the man's sleeve, panted, "H'ya, Glennon? Tell this flatfoot I'm okay, will you? He wouldn't listen to me!"

Inspector Glennon scowled at Nick, and grudgingly said to the cop, "It's all right. Get back there and hold that crowd."

Then the inspector took Nick by the arm and urged him into the house. "You're just the baby I been looking for, Ronson. There's something stinks in this whole business, and you're the fair-haired boy that knows all the answers!"

"Sure," said Nick. "I know all the answers. Any time you're stuck, just ask me. Only suppose you tell me what's happened around here?"

Glennon looked down from the height of his six-foot-two to Nick's measly five-foot-ten, and said, "Nothing's happened, baby. Nothing—at—all!"

He piloted Nick into the living room, and Nick gasped. The living room looked like a temporary field hospital. McGuire lay stretched on the sofa, groaning, while a white-coated interne wrapped bandage around his head.

Munsey, one of Nick's operatives, sat in the easy chair while another interne taped his arm. The body of the Chinaman whom Deming had killed was still on the floor next to that of Frayner, the secretary. Both were covered now.

Nick's other operative, Joe Brody, was standing by the couch trying to help the interne bandage McGuire's head. Joe Brody had his right trouser leg rolled up above his knee, and his leg was plastered up with gauze and adhesive tape.

Inspector Glennon let go of Nick's arm and said, "Well?"

Nick said, "What was it, Joe, a raid?"

Joe Brody turned from the couch and grinned sheepishly. "Just that, boss. The Chinks took us unawares. I was in here with Deming, and Munsey was outside at the door. McGuire, here, was keeping Deming and me company until the morgue wagon came for the stiffs."

"So what happened?" Nick asked impatiently.

"So the first thing," Brody went on, "we heard a battling around at the outside door, and a shot. So I get up to take a look-see, and just at that minute three wild Chinks bust in here with a sawed-off shotgun, and let fly without a single word. It got us all except Deming who was sitting in that chair over there, out of range. Then when I was on the floor with this stuff in my leg, I tried to go for my gun, and one of the Chinks covered me. So I had to lay there while they dragged Deming out."

Nick's eyes were smoldering. "Nice!" he grunted. "Fine protection we gave Deming! What happened to him?"

Glennon coughed. "They took him away in a delivery truck marked, 'Fancy Groceries.' There was an alarm out for the truck inside of five minutes, but it did no good. We found the truck down on the West Side, abandoned. They must have switched to another car."

Nick asked, "Did Deming have that jade figure on him?"

Brody shook his head. He took the two pieces of jade out of his own pocket. "No. He had given them to me to hold. And the dopes never stopped to make sure he had them. I guess they were a little nervous, even with the riot guns."

Nick snatched up the two parts of the jade figure. His eyes glinted.

Glennon growled at him, "Look here, baby—what's this all about? Where were you while this was going on?"

Nick laughed mirthlessly. "Where was I? I must have been at a movie. Or maybe I was having my nails manicured." He turned to go. "Take Munsey home when he's fixed up, Joe. And don't feel too bad about it. I should have put an army in here instead of just two guys."

Glennon's thick arm came up to bar his way. "Hold everything, baby! Where the hell do you think you're going with that jade! And where the hell do you think you're going—anyway?"

Nick stopped short and glared at him. "I'm gonna earn my five grand, you dope, by getting Deming out of one hell of a pickle. You should be the last one to stop me. I'm doing cop's work for the department, and all I get is abuse!"

"All right, all right," Glennon soothed. "Don't get huffed up. That jade figure is evidence, an' we'll need it. You can't take it away like that."

"This jade figure," Nick said slowly, "is what is going to save the police department a hell of a lot of razzing. Because it's going to bring Deming back with a whole skin. Do I get it, or don't I?"

Glennon stared at him stonily for a long while, then shrugged. "You're a hard guy to get along with, Ronson, but I got to play this your way. You're in the saddle. You wouldn't want to take me in on the know with you, eh?"

"I wouldn't," Nick told him.

Glennon sighed. "Go ahead, then." His brows came together, and he poked a finger under Nick's nose. "But if you muff this, and let Deming get bumped, I'll ride you out of town—and don't you forget it!"

Nick pocketed the jade, grinned across the room at McGuire who was sitting up on the couch looking like a Turk with the bandage on his head and a scowl on his face. "So long, Mac," he called, and went out with a mock salute to Glennon.

OUTSIDE, HE SAW the same cab driver who had brought him to the house. The driver grinned, and said, "I figured there'd be some sort of a ride back, so I hung around."

"All right," Nick grunted. "You get a good ride. Take me through the Holland Tunnel to Hoboken—and squeeze the minutes!"

At the corner of Ninth and Peasley, in Hoboken, Nick got out of the cab and said, "If you're looking for more business, you can wait around. I might be coming back."

The driver grinned, showing a hole where two teeth were missing. "I'll wait. You seem to be the kind of a guy that always comes back."

Nick left him and walked up past two or three buildings till he came to the dirty plate glass window on which was lettered:

Sam Mee Hand Laundry

There was a light in the store, and three undersized yellow men were working away industriously, with the sweat pouring down their necks and soaking their undershirts. They were all south of China boys, meagre of build, but wiry, and dangerous in a fight.

One of them came behind the counter when Nick entered, looked at him expectantly, as if waiting for him to produce a "tickee." But when he got a good look at Nick, his face became blank, devoid of expression. His body seemed to go taut.

Nick said, in Cantonese, "It is many months since I have seen you, Sam Mee. Your health is good, I trust?"

The other two Chinamen looked up from their work when they heard the fluent flow of sing-song syllables coming from the white man's mouth. Sam Mee did not show by a single flicker of expression that he understood what the detective had said. His hand stole along underneath the counter, while his eyes remained locked with the visitor's.

Nick saw the movement out of the corner of his eye, and shook his head reprovingly. "The wise man knows when he has met his superior," he quoted in Chinese. "Do not try to press that button which will warn those inside, Sam. You remember the time that I saved you from a murder charge? You remember how fast my shooting was then? I can still shoot, Sam."

He spoke very softly, but Sam Mee stopped the motion of his hand, brought both hands to the top of the counter.

"I remember," he answered, "the service you did me, thereby placing the whole Kung Tong in your debt. But this is a matter that is deeper than the life of any of us. My brother has told me about your visit to the tong house, how you chose to take the other side. He thought you were killed there, but I see he was in error. Now that you are still alive, I beg of you, do not go behind the rear partition tonight, for you will exhaust the patience of the gods. It will surely mean your death, and I will be sad."

Nick wagged his head from side to side. "Sorry, Sam, but I got to see this through."

He walked sideways toward the rear of the store, keeping an eye on all three of them. At the rear wall he felt around with his hand until he found a button. He pressed it, and a section of the rear wall slid open. He stepped through, and the sliding door closed behind him.

He was in a lighted, bare room. A wiry yellow man sat before a closed door at the far end. The yellow man snarled, his hands moved like lightning, and a knife came hurtling through the air. But Nick was already on his knees. The knife imbedded itself in the closed panel, and the Chinaman reached for a gun.

Nick flashed his own out of its holster, covered the other. The Chinaman froze, hand inside of his shirt.

Nick said in the other's tongue, "You are not ready to go to meet your ancestors yet. Do not draw that weapon."

His words were convincing enough, for the Chinaman took his hand slowly out of his shirt, raised it and the other in the air. Nick came up close to him, said in English, "It hurts me to do this, brother, but you know how it is!" His left fist crashed against the Chinaman's chin, and the hatchet-man went down in a heap with a muted groan.

Nick gripped hard on the knob of the door the hatchet-man had been guarding, and turned it slowly. Then he pulled it toward him very gently. The door opened.

Through the slight crack thus made, Nick could see a room luxuriously furnished in oriental style. But he could only get a view of a small portion of it. He saw a black-garbed yellow man stooping intently over something that might have been a table.

Then he heard a smothered cry of agony, and tore the door wide open, stepped in, gun at his hip.

THERE WAS A table in the center of the room. Deming, stripped to the waist, was strapped to the table. Charlie Mee was standing close by, regarding the proceedings with a benign expression.

The black-garbed hatchet-man, Nick now saw, was one of three around the table. He was holding a strange sort of thing that looked like a pin cushion with the pins reversed, the points sticking outward. The cushion was attached to a bamboo handle, and just as Nick stepped into the room, the hatchet-man had finished sweeping it down across Deming's naked chest in a raking blow that caused the pins to scrape bloody furrows in the jade collector's body.

There was a bandage over Deming's eyes, and he strained against his bonds in agony.

Nick said nothing, just swung his gun in an arc to cover the four yellow men. One of the black-clothed ones made a motion to go for a gun, but Charlie Mee, with a movement that was surprisingly swift for so fat a man, put a restraining hand on his arm.

The hatchet-man let his hand drop to his side, and stared at Nick out of narrow, wicked eyes.

Charlie Mee walked around the table, came close to Nick, with his hands spread out, palms up. He said very low, in Cantonese, "You are a man of miracles. I was aware that you knew of this place, but I thought that you were killed; my heart is glad now that you were not. Since you seem to have us at your mercy, I ask you to wait another moment; you may learn something that will surprise you. Please answer me in my own tongue—I do not wish that Deming should know you are present."

Nick looked into the fat man's eyes, and shrugged. "I will wait, and see what I shall see," he answered. "But I am not to be taken unawares."

Charlie Mee nodded wordlessly and returned to the table on which the blindfolded Deming was strapped. He spoke to him in English. "Where, my friend, is the image of Kung Fu-tsu? Before we go on with the Death of a Thousand Cuts, you have another chance to speak."

Deming groaned. "I tell you, I haven't got it! I gave it to that private detective. Get him. If you torture him, he'll give it to you. God, let me up! I can't stand any more!"

Charlie Mee bent lower over him. "Tell us, then, once more, what happened in your house when you killed the brother of the Kung Tong—not the story you told the police and Mr. Ronson, but the true story!"

Deming spoke with difficulty. His chest was heaving, little rivulets of blood were running down his body from the cuts onto the table. "God! I've told you that already. Can't you let me alone?"

Charlie Mee said patiently, "There is a man here whom the Tong holds in high esteem. We wish him to hear the story from your own lips. Speak quickly, and we may spare you further—er—affliction."

"All right," Deming moaned. "That Chinaman had half of the Confucius, and I had the other half. He wouldn't sell, he wanted to buy my piece. He brought his part to my house to compare it—I got him to do it, making him think I was willing to sell. And when he came, I killed him; killed him, and took his half. Together, the two halves make the most precious piece of jade in the world. I would have killed a hundred men to own the whole thing!"

Nick's eyes opened wide while Deming spoke. He took a step toward the table, his face purpling, but he stopped as Charlie

Mee bent lower and ordered, "Repeat now, the part about the secretary."

"I killed Frayner, too," Deming croaked hoarsely. "Frayner came in just when I shot the Chinaman. He saw me do it. I hit him on the head, and then stabbed him with the Chinaman's knife. Then I touched the Chinaman's fingers to the safe and made it look like robbery!" His body sagged weakly in the straps. "Now, you devils, let me up," he gasped.

Charlie Mee straightened up over the table, and his eyes met Nick's. Then he waved the three hatchet-men back. The one with the pincushion went to a corner and put it away.

Charlie Mee said to Nick, still in Cantonese, "You see, my friend, the nature of the cause you have espoused? I could not explain to you before because the laws of our Tong forbid us to speak of our wrongs to one of an alien race, even if it means death to those we love. We must work out our own vengeances." He smiled a little. "But I have violated no Tong laws. I told you nothing. This man has spoken for me. Now you know."

Nick slowly put his gun away. From his other pocket he took the two jade pieces, laid them together and handed the image to the fat man. "This is yours," he said.

Charlie Mee took the icon, and for the first time he smiled. "I was desolated when I had to order you killed, but the Tong comes before all else, as you well know, who have yourself lived among my countrymen. Had you died, I intended, when the image was recovered, to follow you into death to seek your forgiveness. I am a happy man."

Nick took from his wallet the check that Deming had given him and tore it to bits.

Charlie Mee looked at the pieces of paper and said, "The Tong knows how to reward its friends. You shall not be the loser for having destroyed that check."

"The man on the table," Nick said sternly, "must be turned over to the law."

Charlie Mee bowed graciously. "We are done with him. He is yours. The price he would have received for his half of the jade shall go to the dead man's relatives as indemnity."

"All right," said Nick. "You deliver him. I'll go ahead and prepare Inspector Glennon."

From the table came a moan, and Deming called out weakly, "What are you going to do with me? What are you going to do with me? God, don't cut me with those pins anymore!"

"You," Nick said in English, "are not going to be cut any more. You are going to burn!"

And he went out to find his cab.

THE HOUSE OF DOOM

Arden X. Pangborn

*Lee Taitt knew that Death walked the dank
and sinister byways of Chinatown—knew
that somewhere in the maze of Yellow Crime
lay the answers to his comrades' deaths,
but never guessed that vengeance lay in a
painter's brush and a penny box of matches.*

DETECTIVE LEE TAITT stood in the tenth floor office
of the police commissioner.

"O.K., chief," he said. "Shoot."

The commissioner leaned back in his red leather swivel chair,
staring moodily across the broad, glass top of his walnut desk.
His bony fingers toyed absently with a yellow pencil; his square
face wore a worried look. Even the criss cross section of lines
about his small, bright eyes—the only service stripes the city
had ever given him—seemed more deeply etched than usual.

"You know why I asked you to report here?"

Taitt shrugged. He was a tall, lean man, almost gaunt. His
arms were long, his shoulders powerful. About him lurked an
air of hidden energy; it was as if he were tense, eager to burst
into sudden violent action.

*Wang Tai crashed back
into the gaping pit*

"Chinatown maybe," he said. "I don't know."

"Chinatown." The commissioner nodded slowly. "Yes, Chinatown." He leaned forward. "Two of our men have disappeared in Chinatown within the last week, Taitt. Monday it was Hazen; Wednesday it was McMorran. We know they got to Chinatown. Both of them were seen there. Then they vanished." He made an upward and outward motion with his two hands. "Utterly. Just like that. We don't know how. We don't know why. But we've got to find out. It may not be easy."

"No, it may not be easy." Taitt's jaw was firm. "But I knew Hazen, chief. We'll tear down Chinatown if necessary."

"Do it your own way, Taitt. You spent several years in China. You know Cantonese and Mandarin and maybe something about the way the Chinese think. That much you've got in your favor. The rest you'll have to work out for yourself."

"O.K. I'll get a room, move into Chinatown. It'll take a little money to do it right. Fifty bucks or so. And it'd be a good idea if you'd shoot some men into the district to make an investigation. Ask a few questions, anyway. Otherwise they'll be suspicious."

"But if you move into Chinatown openly, you'll be spotted right away."

"Maybe." Taitt shrugged again, and his eyes took on a sparkle. "Then, maybe not. We'll find out. But I've got an idea. I used to paint some over in China, mostly pretty bad landscapes. I'll pose as an artist. Maybe they'll think I'm just crazy. If they do, so much the better."

"And if they don't—well, you know the answer, Taitt." He rose from his chair, almost impulsively shoved out his hand. "I'm counting on you, counting hard," he said. "The whole force is. Go to it—and good luck."

Taitt grinned to himself as he set up his easel on a corner in the heart of Chinatown at 9 o'clock the following morning. The natives were about to see some of the world's worst painting, he admitted inwardly. He arranged his canvas, his brushes and his oils. Then he made a show of studying the light, the perspective, the colors. Presently he began to sketch.

About him a stream of bland, yellow faces eddied and swirled. He had been wise enough not to don beret and smock, but even in his rough tweeds, badly in need of a press, he attracted plenty of attention. He didn't mind the staring eyes, however, nor the smiles, nor the occasional jibe in Cantonese that reached his ears.

After all, to attract attention was really a part of his plan. He must establish himself as an unsuspicious character as rapidly as possible. Otherwise he could not hope to mingle with the Chinese without arousing suspicion. They must become accustomed to seeing him in their midst and to accept him as an artist—as a would-be artist, at least. Then there might be some chance of his picking up a clue, a hint—some chance remark in the language they would think foreign to him, a bit of gossip perhaps. It was a thin hope, but an only hope.

So he daubed with determination, keeping his eyes and ears open and hoping that the result on his canvas would not be too bad.

His subject was a row of little shops, picturesque in a mild way with their gold and scarlet signs, their mottoes in Chinese characters upon window and doorpost, their motley display of goods for sale. There was a meat shop, with its long strings of browned pork and salt fish showing in the window; a jewelry shop, with its bits of rare old jade and rings and earrings of hand wrought gold; a clothing shop, with silks and satins from the bazaars of Canton and Shanghai.

When Taitt finally folded his easel for luncheon, he grimaced at his work. But then, he consoled himself, the Chinese might think it modernistic. Besides, no one had shown any doubt of his sincerity, which was the most important thing.

He moved his easel twice the next day, each time picking out a crowded section of the colony for his labors. Fewer and fewer Chinese halted to peer at him in wonder as the hours dragged on, but Taitt kept doggedly at it. He knew the time had not yet come to cease his task, to risk any show of curiosity. Another day, perhaps.

IT WAS ELEVEN o'clock on the third morning when Taitt, daubing at his fourth square of canvas, looked up just in time to see a man across the street turn into one of the shops taking form beneath his brush. There was nothing particularly unusual about the man. Had it not been for his own task at the moment, Taitt probably would not have noticed him at all; certainly he would not have remembered him if a second man had not entered the same shop a moment later. Then Taitt recalled that both of the men were white.

He jabbed his brush into a spot of green paint and made a sweep across the canvas. It was a matter of no consequence, he told himself. Plenty of white men have legitimate business in Chinatown. Presently, however, he realized that neither of the men had reappeared. Meanwhile, other men were entering. The newcomers were Chinese. Taitt found himself counting them. There were four. They, too, all remained inside.

A few minutes after the last one had entered, a little, fat Chinese with an apron tied around his middle padded out of the shop, fiddled for a moment with some ropes at the side of the door and slowly lowered a bamboo curtain over the dusty, plate glass window. Then he padded back, pulled another curtain over the glass in the door and vanished inside.

Taitt's brush paused in mid-air. His forehead wrinkled. The man was closing shop with his customers inside in the middle of the morning! It didn't quite make sense.

Taitt's interest in his art lessened with rapidity. His eyes lifted to the name on the red bricks above the window. "Peking Merchandise Company", he read. In Chinese characters beneath the faded black of the firm name was a long motto: "May heaven bestow peace and happiness and may clouds of trade gather around the business carried on here."

He was still wondering what that business might be when, half an hour later, the fat little Chinese in the white apron came through the door again, lifted the bamboo shades, and, without the slightest change of expression upon his round, yellow face, retired once more to the interior.

Taitt made up his mind quickly. He folded his easel, picked up his paint box. There might be nothing unusual about the Peking Merchandise Company, nor the business transacted with so much secrecy behind its bamboo curtains, but it wouldn't hurt to investigate.

He crossed the street, turned toward the shop. Directly ahead of him, a thick-shouldered man in a light gray topcoat whirled suddenly, let out a cry. Taitt jerked to a halt, his free right hand darting toward his shoulder holster. Then he cursed himself for a fool. The man was not in danger. He was wobbling on his feet; there was something wrong with him. Even as Taitt realized his error, the man stumbled, clawed wildly at air and went down in a heap.

Taitt was at his side in an instant, bending over. Already a crowd was forming. Taitt dropped his easel, grasped the man's shoulders, turned him over. A gasp escaped his lips:

"Markel!"

It was Markel, all right—Gus Markel, G-man and implacable foe of crime. Taitt had worked on a case with him once; that had been a long time ago, but there was no mistaking those square rugged features, those bushy brown eyebrows. Taitt remembered him well. Everyone who ever worked with Gus Markel remembered him—remembered him as brilliant, fearless, incorruptible.

So it was that Taitt gasped when the name came to his lips, for Gus Markel would work on no more cases. Warm, sticky red gushed from a gaping hole in the side of his neck and the muscles of his face jerked convulsively from shock. Taitt knew instinctively what had happened. The ravages of a soft nosed bullet were too plain to be mistaken. From somewhere close had come a leaden missile from a silenced weapon. That missile had spelled death.

Markel was still breathing, but he could not hope to do so for many moments. His eyes fluttered open as Taitt bent over him. It seemed that recognition flashed for the briefest instant across his rugged features. His lips moved. There was no sound at first. Then three syllables came in a tortured whisper:

"Ng sup chut. Ng sup chut." He paused and his labored breath was like wind blowing through a field of straw. "Fifty-one. Fifty-one!"

He stiffened suddenly, then relaxed. Taitt rose. It was all over. A siren sounded close at hand. Someone had called headquarters. Taitt pulled himself together. It would not do to be recognized here by police. He hesitated a second, then turned, picked up his easel and paints and disappeared into the crowd.

"Fifty-one!" The number ran over and over in his mind as he worked his way through the throng. His mouth was strangely dry, his face hot. "Fifty-one!" What had Markel meant? Or had he meant anything? Had he been merely mumbling in the delirium that comes before death? But no, he had whispered the figure in Chinese first. *"Ng sup chut!* Fifty-one!"

Taitt found himself free of the crowd. Suddenly he realized he had completely forgotten the original object of his mission.

The small, green door of the Peking Merchandise Company was only a step away. He crossed the threshold.

The fat Chinese with the white apron was behind the counter, peering through the dusty glass of his window at the milling pedestrians outside. His yellow countenance lacked any indication of emotion as he turned to face his customer.

"What was it?" he wondered aloud.

"Man killed, it looks like." Taitt's sharp, blue eyes circled the shop. "Shot, I guess. Got any matches?"

The fat Chinese bent under the counter. "Too bad," he said. He brought out a red and white box, laid it on the counter.

Taitt lighted a smoke, flipped the match at the doorway. Nothing very suspicious so far, he decided. The shop was typical—small, dimly lighted, none too clean. A dankness was in the air and a mustiness in the goods on the many shelves. The abacus at the fat little proprietor's right hand seemed little worn from use, the proprietor himself but little worn from worry about it. A copy of the Chinese daily paper lay crumpled on the counter. At the rear, two doors led off into the inner regions of the building.

No, nothing suspicious so far, Taitt thought, but what had become of the six men who had entered and failed to reappear?

"You knew him, perhaps?" suggested the Chinese, motioning with one arm toward the street.

Taitt shook his head. "Never saw him before," he said. He dropped a coin on the counter. It would not do for him to linger too long, to seem too interested. "Thanks." He turned to go.

AS HE DID so, a roar of laughter came from somewhere

behind the thin partitions at the rear. Instinctively, he turned again. One of the doors at the rear had swung open. One swift glance and the door banged shut again, but Taitt saw enough in that single flash to make him laugh at his own suspicions. The mystery of the men was solved. They were gathered about a green covered table and before them were the ivory faced pieces of a mah jongg set!

The fat little Chinese followed Taitt to the door, smiling and nodding his round head energetically. "You come again," he suggested.

"Sure," said Taitt.

He went outside, stood on the sidewalk. The police ambulance had come, taken away the body of Markel. The crowd had begun to disperse. Taitt felt strangely lost. Two detectives had vanished; a G-man had been slain on the street in broad daylight. Two jobs and he didn't quite know where to start on either one. He had no contacts, no stool pigeons, not even a clue.

He paused on the curb, staring moodily into the street while he finished his cigarette. What made him turn back to glance once more at the shop, he never knew. Perhaps it was that instinct which good dicks have, that instinct which solves more cases than all the fancy sleuthing in the world. At any rate, he did turn back. He turned, and froze.

Above the dingy doorway where the dull green paint had best withstood the ravages of time and weather was the shop's street number. It was in tiny figures of faded black, but had it been in blazing lights a foot in height it could not have shocked Taitt more. The number was fifty-one!

Taitt started back toward the shop, then hesitated, shook his head. After all, he had nothing on the fat little Chinese. The fact that Markel had died mumbling the number of the shop would mean less than nothing in a courtroom. He changed his mind, strode off down the street; but his eyes were narrowed to slits and a hard glitter shone in them as he made his way back toward his room. Already a plan was forming behind those eyes.

Darkness had fallen over Chinatown. A few lights gleamed brightly from the windows, but the noises of the narrow streets were quieted. Along the darkened sidewalks, shadows slipped occasionally, but even these were few in number. The whole atmosphere seemed subdued and strangely silent.

Taitt hitched his automatic forward in its shoulder holster as he turned into the alley. Above him through the thin slit between the tops of the buildings he could see the soft blue of the night sky. From somewhere came the moody melody of a three-stringed guitar, the *san hsien,* and the melancholy, piercing notes of a transverse flute. Something in the weird, distant music sent a little chill up his back. He shrugged off the feeling, let his fingers rest for a moment on the butt of his weapon. It was cool to his touch.

He had come now to the rear of the building which housed the Peking Merchandise Company. There was but one door in the flat brick wall and it was buried in heavy shadow. He approached cautiously, tried the knob. It was locked. Then his eyes, lifting, rested upon a small window above the door. He climbed, resting his foot on the knob, and his long fingers pressed the pane of glass. It gave under his touch. A smile touched his thin lips. He pulled himself up, squeezed through the narrow opening. As lightly as some jungle animal, he dropped. There was a rustle of sound, nothing more. He paused, listening.

Ahead of him all was blackness, all was silence. He took a step forward, wondered if he dared risk a flash, decided against it. Presently his eyes became more accustomed to the gloom. He realized he was in a narrow hallway. He felt his way cautiously toward the front of the building.

The slowness of his advance undoubtedly saved his life. His exploring foot suddenly encountered space. Where the floor should have been there was no floor. Taitt's heart thumped in his chest. In the blackness, the yawning hole was only a little blacker than the floor itself. He would never have seen it. He stooped, examined the trap. It was nearly three feet square. In the Stygian depth below, he could see nothing.

He stepped back, leaped. The rubber soles of his shoes thumped lightly on the other side. Now his advance was even more cautious.

He came presently to a stairway. He hesitated a moment, then climbed upward. At the head of the first flight, he came to a door. It was locked. To try to open it would be to risk detection. He decided against it, moved back down again. His search led him in another moment to the room in which he had seen the six men playing mah jongg. From this room a doorway opened to the cellar.

The musty reek of damp earth and decaying wood assailed his nostrils as he descended. There was another odor, too—the unmistakable, pungent odor of burned opium. A dim light glowed dully in the distance, throwing a yellowish dusk in a circle about it.

The cellar had been divided into roughly constructed rooms,

Taitt saw. From one of them came voices. He crept close.

How many men there were behind the flimsy door, Taitt could not tell; four, at least—perhaps five. Some of them were speaking in Cantonese. Their tones were muffled and Taitt followed their conversation with difficulty. There was something about girls, smuggling. Then another voice, harsher than the others, broke out in English:

"Quit talkin' heathen, will yuh? Me and Bill's in on this, too. We got a right to know what's going on."

"Peace. Wang Tai will be here presently. Wang Tai will give orders."

Taitt felt a queer sensation come into the pit of his stomach. Wang Tai! Taitt had never believed that Wang Tai really existed. He had heard the name before—often. The Chinese generally blamed Wang Tai for all the crime in Chinatown, but they all admitted under pressure that they had never seen him, had never, as a matter of fact, really known anyone else who had ever seen him.

THE POLICE THOUGHT of Wang Tai as a mythical creature coined by the imaginations of the Chinese to explain what was otherwise inexplicable. And yet these men spoke of him as of flesh and blood. Wang Tai would be here presently! Wang Tai would give orders!

"He will bring with him six tonight," a smooth, oriental voice was saying. "They are already sold to the Pavilion of the Lotus Blossom. That will be a thousand dollars apiece for profit."

"O.K., O.K.," another voice agreed impatiently. "I'm not squawking about the price, am I?" This was the white man's voice. "How about a hand of fan tan?"

Taitt turned on his heel. Earlier in the day he had had nothing on which to base an arrest. Now he had plenty. He knew no details, true, but that could come later. He would organize a raiding party, wait for the arrival of Wang Tai, then—

The floor slipped suddenly beneath his feet. A gong boomed through the cellar, bright lights flashed on. He had stepped on a loose board, a board he had somehow missed when he had approached earlier—and that board had been wired to give warning. Instantly doors banged open. There were running footsteps, a shout.

Taitt's hand swept toward his automatic, then dropped. It was no use. Two burly Chinese with thirty-eights in their yellow fists were at his side. He was trapped. He shrugged.

Others crowded around. There were six, all told. He recognized the two white men who had entered the Peking Merchandise Company just before the death of Jim Markel. The other four might have been the Chinese who sat at the mah jongg table. He could not be sure. He looked for the fat little shopkeeper, but the latter was nowhere in sight.

One of the Chinese grinned evilly at him. He was a thin, dark man with heavy lips, hollow cheeks and a scraggly beard.

"Wang Tai will be pleased to welcome you," he said. He motioned the two with the automatics. His voice was cold. "We will take him to the upper room to await the orders of the master."

The upper room—there was something in those words, the tone in which they were uttered, that chilled Taitt's blood. He knew the Chinese, knew what devilish tortures they could devise, knew their calm acceptance of the death of their enemies. What unknown horror awaited in that upper room of which this thin one spoke so glibly?

One of the men ran hands over his body, took his automatic. Another prodded him in the back:

"Move!"

They climbed to the first floor, then up the flight at the top of which Taitt had found the locked door. Someone fitted a key into the lock and they went on. It seemed an interminable climb, but Taitt, counting the flights, knew there were only four.

He wondered vaguely what might be on the floors that they passed, but there was no way for him to tell. Lofts, perhaps, owned no doubt by the mysterious Wang Tai who would arrive presently with his cargo of six slave girls for the vice den of the Lotus Blossoms.

They came at last to the upper room. It was a small room, thick walled, tightly locked. Inside, one of the Chinese touched a light switch. Brilliance flooded the tiny quarters and Taitt felt a little shudder run through him. There was something faintly horrible about the room, something he could not describe. Perhaps it was the heavy, velvet drapes of black that surrounded the walls, funereal drapes, gruesome with suggestion.

Or perhaps it was the grotesque, pagoda-like shrine which faced the door, with its tablets, its incense pots and its image of the evil-visaged God of War. Above the shrine, two skulls, white and shining, grinned vacantly. Below were smaller figures, the Gods of Wealth—all five of them. In the deadness of the air, the odor of stale incense and burned tallow lingered.

This was a ceremonial room. The bamboo mats before the shrine proclaimed that fact. Into them had been woven in brilliant scarlet the characters Wang and Tai. Mats such as these could be used for no ordinary purposes, Taitt knew; the Chinese reverence for their written language would not permit such sacrilege.

The thin, dark man had moved behind a drape. He came forth holding in his skinny fingers a length of fine, silk cord. He uttered two sharp words in Cantonese.

"Tie him."

It did not take them long. Taitt found himself lying on his back, his arms and legs securely bound. The fine cord cut deeply into his wrists.

"There will not be long to wait," the thin one promised. He motioned the others ahead, closed the door. Taitt heard the lock click into place.

For a long moment, he waited, listened. Then he rolled upon his side. He had been bound before. The bindings held no terrors for him. By rocking back and forth, rubbing his leg across the floor, he gradually worked the objects from his right side trousers pocket. There was some string, a handkerchief, a couple of dimes, the packet of matches he had bought from the fat shopkeeper, a cigarette lighter. It was the lighter he wanted. With his teeth he set it upright on the floor; with his chin he pressed the trigger. Tiny flame appeared on the wick. The trigger did not snap back.

Taitt twisted, maneuvered his hands behind him. He could not see what he was doing and the flame licked at his wrists, but he gritted his teeth and stretched the silk cord tight.

Abruptly the flame found its mark. Taitt felt the fine silk snap. His hands were free. A grim smile crossed his face as he touched the lighter to the cord about his ankles.

HE CROSSED THE room with rapid, silent strides and pressed his weight against the door. The lock was solid. He was gathering himself for an assault against the heavy panels when voices came to him from the other side. The men were coming back!

Taitt's mind raced. But one thing remained for him to do. He retreated, dropped to the floor, fastened the cord loosely about his ankles, shoved his hands behind him. A casual glance would not divulge his secret.

The door swung open.

Taitt grunted to himself. Wang Tai had come—Wang Tai, the terror of all Chinatown! And Wang Tai was only the fat, little shopkeeper with the smooth, round face who sold a box of matches for a penny!

But there was something different about him now as he stood in brocaded jacket and silken trousers, his western clothing discarded. His dark eyes were mere slits, beady, brilliant. His oily face was drawn in tight, cruel lines. Even his voice seemed harsher when he spoke.

"So our tableau of the mah jongg table did not fool the white detective. It is unfortunate, most unfortunate. But not for Wang Tai." He paused a moment, the sneer on his thick lips unhidden. "The white detective should remember the wise man does not leap into the river until he has learned to swim."

Taitt gritted his teeth, but said nothing. His eyes roved the faces of those who had followed Wang Tai into the room. He found there only brutality and hatred.

"The business in slave girls is too good to be interrupted by the meddling of a few police. Two of your men have tried it; they have disappeared. You will disappear, also. The gods have smiled kindly upon the humble person of Wang Tai."

He turned abruptly, crossed to the shrine, stooped and opened a scroll-worked panel. He brought out a number of tiny, yellowish candles, placed five of them upon the altar— one before each of the five Gods of Wealth. The thin Chinese with the sunken cheeks touched a match to blackened wicks.

"And Jim Markel, the man who died in the street," Taitt rasped, "I suppose you killed him, too?"

Wang Tai's slitted eyes flickered evilly. "He should have vanished like the others," he gritted. "Only there was not time."

The thin one had placed incense before the evil faced God of War. Twin spirals of the blue-gray smoke crawled upward toward the blackness of the velvet covered ceiling.

"He would have reported a valuable secret," Wang Tai went on. "It was necessary to act quickly. With you, it shall be differ-ent. There will be time for the ceremonies."

The ceremonies! What sinister rites did those two words portend? What horrible murder had they planned for him? Taitt held a grip upon himself. It would not do to lose his head.

The candles lighted, Wang Tai approached his captive. His thick lips drew back over yellow teeth, his dark eyes gleamed. With the swiftness of a serpent's tongue, his right arm moved. From somewhere beneath his baggy jacket came a knife.

Taitt stared unblinking at the glint of light upon the polished steel. The blade was long and slender; its hilt was stained a muddy brown, as if from blood, long dried.

Suddenly Wang Tai laughed. It was not a pleasant sound. "No," he gloated, "you shall not die so easily as this. The knife is merciful." He bent and with a single motion split the cords with which Taitt had retied his own feet.

"Come!"

Taitt did not move. The two Chinese with the automatics jerked him to his feet, prodded him forward.

Wang Tai pulled back a drape. They were in another room, a room with neither door nor window. In its center was a railing nearly six feet square. Wang Tai leaned upon the railing, pointed downward. Taitt looked, saw space. A shaft had been constructed so it pierced the building, like a light well, to the lower floor. Wang Tai pressed a button. Far below, a light flashed on. The shaft, Taitt perceived, had been walled in from fourth to second story. It opened in the ceiling of the room behind the little shop, he judged.

Now Wang Tai pressed another button. Taitt felt the hackles rise upon his neck. The floor of the room four stories below had parted, had drawn back in two sections to disclose a brick-lined well beneath the shaft. The odor of moist quicklime came faintly to his nostrils.

It was clear to him, as clear as if Wang Tai had spoken. This was the way Wang killed his victims—flung them as a sacrifice to die in hammered pulp against the distant bricks. The quicklime in the gruesome pit would do the rest.

"You will find the bodies of the other meddling white detectives when you go to join them," Wang Tai murmured.

Taitt tensed. He fought an almost overwhelming urge to leap, to feel his fingers sink into the fatness of Wang's neck. It would be suicide, he knew, but worth the price if he could take Wang with him. But Wang Tai might escape. Besides, no one had yet discovered that his hands, clasped tightly behind him, were free. A better chance might come.

They went into the other room. The white men were gone.

Only the Chinese remained. That made five of them. Two had automatics. Wang Tai had a knife. The others might be armed, might not. Taitt could not tell.

They flung him to a sitting posture against the drapes. Wang Tai spoke in Cantonese. The thin cheeked man placed holy mats before the shrine. Wang dropped upon his knees, bowed low, touching his forehead to the floor. He muttered a prayer, strange, unintelligible, while the others—all except one who kept his automatic trained upon Taitt's forehead—followed his example, bowing in unison.

Taitt knew the time to act had come. If only that lone guard's vigilance would waver!

As he lay there waiting, scheming, he realized abruptly that his fingers, held behind him, still clasped the lighter which had freed him from his bonds. A grim smile creased the corners of his eyes. The lighter was his answer. He flicked it, felt his hand grow warm. His fingers, moving backward, found the velvet drape.

FOR A MOMENT nothing happened. Then a tongue of flame licked upward. The dry cloth flashed with a streak of climbing fire.

The lone guard roared a shout of warning. His eye, caught by the rising blaze, swept upward. In that second, Taitt tensed his muscles, leaped. His plunging body caught his captor just above the knees. His two hands grasped the other's right wrist as he tumbled backward. The automatic came free, clattered to the floor.

So sudden was the move that the others in the room seemed stunned. Taitt scooped the weapon up as Wang Tai, faster to

recover than the others, flung his slender bladed knife. The
sharp steel whispered in Taitt's ear as it crossed his shoulder a
scant inch from its mark.

Taitt whirled and jerked his trigger. The weapon clicked but
did not fire. He jerked again and this time lead belched forth,
but Wang Tai had fled to safety behind the heavy shrine. From
somewhere close an automatic roared. Hot lead clutched his
sleeve. He twisted, saw a leering yellow face, took rapid aim.
The Chinese with the automatic grunted once and went down
with a red stream gushing from beneath his chin.

Now the others had recovered from their shock. Taitt met
their charge, his weapon spitting death. He felt fire sear his
left arm, felt cold steel graze his thigh. But they were wild,
excited, aiming recklessly. He swung his automatic, saw the
hollow cheeked Chinese stagger backward clutching at his
stomach. He saw another go down with a great hole where
an eye had been. His bullets gone, he clubbed his weapon, felt
bones crunch beneath its crushing blows.

Then abruptly he realized he stood alone. He paused a
second, panting, his eyes upon the wreckage he had wrought.

The scene sent a little shudder through him. There is something horrible in violent death, even to one as used to it as a
homicide detective. He brushed a lean hand across his hot,
wet forehead. Then he thought of Wang Tai. He leaped for
the shrine. But Wang had fled.

Taitt found him in the inner room, crouched against a wall,
his fat face crazed by fear, his dark eyes gleaming madly.

"All right, Wang Tai," he grunted. "The game's up. Come
along."

But Wang Tai knew that only death awaited him. He hurled

himself at Taitt with fury born of terror.

The suddenness of the attack caught Taitt by surprise. The hurtling body of the Chinese threw him backward. He fell, his head banging hard against the floor. Red spots danced before his eyes. He tried to roll, but Wang Tai was on top of him, his fat hands tearing at his throat.

Taitt felt hot, reeking breath upon his face. He felt the clutch of maddened fingers upon his windpipe. He had not realized how little strength was left to him. Even his brain worked slowly. A horrible burning was in his chest and the room whirled about him in dizzy circles when the idea came. He brought his legs up under the fat man's body, shot them out with all his ebbing strength, like pistons. The move flung Wang Tai back.

Then they were on their feet and Wang Tai charged again. Taitt saw him coming through a haze of scarlet. He shook his head, clenched his teeth. As Wang closed in, his right fist swung. All his weight was in the blow. It caught Wang Tai squarely. Blood spurted from a broken nose as Wang stumbled back.

There was a sound of ripping wood, a piercing shriek. Then silence. Taitt shook his head again, and only then did he realize Wang Tai had vanished.

Taitt regained his breath and ran back to the outer room. The fire had swept the drapes, burned itself out.

As he stooped to retrieve his automatic from the Chinese who had taken it from him, racing footsteps came to his ears. He straightened quickly, the gun in his fist. He had completely forgotten the two white men!

They burst into the room with weapons drawn. But Taitt

had reached the wall beside the door. He hugged it as they hurried in.

"O.K., boys," he growled from behind them then. "Grab air."

It was nearly two hours later, and Taitt's wounds were wrapped in yards of bandages, when he stood once more in the tenth floor office of the police commissioner.

The commissioner leaned back in his red leather swivel chair, his gray eyes speculative.

"You know, Taitt," he said at last, "we've got an electric chair in this state. From what the boys tell me, you apparently didn't know about it. Anyway, I'm glad you saved the two of them for it." He shoved a box of cigars across the broad, glass top of his desk, flipped back the lid.

"They spilled the works," Taitt reported. "Wang Tai had a first class racket smuggling slave girls in from China by way of Mexico. Hazen and McMorran both got wise somehow and Wang Tai murdered them. The same thing happened to Markel, only he got his on the street."

The commissioner nodded. His face was thoughtful. "I've got an idea, Taitt," he said at last. "That's why I asked you to come in. We've had a lot of crime in the last six months in Chinatown. From now on, that's your job—to stop it."

Taitt grinned. "O.K., chief," he said. "I'll like that."

"I thought so." The commissioner rose. "And by the way," he added as an afterthought, "you'd better turn in that shield of yours. You'll be drawing a new one when you're ready to go back to work. It'll have the word 'Sergeant' on it."

CORPSES IN CHINATOWN

William Hines

On Quincy Street, Stub Samson, was a peg-legged bum, wanted by the police for murder; at City Hall, Paul Van Cleve was a polished gentleman and the smartest D.A., Mason City ever had. Were there any who suspected that both men were really one and the same? Paul knew there were—when the blood of an old Chinaman stained his office floor and a scurrying crab gave warning of wholesale death!

1

Death Walks In

PAUL VAN CLEVE looked down again at the card in his hand. *Joseph B. Cowdrey, Private Investigator.* He looked back up at the man who had presented it, a man who stood with his gloved hands flat on Van Cleve's desktop, staring. Van Cleve grinned. He knew he looked too young for his job; that his wavy blonde hair and horn-rimmed glasses made him look more like a Sunday school teacher than the crusading district attorney of Mason City.

"They say you're an honest man, Van Cleve," Cowdrey had the look of a lawyer with the witness for the opposition on

the stand. "Then why is it that Chinatown is running as wide open as it ever did?"

On Van Cleve's side of the desk, Webb Wottles, chunky police lieutenant attached to the district attorney's office, jumped to his feet. "Listen, Mister!" His voice was red as his face. "I don't like the way you said that! Suppose you tell us who you are before you start throwing your weight around in the office of the best D.A. Mason City ever had!"

"Perhaps you didn't hear me the first time, Lieutenant."

There was an instant of hesitation; the hairbreadth second of surprise Samson had counted on....

Cowdrey's tone was polite. Too polite, Van Cleve thought. "My name is Joseph Cowdrey, and I have been secretly employed for several months as an investigator for the Good Government League. In case your memory needs jogging, the Good Government League put the present administration into power, including Mr. Van Cleve. A few months ago this organization hired me to get them the facts. Before I give them those facts, there are a few questions I should like to have Mr.

Van Cleve answer. And since there is an election coming up, I thought Mr. Van Cleve might be glad to listen to what I have to say."

Van Cleve smiled at his visitor. It was almost a friendly smile. "Don't you mean—*do* as you say, Mr. Cowdrey?"

"I can see you're as smart as they say, Van Cleve. You get the point."

"And that means—clean up Chinatown?"

Cowdrey nodded. "It means get rid of Too Fung. You've done a fair job of cleaning up this city, all except Chinatown. That's the sore spot. That's the one place you've made no attempt to touch!"

Wottles, explosive with rage, started to speak. But Van Cleve silenced him with a wave of his hand. "Too Fung lets lotteries run in his district," Van Cleve said slowly. "And I think there's some fan-tan and a few dice games. But it's a pretty clean district. No trouble's ever come out of Chinatown...."

The sound of raised voices came from Van Cleve's outer office. A woman's voice said: "But you can't go in there! Mr. Van Cleve is in…" And then the woman stopped talking, and screamed.

The door from the outer office opened, and a little Chinaman stepped inside. He wore a derby hat and a cast-off Chesterfield coat several sizes too big for him. His lips and chin were red with blood that flowed in rivulets down each side of his Adam's apple. He stopped just inside the door, his legs buckling as if they could carry him no farther. His eyes sought Van Cleve, seemed to plead with him. Then, dramatically, and as if with his last ounce of strength, the Chinaman threw his coat open.

He wore trousers, but no shirt. And his upper torso was

streaming with blood that ran from grooves cut vertically in his flesh, grooves such as might be made by the claws of a tiger. Behind him wound a bloody trail that led into the outer office, where a girl stood with her hand over her mouth, her eyes popping with horror.

The little yellow man weaved, toppled into the stream of his own blood, lay face down in the growing pool. His derby fell from his head, brim up.

Van Cleve, Wottles, and Cowdrey were all on their feet, and for some reason they stared not at the Chinese, but at the derby hat. It rocked gently on its curved crown, as was natural. What was not natural was that the speed of the rocking movement was increasing instead of decreasing. It was as if the derby possessed a volition of its own.

THE GIRL IN the outer office screamed again as the hat rocked onto its brim, tilted toward her. The men around the desk saw a claw reach out from behind the hat. The claw opened, closed, felt its way forward. Behind it came a crab as big as a man's hand. The crab scuttled sideways a short distance, surveying the scene suspiciously with its greedy, telescope eyes. It stopped at the edge of the bloody puddle beside the Chinaman's head, lifting its legs gingerly. It dipped a claw into the viscous blood, slid its mouth open, and began to feed.

Van Cleve's lips twitched, and sat down suddenly. He opened his mouth as if to speak, closed it again. Wottles and Cowdrey, too, stared at the crab, held silent by the sudden horror.

Then Wottles found his voice. "How… how did he get in, Frances?" His Adam's apple bobbed as he circled the bloody corpse and the gorging crab on his way to the outer office.

"How do you think, Gumshoe?" She tried to sound flip, but the rouge showed in bright circles on her chalk-white cheeks. "In the door. He… he went right across the room to Mr. Van Cleve's office. I started to tell him Mr. Van Cleve was in conference, and then I saw… the blood."

"Call Homicide. Right now." Wottles' eyes were on the crimson trail of blood meandering across the brown linoleum floor. He followed it to the outer door.

F'goshsake, Webb!" Frances looked back at the crab, looked quickly away again. "Aren't you gonna do anything about… that crab?"

"Leave it for Homicide!" Wottles yelled back at her as he stepped out of the office. "Don't touch a thing! I'll see if I can find out where this guy come from."

Frances picked up the telephone, dialed the right number the second time, put through the call.

"You were saying… no trouble's ever come out of Chinatown, Mr. Van Cleve?" Cowdrey grinned, but the edges of his mouth trembled a little.

Van Cleve didn't seem to hear him. He stood up, had a hard time finding the end of his cigarette with the flame of a silver lighter. "You'll excuse me, Mr. Cowdrey. All this has unnerved me a little." He picked his way past the corpse and the crab with steps that were almost mincing, started toward a private exit that led directly toward the hall. "I'm not feeling well, Frances," he called to the girl in the outer office. "You and Wottles and Mr. Cowdrey tell the homicide squad everything we know about this." He opened the door, paused. "And will you call Miss Plenover and tell her I'm frightfully sorry, but I won't be able to take her to the opera tonight? That I'm not…

ah… feeling very well?"

"I can't believe it!" Cowdrey told the office girl a moment later. "So that's Paul Van Cleve, the daring prosecutor who has cleaned up Mason City! Paul Van Cleve, the scourge of the underworld; Why, he hasn't the guts to break up a game of rummy in an Old Ladies' Home!"

Frances pulled the gum out of her mouth, stuck it firmly beneath her desk. "You listen to me, Mister. Sometimes it doesn't take guts. Sometimes it takes brains. That's what Paul Van Cleve's got. He knows more law than all the rest of the lawyers in this town, and don't you forget it!"

VAN CLEVE WAS hurrying down Grover street when the sporty roadster glided to a stop beside him. "Paul!" called the girl behind the wheel. She had to repeat it. "Paul!"

He turned his head toward her. She was sure he saw her, yet he took two or three steps more before he stopped, came slowly over to the edge of the walk. "Pat!" His eyes took her in in spite of himself. It was always hard for him to believe that she was as beautiful as she really was.

"I decided that you were going to take me to dinner. I was just going to pick you up at the office." Her eyes were warm and friendly and a little mocking. "I'm certainly glad to see that you're careful about stopping when strange girls yell at you."

He tried to echo her bantering tone in his laughter, but it sounded forced, even to him. "No dinner tonight, Pat. No opera, either, I'm… I'm feeling simply rotten. A bad headache…."

"You poor thing!" she chimed. "Hop right in and I'll take you…."

"No," he said, really feeling utterly miserable. "Thanks. But there are several places I have to stop and...."

"So you're standing me up? The old run-around." Her tone was still bantering, but a chill had crept into it. "Is it a brunette, Paul? Do you like them better?"

"No, Pat! I swear by all that's holy...."

"This has happened before, Paul." Her voice was suddenly all serious. "I think I know you, and then suddenly you become vague and mysterious. You'll tell me what it is someday, won't you?" Her car suddenly shot away.

He stared after her only for a second, then hurried doggedly on down Grover street, crossed at Scranton, went over two blocks to Geary. A blind man with a hat full of pencils was standing in front of the decrepit office building in which Van Cleve still maintained the office he'd used while in private practice. He dropped a four-bit piece in the blind man's hat, wondering for a moment at the beggar's being on such a poor corner, then went on up the stairs to the second floor.

He turned his key in the lock of the door marked PAUL VAN CLEVE, ATTORNEY AT LAW. Inside, he locked the door behind him. It was late afternoon, and dark in this stuffy little office with the drawn shades. But he did not turn on the light.

He stepped sure-footedly through the darkness to the side of the room. His fingers felt the surface of the knotty pine panels, and presently a panel slid aside, and he stepped through. He pulled the panel closed, made sure the lightproof blind was drawn, its edges taped as usual, before he turned on the light.

He stood in a small enclosure which once had been a lavatory, but which he had remodeled for his own uses. There was a chair, and opposite the chair a mirror. On one side of the mirror an underarm holster of supple leather hung on a nail. From the holster protruded the black butt of a .44 revolver. On the other side of the mirror hung a suit of heavy under wear, a hickory shirt, a tattered mackinaw, and a pair of blue denim pants with one leg cut off at the knee. On the floor was a very dirty tennis shoe.

Van Cleve sat down opposite the mirror, pulled the horn-rimmed glasses from his nose, took off the double breasted dark blue business suit, hung it up. He slapped his right leg thoughtfully, and the sound of the slap was tinny. Even in color it looked like a flesh-and-blood leg. It was a good leg, he thought. Particularly that trick knee. He'd never had a gam with as good a knee. Well, it ought to be good, for six hundred dollars. He was proud of that gam, proud of the fact that nobody suspected.

He loosened the straps that bound it just above the place where his knee would have been, put the aluminum leg in a cabinet at his left, took out a wooden peg leg, strapped it on. Then he changed the rest of his clothes, tucking the flap of the right trouser leg down around the stump, to cushion it a little. He rubbed perfumed hair dressing into his unruly, wavy hair until it was tight against his scalp, dark with grease. He strapped on the holster, checked the loading of the .44, and slipped on his mackinaw.

2

Beware the Crab

HE LOOKED INTO the mirror. He was no longer Paul Van Cleve, socially and politically prominent district attorney of Mason City. He was Stub Samson, a murderer wanted by the police, a hoodlum, denizen of Mason City's underworld.

He hated having to assume this role again, he told himself, hated the fact that a crab and a little Chinaman who'd been tortured to death had forced him once more to become Stub Samson. But in his heart he was glad. For the clothes of Stub Samson felt more natural to him than the clothes of Paul Van Cleve, and he knew that there was that within him which would always send him back to being Stub Samson now and again. For he had been Stub Samson long before chance and the years had disguised him as Paul Van Cleve.

He must have been born somewhere near Quincy street, for the sights and sounds of that thoroughfare were among his earliest recollections. His mother he remembered only dimly, for she had died before he was old enough to remember much. He had been 'adopted,' and had run away from the woman who beat him; lived off handouts from Quincy street tavern keepers, eaten out of their garbage pails, drained the dregs from their bottles. He had spent some months in a 'house of correction,' and had run away, back to Quincy street.

It was on Quincy street that he had lost his leg when he fell beneath the wheels of a street car while hooking a ride.

They had taken good care of him in the county hospital. He was eight years old, and it was then that they started to call him "Stub."

At eighteen he was tough even in the uncritical lexicon of Quincy street, and the cop on the beat looked forward to the day when society would rid itself of Stub Samson by putting him behind bars.

It happened one night when he was on his way from one bar to another. In the middle of the block, where the lights were dim, a big man caught up with the girl walking ahead of him, grabbed her arm. The girl tried to pull away, and the man pinned her arm in back of her, put a hand over her mouth. Samson tapped the man on the shoulder. "Listen, Mister." He said it softly, out of the corner of his mouth. "Leave her be."

"Keep outa this, you peg-legged son!" the big man snarled. And Stub Samson slipped on his brass knucks and belted him one.

It was later, when the police caught him, that Samson found out that the girl was Nancy Too Fung, daughter of the Lord of Chinatown, that the man was Gilhooley, a party payroller of some prominence, and that Gilhooley had died from a fractured skull.

Through a miracle no greater than cutting steel bars with a hacksaw, Too Fung's men broke Samson out of jail. For months Too Fung kept Samson hidden in a secret room under Quincy street itself, tutoring him in all the education he had missed. Stub Samson learned quickly. Too Fung sent him to other cities, to special tutors, private schools, and then to college and law school. It was as Paul Van Cleve that Stub Samson came back to Mason City to practice law, and as Paul Van Cleve that he had been elected District Attorney.

This was not the first time that he had returned to Quincy street as Stub Samson. For he had found that in that role he could get information and accomplish ends that could not be gained officially. It was dangerous, for since there were those in the underworld who remembered him, there were those on the police force who remembered, too.

NOW HE SLIPPED a sheathed case knife into an inside pocket. That knife had gotten him out of many a tight spot, and might again. He turned off the light, pulled the masking tape away from the window casing, pulled up the shade and opened the window. He looked each way down the alley, to where the lights glowed in the murk. It was clear both ways. He climbed out onto the telephone post which jutted up beside the window, pulled the shade down, closed the window, and crawled down to the alley, keeping his body between the building and the post.

The rubber pad of his peg thumped softly on the cement as he hurried toward the street. The blind man who had stood at the entrance to the building worried him, and Stub Samson wondered if he still stood there. But there was no time to find out. If Samson were right, the death of the little Chinese in his office meant that life or death for those he loved depended on how quickly he could get to Chinatown.

But at the mouth of the alley the blind-man came suddenly out of nowhere to stand in his path. "Buy a pencil, Mister?" he whined. "Buy a pencil?"

Samson stifled an impulse to push the beggar out of his path. Probably the guy really was blind. Samson stepped aside, said: "Sorry."

The limousine was almost opposite the alley mouth before Samson saw it. It was coming fast. Samson threw himself flat, swept out the .44 in one movement, his ears tuned for the *rat-tat* of machine gun fire.

None came. The back door of the limousine flung open. Something came hurtling out, rolled to within a few feet of Samson, and the limousine was gone.

The blind man, too, was gone. Samson picked himself up. He was alone in the alley with the thing which came out of the car. He looked down at it.

The street lights faintly illumined a cadaver which, from the odor, had been a cadaver for several days. It still had the general shape of a human body—torso, legs, arms, head—but that was all. It had no skin, and yet it was not bloody. There was no more blood in it than in a piece of well-done pork. It was pockmarked with many hills and valleys, as if it were a contour map designed from human flesh by greedy mouths.

What had been the cadaver's mouth was now a dark hole set in the center of a mass of shapeless flesh. Samson felt cold creep down his spine as that shapeless flesh seemed to move. It was as if the corpse were about to speak… with lips that were no longer lips!

And then a tiny claw reached out from the aperture which had been a mouth. After the claw came a crab a little bigger than a silver dollar. The crab scuttled sideways across what had been a cheek, lifted its pincers delicately, began to tear away morsels of flesh, carry them to its mouth.

Samson fought to keep his belly down. The gun was still in his hand. He couldn't help pulling the trigger any more than he could help taking his next breath. The crab was only four feet away when he shot. The crab went all to pieces.

The report of the gun filled the narrow alley like the sound of cannon. Stub Samson fled the sound, into the next alley, and the next, toward Quincy street and Chinatown. He was frightened. The "blind" man was a finger man. He had seen him go into the office building as Paul Van Cleve; he had seen him come out of the alley as Stub Samson. The "blind" man had fingered him not for death, but simply so that his employers could dump that horribly mutilated corpse at Stub Samson's feet.

Why? Why had they not killed him when they had the chance? Why had they sent Ho Wen, who had tutored Samson in the old days, and was more like a father than instructor, to die in Paul Van Cleve's office? Samson could not even guess at the answers. But one thing was obvious: Whoever was responsible for these deaths must either know or guess that Stub Samson and Paul Van Cleve were one and the same person! And whoever knew or even guessed at that held aces in this game of death.

THERE IS A side entrance to the Shanghai Restaurant few people know about. The light over the door was broken long ago, and no one has ever seen any reason to replace it. Hugging the shadows, Samson came out of the alley toward this door, tapped softly three times with the flat of his hand.

The door slid open, and shut again in a split second. Stub Samson stood inside, shaking the hand of Chang Wat Duck.

"Velly glad see," nodded the Duck, tucking his arms back inside his long silk sleeves. "Much tlouble. Need Stub Samson much. Glad see."

"What's the trouble, Chang?" Samson asked as he stumped up the steep stairs behind the Chinese.

"No talk." The Duck shook his head. "You make much talk bymeby with Too Fung." He rapped softly on a door at the head of the stairs, and the door swung open.

The ceiling of the room was sixteen feet high, and looked higher. The walls were hung with Chinese tapestries and pictures, and from the ceiling hung a carved jade lamp, faintly glowing. At the end of the room was a carved teak desk, and behind it sat Too Fung. The ceremonial robes and trappings of his fathers were not for Too Fung. He wore a double breasted business suit, and his jet black hair and smooth almond-colored skin belied his age.

The Lord of Chinatown looked up. His face held no expression at all, and there was no sign of recognition in his bright black eyes. "Who is this person you bring unannounced into my study?" Too Fung asked the Duck.

Samson and the Duck both stared. They knew that Samson was more than a son to the master of Chinatown. For a wild second Samson thought that this was not Too Fung, but a stranger masquerading as the venerable Chinese. Then the Duck broke into a torrent of Chinese. Too Fung held up a hand to silence him. He rose from his chair, stepped from behind the desk. The movement was made casually, and yet Samson sensed a purpose behind it.

"Enough!" said Too Fung. "Take the intruder away. Let him tell you his business in the usual way. Then, if I wish to see him, let him make an appointment."

It was too deep for Samson. He took a step toward the door. On the other side of the room, Too Fung took a step to the side. And then Samson got it. *Too Fung was keeping himself between Samson and the red dragon-embroidered curtain that hung at the window.* Ever so slightly the curtain stirred, as if with a breath of wind. But there was no wind! Samson cursed softly to himself, leaped quickly to one side, so that Too Fung no longer stood between him and the curtain. As he leaped, he swept the .44 out of its holster.

"Come out from behind that curtain, you!" he said, and threw himself flat on the floor. The roar of the gun beat at his eardrums, and at his temple the cold feel of the air impacted by the bullet made him instinctively duck. It was that close. Then the sound of shots from his own gun blended into one continuous roar, and the gun was suddenly warm in his hand.

The dragons on the curtain leaped into a dance. The curtain bellied out, tore loose from the rod, collapsed. A man with a bloody head writhed there among the green dragons. A revolver skidded out across the floor from the tangle of man and curtain, and the man's hands clutched spasmodically at the cloth, like gobbling mouths. And then the hands stopped clutching, and the man was still.

3

Blind Alley

SAMSON PULLED HIMSELF to his feet, reloaded his gun before he holstered it.

"A thousand thanks from your unworthy servant for saving me from this eavesdropping dog." Too Fung calmly returned to his chair behind the teakwood desk.

"It is you, oh Illustrious One, who have added to my indebtedness to your own honorable self by attempting to save me from this well laid trap." Samson grinned, and then his face sobered. "Ho Wen died in my office," he explained. "I knew therefore that there was trouble here. How did this one come into your chambers?"

"M'to Chang, my youngest daughter, was gone from her room this morning," Too Fung said. "This man had news of her. He said she was held by one who calls himself the Crab. The police came to ask concerning Ho Wen. This one hid behind the curtain, saying that if I revealed him to the police, or mentioned M'to Chang's absence, then surely she would die the most horrible death."

"And so you pretended not to know me, in order to save me from the one behind the curtain." Samson's face was grave. "And in killing this skulking dog, I have unloosed the wrath of his master upon your daughter! What does he want of you? What does the death of Ho Wen mean?"

Too Fung shook his head.

There was the sound of hammering on the door, and a voice shouted: "Open up there. In the name of the law!" The panel of the door buckled in a little as a shoulder heaved against it.

The police had heard the shots!

Samson stumped across the room to the opposite door, put his hand on the knob. And then it, too, resounded with the boom of a fist on the other side of the panel. He was trapped! Wildly, he looked back across the room, saw the door there bend inward again. Another second, and the police would be in the room, and Stub Samson would at last be in their hands.

It meant the end of Paul Van Cleve, the end of Stub Samson. But, more than that, it meant that he would be put away where he could give Too Fung no help in saving his daughter from whoever or whatever the Crab was.

Chang Wat Duck's hand went into his sleeve, came out with a long curved knife, and the Duck came to stand by Samson's side.

"No, Chang!" Samson whispered fiercely. "Not that way!"

The Duck swung the knife in a glittering arc, and smiled benignly at the door, which chattered with the tattoo of fists.

"Call him off, Too Fung!" Samson said desperately over his shoulder. "If you turn him loose on these cops, he may carve our way out of here, but you won't be safe this side of China."

"Come here, Chang," Too Fung sighed, and the Duck reluctantly thrust the knife back into his sleeve, folded his arms, went to stand beside Too Fung. But Samson saw that Too Fung's hand was beneath the desk top. His fingers, Samson knew, were on the buzzers which would bring tong men swarming in when the alarm was sounded. For Too Fung knew what it meant if Samson were captured, and Too Fung was a loyal friend. He would sacrifice everything if it were necessary to save Samson, and once Too Fung's hatchet men went for the police Too Fung was through.

Samson knew that there was no time to argue, and no use to argue if there were. His fate and Too Fung's hung on the next few seconds.

He waited till the door shivered again from the thrust of a shoulder, then he threw back the bolt on the door, jerked it open. Wottles, who was ramming once more at the door, was taken completely by surprise. He charged through the suddenly opened door, tried to hurdle Samson's out-thrust foot, missed, and hit on his chin. Just behind him was a cop in uniform, a gun in his fist. Samson's peg leg struck like a snake at the cop's gun wrist, connected, went on home to the cop's solar plexus. The cop grunted and folded up, and Samson leaped over him to the stairway. From the room behind he heard the crash of the other door being broken in, the thud of feet, the booming sound of voices.

He took the first flight of stairs in one step, and lit with too much weight on the peg. It had been awhile since he'd worn that stump and he'd forgotten just how to handle it. He winced with the pain in his stump, took off for the next flight of stairs.

He misgauged it. The peg caught on a step half-way down. Samson went head-over-heels as a police .38 roared heavily and a bullet split air where his head had just been. Behind him the broken plaster patted on the treads as he kicked against the stairs like a swimmer making a turn, sailed headfirst out a door being held open for him by a grinning Chinese.

He kept his body low, his peg swinging in great circles from his hip, his good leg driving it along. Halfway down the alley he glanced half-fearfully ahead to his left, grinned as he saw that things were still as they were when he was a kid. They never had remembered to close the lid on that garbage box as the city ordinance provided. He dove for the box, trying to forget a night like this years ago when he had found it full of broken bottles.

He lit with a stifled grunt in the bottom of the almost-empty refuse box, and blessed the efficiency of the city's sanitation department. Boots hammered down the back steps of the Shanghai restaurant, pounded on down the alley past his hiding place. Police whistles shrilled, and a gun barked as some cop pulled a trigger just for the hell of it, as far as Samson could tell.

SAMSON WAITED, STIFLING the impulse to crawl out of the box as the noise of pursuit faded away. After a while came the sound he knew must come: The slow tread of feet approaching each other from each end of the alley. The sounds met just opposite his box, stopped there.

A voice said: "Any luck, Mac?"

A second voice answered: "Not a smell. That Samson must be a magician. God, will the papers pan us for this! We catch Samson right on the kill, have him all bottled up, and then he gets away!" Samson held his breath. If it had not been for the thin boards of the refuse box he could have reached out and touched the two policemen.

"That Chink must have him hid somewheres."

"Hell, we took the place apart. He ain't there."

"Maybe he got away through some underground passage."

"Underground passage!" The cop snorted. "You been readin' stuff. I tell you we took the place apart, and he ain't in there. And listen." The cop dropped his voice "I got it straight that Stub Samson is the Crab!"

"No!"

"Sure. Who else? You know what they found beside the body of the guy Samson plugged? A crab! Samson must of left it there, and it's the same trademark he left with the Chink he killed. He just didn't have time to carve this one up, that's all."

"And we let the dirty son get away!" In the murk over his head, Samson saw the flare of a match as the cop lit a cigarette.

Samson hugged the bottom of the box. A match flare was all they needed to see him hidden there.

"I wouldn't like to be in the D.A.'s shoes right now!" The cop tossed the lighted match into the refuse box, and for an instant Samson's hiding place was lit as if by a star shell. The match went out as it spiraled to the bottom of the box. For a moment Samson couldn't believe that they hadn't seen him.

"Funny, nobody knows where the D.A. is. I was in the station when a call come in from this broad he's sweet on—you know, the mayor's daughter—saying that a messenger had delivered a florist's box to her. When she opened it, there was a bloody crab inside. We tried to get Van Cleve, but couldn't raise him anywhere. His office said he'd gone home with… get this now… with nervous indigestion." The cop gave a nasty laugh.

The second cop spat into the box. "If this Van Cleve ever run into Stub Samson like we did tonight, he'd be drinking his bromos out of gallon crocks."

Both cops laughed as if that were the final word on Paul Van Cleve, and walked away from each other, back to their posts at the end of the alley.

Stub Samson, crouched in the box, clenched his fists. It was hard to restrain himself from jumping out of that box, and taking his chances on getting out of the alley. But there were only three ways to get out; through one of the alley entrances, or through Too Fung's restaurant. The police had all those exits blocked. The moment they saw him it was their guns against his. And Samson didn't want to kill a cop. He particularly didn't want to kill a cop who was simply trying to do his duty in trying to rid the town of a brutal murderer whose trademark was a living crab!

SAMSON SMILED BITTERLY as he realized how completely he had been caught in the net of circumstances. Now the police had not only the old murder charge on which to crucify him, but not without cause they had credited him with these bestial murders which would shock the city!

And Pat had been threatened with one of the bloody crabs! Samson thought of her lovely body mutilated like that of Ho Wen, or the nameless thing which had been dumped in the alley, and he shuddered. As to the identity of the murderer or murderers he had no clue except the fact that they were striking closer and closer to him. And suddenly a portion of this pattern of murder assembled itself a little more clearly in his mind.

Ho Wen must have been brought to his office by the murderer. And that murderer must have *known* that Paul Van Cleve and Stub Samson were one and the same person! For the "blind" man in front of his office had obviously known. Why else would he have been waiting in the alley to act as finger man for the car? And the master mind behind this must also have known that the death of Ho Wen in Van Cleve's office would force him to assume the identity of Stub Samson so that he might visit Too Fung in Chinatown. The man behind the curtain might have been a dupe planted there by a master who knew that Stub Samson would kill him, who knew it so well that he had his dupe carry a crab in his pocket, a crab which would point to Stub Samson himself as the murderer of the others!

Thoughtfully, crouched there in the darkness, Samson caressed the butt of the gun in his holster. The details of this intricate plot were hazy, and altogether it was damned little to go on. The end of the little drama this murderer had arranged was probably to have come when the police captured Samson in Too Fung's room. Luck had been with him in escaping that trap.

Now they had threatened Pat. With every cop in town looking for Stub Samson, he could be of no help to either Too Fung or Pat in that role. The next move was to get back to his private office, back into the role of Paul Van Cleve so that he could fight for the girl he loved more than life itself.

He had to get back to Pat! Crouched there in the box, Samson chafed with impatience. The cops guarding the alley would be called off as soon as their superiors decided that the bird had flown. That decision must come in a few minutes now. Samson wondered how long he had been there. Minutes? It seemed like hours.

And then the voice of Webb Wottles boomed from one end of the alley. "He didn't get away, McGovern! There's a net around this block even that greased eel couldn't slip through! It's dollars to a dog biscuit he's right here in this alley!"

"In this alley! Where?"

"Think, man, think! Why couldn't he have jumped into one of those trash boxes? You look there?"

"No. You told me to stay right here at the end of the alley."

"That's the trouble with this department! No initiative!" Wottles shouted. "Come on, let's comb him out!"

Down at the end of the alley, Samson saw a flashlight played into a trash box. Dimly, beyond it, he could make out the shadowy figures of many cops, that of Wottles in the van, shorter and wider than the rest. More cops were at the other end of the alley.

This was the showdown. Pat needed him as never before. He

felt himself responsible for the threat against her life. And it could be only seconds now before the law would have him in a spot in which he could never help Pat!

Something brushed Samson's shoulder. The tautness within him released itself in a swing of his fist at the thing. It was soft to the touch of his knuckles, unresisting as his fist drove it away. Cautiously, curiously, his hand went out for it. It was a rope! From above some unseen benefactor had sent him this way of deliverance. He pulled down on it, harder and harder. It held! It would carry his weight!

For a second he wondered whether he could still go up a rope hand over hand, and then he was doing it, his good leg and his peg thrusting against the brick building, his arms and shoulders carrying most of his weight. He went up ten feet in about as many seconds. His hands touched the bottom rung of a fire escape. He pulled himself on up, rested with his good leg crooked around an iron rung. His breath whistled so loudly he thought the police in the alley below must hear it. He cursed himself for getting so soft as he pulled the rope up after him.

THE POLICE WERE almost at the box. He hung there like a giant spider, waiting, crossing his fingers against the chance that one of the dancing spotlight beams below would suddenly swing upward, pinning him there. To his left was a window, and for a moment Samson thought it might be a way of escape. He peered around the edge of the brick to see a cop staring out the window, Chang Wat Duck just leaving the room. Samson ducked back hurriedly. It was undoubtedly the Duck who, knowing his predicament, had managed to drop the rope down to him. But there was no hope of escape through the building. It was filled with cops.

4

———

Claws of Death

THE FEET OF the police scraped the cement below. Their flashlights probed the box where he had been a few moments before. Samson's heart seemed to stop beating for an instant as he waited for the stab of light which would be followed so swiftly by the inevitable stab of lead.

And then Wottles' harsh voice sounded above the other sounds of the men below: "All right, boys! All right! This ain't the only trash box in the alley! Do you think six of you can see into that damn box better than one?"

The cops moved away. Stub hesitated. He could go on up the fire escape to the comparative safety of the roof. Or he could drop back down into the alley. The guard at one end of the alley had been pulled in by the search, and Stub was fairly sure no other guard had been posted there. It might be the longest chance, but it was the quickest one. He thought of Pat Plenover, and of what the body of Ho Wen looked like. The rope burned his hands as he slid to the ground.

He went swiftly down the shadows of the alley, across the dimly-lit side street, following alleys and little-used thoroughfares, until he stood across the street from the building which housed his private office. A few feet away from the store entrance in which Samson stood a cab was parked, the driver reading a newspaper spread across the steering wheel. In front of the entrance to the office building a limousine stood. It looked suspiciously like the limousine from which the cadaver had been tossed. There was someone in the driver's seat, two or three dim figures behind him in the rear.

A roadster which had a familiar look pulled up behind the limousine. A girl stepped out onto the sidewalk, turned her head as if looking for someone. A man with a bulky package and a suitcase emerged from the dark entrance of the office building, spoke to the girl, then opened the back door of the limousine. The girl put one foot on the running board.

As she did so, she turned her face so that the flickering light from a neon sign fell full on it. It was Pat Plenover!

Samson's hand leaped from beneath his coat with the .44. But Pat stood squarely in the line of fire. Samson hesitated. And then Pat and the man with her were in the limousine, and the limousine was flashing away from the curb….

Samson dropped the gun back into its holster. Too dangerous to try for a shot with Pat in the car. He leaped for the cab at the curb, jumped into the seat beside the driver, swept the newspaper from under his nose. "Follow that car!" he ordered. "And drive like hell!"

The driver looked at Samson, looked at the dirty mackinaw, the blue demin pants, the wooden leg, at the pale blue eyes burning at him from a dirty face.

Ahead the limousine was halfway down the block. Samson fished a ten dollar bill from his shirt pocket. He waved the bill in front of the driver's eyes.

The cab started with a jerk that almost threw Samson out of his seat. The limousine swung to the left. But the cab, in high now, was picking up speed. "Just keep it in sight," Samson ordered. "Don't get too close." His hand was on the butt of the gun and the butt was slippery with sweat.

Rubber shrieked on cement as the cab took the corner. The wrong way! The limousine had gone to the left. The cab driver had swung to the right.

"What the hell!" Samson yelled.

And then he felt something hard jab the back of his head. "Bring your hand out, Samson," a cold, hard voice demanded from the rear seat. "Without the gun. Now put both hands in sight and keep them there."

SLOWLY, SAMSON UNCURLED his fingers from the butt of the gun, pulled his hands into view. The cabby grinned as he pulled to the curb, stopped. Still grinning, he reached beneath Samson's coat, pulled out the gun.

"Check his other pockets, Joe," the voice ordered. "They say this guy is a rat."

The cab driver shook him down, found the case knife in an inside pocket. "Didn't I tell you he was a rat?" the voice from the rear inquired.

Samson sat with his hands stiff beside his shoulders, his eyes keen on every movement of the cab driver, watching for a break. But there could be no break with that gun muzzle hard against the back of his head! He cursed himself for not suspecting the cab had been planted there. It had been so convenient… too convenient!

He felt the muzzle leave the back of his head for a split second, and in the next second felt it whip down sickeningly just behind his ear. His head lolled to one side. Desperately, he tried to hold on to consciousness as the cab driver tied his arms and legs, then hauled him out of the front seat, shoved him on the floor in back.

The man in back was wiping the blood and hair from the muzzle of the gun onto his shirt. He was a big man, swarthy and grizzled, with a scar that slanted from beneath his left eye across the hollow of a broken nose. Samson recognized him from the pictures on F.B.I. circulars.

Huddled there on the floor, Samson shook his head, trying to clear it of the terrible ache. He could feel the warm wetness of blood running down his cheek, taste the salt of it in his mouth. "Manny Funkhouser!" Samson exclaimed. "I think you'll find the cops tougher here than in Chicago, Manny."

Manny kicked him in the face, kicked him again, and laughed. "You might find the cops sort of tough here yourself, Samson. Fact, I'm all in favor of dumping you on the steps of some precinct station, and letting the cops work you over. But the boss insists that you meet The Crab!"

Suddenly Samson understood something that he had wondered about. He could tell from the sound of traffic and frequent stops that they were going through midtown and he had wondered why they hadn't gagged him. Now he knew. They figured that he was even more anxious than they to avoid any contact with the police. The hell of it was, they were right!

"The girl… the girl who got into the limousine." No longer could Samson resist asking the question uppermost in his mind. "Where are they taking her?"

Manny looked at him curiously. "For a peg-legged gutter rat, you're damned interested in that girl, now ain't you? Well,

I wouldn't be surprised but what you and her would meet The Crab together.

Traffic noises were not so frequent. From the smell of salt in the air Samson knew that they were somewhere on the waterfront. The cab bounced a little as it went up an incline, and it grew suddenly darker. Walls echoed the hiss of tires on pavement, and Samson knew they were in a building.

Manny and the cab driver climbed out, slammed the door behind them. Samson lay on the floor of the cab, staring up toward its roof. It was too dark to see even that. The air had a damp, musty feel to it. Out of the darkness came a low mumble of men's voices, the occasional scrape of feet on the cement beside the car. Samson tugged at the bonds which held his wrists together, and the persistent ache in his head throbbed with fresh pain.

SOMEWHERE A DIM light went on, and the blackness washed out to a dirty gray. The door at Samson's feet opened, framing Manny Funkhouser's hulking silhouette. One of Manny's hands circled Samson's good leg, dragged him out of the car. Samson held his head up stiffly, took the jolt to the floor on the back of his neck.

Manny dragged him across the floor, and through the gloom Samson could sense the shapes of men watching. Just ahead, a figure stooped to pull open a trap door. Manny pulled Samson to the brink of the opening.

"So long, tough guy," Manny chuckled. And there came a soft answering chuckle from those other shapes in the darkness.

Manny stepped across the opening, pulled Samson across it. For a second Samson hung there, suspended over the black maw beneath. And then Manny let go.

Samson couldn't break his fall with hands or feet. He lit on his side with a jolt that knocked the breath from his lungs, made his senses swim with pain. But he didn't pass out. Not quite. He could hear the lap of waves not far away, and a soft hissing sound that made him instinctively shudder. He tried to pull himself into a sitting position, eyes straining to see through the darkness. He realized with a shock that he hadn't moved a muscle. He tried again, failed. The fall had paralyzed his body.

His ears sensed the sibilant movements of the things in the dungeon with him. Worst of all was the odor; worse than the stench of a stagnant backarm of sea. It was the odor of death, of death and corruption.

Something wet and clammy brushed his cheek. Shuddering, he tried to twist away from it, and couldn't. And then someone moaned. He almost welcomed that moan. There was another human being here!

And then he remembered Pat. He tried the word not knowing whether he could even speak aloud. "Pat!" He called her name into the darkness with a little prayer that it would not be she who answered; that she had met death more quickly and kindly than whatever it was which awaited them.

"Who… who is it?"

"Paul," he almost said, and then remembered. "Samson, lady," he told her. "Stub Samson."

"Oh!" she gasped. "The murderer!"

"That's wrong, Miss. I ain't no murderer. But I guess it don't make no difference now to either of us."

"They've got you too?" He could hear her teeth chatter. "You're not… one of them?"

"They got me too."

The stench of death was strong in his nostrils, and he knew that death was close for both of them. If he could only get to her side, tell her the whole story of who he was, tell her again that he loved her before death came....

"Didn't... didn't you call me... Pat, Mr. Samson?"

The words of explanation were on the tip of his tongue. And then, in the ceiling above, a light bloomed. Pat lay bound hand and foot, her eyes on Samson. He saw the shudder of revulsion at the sight of him pass over her face, and the words died on his lips. It was better that she remember him as Paul Van Cleve. She must never know.

He forgot that his head and face were covered with blood. With the supersensitiveness of the cripple, he thought only that now she was seeing one-legged Stub Samson as he really was, and that the sight of his deformity disgusted her.

And then, as his eyes left hers, horror drove all other thoughts from his mind.

THE WALLS OF the dungeon in which they found themselves were made of cement. Along the outer wall a stagnant backwash of the sea made a puddle which lay over a third of the dungeon's floor. Lying in the puddle, half-hidden by the water, were the dead bodies of men and women.

The soft hissing sound Samson had heard was the sound of the movements of swarms of giant crabs, feeding on those bodies! Hurrying as if their feast might momentarily be snatched away from them, the claws of the crabs ripped the flesh from the unresisting carcasses of the dead, stuffed it into their mouths.

A big crab made a sidelong dash toward Pat. Her face paled, and the skin of her throat stretched tight as a drum. "Don't!" she whimpered. "Don't… let it…!"

The crab hesitated, waved its claw angrily as if she had cheated it by not being dead, scuttled back to the body from which it had come. From what was left of it, Samson could tell that it had been the body of a woman. On the little finger of what was left of the woman's right hand was a ring with a square-cut emerald. Samson would have known that emerald anywhere. It was the body of M'to Chang. Too Fung's youngest daughter.

From the south wall came the sound of an opening door. Through a doorway in the center of the wall opposite came Manny Funkhouser, the cab driver, and a third thug. They carried a rough wooden table which glistened darkly beneath the light overhead. None of them spoke as they set the table down, stepped back to stand against the wall, but their eyes watched the doorway in evil expectation.

Samson's eyes followed theirs to that open door. Beyond it lay only blackness, a blackness which held the answer to the horror that had been and was to be.

And then it stood there, embodied. There was a black hood, with two eyeholes which revealed the circular whiteness of the flesh around the eyes, and the dark eyes themselves. Below that was a white shirt, with sleeves rolled up over white, hairless arms, and a pair of light tweed pants.

Pat gasped: "Oh! Oh, dear God!"

Samson turned his head toward her. It hurt, but it turned! The paralysis was leaving him! "Add it all up, and what have you got?" he told her. "Just another thug in a mask."

The man in the doorway spoke. "Put her on the table, boys."

Funkhouser and the other two lifted the bound girl, laid her on the table. She tried to twist away from them, sobbing with effort as they strapped each arm and leg separately to the table.

"Now… my gloves," said the man in the doorway. He held his hands stiffly before him, like a surgeon about to don rubber gloves.

Funkhouser stepped in front of him, fitted something on to his hands, stepped away again. Samson saw that the hooded man had indeed been fitted with gloves, gloves the fingers of which terminated in glistening steel blades six inches long!

He moved his fingers, and there was a faint rasping tinkle of steel on steel as blades met. He gestured with one metal claw toward the gorging crab. "Progress," he purred softly, "is nothing but man's improvement on nature."

5

Death Wears a Peg Leg

SAMSON TWISTED HIS good left leg, stretched it out, out until it seemed as if the hip would leave its socket. He sweated with the pain, but thanked God he could move a little now! The eyes of Manny Funkhouser and his henchmen, avid with bloodlust, were on the man in the hood. And then Samson felt something give, and knew that his peg leg had slipped the noose which bound it to his left. A peg leg, he thought grimly to himself, was sometimes mighty handy. His bound hands still held him prisoner, but just getting those legs free was something.

The man with the claws stepped over to Pat, strapped so securely to the table. She screamed in utter terror as he hooked his fingers, thrust the dreadful talons slowly toward her face.

"Scream as much as you please, my dear," he chuckled.

Pat bit her lips until a bright drop of blood oozed from beneath her teeth, flowed like a vermilion tear down the white velvet of her chin. Once more the monster who stood over her reached for her with his murderous claws, then hesitated again. "I think Mr. Samson will enjoy this more if we present him with his little gift before we begin." All eyes were suddenly on Samson, and he lay very still. "Manny, will you bring it in?"

Manny, a wide grin on his face, stepped outside for a moment. When he returned, he carried a suitcase in one hand, and in the other he carried… an aluminum leg!

There was no mistaking that leg. Samson knew it as well as he knew his own right hand. Hell, it was as much a part of him! It was his leg! It was his own beautiful gam with the lovely trick knee, the gam that had set him back six hundred dollars, and was worth every cent of it!

"What, Mr. Samson?" the masked man asked sarcastically. "No speech of appreciation for this lovely gift which will hide your deformity? But perhaps you do not entirely understand. In the suitcase is a suit of clothes, and a few other personal things which are… or were… the property of a prominent young lawyer in town. Perhaps you can guess his name. When we are through with Miss Plenover, and have left her body for the crabs to finish, you might think that we intend to treat you in a similar way. Have no fear, Mr. Samson! We are more subtle than that.

"We will leave you locked in this room with what is left of

Miss Plenover, with the crabs, with this aluminum leg, and with the suitcase. Ah! I think you begin to see. Then we will call the police, and you may rest assured that we will see to it that you do not have time to escape before the police arrive. The police will find these elements I have mentioned: You, Stub Samson; these claws, which I anticipate no further use for; the body of Miss Plenover; the crabs; the suitcase; the aluminum leg. After the best minds of the police department have tussled with the problem presented by these rather interesting clues, I imagine they will arrive at a solution. And I think you need no prompting to know what solution."

Manny Funkhouser and his two henchmen laughed delightedly. And Stub Samson cursed them in a way that delighted them even further.

Remembering Pat, Stub glanced toward her. Did she realize what this meant? Did she know now what these men knew: That he was Paul Van Cleve, and that he was going to be framed for the crimes these men had committed? That when the fact that Stub Samson and Paul Van Cleve were the same person was discovered, that his word would be taken as worthless? That it meant the whole reform administration would be discredited, defeated in the coming election, and that corruption would once more rule the city?

But Pat's eyes, as they met his, held only fear and bewilderment. Once more the keen-edged talons started toward her, and the eyes of the masked man's minions hung hungrily on every glint of the blades.

INSTANTS WERE PRECIOUS. Samson bent his good leg back as far as it would go. Stretching, he could grab the heel of his shoe with the fingertips of his bound hands. A stout razor blade was buried in the heel of that shoe, put there long ago for just such a contingency as this. Sawing the cords with the edge of the blade, Samson didn't even feel the pain of his slashed wrists.

Pat screamed. Samson didn't look up. There was the chance that one of the criminals might glance his way, see what he was doing. But there was no time for circumspection. His hands were free! Squatted on his left hunker, Samson's right hand flashed to the tip of his leg, twisted it, and swept a stout sword from the hollow center of the leg!

"Look out!" yelled the thug at Funkhouser's left.

There was an instant of hesitation, the hairbreadth second of surprise Samson had counted on.

The cab driver's draw was first, his gun almost level as Samson's blade swept toward him in a shining arc. The tip of the sword caught the cab driver's gun hand at the knuckles. The gun dropped. Four fingers dropped, too. The cab driver was screaming, his left hand cupped over his right to stem the spurting blood, as the second thug pulled the trigger. But the deadly tip of Samson's blade, swinging up from the cab driver's hand, had sliced across the second gunman's throat, just deep enough to catch the jugular. The report of the gun slapped deafeningly against the walls as the gunman fell, the bullet grooving the cement floor three inches from Samson's good foot.

Samson's first swing of the sword had carried him around in a complete pivot, to find Funkhouser facing him four feet away, the muzzle of his revolver centered between Samson's eyes. Samson rolled away from the shot as a boxer rolls away from a blow. Something stung his cheek as the report of the gun beat at his eardrums, and his lunge carried the biting steel into Funkhouser's belly.

It happened so quickly that the masked man still stood at the other side of the room, claws poised above Pat's body. Samson held the sword like a javelin, its tip aimed at the masked man's heart. "Don't move!" Samson growled. He was afraid to hurl the sword… afraid that it would not take the life of the masked man quickly enough to prevent his burying those steel talons deep in Pat!

"Don't move yourself!" the masked man said silkily. You're covered from behind! Drop that sword!"

"Look out!" Pat screamed. "Behind you! A gun!"

THERE WASN'T TIME to think about it. Samson flung the sword, whirled to face the new menace as he threw himself sideways to the floor. It spoiled Samson's aim. The sword went low and to one side, pierced the masked man's side just beneath the lowest rib, pinned him to the wall. The masked man screamed.

The thug whose fingers Samson had cut off lay on the floor, the bloody stumps of his right hand pressed hard against the filth of the floor. In his left hand was a revolver. The revolver swung with Samson's movement, centered on him again.

The gun boomed. For an instant Samson wondered why it didn't hurt, and then he saw the side of the gunman's head mushroom out like earth lifted by a charge of black powder. The gunman's hand was suddenly limp, and his unfired gun slipped to the floor.

Chang Wat Duck stood in the doorway, smoke drifting

upward from the muzzle of his gun. The eyes of the Chinese filled with horror as they went slowly around the room.

Behind the Duck stood other Chinese, dressed in the long sleeved black shirts of the tong. Gravely they surveyed the room, filtered into it, as Samson untied the leather thongs that bound Pat to the table. She had fainted, but her pulse was strong and sure.

"I owe you more than I can repay in a thousand lifetimes," Samson told Chang Wat Duck.

"It is nothing," the Duck murmured, his arms folded as he surveyed the carnage. "I owe you instead a thousand pardons for stealing the honor of complete vengeance from your hand."

Stub Samson stood with his legs wide apart, his arms on his hips, and laughed. "Cut it out, Chang! You know darned well I'd be dead right now if you hadn't nailed that bird. How'd you get here?"

"I sent one of my men to follow you. He returned to tell me you had taken a cab to this address. We followed. There were men upstairs."

"You have trouble with them?"

The Duck smiled grimly. "I said there *were* men."

Samson stepped to the cringing, sobbing figure impaled by the sword. He jerked the taloned gloves from his fingers, pulled the hood from his head. It was Joseph Cowdrey!

Silently, the Chinese formed a tight semicircle around him. Samson pulled the sword from Cowdrey's side. "Barely nicked him!"

"M'to Chang?" the Duck asked.

Silently, Samson pointed to the emerald ring on the finger of one of the crab-eaten corpses. The eyes of the Chinese followed

Samson's pointing finger. And then they began to tighten the half-circle they had made around Cowdrey. Cowdrey began to whimper. "Stop them!" he screamed. "For God's sake, Samson, make these yellow devils stop!"

The Duck looked at Samson. "I think you should take Miss Plenover and leave here," he said. "The Chinese have methods of dealing with dogs like this one...."

Samson's eyes locked for a moment with Chang Wat Duck's. Then Samson looked at the mutilated bodies lying there in the filthy water of the sea, at the giant crabs. He looked back at the Duck and nodded. "In an hour I shall call the police," he said.

PAUL VAN CLEVE was in his office early the next morning. There was tape over his right cheek, more tape on the back of his head, and he moved a little stiffly, almost painfully, as he settled himself with the morning paper before him.

"MURDER RING SMASHED" declared the headlines spread over the front page above a picture of Pat Plenover. "MAYOR'S DAUGHTER ABDUCTED, SAVED BY WANTED MAN."

The rest of the story was almost a direct quotation from Pat Plenover. She told how she had been sent to a certain address because of a message which purported to be from her fiancé, Paul Van Cleve; how she had been kidnapped; how Stub Samson had been thrown into the same dungeon with her, and a graphic description of his fight to save her life.

She told the reason for the wave of horrible murders as explained to her by this derelict who had rescued her: Joseph Cowdrey had worked his way into the inner council of the

Good Government League in order to destroy it. Cowdrey was a criminal with important gangland connections in cities on the eastern seaboard. He intended to discredit the Good Government League with murders for which Chinatown would be apparently responsible. With the Good Government League out of power, he himself would be able to establish profitable vice dens....

There were several puzzling details, the story continued, for Miss Plenover had fainted at the height of the battle between Samson and the criminals. In addition to the dead in the room in which Miss Plenover had been kept prisoner, the bodies of several men were found on the main floor. All of them had their throats cut, and while all of them carried guns, none of the guns had been fired.

In contrast to the other bodies, that of Cowdrey showed no marks except that of a stab wound in his side, which the coroner declared could not possibly have caused his death. And yet from the expression on his face he had died in agony.

Mention was made of the fact that Paul Van Cleve, District Attorney, had been injured in an automobile accident while on his way to the scene of the battle.

There was a knock on the office door, and Webb Wottles strutted in. "Well, Paul, we got 'em," he exulted.

" 'We?' " There was a twinkle in the eyes behind the horn-rimmed glasses.

"Of course!" Wottles looked hurt. "Confidentially, Stub Samson has been working undercover for the department for some time."

"But how about the fight with him last night in the Shanghai restaurant, and the murder charge?"

"Just a smoke screen, Paul, a smoke screen. It led them right into the trap."

Van Cleve extended his hand. "Congratulations, then, Webb! I do resent the fact that you didn't let me in on it, but I suppose you had to preserve the utmost secrecy."

Wottles beamed as he took the extended hand. He was very happy. So was Paul Van Cleve.

THE CHOKING CHALICE

Frank Gruber

From the golden tankard of the great Tartar warrior, Genghis Khan, men drank and lived or—more often—drank and died. Jud Stanton did not know the secret of the ancient chalice and its devil's brew but now, as it was being thrust to his lips, he could do nothing but pray—and drink deeply.

HAVING LIVED THE first seventeen years of his life in China, a Chinese funeral was no novelty to Jud Stanton. Professional mourners, relatives and friends of the deceased parading with hideous masks, shooting off firecrackers and scattering millions of bits of paper to the winds—It was all familiar.

Stanton knew that each bit of paper had a hole or two in it, through which the devil must pursue a tortuous path before enabling himself to reach the soul of the departed one.

This funeral was in San Francisco's Chinatown, and Stanton's only reason for being present was an anonymous telephone call. A Chinese voice had spoken one phrase to him. "Attend the funeral of Charley Ho." Working on a Chinese case at the time—an exceedingly baffling one—Stanton took the tip to mean that the funeral might provide him with some clue.

He threaded his way through throngs on the sidewalks and kept pace with the funeral cortege. They apparently intended to parade in this fashion all the way to the docks where the coffin was to be loaded on board a ship, then taken to China for burial. The dead man had been wealthy, he and his surviving brother, Harry Ho, having owned the largest importing business in San Francisco.

So far Stanton had seen nothing which could have prompted the anonymous tip. The funeral was noisy, but orderly—

Scarcely had that thought crossed Stanton's mind than a half-dozen hideously masked men forced their way through the sidewalk throngs and surrounded the carriage containing the ornate, gilded coffin.

A chattering storm of protest went up from the pallbearers. Even as Stanton started precipitately forward, a knife flashed in the sun. The crowd hampered Stanton for a moment. When he was able to force his way out to the street he was startled to see that two of the attackers had dumped the coffin from the carriage to the street. Mourners yelled and screamed, and the attackers flailed out furiously with knives. One of the two who had dumped the coffin to the pavement jerked it open, reached in and suddenly brought forth—a gold cup!

Stanton gasped, almost missing a step in his headlong charge. It was the cup of Genghis Khan, that had been stolen from the apartment of Roderick Mallory two weeks ago and for which Stanton had been scouring Chinatown.

STANTON WENT FOR his .32 automatic which was snuggled in a shoulder holster. As it leaped into his hand, the man with the gold cup uttered a shrill yell. His cohorts suddenly ceased fighting and surrounded him. The half-dozen men hurled themselves at the crowd on the sidewalk. Stanton, still forty feet away, stopped in his rush. His arm swung up. His trigger-finger took up the slack, squeezed.

The .32 roared. A bullet smashed into the thief's shoulders, knocked him forward to his knees. The gold cup flew from his hands and landed in the gutter with a metallic clang. The effect of the shot on the surviving members of the attacking gang was miraculous. Almost as one man they wheeled, looked at Stanton steadying the automatic for another shot, then with howls of terror split and scattered.

Stanton swooped down, caught up the gold cup and charged the sidewalk crowd. Pandemonium reigned. Chinese, who had seen the grim tableau, scrambled to get out of his way.

Not so the pallbearers and mourners. They had been taken by surprise by the attackers, but during the fight their forces had gathered. By the time Stanton had retrieved the cup, more than a score of the mourners had assembled. Now they launched themselves in a solid phalanx at him.

The threat of Stanton's gun forced the shrieking throng to break apart enough to let him pass. But the mourners' phalanx was too big for the opening. Like a wave they struck the break-water of the crowd, fell back. Stanton forced himself to a store doorway and leaped inside, gun still in his hand.

A wild-eyed young Chinese took one glimpse at him and ducked discreetly behind the counter. Stanton darted through the store into a rear room. He gave a gasp of relief as he beheld an open window leading to a small yard in the rear. He literally dove through the window and landed in the yard on hands and

knees, an excellent position for a running jump at the board-fence at the rear of the yard. He was just scaling it when he heard yelling inside the store.

He was over the fence on the other side of the alley before the pursuers reached the yard behind the store. It was a simple thing then to dash through another store and out to the next street. There, luck proved with Stanton. A taxi was just cruising past.

Stanton piled into the cab, emitted a tremendous sigh of relief and leaned back against the cushions. This was his first opportunity to examine the gold cup. It was ornate, standing more than six inches and made of heavy, beaten gold, more than a quarter inch thick. Two jade inlays were on the cup, one of a falcon and the other, directly opposite on the other side, of a dove. The workmanship was exquisite, evidently having been made by a medieval craftsman of genius.

Stanton had been told that this cup had been owned by Genghis Khan, mightiest of all Chinese warriors, and he did not doubt it. No one but a king, or an exceedingly wealthy man, could have owned it.

Now that the cup was safely in his possession, Stanton began to think about his situation. The police and papers would no doubt make a great to-do about the funeral and fighting. Stanton did not worry about his own part in the affair. He knew that the Chinese are the closest-mouthed people on earth. He was a familiar figure in Chinatown, and probably fifty people had recognized him during the fight— but he believed not one would reveal his name to the police. When they had time to think it over, the relatives and friends of the deceased Charley Ho would know that he had fought against the coffin raiders.

Now he must get the cup into the hands of its legal owner— Roderick Mallory. After that, it was Mallory's affair. He would no doubt take precautions so that it would not be stolen from him a second time.

RODERICK MALLORY'S APARTMENT on Geary Street was a considerable distance from Chinatown, but the interests of the assemblage gathered for dinner were very definitely Chinese. Mallory, the host, had explored sections of Mongolia and Tibet no other white man had ever seen. His partner, Gordon Selkirk, had been with him on several expeditions and was also a specialist on China, although not as expert as Mallory.

Tse Ming, dignified Chinese of middle age, seldom strayed from the streets of Chinatown, where he was the unofficial mayor and most important Chinese in San Francisco.

Harry Ho, bland and Americanized, was a millionaire several times over, but his money had been made in Chinese trade.

The other guest—Jud Stanton—knew more about China than anyone present. He was a keen student of all things Chinese.

Stanton had wondered somewhat about this dinner. He had returned the cup of Genghis Khan that afternoon, and the explorer had been delighted. However, at once his former attitude of wanting the cup back, with no questions asked, disappeared. Now he very definitely wanted to ask questions. That was the reason for the dinner.

During the dinner, Mallory talked brilliantly to his guests on many topics. He was a big, fine-looking man of about fifty, but could easily have passed for forty. The dinner was a splendid one—only one thing missing. Stanton noted there was no wine. As a cosmopolitan, Mallory should have served liquor of some sort. As a host entertaining Chinese, the absence of wine was decidedly a breach of etiquette.

The absence of liquor was explained when everyone had finished eating. Roderick Mallory shed his affable manner and became brusque. "Gentlemen, you have probably wondered why I was so urgent about your having dinner here this evening. I shall now explain."

He paused, looked about the table. Stanton noted that Selkirk's face was becoming florid. He seemed to be angry with Mallory. Stanton guessed that Selkirk knew what was coming.

Mallory went on: "All of you know that I brought with me from Mongolia a priceless relic—the cup of Genghis Khan. I discovered in a remote monastery in Mongolia and purchased it from the monks. The cup is authentic, beyond a doubt, and as a relic alone is easily worth fifty thousand dollars. But, to gentlemen like you, men of wealth and influence—Mongols— the cup might easily be worth several times fifty thousand.

"You can imagine, therefore, how dismayed I was two weeks ago when the cup was stolen from this apartment—and how glad I am that it was restored to me this afternoon, by my good friend, Mr. Stanton."

Among a strictly Occidental gathering, such news would have created at least a murmur. But here, it provoked merely an impassive glance at Stanton from Harry Ho. Tse Ming did not even take his eyes from the face of Roderick Mallory.

Mallory continued: "Peculiar circumstances surround the recovery of the cup. It was enclosed, I am told, with the remains of your honorable brother, Mr. Ho—and, but for intervention, would have gone to China. I would like to know about that, Mr. Ho. Did you have knowledge of the cup being in the coffin of your brother?"

Bland Harry Ho waited discreetly for a moment, then replied in a clear, flawless, voice. "I did not, Mr. Mallory. And I, too, am deeply grieved that it was found there. Not because it might cast reflections upon me, because I can bear that, but because it defiled the dead body of my honorable brother—and that cast reflections upon his spirit. I am greatly interested in knowing how the cup of the great Khan got into my brother's coffin."

"And you, Tse Ming?"

The dignified Chinese leader answered without hesitation, his words strongly accented, but his English good. "I had heard of the cup, of course, but how it got into the coffin of the Honorable Ho, I do not know. The dead thief—for whose death I pay my respects to Mr. Stanton—was a member of the—ah—unnamable tong of the thieves and undesirables. I intend to look further into the doings of this tong—but at the present time, I am sorry, I cannot give you any information."

STANTON KNEW WHAT Tse Ming meant by looking into the doings of the outcast tong—tong war. He shook his head. He wished Mallory would drop the whole affair. He had his cup and should be thankful for it.

Mallory had no intention of dropping the matter, however. His lips merely tightened, and he struck a bell on the table before him. A squat Chinese servant, dressed in brocaded black silk, padded into the room.

"Kang, the wine," Mallory ordered.

The servant bowed and padded out of the room again. A square box stood on the table before Mallory. As the servant left for the wine, Mallory raised the lid of the box, reached in and lifted out the cup of Genghis Khan.

"Inasmuch as no one here seems to know anything about the matter, I wonder if you will submit to a test?"

Gordon Selkirk rose abruptly to his feet. "Just a minute, Rod," he snapped. "I think you're carrying things too far."

"Perhaps," sneered Mallory, "you are afraid to take the test?"

"Of course not," retorted Selkirk, "but it's silly—absurd."

"You are not a Chinese," said Mallory. He turned to the others. "All of you know the legend of this cup. Genghis Khan used it only when he entertained chieftains or princes with whom he was making treaties. This chalice was supposed to have extraordinary powers. Genghis Khan and the guest both drank from it. If the guest were honest at heart, nothing happened. But if he were lying, planning to double-cross the Khan while professing friendship, the cup would reveal the fact—because the drinker immediately fell dead. Do you think the legend an absurd one, Mr. Ho?"

Harry Ho shrugged. "Genghis Khan lived eight hundred years ago."

"That's right," agreed Mallory. "But his memory still lives in the hearts of all true Mongols. To them he will always be their greatest idol. Do you revere the memory of Genghis Khan sufficiently to drink from this cup, Honorable Tse Ming?"

The silence before Tse Ming answered was a long one, but finally the old man spoke firmly. "I do. I believe in the legend of the sacred cup."

"Good!" exclaimed Mallory. "Kang!"

THE SERVANT HAD reentered the room and stood beside Mallory with a large bottle of amber wine. Mallory held out the gold cup and the servant poured almost the entire contents of the bottle into it. Stanton watched the proceedings closely.

Mallory faced his guests again, then struck by a thought, spoke to the servant, "Kang, as long as we are doing this in the royal-Mongol fashion let us do it properly. The servant should always drink first from the cup—just to make sure the master is not being poisoned."

Kang seemed to tense. "Poison in wine?" he exclaimed. "Then Kang no want drink."

"Drink!" ordered Mallory sharply, forcing the gold chalice into the servant's hands.

Kang accepted the cup, looked about at the guests, then drank. Stanton could see his Adam's apple go up and down as he swallowed.

Mallory was satisfied. He took the cup from Kang and raised it. "As host, I drink next." He tilted the cup to his lips, swallowed—and the cup dropped from his hands to the table, spilling the wine over the white tablecloth. Stanton half rose in his chair, for the eyes of Roderick Mallory seemed to be bursting from his sockets. The man's jaws worked horribly. Then he gasped: "I've been—"

A cough choked him, and he doubled forward. His head hit the table-edge, bounced up and the big body slid to the floor.

The dramatic climax brought all about the table to their feet. Even old Tse Ming paled. But it was Stanton who was the first to reach Mallory. He dropped down on his knees, looked into glazed eyes and knew that Mallory was dead.

He rose to his feet. "He's finished," he announced.

"Dead?" cried Gordon Selkirk. "He-he can't be. Why, Kang drank first. Kang—how do you feel?"

Stanton looked sharply at Kang. The servant's eyes darted about, and his lips worked nervously, but it was obvious no poison had affected him. "I—I feel all right," Kang gasped.

"But, sirs, how could he have been poisoned? The wine was good. It came from a new bottle."

A look of vague alarm came into Selkirk's face. "I wonder if there could be something to what Mallory said—about that Genghis Khan cup?"

"Don't he absurd," Stanton cut in shortly. "As Mr. Ho pointed out to us earlier, Genghis Khan died eight hundred years ago. If there was some truth in the old legend it was the result of clever chicanery—the great Khan merely dropped poison into the cup after he was through drinking."

"That's it!" cried Selkirk. "Kang dropped poison into the cup after he drank."

"No!" screamed the servant, Kang. "I no put poison in glass. I—"

"Don't get excited, Kang," Stanton said soothingly. "I was watching closely and I'm sure you didn't drop anything into the cup. No, there must be some other explanation. What's your opinion, Honorable Tse Ming?"

The mayor of Chinatown looked bland. "My opinion is that it is better to call the white police."

Stanton frowned. "You're right, but I'm going to come in for some razzing. Me—a private detective—and someone poisoned before my very eyes."

"It has not yet been established that Mr. Mallory was poisoned," said Harry Ho softly. "Perhaps, it was heart failure—the excitement."

Stanton whistled softly. "You may be right, Mr. Ho. We've been taking too much for granted. Just because of all the talk about the cup and the poisoning. Mr. Selkirk, did Mallory ever show symptoms of apoplexy?"

Selkirk's forehead wrinkled. "He did, on several occasions. In fact, he had a thorough physical examination after his return from this last trip. The doctor told him he was through leading a rigorous life."

Stanton breathed freer. Of course, Mallory had died from apoplexy. That was the logical explanation, and it simplified things a great deal. He shook his head and looked around the room. "I'll phone the police. Kang, where's the phone?"

The servant pointed to the adjoining room. "In there, Mr. Stanton."

Stanton nodded and walked into the next room. He found the telephone on a table against the wall and dialed headquarters. Briefly, he explained to the desk-sergeant what had happened. Then he put down the receiver—and the lights in that room and the adjoining one went out.

STANTON STOOD STILL a moment. In the next room he heard swearing and a choked scream. His hand went to the gun in his shoulder holster.

A black shadow flitted through the door leading into the room. Stanton's hand tightened on the trigger. He heard slithering footsteps and lowered himself cautiously to his knees.

He was so tensed that the report of a gun in the next room caused him to jump. Then there was a rush of air, and a heavy body collided with his. Stanton was bowled over backward. In falling, he lashed out with his gun, felt it strike yielding flesh. Something exploded against the side of his head, and lightning flashed to his brain. Stanton knew that he pulled the trigger of his gun, for he heard the report of thunder. But that was the last he did hear for some time…

THE NEXT THING he knew, his eyes opened in a brilliantly lighted room and he looked up into a grim-jawed face. He shook his head and blinked his eyes. "Ramsey?" he gasped. "When'd you come here?"

Lieutenant Ramsey scowled. "You called for the cops—and here I am. Been here ten minutes, trying to wake you up. What happened?"

Stanton struggled to his feet and became conscious of blinding pain on the left side of his head. He put up his hand and felt something wet and sticky. "You found Mallory?" he asked.

"Yeah," growled Ramsey. "Heart failure. But what laid you out? Bang your head against a door?"

"I'll tell you about myself in a minute," said Stanton. "First let me get things straight—about Mallory. You say heart failure? How do you know?"

Lieutenant Ramsey jerked a thumb at a corpulent man in civilian clothes. "The doc says heart failure. He ought to know."

Stanton took a couple of steps toward the medical-examiner. "It couldn't possibly be poison, Doctor?" he asked.

The medical-officer shrugged. "Symptoms indicate heart failure. Of course, it could be poison—there are drugs that have the same reaction on a corpse as heart failure, but it would take a post mortem to tell."

"What makes you so sure it's poison?" barked the police lieutenant.

Stanton shook his head. "Where are the others?"

"What others?"

"The other guests. Tse Ming, Harry Ho, Selkirk—and Mallory's servant." Ramsey shook his head. "You and the corpse were the only ones here when we came. And we musta' got here inside of ten minutes after you phoned."

Gone—Selkirk, Tse Ming, Ho and Kang! They had all lit out. Why? The servant had been in a tight spot—it was understandable that he would try to make his getaway. But the others were wealthy and substantial citizens. They didn't have much to fear from a routine investigation—not if Mallory had really died of heart failure. After the attack upon him, Stanton was unwilling to admit it had been heart failure.

"All right," he said to Ramsey. "Call it heart failure. I guess it was. And there wasn't any use of the others staying here."

"Yeah—but who conked you?"

Stanton's lips tightened. "I guess I had too much to drink and there was a bit of a misunderstanding."

Ramsey growled in his throat. Stanton followed him into the other room. The remains of the dinner were still on the table. Stanton pressed his hand on the tablecloth before what had been Mallory's place. It was still damp from where the wine had spilled. The cup was gone. Stanton wasn't surprised.

He knew China. He knew that Genghis Khan was revered as a saint in Mongolia. A Mongol in possession of the great Khan's legendary cup could get about anything he wanted. Ho and Tse Ming were Mongols. One or the other might want to return to China.

The wagon had taken away the body of Mallory. Lieutenant Ramsey was ready to leave with his policemen. "Want a lift downtown?" he asked Stanton.

"No, I think I'll walk to my lodgings."

"O.K., I'm leaving a copper here."

Stanton followed Ramsey outside. He watched the policemen drive off, walked a few feet up the street, then returned to Mallory's place. He rang the bell, and the policeman let him in. "Lieutenant Ramsey said it would be all right for me to look about a bit."

The policeman had seen Stanton on friendly terms with Ramsey. "O.K., Mr. Stanton. Help yourself."

Stanton walked straight to the bathroom and searched the medicine cabinet. He found iodine, headache powders and other drugs, but none that seemed deadly. Next he went to Mallory's bedroom, searched the dressers. The result was a failure. Then he slipped into the small room of Kang, the servant. He hadn't expected to find any poisons in Mallory's room, didn't expect to find any in Kang's room, but he might just as well clean up this trail before going on to others. Stanton was always thorough in his work. That was why he usually produced results.

Stanton's detective business was exclusively Chinese. There were plenty of detectives in the city who handled white man's cases. Competing against them, Stanton would have been merely another detective. But there was no other white detective who could speak Chinese, who knew the ways of the Chinese and possessed their confidence.

Stanton ran rapidly through the little closet in Kang's room. He was somewhat surprised to find excellent silk-padded robes, a brocaded suit of Chinese clothes and an expensive American suit of clothes. Kang, like the modernized Chinese, went in for good clothing, the latest and most daring men's styles—and wasted it all in cheap taxi dance-halls, trying to impress white girls.

But it was in Kang's dresser that Stanton found something

interesting. It was a thick American book and the title of it was *Genghis Khan*. So the servant was interested in Genghis Khan! There was a name on the fly leaf—*William Kang*. Underneath was a Chinese ideogram, painted on with brush and ink. Stanton frowned as he read it. It was a compound Chinese name. *Temu-Jin. Temu-Jin* meant "perfect warrior."

Stanton returned the book to the drawer, pulled out the next one. But then he shoved it back and withdrew the book again. He ruffled the pages, read. Five minutes later he slammed the book shut and returned it to the drawer.

In the other room the policeman said to him: "Find anything interesting?"

"Not a thing, officer. I'm leaving."

OUTSIDE, STANTON WALKED swiftly to the corner. He waited there a moment or two, hailed a cruising cab. Ten minutes later he paid it off in front of his own apartment house on Lombard Street. He hurried up to his bachelor's apartment and entering, immediately picked up his telephone.

"Chinatown Exchange," he said into the mouthpiece. A moment later a voice greeted him in English.

"I wish to speak to the Honorable Tse Ming," Stanton said in Chinese.

The San Francisco Chinatown Telephone Exchange is perhaps the most amazing in the world. Many Chinese do not have phones in their lodgings—but say a Chinese name to a Chinatown Exchange operator, and the owner of that name will get to a telephone. Perhaps the message is relayed a dozen times, but eventually—and in amazingly short time— the person sought will be found.

It took the operator less than three minutes to report to Stanton. "I am very sorry, sir, but we are unable to reach the Honorable Tse Ming. His residence reports that earlier in the evening he went to have dinner outside of Chinatown. Inquiry at this place"—the girl hesitated, then went on—"reveals the information that a policeman is the only person there, Tse Ming having left some time ago. Do you wish to leave a message that Tse Ming is to call you when he reaches home?"

"No," said Stanton. "Thank you very much."

More than an hour, and Tse Ming had not reached his home—and that was unusual for a man as important as Tse Ming. He usually managed to let his whereabouts be known to his household. He was always in demand by someone or other.

Stanton slumped into his chair, put his head into his hands and stared at the floor. After a minute he became aware of his aching head and went into the bathroom. He washed the dried blood from the wound, found that the bruise was not serious but that there was a big blue lump on his left temple. He started to put adhesive tape over the wound, then suddenly gasped.

He dropped the adhesive tape, sprang into the other room. He caught up his coat and hat, bounced across the room to his desk and rummaged about for a moment. He brought out two guns, a .32 automatic and a .25. The .32 he put into his shoulder holster. The .25 he strapped to the calf of his right leg.

FIFTEEN MINUTES LATER Stanton paid off a taxi-driver near the Fort Mason docks. He walked swiftly toward the shadowy sheds on the long wharves. There were several dock watchmen about. Stanton stopped one of them. "A vessel sailing for China—where would it be?"

The watchman scratched his head. "That'll be the Chink funeral-boat. Imagine a boat going to China just to take the corpse of some rich Chink! Funny people these Chinese."

"That's the ship I want. Where is it?"

The watchman pointed. "Over there by Pier Twelve."

Stanton nodded and started off. He saw the riding lights of the ship when he reached Pier 12. He saw a scurrying figure or two on the boat. Stanton had a hunch that the ship was due to sail soon. He hurried his step—and then a figure slipped out of the shadows. Stanton stopped and the hand holding his gun came out of his pocket. "Who are you?" he called out.

"F'liend," replied a singsong voice.

"Well, keep your distance," said Stanton. "I don't like my friends to come too close in the dark."

"You go *Samu Maru?*" asked the shadowy figure.

"Yes, this it?"

"It is. I am sailor on it. Ship owned by Honorable Harry Ho."

"That's right. Well, if you're a sailor lead the way. I'll follow."

"Hokay!" said the voice.

The man padded ahead of Stanton. He followed a dozen feet in the rear, gripping the automatic. Up to the ship and across a short gangplank. Stanton stepped on the ship and walked into the arms of two very brawny Chinese. Before he could even fire a shot, his gun was smashed from his hand and he was held helpless, a huge arm about his throat, a pair of muscular hands around his knees. His feet were swept out from under him and he was carried in that fashion down into the cabin of the ship.

There he was thrown to the floor. "He came, master!" said one of the men who had captured him.

Stanton, choking from the strangling arm, looked up into the face of Kang, who had been Mallory's servant. The Mongol was dressed in a brocaded mandarin's gown and looked very unlike the meek servant of that afternoon.

"Welcome, Mr. Stanton. You're just in time to join us at dinner."

Stanton looked in the direction of Kang's gesture and gave a start. For there, around a table, sat Tse Ming, Selkirk and Harry Ho.

He rose to his feet. "I shall be delighted to join you at dinner."

"Then take this seat at my right," motioned Kang.

Stanton walked over to the table, sat down. Kang sat down beside him. The two Chinese who had captured him, took up posts by the door. One held a huge six-shooter, the other a wicked cutlass.

KANG SAT AT the table-head. At his right was Stanton, at the left Harry Ho. Tse Ming sat beside Ho, and Selkirk beside Stanton. Selkirk's blustering manner was gone. He was nervous and constantly moistened his lips. Harry Ho and Tse Ming, as usual, were impassive.

The cup of Genghis Khan stood before Kang, and the Mongol regarded it chucklingly. "Once before today, you honorable gentlemen were asked to drink from his cup. One of your number drank and died. I drank and lived? Why?"

"I do not know why," said Harry Ho, coldly, "unless you yourself dropped the poison into the cup after you drank."

Kang shot a baleful look at Ho. "I did not," he retorted promptly, "and for that inference, you, Honorable Wealthy Ho, shall have the pleasure of drinking first tonight."

Selkirk exclaimed. "You are going to force us to drink from that cup?"

Kang smiled thinly and looked significantly at the pair of stalwart henchmen standing near the door. "No—I shall not *force* you to drink. But perhaps you will want to drink." He shifted his eyes to Stanton. "Before we go on, I should like to know just how you stumbled onto the information that I was taking this ship out of here."

Stanton shrugged. "It was because you wrote a name in a book; the original name of Genghis Khan—*Temu-Jin.*"

Kang started. "You—you know that?"

"Of course," Stanton replied. "I've studied my Chinese history. Genghis Khan as he is known today didn't take that name until late in his career, after he'd conquered most of China. Before that he was known as *Temu-Jin.* He called himself Genghis Khan—which means "perfect warrior"— when he became so inflated with his ego that he considered himself invulnerable. Like some other conquerors of history Genghis Khan was an unbelievingly bloodthirsty barbarian. He—"

"Stop!"

Kang leaped to his feet so suddenly his chair flew backward. "Fool!" he thundered. "How dare you defile the name of the greatest man China has ever known—the man whose name I also bear? Yes, my name is *Temu-Jin,* and I am a true descendant of Jenghiz Khan! I am the rightful ruler of all Mongolia right now."

Stanton leaned forward. "That's why you wanted the cup?"

Kang's eyes flashed fire. "Of course. Once I get into Mongolia and the news of this cup gets around, the Mongol hordes will gather. We will sweep the Japanese out of Munchukuo, then we'll go south, take possession of all China. And from then—"

"Before then you'll face a firing-squad," Stanton cut in dryly.

Kang smacked his fist on the table. "Enough. I was going to compel Ho, the money-grabber who thought himself worthy of the cup, to drink from it first, but now, Mr. Stanton, you shall have the privilege. Sing!"

One of the Chinese left his position by the door, went to a sideboard and brought a bottle of wine to the table. Kang took up the gold cup, held it out. The servant, Sing, poured it almost full. "We will follow the correct procedure with the cup," Kang said, sneering. "Sing, you drink first!"

Almond eyes flashed, but Sing took the cup. It trembled in his hands, and wine spilled to the floor. Then, suddenly, the servant put the cup to his lips and took a big gulp. Nothing happened. Kang took the cup, smiled mockingly and drank. Again heads craned forward, but again nothing happened.

"All right, Mr. Stanton," said Kang.

Stanton reached out for the cup.

Well, this was the finish. He couldn't drink the wine, he knew that. Kang's eyes told him that to do so would be death. To refuse—also meant death.

Three to one—and four or five upstairs. The little automatic in his garter holster held seven waspish slugs. By a surprise attack he could perhaps win out down here. Upstairs was something else.

Stanton looked at the cup. The side with the jade dove inlay was toward him. The symbol of peace—if his heart carried peace he would drink and live. Mallory had drunk from the side of the dove. Stanton had noticed that. He had died. But wait—Just now both Sing and Kang had drunk from the falcon side. Why—Stanton gasped. Of course, that was it!

"All right," he said quietly. "I'll drink."

Beside him, he heard Selkirk draw in a sharp breath. Stanton lifted the cup to his lips—then turned it around to the falcon side and drank!

IT WAS RED wine and Stanton, tasting it, felt sure that there was no foreign agent in it. He handed the cup back to Kang, looked into the Mongol's eyes. He saw fury, knew he'd guessed right. The Mongol spoke with an effort. "You are fortunate, Mr. Stanton. Very well. Honorable Ho, will you drink next?"

The bland Chinese merchant showed emotion for the first time that day. His eyes flashed, and his lips seemed to tremble. "I—I do not want to drink."

"You are afraid," jeered Kang. "Yet you were brave enough to steal the great Khan's cup from the white man."

"Ah," said Stanton, "now it all comes out. Ho, you stole the cup and intended to ship it to China in your brother's coffin, intending to follow later, I suppose?"

"If a true Mongol had not been in his employ, he would have succeeded," said Kang grimly. "Imagine a fat low-caste like himself ruler of the Mongols?"

Harry Ho wilted under the abuse. "I have much money, *Temu-Jin.* I will pay—"

"Bah!" snorted Kang. "I will get money in Mongolia. My men have taken your ship. We don't need you. Drink!"

Harry Ho looked into the relentless face of Kang and capitulated. "Very well," he said in a trembling voice.

Stanton slumped down in his chair. His hand went to his leg, pulled up the trousers. He pulled out the little automatic and brought it up into full view.

"Drink from the falcon side, Mr. Ho," he said quietly.

Kang lunged forward. "You—you American dog. Sing, kill him!"

Sing looked at the little gun in Stanton's hand and his teeth bared. He hunched his shoulders and started toward Stanton. Stanton calmly shot him through the face. Then, as the big man was swaying on his feet, he turned and sent a tiny bullet smashing through the other guard's right arm. The cutlass clattered to the floor, and the man let out a moan.

"Selkirk," cried Stanton. "Get the gun. The others will be charging down here in a minute."

Kang sprang from the table and charged for the sideboard. Stanton shot him through the kneecap. The Mongol broke in his stride and plunged forward. His face struck the edge of the sideboard, and blood spurted.

Upstairs, Stanton heard yelling and pounding of feet. "Quick," he cried. "Step to one side. They're coming down. Selkirk, grab that gold cup!"

The explorer tore the cup from Ho's quaking hands. Tse Ming padded to one side.

"No shooting unless I give the word!" Stanton cried. "I've got another plan."

Feet pounded on the stairs. Stanton stepped across the moaning Kang who was sitting on the floor and clutching his wounded knee. He put the little automatic up against the Mongol's head. Men piled into the room.

"Stop," thundered Stanton. "One more move and I shoot *Temu-Jin*—the descendant of Jenghiz Khan."

"Kill them!" screamed Kang.

The men stood blocking the doorway. They held guns ready, but they were bewildered. Kang had sold himself to them. They really believed that he was a descendant of Genghis Khan. Even those who didn't were true Mongols and believed in the sacred cup of Genghis Khan.

Stanton saw their eyes go to Selkirk, who held the cup, and a brilliant thought hit him. They might be willing to sacrifice Kang, but—

"Selkirk," he cried. "If they make a move, throw the cup through the port window—into the sea, where it'll be lost forever."

"No," babbled the leader of the Mongols. "No—do not throw away. I—we surrender."

"Then throw down your guns!" cried Stanton. "And round up every one of your men on this ship."

Selkirk had caught the importance of the act and had stepped to the porthole. He stood a couple of feet away from it, hands poised to heave the cup through it.

"Don't listen to—" began Kang. Stanton stopped him by cupping the little automatic in his palm and smashing it down on Kang's head. The Mongol collapsed.

That was the end. The leader of the pirates tossed his gun to the floor. The others behind him followed suit. In five minutes everyone aboard had surrendered.

STANTON EXPLAINED THINGS in the cabin. "Kang may actually be a descendant of the great Khan—that I don't know. I do know, though, that he came to America for the express purpose of stealing the gold cup. He was fortunate enough to get a position with Mallory, but before he could steal the cup, Ho beat him to it. One of Kang's pals was in Ho's employ, and that's how Kang got to grabbing the cup. There's one thing, though, that I don't understand. Who was it tipped me off to attend Charlie Ho's funeral?"

Tse Ming murmured: "I have many friends. Rumor reached me"—he shrugged, then went on—"but there is one thing else. The poison?"

Stanton picked up the cup of Genghis Khan. "I tumbled to that when I saw Kang drink from the falcon side. Look." He tilted the cup in the direction of the falcon inlay. Nothing happened. Then he tilted it to the dove side. The watchers gasped. Now that they were looking for it, they saw a tiny needle shoot out at the lip of the cup. "That's how Genghis got rid of bothersome chieftains and princes. Poison. Of course, those who proclaimed peace always drank from the dove side. Kang discovered the secret and filled the needle with fresh poison. Well, if I have any influence with Mallory's relatives, this cup goes to the Chinese Museum in Peiping. It's too dangerous in private hands."

THE HEADLESS IDOL

Sidney Herschel Small

*A Dying Man, a Headless Idol and the
Flight of a Bee Tell Wentworth a Tale of
Frightful Crime and—Kong Gai!*

1

The Missing Children

"AND WHAT I don't know, I can't tell you," said Captain Dunand, attempting honestly to answer the shrewd queries of the reporters as he sat behind his desk in San Francisco's Hall of Justice. He went on doggedly, "You boys seem to think I'm trying to get out of making an arrest. That ought to make you happy, because as long as the Whitcomb case remains unsolved, your papers can keep on calling me a doddering old fool—"

"Then you refuse to admit that Whitcomb and his three children are victims of a gang outrage?" demanded the *News-Call* reporter. "You refuse to admit that they are being held for ransom? You refuse to admit—"

"I'm not admitting what I don't know," persisted the gray-haired captain of detectives. "Not if you keep after me all day, boys."

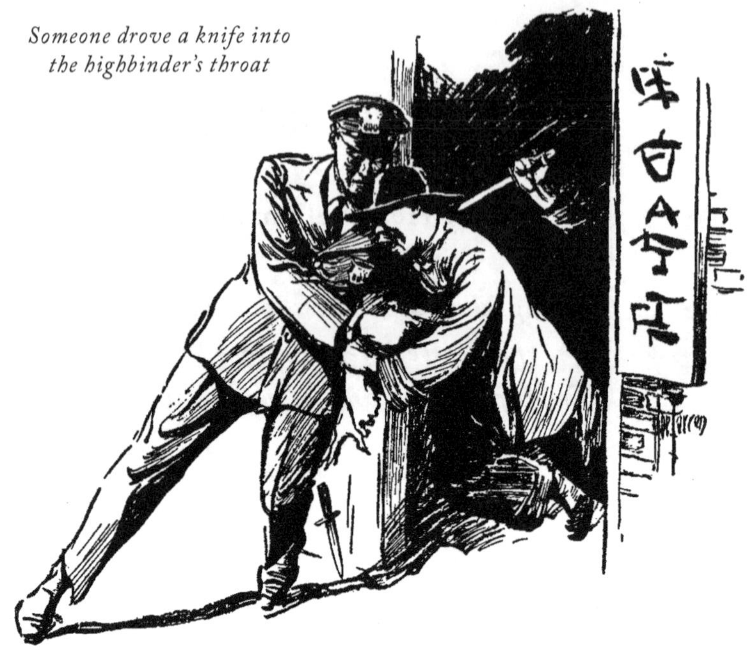

The *Enquirer* man drawled, "We've been after you six days, cap, and you haven't come across with one printable line. You play with us, and we'll play with you. The public have a right to know what's being done to clear up Whitcomb's disappearance. They're pretty worked up about it, too. A man and three youngsters can't vanish without leaving some sort of clew—"

Captain Dunand stared out of the window, and blinked as the last rays of sun glinted off the roofs of Chinatown and were reflected into his eyes. He said finally, "I agree with you, Haynes. I don't want to fool anybody, except the criminals involved in the case. The department had one clew, and gave it to you."

"The fellow who came to Whitcomb's office and threatened him?"

"That's the man. Martin Cravens."

"Well," insisted Haynes, "how about finding him in time for my next edition?"

Dunand said wearily, "I told you boys that if you plastered his name all over the front pages he'd go into hiding."

"Well, how 'bout the chauffeur of Whitcomb's machine, cap? He'd do to keep our jobs for us."

Dunand was about to reply that the department was making every effort to find the missing chauffeur when he heard a whisper, followed by a laugh. He asked abruptly, "What's funny, Haynes? Let us in on it."

"I just said it was too bad it wasn't a couple of elephants your dicks were looking for, cap. They could probably find a pair of elephants, provided the animals stayed on Market Street—"

Leaning back in his chair, Dunand said, "Let's go over this thing, boys. And"—solemnly—"anything I may say isn't for publication. Right?"

The oldest reporters pledged their words with a quiet, "Shoot, captain."

"Six days ago," Dunand began, "Ronald Whitcomb left his house and went to his office. He arrived at nine o'clock, about. A few minutes later the man Martin Cravens, a clerk at the Consolidated Oil, came to see him. There was an argument. It seems that Cravens had bought stock on Whitcomb's say so, and lost his shirt. Cravens said some dangerous words; he was heard to say them by people in the outer office."

"We know all this, cap!"

"Wait. Let me finish, Haynes. Cravens leaves, promising to get even. At a few minutes past ten, Whitcomb's own car takes him away.

"Then we learn that somebody telephoned his home, ordering the three children to come to Maginn-Duane's, the department store, and meet their father. The children are taken there in a taxi—"

"What taxi, cap?"

"Not the one phoned for," said Dunand, "because the maid at the house said a second cab came, a few minutes after the first one. Let me go ahead, boys, will you? You know all this, anyhow.

"THE CAB DIDN'T go to the department store, so far as we can learn. Whitcomb is gone. His three children are gone. It looks like the work of a number of men, but there's been no demand yet for ransom. Martin Cravens couldn't do it by himself. He's only a clerk, and, as you boys've found out, a fellow with a good reputation.

"Whitcomb's chauffeur is also an honest man; been with him eleven years. So I tell you that it looks to me like the work of a gang of men, just as you fellows have been trying to get me to say, but"—his big finger waving at the listeners—"I want it to appear as if all suspicion is on this man Cravens! If he's in with a gang, I want 'em to push him forward when the time comes for dickerin'. In other words, boys, I want the department to appear dumb, and according to you fellows that ought to be easy."

"Do you realize, cap, that you've not told us a single new fact?"

"I've never lied to you, boys, and I'm not starting to do it now!"

The *News-Call* man said thoughtfully, "We've all printed stories that it looks like a gang outrage, captain."

"Sure. But the department hasn't backed up your statements."

Haynes said suddenly, "We're not blaming you, cap, but our city editors are all riding us to get some sort of story. Here's an idea. Why don't you put Wentworth on the case? It would let us print a lot of hooey, and we'd get by with it, and in the meantime put the real gang clear off any notion that they're suspected. Let us cook up a tale about the trail leading to Chinatown! We can use Wentworth's photograph, and rehash some of the stories about arrests he's made. Be a good guy, cap. All you got to say is 'Sergeant Wentworth has been assigned to the Whitcomb case' and we'll do all the necessary fiction writing."

"Wentworth's only the patrolman on the Chinatown beat," said Dunand.

"I'll leave it to the boys."

"You said it," agreed the newspaper men in chorus.

Dunand instantly attempted to retreat behind his last line of defense: "Then I wasn't talking for publication," he growled.

"No go," the veteran police reporter decided fairly. "You're protected in anything you said about the Whitcomb case, but this came later. If Haynes wishes to use it, he can. We all can, and we all probably will, because we haven't anything else to turn in. It makes a good yarn, and can't do any harm."

"If I assign Wentworth to the case for one day, does that satisfy you?"

"One minute'll satisfy me," grunted Haynes. "Now, call Wentworth up here, and let us talk to him."

Dunand was trapped, and knew it. He reached for his desk telephone, and said into the transmitter, "Chinatown squadron. Manning? Dunand. Is Sergeant Wentworth in? He is? Tell him I want him. Eh? Yes, I'll speak to him on the phone first—"

There was a pause, and then the captain of detectives said, "Hullo, sergeant. I want… hullo… oh, it's you, Manning? What? Busy? Well, let me talk to him on the phone. There're some newspaper men here, and they want a word about the Whitcomb case."

Silence again; when Dunand said, "I'm listening, Manning. He said… what? Oh, he said that, did he? Hmm, well, well, well." A slow grin was spreading over the gray-haired captain's stolid face. "Very well, Manning," he concluded. "Just say to the sergeant that I'll wait for him here."

HAYNES WAS LOOKING at his watch. "Have him make it snappy," he said, as Dunand replaced the telephone. "I've got a suburban edition to make, cap."

"Sergeant Wentworth said he was busy," said Dunand placidly.

"Say, who's in charge of the bureau? You, or Wentworth? How long've I got to wait?"

"It takes a long time for boiling water to freeze," Dunand told him calmly.

"Meaning Wentworth said I could wait until hell froze over?"

The gray-haired captain of detectives said softly, "Something like that."

"Put into words, Wentworth isn't coming up to let us talk to him, and you are not assigning him to this case!"

"Something like that," repeated Dunand, smiling broadly. He watched Haynes scrawl a few words on paper, and then said, "And that isn't news, is it?"

"Want to hear what I'm phoning to my office? 'Dunand refuses to assign Detective-Sergeant James Wentworth to

Whitcomb case. Detective bureau apathetic.' And what will the Police Commission say to that, cap?"

"I haven't refused to assign Wentworth to this case, have I?"

The oldest of the police reporters took charge.

"Captain," he said, "we aren't getting anywhere. We aren't getting any news, and you aren't getting the abductors of Whitcomb and his youngsters—"

"Who said we weren't?" demanded the captain.

Every reporter put two and two together. Several of them stood up.

"Where're you going now?" Dunand asked.

"To telephone our papers that Wentworth has uncovered a clew!"

Dunand said urgently, "Boys, he… he hasn't uncovered anything. Be reasonable!" The honest eyes of the captain clouded, and then he went on glibly, "Wentworth's only checking on some data just brought in—"

"What data?"

And so the wise chief of the detective bureau began to lie for one of the few times in his life: "We picked up a vag, just a little while ago, boys. I'll give you his name in a minute. He was standing outside the Whitcomb Building, and he saw a big green touring car with the side curtains all on, and while the machine was in front of the building he thought he heard a child cry, and then Whitcomb came down, very excited, and got in the green touring car, and…."

Three full minutes it took the captain to complete his fairy story. When he had finished, and the reporters had hurried out to get in touch with their various city desks, Dunand lifted the telephone again.

He was connected with the Chinatown squad room, and said to his sergeant of detectives in charge of the Chinatown detail:

"I've done more lying this evening than I've ever done before, Jimmy. It's safe for you to come up now, boy. And if you haven't picked up a real clew—which is why I lied, to keep you and whatever you've found out away from the papers until we get a chance to act—I'm going to send you out to the Sunset district where you can pick buttercups!"

2

Wentworth's Clew

IT WAS ONLY a few minutes before a lean young man in the uniform of a patrolman stepped quietly into the captain's office. It was only a few minutes, but in that time Dunand had firmly denied the pleas of two city editors, who wanted pictures of the "vagrant" who was supposed to have seen the abduction, and who promised all sort of influence being brought to bear on the captain's gray head when the requests were refused.

The Whitcomb case had been on the front page for just a day short of a week. The city was aroused, not only because of the disappearance of the wealthy Whitcomb, head of the brokerage house bearing his name, but also because of the obvious abduction of the small Whitcomb children. Rumors—terrible rumors—were on every lip. In the meantime the police were not able to produce the man Cravens, who had threatened Whitcomb the morning of the disappearance, nor to find the Whitcomb automobile and its chauffeur. There was flaming talk, aided and abetted by the newspapers, which the administration did not find pleasing. Coals were constantly being dropped on Dunand's head—and he could do nothing about it save keep after his men. Almost the entire department was on the Ronald Whitcomb case, but not a man had learned a single essential fact, nor picked up the trail of the clerk Cravens.

It was freely admitted that Cravens had just cause for anger against Whitcomb. The millionaire broker had advised Cravens to buy several varieties of stocks—or Whitcomb's office had advised it, which was the same thing—and Cravens had lost his savings. But that was not unusual. Many others were in the same fix, and through no real fault of Whitcomb's. Had Cravens taken a good punch at the broker, San Francisco would have said, "Served him right!" and laughed about it. But kidnapping three children, as well as Whitcomb himself, was a different matter.

The department was baffled. Here was what appeared an obvious crime, with the criminal known, and yet they were unable to produce the man.

All of this was in Dunand's mind as he said, "Sit down, Jimmy. I've lied hot and heavy to give you time, lad. Now, let's hear what you've picked up."

Wentworth said soberly, "Yes, sir. It isn't much, but it's a clew—"

"It'd better be," Dunand snapped. "Or the department'll be in a fine mess. I'll be the judge. What is it?"

The youthful sergeant of detectives reached into his trousers pocket, and as he withdrew his hand said gravely. "I'm afraid I'll have to be the judge, sir. It's in my line… this is it."

"That? What's that?"

Dunand stared at the object in Wentworth's hand.

It was small, no larger than an apple, which, at first glance, it resembled. A closer look showed that it was the body of an idol of some strange god, with the arms folded, and the legs drawn up. The image was of carved wood, and very old; so old that the surface was smooth, brown, and polished.

WENTWORTH SLOWLY TURNED the curious little talisman between his fingers, so Dunand could see where the head had been. Here the wood was much lighter in color, as if it had not been exposed long to the air, nor been handled much. And where the head of the idol had been severed, there was painted three tiny white flowers, no larger than the heads of matches, but delicately, beautifully done.

"That's your clew?" Dunand said wearily. "That's why I lied for you?"

Wentworth said swiftly, "That's it, chief."

"I suppose," the captain went on bitterly, "you found it in Chinatown, rolling along the gutter? Or—"

"I took it away from a *bo' how doy* who was hop-crazy, sir. If you'd seen him fight when I found it—"

"You mean fight because he was full of hop!"

"—you'd have known yourself that it was important," Wentworth finished.

The captain stared at him, and then laughed shortly.

"I'll get you a radio job, Jimmy," he said. "Bed-time stories. But tell it to me. Maybe I can give it to the reporters! It's a wilder yarn than I gave 'em, and I didn't think that was possible."

Wentworth stroked the image.

"An idol is beheaded only when a kidnapping has been accomplished," Jimmy said softly. "The kidnapper himself does it, for several reasons. It prevents the god of Life from seeing where the kidnapped person is taken. It prevents the gods of evil from enacting vengeance on the kidnappers. And, lastly, it's supposed to protect the kidnappers from capture, which, in China means they'll be beheaded with dull knives, because everyone in China wants to see kidnappers harshly and painfully treated—"

"And because of this you want me to believe that Whitcomb was abducted by Chinese!"

"I don't know about Whitcomb," said the sergeant of detectives who had spent his youth in China, "but I'll swear anywhere that the three little white flowers painted on the neck of the idol represent three children, and three white children at that."

For a long moment Dunand stared at the curious, outlandish headless idol in Jimmy Wentworth's hands, and then he snapped to action:

"What's the Chink say?" he roared. Forgetting that he knew no word of Chinese, and that only Wentworth spoke the dialects like a native, Dunand shouted, "Bring him up here! I'll talk to him! I'll find out where the Whitcomb children are! I'll... I'll... what'd he say?"

"He's dead, chief," Wentworth said.

"What? Did he talk?"

"You'd better let me explain, sir. I was finishing my beat, with an eye on Number Eighteen Eleven Waverley, because there's been hop sold there, when I heard a racket. Some Chinese were attempting to persuade another Chinaman—

this one I found—not to go somewhere. He was so full of dope—that is, he wasn't past the dream stage, and wasn't out cold—that they couldn't do anything with him. He rushed out, and I thought I'd have a look-see just why they didn't want him going places.

"I stopped him—and it took a gun in his belly to do it...."

Dunand could see what had happened. Wentworth in a dark doorway. The 'binder, drug-crazed, leaping down a rickety stairway and into the street, murderous, deadly, to anyone who would confront him. Wentworth stepping before the Asiatic, gun out. A few sharp words, the flash of a knife...

"You shot him, Jim?"

"No," Wentworth said quietly. "I took his knife away from him, and intended to book him as disorderly, just as an example to the hop-joints to keep their customers inside until they'd slept it off, when some other Chino slipped up, and before I had a chance to shift my grip, he drove a knife into my man's throat... and that's hatchetman-way of saying 'Nobody talk!'"

"Get the murderer?"

Jimmy Wentworth said. "He was gone before I could get blood out of my eyes."

INTO DUNAND'S EYES crept momentarily a look of fear, the fear of the unknown, of the mysteries of Chinatown, which only his youthful sergeant fully understood.

"Ah," said the captain. And next, "The dead man, Jimmy... was he...."

"One of Kong Gai's hatchetmen? No! That's the curious part of it. My guess is that he's a new *bo' how doy*, earning his spurs, and not considered bad enough to be a brother of the snake.

Some real Cobra knifed him, to make sure he didn't talk… and there's my clew."

"Put in simple words, you're trying to tell me that Kong Gai has a hand in the Ronald Whitcomb case?"

Wentworth said, "I'm telling you, chief, that the dead man had a hand in kidnapping three white children."

"Rubbish! If Kong Gai were kidnapping for money, he wouldn't take the father, too!"

Jimmy Wentworth looked out of the window. He said thoughtfully. "Not in America. But in China, chief, when ransom is demanded, one of the favorite ways of getting it is to take two people—a man and his father, for example, and… I hate to say it!… and torture the father until… the son is willing to pay any amount. And… well, you can see how this might be…."

Shivering, Dunand said, "You mean they'd torture Whitcomb's children until the father, Ronald Whitcomb, would pay? I… of course you mean it. Kong Gai! It's the sort of thing he'd do! But why should he pick Whitcomb? There are wealthier men in the city. Whitcomb's rich, but there're others with more money. Why Whitcomb, Jimmy?"

"I thought about that," Jimmy Wentworth admitted. "The only answer I can give is that shown in Whitcomb's list of customers. You had a copy of that, sir, and I looked it over. There are a few Chinese names on that list. Kong Gai might have had Whitcomb's house invest money, and have lost it in the crash, and this is Kong Gai's way of getting both money and revenge…."

"I'll tear Chinatown apart," Dunand growled.

"And scare 'em somewhere else," Wentworth said. "Not that

I have anything to suggest, chief. All I can do is to keep my eyes open. And I'm grateful that you kept the newspaper boys away. One hint that Kong Gai is involved, and the lives of the four, father and children, won't be worth the price of a flower like those painted on the idol's neck...."

While Dunand's brows drew together, as the keen old captain fought to find some plan, Wentworth held the headless idol under the light on Dunand's desk.

"Look at the little tiny lines painted on the petals of the flowers, sir," he said. "The Chinese are marvelous artists, aren't they?"

"I don't give a damn what kind of artists they are! And neither should you, Jimmy Wentworth!"

"I was just wondering—"

The telephone rang sharply; Dunand answered it with his customary: "Dunand. Who's this?" and then listened.

If Wentworth had not been bent over his strange wooden idol, he would have seen his chief's face change from inattention to surprise, to astonishment, and then to fierce satisfaction. Dunand listened intently, and then said, "We'll be right there. Nobody's to see him. We're on our way."

Dunand stood up happily.

"Kong Gai," he chuckled. "Kidnapping. Baloney. Here's the end of the Whitcomb case! Ronald Whitcomb's in the Forest Park Hospital, Jimmy. Mulloy phoned. Found him 'dazed.' Blah! I'll bet his accounts are all wet, and he's been usin' customers' money. We got Whitcomb, and I'll bet he took his three children with him and intended to run off and then got cold feet about taking a trip to Peru. Dazed! Hooey! And you, Jimmy Wentworth, and your three flowers!"

Wentworth looked up, almost as if he hadn't heard the gleeful speech.

"Now, what's the matter?" demanded his chief.

"I was wondering why the petals of the flowers are marked, veined, the wrong way. When you look closely, the tiny black lines, the veins, are painted like those on… well, on a bee's wing."

"A bee's left ear," suggested the jubilant captain of detectives. "You been taking hop, too, Jimmy? Come along with me. A breath of air'll do you good. Maybe it'll make you stop dreaming about Kong Gai."

3

The Man the Bees Stung

OFFICER MULLOY WAS standing on the fourth floor of the hospital, trying to appear as if he didn't realize that the nurse at the desk was red-headed, pretty, and Irish, and as if he had forgotten that at home there were seven little Mulloys, and Nora herself, who would stand for no nonsense.

He saluted briskly as Dunand and Wentworth stepped from the noiseless elevator, hoping that the nurse could see the breadth of his shoulders.

"Found him wanderin' on Forest Parkway, sir," he said. "Red in the face he was, and that's no lie, but whether it's drinking he was I couldn't say. He was goin' this way and that, and I says, 'Think shame to yourself, man, out on a street where th' children is playin'. But he only looks at me. At first I thinks he's far gone in a drunken spree, and then I see his eyes. And like no human eyes was they, sir! And—"

"And you brought him here," said Dunand crisply.

"No other way could he have come, sir. For he fell right down before me eyes, he did, and I stop the first machine I see, and—"

"Good work, officer. Which room is Whitcomb in?"

"The one behind me, sir. But a nurse says he's a very sick man, sir, or I'd have verified me suspicions—"

Dunand said sharply, "You aren't positive it's Whitcomb?"

Officer Mulloy drew himself up.

"And don't he live on this beat, sir? Many's the time I see him being drove home from work. I meant me suspicions about th' drink an' all—"

Dunand nodded, looking about. He said, "There's a nurse, officer. Please ask her to go into Whitcomb's room and tell the doctor I'm here, and that I want to see Whitcomb immediately."

Nothing loath, Mulloy marched to the little alcoved desk and delivered the captain's request. The nurse first telephoned her superintendent for permission to enter the sick room for the police, and, being given this, hurried across the hall. She reappeared in a moment and spoke briefly to Mulloy, who trudged back to his superiors.

"She says will you come with her to th' room," said Mulloy. "An' she says he's a sick man, is Mr. Whitcomb. And"—grinning broadly—"she wants to know if th' young felly, bein' you, sarge, is a college boy working on th' force for experience, an' I didn't have th' heart t' tell her what a tough felly you are."

Jimmy Wentworth glanced swiftly at the pretty nurse, and her heightened color told him that she knew Mulloy had repeated what she had said.

The two detectives followed her into the sick room.

On the bed lay a man in middle years. His face was gray, what little the men from Headquarters could see. Most of it, and the entire forehead, was covered with what appeared to be thick towels, but were ice bags.

One hand was visible, and Wentworth's first impression was that the skin must have been immersed in water, for drops stood out on it.

It was obvious that Whitcomb was indeed a man in peril of death.

A DOCTOR AND interne were drawing blood from the exposed arm, with several nurses assisting. The operation was completed, and the bandaging finished, before the house doctor had one of the girls strip off his rubber gloves. He said, "Have fresh ones ready. One of these broke," and then came to the detectives.

"From what the officer said, I understand this is Ronald Whitcomb," Dr. Lyle said quietly. "The hospital has already put in a call for his personal physician, but we didn't dare wait for his arrival. Whitcomb is in bad shape, sir."

"My name's Dunand," said the grim captain. "This is one of my sergeants. First thing; Whitcomb will recover?"

"Probably. Thanks to your officer, captain. By bringing him here promptly, he undoubtedly saved his life."

Wentworth asked, "What is wrong with him?"

"Heat apoplexy, I believe. You call it sunstroke, sergeant. Whitcomb's a heavy, full blooded man. They are most susceptible. Especially if they've been subjected to any kind of physical or mental strain."

"Never heard of anyone in San Francisco being sun struck," Dunand muttered.

"It isn't entirely a matter of heat, captain. He may have been wandering aimlessly about without a hat, you know—"

"Had he been drinking?"

"I shouldn't say so."

"You are positive of your diagnosis?" Wentworth questioned.

The doctor smiled. "Just about as positive as is ever possible," he countered. "The man is unconscious. Spasmodic, jerky breathing. Hands and face cold to the touch, but, as you can see, covered with excessive perspiration. Flickering pulse. Dr. Jaynes finds faint heart beats, about a hundred and thirty to the minute. Pupils insensitive to the light. All the signs of heat apoplexy. We've bled him, and packed his head in ice. In my opinion, he ought to recover."

Dunand said briefly, "Sounds logical. You ought to know."

"Has he been conscious at all?" Wentworth asked.

"No, sergeant. Nor will he be for a day or so. He will lie there without movement whatsoever. That's typical of sunstroke."

"Do any harm if I looked carefully through his clothes?" Wentworth asked in the same level tone.

"Not the slightest. I'll have Dr. Jaynes and a nurse see that his arm is not disturbed. Help yourself, sergeant."

Dunand understood what his subordinate was after; some shred of clew which might indicate that Whitcomb had been abducted, or had not been abducted. Something to tell of the whereabouts of the children. He nodded agreement to Wentworth's unasked question, feeling that the matter should be cleared up immediately.

Jimmy Wentworth stepped to the side of the high metal bed

on which Whitcomb lay, covered only with a rubber sheet, which was drawn down. The broker still wore his shirt, so hastily had the hospital people applied first aid for sunstroke, and before Wentworth began his investigation he looked about for coat and vest.

"In the closet," a nurse told him.

"Please get it," Wentworth requested. No sense in disturbing the unconscious man at all if the upper garment would reveal what he sought.

The youthful sergeant of the Chinatown squad had his hand in the inner coat pocket when he heard a strangled cry, terrible in the silent room, followed instantly by an ejaculation of surprise from one of the doctors. Wentworth turned round instantly to look.

Whitcomb's mouth was open now. His eyes were open also. A horrible rigidity had straightened his arms and legs.

THE SICK MAN groaned deeply, and before Dr. Lyle could take the hypodermic which an attentive nurse was handing him, Whitcomb began to shout incoherently, to rave and toss his arms and shoulders about on the bed. Nurses and doctors hastened to hold him down as he struggled, and then Dr. Lyle shot the needle home. For a full minute more Whitcomb struggled furiously, crying out a jumble of meaningless words which ended in a shriek: "No more!"

And then complete silence, as the powerful drug stopped the raving.

Whitcomb's face now was as gray as ever, and the man lay as if dead.

"Well," said Dr. Lyle. "Well. Another diagnosis gone to

the devil." He growled a long string of orders, and the room became very active as the interne and nurses hurried to put them into effect.

Wentworth said quietly, "So it isn't sunstroke, doctor?"

"It is not," Dr. Lyle told him soberly. "Not when he acts in such a manner." He looked at his watch. "I wish Dr. Henderson—Whitcomb's physician—would hurry and get here. Because—"

"Because you think the man is not going to recover?" broke in Dunand shrewdly.

Dr. Lyle shrugged.

"I've done enough guessing," he said briefly.

"Will you guess what is wrong?" Jimmy Wentworth suggested.

"Don't need to guess—now," said the physician. "Not about that. I know. It's a rare case, gentlemen, and between ourselves there isn't much we can do about it. To put it plainly, Whitcomb is going to die from insect stings."

"What?" grunted Dunand. "First you said sunstroke, and now you talk about bugs!"

"Not bugs. Wasps."

"Or bees?" Jimmy Wentworth said softly.

"Or bees," agreed the medical man. "Either one. The early symptoms are exactly the same as heat apoplexy. Exactly, when there are no swellings, and that's often the case. Now you'll excuse me, please. There are a lot of things we can try, and we'll try them all, but Ronald Whitcomb is going to die without recovering consciousness just the same."

Captain Dunand stared at the dying man, and from him to Wentworth. No word was passed, but both were thinking the selfsame thing. That the petals of the little white flowers painted on the headless idol were veined in black like the wings of bees—and the image had been found on the body of a *bo' how doy*—a Chinese 'binder, a killer, a hatchetman, who had himself been murdered before he could say a word to anyone.

4

—

The Charge Is—Murder

THE FIRST EXTRAS were out by the time Dunand and Wentworth returned to the Hall of Justice, after having left word at the hospital to be informed of Whitcomb's death, or any change in his condition. Dr. Henderson, Whitcomb's own physician, had agreed with the second diagnosis of the hospital medical men, and agreed also that chance for recovery was almost impossible. All the physicians were positive that Whitcomb would not recover consciousness, but just the same Dunand had not left until two men from the department were in the room, ready to take down any word, and, if possible, to ask the questions Wentworth had told them to ask.

The headlines just about told the story:

WHITCOMB FOUND;
CHILDREN STILL MISSING

MILLIONAIRE IN DAZE AT LOCAL HOSPITAL

POLICE REFUSE TO ALLOW WEALTHY BROKER TO TALK

Which Ronald Whitcomb, at death's door, couldn't possibly

have done, but which held off the newspapers as to the manner of the broker's dying for a few hours.

Down in Captain Dunand's office, gray haired chief and black haired sergeant sat staring at the envelope they had taken from Whitcomb's pocket. They had already read the letter a dozen times. It was typewritten on fine paper, with the sheet cut in half to remove a letterhead or address, and said:

The enclosed check, signed by myself, is to be honored when presented for payment by any official of the Whitcomb Investment Company. The check is to be cashed in five and ten dollar bills, and these are to be taken to whichever place is designated at a later date. If the police accompany the person bringing the ransom money, when he is told where to bring it, my children will be put to death. It is my order and wish that these requirements be exactly carried out.

The communication was signed by Whitcomb. The check, attached to the letter, was for one hundred thousand dollars.

Dunand said slowly, "Not much to go on, Jimmy. We'll have men at the Whitcomb Company tomorrow. And tap their phones. Only...."

"Only you're a man," said Wentworth, "and you don't want the children hurt."

"No. I don't want them hurt, lad. You... you still think this means Kong Gai?"

"I do, chief. Now more than ever. No one save a fiend like that Chinese would send a father with the ransom note for his children, knowing full well that he would not be able to tell where the youngsters were. And what has been done to Whitcomb will make anyone anxious to get the children out of the hands of such monsters."

"I don't understand it," muttered the head of the detective bureau.

"According to the doctors, Whitcomb was stung and stung until he became almost unconscious. Somewhere along the line he signed the demand for ransom and the letter. Then the devils allowed him to partially recover consciousness, put him in a machine, let him off somewhere near his home while—according to the doctors—he could just stagger about, but was to all intents already a dead man."

"And if he hadn't raved, everyone would have thought he'd died from apoplexy!"

"There is no perfect crime," Wentworth said slowly. "At least, not yet. Given time, Kong Gai the Venomous One may find it. Through his opium sales, he has his coils about some renegade physician. That's sure. That's where he must've picked up the bee sting idea. He has his slimy coils everywhere, captain! He—"

THE TELEPHONE RANG briskly, and Dunand said, "Damn reporters. Or a city editor. I hate to answer it."

He spoke gruffly into the receiver: "Dunand. Well?" and then said excitedly, "Splendid! Congratulations, sheriff! Bring him right up here!" As he hung up, he said to Wentworth, "Cravens's caught! Down in San Bernardino county! The sheriff's office kept it under cover, and they've got him downstairs now."

"And what good is that going to do?" Jimmy Wentworth demanded. "I suppose you think Cravens tortured Ronald Whitcomb?"

"No, but he might be a tool of a gang. Perhaps"—magnani-mously—"Kong Gai's tool."

"If he were, you'd find him in the bay with his throat slit."

This time Wentworth reached for the telephone, for Dunand was snapping off the desk light, and pressing another button which would cause all the brightness in the room to fall on Cravens when he was brought in for examination; the China-town detective sergeant answered the ring with a voice so like his chief's that Dunand was forced to smile.

"Dunand," said Wentworth. "Well? Oh, hello, Williams… you did, eh? And it checks? Thanks. I'll tell the captain."

As the door opened, Wentworth said curtly, "Williams reports that the sample of ransom letter paper we gave him coincides with paper used by the people where Cravens worked, sir."

"Very good, sergeant," said Dunand.

The captain nodded to the three deputies and the under-sher-iff who shoved a thin young man into the room. Not until the four, prisoner and captors, were in the spot of light did Dunand speak. He said, "I think it's safe to take off the handcuffs, boys."

"We took no chances, cap," said Undersheriff Egan. "Not with this boy."

"Tough, is he?"

"Say! He wouldn't come across with a word! We says, 'The sooner you tell us where Whitcomb and his kids is, the better it'll be, bud,' but the punk won't open his head."

"Why were you in San Bernardino?" Dunand asked quietly of the prisoner.

Cravens lifted his head. The eyes were circled with black, with fatigue, and the young man's face was very pale.

"You wouldn't believe me," he said at last.

Dunand looked out of the window. It was black outside now. High on a roof in Chinatown a lantern glowed, like the single eye of a five-legged dragon. Dunand carefully drew open a drawer of his desk, took out a box of cigars, and handed them about to the deputies. He selected one for himself, cut the end, was about to put it in his mouth, when he roared suddenly:

"Where are the children, Cravens?"

The prisoner shivered, but his eyes met the fierce gaze of the captain.

"I don't know," he said.

Dunand waved the ransom letter in front of Cravens.

"When did you write this?" he asked.

"I didn't write it."

"It is on paper from the company you worked for!"

Cravens bowed his head, but remained silent.

A third time the telephone rang, and again Wentworth answered it. He spoke now for the first time, gently; "The charge had better be changed, captain. From kidnapping to murder, Whitcomb is dead."

Dunand shifted ground subtly.

"You can be cleared of murder," he said to the frightened prisoner. "If you will give us the names of the gang, and tell where the Whitcomb children are, I will do my best with the District Attorney."

"I didn't kill Whitcomb," said the exhausted man, "and I didn't kidnap his children—"

"Give an account of your actions for the past six days."

"You won't believe it," repeated Cravens.

"Tell us anyhow," said Jimmy Wentworth.

THE ACCUSED MAN looked at him, seeing only a fellow no older than himself, in a patrolman's uniform.

"What's the use?" the prisoner muttered.

"Because I might believe you," Wentworth told him gravely.

Cravens' head was hanging; he looked so guilty that Dunand was about to roar at him again, and then the prisoner began to speak jerkily.

"I went to Whitcomb. I admit it. I'd given him three thousand dollars to invest. He put it in speculative stocks. I wanted bonds. I told him I'd… I'd…."

"You can leave out what you told him," said Jimmy Wentworth. "Because anything you say can be used against you. Tell us why you left the city."

"I didn't leave the city," blurted Cravens. "I was taken away! In a machine. I've been kept doped. You can see"—he pulled up a sleeve—"you can see where I've been doped!"

Wentworth did not intend asking who did it, lest the prisoner say, "Chinese," and the deputies repeat it outside the Hall of Justice. So he said, "And you came to in San Bernardino county?"

"I woke up on the side of a road, and that's all I know. I never even knew who took me away! I never heard them speak. I was blindfolded after they slugged me—"

"Where?"

"Just as I came out of the Whitcomb Building! I had walked to the curb, and turned around and shook my fist at the building. I wanted to tell the world what I thought of them all! I said something… crooks, you know… not very loudly, perhaps… and then just as I stopped, because there was a car at the curb, somebody said something I didn't catch, and I was banged over the head. That's all I remember, although I must have been yanked into the car—"

"Bull," growled one of the deputies. "Trying to tell us you were kidnapped yourself, on a downtown street!"

Wearily, Cravens said, "I knew nobody'd believe me. I remember, too, that when I shook my fist toward the building there didn't seem to be many people in sight; a couple of men and women walking the other way, with their backs in my direction, but no one saw me shake my fist—"

"One person saw you," said Jimmy Wentworth. "A person I'm looking for myself."

"You mean—you know—who hit me? Who carried me out of the city? Who got me in this terrible mess?"

"When we find him, we'll find the same man who killed Whitcomb and stole the children."

THE DEPUTIES STARED at the lithe, youthful figure in patrolman's blue. Finally Undersheriff Egan blurted, "You can't talk us out of th' reward for th' kids' recovery like that, off'cer! Cravens is guilty as hell. He threatened Whitcomb, didn't he? He wrote th' ransom note on his company's stationery, didn't he? He ran away, didn't he? We caught him, and there's a five thousand dollar reward for doin' it—and it's goin' to be ours!"

"You're wrong," Wentworth said.

"We'll see what the newspapers say about it! I kept the capture quiet to give you city bulls a chance to make some more arrests, maybe, but now I'll tell what I know. Then see where you get off if you let Cravens go!"

"We aren't letting him go," the Chinatown detective-sergeant said soothingly. "We're keeping him for his good, and for our own. If you tell the newspapers, you will excite public opinion so greatly that Cravens, an innocent man, will be hanged. You don't want that, do you, sheriff?"

"No," said Undersheriff Egan, after a long pause. "But I don't want to see the boys done out of a just reward, neither! I want some kind of assurance that you got another clew——"

"I give you my word," Jimmy said simply.

Again the deputies all looked over the slim figure in blue.

"Yeah," said Egan. "Your word. And who might you be, officer?"

"My name's Wentworth," said Jimmy.

A third time the men from the southern end of the state stared, this time in utter astonishment. Then one of the deputies ejaculated, "Wentworth! A kid like you! I don't believe it!"

Captain Dunand said soberly, "He's Wentworth, boys. Rated as sergeant of detectives—"

"Wentworth of the Chinatown Squad," muttered Egan. "Well, well, well… I'd like to shake your hand, sergeant! If the case is in your hands, I won't say a word! When'll you make your arrests, sergeant?"

Jimmy Wentworth's heart beat more rapidly. He knew on what a slim chance he based his conclusions—little more than flowers painted on the neck of a headless idol, and what common knowledge he possessed about bees—but was convinced that he was on the right trail. At all events, he was convinced of Cravens' innocence, and that was sufficient to make him say quietly:

"Perhaps tomorrow, boys, if all goes well."

5

The Bee's Flight

WENTWORTH HAD LITTLE sleep that night. Bees! He had to learn about bees, and with that thought in mind routed out an expert at the state university across the bay. To him Wentworth listened carefully, making notes again and again; he left with the scientist's assurance that his original conclusions, if faulty in detail, were correct in all major analysis.

These were simple. Bees were hungry little things. Bees didn't like smoke. Bees died if they did not receive adequate fresh air. Bees became angry when cooped up. Bees could get out of any crevice, and would if they had the chance. Lastly, bees would always return to their hive, or wherever they were being kept, if they had been brought a considerable distance from their original hive…

And Whitcomb had died from many bee stings, died under torture.

Only Kong Gai the Deadly would have thought of sending a man to deliver the ransom demand for his children. Only Kong Gai's mind would consider such a thing a joke, and something to be proud about.

Wentworth believed that the little black lines, like the markings on a bee's wing, had been made on the headless idol to further protect the 'binder carrying it from vengeance of a god or devil not even Jimmy knew—some awful being of the underworld who, in addition to riding on a dragon, in addition to breathing fire and bearing ten swords in ten bands, also could kill by stinging men to death… that must be the reason why the white flowers—representing the kidnapped children—were so painted. To propitiate the god.

At eight-ten in the morning Wentworth marched into the bowl shop of the Wangs, who had more than once assisted the department. He found old Wang Yu behind his counter, and, after bowing and hoping that the ancient's health was good, asked for the son, Wang Chen-p'o.

Old Wang clapped his hands thrice, and a Chinese dressed in American clothing instantly appeared. Without a word or look toward Wentworth, Wang Chen-p'o said, "And what are my honorable father's commands?"

"Here is our friend," said old Wang, indicating Wentworth. "I have none, except to have demanded your presence."

"Hi, Jimmy," grinned Chen-p'o, without apology, since he knew that his friend understood the Conduct-Toward-One's-Father. "What do you want now? Everything is quiet on the Eastern Front, so far as I know—"

"How many youngsters are there in the Wang family?"

"Thinking of adopting one of them, Jimmy?"

"It's Saturday," said Wentworth, "and I thought maybe some of them might want to earn money to buy duck's-egg cake."

"They all have the Yankee spirit," laughed Chen-p'o. "What do they do in order to make enough to get good and sick? They're ravenous little devils, Jimmy. They can eat you into the hospital. Shoot!"

Jimmy said lightly, "They hang around their windows, Chen-p'o, where the lily-pots are, and when they see a bee, they catch it and put it in a box. One bee, one dollar."

"Bees in Chinatown? Say, these youngsters aren't dumb, Jimmy! They know better than to try such a game."

"I think some of them may catch a bee or so, old man."

Wang Chen-po scratched his chin, and before he had finished his father cackled in Cantonese:

"You waste time, my son. Inform the grandchildren of Wang Yu that bees are desired, in the shortest time possible. Our white friend does not joke."

"That's right," Jimmy said, after bowing to old Wang. "And if the kids'll catch bees, maybe I'll catch…"

HE BECAME SILENT. Both Chinese knew what he meant, but neither blinked an eye. Kong Gai! Every decent Chinese hated the terrible leader of the Snake Brotherhood. No man's life was safe while the King Cobra lived.

"I'll see what can be done," Chen-po said quietly. "The kids are to be careful that they aren't seen, eh? And to say nothing about it?"

"That's it," agreed Detective-Sergeant Wentworth. "I'll go around my beat, and drop in just before lunch."

It was almost noon when Jimmy Wentworth leaned against the old bricks of the cathedral on the southerly boundary of the Asiatic district, and pulled from his rear pocket a thick newspaper. He stood there, apparently reading, but his right hand was shrewdly busy inside the paper. For Wentworth was attempting to put into practice what the bee expert had told him… would it work?

Inside the paper was a thin box, in which was a bit of honeycomb. The end of the box, fashioned that morning, very early, in the basement of the Hall of Justice, could be slid up or down, enough to permit a bee to escape. And in the box were five bees, collected by the grandchildren of old Wang as the little insects had sought pollen from the white and yellow china lilies...

Five bees!

Would the little winged workers lead the way to the venomous Kong Gai?

Wentworth felt something soft crawl along his finger, inside the paper, and a moment later a bee crept out, remained motionless an instant, and then flew up. The detective-sergeant tried to follow the bee's eccentric circles and oscillations. Each time, as the bee swung above the newspaper concealing the honey in the box, it seemed to sway to one side, so that the honey was at the edge of its circle instead of the center, as if the bee were throwing a loop about the sweet to make positive of its exact location. Then, in a straight line, it darted northeast.

Wentworth's eyes instantly sought the clock on the old cathedral. Four minutes to twelve. He stood there quietly, reading his newspaper, as if waiting until twelve to go for his lunch.

A moment before the clock boomed the hour, a bee hovered over Wentworth's head, and, after one swoop, again crawled to the concealed box in the newspaper. Wentworth could hear its excited humming and buzzing as it tried to enter the box, but he did not open the slide, lest another bee escape. Instead, he again glanced at the clock; one minute to twelve!

The bee had been gone three minutes. The bee expert said that a minute and a half was consumed by a bee delivering the pollen at the hive. That meant the bee had spent less than a minute going to... where?... and less than a minute returning. A bee could fly a mile in five minutes. Therefore the place where it went could be no more than a block or two away... in a northeasterly direction!

The captive bees, laden with honey, buzzed in the little box as Wentworth marched along his beat, as if he had decided to make one more round, and, as he often did, go to his lunch at one instead of twelve.

Wentworth paused the second time before the basket shop belonging to a member of the Wang family, where no questions would be asked, and repeated his performance. Again he timed the greedy bee, which, like its fellow, had difficulty in obtaining food in the city where it had been brought. Again he checked the direction of flight. Twice more he did this, until he had but one bee left.

Then he walked calmly along the street where the lines had crossed; where the bees seemed to be going. Even allowing a half minute leeway, it seemed probable to the detective that the location of the hive must be in the middle of the block somewhere, and as he reached it he let the last bee escape.

Again the bee circled, but this time darted straight up. Wentworth looked with an air of disinterest, and saw that the windows of the third story were boarded up. As if, according to Chinese custom, someone had died and the body had not yet been shipped to China. No unusual occurrence—except because of the flight of the bee! And as his eyes lowered, and he shoved his newspaper into his hip pocket again, he caught an opened wicket in a basement door across the street… 'binders, watching! Kong Gai's men.

As if he had not seen them, Wentworth crossed the street, entered a drug shop, and, by pointing, was sold a packet of cigarettes. He put these in his pocket, and then strode leisurely up the street. When he turned the corner, he pulled out his watch—in case he was being spied upon—and then walked slowly up the long hill, out of the district, as if now going for food.

HE WAITED UNTIL he was two blocks from the district, and then entered the first apartment house.

"A telephone, quick," he told the switchboard operator in the lobby. "No, not one here. In an apartment. And if anybody comes in, or you see anyone looking in, you haven't seen a cop come in. Get that!"

The operator took Wentworth to a ground-floor apartment, and the sergeant called Headquarters immediately.

He was given Dunand at once.

"It's Number Ninety-one Ninety-two Fish Alley, sir," said Wentworth eagerly. "No mistake about it. Three boarded-up windows, third story. Which makes the bee expert correct. He said the bees wouldn't be active, nor sting, if they were kept in any cold dark basement…."

"We're ready," snapped Dunand.

"Tell 'em to go along Stockton street, chief. To Sacramento. Down two blocks. Left turn to Fish Alley. The seventh house. That's the one. Middle of block, right hand side. I'll swing on when they turn off Stockton."

"Better get goin'," ordered the gray haired captain. "I'm givin' th' order to start, boy!"

6

Kong Gai Laughs

THE BLUE-CLAD PATROLMAN making his regular beat on Nob Hill saw the hurrying figure of a fellow officer, and ran to meet him; when he saw who it was he said:

"What's up, sergeant?"

"Plenty," said Jimmy swiftly. "When you hear a racket—you'll hear it—come along and see!"

With that he hastened back toward Chinatown. At the corner of Stockton and Sacramento, near the mouth of the tunnel where he had once found a murdered flower girl killed by Kong Gai, he paused, and then turned northward, walking slowly along the pavement, stopping to play with a Chinese urchin in pink jacket and red pantaloons; he did this until he heard a sudden roar, coming from the tunnel.

A moment later hook-and-ladder Number Fifteen roared out of the tunnel, siren wailing and engine humming a high tune. Behind it Wentworth saw a red-and-gold hose wagon, with men in fireman's blue hanging to the sides....

Chinatown gaped, wondering where the Fire God was striking. As the hook-and-ladder slowed, and swung around the corner, barely missing the lamp-post on the sidewalk, Wentworth leaped to the side.

Nobody would think anything of that. It was a policeman's duty to get to a fire as rapidly as possible.

Wentworth heard someone next to him shout, "Nice goin', sarge!"

The deep voice was that of Officer Reilly, holder of the department's record for marksmanship, and no fireman at all. Only the driver, and the rear wheel-man, were from the fire department. Every other person in slicker, or in blue uniform, was a member of the riot squad....

Down one street! Left turn! The scream and squeal of brakes and tires, and a sudden noiseless operation that shot the first length of mechanically operated ladder into the air, in front of the windows of the house Wentworth had told about.

A spying 'binder popped his head out from the basement across the street. Officer Reilly waited until he saw the flash of metal, and the raising gun, before he drew trigger. The sound of explosion was covered by the roar of the hose wagon's engine as it drew up beside the hook-and-ladder.

Men were already running up the ladder. The first two were axe-armed, and the raising ladder took them to one of the windows. As an axe crashed against the barrier, Wentworth, followed by other men, swung to the building-side of the ladder, and continued frantically up to the roof.

Wentworth's head cleared the coping first, and almost the same instant his gun roared. He saw a 'binder leap high in the air; saw others turn and level drawn weapons, and then the riot squadman behind him had shoved the nose of the deadly chopper across the coping, and the rat-tat-tat of the little gun sprayed death over the Chinese.

Wentworth knew there was not a moment to be lost. While some of the *bo' how doy* were still trying to get a bullet into the slim target afforded by one eye and a bit of forehead of the man operating the chopper, Wentworth pulled himself to the roof. He felt the sting of hot metal in his shoulder, and the impact half swung him about.

Nothing better could have happened. Had he continued straight forward, he would have been riddled with bullets.

Jimmy Wentworth, the smiling young detective-sergeant of the Chinatown squad, had gone berserk. Here was a chance to get his hands on Kong Gai! He made one leap, notwithstanding the pain in his shoulder, and fell through what had been a skylight, but had been changed to a row of light slats, to give the bees air at times. The stairway to the roof was ten feet further along the roof. For a fraction of time something seemed to stay Wentworth's fall—a black curtain of heavy silk, which had been used to cover the opening most of the time—and during it he managed to squirm about….

The silk ripped, and Wentworth fell, landing on hands and knees. His gun was up at the very time of impact, up, and blazing at a black-clad figure.

A shrill, sweet voice screamed, *"Hola!* Get him, snake-brothers! It is the white fool himself! Get him for Kong Gai!"

WENTWORTH'S HEART STOPPED as his eyes and gun flashed up. He expected to die now, but if only he could get one shot at the King Cobra, and end his reign of terror! Then, so swift that it bit into Kong Gai's last words, he heard the tapping sound of the chopper at work, searching out corners of the room in a vain effort to get the Venomous One.

Jimmy's head began to work sanely again. He yelled, "Look out! The kids are somewhere here—"

"They're behind you, sarge," shouted the machine gun officer. "All's O.K.," and he alertly kept the muzzle of the chopper moving, ready to fire.

Despite this assurance, Wentworth waited. Would Kong Gai, from some clever point of concealment, kill him now? It could easily be done....

The sweet voice droned on, "Your eyes, oh white fool, I will tear out with my fingers! Your mouth I shall sew together, so you cannot destroy my sleep with your screams when we cut your body apart, inch by inch, and put little serpents to feed on you while you are still alive! The day will come soon! I could kill you now, but that is not my way of killing!"

A storm of bullets from the chopper ended the terrible promise. Then all was silent, save the hammering of axes and the stamping of feet.

For the three closed windows had not shown the room in which the kidnapped white children had been found, and when the officers smashed inside they found only a place of awful worship, with a great naked headless idol surrounded with crushed white flowers and many impaled dead bees, killed as sacrifices after they had served Kong Gai's horrible torture of Whitcomb.

And a row of the little insects which, maddened, had stung Whitcomb to his curious death, was found about a sheet of paper before the idol. On the paper was a statement of the account of one Sam Gee Quong, who had lost several thousands of dollars in the stock market. And it was easy to guess that Quong was only another name for Kong Gai, and why the Venomous One had picked Whitcomb to kill, and his children to be held for ransom....

Jimmy Wentworth's shrewd deductions had been close enough, and had led the riot squad to the building itself, if not to the inner room. The other room must have been the chamber in which the bees had been kept, and a search at once found a small, makeshift hive, with a volume of instructions on bee-keeping beside it. The constant burning of incense in the other room made it impossible to keep the bees there, save when it was intended to let them sting someone…Whitcomb.

Kong Gai had lost the children, and seven hatchetmen to boot. Four more were caught alive, but wounded. The remainder of the Brotherhood had escaped along some secret passage.

Captain Dunand felt that only Wentworth's mad promptness in leaping to the roof in face of the 'binders' bullets had prevented the Cobra Men from rushing off with the children. Apparently it had been Kong Gai's command that the children be carried to the roof, and to some secret hiding place. That would be Kong Gai's way, too—not taking any chance that the police might follow the children along his own secret tunnel deep into the dark places of Chinatown. He cared for his hide, did Kong Gai, and took no chances.

"If we'd nabbed Kong Gai, this would have been perfect," commented the gray haired captain, as he surveyed the strange, terrible headless idol, supposed by the Chinese to protect those who kidnap children, and before which the Snake Brotherhood had bowed low.

"He was here," said Wentworth quietly.

"See him?"

"No. Heard him."

Captain Dunand said thoughtfully, "Say things, did he?"

"Some day," Jimmy answered, "we're coming face to face. Then…we'll see."

Kong Gai's horrible laugh shrilled in the room.

"We'll see!" screamed Kong Gai in English. "Yes! We'll see!"

Try as they might, the riot squad could not find from what vantage point the fiendish Kong Gai had spoken. Once more the Evil One laughed, and then the room of the Headless Idol, with its crushed white blossoms and dead bees and streaming incense bowls, was as silent as death.

THE PAIN ROOM

Hugh B. Cave

*Through the torturous, unclean drizzle of
Chinatown walked Paul Maury, pain-
wracked and seeking with bloodshot eyes…
Had the loved one he sought died mercifully,
or did she lie in some fiend's torture-room,
a prey to all the torments of the damned?*

1

Grace Lost

UNAWARE OF THE drizzle that had long ago drenched
him to the skin, Paul Maury walked slowly, wearily along the
cluttered sidewalk and stared ahead with bloodshot eyes at a
green-glowing neon sign that blurred through the murk.

The thought came to him, dully, that he had been walking
thus for days. More than a score of times he had turned in
beneath that green sign and dragged himself up those winding black stairs.

Bickford Street was dark now. And black water ran in deep
gutters, through mounds of sodden refuse that gave off an evil
stench. Ocher-glowing windows, opened against the sultry
rain, gave out murmuring voices intoning Oriental words. And

ahead, near the street's end—the end that wormed its way deep into the soul of Chinatown—glowed that green neon sign:

THE GREEN ROOSTER

Nothing else. Nothing about shadowed booths with unclean tablecloths and sloe-eyed waiters. Nothing about dancing to the grotesque wail of popular American music rendered by a five-piece Chinese orchestra. Nothing about Wen Lee, the large-bellied, perspiring proprietor who looked at one and smiled, showing uneven yellow teeth, and made one feel suddenly as if a bloated, sluggish thing had crawled out of darkness, assuming human shape for ominous reasons of its own.

Nothing about Grace Maury—Paul Maury's sister—who three nights ago had walked up those sinister stairs, into that dimly lighted place of Oriental shadows, and—*never walked out again!*

Maury slouched on, heedless of his surroundings. Out of the drizzle, a uniformed shape moved toward him; Irish lips frowned and opened to make words.

"Listen, Mister Maury. This ain't goin' to help any. For hours I see you trampin' the streets like you was a ghost. Why'n't you go home and get some sleep?"

Maury stared. Go home and sleep? That sounded funny. Officer Ryan meant well, but…

"I've got to find her." He had mumbled those same words, to himself and to sympathetic questioners, at least a hundred times during the eternity of the past three days. He had many friends, none of whom could help. Being in charge of the

Mission on Huyler Street had given him open sesame to places in Chinatown where other white men were not welcome; but even that had not helped.

Hour after hour he had walked the streets, from one dive to another, searching. And not finding her.

"Listen," Ryan said again. "Alone, you can't do nothin'. The police are doin' all they can; you know that. Go back to the Mission and stop prowlin' around like this."

"I can't go home. I've got to find her."

"But good God—"The officer put strong fingers on Maury's arm. "Where you bound for now?"

"There." Paul Maury pointed to the green neon sign.

"Again you're goin' in there, just to sit around and look?"

"Yes." Wearily Maury shoved forward.

The green sign glowed above him as he pushed open the door. His damp hands pawed the wall; his feet scraped on dark, dirty stairs that snaked upward toward a dim green light and a closed door.

It was a place of paradox. Up these stairs came young men and young women from the Back Bay, from Beacon Hill, seeking the ultimate thrill. Up these stairs, with far less laughter and merriment, came whisper-footed Chinese, sallow-faced denizens of the underworld, to pace silently into Wen Lee's back room and bend above gambling tables.

Silently, Maury pushed the door open, slouched across the sill. A slant-eyed waiter came toward him through a murk of green-glowing cigarette smoke. The waiter stopped, stared, made a shrugging movement with his thin shoulders and glided back toward a table where girls were giggling, young men talking in loud voices.

Here in Wen Lee's Green Rooster, Paul Maury was not wanted. Three days ago he had been a well-dressed, clean-shaven young man with a face that smiled easily and shoulders

that were normally straight. Now he was a drenched, disheveled scarecrow walking in a world of his own, a world of darkness and despair. And Wen Lee had no use for derelicts.

But knowing what he had been, they left him alone. Unmolested, he walked to an empty booth, slumped down and put his head on his arms. People stared holes in him. A girl across the way laughed drunkenly. The orchestra played.

AFTER A WHILE, Paul Maury pulled his head up and peered around him.

He stiffened then. The glint that came suddenly into his eyes, as his gaze focused intently on a table in the opposite corner of the room, was a glint of savage hate. Lurching, he pushed himself erect and stumbled forward, made his way around the small dance area. Not once did his gaze quit the table, or leave the well-dressed, sallow-faced youth and the dreamy-eyed girl who sat there.

The youth looked up as Maury approached. His face paled. The girl, sitting across from him, stared at Maury in wide-eyed bewilderment.

Paul Maury stopped, gripped the table-edge with both hands and glared into the young man's face. Words jarred from his lips. Harsh, rasping words.

"So you're back again! With a girl, as usual. Just three days it took you—to find another girl and bring her to this filthy hangout of yours!"

The sallow-faced youth made mumbling sounds, glanced nervously at the girl.

"Aw, lay off," he growled. "Just because you've gone nuts, you don't have to take it out on me. I've told you a dozen times it wasn't my fault your sister didn't come home!"

Under its growth of stubble, Maury's face went sickly white with rage.

"You—filthy—beast!"

"Aw, go fly a kite. Your sister didn't mean nothin' to me anyway. Lay off me. Scram."

Maury rocked on stiff legs, stared through a red mist of rage and strove to regain control of himself. The sallow-faced youth exhaled noisily with exaggerated impatience; the girl turned from Maury's gaze and said indifferently: "Say, what *is* this, Ricky? Is he crazy?"

"He's nuts. I took his sister out three nights ago, and brought her up here to show her a time, and he's blamin' me because she didn't come home afterwards."

"You mean… something happened to her?"

Ricky shrugged, deliberately ignored Paul Maury as he answered. "All I know, honey, is that the girl and me was sittin' in here, and Wen Lee brings her a note. She reads the note, and excuses herself for a minute, and goes out the door. For more'n an hour I hang around waitin' for her to come back; but she don't come, so I scram." He jerked his head around, glared at Maury. "Listen. Be a good guy and get the hell out of here. I'm entertainin' a lady."

Paul Maury said again, thickly: "You—filthy—snake! What my sister ever saw in you to make her come to this place—"

Jangled nerves gave way. Paul Maury's pent-up emotions abruptly burst the stopper. His voice went shrill, spewed forth with a hoarse bellow that reverberated wildly through the room as the orchestra ceased playing.

"And now you're here with another innocent girl who doesn't know the kind of dirty beast you are! By God, if it's the last thing I ever do, I'll tell her—"

The Green Rooster was suddenly still as death as a heavy hand clamped down on Maury's shoulder from behind, jarring him backward. Thick fingers twisted viciously around his arm, dragging him about.

White-faced, breathing hoarsely, he stared through a crimson haze into the face of the man who had lunged forward to seize him.

It was an ugly face—one that Paul Maury had peered into many times before, and many times wondered about. The massive body attached to it was attired in a waiter's uniform; but Big Willie Mung was no waiter. For that matter, though Willie Mung's face was sallow of complexion, with eyes a little slanted, he was no Chinaman.

Willie Mung had another name and another nationality. The nationality was Italian; the name, Angelo Silva. And more than once Paul Maury had wondered why Angelo Silva, a Harrison Avenue mobster of ill repute, should be working for low pay in a cheap dive like Wen Lee's Green Rooster.

But those thoughts did not come now. The face that glared into Maury's own was convulsed, black with anger. Guttural words came through Willie Mung's lips.

"*Get out!* Already you been told a hundred times to get out and *stay out!* Maybe you think this is a hangout for tramps!"

Something in the rasping snarl of that voice cleared the scarlet mist that hung before Paul Maury's eyes. He sucked breath slowly, stood stiff.

"Take your filthy hands off me!"

For answer, the big Italian let go with one hand, balled the hand into a murderous fist and drove it with sledge-hammer force into Maury's chalk-white face! The blow slammed Paul Maury's scarecrow body backward in a staggering heap, spilled him against the booth-table.

The girl in the booth screamed. The sallow-faced Ricky reached out sneeringly and pushed Maury's bloody head away from him, allowing the sprawled body to slide to the floor in a limp heap.

Big Willie Mung, official bouncer for the Green Rooster,

wiped a greasy hand backwards across his curled lips, strode swaggeringly across the dance area and said to a gaping waiter: "Go outside and bring in a cop."

And Wen Lee himself, standing in the dim doorway that led to the kitchen, folded fat hands over his protruding stomach and smiled a thin-lipped oily smile of sinister satisfaction.

ALMOND-SHAPED EYES, NOT sinister but filled with a warmth of sympathetic understanding, were gazing into Paul Maury's bloodshot orbs when he blinked them open after fighting his way back to consciousness. A yellow hand with delicately pointed fingernails reached out and pushed a tangle of hair out of his eyes. A low voice said softly: "There is nothing to fear, Mr. Maury. Please be at ease."

Maury pushed himself up on stiff elbows and stared around him. He was no longer in the Green Rooster. Here were four painted walls, a butt-scarred desk with a lamp hanging above it, and a group of men standing about the wooden bench that supported Maury's battered body.

He exhaled slowly as he recognized his surroundings. Often he had been here before, in connection with his work at the Mission: sometimes to ask assistance, sometimes to plead for unfortunates who had strayed from the straight and narrow. This was the Twelfth Precinct Police Station, on Harrison Avenue. And the uniformed officer leaning there against the desk was Pat Ryan, the same Pat Ryan who had accosted him earlier tonight.

But these almond-shaped eyes that were staring—Maury remembered and felt relieved. All Chinamen were not like Wen Lee. This one was not Wen Lee's type at all, but a well-dressed, gently smiling, middle-aged Oriental whom Maury had met before at the Mission.

This was Li Tsan, refined and educated and wealthy. Li Tsan, who lived somewhere beyond the evil borders of Chinatown, yet came here to donate money to the Mission, and to plead for the cause of his people. Li Tsan, cultured and soft-spoken and owner of one of the city's largest importing houses. A good man.

Even now Li Tsan was saying softly: "There is nothing to fear, Mr. Maury. We are your friends."

Maury put a trembling hand to his face and wiped blood away. "Who brought me here?"

Pat Ryan blurted: "I did. It was me that was poundin' the beat when that lousy Willie Mung sent out for a cop. By the saints, Mister Maury, you'll know enough now to take a dumb cop's advice and let the police handle this. Next time, they'll be killin' you!"

Maury sat up, put his head in his hands and would have slumped back again in sudden dizziness had not Li Tsan put out a hand to hold him. In the swivel-chair behind the desk, another uniformed figure leaned forward.

"You'd better go home, Maury."

"Go—home?"

"Home. We know how you feel. But we're doing all we can, and you're only making things worse by prowling around, getting into trouble like this. Li Tsan here says he'll pull all the strings at his command, and he has plenty. If anybody knows anything about your sister, he'll find it out. The place for you is back at the Mission."

Maury shuddered. It was good advice; coming from Captain

Dan Clark, it could be nothing else. Dan Clark knew Chinatown, knew the ways of those slow-footed denizens of the underworld who were in all probability responsible for Grace's disappearance.

But—go home? Home to a sordid little Mission building where the ghost of her face would be in every empty room, in every walking shadow? They—they didn't understand.

"I can't," Maury groaned. "Oh God, I can't! I've got to *find* her!"

"That is true, my friend." It was Li Tsan who answered, and the Oriental's soft voice had a soothing effect on Maury's jangled nerves. "But in your present condition you can do nothing. It is best to go home, to sleep. And then, when the body is rested, you may go forth with new strength. Meanwhile, all of us will do our best, our very best."

Maury nodded, moved his head up and down as if it were weighted with lead. "I—I'll go home." He stood up; dully he scuffed like an automaton to the door. "Yes, I'll go home—for a while—and sleep."

Behind him, Li Tsan sighed softly, as if relieved, while Captain Dan Clark and Officer Pat Ryan exchanged glances of silent compassion.

2

The Empty Room

AN UPTOWN CLOCK was striking three a.m. when Paul Maury turned from Harrison into Huyler and walked sluggishly toward the shabby red-brick building that lay between darkly silent wooden tenements. His gaze was on the unclean sidewalk; his feet moved mechanically. When at last he came opposite the doorway, his scarecrow body twitched with a convulsive shudder, and he stared.

This was the Mission. It had no other name. It had been Grace's idea, and he himself had purchased the building for her, made it into the kind of place she wanted. Here, because of the charm and loveliness of a twenty-year-old girl, had come human derelicts, riffraff of the underworld, to find a new lease on life. Here had come men and women who were hungry, ill in mind and body… and Grace Maury had been their Good Samaritan, sending them away with a new light of hope in their eyes.

Now—she was gone. In a moment of weakness she had yielded to the advances of a slick-tongued beast who called himself Ricky Lester. With him she had gone to the Green Rooster, for a "thrill." And she had never returned.

Sluggishly Maury climbed the stone steps. He dragged the door shut behind him, thumbed a light-switch in the wall and shuffled along the corridor, past the tiny office that had been his sister's. Once he stumbled, had to cling to the wall to hold himself up. From the far end of the corridor—the end that led to a flight of rickety stairs winding down into a basement soup-kitchen and reading-room—came a scrape of clumsy footsteps. A bulky form took shape, advanced toward Maury's suddenly stiff figure. Then Maury relaxed, as a drawling voice rolled between the corridor's walls.

"That you, Mistuh Maury suh?"

"What is it, Alexander?"

The man came forward, peering. He was a Negro, big-boned and moon-faced.

"You's sure been gone a long time, Mistuh Maury. They's a young lady done come here to see you ages ago."

"A—young lady?"

"Yas-suh. F'um the way she spoke, I reckon she knows you real well. I told her you might not be gettin' home till dawn, like you did last night, so she lay down on the couch in your office and I reckon she's asleep in there."

Dully Maury thanked the Negro caretaker, paced along the corridor and hesitated before the door of his own office. Shaking his head dazedly, he pushed the door open, stepped over the threshold.

George Alexander had been right: a woman was sleeping on the couch against the wall, under a lamp that cast its yellow glow over her slender form. Maury stood and stared at her, stared wide-eyed at the attractive, softly-featured face that was turned toward him. Then, sobbing, he stumbled forward, spoke the girl's name in a hoarse whisper.

"Ruth! Thank God—"

The girl awoke as he went to his knees beside the couch. With a start, she opened her eyes, looked into his stubbled face; then, even as his arms went out to embrace her, she was in them, holding him close, hard. Words came from the lips that were pressed against his throat.

"Paul—oh, you poor boy. I had to come, after the letter you wrote!" She drew his head down and held it in her arms, so that his sobs were smothered against the smoothness of the clinging silk that covered her breasts.

"Tell me about it, Paul. Tell me everything."

He told her, pouring it out as he had longed to pour it out to someone who could understand. This girl would understand. She had known Grace. She had promised, months ago, to become Paul Maury's wife.

He told her, and when at last he was done, she put her lips to his.

"It will be all right, Paul. It *must* be."

"Yes, it will be—all right." Something about this girl made him believe it. "The police and Li Tsan—they'll help us. And in the morning, I'll go out again—" He stopped, stared at her. "You mustn't sleep here, dear. Grace—Grace's room is empty, upstairs. I'll show you…"

She followed him out of the office, along the corridor and up a flight of dim stairs where he gripped her arm to keep her from stumbling. A night-light glowed in the upper hall, revealing closed doors. Maury opened one of these, touched a light-switch inside, and turned again to take the girl in his arms.

"You've made things seem so different. I—I think I was on the verge of going mad, Ruth."

Ruth Wells looked up into his emaciated face and found courage enough to smile. "You're not going mad, dear. We're going to find Grace, tomorrow."

He would have clung to her for an eternity, but she kissed him, slipped gently from his embrace.

"Good-night, Paul."

The door closed. Maury walked slowly away from it, groped his way along the corridor and went into his own room.

Removing his ragged clothing was an effort. When at last he extinguished the light and sprawled out on the bed, his eyes closed and refused to open again. Sleep claimed him…

IT WAS A different Paul Maury who awoke, hours later, with a sudden fearful sensation that something sinister, something evil, had awakened him. Sleep had removed the chalky whiteness from his face and paled some of the crimson in his eyes. Every nerve alert, he pushed himself off the bed, stood rigid.

Something… some alien sound…

It came again, furtively. A soft whisper of slow-moving feet in the corridor outside… Abruptly, Maury stepped backward in darkness, reached out and pulled open the drawer of the table behind him.

When he toed his way silently to the door, one hand gripped a police thirty-eight.

Captain Dan Clark, of Precinct Twelve, had given him that revolver more than a year ago, with the laconic comment that Chinatown was Chinatown. "You're not a cop, Maury, but in your particular job you're apt to meet things that even cops don't come across."

Noiselessly, Maury inched the door open, put a foot on the threshold. In the semidark hallway, the whisper of approaching footsteps had ceased, leaving a pregnant silence doubly ominous.

And then, very suddenly, a door jarred open and a scream of chilling terror spewed through the silence!

The whiteness was back in Maury's face as he lunged forward. Above the sucking intake of his breath that scream of terror from a girl's lips filled the corridor with shrill reverberations. Maury's feet pounded the floor, carried him in a headlong rush toward the open doorway ahead, where hours ago he had clung to Ruth Wells in a good-night embrace.

The girl's scream crescendoed to a shriek. Paul Maury forgot caution and hurtled blindly over the threshold.

The sill itself saved him from annihilation. Tripping him, it sent him off balance, threw him forward with both arms outflung. In the dark of the chamber, a whirling object missed his lowered head by inches and imbedded itself with a dull thud in the side of the door-frame. Head foremost, Maury crashed into a dark shape that leaped backward to avoid him.

Faint light came from the room's one window. Near the bed at the far end of the room, a second dark shape was struggling with something white, something that gasped and sobbed as it fought frantically for freedom. That white shape, writhing in the embrace of black-garbed arms, was Ruth Wells.

Paul Maury needed no more to fire the madness in his heart. His own assailant lunged forward a second time, robed arms outflung to drag him down. The revolver stabbed up in Maury's fist, belched thunder as it drove lead into the man's hurtling body. Then he whirled, leaped clear of that screaming shape and flung himself toward the bed, toward the black-gowned Oriental viciously endeavoring to subdue Ruth Wells.

The Oriental whirled, made a quick downward movement with one stabbing hand and snatched a gleaming thing from the belt of his flapping trousers. The weapon made a whining sound, lashed out with snakelike quickness and missed Paul Maury's shoulder by fractions of an inch.

The thing was a hatchet, razor-sharp and light. Paul Maury's gun-wrist jerked up beneath it. The heel of the blade made grinding contact, broke flesh and sent nerve-killing pain through Maury's arm.

The gun spilled from his paralyzed hand and fell to the floor. With a vicious whine the hatchet rose again; the black-garbed Oriental surged forward.

BUT PAUL MAURY was not done. Lunging, he drove his good fist with pile-driver force into the midst of that snarling face. The Oriental staggered, lurched against the edge of the bed and went off balance, clawing darkness. Maury leaped, savagely hurled blow after blow.

Sobbing, sucking breath in sharp whines, the Chinaman reeled clear, and raced in blind terror toward the door.

Maury stood swaying, staring as the fleeing shape crossed the threshold. On stiff legs he turned, reached out with both hands to take hold of the limp shape that lay upon the bed. Fiendish fingers had torn the white silk slip from the girl's slender body, exposing the paleness of her shoulders, the smooth curves of her breasts and the white firmness of her thighs. Sharp nails had dug deep, leaving bloody scratches.

Ruth Wells had fainted…

Hate blazed in Maury's eyes then. The blood-mist returned, blinding him as he swung about and hurled himself toward the door, after the hatchet-man who had escaped. Reaching the hall, he sped down it, heard a pounding of slippered feet in the corridor below. A door jarred shut.

Maury groped down the dim stairway and lurched along the lower hall.

And behind him, above him, in the shadowed upper corridor, a silent shape moved slowly, furtively toward the open door of the room where Ruth Wells lay unconscious…

But Maury did not see that slinking shape as it tiptoed silently across the threshold. Intent only on the door that led to the street outside, he thrust out a trembling hand, jerked the barrier open.

In the street, with cold night-air whipping his face, he stood wide-legged, peering both ways along the unclean sidewalk. The sidewalk was deserted; the street itself was empty. The fleeing Chinaman had vanished, leaving only a street of mocking shadows and patches of yellow light thrown by far-apart street-lamps.

A savage oath came to Maury's lips, died there as he realized its futility. The hatchet-man had escaped. For Paul Maury to prowl the streets of Chinatown looking for him would be both useless and dangerous.

Wearily he turned, recrossed the threshold and pulled the door shut behind him. As he climbed the stairs his thoughts were black, bitter, full of a realization that this night's ugly business included something more than just two murderous hatchet-men of the underworld.

Chinese hatchet-men were professional murderers, kidnapers, and worse. Their services were for sale. Someone—someone probably connected with the disappearance of Paul Maury's sister—had hired those two black-garbed fiends to creep into the Mission and lay hands on Ruth Wells.

Who? Maury was not without suspicions, despite his inability to find proofs. There was Wen Lee, for one, and the sallow-faced youth called Ricky, and the Italian mobster who worked under the name of Big Willie Mung…

Scowling, Maury paced into the room where he had left Ruth Wells unconscious on the bed. He swayed, stood staring. Then a hoarse sob came from his quivering lips, and he lurched forward.

The bed sheets were crumpled, thrown back in disarray. And Ruth Wells' near-naked body no longer lay there. The girl was gone!

3

—

The Whistling Death

COLD FEAR WIDENED Maury's eyes as he stared into every corner of the room. Sweat stood out upon his face. He stumbled away from the empty bed and blundered from one side of the room to the other. But save for the body of the Chinese he had shot, the chamber was empty; the only sound in that room was the hammering of his own heart.

Shrill words rasped in his throat as he stumbled to the doorway and leaned there with hands white against the frame.

"Ruth! Oh my God—*Ruth!*"

The name rolled back to him in mocking echoes.

"*Ruth!*" White-faced, he went down the hall, pawed his way to the head of the stairs and lurched down them. In the lower corridor he turned once more, stared with bloodshot eyes and bellowed again the girl's name. Maddening echoes shrilled back to him…

Something snapped in his mind then—something born of a dull realization that he himself was to blame for the girl's disappearance. Because he had left her alone and raced insanely after a fleeing Chinaman who was merely a pawn of some fiend higher up, Ruth had become the prey of that same nameless fiend. First Grace… and now Ruth Wells.

Tears were in Maury's eyes as he lurched along the hall, yanked open the door leading to the basement, and shouted the name of the Negro caretaker. Perhaps Alexander had seen, had heard some slightest thing that might throw light upon the darkness. But no answer came to Maury's shouts. And when he descended the stairs, turned on lights and prowled frantically through the stone-floored chambers in the basement, he found nothing. The tiny room where Alexander usually slept was vacant.

Maury put both hands to his head, swayed with the icy fear that was growing to gargantuan size within him, and moaned aloud: "She's—gone. Gone the way Grace went. God have mercy…"

After that, he was not sure where he went or what he did. For a time he wandered about the Mission, upstairs and down, staring wide-eyed into shadows, whispering the name of the girl he loved. Then he was outside in the street, walking lifelessly through a cold drizzle that clung to him with clammy hands.

Murky dawn was breaking the darkness when he finally climbed the steps of the Twelfth Precinct Police Station.

He talked, then. Slumped on a wooden bench with Captain Dan Clark bending above him, he blurted out words, continued to blurt them out until his hoarse throat would yield nothing more than a cracked whisper.

Dan Clark gripped Maury's shoulders hard, then, and said sternly: "Snap out of it. Go back to the Mission, in case she returns there. In ten minutes I'll have every available man looking for her."

"You—won't—fail?"

"We'll find her or we'll rip this whole bloody district apart! Now get out of here. Go home!"

Home? The word brought a bitter snarl to Maury's lips as

he descended the station steps. Home?—with Ruth Wells, the girl who had promised some day to make him a home, now in the hands of black-souled Orientals to whom a white girl was merely something to be sold, sold into some foul den of vice where she would become the plaything of sex-hungry horribles…

He laughed drunkenly, stopped laughing as a shudder shook him from head to foot, chilling his already cold body. Through gray daylight he made his way along Harrison Avenue, turned into the street that harbored Wen Lee's Green Rooster. There were other places more important than home…

His hand went into his pocket, seeking the police thirty-eight that Dan Clark had given him long ago. Then he remembered: the gun lay on the floor of the room Ruth Wells had occupied, back in the Mission.

For an instant he hesitated, stared ahead at the green neon sign that marked Wen Lee's place of shadows. It would be madness for Paul Maury to enter there now without a weapon. Scowling, he turned from Bickford Street into Huyler and made his way back to the Mission.

THE HATCHET THAT had missed him by inches was still wedged in the doorframe of Ruth's room; and Maury frowned at it, shuddered a little as he paced past it on his way out of the chamber. In his pocket lay the gun that had already belched death—death to the black-garbed Oriental who lay in a contorted heap just inside the door.

In the street again he stopped, narrowed his eyes. An expensive car now stood at the curb, and a smallish well-dressed figure was stepping onto the sidewalk. The man spoke Maury's name as he came toward him; and Maury gazed, with a sensation of sudden relief, into the sober face of Li Tsan.

The Chinaman's hand was extended. Maury gripped it, felt courage pour into him through the firm clasp of those slender fingers.

"My friend, you are in trouble," the Oriental said. "Captain Clark has telephoned me about it. I have come to learn what I can do to help."

Maury licked dry lips, said slowly: "God knows I need help, Li Tsan."

"And it is I who may be able to render it."

"Maybe. I don't know." Maury clenched both hands, glared toward Bickford Street. "Right now I'm playing a hunch, playing it alone. If it fails—"

"You are going somewhere?"

"I'm going to make a certain filthy beast do some talking! If he refuses, God help him!"

"To whom," Li Tsan said softly, anxiously, "do you refer?"

"Ricky Lester!"

"But that is dangerous, my friend. If you go to the Green Rooster, where he spends most of his time, you walk into danger. If you antagonize such evil characters as Wen Lee and Willie Mung—"

"If they get in my way," Maury growled, "I'll commit murder!"

"But it is better to be cautious, my friend. In Chinatown, the person who is headstrong sometimes plunges himself into dire trouble!"

Maury nodded, muttered grimly: "I'll take that chance. If I fail, Li Tsan—if I get one of those bloody hatchets buried in my head— you and Dan Clark will have to find Ruth. Ruth—and Grace."

He swung about, strode swiftly away from the anxious-faced Oriental. Somehow, Li Tsan's quiet words of warning had calmed the madness in his heart. When he climbed the dark stairs of Wen Lee's Green Rooster, ten minutes later, he was fully aware of the dangers confronting him, and grimly determined to carry out the plan forming in his mind.

That plan concerned Ricky Lester. Lester was the one who had lured Grace into the Green Rooster. And Paul Maury was certain that Lester knew something, despite the fact that the police had failed to unearth anything of importance after questioning Lester for hours.

A green light was still glowing above the upstairs door. Inside, the shadow-ridden place was deserted; booths and orchestra-platform were empty. Maury paced across the waxed area toward the door leading to the kitchen.

Without doubt, Ricky Lester would be here. Lester slept during daylight hours, and did his sleeping in one of Wen Lee's back rooms.

The kitchen door swung open as Maury advanced. Wen Lee himself bulked there on the threshold, peering through narrowed eyes and turning thin lips into an unpleasant scowl.

He came forward slowly, and said with Oriental sluggishness: "What is it you want? Why you come here at this hour, after everything over and finished with?"

Maury stood wide-legged, stared straight into the man's ocher countenance. "Take me to Ricky Lester."

"Uh?"

"You heard me, Wen Lee. I came here to see Lester."

"If you come here to make trouble again, I call the police very quick!"

"What trouble I make depends on you, not me. I said take me to Ricky Lester!"

Wen Lee hesitated, lowered his head and took note of the fact that Maury's right hand was hidden to the wrist in a coat pocket that bulged slightly outward. With a slow shrug then, he said: "Very well. But if you make trouble, I go to the police and have you arrested."

He walked back through the doorway, traversed the kitchen with a slow waddling gait. The place was hot; slant-eyed Chinamen moved sluggishly about, shirtless and perspiring. Unlovely eyes took in Maury's every movement as he trailed his guide.

A swinging door opened, swung shut and kept swinging with a sound like the thumping of Maury's heart. Silently he trailed Wen Lee along a shadowed corridor, stopped at a safe distance when the Oriental paused before a closed door and rapped with yellow knuckles. Inside the room a voice grumbled in answer.

Wen Lee opened the door, peered inside and said quietly: "Someone is here to see you. It is unpleasant at this hour, but I have no choice." Standing back, he waited for Maury to enter.

Stiffly, Maury crossed the threshold, turning slightly so that the Chinaman did not for an instant go unwatched. The door closed; sandaled feet whispered away from it along the corridor outside. Gripping the revolver in his pocket, Maury paced slowly toward the sallow-faced youth who sat on the bed.

JUDGING FROM APPEARANCES, Ricky Lester had but recently sprawled out on the bed half dressed. He gaped as Maury advanced—continued to gape as Maury dragged a chair close to the bed and stiffly sat down.

Paul Maury leaned forward, toyed with Dan Clark's thirty-eight and said savagely: "Now you're going to talk. Understand? You're going to *talk!*"

Ricky Lester stared at the gun and went white. He did not snarl his answer. He was not the same Ricky Lester who had sat, with a girl, in one of the Green Rooster's booths a number of hours ago and sneeringly told Paul Maury to go to hell. The gun made a difference. At sight of that menacing weapon, Lester's eyes bulged with fear; the yellowness of his soul came to the surface. In a whimpering voice he said almost inaudibly: "What—do you want?"

"You know damned well what I want!"

"My God, I don't! I swear I don't know nothin'!"

Maury curled a forefinger in the trigger guard of the revolver and stared straight into Lester's bloodless face. "Listen, Lester. Either you talk—either you tell me all you know about what happened to my sister and Ruth Wells—or you'll never talk again."

"You wouldn't do that to me! My God, I never done nothin'! It ain't my fault if your sister—"

"You heard what I said."

Ricky Lester shuddered, seemed unable to take his gaze from the menacing hole of the gun. Beads of sweat formed on his forehead and gleamed there.

"I—I don't know nothin', I tell you. For the love of God—"

Maury's finger tightened on the trigger. Tightened slowly. "I'll give you just ten seconds, Lester. Then I'll kill you and leave you here. One... two..."

Ricky Lester shot a quick, frantic glance at the closed door and made a sobbing sound in his throat. His twitching mouth made whispered words.

"Don't! Don't shoot me, Maury! I—I'll talk."

Maury stopped counting. "Go ahead, then. I'm listening."

"What—do you want to know?"

"What happened to my sister? Where is she?"

"I don't know where she is," Lester sobbed. "Honest to God, I don't. All I know is, I was told to bring her to the Green Rooster that night."

Maury's face paled. He had hoped against hope, prayed to a merciful God that his suspicions might have no foundation. Now the chalk-faced rat before him was corroborating those suspicions, whining out words that were transforming hellish thoughts into realities.

Behind Maury, the knob of the door turned slowly; the door inched open without creaking. But Maury did not see. Leaning forward, breathing so hard that his chest swelled with every sucking intake, he snarled savagely: "Who told you to bring my sister here?"

"My—my boss," Lester whined.

"*Who?*"

"You wouldn't know him even if I told you. Honest to God, I ain't never come face to face with him myself. All I know is, he supplies girls for some of the Chink hop-joints in different cities, and he has different guys workin' for him, and—"

Again Maury's trigger finger tightened. "I asked you *who!*"

Lester's answer was a whine of terror. "My God, he'll kill me if I tell on him! I don't dare!" Wide-eyed, he stared at the gun, tried to squirm backward away from it. Sobbing like a terrified child, at last he whined out: "I—I'll tell. Only for God's sake don't tell no one who told you."

Maury said savagely: "Who is he?"

"I—I'll tell you. He—"

Paul Maury heard a whistling noise over his head, lunged sideways. But the weapon was not intended for him. Turning once in mid-air, it sped true to the mark, buried itself in the precise center of Ricky Lester's face! More than three inches of razor-sharp blade ate through flesh and bone. Handle downward, the hatchet quivered in its living target.

A single shriek of agony spilled from Lester's gaping mouth. In a contorted heap he sprawled backward over the bed, and the bed was a lake of blood even before he ceased writhing, ceased clawing with both hands at the hatchet-handle.

Stiff as wood, Paul Maury stared, unable even to lean forward in his chair. Eyes bulging, brain numb with horror, he gaped at the fountain of crimson blood that spurted from what had been a human face. Then, his own face white as paste, he turned slowly in the chair, groped to his feet and peered at the door.

The door was open but the doorway was empty.

4

The Torture Room

RICKY LESTER WAS dead, had been murdered because of his willingness to confess the name of his employer. The confession had died with him. And the doorway, the doorway which had vomited forth that murderous hatchet, was now an empty rectangle of shadow, mocking Maury as he paced stiffly toward it.

He walked with both hands in front of him, one of them gripping Dan Clark's revolver…

But the corridor was empty. Warily, Maury prowled down it, pushed open the swinging door that led to the kitchen.

Near-naked Chinamen were still working, as if unaware that anything had happened. In a straight-backed chair tipped against the wall, Wen Lee sat dozing, his eyes closed. At a small, linoleum-covered table in one corner, Big Willie Mung was eating from a deep dish filled with Chinese food, his head and shoulders hunched over the plate.

The man looked up, glared a moment as Maury walked slowly across the kitchen. Without speaking, he turned his attention once more to the food before him. Wen Lee did not stir.

Maury kept going, forced himself to walk without haste. That, in itself, was an effort; cold fingers played on his spine, urging him to lunge wildly toward the door that seemed miles distant. His heart was hammering; breath stuck in his throat as he advanced. But the denizens of Wen Lee's Green Rooster made no attempt to stop him.

The door closed behind him. Not until then did he realize that his hand still gripped the revolver. A moment later, when he was descending the stairs that led to the street, he dropped the gun into his pocket and breathed deeply for the first time since that whining hatchet had ground into Ricky Lester's face.

Then, pacing slowly along the cluttered sidewalk of Bickford Street, he tried to think.

Think? Think what? An hour ago he had known where to

turn, what to do. But that murderous hatchet had brought defeat at the very moment of triumph.

There was only one thing to do—now. That was to seek Li Tsan. Li Tsan knew many things. Perhaps he would know the names of certain men who had been Ricky Lester's associates…

With quick steps, Maury strode across Bickford Street, headed back toward the Mission. But Li Tsan's expensive car no longer stood there at the curb. Instead, as Maury approached, the bulging form of George Alexander, the Negro caretaker, came lumbering toward him from the doorway; and the Negro's big face was twitching with emotion as he reached out to grip Maury's arm.

"Mistuh Maury! I been lookin' all over ever'where for you!"

Maury stared, said stiffly: "What—has happened now?"

"Ain't nothin' happen just *now*, Mistuh Maury, only I been lookin' for you to tell you where they done took your girl!"

"You—what? You know where they took her?"

"Yassuh!" Alexander's eyes bulged as he jerked up a heavy arm and pointed.

"I follered 'em and seen the place they went into, and—"

"Take me there!"

The Negro gulped, moved his big head up and down violently and began walking. At the same time he talked, mumbling words. "I ain't sure what kind of a place it is, Mistuh Maury. Believe *me*, I don' want to know *too* much! All I know—"

"For God's sake," Maury blurted, "hurry!"

The Negro moved forward at a lumbering, ground-eating gait. His course took him down Huyler Street to Harrison, along Harrison to a break in the sidewalk where an alleyway ran between walls of dirty red brick.

Stopping, Alexander pointed again. "Tha's where they went, Mistuh Maury. Right in that there doorway."

Maury peered around him, scowling. This narrow alley, running darkly between frowning walls, was evidently a rear entrance to the buildings on both sides. One of them was a warehouse of some sort, the other a block-long structure harboring stores and small tenements and perhaps other things less innocent. There was a door at the deep end of the alley… a closed door with a frosted glass globe bracketed to the wall above it. And George Alexander was pointing.

Slowly, without thinking, Paul Maury paced forward, prowling deeper into the alley where perpendicular walls cut off any breath of air from outside. At the alley's mouth, George Alexander was standing motionless, gaping; and when Maury turned, the big Negro shook his head, made mumbling sounds of fear.

With a shrug, Maury advanced alone. Reaching the door, he put a hand on the knob, sucked breath as the door swung inward under pressure. Ahead of him lay a black-floored corridor dimly illuminated by twin bulbs in the high ceiling.

Revolver in hand, Maury toed silently forward.

Twice, before reaching the door at the far end of the passage, he stopped and stared around him. There was no sound, no sign of movement in the semi-dark.

His outthrust hand found the door, pushed it open. When he released it, after stepping over the sill, it swung shut with an ominous click that made him whirl around and grip the knob again. Then he knew the meaning of fear, knew that somewhere in the darkness ahead human eyes were watching him, checking his every movement.

The door was locked. He was a prisoner.

AND NOW THERE was no light. Whatever dangers lay before him, lay lurking in darkness impenetrable. Stiff as wood, Maury waited, stared with enormous eyes into the gloom. Ahead of him a dim light winked on, glowed like a beacon in the dark. A voice came out of nowhere.

"There is no danger, Paul Maury. At least, there is none yet. You are at liberty to enter and inspect my humble abode. Come!"

Strange, that voice! It seemed to emanate from no single source, but from all directions at once. And it had a familiar ring to it, a gloating, purring quality that caused worms of dread to crawl in Maury's veins.

His stiff fingers gripped the revolver more securely. Slowly he moved his feet on the dark carpet that extended before him. Step by step he approached the yellow glow of the light.

"I believe, Mr. Maury, that my home will delight even so distinguished a guest as you. When you have come another twenty steps, stop and look about you."

Twenty—steps. That droning voice had a power to make Paul Maury obey. Mechanically he counted the falls of his feet, continued on past the light and came to a slow halt, aware that he had walked beyond the corridor's end, through a doorway and into some kind of room beyond.

Then, abruptly, the darkness was gone. A chandelier above him threw out an amber glow from dozens of tiny bulbs. And Paul Maury stared, gasping his amazement!

This was no Chinatown den! It was a room as luxurious, as beautiful, as any to be found on Beacon Hill! Warmth and beauty were on all sides, in dull-gleaming shapes of heavy furniture, in dark-patterned Oriental rugs, in huge wall-covering tapestries. Silk-shaded lamps, strangely Oriental in design, glowed palely; a massive fireplace loomed in one broad wall; fantastically shaped Oriental antiques stood on teakwood tables.

Speechless, Maury turned a slow circle, moved forward. And in the room with him that gloating voice spoke again.

"This is merely one room of many. All are at your disposal, until I am ready to make your acquaintance more intimately. But be warned, Paul Maury! Beauty is sometimes treacherous. Beware lest you touch certain innocent-seeming objects which were designed to cause violent and terrible death. The table toward which you are now walking, for instance… it resembles mahogany but is fashioned of metal, and the floor surrounding it is fashioned of metal also. If you should touch that lovely table, you would be unable to retreat until many thousands of volts of electricity had ceased devouring you! Death is on all sides…"

Maury's face blanched. With a convulsive jerk he stepped backward, stood staring at the massive table. A shudder shook him, left him limp, breathing hard.

Then he caught himself, walked toward a fantastically shaped urn that stood near the tapestried wall. The thing stood shoulder high on its pedestal, and the pedestal itself, as well as the urn and the serpentine handle that curled out from it, were of hammered iron.

The voice had gloatingly declared that the huge table in the center of the room was charged with electricity. If so, things would happen if the iron urn were hurled, pedestal and all, against the table, striking table and floor at the same time…

Grimly Maury paced forward, reached a hand toward the snake-shaped handle.

"It is dangerous to do that, Paul Maury! Look closely. The rim of that particular handle is fitted with tiny needlepoints of steel. And each of those tiny needles has been dipped in sufficient poison to destroy the human body in less than five minutes. Five minutes of unspeakable agony."

Maury's outstretched hand stiffened; slowly he drew it back again, stared at the urn as if it were a thing alive. Blood ebbed from his face, left his eyes bulging in a chalk-white mask. Leaning forward, he saw the tiny needle-points on the inside rim of the iron handle.

"You see, I am not bluffing," the voice intoned mercilessly. "Death is everywhere, in many different forms. But I shall leave you now to your own devices, Mr. Maury. There are other rooms besides this one. You may wander about at will, enjoying yourself as you see fit. But remember: there will be no further warnings. If you stumble upon any of my death-devices in your wanderings, I shall not prevent you. I shall be pleasantly busy, amusing myself with what I was doing before you intruded."

Then the room was silent. And as Maury stared about him, rigid with dread, each separate object of furniture, each glowing light in the chandelier, seemed to be leering, gloating in evil triumph.

Slowly, very slowly, he turned, stared back at the open doorway through which he had entered. His stiff legs took him forward; he stopped again, stood staring over the threshold into the corridor through which he had walked into the trap.

That corridor led to escape, to freedom!

He took a step toward it. His gaze swept the threshold and

he stiffened to a stop. The threshold and the floor on both sides of it were of sheet iron, uncovered by carpet. Sheet iron—that might carry a death-dealing charge of current!

With a low sob, he stepped back. Moments ago, the owner of the voice had allowed him to enter through this same doorway. Now the threshold was a place of death.

Trembling from head to foot, he retreated, turned and paced stiffly across the room again, avoiding contact with the objects of furniture that lay in his path. His eyes were wide, studying each seemingly innocent shape as he paced past. In another moment he had crossed a wooden threshold and was standing in a second luxuriously furnished chamber similar to the first.

He moved forward, stopped. From somewhere ahead, beyond the wall that confronted him, came a dull moaning sound that caused him to stand rigid, listening. The sound stopped, began again after a nerve-racking interlude of silence.

Somewhere a woman was sobbing, groaning in pain!…

HE MOVED FORWARD again. As if reading his thoughts, that detached voice droned toward him through the silence.

"Perhaps you had forgotten why you came here, Mr. Maury. You were seeking your sister, were you not? And the young woman who was removed from the Mission? If you are still interested, let me suggest that you inspect the couch in the room where you are now standing."

Maury gaped. Against the wall stood a large, mahogany-legged couch covered with drapes of silk—red and black silk bearing brocaded dragon-designs. He moved toward it, went suddenly cold as his narrowed eyes discerned what lay there. Silken drapes concealed it, but beneath those thin layers of silk the outlines of a human body were visible.

Fingers of icy fear gripped his heart as he leaned forward, slowly drew the drapes aside. Then a blinding wave of agony went through him; his lips opened to release a sob that came from the depths of his soul. On his knees he stared into the face of the naked shape that lay before him. Scalding tears ran from his eyes. His hands clenched so hard that blunt fingernails ate into the flesh.

That naked shape was a thing of horror, and it was a woman. Face up, the girl lay on the couch, her head lolling, her arms folded below the ruptured flesh of her young breasts. And Maury's agonized gaze, traveling slowly over the girl's body, saw evidences of the horror that had brought death.

Somewhere—somewhere he had heard of the Death of a Thousand Cuts, that hellish, Oriental torture in which sharp knives made a horror of the victim's nude body, removing fingernails, eyelids, lips... and continuing slowly, relentlessly, until death stilled the victim's agonies. And this girl on the couch... this girl was Paul Maury's sister!...

Mutely he stared down at her, buried his face in his hands and swayed on his knees, sobbing out the torment that was in his heart. His... sister... the girl whose loveliness and kindness had been expended in making the world a happier place for others. Never in her life had she raised a hand to harm any living thing. And now...

Through the numbness that possessed him, he was aware that the voice was once again addressing him. The same gloating voice, even more triumphant now.

"You see, Mr. Maury, your sister refused to obey my wishes;

that is why she died. She is not the first… As Ricky Lester informed you, I have dealings with many attractive young women. They are brought to me, and if they are willing, I sell them to customers of mine in many large cities.

"But they must be willing. My customers have no desire for women who do not return the love that is bestowed upon them. Therefore, before sending a woman out of this house, I inform her of what is expected of her and ask if she entertains any objections. Some do object, and then I am forced to use persuasive methods to bring about a change of heart. There are many methods. And if all of them fail, what of that? I have still had the pleasure of trying; and what more could a man desire?"

Maury sucked breath, rose slowly to his feet and turned to face the wall from which the voice seemed to be coming. Savagely he reached down, took his revolver from the couch where it had slipped from nerveless fingers. His face was white with madness, his unblinking eyes alive with hate, as he paced stiffly forward.

The voice stopped him. "You are angry, my good friend? You think I am a heartless fiend to have taken the life from your sister's lovely body? Ah, but it was a pleasure to work with her. It was a delight to be so close to that charming body, to watch it writhe in agony and to hear the screams that came from those lovely lips. But that is nothing, nothing at all. Would you see more? Before I kill you, would you care to look once more into the face of the girl who has promised to be your *wife?*"

Maury's answer was a lurid curse, a savage, screaming oath that spewed from bloodless lips. Oblivious to danger, he lurched blindly forward, clawed his way toward a door in the opposite wall. Not until his outstretched hand was within inches of making contact did he realize that the door was a barrier of iron, and that the floor in front of it was a sheet-iron plate. Then, staggering back, he stood swaying on widespread legs, sobbing noisily.

"You have excellent self-control, Mr. Maury," the voice intoned. "I am disappointed. I had hoped to see you lunge against that particular door. It is the door of my amusement-room, and I would have been amused by your death-agonies!"

Maury caught a grip on himself, forced his rigid body to stop shuddering. He knew now why men went mad, why they became raving, screaming idiots. In a little while, he, too, would be like that. Already a strange sensation of dizziness was surging through him, filling him with a desire to shriek out gusts of laughter.

"Beside you, in the wall," the voice informed him droningly, "is a circular steel plate, Mr. Maury. It will not harm you. Open it, and you may have the privilege of enjoying, with me, the pleasant sufferings of a young lady who has proved to be very obstinate. She has refused to accept my terms, and I am endeavoring to make her change her mind. You are at liberty to watch the transformation."

Maury paced forward, inches at a time. His hand touched the steel plate, froze there as a new surge of dread stabbed through him. Slowly he drew the plate open, stared through the aperture.

But he was immune to further horror. The sight that met his gaze merely served to drag a new groan of anguish from his twisted lips.

The aperture before him penetrated the wall and afforded

a view of the chamber beyond. A view, at least, of enough of the chamber to cause a red mist of horror to form before his eyes. A white wall stared back at him, and a low white table surmounted by an apparatus that looked like something out of a chemist's laboratory.

On that table, strapped to it with leather thongs that ate into pale flesh, lay an almost nude body, a girl's body, writhing in torment. And Maury's lips released a lurid shriek as he looked into the girl's face and saw that it was Ruth Wells!

5

Poisoned Barbs

NEAR NAKED SHE lay, face up on the torture-table, her arms extended behind her, wrists and ankles rigidly bound to iron rings on the table-edge. And the apparatus above her was in motion, gliding slowly, relentlessly back and forth, back and forth.

Stiff with horror, Maury stared through the opening, clung to the wall beside him in an effort to repress the violent shuddering of his rigid frame. Moments passed before he realized the full scope of the torture-machine, before he saw the thing in action.

It resembled a dentist's drill, a drill whose needle was no needle at all, but a cone-shaped funnel, releasing tiny drops of liquid. Continually in motion, that unholy funnel traveled in a slow circle above Ruth Wells' body. Now a drop of liquid fell, landing with a tiny splash on the girl's rigid forehead. Slowly, inexorably, the funnel swung in its circle, while another bead of moisture formed at its needle-sharp point. Then that bead descended, making contact with the gentle slope of the girl's alabaster breast.

A third drop fell… splashed on the victim's bare abdomen. Slowly, fiendishly, the funnel circled above her, releasing its drops of liquid at sixty-second intervals. And with each touch of that liquid, Ruth Wells writhed in moaning agony, strained helplessly at the leather thongs that encircled her wrists and ankles.

Dully, vaguely, Maury realized that the hideous torment before him was an outgrowth of what the Orientals called the water-torture. Drop by drop that hellish liquid fell upon the victim's bare body, moving from forehead to breast to abdomen, abdomen to breast to forehead.

At first those falling drops would mean nothing, would cause no pain whatever. Then, as hour after hour of slow torture went by, each drop would become a falling sledge, striking its way into the victim's nervous system. And while each succeeding ball of moisture formed on the cone-shaped funnel above, the victim would stare with terror-filled eyes, watching the tiny globule gain weight, dreading its inevitable release.

Then the drop of liquid would fall… would strike with a force that felt like the blow of a hundred-pound weight. And the victim would shriek in agony, scream out words of supplication. The Chinese water-torture…

No other torment in the sadistic repertoire of the torturers was so slow, so hideous. And Ruth Wells must have been enduring it for hours, moaning and sobbing as each drop made contact with the satin-smooth flesh of her body. In a little while more, those moans and sobs would become shrieks; that near-nude body would writhe in agony unspeakable.

Maury could stand no more. Sick in soul and body, he staggered back from the aperture, stared down at the revolver clenched in his fist and drove his ice-cold body toward the iron barrier that marked the entrance to that room of horror. And once again, as it had done many times before, the droning voice of the torture-master stopped him.

"You are shocked, Mr. Maury? Ah, but that is half the pleasure! For me it is a pleasure to watch you, as I am able to do through ingenious tubes that allow me to look into every room of this lovely house of mine! Why do you hesitate, my friend? You know where I am—you know that I am standing here in this room of divine pleasure, on the far side of the door you are now facing. Why do you pause? The door can do no more than kill you!"

A throaty chuckle accompanied the words, and the voice began again. "In a little while your sweetheart will yield to my persuasions, and agree to go willingly into the arms of yellow men who will delight in making love to her. She is lovely, no? She will bring a fine price, this girl! And you—you will have lost a sweetheart, but what of that?

"Do you wonder who I am, Paul Maury? It grieves me that you may never learn the truth. This much I may tell you—I have many men in my employ. Your own servant, your George Alexander, is a hireling of mine. It was he who brought Ruth Wells here, after two of my hatchet-men had failed to complete their assignment. And did you not realize, when you yourself came here, that the Negro who led you was merely obeying my orders?"

The chuckle became a triumphant laugh. Then the voice changed tone.

"You will die presently, Paul Maury. But first I am allowing you to watch the transformation that is about to take place in the girl you love. She has been very stubborn. But in a very little while now she will yield to my wishes; she will agree to be sold into the arms of yellow men who will admire and love her devotedly."

THE WORDS DRONED into silence. Paul Maury stood wide-legged, glaring through a crimson mist at the iron door. That door was all that held him from the throat of the monster in the torture-room. And the door was of iron, with an iron threshold. If he touched it…

In blind fury he flung himself backward, stripped off the coat that enveloped his heaving shoulders. A wooden table stood near him, within reach. Savagely he jammed the revolver into his pocket, seized the table in sweating hands and flung his coat around two of its heavy legs, then heaved it from the floor and advanced with it.

"Be careful, Paul Maury! If you let madness get the best of you…"

Madness had already eaten its way into Maury's heart. Swinging the table high, he advanced with stumbling steps, hurled himself straight at the iron barrier.

Again and again, in savage fury, he smashed the heavy table against that massive block of metal, struck with all the strength in his lame shoulders. But the blows had no effect. When at last he slumped back, the obscene voice beyond the door was still chuckling, still laughing softly in triumph, and the table in Maury's hands was a jagged mass of splintered wood.

An animal glare came into his eyes then, as he stood stiff, holding the wreck of the table in his bleeding hands. Nothing mattered except the door that confronted him, the iron barrier that was holding him from the fiend beyond it.

Animal cunning took possession of him, ate into his brain. With a sullen grunt, he hurled the shattered table aside, clawed the revolver from his pocket and took savage, deliberate aim. Four times his curled finger jammed the trigger; four times the gun belched thunder, filling the room with staccato reverberations. When the mad echoes died away, the lock of the door was a twisted, shattered mass of metal. Once again Maury gripped the legs of the table and lunged forward.

And this time, as the wooden bludgeon made contact, the door groaned open, jarred back on its hinges and left a gaping aperture for Paul Maury to hurtle through!

He went headlong, clearing the sheet-iron threshold in a single savage lunge, without touching floor or door-frame. He righted himself with a desperate twist of his shoulders, snarled erect.

Ahead of him, separated by ten yards of floor, stood the white-legged table that supported Ruth Wells' nude body. And beside that table, crouching like a deformed ape, stood a sinister, staring shape that was the owner of the voice.

Maury stared, too. With an animal growl rumbling in his throat, he hurtled forward, whipped up the revolver in his fist and jerked the trigger. The hammer clicked on an empty chamber. Snarling, he flung the gun aside, extended both hands as he continued his mad lunge.

A gleaming blade, snatched from the torture-table by stabbing yellow fingers, leaped to meet him. Whining, the steel shaft missed his lowered head by inches, thudded into the wall behind him. Then the monster lunged. An upthrust yellow hand swung high, gripping a gleaming ribbon of steel.

Paul Maury met the attack by hurtling under it, driving a clenched fist into the face of his snarling assailant. The fist ground home, drew blood from that convulsed countenance. Maury's left hand shot forward, clamped over the descending knife-wrist and twisted with such savage force that the knife slid from paralyzed fingers.

Then, locked in an embrace of madness, Maury and the torture-master staggered blindly across the room.

They fought like animals. The ocher-skinned fiend used pointed fingernails to rip flesh from Maury's face, employed knees and feet in a savage attempt to disembowel his white adversary. Maury used fists, drove them blindly, viciously into the Chinaman's lunging body. Across the room they reeled, away from the table where that hideous torture-machine was still inflicting agony on Ruth Wells' near-naked body. And the Oriental, endowed with the cunning of his kind, carried the conflict his own way, toward the sheet-iron threshold over which Maury had entered the death-chamber.

It was a cunning move, that. Stumbling clear of Maury's flailing fists, the Chinaman feigned weariness, rocked backward with groaning sounds in his bloody mouth. Paul Maury hurtled toward him. The Oriental lunged sideways, cleared the threshold and the death-dealing iron plate in a tremendous backward leap. But Maury cleared it after him, missed death by inches and sprawled on hands and knees in the room beyond.

Animals… fighting desperately for the right to kill! The growls that issued from Maury's throat were inhuman sounds of madness, hunger. The hissing sobs that came from his adversary's lips were exploding grunts of sadistic hate.

Away from the death-door the two men staggered, now tangled in murderous embrace, now separated by crashing mounds of furniture.

An upthrust knee stabbed Maury's groin, brought a shriek of agony to his lips. The heel of his hand made contact with snarling lips, tore yellow flesh as it raked upward to the Oriental's eyes. A sledge-hammer fist sent the Chinaman reeling, hurled him through the doorway leading to the room where Paul Maury had first known terror.

Cunning came into the Oriental's almond-shaped orbs as he regained balance and stood on stiff legs. Less than three yards behind him the carpet ended, the floor became a surface of bare metal supporting the death-dealing table which Paul Maury had cringed from once before. Arms outthrust, the Chinaman awaited Maury's charge, set himself to leap sideways.

But Maury whirled in another direction.

Too late, the Chinaman divined his intent, hurtled forward to stop him. But Maury's hand had already closed over its objective, already clamped around the base of the iron urn with the needle-barbed handle. The heavy pedestal swept up, shot from his fist as the Oriental lunged backward with a shrill scream of terror.

True to the mark, the iron handle ground into the Chinaman's face, ate its way through ocher flesh and hurled the man backward. Poisoned needles stabbed home, brought a lurid shriek from lips that writhed open in agony. Clawing blindly, the torture-master reeled on crooked legs, lost balance.

Screaming, the Oriental fought frantically to straighten his staggering body. But the effort came too late. One stumbling foot made contact with the iron floor; writhing shoulders crashed against the table.

CREATION UPENDED. A livid glare of light enveloped man and table and floor, blinding Maury's wide eyes. Like a propped-up corpse, the Chinaman remained rigid, shoulders jammed against the iron edge of the table, arms extended stiffly toward the metal floor. Lightning shot from his fingertips, crackled floor-ward in livid streaks of fire.

For ten seconds a living hell enshrouded the Oriental's rigid body; a grinding, screaming cacophony smothered the shrieks that welled from his lips. A stench of burning flesh filled every corner of the room.

Then, flung aside by the unholy current that had destroyed him, the Chinaman pitched free, lurched two steps forward and fell in a grotesque heap at the edge of the carpet. And Paul Maury, white-faced with horror, paced slowly forward to stand above the contorted body, and stared down into the man's blasted face.

It was a familiar face, a face that Maury had looked into many times before. It was the face of the man who had claimed to be Paul Maury's friend and the friend of Captain Dan Clark. That blackened countenance, staring up in hideous death, belonged to Li Tsan!

Maury shuddered, would have continued to stand there, staring, had not another sound invaded his consciousness. The sound came from the torture-room, moaning its way from the lips of the girl who lay there in agony.

She was still moaning when Paul Maury stumbled to her side a moment later.

He looked down at her, looked up at the torture-machine that was still moving relentlessly in its grim horror-circle. Savagely he dragged the table clear, unstrapped the leather thongs that held Ruth Wells rigid. Then he stumbled back, holding a near-naked, sobbing shape in his arms—and the girl was saying in a whisper that was almost inaudible:

"Thank—God, Paul! Oh, thank God, you found me!"

He lowered her to the floor, stared at her as he gently rubbed the livid welts made by the table's leather thongs. Mechanically at first, then hungrily, his lips found hers. When he spoke again, it was to say anxiously:

"I've got to get you out of here! But how? That damned current..."

The girl's hand found his arm and clung there reassuringly. "It can be turned off, Paul. The switch in the wall behind you—I saw him use it..."

He lifted her from the floor, turned and scowled at a black-handled, copper-jawed switch in the white wall. His hand went out, dragged the thing slowly downward.

Then, with one arm about the girl's waist, he led her to the door, walked with her into the adjoining room and covered her nakedness with a silken drape from the couch.

Standing there beside the couch, he stared down at another near-naked shape, leaned forward and gathered the limp form in his arms. A sob shook him; tears were in his eyes as he turned.

"I—I can't leave her here," he mumbled.

Ruth Wells said nothing. Silently she followed him across the room, through the chamber where lay a blackened, contorted thing that had been human. In the dimly lighted corridor leading to the night outside, she looked into his face, saw the anguish there, and said quietly for the sake of speaking:

"The police will have to do the rest, Paul. Li Tsan had many men working for him—Wen Lee, Big Willie Mung, George Alexander and others. He bragged about it while he was gloating over me. White-slavery is—is a terrible thing. And when an intelligent, educated man like Li Tsan turns into a sadist…"

The outer door closed behind them. Slowly, Maury led the way through the alley, stopped under an arc-light that burned above the Harrison Avenue sidewalk. What time it was, he had no idea, did not care. He and the girl beside him would go first to the police station, and then, in a little while, they would be back at the Mission, alone together.

And then, what? Dully, he gazed down at the limp shape in his arms, raised his head and peered into Ruth's pale face.

"You and I," he said. "You and I will go away from here—together—to forget."

Uptown, the bell in the clock-tower of Park Street Church struck a single, solemn note, smothering Ruth Wells' whispered word of agreement.

LEAD POISON

Frederick Nebel

It wasn't that the big dick from Cosmos couldn't coöperate with the police—it was just that he didn't relish cutting Sergeant Brice in on the reward melon. However, when the life of his pet Chinese op hung on whether he played ball with the cops or not— Well, that was a horse of another hue, and to hell with the reward! If it meant saving Sam Chang, Cardigan could stop being a one-man team in a trice and pal up with all the thick-headed coppers in creation—for a minute anyhow.

1

Chop-Spot

CARDIGAN DRIBBLED TOBACCO from a cotton sack into a piece of rice paper, nipped the sack's drawstring between his hard teeth and yanked the sack shut, let it drop to the table. He rolled the cigarette into a neat cylinder and looked out through the window of the Pearl of Nanking Café, down onto Grand Avenue. A few pedestrians dug head-down through the raw wind of a dark San Francisco night.

Cardigan's eyes were idly focused on as much as he could see of the man who had been standing across the street for the past half hour. The shadow of a wooden awning masked the man as far down as the hips; below that, Cardigan saw the skirt of a dark overcoat, trousered legs, a pair of shoes that sometimes reflected the light of a nearby street-lamp. The Cosmos op figured that if the man were waiting for someone he'd be much warmer back in the recessed doorway between the two shop-windows.

"All right," he said, "I'll try again. Where's Tom Gow?"

THE GIRL SITTING across the table from him was Chinese, dressed exquisitely in American clothes. They were the only ones in the small second-floor dining-room of the Pearl of Nanking Café. Mae Ling had a smooth triangular face, penciled eyebrows, neatly rouged lips. She said, for the sixth time, "I don't know," her eyes averted, her hands clenched in her lap.

Cardigan flashed a match on his thumbnail and lit up. His eyes, dark, probing, moved beneath shaggy brows. "I told you to come to my agency office in Market Street," he said. "You begged off. You made the date for here, when I said you'd bounce into trouble if you didn't see me. Why here?"

Her pretty lips contracted. "I—I just didn't— I was afraid, I guess. In a public place, like this, I feel safer."

"What was there to be afraid of?"

"I didn't know you."

He leaned heavily on his elbows. "Tom Gow was running around with Berkman and Finger in Los Angeles a month ago. We got that tip from the L.A. branch of the agency. This Siamese throne-chair was shipped up from Los Angeles two weeks ago, after that movie company took some shots of it. It was put on exhibition here in the Jerris Gallery. Three days ago it was bought by Ludwig Hertz. He paid down a three-thousand-dollar binder, with the understanding that the rest of the amount, ninety-seven grand, was to be paid on delivery at his place.

"The chair was called for by the express company in an armored truck. The truckmen wore regulation uniforms but they'd held up and conked the real truckmen and taken the necessary papers away from them. Bushman, the guy at the gallery, had no way of knowing. The two men seemed O.K. They carried out the chair. Now Bushman's a nut on taking pictures. The removal of that throne-chair was a big event to him, and he leaned out the window and took a picture of it being

He reeled and together they clattered down the steps.

lifted into the truck. The picture shows only the tops of the truckmen's heads, the tops of their caps—no faces. But standing on the curb near the truck, it shows a Chinese and part of his face—a snappy dresser. He's blurred a bit, but if it ain't Tom Gow I'll eat my hat. I want to know where he is. You know."

"I don't."

Cardigan said: "Sam Chang, our only Chinese op, cased your apartment. Down between the pillows on your sofa he found a Pullman stub for a berth from Los Angeles to here. The stub's dated the day after the throne-chair was shipped north. You didn't go to Los Angeles at that time, I can prove it. A check-back shows Tom Gow packed up and left his hotel room in Los on the same date as the Pullman stub. Things add—they add up, kid."

Her eyes were fixed on his tie. "They add up because you make them add up. I tell you I haven't seen Tom in two months. I don't know where he is. That's final."

"Your neck, it is!" he growled. "Listen, Mae, you ain't a bad charmer. You've got no police record. We've figured it out that you make a pretty good living posing for illustrators. But you're going to get a record, Mae, if you don't come clean with me. You're going to get it quick. We know Tom Gow likes to drink Pernod—he drinks nothing else. We know that the morning of the day he arrived you went around to a store and bought a bottle of Pernod. Next day a tailor cleaned a suit for a guy of Tom Gow's description. The suit had Pernod stains. It adds, Mae!"

"Just because you add it. I'm leaving."

"Sit down," he grunted.

Her jaw shook as she stared at him.

He said: "I told you—you're heading for a police record. You can avoid it by coming clean with me. If you don't, I turn you over to Dave Brice of the Chinatown Squad—now!" His palm slapped the table.

She grimaced, shook her head. "No—no—don't do that!"

"Hell, do you think I want to?" he demanded. "If you'd stop giving me the run-around, I'd see you wouldn't be touched. But I'm not going to finagle Dave Brice for a dame that won't spring information to me."

Her shoulders were shaking. She said in a small, clogged voice: "Let me think…." From her purse she took a cigarette, slipped it between her lips and struck a match, lit up. She waved the match out and dropped it to a tray.

Cardigan moved suddenly. His big feet dug against the floor and he heaved the table, knocking Mae to the floor, and threw himself sidewise and downward as the explosion of a gunshot mingled with the crash of shattered glass. He spun while kneeling, sprang to the next window, saw a dim flash of glass beneath the wooden awning across the street, as if a door had swung. Wind was whooping in through the broken window alongside the table.

HE WENT DOWN the staircase, four steps at a time, reached the street and sped across to the darkened shop. His left hand fell on the doorknob as his right whipped out his gun. The door opened as he turned the knob and he went in fast, bent way over, scraping his knees. His left hand groped upward, found a light switch, turned it. A center light sprang on, revealed a small curio shop. In the rear, a heavy bead curtain was swaying slightly, as if someone had recently brushed it aside in passing. Cardigan went toward it at an angle, came up on the left side of the doorway and gave the curtain a sweep with his left hand.

Nothing happened. He could feel a cold draft pulling, and peering around the door-frame, through the bead curtain, he saw a door half open and beyond the door the indistinct dark outside. His big shoulders flayed the bead curtain on his way through to the small rear room. He stepped into the alley beyond, heard the drum of running feet, saw nothing. Moving farther into the alley, he strained his ears—took a chance and turned left, broke into a run. He reached Grant Avenue, stopped, knew he had lost his man. Turning, he tramped back down the alley, found the rear door of the shop and stepping in, saw a stocky Japanese dressed in a heavy silk robe, sandals and a nightcap. The man looked angry, surprised and puzzled all at once.

"You own this place?" Cardigan said.

"Yiss."

"Was your front door locked when you closed up and went upstairs?"

The Oriental nodded, said: "Yiss. Yiss, sar." He put a finger to his chest, then pointed to Cardigan and said: "You, sar, pol-eece?"

Cardigan took a short-cut—he nodded.

The other bowed. "So sorry."

Cardigan explained: "Man open your door. Man shoot. Man open your door. I chase. Anything stolen, you report."

The man giggled. "So sorry."

Cardigan gave it up. He went through the shop, out into Grant Avenue, and saw a crowd gathered across the street.

The ground floor of the building housing the Pearl of Nanking Café was occupied by a provision shop, at this hour closed. Cardigan shoveled with his shoulders through the crowd, went up the inside stairway to the dining-room and saw the Chinese owner throwing a fit because of the broken window. Two uniformed cops were listening to him. The girl Mae Ling was not in sight. At Cardigan's entrance one of the cops turned.

Cardigan said, "Hi," and went across to get his hat and over-coat.

"Hey," said the cop who had turned.

"Yeah?" Cardigan said, bundling into his shabby ulster, slapping on his shapeless old fedora.

"You was at that table with—"

"A gal, yeah," grinned Cardigan.

"So what?"

"So… what?"

"Where's the gal?"

Cardigan chuckled roughly. "Hell, officer, I'd like to know."

The cop said: "A Chinese gal."

"Sure. And a looker, too."

"Say, are you trying to be funny?"

"No."

The cop said: "Chin Fu here says a shot busted the window, you ran out, and the gal ran out after you."

"Right—except she didn't follow me. She took a run-out powder on her own."

The Chinese was going on and on, almost weeping, about the broken window.

"Who was the gal?" asked the cop.

"I don't know," Cardigan said. "A pick-up. I picked her up on the corner of Grant and Pine. I didn't know she had a gun-mad boyfriend. Well, nobody's hurt, so I'll be going."

The cop got in front of him. "Not so fast, mug. If it was just as simple as that, why'd you leave your hat and overcoat and the dame and line out of here?" He slapped Cardigan's pockets and pulled out Cardigan's gun. "Ah, a gat!"

"Yeah. Now—look in the inside pocket and you'll find a license to carry it."

The cop looked. He found the license and also Cardigan's agency card. He handed them back, handed the gun back, and said: "All right, fella. If it don't pan out, we'll know where to find you."

His face showed that he was not quite satisfied with Cardigan's explanation, and while he was still hovering over his own doubts, Cardigan said: "Well, goom-by, boys. School's out."

2

The Punk in the Lobby

WHEN CARDIGAN ENTERED the Cosmos Agency office in Market Street it was ten to ten. Magruder, the night man, was standing in front of an olive-green steel filing-cabinet, thumbing through an index. A green eyeshade was askew on his forehead and a heavy curved pipe dangled from his teeth.

Sam Chang was sitting on a desk, dangling a spatted foot and reading a letter. He was a compact man, about five foot ten, big-handed, wedge-jawed, with clipped black hair that stood up like the bristles of a hairbrush. His brown worsted suit, tan silk shirt, wine-colored tie blended nicely. He was neat, muscular, with close-lidded slant eyes above which were tufts of coarse black hair. He looked up, said, "Hello, Jack," smiled, tapped the letter. "My wife left Shanghai. She's on her way home. Ask me if I'm glad."

Cardigan grinned. "You glad, Sam?"

Magruder spat, snorted. "Glad! The ape's been carrying on like a two-year-old ever since he opened the letter."

Sam Chang, still smiling, folded the letter and put it away in his pocket. "Three months is a long time," he said, rubbing his palms together. "She wants to be remembered to you, Jack." He chuckled. "She says you should take care of me, see I don't get hurt."

Magruder said: "Yah, stick around that Irish mug and you'll wind up in so many pieces some day it'll take an expert to put you together again."

"What's eating you, sour puss?" gibed Cardigan.

Sam Chang said: "He's just Scotch, that's all. He's been sending away for free samples of tobacco for years—never bought any in his life—and he's sore because one of the companies finally got wise."

"Yah!" snorted Magruder.

Cardigan dropped down into a swivel chair, said: "Sam, I met Mae Ling."

Sam Chang looked down at him. "Yeah?"

Cardigan told what had happened.

Sam Chang's face grew very grave. "Here's something else, Jack. About half an hour ago I heard that Dave Brice picked up young Charley Sun. He's a clerk in the office of the express company that contracted to move the throne-chair."

Cardigan squinted. "Why'd they pick him up?"

"Because they found out that two hours before the truck was to pick up the chair, Charley Sun left the office for fifteen minutes. He went around the corner to a drug store. The clerk there remembered seeing him come in and go to a telephone booth. It's a dial phone. They couldn't trace the call and Charley won't tell 'em who he called." Sam Chang stopped, but his manner indicated that there was more to tell.

"What else?" Cardigan asked.

Sam Chang didn't look happy. "Last Saturday night I saw Charley at the Oriental Music Box with Mae Ling."

"Dave Brice know that?"

"No. We're the only ones know about Mae Ling. Jack, it's tough about that gal. My wife ain't going to like it if we get her slammed in the can for conspiracy. They went to school together and Anna always liked her."

Cardigan bent a stern eye on him. "That make any difference to you?"

Sam Chang looked at the floor. "I'm working for you, Jack. That's your answer."

"That's all I want to know. Mae looks like a nice kid but it was Mae who put me on the spot tonight. When she lit a butt and then waved that match—that was a signal. When a gal, Chinese or any other, goes ga-ga over a guy, it don't matter whether the guy's a heel or not. Tom Gow's a heel. Mae made that date with me because she was scared. She didn't know how much I knew, and she was afraid of the cops. When she saw I meant business, when I told her I'd turn her over to the cops if she didn't tell, she waved that match and the guy across the street took a shot at me. Charley Sun supplies the missing link—how those guys knew what truck was to make that transfer, and at what time."

"Charley Sun won't talk."

"The gal will—the next time I lay hands on her. The insurance company that underwrote that chair has been a good client of ours for ten years. We can't let 'em down. And," he added, "Ludwig Balm is offering, on his own, two thousand bucks reward for the recovery of the chair. I got a sick buddy back east that was shot up in the war and ain't ever been well since. He could use some of that dough. Come on—let's go."

"Where?" said Sam Chang, getting off the desk.

"Mae Ling's place."

"She won't be there."

"I want to give it another casing."

Sam Chang smiled. "Checking up on me?"

"Don't be an Airdale. Something new may have turned up since you cased it last night."

Magruder said: "Hey, you guys. On the way out, stop in the greasy spoon next door and tell the Greek to send up a milk bottle full of coffee and six lumps of sugar."

"Sweet tooth, huh?" said Cardigan.

Sam Chang said: "He uses two lumps and takes the other four home. Then he tries to get a rebate on the milk bottle."

"You're a liar," rasped Magruder. "I take the six home. I don't use sugar myself."

CARDIGAN OPENED THE hall door, the wind at his back, flapping the loose skirt of his ulster. Sam Chang followed him in, closed the door and shut out the wind and the sound of it. The hall was warm. A light, amber-shaded, glowed from the ceiling. Sam Chang moved ahead of Cardigan, motioned with his chin and climbed a narrow, heavily carpeted stairway. In the hall above were half a dozen closed doors, all painted a glossy yellow. Wordless, Sam Chang went to one of the doors, knocked, listened. He peered through the keyhole, straightened and said: "Dark."

Cardigan nodded, gestured with his forefinger toward the keyhole. Sam Chang took out a ring of keys, chose a master key, worked with the lock for half a minute and then felt the key bite; turn. He opened the door, reached in and turned on a light.

It was a small apartment of two small rooms—the smallest Cardigan had ever seen. He twisted among the pieces of furniture, picked up cushions, slapped them down again. He rolled down all the shades to see if anything had been rolled up in them; looked back of pictures on the wall. On a small oblong table stood the photograph of a young Chinese woman.

"Your wife," said Cardigan.

Sam Chang nodded.

Cardigan picked it up, said: "I'll take it. No use getting her involved, if the cops land on this place."

He rifled a small knee-hole desk, swiftly, completely, closed all the drawers and got up and went into the tiny bedroom, turning on a light there. He looked under the pillows, the quilts, the sheets, the mattress. The bureau drawers were next, then in the small dressing-table; then the closet and the coats, the shoes, the dresses in it. It took him only two minutes to case the bathroom. Then he opened the windows, looked out to see if anything had been hung outside; closed them, and looked under the rugs.

He stood up, his face red from having bent over, and said:

"Well, nothing, Sam." He stood looking around the room, took out papers and tobacco and began rolling a cigarette. "Now look, Sam. She may come back. You never can tell. I want you to stay here tonight. Turn the lights out, lock the door, and wait. If she comes in, don't argue here. Just take her over to the agency office in a cab and give me a ring at my rooms and I'll come over."

Sam Chang said: "What do you want me to do if the police should happen to come in?"

"How can they? They don't know about Mae." He went to the door, turned to say: "If they do pile in, it'll mean they do know something—so you'll have to say you had a tip she was mixed up in it."

Sam Chang didn't look very happy.

CARDIGAN LEFT THE small apartment, clopped his big feet down the stairs and pushed out into the street. The wind slammed him and he turned up his ulster collar. He walked three blocks, stopped in a telephone booth to make a call, and then caught a taxi cab. He rode Kearny to Post, and Post to Mason, where he got off. He went into the wind up Mason until he came to the Tareyton Court, whose bronze-and-glass door he pushed open; crossed the deserted oval lobby and stood watching the elevator clock tick off floors. Presently the bronze shaft door opened and Cardigan entered the empty car, said: "Six." The slick-haired Filipino boy tooled the car upward, cushioned it to a stop at the sixth.

610 was five doors from the elevator and Ludwig Balm himself opened the door and said: "Thoughtful of you to phone first, Mr. Cardigan. Come in."

"I figured you might be out."

"I'd just come in, as a matter of fact. I'm having coffee and brandy. Will you have some? Leave your things right here."

Balm was fiftyish, a heavy, hard-bodied man with a big, pink-cheeked face, a large nose, plump jowls. His brown hair was thick and without a part, It flowed backward from a wide fore-head. His eyes were large, sharp, alert behind rimless eyeglasses. The clothes he wore were dark, almost elegant. He put a hand out, palm upward, indicating the way to the living-room.

A woman was bent over a small table, pouring coffee.

Cardigan hesitated, said out of the side of his mouth to Balm: "Listen, I'm butting in...."

"Not at all.... Marya, this is Mr. Cardigan. Marya Rutlov, Mr. Cardigan."

Cardigan nodded and the woman, in her late twenties, straightened, dipped her head and gave a V-shaped smile that showed small, incredibly white teeth.

"This is an adventure," she said. "How do you do."

"He'll have some coffee, Marya. Do the honors."

"Half and half?" she asked, indicating the brandy bottle.

Cardigan nodded. "Yeah—about."

She had hair the color of copper. It was pulled tight on her shapely head and rolled into a taut knot just below and back of her left ear. She wore a high-waisted blouse and a drape skirt and she was fairly tall, and built. Her eyes were dark, smiling, but seemed to wear a protective veil.

"You have news?" Balm asked, bending an interested eye on Cardigan.

"I got a man planted at an address that might turn up news."

"Here in the city?"

"Chinatown."

Cardigan took a cup of coffee from Marya Rutlov, then took a glass of brandy and poured it into the coffee. He said to Balm: "I stopped by mainly to find out if you heard about the cops picking up Charley Sun, a Chinese lad from the express agency."

Balm looked surprised. "No, I've heard nothing."

"That's what I wanted to know. It means they didn't get anything out of him—yet."

Marya Rutlov said: "You seem pleased."

"Maybe," Cardigan said. "But I figure that reward's as good in my pocket as anybody else's. I'm not in this business because I like it."

Balm laughed, his jowls shaking. "I like your frankness, Mr. Cardigan. It's refreshing." He touched a corner of his mouth with his handkerchief. "But if the police have this—what's his name?—Charley Sun, it seems as though they have an ace."

"There's four aces in a deck," Cardigan grinned, "and a queen kicking beats a jack."

"*M'm,*" mused Balm.

Cardigan set down his empty cup. "I've got to beat it. I'll report to you from time to time."

"Do that. But I am, by the way, taking a trip. However, I'll post the reward at my bank. I've a reservation on the Honolulu Wing for tomorrow. Flying to Hawaii on business. I'll be back in a fortnight. Luck, old man!"

Marya's eyes shimmered darkly as she smiled, raised her cup. "Luck, Mr. Cardigan."

"Thanks a million," said Cardigan.

HE GOT HIS hat and overcoat and went out into the corridor, down to the elevator bank. The marker showed that the car was at the top floor. Cardigan buzzed for it, waited a minute, and when the marker did not move, took the stairway down. As he walked across the lobby he saw a youth sitting on one of the divans reading a newspaper. Cardigan went on to the door, pushed against it, then stopped pushing and turned and went back into the lobby. His eyes were keen with thought as he went toward the divan. He sat down on the divan alongside the youth, who did not take his eyes off the paper.

"Pinky Bellmont," Cardigan said.

The youth turned his head slowly, gave Cardigan a blank look, turned a page of his newspaper and went on reading. He was thin, of medium height, with bony white fingers, a bony sallow jaw, and pink cheeks. He weighed about a hundred and ten. Yellow silky hair showed beneath the brim of a green velours hat. His clothes were cheap, flashy, and he wore grain leather shoes and tan spats, pearl-buttoned.

Cardigan wore a half-smile of grim amusement. "What've you been doing since they won't let you ride horses anymore?"

"Move on," said Pinky in a bored voice.

"Or since they let you out of the can in San Diego?"

Pinky read intently.

Cardigan said: "Don't tell me you live here."

Pinky sighed, read on.

"Don't you find it cold in San Francisco?" Cardigan asked.

"I find that a bad smell has suddenly come in this lobby."

"Sure. You opened your mouth once. Now you've opened it twice and the smell is worse. Why don't you wash it once in a while?"

Pinky looked blankly at him. "Move off."

"I suppose you came in here to get out of the cold."

"No. I just killed six guys down the street and cut the throats of six kids. Move off."

Cardigan said: "The more you open your mouth the worse the smell gets. Not even your best friends will tell you." He stood up, said, "Keep your feet clean, Pinky," and went out.

Three blocks away he entered a drug store, crowded into a booth and called Balm's apartment. He said to Balm: "Just for your own information, I saw a young punk down in the lobby of your apartment house. It may mean nothing at all. I just thought I'd tell you…. Why, he's about five-feet-eight. Thin as a rail. Dark green hat, blue overcoat, blue suit. Narrow face, pink cheeks. About twenty or twenty-one. Pinky Bellmont's his name. He used to be a jockey…. Don't mention it."

He took a streetcar out to his place on California Street—he always used the same address when he was in San Francisco—two plain rooms in a plain old house. It was economical, and he was a working man.

3

Lead Poison

WHEN THE TELEPHONE bell jangled, he rolled over in bed, pulled on the bedlight and, picking up the phone, saw that the hands of the tarnished old alarm-clock pointed to two A.M.

"Yeah?" he yawned into the mouthpiece. "Oh, hello, Sergeant.

Don't you ever go to bed?… Sure I was asleep…. Now is that nice?… All right, spill it. It's probably screwy…. All right, don't like it. You can't wake me up at two in the morning and expect me to be cheerful." He sat up in bed suddenly, his hands tightening on the instrument. "When?" he muttered. "Yeah…. Who called you?… No, never mind. I'll come over."

He hung up and swung out of bed at the same time. His worn cotton pajamas were twisted around his body and one of his pajama legs was bunched up under his knee. He stripped, bleary-eyed with sleep; got into his undershirt and shorts and going into the bathroom doused his face with cold water. He took one sweep at his hair with a comb and considered himself groomed. In five minutes he was dressed.

California Street was a wide, deserted thoroughfare. He saw neither streetcar nor taxi. The wind was raw, damp, and cut him to the bone. He started walking east, his hands dug into his coat pockets, his head bent deep against the wind. When he had walked three blocks a nighthawk taxi creaked around a corner and Cardigan winged it, told the driver where to go.

"And step on it, pal."

CARDIGAN CLIMBED OUT of the cab a block from the place, paid up, and went ahead on foot. Outside the house where Mae Ling lived, a small group of men huddled, curious and murmuring. Besides the ambulance, there were two small inconspicuous cars. A cop was leaning against the iron handrail of the front steps. Cardigan slanted past him, climbed.

The cop turned, poked him in the small of the back with a nightstick and said: "Hey, you live here?"

Cardigan, angered by the jab, turned and growled: "Look out

how you use that stick, copper!"

"You want it used on your head?"

A voice said from an upper window: "What's going on down there?"

Cardigan looked up. "A jumpy cop, Sarge."

"Oh, you, Cardigan? Get up here!"

Cardigan plowed into the hall, climbed the stairs and found the upper corridor littered with half a dozen uniformed policemen. Mae Ling's door was opened and Dave Brice appeared there with a pearl-gray Stetson on the back of his head. His suit was gray and although it was well pressed it still looked baggy. He wore a green-striped silk shirt and a black bow tie. A big-boned man, he was broad as a garage door, with leathery skin, big hard white teeth and a jaw like a spade.

He said: "They're just about to take him out."

"Look out," said Cardigan, and twisted past Brice into the little living-room.

Sam Chang was on a stretcher and two men were lifting it. The Chinese op's eyes were closed but his body was writhing in agony, sweat was pouring down his face. Cardigan moistened his lips, said in a low voice that he suddenly found clogged: "Where'd they get him?"

The ambulance doctor said: "In the arm—left arm."

"But—hell, he's in agony!"

"Yeah," the doctor said. "And he can't talk. Something goofy. The wound's a minor one but—" He shook his head. "I dunno. I got to get him to the hospital quick. It's beyond me."

Cardigan said: "Sam—Sam—"

"No soap," the doctor said. "He can't talk. Look out, buddy. It's a hurry-up case."

Cardigan stepped aside, watched them carry Sam Chang out. Dave Brice watched too, and when they had got Sam Chang into the corridor the sergeant closed the door, put his palms together, pressed them against each other and took four long strides the length of the room.

Detective Adolph Bodenmeyer came out of the bedroom polishing a pair of steel-rimmed spectacles. He put them on, dipped his fat head toward Cardigan and mumbled something.

"What?" said Cardigan.

Bodenmeyer mumbled, gestured.

Cardigan shrugged.

Dave Brice said: "Bodie's embarrassed. He was taking a snooze when this call came in and we got away so fast that Bodie forgot his false teeth—left them in a glass of water."

Cardigan was toeing a spot on the rug. "This where Sam Chang was found?"

"Yeah." Brice sat on the arm of the divan and eyed Cardigan shrewdly. "The guy in the apartment downstairs heard the shot at half past one. He's an old guy, a tailor. He heard, right after the shot, somebody run down the stairs. But he didn't look out. He was scared. He rang us. What was Sam Chang doing here?"

Cardigan said: "I'd like to know."

"Was he working on the throne-chair case with you?"

"Yeah."

"And you don't know what he was doing here?"

Cardigan shook his head. He said: "Maybe he tailed somebody here. He must have."

Brice stood up, took a look out the window, then turned and said: "What about that business in the Pearl of Nanking Café?"

"Oh, you heard about that, eh?" Cardigan said.

BODENMEYER GESTURED AND made some unintelligible sounds and Dave Brice said irritably: "Either go back and get your teeth, Adolph, or shut up." He slapped his blue sharp eyes at Cardigan. "Sure I heard about it. It's my business to hear about things in Chinatown five minutes after they happen, sometimes five minutes before. Who was the dame?"

Cardigan shrugged. "A pick-up. I thought it'd be fun."

Brice moved his body inside his clothes as though it itched. "Trying to fox me?"

"I wouldn't fox you, Dave."

Brice grinned, showing most of his big hard teeth. "No you wouldn't!" He grunted sardonically. "I hear that the minute the shot busted the window you uncorked for the door and was down in the street before all the glass stopped falling."

"Why not? If a guy takes a swing at me with a gun—"

Brice took the wings of his tie between his fingers and put his head far back without taking his eyes off Cardigan. "Jackie, my boy, you half-expected that shot. When it happened, you uncorked for the street—you wanted that guy. You missed him and when you got back to the Pearl of Nanking Café the gal was gone. If the guy was the gal's guy and you figured, as you said, that he took a shot at you just because he was jealous, you wouldn't be dope enough to go out as fast as you did after him."

Cardigan spread his palms. "That's the way it is, Dave."

Brice gave him a long hard stare. "This is the way it was, fella. Let me figure it out this way. You offer the gal a bribe for some information and take her to the Pearl of Nanking Café. She's being tailed by a guy who sees you and the gal go in and he figures she's going to spill to you, so he takes a shot at her. You slam out after him but don't get him. The gal's gone when you get back, so you get Sam Chang to find her. Chang gets a line on her through some of his Chinese friends and comes here to get her. She thinks he's somebody sent by Tom Gow to polish her off and she shoots first."

Cardigan said: "If that's the way you figure it out, Dave, all right. You're a better man than I am."

"The thing is," Brice said slowly, incisively, "that I have to figure it out, but you know—*you know.* The dame that rents this apartment is named Mae Ling. I never heard of her. But I never heard of Charley Sun, either, until we picked him up. He's the clerk at the express company." He set his jaw, squinted one eye. "I've been patient with that guy, but now I'm going back and slap him silly."

Cardigan said: "What makes you think there's any connection between him and the girl that owns this apartment?"

"Don't ask foolish questions. We pick him up because he makes a phone call just before the throne-chair is to be moved. You're working on that case—and you're with a Chinese girl in a restaurant when somebody takes a shot at you. Then Sam Chang is found shot in a Chinese girl's apartment. It's good enough for me, Jackie. If you don't want to play ball, I'll play myself."

Cardigan shot at him: "Don't forget, baby, that as soon as that throne-chair was stolen I went around to you and offered to work on it with you. You stuck your big nose in the air and said, 'I don't need any kibitizers'." He added in a lower voice: "Since then, Balm's offered a cash reward, and I see you've changed your mind."

Brice's eyes looked chill. "And I see you've changed yours, too. Now you're a male Garbo and want to be alone. Well," he said, his voice rising angrily, "be alone! Go it alone! I don't need your help! To hell with you!"

"That's all, Dave?"

"I could say the same things over in dirtier language, you big bum!"

"Save it for the gutter, Dave—it drains off faster."

Cardigan turned, stepped on something that rolled beneath his foot. He bent down and picked up a small, round black button studded with a metal eyelet.

Brice said: "What's that?"

Cardigan dropped it into the sergeant's palm and Brice said: "H'm. Button off a woman's shoe. The Ling woman...."

He looked up narrowly at Cardigan. "Gonna be a hold-out, huh?"

"I'm a big bum, huh? I'm a kibitzer, huh?"

Brice rasped: "Hell, don't be a sorehead! A guy's liable to say things when he's mad."

"What are you doing now, sucking around?"

Brice's eyes flashed. "Nuts to you!" he exploded, and turned on his heel.

CARDIGAN SAT ON a metal-frame chair in the receiving-room of the hospital. It was four in the morning. A white-shaded light glowed on the white wall. Another light, green-shaded, glowed on a flat-topped desk. The big op had not removed his overcoat. His head was forward, his chin on his chest, and he dozed fitfully. A white-coated interne came in, took off his glasses and sat down, shaking his head.

"No luck yet," he said.

Cardigan's head bobbed up. "The other doctor get here?"

"Yes. He can't make anything of it. Both agree that it's a poison of some kind but they haven't been able to recognize it." He added: "They've got the bullet out. It's impregnated with the poison."

Cardigan said: "I knew a tough dago in Kansas City who used to rub garlic on his bullets."

"Oh, we've had cases like that—but never one like this."

"You think he'll pull through?"

The interne gave a short laugh. "If we knew the nature of the poison, it'd be a simple matter. But he's in agony. The wound's really nothing at all—but this poison has started into his system and we can't—"

A nurse came in, said, "Baggot's licked," and went out by another door.

"*H'm,*" the interne said.

"Listen—" Cardigan stood up. "What are you doing, dragging in any doctor off the streets that isn't busy?"

The interne smiled compassionately. "Brother, Baggot's good."

"There's good and there's excellent. How about Stedter?"

"He's a Seattle man."

"I don't care where he is. Get him…. Don't be afraid. I'll raise the dough somewhere. Tell him to grab a plane."

Baggot looked in, said: "It looks pretty bad, Mr. Cardigan. I'm calling in two colleagues. Just reached one in Sausalito and the other's on his way over."

The interne said: "Cardigan's set on Stedter."

"Stedter's tops!" Baggot said earnestly. He looked at Cardigan. "That true? You want Stedter?"

"Sure I want Stedter!"

Baggot cried: "Swell! I'll phone him myself!"

"That sounds like action," Cardigan muttered. "I'm going out and tank up on coffee. I'll be back."

HE FOUND A lunchroom five blocks away, its windows steamed up. The place was empty except for a couple of taxi-drivers and the goose-necked counterman, his bare arms covered with tattoo designs.

Cardigan said: "Two mugs of coffee and don't put any milk in them."

He thought of Sam Chang's wife on her way home and wondered how he could ever face her if Sam died. He knew he should never have planted Sam in that room—he should have stayed there himself. The coffee came and he drank it—black and thick and hot. It burned his insides. Instead of slamming out after that lad who had taken a shot at him in the Pearl of Nanking Café he should have stayed with Mae Ling.

When he returned to the hospital the nurse said: "Why don't you go home? You can't do any good here."

"Why don't you mind your own business?" he grumbled, flopping to a chair.

"All right, be nasty!"

He shook his head. "Excuse it, sister. I didn't mean it." He made a face, as if he were all mixed up. "I should never have let that guy—" He broke off, shook his head.

"Go ahead—go home," she urged. "He's unconscious now," she added. "There are four doctors in conference now. They're doing the best they can. Stedter's unable to come—he's deathly ill. Go on, be a good egg—go home and get some sleep."

He stood up again, muttered: "I guess you're right."

He went out and walked five blocks in the empty, windy darkness; then stopped, thought for a couple of minutes and turned and walked back two blocks. He crossed the street, cut through an alley, walked three more blocks and pushed into a police station. To the man at the desk he said: "Brice in?"

BRICE STRADDLED A chair, his arms draped over the back of it. He wore a heavy long-sleeved undershirt and one strap of his suspenders was up, the other down. His hair was tousled and he looked fagged out. Bodenmeyer, his mouth now glaringly full of false teeth, had his collar off and his sleeves rolled up. He sat at the desk drinking black coffee from a tin can.

The Chinese sitting on the straight-backed chair, strapped to it across the chest, was Charley Sun. Two powerful lights streamed into his face and his skin looked chalk-white. He was thin, tall, and at present looked only half conscious.

Cardigan, closing the door and leaning back against it, said: "Got him pretty well sapped, huh?"

"I ain't laid a hand on him," Dave Brice growled. "And I don't know who's more worn out, me or him. The kid can take it—plenty." He looked Cardigan over from head to foot with sultry eyes. "I don't remember inviting you here."

Bodenmeyer said: "Now, Dave—now, Dave."

"You pipe down," Brice told him. "Teeth or no teeth—you always say nothing better than any guy I know."

Bodenmeyer said to Cardigan: "Dave is upset. Whenever Dave is upset—well, he is upset. Have some coffee, Cardigan."

Cardigan shook his head, and to Brice, "What'd you get out of Sun?"

Brice cackled. "What'd I get out of Sun!"

Cardigan went across the office and stood in front of the Chinese. "Boy," he said, "Sam Chang might die—he will die if they don't find out what kind of poison's on the bullet. So far, only an old Siamese throne-chair's been stolen—or about a hundred thousand bucks. If Sam Chang dies"—he dropped his voice dangerously—"that'll be murder. Murder, Charley Sun. That's different. Savvy?"

Charley Sun's head rolled from side to side and the whites of his eyes shone as his lids rolled up and down fitfully.

Cardigan said: "Last Saturday night you were at the Oriental Music Box with Mae Ling."

Brice jumped up, his lips whipping taut. "Where the hell did you find that out?"

"Sam Chang found it out a few hours before he was killed."

Brice boiled. "You—you told me you didn't know—"

"Quit butting in," Cardigan said. He said to Charley Sun: "I made Mae Ling meet me. She was afraid to come to my office so we met at the Pearl of Nanking Café. I wanted to know where Tom Gow was. She knew but she wouldn't tell. When I threatened to turn her over to Dave Brice she signaled a guy in the street and he took a shot at me. Mae disappeared and I didn't get the guy. Sam Chang and I went to her apartment and I planted Chang there in case she came back. The cops found Sam Chang shot in her apartment."

Dave Brice looked very dark and forbidding. He snapped: "I knew you were lying the pants off me before! Damn you, Jackie, I got a mind to toss you in the can!"

"If you've got a mind, Dave, use it—and shut up. I've thought things out. I wanted that reward—sure. But to hell with it now.

To hell with the throne-chair. I've got to save Sam Chang—
and I'm taking water—I'm telling you just how much I know."

"So you can't get along without the cops after all."

"I probably could—but I'm not taking the chance. I can't
afford to take the chance, with Sam Chang dying by inches.
If you want to crow, Dave, crow. I can take that, too. I can take
anything—so long as there's a chance of saving Sam Chang."

Dave Brice stared. Then he exploded: "By cripes, I didn't
think it was in you! I didn't think you had the guts ever to back
down an inch!"

"Ah, sure you did," chimed in Bodenmeyer. "Only a coupla
hours ago you said it was tough you and Cardigan was both so
bull-headed—that together, you two guys could—"

Brice barked: "I wish you'd lose your teeth for good! Give
you a pair of teeth and—"

"You heard me, Charley Sun," Cardigan was saying dully.
"Who did you phone? We've got to know. We've got to know
if Tom Gow and Berkman and Finger are really in this city.
We've got to find Mae Ling. We've got to find the guy that
fired that shot that wounded Sam Chang—or if it was Mae
Ling, we want her. It'll be murder if Sam Chang dies."

Charley Sun groaned.

Cardigan added grimly: "And if he dies—there'll be death
to pay for it—you and Mae Ling and the others."

"Not—Mae Ling," panted Charley Sun. "I phoned—
phoned—" He groaned, pressed his eyelids together and
writhed in the chair. "Not Mae Ling!" he sobbed.

"Who?"

Charley Sun gritted out: "Marya… Rutlov.…" He slumped
in the chair, his mouth falling open loosely.

"*H'm,* he has passed out," observed Bodenmeyer gravely.

Brice barked: "Who the hell is Marya Rutlov?"

"I know," Cardigan said quietly.

"You know! It seems to me that you know an awful lot!"

Bodenmeyer got up. "Listen, we better bring Charley Sun to, so we can—"

"There's a faster way, kid," Cardigan broke in. "Put some clothes on, Dave."

Brice snapped to it, flung at Bodenmeyer: "You stay here with Sun."

4

Button—Button—

IT WAS FIVE past five in the morning when Cardigan knocked on Ludwig Balm's door. Dave Brice, smoking a rank cigar paced up and down the corridor—six paces one way, six another—his baggy pants flopping around his knees.

When, a couple of minutes later, the door was opened, Brice stopped pacing and Cardigan said: "This is a screwy hour, Mr. Balm, but…."

"What's wrong, what's wrong?" Balm asked, his face still dulled by sleep, his hands knotting the belt of his robe.

"Plenty," said Brice.

"Must be, must be," said Balm concernedly. "Come in, come in, please." He rubbed his eyes as they walked in. "Gad, I must have been sleeping hard. I need an eye-opener. You men like one?"

They shook their heads and Balm, padding into the living-room, poured himself a tot of whiskey, downed it neat.

Cardigan said: "This Marya Rutlov—the woman I met here—where does she live?"

Balm's eyes popped.

Dave Brice said: "Charley Sun made a phone call to her before that damned throne-chair was shipped."

"Sam Chang," said Cardigan, "an op of mine, was shot after midnight in a Chinese girl's apartment. With a poisoned bullet. He's paralyzed—can't talk—and so far the doctors haven't been able to name the poison. We're working fast. Got to. If we don't find out the poison, it means Sam Chang dies. That phone call was Charley Sun to the Rutlov woman."

Balm, his face blank with amazement, sat down. "Excuse me, gentlemen—but this is a shock."

"How long you know this woman?" Brice asked.

"Why, I've known Marya several years. It can't possibly be true—what you say. The Chinese boy must be lying."

"I don't think so," Cardigan said. "You pull a name like Mary Smith out of the air—but not one like Marya Rutlov. Where's she live?"

Balm kept shaking his head as if unable to understand. Then he stood up, said angrily: "We will all see! I'll go with you, gentlemen! I'll be dressed in a few minutes. Excuse me."

He spun and strode heavily, angrily across the living-room, disappeared in regions beyond. Four minutes later he reappeared putting on his overcoat.

"Let us go, gentlemen," he said grimly.

They went down in the elevator and out into the windy street. A Bureau sedan was parked at the curb and Brice got in behind the wheel, Cardigan followed Balm into the rear and Balm said: "Telegraph Hill. Out Stockton and up Filbert. I still think there's a mistake, gentlemen—but if there isn't"—he hardened his voice—"I want to be in on the showdown."

Brice opened the throttle wide and the sedan roared through the deserted streets. Turning into Filbert, he shifted back to second and then, as the grade stiffened, into first. Filbert dead-ends near the top of the hill and beyond that are many small frame houses and careening footwalks of wood. Brice cramped the car into the curb, braked and locked it. Balm was the first out, and smacking his gloved hands together said: "Now we climb."

THEY CLIMBED WOODEN steps, went along a level footwalk, then climbed some more, switch-backing. Soon they were on the very top and could see, far below, pier lights and harbor lights and the sweep of the Embarcadero. Balm took an off-shoot of one of the main foot-walks and his feet knocked onto a small porch. There was no light in the bunga-low, but after he had knocked several times a light sprang on somewhere in the rear and a moment later another sprang on in front. The door was opened by Marya Rutlov. She had a black-and-red kimono wrapped around her and was pushing her hair back.

"What an hour!" she groaned.

Balm said: "Yes, my dear. What an hour. I have with me Sergeant Brice of the Chinatown Squad and Mr. Cardigan of the Cosmos Agency."

"This must be interesting," she said. "Come in and let me comb my hair."

They went in and Cardigan said: "Better skip the hair-comb."

"But, goodness, I look a mess!"

Balm said: "Marya, this is very serious. Sit down and listen to what they have to say." He took a seat himself, folded his hands, pursed his lips and eyed her speculatively.

Cardigan said: "Miss Rutlov, the Chinese boy, Charley Sun, sprang. He said he made that phone call to you. Phoned you before the express-company truck was to pick up the throne-chair."

She leaned back. "Ah, poor Charley—"

Balm leaned forward.

"Well?" demanded Dave Brice.

Marya Rutlov looked up at him, shrugged. "Well, if he told you, why should I go over it?"

"He fainted just after he mentioned your name," Cardigan said. "We didn't wait till he came to. Sam Chang's dying by inches and we can't lose a minute."

She sat up, her eyes opening wide.

"What is this about Sam Chang?"

Cardigan told her.

She laughed. "You should have got the whole story from Charley Sun. Go back now and get the whole story from him."

Dave Brice shook his head. "You tell us—and we'll check up from him."

She leaned back again, weary, a little bored. "Charley Sun is a young fool," she said. "He did telephone me. Do you know why? I'll tell you. It has nothing to do with all this. Now and then I do a little painting, and a Chinese girl named Mae Ling has posed for me. Charley Sun is in love with her. Sometimes he would come here with her. But he was afraid she was running around with bad people and it so happened that on the day before the robbery he came to me and said, 'Miss Rutlov, you are a woman and maybe you can help me. I love Mae Ling but I am afraid she is seeing people who take advantage of her. She says no. But you are a woman and maybe you can find out, so that I can protect her.' I said I would try and told him to call me next morning. Mae Ling would tell me nothing. I told him that on the phone and he thanked me and asked me please never to mention it to anybody. That is all. It's very unfortunate if Mae Ling has got in trouble, because Charley Sun loves her."

Dave Brice crossed to the phone and called his office. "That you, Adolph?" he said. "Has Charley Sun come to?… What did he say?" Dave Brice listened, nodding, making faces, grunting. Finally he hung up, looked at the woman. "It checks," he said. And to Cardigan, "Well, we're back where we started, or maybe further back."

Cardigan looked haggard. He was desperate. He thought of Pinky Bellmont, the punk he had seen sitting in the lobby of Balm's apartment house. They might try to pick up Pinky. But just because you happen to see a punk sitting in an apartment-house lobby, you can't call him guilty. However, he was desperate. No thought of the throne-chair entered his head. He was thinking only of Sam Chang, a quiet, able operative—and of Sam's wife on the way home from China.

HE SAID: "THEIR stories check but, damn it, they shouldn't! For those guys that swiped that throne-chair knew what truck was to pick it up, and at what time. Damn it to hell, Charley Sun was the clerk in the office—he knew. The guy at the museum knew. Mr. Balm knew, of course. Who else knew?

Maybe a listening-in telephone operator." He looked at the woman. "Maybe you knew."

"I'm sorry," she said. "I didn't."

"Mae Ling," muttered Brice. "That's the gal we want. We get her and we get the mob."

Cardigan's jaw was sticking out. "Take this woman to the station-house and make her face Charley Sun. She knows Charley Sun and she knows Mae Ling."

Dave Brice said: "Don't be a fool."

Cardigan's face was burning, his voice was hoarse, heavy. "Her story's too pat. So is Charley Sun's. And while I'm being a fool, let me go whole hog. Pick up Pinky Bellmont."

"Pinky Bellmont ain't in town," Brice said.

"Pinky Bellmont was in the lobby of Mr. Balm's apartment house last night. I figured him too small a punk to be mixed up in anything like this—but pick him up."

Dave Brice said: "All right, we'll pick up Pinky—but I'm not dragging this woman down to the station-house just because you've gone haywire. Come on. Let's beat it."

Balm stood up, shook his head, saying: "I'm afraid Mr. Cardigan is very upset."

"Of course, I'll go along," said Marya Rutlov, "if I can be of any help."

Brice said: "No, never mind. Just stick around town. We'll give you a ring if we need you." He grabbed Cardigan by the arm. "Out, big fella. Don't let a bum steer get you down. Can we drop you off, Mr. Balm?"

"Yes, I wish you would," Balm said. And to the woman, "I'm sorry, about this, Marya—but it had to be done."

Cardigan would not be hurried. He rolled a cigarette, stuck it between his lips, picked up a book of matches that lay on one of the window sills and, lighting up, waved the match out and tossed it into a tray. He muttered: "O.K., Dave."

Marya Rutlov said: "It's silly to be mad. I have some brandy here. Won't you have some brandy, all of you?"

"Well, that's very nice," said Dave Brice, grinning.

"Nix," said Cardigan. "Come on, Dave—you wanted to go, now let's go."

Marya smiled and came over to take Cardigan by the arm. "Do sit down."

"Lady, I got an op of mine dying—and I'm not sitting around swilling brandy meanwhile."

Her voice chided: "Please—please, now, Mr. Cardigan."

"Just one—come, come," said Balm largely.

"Yeah, just a quickie," Dave Brice said, "and then we'll trot along."

The woman was pressing on his arm. "Don't be a child, Mr. Cardigan. A big man like you!"

Balm said, "Stuffy in here," and opened the door, inhaled deeply, turned and said in a loud, laughing voice: "Don't worry about your man, Cardigan. Everything will turn out all right. Yes, yes, indeed."

Cardigan pushed the woman away. His thick brows forked above his nose, his eyes glittered. He lunged across the room, thrust Balm aside and dived out to the porch. In the dawn gloom he saw something move on the boardwalk about twenty yards away. He barked: "Hey, you!"

He heard the sudden flight of feet on wood. He set off at a bounding run, heard feet drumming on the wooden steps; heard the feet miss, clatter, struggle to regain their balance.

Cardigan pulled his gun and yelled: "Freeze—or you get it!"

He ran into a man who chopped with a gun, kicked with a foot whose shoe glinted. The foot missed but the chopping blow landed on Cardigan's head. Sparks seemed to burst inside his head and as he reeled he grabbed hold of the man and together they clattered down the steps to the first landing. The man was like an eel, fast and slippery. He squirmed free and leaped, but Cardigan, on his side, slapped at the man's ankle, brought him down so hard that the wooden landing shook. He lost his gun as he fell on the man but instead of trying to recover it clubbed the man with his fist, banging his head back against the wood. The man's hat flew off, he kicked upward with his knees. Cardigan slugged him again, ripped the gun from his hand.

DAVE BRICE WAS pounding along the footwalk. Another figure leaped over the edge of the footwalk and said: "Stop in your tracks, Brice."

"Like this," said Brice, firing. The newcomer fell against the railing, his knees wobbled, his gun fell. Dave Brice grabbed hold of him, held him up. He yelled: "You all right, Jackie?"

Cardigan was hauling his man to his feet. "Yeah," he said, and slammed his man along the boardwalk, picked him up and dragged him onto the porch, flung him into the bungalow living-room.

"Goodness!" said Ludwig Balm.

Brice came with his man, walking him in, then let him go and watched him crumple to the floor.

Cardigan was breathing heavily. "You got Pinky Bellmont, Dave. And I got—"

"Tom Gow."

The Chinese lay on the floor, his fingers clawing at the carpet, his breath beating through his lips. Marya Rutlov was backed against a wall, her eyes staring.

Cardigan leaned down, pulled up the cuff of Tom Gow's left trouser leg. Tom Gow wore patent-leather shoes with cloth uppers, buttoned. One of the buttons was missing. Cardigan said: "Remember that button we found in Mae Ling's room?"

"By cripes!" exploded Dave Brice.

Cardigan lifted Tom Gow to his feet, shoved him against the wall and said: "Quick, fella. You shot Sam Chang with a poisoned bullet. He's dying. We've got to know the kind of poison, to save him."

"I didn't," choked Tom Gow.

"Brother, I'm not going to monkey around long with you." He hefted the gun in his hand. "This is your gun, Tom Gow. I'm going to test it on you if you don't come across."

Dave Brice snapped. "Spill it, Tom!" and went across and whacked him on the jaw. He whacked him again and said: "Spill it fast, baby!"

Cardigan grunted, "Look out, Dave," and went up very close to Tom Gow, the gun leveled. "I'm not going to shoot you in the belly, Tom. I'm going to shoot you in the leg—a minor wound. Then we'll see where you got the poison, what it is."

Tom Gow gagged. His eyes bulged as he watched Cardigan move the muzzle of the gun downward for a leg shot. Tom Gow began to shake. Sweat beaded his face and his lips trembled. He pressed back against the wall, his arms out, his fingers scraping against the plaster.

Ludwig Balm cried: "Put your hands up, Cardigan—and you, Brice!"

Cardigan spun and fired at the same time and the small room seemed to bounce with the explosion. Balm stumbled and his gun went off three times, the bullets slamming into the floor at Cardigan's feet. Tom Gow jumped and Dave Brice knocked him cold with a blow on the ear. The woman slumped sighing to the floor. Balm dropped his gun and fell face down on a divan, choking: "Get me a doctor—"

"What's the poison?" muttered Cardigan.

"Get me—quick—a hospital. I'll tell—doctor. Agony—will be awful in half—hour—sooner maybe—"

Brice clipped: "Better not argue, Jackie. You gotta save him to save Sam Chang."

"Right," Cardigan grunted. "I'll carry the bum."

"I'll stick till I can get some cops here," Brice said. "How the hell'd you know those guys were outside?"

Cardigan, shouldering Balm, said: "I didn't. But I accidentally waved a match by that window when I lit that butt. From that minute on the dame and Balm tried to hold us here. Balm must have phoned her or the heels, when he went to get dressed before at his apartment. I figure now she would've waved a match if we'd collared her, and the heels would have come in. We didn't collar them, so no match—until I waved it by accident. Same signal as at the Pearl of Nanking Café."

5

One-Grand Taxi Fare

MAGRUDER WAS SITTING on his desk in the Cosmos Agency office when Cardigan strode in, went to a mirror, looked at his left eye, which was slightly discolored, and said: "Well, thank God, Sam Chang's out of danger. Balm knew the poison—he was the one poisoned the bullets. We got the throne-chair about half an hour ago. They'd lugged it aboard a fishing schooner, the *Pacific Shark*. Me and Brice and a dozen cops. Got Berkman and Finger there, too—and found Mae Ling there. They'd tied her right in the damn thing. Afraid she'd squeal, I guess, if she got away. I had to shoot a couple of the Chink crew that were guarding her."

"Balm was plenty smart, I guess."

"Plenty." Cardigan nodded grimly. "It was neat work, most of it—and the whole thing might have come off O.K. if Tom Gow hadn't fired that shot at me through the window of the Pearl of Nanking Café. Mae Ling hadn't bargained on that. She did meet me because she was afraid but she didn't bargain on gunfire. When Tom Gow came up from Los Angeles with Berkman and Finger he went right to see Mae Ling. They used to run around together but Tom Gow knew she was going with Charley Sun. He knew that the express company Charley Sun worked for always handled shipments to or from the Jerris Museum and he wanted Mae Ling to get Charley to tell her when the throne-chair would be moved next. She

wouldn't, of course. He left, but he came back later and said
he'd made a deal with Charley Sun himself. She went and
confronted Charley and he denied it, but Tom Gow told her
Charley would have to deny it and that if she said anything to
the cops, or to anybody, it'd be tough for Charley.

"Balm was back of it. Balm knew Pinky Bellmont from Cali-
ente days and told Pinky he'd like to get hold of two or three
guys to help pull a deal. Pinky wrote Tom Gow and Tom and
Finger and Berkman came up from Los Angeles. When they
couldn't reach Charley Sun, Balm got this bright idea. Tom
Gow kept telling Mae Ling that Charley was involved and he
kept telling Charley that Mae was involved; in that way, he
kept Mae and Charley anxious about the other and neither
one would tell on the other. It was Tom Gow who advised Mae
to meet me when I asked her. He said that if I showed signs
of arresting her she should wave that match by the window
and he would make a phone call to the Pearl of Nanking that
would take her from the table—and then she could skip out.
But Tom Gow took a pot-shot at me instead. When Mae ran
out Pinky Bellmont, who was up the street, picked her up and
gave her over to Finger and Berkman. They took her aboard
the schooner, afraid she'd break up. Pinky and Tom Gow tailed
me and Sam Chang. Pinky tailed me away from Mae Ling's
place and Tom Gow went up and shot Sam Chang. Pinky was
to kill me, but he held off until he could get a load of dope and
enough courage.

"The phone call that Charley made to Marya Rutlov was
sincere on his part. But Marya told him to make it at that time
so that if things jammed up, he'd be accused of complicity. She
knew at what time the throne-chair was to be moved because

Balm had told her. It was clever of Balm. He pays down three thousand bucks in cash, he even offers a reward—which he knew he would never have to pay. The schooner was to start out westward with the throne-chair. Balm was to fly to Honolulu and get another schooner to meet the *Pacific Shark*, take off the throne-chair and then sail with it to China.

"Mae refused to tell me anything about Tom Gow because she was afraid that would lead to something about Charley Sun. And Charley hung back about explaining the phone call because he felt that would lead to something about Mae Ling. Tom Gow had planted so much suspicion in Mae's and Charley's minds—about each other—that the poor kids were ga-ga with doubt. It was a swell sight, seeing them again—and both on the level."

Magruder grunted. "It's all swell, except for once in your life you got dished out of a reward. You and Dave both!"

"Yeah?" said Cardigan, laying down ten one-hundred-dollar bills. "Balm offered a reward, he advertised it. All those doctors over Sam Chang cost dough, so I charged Balm taxi fare to the hospital. A thousand bucks taxi fare, baby. You're not the only one around here with dash of Scotch."

Copyright Information